A VEIL OF SPEARS

BRADLEY P. BEAULIEU

A VEIL OF SPEARS

Book Three of
The Song of the Shattered Sands

DAW BOOKS, INC.

DONALD A. WOLLHEIM, FOUNDER
375 Hudson Street, New York, NY 10014
ELIZABETH R. WOLLHEIM
SHEILA E. GILBERT
PUBLISHERS
www.dawbooks.com

This one's for Rob, for being a friend,
for grounding me when I needed it.

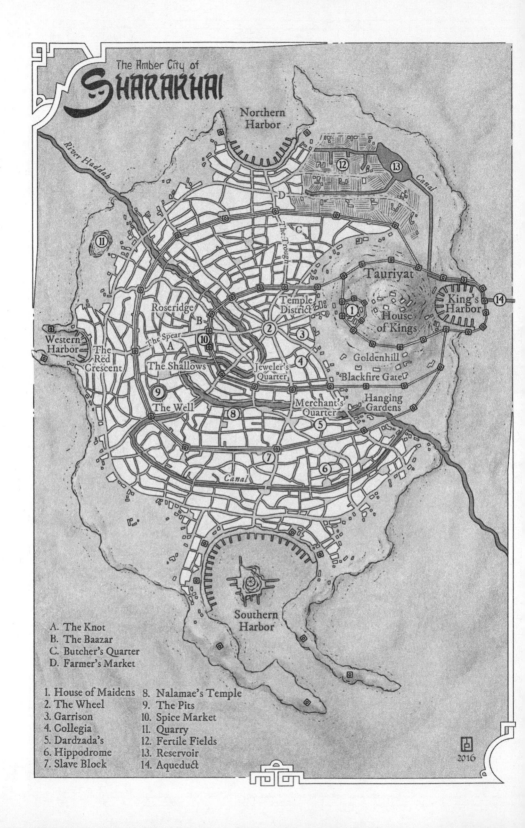

The Amber City of
Sharakhai

Northern Harbor

River Haddah

The Trough

12

13

Canal

D

C

11

Tauriyat

Temple District

1

House of Kings

King's Harbor

14

Roseridge

B

2

3

The Spear

A

10

Western Harbor

The Red Crescent

The Shallows

4

Jeweler's Quarter

Goldenhill

Blackfire Gate

9

The Well

8

Merchant's Quarter

5

Hanging Gardens

7

6

Canal

Southern Harbor

A. The Knot
B. The Baazar
C. Butcher's Quarter
D. Farmer's Market

1. House of Maidens
2. The Wheel
3. Garrison
4. Collegia
5. Dardzada's
6. Hippodrome
7. Slave Block
8. Nalamae's Temple
9. The Pits
10. Spice Market
11. Quarry
12. Fertile Fields
13. Reservoir
14. Aqueduct

2016

Chapter 1

ÇEDA KNELT IN A CAVERN beside a pool of water, deep beneath the desert's surface. The cavern's darkness enveloped her, as did the chill air. It smelled clean here, unsullied, a place that might have remained hidden throughout all the history of the Kings of Sharakhai, perhaps longer.

In her hands she held a thick, golden bracelet. She turned it over, again and again, feeling its weight, touching the oval stone, roughing her skin against the intricate designs worked into the gold.

"Speak to me," she said. "This time, speak to me."

The echoes went on and on.

The bracelet had once belonged to King Mesut, the Jackal King, but now it served as an indictment of all the Kings and even of the gods themselves. It was not the band itself that provided evidence of their treachery, but the onyx stone. Even now she could feel the souls of the seventeen dead asirim within it, clamoring for freedom, pleading for their release. Çeda was desperate to give it to them, but after six weeks of trying she still had no idea *how*.

On the night of the great battle in King's Harbor, Mesut had summoned them forth as wights and set them against Çeda and Sehid-Alaz, the King of the thirteenth tribe, the crowned asir who had kissed her and set her on this strange new path. It had been a desperate moment, but she'd managed to sever Mesut's hand and take the golden band from him. She'd pleaded with the ghostly souls to take their revenge against Mesut, and they'd answered, descending on Mesut like buzzards. Each rake of their terrible claws had brought them exultation, a taste of their long-awaited revenge, but the joy had been short-lived. No sooner had Mesut succumbed to his wounds than they'd been drawn back into their prison and chained once more. The trick to freeing them had eluded her ever since.

"By your grace," Çeda whispered to the goddess, Nalamae.

Cleaving open her mother's flame-shaped locket, she took out the last of her adichara petals. Her mouth watered at the floral scent, and when she placed it beneath her tongue, the mineral taste rushed through her. It warmed her limbs, drove away the cold humidity of the cavern in a way that a fire never could. Clipping the locket closed, she breathed deeply, closed her eyes, and welcomed the sensations that came.

She felt the asir, Kerim, somewhere high above her. He was outside the cavern, roaming among the rocks, she guessed. He seemed reticent, as if he were hiding his thoughts and emotions from her. He didn't like the bracelet. He'd told her so. She could feel the revulsion within him, though whether it was from the constant reminder of his own fate, or concern for the souls trapped within, she couldn't say.

Opening her mind further, she beckoned the souls nearer. When they retreated, she searched for the onyx's boundaries, tried to define them in some way so that she might learn more about the souls within. But as it had every other time she'd done this, the gemstone felt unknowable—a star in the sky, well beyond the ken of mortal man. When she'd taken petals in the past, in or near Sharakhai, she could always sense the blooming fields and the asirim below, trapped in their sandy graves. Even now she could feel them, far, far to the west of the cavern where she and Kerim now hid. She'd thought by using the petals she would feel the asirim in the onyx. She'd hoped to be able to puzzle out its secrets, to use the asirim's shared bond to free them from their prison or, failing that, simply *speak* with them as she did with Kerim. To no avail. She'd been rebuffed over and over again. Not once in the weeks following the great battle in King's Harbor had she felt nearer to her goal.

"Speak," she said, that lone word echoing in the cave. "But one word, and I'll know this is not a lost cause."

Her only reply was a miasma of anguish, fear, confusion, and hatred. The same as always.

Her concentration was broken, as it was so often of late, by the growls and yapping of wolves. She was tempted to simply let it go on, but when the sound became more fierce, and she felt panic emanating from Kerim, she pulled away from the souls in the bracelet.

"Forgive me," she whispered, and rushed up the winding tunnel toward the sun.

She was out of breath by the time she reached the cavern's entrance where, spread before her in a protective fan, were her pack of maned wolves. They'd placed themselves between Kerim and the entrance to Çeda's cave. Directly before Kerim's crouched form was Mist, a white wolf, hunkered low, ears laid back, teeth bared as a deep growl issued from her throat. She was the very wolf Çeda had stumbled across with Emre on her first trip to the blooming fields, the very wolf that had healed Çeda and led her here so she could recover from her wounds and decide what to do next

"Kerim!" Çeda said as she approached.

Kerim didn't acknowledge her. He was staring at Mist, his jaundiced eyes wild and nervous, as if he couldn't understand how he'd come to be here. His disorientation had been getting worse the longer they hid from the Kings' forces.

Kerim, back away.

As she came near, the maned wolves closed ranks, blocking her path. The largest among them, the scarred one she'd named Thorn, was padding behind Kerim. Though the pack tried to stop her, Çeda pushed her way through them, then charged at Thorn, waving her arms as the wolf darted toward Kerim, silent, teeth bared.

"Thorn, no!"

Kerim turned, arms raised, just in time for Thorn to claw him, to tear at his shriveled, blackened skin. Kerim could have killed him with one blow—the asirim were inhumanly strong—but he didn't. He backed away, warding off Thorn's advances with arms and hands spread wide. But the danger was far from over. While she'd been focused on Thorn, Mist had padded to Çeda's left, clearing a path to Kerim.

"Back!" Çeda cried, putting herself between Kerim and the white wolf.

Mist's eyes flicked between Kerim and Çeda, but she obeyed, and Çeda ran to stop Thorn.

Kerim wailed, his bloodshot eyes wild with fear. He swung wildly, angrily, at Thorn. Çeda heard a thud as Kerim's fist struck the wolf's massive head. Thorn was the largest among the wolves—with his long legs, his head was higher than Çeda's—yet he was flung aside by the force of that blow. It brought on a fierce yelp and a renewed fury that drove the entire pack to close in. Their heads were low, growls rumbling from between their bared teeth. They'd listened to Çeda until now, but with Kerim's attack on their leader, they were ready to excise this hated member from their pack once and for all.

Çeda pulled at Thorn's black mane. "Leave him alone!"

But Thorn rounded on her and charged. Jaws snapping, he caught her wrist. She managed to snatch her hand away, but caught several deep gashes while doing so. She stumbled backward and fell as Thorn advanced, snapping at her ankles as she tried to kick him. He'd just managed to clamp his jaw over her calf when a blur of ivory flew in.

Her leg was freed as Mist and Thorn growled, grappled, and rolled in the sand. The other wolves looked on, their eyes intense as they studied the two wolves locked in battle. It grew so fierce Çeda thought they would kill each other, but when Kerim turned and began sprinting over the sand away from them, the wolves finally disengaged.

In moments, all their growling and yipping and yowling stopped. They panted, wary but content in Kerim's absence. Thorn was the most animated among them, alternating looks between Çeda and Mist, but then he loped off, heading into the shade of the rocky overhang near the cave entrance, where he dropped down and watched, as if daring any to come near and challenge him, Çeda included.

Mist padded closer to Çeda and licked the blood welling from her wounds. They immediately felt better, just as her injuries had weeks ago. Mist did the same to the puncture wounds along Çeda's calf while Çeda raked her fingers through Mist's cloudy mane. "Thank you," she said, then limped after Kerim.

She followed the footsteps and the trail of black blood left over the sand, weaving her way between the sentinel-like pillars of rock. She found him a quarter-league away, sitting cross-legged between the dunes, knees hugged to his chest like a child lost in the desert.

She crouched by his side, careful not to touch him but close enough that he could feel her warmth. "You don't have to stay." She waved her arm to the dunes. "You can go, flee into the desert. Surely, somewhere in the Great Mother you might find peace."

She didn't want Kerim to go. Not truly. She wanted to free him or, failing that, find a way for him to have his revenge on the Kings, and how could she do either of those things if he left? But his misery was so great she had to try.

His only response was to swivel his head and stare at her left wrist, where Mesut's thick gold band rested. Çeda felt the souls in the onyx gemstone, though muted, as they always were in the sunlight. As if he couldn't bear to think about them any longer, Kerim lifted his gaze to meet hers, a silent plea, and then looked to the sword at her side. Her ebon blade. She put her hand on the pommel, knowing that he'd contemplated this, his final release, since leaving Sharakhai.

"I will give it to you, if that's what you wish."

Kerim opened his mouth to speak. A long wheeze came out. He swallowed and tried again. *"I . . ."* he said, the lone word coming out in one long rasp. *"I would . . ."*

She stood and with clear intent laid her hand over the leather grip of River's Daughter. "This?"

He nodded.

Çeda's heart pounded loud in her ears. She didn't wish to be alone out here, nor did she wish to end a life that might help others to win their freedom, but she meant what she'd said. No one deserved a life like Kerim's.

And yet . . .

"You must say it, Kerim." She licked her lips, praying he would say no. "I can't do it unless you say it."

Kerim stood, the blackened skin of his forehead wrinkling. *"I . . ."* he said again, but then he turned sharply to his left, and Çeda followed his gaze.

Beyond a dozen clutches of standing stones, she saw it, a sleek ship, lateen sails cutting a line across the horizon—a royal yacht, from the looks of it. It was not headed directly toward them, but a crewman atop the vulture's nest might see them at any moment.

She crouched, pulling Kerim down with her. Her fingers became sticky with the dark, drying blood on his arm.

He looked at the blood, lifted his gaze to the ship in the distance, then regarded Çeda once more. *"I cannot leave you."*

She was tempted to ask if he was certain, only her relief was so great she couldn't find the words. "Come," she told him. "We shouldn't linger."

As they headed low and fast toward the cave where the pack had gathered in the shade, she felt Kerim's worry growing. He'd managed to resist the Kings' call thus far, but could he if a Maiden were close and summoned him, or worse, a King? Ahead, Mist was digging in the sand, most likely for a lizard to eat, or to give to Çeda, but stopped when Çeda came near. Her ears perked and her head lifted. Perhaps sensing worry in Çeda even as Çeda felt it in Kerim, Mist returned to the shade of the rocks and lay beside them.

A pack once more, they huddled close, while in the distance the yacht drifted across the horizon. It adjusted course once, and Çeda thought they'd been spotted but, thank the gods, it merely continued in a straight line.

When the sails were nearly lost, Çeda breathed easier, but Mist was still tense. She gave a soft yip, staring at the rocks above them, then huffed and nipped at Çeda's wrist. Wary, Çeda stood and, silent as a scarab, climbed the rocks, gained their flattened top, and crawled to the far lip.

On the sand below, a hundred paces distant, three skiffs huddled behind a cluster of stones. Three women and a man with a long, sandy beard stood nearby. They watched the horizon, where the tips of the yacht's masts could still be seen, wavering in the heat.

Four to man three skiffs? Çeda thought. *There must be more crew.*

The typical minimum was two to a skiff, but given how much gear she saw inside the hulls, likely a dozen had come. The footprints she saw heading away from the ships confirmed her fears.

She'd grown out of practice with feeling for the hearts of those around her. She tried now, clumsily, and realized too late there were others nearby, some working their way around the bulk of the rock she lay upon—

"Stand," came a voice behind her. "Slowly."

She stood and turned to find a woman and a man only a few paces away, both holding shamshirs. Çeda lifted her hands in peace as the stiff wind tugged at their amber thawbs. Their faces were hidden by the veils of their turbans, but Çeda recognized contempt when she saw it.

"Your sword," the woman said. "Carefully." She wore a black turban with thread-of-gold embroidered throughout. The small coins adorning the fringes clinked softly in the wind.

"I am not yours to command," Çeda said, lowering her hands until they were loose at her sides.

"Fool girl," the man said, stepping forward, ready to poke her chest with the tip of his shamshir—a warning meant to draw a bit of blood if Çeda refused to comply. He did it sloppily, betting she'd be cowed, but in this he was sadly mistaken. Before his blade could touch her she spun and slid alongside the path of his swing. He tried to recover, but she was inside his guard now and moving quickly. As he pulled his shamshir back, she gripped the blade near the hilt with one hand, his wrist with the other, and followed his movement. She guided the sword back and up, twisting beneath it and controlling him so that his body effectively blocked any advance by his female companion.

She had more than enough leverage to snap his wrist or dislocate his arm, but she merely flipped him over his extended arm, taking his sword from him in the process.

The woman advanced with a good deal more prudence, but Çeda wasted no time. Gripping the shamshir with both hands, she beat the woman's initial swing up, dodged when the expected downward swing came, and brought her shamshir down across the woman's sword with a mighty two-handed chop. The woman lost her grip on it, and the sword clanged loudly against the stone.

Things were escalating far too quickly, but when the woman made the foolish decision to reach for her lost sword, Çeda had no choice but to hold the man's shamshir against her throat. Thankfully, she took it no further, choosing instead to stand and back away, hands raised.

Without taking her eyes from them, Çeda crouched and picked up the fallen blade. "Who are you?"

It was the woman who answered. "You've no right to come on our land, steal our water, and ask us questions."

After considering that for a moment, Çeda said, "You're right." She flipped both swords, one in either hand, so that she held them by the blade, then held them out. The woman accepted hers cautiously; the man leaned forward and snatched his angrily.

Neither, thankfully, advanced on her.

Çeda pulled the veil from her face and bowed her head to the woman. "My name is Verrain, and I've come from Sharakhai. I lost my skiff to slipsand two weeks ago and have been here ever since, hoping . . ." She waved in the direction of the skiffs beyond the rocks. "Well, hoping someone might come."

Kerim was in the cavern, his fear for Çeda spiking. *By Rhia's grace, remain silent,* she bade him. *Hide deep in the cavern unless the need is great.* He was poised to howl, to come bursting forth from the tunnel's entrance. If that were to happen, blood would flow, and it likely wouldn't stop until many had fed the sands with their lives.

The woman's brows pinched in a frown, but then something caught her attention, and her eyes drifted down toward the cavern's entrance. Çeda risked a glance back. Just entering the swath of shade were a dozen men and women, dressed in similarly pale thawbs and black turbans. A few, like the woman, wore turbans with coins woven into the fabric. Others wore conical helms with patterned scrollwork and a curtain of chainmail along the sides and back. They'd heard the clash of steel, no doubt. Now they'd spotted the wolves and were watching them warily. A few were drawing bows from their backs and stringing them. Three had broken away and were making their way toward the top of the rocks, but when the woman in the thread-of-gold turban held up her hand, they stopped and waited.

Kerim, praise the gods, remained silent as the woman regarded Çeda levelly, thankfully with more curiosity than enmity.

"And the wolves?" she asked.

"They were here when I arrived. We've been sharing the water."

"Then you won't mind if we kill a few?"

"I'd rather you didn't."

The woman considered for several heartbeats before she too removed her veil. Staring back at Çeda was a stern, weatherworn face with blue tattoos marking her cheeks, forehead, and nose. She sheathed her sword and motioned the man to do the same. She kept her right hand on the hilt of her shamshir, however, a warning that in the desert, trust was a commodity bought with truths.

"How does a Blade Maiden find herself in the lands of Tribe Salmük?"

"I'm no Maiden." A simple enough statement, and true. "I stole both the dress and the blade."

"The Maidens are hardly in the business of misplacing their dresses, and even less of losing their blades."

"True, but nor do they complain much when their blood has fed the Great Mother."

The woman's eyebrows rose as she glanced at the man beside her. "You expect me to believe you killed a Blade Maiden?"

"I do." Çeda watched carefully for their reactions, especially the woman's. Çeda had two choices for how to proceed: either to mark herself as an enemy of the Kings or not. Depending on the loyalties of Tribe Salmük, or at least the band gathered around her, she might be choosing wrongly, but she suspected not—the way the woman had reacted to her claim of killing a Maiden had smacked of being impressed.

"Perhaps by now," Çeda went on, "word of a battle in Sharakhai has reached your tents. I took part in it. I fought the Maidens and the Kings."

The woman jutted her chin toward the horizon, where the yacht had disappeared. "That ship was searching for *you*, then?"

Çeda nodded. "They've been chasing me for weeks."

The tattoos at the corners of the woman's eyes pinched as she took in Çeda anew. "You're a scarab?"

A scarab of the Moonless Host, she meant, a soldier in the fight to bring down the Kings. "No," Çeda replied, "but our interests align."

As the woman turned to the man, something changed below. Thorn emitted a low growl, and was moving toward the nearest of the desert folk, a man who held a bow with an arrow nocked and sighted. Çeda whistled sharply, urgently, and thankfully Thorn went silent and slinked away.

The woman took this in, one eyebrow raised. "They were here when you arrived, you said?"

Çeda shrugged. "We've come to an accord."

Now both her eyebrows rose, and she laughed. "I daresay!" She weighed up Çeda for a moment. "You'll remain here." And with that she headed down along the sloped stone, motioning the man to follow.

When they reached the other desert folk, they spoke together for a time, softly enough that the strong wind hid their conversation despite the adichara petal Çeda had taken. The woman was doing most of the talking. Now and again some of them would look up toward her. The man at one point gesticulated wildly to the north—the place where Tribe Salmük was gathered, perhaps? When the conversation died, the woman waved Çeda to approach, and Çeda made her way down to the level stone beyond the cavern entrance, her heart pounding so strongly it was sending Kerim's fear to new heights.

Stay, Çeda said as calmly as she could manage. *All is well.*

She heard his soft moan from the cavern's entrance, but luckily no one else did, mixing as it did with the sigh of the wind.

When Çeda came to a stop before the gathered tribesman, the woman clasped her hands before her and bowed her head, a gesture of peace in the desert, a gesture Çeda quickly mirrored. "My name is Beril," she said, "and you are welcome in our lands. Our shaikh is only a day's sail distant. I hope you'll come to speak with him." She looked Çeda up and down. "I suspect you could use the food, and we could use tales of the city."

"A trade, then?" Çeda asked.

The woman named Beril tilted her head in acknowledgment, but not without a wry smile. "A trade."

Çeda couldn't remain out here with a pack of wolves and live on lizards and beetles forever. Accepting Beril's offer would mean that she would be parted from Kerim, at least temporarily, but it couldn't be helped. She'd spent these weeks in the desert waiting for the dust to settle in the city, using that time to learn more about Mesut's bracelet to free the souls within, but the time had come to move on. She had to return to Sharakhai, and soon. There was so much to do, not the least of which was learning more about the bonds that chained the asirim. In Kerim she had found one who could resist the call of the Kings. Might she find more? Might she be able to help them break their bonds once and for all? It must be so. They'd been weakening for centuries; she just had to find a way to exploit it.

And there was the silver trove to consider, the thing she felt certain her

mother had gone to find the night before she'd been captured and killed by
the Kings. Dardzada, her foster father, had thought it a mirage. In the end,
her mother had too, but Çeda would know the truth of it. She had to try to
retrace her mother's steps on Tauriyat that night.

Lastly, there were the Blade Maidens. She needed allies. And what better
way to gain them than by turning one of the Kings' greatest strengths to her
advantage? There was Zaïde, but the time had come to try to gain more, to
convince others outside the thirteenth tribe that the Kings' story—of the
asirim being holy warriors who'd sacrificed themselves on the night of Beht
Ihman—had always been a grand, sickening ruse.

Still, this was no easy decision. Would Beril's shaikh be friend or foe? In
her time with the Blade Maidens she'd learned much of Shaikh Hişam, the
leader of Tribe Salmük these past thirty years. He was petty and fought the
neighboring tribes fiercely, wielding his control over access to the trading
paths to Malasan like a cudgel. Still, he had no great love for the Kings of
Sharakhai. He likely wouldn't turn her in for ransom, not without hearing
her tale and weighing what she might have to offer his tribe. He might even
supply her with a skiff.

"Very well," Çeda said, "I will gather my things."

And so Çeda did. The desert folk went to the underground cavern and
filled bladders with water. Kerim, blessedly, had retreated deep into the darkness. She could feel his long-quieted anger awakening once more, as if the
presence of strangers had rekindled that most inescapable part of being an
asir: hunger for the blood of mortal man.

You've held it at bay for this long, she told him. *It will keep a while longer.
Stay where you are, Kerim, but be ready to follow once we've left.*

Soon Çeda was led to the skiffs hidden among the rocks. The wolves
followed her for a time, Mist padding ahead of the others, yipping and jumping occasionally as if she wanted to play. Çeda knew that wasn't it, though.
Of course it wasn't.

Çeda scrubbed the fur behind the wolf's ears, then knelt and hugged her,
digging her fingers deep into Mist's gray mane. "We'll see one another again,"
she said, kissing the wolf on the muzzle. Then she whispered, "Thank you for
saving me."

They left soon after, sailing away across the sand, Mist watching long after the other wolves had peeled away. Soon she had shrunk into the distance, becoming lost altogether as clusters of rocks intervened. They sailed for the entire day, the crew strangely silent. They watched the horizon intently, wary of the royal yacht perhaps, or rival tribes.

"I've heard tales of Hişam," Çeda said as they ate flatbread laced with onion and leek. "They've all said he's a good man, a just leader."

Everyone in the skiff stiffened, sending sly glances at one another; all but Beril, who held Çeda's eye with a steady gaze. "Hişam is dead."

Çeda felt as if the sands were shifting beneath her feet. "My tears for your loss," she said, making sure to meet every grim eye turned toward her. Hişam was childless, which might have put the succession of the tribe in question. Did that explain their tenseness? "Who leads your tribe now?"

"You'll see soon enough," Beril replied.

From that point on, the tone of the voyage shifted. Çeda no longer felt like a guest, nor even an interloper on their lands, but a prisoner. Her immediate thought was to run or to fight if necessary—with Kerim, who followed a good distance behind the skiffs, she stood a good chance. But if she were to survive out here in the desert, she needed to know more about the tribes. She would see this man, this shaikh, and see what he was about.

Near nightfall, a cluster of ships seemed to lift along the horizon. They'd gathered by a large outcropping of stone that looked like a chipped axehead sticking out of the sand. As they came closer, groupings of tents were revealed. Three horses were tied to stakes near the largest ship. People moved about. A fire blazed at the center of the camp.

As their skiff approached, Beril motioned to Çeda's belt. "I'll take your sword until you've spoken with our shaikh."

The others watched, ready. What could Çeda do? She'd known they would ask, and yet the idea of giving up River's Daughter, the very symbol of a Blade Maiden, so repulsed her she considered challenging Beril to take it from her. But the shaikh had no reason to do her harm. If she were careful she should be able to gain his trust, a thing that would be impossible were she to resist. So she slipped the sword from her belt, scabbard and all, and handed it to Beril, who nodded sharply, relief clear on her hardened face.

After they'd anchored near the larger ships, Beril entered one of the largest of the tents near the fire, taking Çeda's sword with her. After a time, she stepped out, waved, and Çeda was led toward the tent, accompanied by four of the desert folk. None had hands on weapons, but they watched Çeda carefully from the corners of their eyes.

Many took note of her arrival: men, women, and children, some preparing food, others working the ships. Most stared with mistrust in their eyes. Those who hadn't noticed Çeda, or weren't interested in the new arrival, seemed joyless, burdened, even in the menial tasks of mixing dough for flatbread, grooming horses, or tending to the ships.

"When did your most gracious lord, Hişam, die?" Çeda asked. It was the only explanation she could think of for the strange mood.

The man walking by her side did not reply, he merely led Çeda, along with the others, toward the large tent.

All around them, the hands at work seemed to slow. All eyes turned to her. In the desert, she felt Kerim—a spike of fear burned suddenly inside his heart, mere moments before a hulking mass lumbered out of the tent. He was a beast of a man. A head and a half taller than Çeda. Arms like haunches of meat. Legs like tree trunks. He wore black armor that might once have been fine but was now nicked, rusted in places, torn near one shoulder so that it hung not-quite-right on his meaty frame. His black hair was matted to his forehead and cheeks, framing humorless, deep-set eyes that gave him the look of one of the terrible hyenas, the black laughers, that roamed the desert.

She knew now why the tribe had acted the way it did, and why fear now filled Kerim's heart.

For Onur, the Feasting King, the King of Spears, stood before her, grinning as if he'd just found his next meal.

Chapter 2

FROM A DARK ALLEY in Sharakhai's cramped west end, Emre studied a window across the street, three stories up, where an old man was methodically setting pistachio shells down into a slowly growing pile. His hands would disappear into the shadows of the room, then reappear in a flash of sunlight with fresh shells, the rhythm revealing how deft he was at shelling the nuts.

Or how bloody hungry he is, Emre thought.

Frail Lemi stood behind Emre, leaning his colossal frame against the mudbrick wall behind him. He cracked his knuckles loudly. "Time to go up, Emre?"

"Not yet, Lemi. Quiet down."

"I know. You said. It's just"—he looked up and down the street, a flash of fear showing on a stark face that all too often projected anger and threat and little else. "I hate being out like this," he said. "Feel like a fucking lamb waiting for the slaughter. You know?"

"I know, Lem. I want to make sure we're not walking into a trap."

Frail Lemi hardly seemed to hear him. "I'm no lamb, Emre."

"I know, Lem."

Shifting his weight, Lemi cracked his neck and glared up and down the street. "No fucking lamb."

Emre kept watching the building—its windows, the roofline, the alleys. Not many walked this street in the Shallows, and those who did knew it didn't pay to linger.

It had only been four weeks since the battle at the harbor, a night the entire city now referred to as Beht Savaş, the Night of Endless Swords. Not much time in the grand scheme of things, but Emre was sure the hunt would continue for months, day by day putting more pressure on the resistance known as the Moonless Host.

There wasn't a night that passed where Emre didn't hear of someone new found hung at the gates of Tauriyat, or face-down in the dry bed of the Haddah, or dragged away for an intimate chat with the Confessor King. He was sure one day he'd return to the hovel he shared with Frail Lemi to find a squad of Silver Spears waiting for them, or hear that Macide, leader of the Moonless Host, had been killed, having miraculously, and perhaps foolishly, remained in the city after his father, Ishaq, had returned to the desert.

Two children ran along the street, each waving a dusty green streamer behind them. It made Emre feel foolish. *Is this what it's come to? Quaking at the sight of empty streets? Seeing ghosts in empty doorways?*

"Come on, Lem. Time to speak to the man."

Despite his bravado, Emre felt as if an arrow were being aimed between his shoulder blades as they crossed the street and entered the squat mudbrick building. It made his skin itch. As he passed into shade, and the breeze flowed along the shade-cooled hallway, he shrugged his shoulders in a vain attempt to ease the feeling. It made his skin itch even more—made him feel a bit of a coward to boot.

He turned and groused at Lemi, "Stop stepping on my heels, will you?"

Frail Lemi looked down, confused. He *hadn't* stepped on Emre's heels, but looked chagrined as though he had. "Sorry, Emre. I didn't—"

"Just give me some space. You're breathing down my neck."

"Sorry, Emre."

Emre felt like a jackass, but said nothing as they took the stairs up to the third floor and walked past a dozen doorways. A month ago these doorways would have been open to allow the breeze to blow through, but today they were all covered by rugs or blankets—all but the last, which was their destination.

"Galliu," he said when he reached the open doorway.

Across the room, in a chair beside the window, a wizened old man sat with a pile of pistachios in his lap. With practiced ease, he took one of the pistachios, split it using an empty shell, and popped the pale green nut into his mouth. "Emre," Galliu said, chewing.

As he spoke, he didn't look toward Emre, nor did he look toward the growing pile on the windowsill as he set another pair of empty shells atop it. He was blind, or near enough that it made no difference.

On a pallet in the corner rested a lone boy, twelve, maybe thirteen years old. The rest of the narrow pallets—fifteen in all—lay empty, bedrolls placed neatly at the head of each.

"One?" Emre exclaimed, wondering what Macide was going to say.

The last time Emre had come here, he'd been paying Galliu to gather volunteers to join the Moonless Host. It had been shortly before the Night of Endless Swords, a night that had seen two of the Kings' caches of life-giving elixirs destroyed. Emre himself, along with Macide, Ramahd Amansir, and Meryam, the Queen of Mirea herself, had gone to Eventide, the palace of Kiral, the King of Kings, where they'd destroyed his cache, while their brother and sister scarabs had done the same to the one in Ihsan's palace. The third, Zeheb's, had been found by the forces of the blood mage, Hamzakiir, before the Moonless Host arrived. Hamzakiir's men had stolen the elixirs, so between them they had robbed the Kings of the bulk of their magical draughts while at the same time shifting a good deal of power to Hamzakiir.

It was a disturbing outcome, to say the least. Hamzakiir had posed as an ally to Ishaq and his son Macide, but had soon betrayed their trust, using his power to siphon off much of the support the Moonless Host received from the shaikhs of the desert tribes and other powerful people in Sharakhai. In the days before Hamzakiir's arrival, the Moonless Host had been beset with trouble, but at least its ranks had been filled with optimism. Now, though . . . Emre stared at the boy on the pallet, sizing him up anew. *Is this what we've come to? One lone, brave boy has answered our call?* Leaning against the crumbling brick wall, legs pulled to his chest, the boy looked small and fragile, and that in turn made this whole endeavor feel like a house of sand ready to crumble the moment the desert winds came howling.

Galliu chuckled at Emre's reaction. "You expected an army?"

"I expected more brave souls to stand up."

"Perhaps the souls of this city aren't quite as brave as you thought."

Emre glanced back at Frail Lemi, who merely shrugged. *One*, Emre thought. *One to add to our cause.* "You told them the new reward?"

Galliu waggled his head. "I did, but they might be worried about you paying. The west end's alive with rumors that it's not Macide who has the money, but someone else."

Hamzakiir. He meant Hamzakiir, who was vying for the hearts of those sympathetic to the Moonless Host. Since dawn had risen on the Night of Endless Swords, he'd been working steadily against Ishaq and Macide, slowly driving a wedge between them and their followers—sowing seeds of doubt that they could free the downtrodden in Sharakhai. He'd promised money as well as protection, but unlike Macide, he'd been able to deliver.

Emre dropped ten sylval into Galliu's outstretched palm and said, "Raise the price to one rahl each."

The coins disappeared. "The price of a life in Sharakhai."

"Save your cheap philosophy," Emre said, waving the boy to stand and follow Frail Lemi from the room. "Just see that it's done."

"Of course," Galliu said as he gathered up the last of the nuts and dropped them into a cloth sack between his feet. He'd kept one in his hand, which he split and ate, but then he did something strange. He placed the shell on the windowsill, but it slipped off the edge, a thing he'd been careful never to do.

Until now.

Emre spun around, suddenly wary. From the hallway he heard the clash of a cymbal ringing over and over. It came from the open window as well, the sound rebounding off the mudbrick buildings. It sounded as if it were coming from their building.

Lemi was leaning out of the doorway, looking down the hall. The boy had inched toward him, and when he saw that Lemi wasn't watching he burst into motion, a knife suddenly raised in one hand.

"Lemi!"

Frail Lemi turned in time to see the boy rushing him. He tried to shy away from the knife, but he'd only managed to take one step back when the boy lunged and drove the tip of the knife into Lemi's chest. The next moment, Lemi had grabbed the boy's wrist and wrenched it upward. The boy cried out, and the knife clattered to the floor. Then, in a blur of movement, Lemi lifted him like a sack of flour and drove him down onto the dry, wooden planks. The impact shook the walls. The sound was like the strike of a battering ram. The boy curled up like a fiddlehead as he fought to regain his breath. In that moment, Frail Lemi grabbed the blood-slicked knife.

"No!" the boy gasped. "I had to!"

But that was all he had a chance to say before the knife blurred and landed with a thump over his heart.

He went stiff all over and gripped Frail Lemi's wrist, mouth agape in a silent plea to the gods for kindness in his final moments.

Emre turned on Galliu as he heard the stomp of boots along the hallway. In a flash of anger, he drew his shamshir. "I name you traitor to the Al'afwa Khadar!"

Galliu, who looked strangely pensive, stared straight ahead. "Depends on who you think is leading the Al'afwa Khadar."

Emre felt a white-hot rage burning inside him. He meant Hamzakiir. Galliu, one of Ishaq's oldest soldiers in Sharakhai, had somehow been turned as well. With one swift stroke, Emre swung his sword across Galliu's neck, knocking him back off his chair and onto the dusty floor, blood spurting from the gash. Pools of his blood collected along the dirty floor, turning it the color of a dusty rose.

A woman's voice bellowed along the hall. "In the name of the Kings of Sharakhai, lay down your arms!"

Frail Lemi stood at the door, his sword in hand, blood flowing down his chest. In another man, such blood loss would seriously hinder him, but not Lemi. He stood, ready to fight, his eyes feral as they searched for a way out. Emre moved toward the window to see how many might be waiting below, but the moment he went near it a black arrow streaked into the room. It caught him with a searing burn across his right arm. He'd only just managed to duck away as three more flew in, all from different angles.

Emre shook his head at Frail Lemi, whose eyes hardened. "I'm no fucking lamb, Emre."

"No," Emre said. "Neither am I." He'd rather die than sit with the Confessor King. But what could they do? Both exits were blocked.

The call came again, "Lay down your arms!"

And now Emre could see her, a Maiden in her black fighting dress, veil, and buckler, the ebon blade in her right hand making her look like a revenant come for its due. There were two more behind her, and a line of Silver Spears behind them.

Emre looked to the window, to dying Galliu, to the boy who now lay lifeless. As Frail Lemi engaged the Maiden and the ring of steel made this already small space feel smaller, a grapnel swung up and hooked over the windowsill. Pistachio shells scattered everywhere. Drawing his knife, Emre rushed forward, careful to stay out of sight of the bowmen. He took a chance, trying to reach out and cut the rope, but the moment he did, an arrow punched through the meat of his forearm, sinking into the wood of the window frame.

Gritting his teeth against the pain, he gripped the shaft of the arrow and pulled up in a sharp, violent arc. The shaft snapped as the rope was cut. Blood streamed down his arm as more arrows thudded into the floor. He'd seen in that split moment how many there were outside: a pair of Maidens and a dozen Silver Spears.

He sat near the window, his back against the wall. With a terrible spasm of pain he yanked what remained of the arrow shaft free of his arm. He shut his eyes as the pain peaked. When he opened them once more, he noticed the state of disrepair in the corner of the room, how badly the bricks were crumbling, and a mad, desperate thought occurred to him.

Rising to a crouch, he shifted closer to the door. Only an arm's reach away, Frail Lemi bellowed with rage as his sword flashed, defending against the Maiden's incredible speed. Emre ignored the fight and ran at the wall, powering one shoulder against it.

Something crunched in his shoulder. Bits of the mudbrick flaked away, but the wall held.

Frail Lemi, retreating into the room, glanced back. His eyes went wide like a child who'd been shown a card trick for the first time. In unspoken concert, he nodded as Emre picked up one of the heavy wooden pallets. Emre's arm burned from the bloody arrow wound, and his shoulder felt as though the bones were being pulverized, but he managed to lift the pallet and run toward the open doorway as Frail Lemi launched three hard, precise blows against the Maiden's defenses and backed away.

Emre drove forward with the pallet, shoving it hard against the Blade Maiden as she tried to enter the room. She was caught off guard, forced back by the massive hunk of wood driving toward her. She braced herself, but too late, Emre shoved her into the hall, crowding those behind her as well.

As Emre picked up his fallen sword, Frail Lemi drove into the wall like a charging akhala stallion. The entire face of the wall caved inward, a wooden beam cracking in two as Frail Lemi, bricks, and a cloud of dust, broke through to a small living space on the opposite side. The support above the wall gave a bit, and more bricks crumbled down into both rooms.

From the floor above, the muffled sound of an old woman's voice shouting in Kundhunese filtered down. A family of five cowered in the room beyond, staring wide-eyed at Frail Lemi and the hole in the wall of their one-room home.

As the Maiden threw the pallet aside and made for him, Emre charged another of the exposed wooden supports. It was dry as bone, and hardly thicker than his arm. He rammed it with his good shoulder, praying to Rhia for kindness.

As the Maiden sliced an arc through the air with her ebon blade, Emre met the support. It splintered as he crashed into it. And the floor above began to rain down.

The Maiden tried to follow, tried to get beyond the falling debris to reach Emre, but Frail Lemi had stood and picked up a heavy iron cooking pot. He swung it by the handle and brought it down with all his might against the Maiden's head. She tried to roll away, but it caught her along the top of her skull with a crunch that was swallowed by the growing stream of debris falling from the floors above.

Emre headed for the open doorway, but Frail Lemi was just standing there, staring at the Maiden's form, his eyes afire.

"Quickly!" Emre hissed, grabbing Frail Lemi's arm and pulling him toward the open doorway. "Lemi, quick, or we're both dead!"

He wasn't sure Frail Lemi had heard him, but a moment later, Lemi's eyes turned to his. The fire in them faded a bit, and he looked around at the ruin they'd created. Then a bit of fear returned, and they sped off, into the hall, following a rush of fleeing men and women and children. Most probably didn't know what they were running from. Few bothered to look back. They just ran, sensing that to remain would be to die. The Shallows had a way of instilling such instincts.

When they came to a set of stairs, Frail Lemi was about to follow the rush, but Emre grabbed his arm. "This way," he said, guiding him to a nearby room. It had a small stove at its center with warm bread spread around it, abandoned in the panic. On the far side of the room was a window and beyond, a space only wide enough for a man to slip along sideways—a victim of the slapdash planning that plagued the Shallows. They were three stories up, but the closeness of the buildings was an asset here. Emre slipped into the gap, one foot on the wall ahead of him, his back against the opposite wall. Bracing himself between the two, he slid slowly down, scraping painfully at times in his haste to reach solid ground.

Frail Lemi came after. When they struck dirt, they sidled quickly along, then squeezed themselves through the narrow gap at the end to reach one of the hundreds of nondescript alleys in the Shallows.

They ran, farther and farther away. The more distance they put between themselves and Galliu's building, though, the more disconsolate Frail Lemi became.

"He was just a kid, Emre. Why'd he have to take a knife to me like that?"

"I don't know, Lem. Things are changing in the city."

Frail Lemi, coated in both his blood and the boy's, didn't seem to hear him. "He was just a fucking kid."

Chapter 3

IN THE QAIMIRI EMBASSY HOUSE, a knock came at Ramahd Amansir's door. "Come," he called.

As the heavy, carved door groaned inward, Ramahd stopped writing. He looked up to find not a servant, as he'd expected, but Amaryllis.

It was winter moving into spring in the desert. The city had been cool, even cold at times, but you wouldn't know it from looking at her. She was wearing the sort of clothes a west-end harlot might wear: a slit skirt that revealed her shapely legs well past her knees whenever she moved, and a sleeveless shirt she'd tied around her waist to reveal her belly and accentuate the curves of her breasts. Both garments were dyed a vibrant mix of orange and ruby red, a match for the dozen ribbons she'd braided into her hair. Together the clothes and the ribbons were a perfect contrast to her dark hair, which cascaded down past her shoulders in curly locks, accentuating a look that was already sultry.

"Can we talk?" she asked.

"Is it important?"

"It's about Tiron."

Ramahd immediately put his quill back in its inkwell. "You found him?"

She took one of the two chairs by the open patio doors behind him. The chair was so large, and Amaryllis so relaxed as she pulled one foot onto the seat, that she looked like a rag doll, tossed there and forgotten. "I found him."

Ramahd joined her in the sunlight, which warmed him to the point of discomfort. "Where?"

"In the Shallows. A drug den owned by a woman known as the Widow." The look that had settled over Amaryllis was one of regret or despair. Perhaps it was both. "He's deep into the reek. He won't last a fortnight if he stays there."

"Did you speak to him?"

"I tried, but he just lay there, staring at the shisha." Amaryllis paused, lips curling in disgust as she gazed through him. "It was a sty, Ramahd. People everywhere, naked, filthy. It smelled like a charnel for the damned."

"Is he still there?"

Amaryllis shrugged. "Probably. He likely paid them ahead so that they'd keep him there, filled with the drug until the coin ran out."

Ramahd pinched the bridge of his nose, remembering the Tiron of old. He'd always been dour, but strong as steel, the sort of man Ramahd depended on in the desert, so far from home. Whatever burden Ramahd had given him, he'd shouldered it and borne it silently.

Until they'd gone to King Kiral's palace, Eventide, on the Night of Endless Swords. That was the night he and Meryam, disguised as Amaryllis, had gone with Tiron, his cousin, Luken, and eleven others to destroy King Kiral's cache of elixirs hidden beneath Eventide. Luken had fallen, ravaged by a demon made from the stuff of nightmares—skinless body, eyeless head, massive, sweeping horns. Meryam, desperate, had fed on Luken's heart and used the power gained to save them all.

Tiron was a hard man, but Luken had been like a brother to him. *Even the hardest men can become brittle in ways that cannot be seen.* His grief weighed heavily, and he finally broke, turning to black lotus and embracing it like a newfound lover. Though he'd tried to hide his growing dependence on it, it quickly became an open secret. Everyone in the embassy house knew, and Ramahd had looked the other way, hoping it would help Tiron forget, that he'd find the will to stop on his own. But after watching him stumble down a set of stairs and hardly notice the pain, Ramahd had confronted him. Tiron grew angry. Angrier than Ramahd had seen him in years. He denied it all, and for a time things had improved, but then Tiron began staying in the city overnight. He'd claimed it was for a girl. A seamstress who created beautiful embroidery. He even brought a few pieces to show Ramahd.

A night here or there turned into days away, and it soon became clear Tiron had found a shisha den somewhere in the city. Ramahd demanded that it stop. Their argument had shaken the walls, and Tiron had stormed out. He hadn't been seen since. That had been two weeks ago.

Ramahd had sent Amaryllis and others to find him—even making inquiries himself when he found the time—but they'd had no word of him until today.

Ramahd glanced at his desk, at the half-finished letter sitting atop the leather blotter. He was working to secure Meryam's power in Qaimir against those who wished for any other to sit the throne. He'd been working to secure her power here in Sharakhai as well. Neither was certain. The work was important. He had a dozen more letters to write before a caravan left for Qaimir in the morning.

But Tiron was important too.

"Let's go and get him."

Amaryllis nodded, and the harried look on her face eased. They were heading for the door when another knock came. The door opened before Ramahd had a chance to reply, and in strode Basilio, the heavyset lord who was Qaimir's primary ambassador in Sharakhai.

Basilio's round face was blotchy, as if he'd sprinted up the stairs. *He looks scared,* Ramahd thought.

Basilio took out a kerchief and patted his forehead dry. "You must come with me."

"It will have to wait for my return."

"Your *queen* requests your presence."

"Tell the queen it is important. She'll understand."

"She most certainly will not."

Ramahd shoved past him.

"Lord Amansir!" Basilio groused. "A messenger has arrived from Eventide. Our queen's presence has been requested and she's of a mind to attend and . . ."

Ramahd turned. "What?"

Basilio straightened himself up. "For some reason"—he pulled his vest down to cover more of his belly—"she requested that *you* attend her rather than me."

Worms churned inside Ramahd's gut. They always did when the precariousness of Meryam's position here in Sharakhai struck him. She wanted to accept an invitation from Kiral, the King of Kings? Gods, if only she'd left the day after the Night of Endless Swords, as Ramahd had bade her. The Kings might have lost four of their number—Azad, Külaşan, Yusam, and Mesut—but they were still more dangerous than a pit of scorpions. Better for Meryam to deal with them from the safety of Almadan. However often she might insist that remaining in the Amber City would lead to better terms, dealing with the Kings face-to-face was an act of tempting fate, pure and simple.

Amaryllis looked as nervous as Ramahd felt. Basilio, his gaze swinging between the two of them, noticed. "Will you not tell me what happened that night?"

It was a rare bit of vulnerability from Basilio, who was always trying to push Ramahd, to exert his authority and ensure that *he* was the queen's most trusted servant. Were they back in Qaimir, Ramahd might have relented and told how he and Meryam had joined forces with the Moonless Host, how they'd stolen into Eventide, and destroyed the cache of glowing blue elixirs that gave the Kings their long life. But they *weren't* in Qaimir, and the danger of gossip was simply too great.

"Take Cicio and Vrago with you," Ramahd said to Amaryllis. "Get Tiron. Take him to the safe house near the pits. I'll come when I'm able."

Amaryllis nodded and left. Basilio, meanwhile, puffed himself up like a pompous peacock. "Keep your secrets then, but I deserve to know why King Kiral wishes to speak with Queen Meryam."

"I don't know, Basilio." Ramahd sniffed, somewhat enjoying the affronted look on Basilio's blotchy face. "But rest assured, the queen will tell you at the appropriate time."

He turned toward Meryam's apartments, but Basilio grabbed his elbow. Rather than do something rash, Ramahd slowed his pace, and when it became clear Basilio wouldn't let him go, he stopped and turned.

When Basilio spoke, it was nearly a whisper. "You know how tenuous things have become in Almadan. I'm doing all I can to keep the hounds at bay. But if we are in danger because the two of you—"

"Our kingdom stands on the doorstep of the desert, Basilio. There is always danger."

"You know very well what I mean."

Ramahd stepped forward until the two of them were chest-to-chest. "And *you* know that to tell you more could endanger you, me, our queen, and the entire kingdom. So keep your bloody questions to yourself and be satisfied with what the queen gives you."

If Basilio's face had been blotchy before, it was a field of red now. To his credit, though, he didn't back away.

He's desperate, Ramahd thought. *I really do need to focus on what's happening back home, and so does Meryam. Soon,* he promised himself, and left Basilio fuming in the hall.

He found Meryam in the coach yard behind the embassy house. He climbed inside the waiting coach and sat across from her as it lurched into motion. With the clop of the horses' hooves mixing with the spray of gravel, Ramahd leaned back into the padded bench. Meryam was propped in the corner of the bench opposite him, wearing a queen's raiment: a stunning copper dress that flared around her hips, hiding to some degree the fragility of her frame beneath.

"You're shaking again," Ramahd said.

Meryam licked her lips, pulling herself taller as a look of embarrassment flashed across her face. "I'll master it ere we sit before the King of Kings."

Ramahd raised his right hand, where he wore a ring with a sharp needle that could be used to draw blood. "Have you need?"

She shook her head, denying his offer even as her shivering became more pronounced. "It cannot be risked. Even after all this time, I'm still not sure how much Kiral can sense of the red ways."

"Some brandy, then." He'd made sure her carriage was always stocked with several bottles of spirits.

"I'd need to be drunk for it to have any effect."

"Perhaps drunk would be better."

"And perhaps a brawling mule would be better than the pestering jackdaw

I find sitting before me." She closed her eyes and tilted her head back until it rested on the bench. "I said I will control it."

Her sharpness had everything to do with how tenuous her position was, but it made the sting no less easy to stomach, not after unrelenting weeks of it.

The coach wound its way higher along the mountainside. They passed palace after palace, and Ramahd wondered at it. Tauriyat had both the look and the feel of power, as if the mountain were made from it. These palaces had stood for well over five hundred years. Together they represented a concentration of power neither the desert nor the four kingdoms surrounding it had ever seen. The Kings were no fools. They used that power to their advantage, negotiating favorable trade agreements, controlling the flow of culture, food, and literature through those accords, allowing only what they'd expressly approved to move from place to place.

Four Kings were dead—Azad, Külaşan, Yusam, and Mesut. To anyone standing in the streets of Sharakhai, the House of Kings would appear as strong as it ever had, but Ramahd knew better. It was a house ready to crumble, now that they'd been robbed of their immortality. How long would the Kings last? Would they age like normal men? Or would they wither away until they looked like the asirim, their centuries of cheating the lord of all things catching up to them in a matter of weeks or months?

Up and up they went. From this vantage the city looked like a grand carpet, an impossibly complicated weave that brought together people from thousands of leagues distant. At last, the wagon rumbled over the drawbridge to Eventide and the city was lost. They pulled around the large circle before the palace doors, where servants in bright finery rushed to welcome them. He and Meryam were led into the palace and up several flights of stairs, an arduous task given how slowly Meryam climbed. She refused all offers of help, though, her face grim. To Ramahd's growing awe, the quivering of her body, which had become so bad he'd nearly asked her to return to the embassy house and reschedule this for another day, had all but vanished.

Your will cannot overcome your failing body forever, Ramahd thought. He could already hear her biting reply. *It can, Ramahd Amansir, for there is work yet to do.*

They reached a grand audience hall, a space made up of blue-veined, marble pillars, of niches filled with stark, stiff-backed statues, of arched domes intricately sculpted. At the far end of the hall, across a sea of patterned, mosaic flooring, sat an empty throne on a daïs. An ancient woman with a sour face stood next to it. The woman was crooked with age. She moved with obvious difficulty as she took three steps down to stand below the throne but still above Ramahd and Meryam.

This was Esmirah, Kiral's daughter and his vizira, a former Blade Maiden. She'd risen to warden, then first warden, then served as a Matron for nearly two decades before being summoned to stand by Kiral's side as his most trusted servant.

"The King will see you shortly," she said as Meryam and Ramahd came to a halt before her and bowed their heads.

She shuffled off toward the door in the corner of the room. As it clicked shut behind her, the sound echoed into the cavernous space, somehow making the space seem larger than it had moments ago. A long bout of waiting followed, and Meryam's quivering returned. She was letting down her guard while they were unobserved, but it became so bad Ramahd took a step toward the line of chairs resting against the nearby wall, prepared to move one so that Meryam could rest.

"No," Meryam said softly. "This is a test, and there will be more to come. Stay where you are, and be wary."

Esmirah returned almost a half-turn later. Meryam's shaking vanished as the imposing form of King Kiral, a man who stood nearly a head taller than Ramahd, entered the room behind his vizira. Standing before his throne, he looked like one of the first men; regal, imposing, even dangerous, with flinty eyes, tightly shorn hair, and a pockmarked face.

When Esmirah bowed and left, Kiral gave Meryam a gesture that could barely be called a nod. "Queen Meryam shan Aldouan, you are well met." He stared at Ramahd as if he were little more than a nuisance. "As are you, Lord Amansir."

"My Lord King," Meryam replied.

Kiral's crown glinted as he sat on his throne, then he spoke in a voice that filled the hall. "It has been some time since we've spoken. It's past time we rectify that, don't you agree?"

"Of that there can be no doubt." Meryam smiled, giving him a pleasant nod. "But forgive me, my Lord King, I don't know that we've ever spoken." Her voice was loud. Strong. No trace of her tremulous tone remained.

"I meant our two kingdoms," Kiral replied easily.

"Ah, of course. But then I wonder, why haven't more of the Kings been summoned? We've always dealt with Ihsan. I'm sure he'd prove invaluable now."

"There will be time to involve Ihsan, after you and I have come to an understanding."

The smile that stole over Meryam's skeletal face was now tinged with a hint of mischief. "Well, *now* we're getting somewhere. On what matter does the King of Kings wish to come to an *understanding* with the Queen of Qaimir?"

"Why don't we begin with your father? How did he die?"

If Meryam was surprised by this, she didn't show it. "You are blunt."

"I've little enough time for many things in my life, let alone niceties. I've read the letter you sent us. I know you told Ihsan your father wished to sail the seas of the Great Shangazi. That you were waylaid by pirates. That your ship was taken and the two of you left for dead." Kiral sat taller in his chair, as if he'd just been insulted. "I would like the true story."

It was a moment before Meryam spoke. It looked as if she was considering how much to share, and how to say it, but Ramahd could tell she was suffering from her condition. Lack of sustenance. Lack of aught but wine and blood. And yet for all his inside knowledge, *he* could hardly tell and was sure Kiral wouldn't see what lay behind Meryam's odd pause. But as he waited for Meryam to speak, he saw how irritated Kiral was becoming. "I will tell you, King of Kings," Meryam finally said, "and then I will make a request. Something you will grant me without hesitation, I suspect."

Kiral looked bored. "Go on."

"You saw the state of my father's body." When Kiral nodded with a tiny movement, as if assent were some precious commodity, Meryam went on. "It was done by the ehrekh known as Guhldrathen. My father was an offering, a way to appease the beast and make it renounce its hunt for the man who had convinced it generations ago to bargain away its power. Do you know who that was?"

To Ramahd's surprise, there was a hunger in Kiral's deep voice as he gave Meryam the name she wanted to hear. "Hamzakiir."

"Hamzakiir," she echoed in satisfaction, "the man the Moonless Host hoped to use for their own benefit, the man *we* stole from them after they raised him from his grave."

"You admit it, then."

"To you, yes." The implication was clear, that she didn't wish for the story to go beyond these walls.

"Name your purpose, then. Why did you seize him?"

"He was about to become a tool of Macide Ishaq'ava and his father, men you and I both despise. It was something we couldn't allow."

"You could have come to us."

She bowed her head, showing just the right amount of contrition. "In hindsight, I would certainly have done so, but Hamzakiir had much to answer for in Qaimir. Now he has even more."

Kiral seemed pleased enough with that answer. "Go on."

She did. She told Kiral how they'd wrested Hamzakiir from the Moonless Host, how they'd returned to Qaimir, how Hamzakiir had bested her and inveigled his way into her mind. The journey to Almadan and the desert beyond was filled with regret, but none stronger than having lost Dana'il, his most trusted man, taken by his own knife in Black Swan Tower after Hamzakiir had found him less than useful.

Then Meryam came to the part of the tale Kiral seemed most eager to hear: Hamzakiir leaving them in the desert for Guhldrathen to find. Hamzakiir had meant all three of them, King Aldouan, Meryam, and Ramahd, as offerings, but it was somewhat sated after devouring Aldouan's heart, and they'd managed to strike a new bargain for their freedom: Çeda's blood if they failed to deliver Hamzakiir.

Ramahd felt his cheeks redden at the memory. *And I sealed the bargain with my own blood.* How foolish it seemed now. The memory of Guhldrathen's hot tongue lapping blood from his fingers made him wonder if the hunger inside him was from simple physical need or from the spell Guhldrathen had worked on him in those moments. He shook the thoughts away as Meryam concluded her tale.

"Desert voyages have not been kind to you and yours." Kiral gave a know-ing smile, which Ramahd wished he could strike from his face.

Meryam stared back, a fire in her eyes. "Nor have the scarabs been kind to Sharakhai."

"The Moonless Host are dying like lambs in the desert."

"Because you've had help," Meryam said.

"Their days were always numbered."

Meryam made a show of looking around the room. "Let us be blunt, my King. Sharakhai suffered greatly on the Night of Endless Swords, and we both know Hamzakiir's betrayal is what has weakened the Host. With his power, influence, and charm, by showing how little Macide accomplished over the years, he has won many of them to his side. You have been hounding the re-mains of the old order since the battle in the harbor, taking what Hamzakiir is willingly giving. But things are about to change again, are they not?"

"That depends on a great many things."

"Such as what happens on your eastern border with Malasan. And your northern with Mirea." Meryam's voice had grown stronger; she was a power to be reckoned with, every bit Kiral's equal. "Such as what Hamzakiir has in store for you all when the Kings grow tired of picking at the bones of the old order."

Kiral had been indifferent, as if this were merely one more burden in his day. But now he leaned forward with the look of a falcon that had just spot-ted a viper slithering toward its nest across the sand. "You said you had a request."

"I do, my King. Do Qaimir the honor of taking this burden from your shoulders. Allow Ramahd and me to hunt Hamzakiir, unfettered, in the city and the desert beyond, wherever his trail might lead us."

Kiral's eyes narrowed, as if this were the last thing he'd expected. "And in return?"

"You will give me Malasan."

A pause. "What did you say?"

"Malasan gathers for war," Meryam replied easily.

"And if they strike, Sharakhai will drive them back across the mountains."

"But why stop there? Why not sweep well beyond the mountains? Only the threat from the other kingdoms holds you back." Meryam clasped her hands tightly. "But were Sharakhai and Qaimir to combine efforts"—her voice dropped to a whisper, and it was all the more chilling for it—"not an army in the world could stand against us. That is what I propose, oh King of Kings. Let us bait those who stand on your doorstep, waiting for you to stumble. Let us draw Mirea and Malasan out. Let us run roughshod over them when they do. And then there will be more than enough to divide between our nations. I humbly request all lands of Malasan we might take, while Sharakhai takes Mirea."

Kiral spent nearly as much time pondering this as Meryam had done. And then in a burst of movement he stood, staring down at Meryam and Ramahd with the look of a mad god. Ramahd was certain Meryam had made a terrible mistake, but when Kiral spoke, he said, "Begin your hunt." He turned and strode toward the door in the corner. "When you've fed Hamzakiir's body to the ehrekh, you shall have your union."

The door boomed shut behind him, echoing into the room. No sooner had the sound faded than Meryam collapsed to the floor. Ramahd rushed forward, cringing as her cheek slapped against the marble.

"Meryam," he whispered, shaking her.

She didn't respond. Her eyes were heavy, her breath coming sharply as if she were in the throes of sickness. "Gods, Meryam." Ramahd took the ring from his finger and used it to pierce his wrist. He held it before Meryam's mouth, worried that Kiral would return at any moment. There was nothing for it, though. After a speech like that, there could be no showing weakness like this. And they certainly couldn't flaunt her ability to use blood magic before the King or anyone else in Eventide.

The blood trickled along Meryam's lips, dripped down to the floor, creating bright red patterns on the polished white and marble tiles. He pressed the wound to her mouth. "Drink, damn you."

Finally, she did. A swipe of her tongue at first, then a suck from the wound. And then she was holding Ramahd's wrist, pressing her warm lips tight against his bleeding flesh. More and more she took, but he refused to let it go too far and ripped his arm away despite the strength that had already returned to her.

Meryam's nostrils flared. Her eyes took in the throne room, as if she hadn't truly seen it until now. "Clean it," she said as she made it to her feet.

Ramahd used his dark sleeves to wipe up the blood, even the little that had slipped between the tiles. Meryam was licking her lips. Ramahd wiped blood away from her chin and cheek until they were both satisfied that they'd left no evidence.

Then, a lord of Qaimir, bloodied by his own choice, and his queen, giddy with the power he'd granted her, left Eventide.

Chapter 4

HIGH IN KING SUKRU'S PALACE, Davud stood before a tall shelf in the room that had been his since he escaped from the horrors of Ishmantep. Bandages, ointments, salves, and other medicinals were stacked along the shelves, all of the highest quality. Many an apothecary in Sharakhai would be proud of such an assortment. It would likely last months and provide care for dozens of patients. Here, it was intended for only one.

Davud took down a roll of bandages and a half-empty jar of thick salve and walked toward the bed at the center of the room, where a woman lay covered from the waist down in a light blanket. The late morning sun was slanting in through the open windows to his right. A gentle wind tugged at the long curtains, throwing shadows across the brilliant marble floor, the ivory blankets, and the still woman, who was wrapped in layers of tightly rolled bandages.

Setting the bandages and salve down, he looked to the man sitting near the door, who watched Davud placidly, as he had every day of the seven weeks since Davud's arrival. He was Davud's primary watchdog, a soldier, Davud supposed, a stocky man twenty years Davud's senior. He had a day's growth of stubble and piercing blue eyes. Most of the guards who patrolled the palace were Silver Spears, sometimes Blade Maidens. This man was different. He was a foreigner, with lighter skin and a sharp nose. Malasani, perhaps. He wore fitted leather armor most of the time, and a hooded cloak when they went outdoors. He was special, though in what way, and why he'd been chosen to watch Davud, was unclear.

"Are you ready to tell me your name yet?" Davud asked.

The man sniffed. The chair beneath him creaked loudly as he uncrossed his legs and put both feet on the floor. "Never you fucking mind. That's my name."

The same answer, more or less, he'd given Davud every day. "I heard one of the other Spears called you Zahndrethus yesterday."

The man glowered. "So why'd you bloody ask?"

"Zahndrethus—"

The man rolled his eyes, his bushy eyebrows pinching menacingly. "Nalamae's teats, call me Zahndr if you're going to call me anything."

"Zahndr. You've seen me do this a hundred times. There's no danger. Couldn't you give her some privacy"—he motioned to the woman lying on the bed before him—"just until I'm done?"

Zahndr stared around wide-eyed, as if he were shocked at his own boorishness, then somehow sketched an elaborate bow while remaining seated. "Why, most *certainly*, my good lord. And when you're done would you like me to fix you some tea and rub your feet?"

"It's for her benefit, not mine."

"Oh?" He made a show of looking over Davud's shoulder. "Well, near as I can tell, she doesn't care. So get on with it."

Davud heaved a sigh. He and Anila had been watched since the moment they'd arrived. What was there to do but suffer it until the Kings came to trust him?

"Anila?" he said softly. The ends of the heavy curtains flapped and scuffed over the floor. "It's time to change your bandages." She didn't stir, nor did she make a move to stop him as he pulled her up to a sitting position. She remained still while Davud, shielding her as best he could from Zahndr's view, began to unwrap the bandages.

Around her head he went, revealing a bald scalp. Her skin, once a healthy copper hue, was darkened—not like the asirim's skin, which was a deep, deep brown, but more a mottled gray. And where once her skin had been smooth and supple, it was now uneven, dry as a sun-cracked riverbed, and nearly as hard.

In the weeks after the devastating events in Ishmantep, where they'd chased the blood mage, Hamzakiir, Davud had hoped her skin would return to normal. Every night he'd prayed to Yerinde to return some of Anila's beauty to her, or sometimes to Rhia that she might be made anew, as the goddess was each new moon. In one of his low moments, he'd even prayed to Bakhi to take her life that she might be granted a new one in the farther fields. He'd convinced himself that if Anila could speak, she would ask to be done with this remnant of a life. Why else had she been silent since the fire that Davud had managed to snuff using blood magic, at the terrible cost of Anila's body?

Over the days that followed he'd been ashamed by the very thought—that he'd considered making this choice for her, and worse, that he'd wondered if he ought to take matters into his own hands.

He continued to unwrap the bandage, tugging it when necessary, wincing at the pain it might cause. He did her arms next, and then, after lifting her arms up, a position she held without comment, unwrapped the one around her chest. As always, he felt supremely conscious of her privacy, of the embarrassment she might be feeling, even if it was masked in silence. The Matrons had asked him if he would rather they do this for him, but he'd only accepted their help for the first few times, so he could learn how to properly tend to her needs. He'd done it every time since. This was his burden. *He'd* done this to her, and he would help her as much as he was able, at least until she was well enough to return to her family's estate in Goldenhill.

The bandages removed, he proceeded to rough her skin with a brush made from the ridge hair of a bone crusher. Anila's eyes reddened, her breath quickened, and tears began to stream down her cheeks. Davud continued to work methodically. The faster he moved, the sooner her pain would end. But he did whisper, "I'm sorry," softly enough that Zahndr wouldn't hear. He knew he said it too often, knew that if Anila could speak she'd most likely scream for him to stop saying it, but the words came practically unbidden. Silent, Anila kept her gaze focused squarely on the rough stone wall.

He brushed all of her exposed skin, even around her face and ears, moving on from each section only after her skin had taken on a rougher, flakier appearance. When he was done, he set the brush down and began peeling. Like dried, sunburnt skin, swaths of it came off at once to reveal dark, shining, indigo skin. *Snakeskin,* Davud remembered thinking the first time it had happened. *The gods have given her snakeskin.*

He buried the thoughts and continued, trying to minimize Anila's discomfort and exposure. Her tears continued, twin rivulets glistening on the black skin of her cheeks. She became cold as the old skin came off every few weeks—indeed, she was starting to shiver already—but he didn't skimp on the final step, which was to clean her with a wet cloth.

When he was done, her skin *gleamed.*

Like a black mamba. Like one of Goezhen's children.

Not for the first time, Davud wished he could speak to Master Amalos about all this. He'd been devastated to learn of his old master's death. Murdered in the tunnels below the city, he'd been told. He missed the man's calm intellect, his ability to reason through problems rather than become frustrated by them. It was something Davud could use more of; his guilt over Anila's injuries was constantly clouding his judgment.

Taking up the glass jar, he rubbed salve over her arms, chest, and back, and finished by wrapping her in fresh bandages. After laying her back down, he repeated the entire process on her legs and pelvis. "They say you'll be done soon enough," Davud said softly as he spread the salve. "That you'll have healed. You can return to your family or, if you wish, remain here with me. The steward said it would be allowed as long as I'm a guest of the Kings."

Just how long that would be, his remaining here as a *guest,* Davud had no idea. The Kings knew he was a blood mage, knew that he'd been given some small amount of training by Hamzakiir. Surely they'd suspected Davud was one of his agents. They might *still* suspect that, despite all Davud had said to convince them otherwise.

The fates will decide, Davud told himself while finishing with her calves and feet. *I'll spend no more sleepless nights wondering if the Kings have decided to murder me.*

In truth, he'd spent little time wondering what the future held. He wanted to make sure Anila was well cared for. There was time enough to worry about his own needs after that, and when she was healed, she would want to return to Goldenhill, not remain in the House of Kings, but in all honesty he couldn't say what her *family* would want. He'd been present the first time her mother and sister had visited. Her mother had been horrified by her daughter's reptilian skin. She'd taken Davud away to speak with him, grateful he'd been there to tell her what had befallen her daughter.

"Has she been cursed?" she'd asked bluntly near the end of their conversation.

What could Davud say? *Of course she's been cursed. And all because of me.*

"I couldn't say," he remembered replying. "Better to speak to a priest than me."

"Which, though?"

It was an echo of his own fears, that cruel Goezhen had touched her.

"Best to begin at Bakhi's," he'd replied.

She'd visited twice more. Both times, whatever small glimmer of hope she had in her eyes had been snuffed not only by Anila's state, but her daughter's cold indifference—to her, to Davud, to the world around her. She hadn't returned. Anila's sister hadn't deigned to come again, and her father had *never* come, perhaps finding himself unable to stand before his daughter after the strange reports brought to him by his wife. Part of Davud wanted him to visit so he could call the man a bloody coward to his face, but another part wanted him there for Anila.

A knock came at the door. Zahndr opened it, and in swept a woman in white robes. After giving Davud a perfunctory nod, the Matron, a terse, middle-aged woman named Kaelira, took in the state of the room. She looked, as always, as if she were the palace steward and had personally assigned Davud to ensure the space was immaculate.

"King Sukru is on the way." She said it so abruptly, and with so little warmth, that it took Davud a moment to understand.

"King Sukru? But why would he—"

She moved to the bedside and inspected Anila's bandages carefully. She might have been pleased—had she not been, Davud would have heard about it—but you wouldn't know it from the sour look on her face. "It isn't yours to question the Kings, though I deem it probable he wishes to speak of your time with the traitor, Hamzakiir." Moving to the same shelf where Davud had taken up the salve, she retrieved a bottle filled with lilac-colored liquid, which she poured into a teapot with a long, thin spout.

Taking the teapot, she returned to Anila's bed and trickled the distillation over the bandages—to hasten the formation of new, healthy skin, she'd told

Davud weeks ago, though what help it might be providing, he had no idea. No matter what they did—debriding it with brushes, applying the salve to her skin, and a half-dozen different distillations to her bandages over the course of her weeks here—her skin retained its midnight hue, its strange, snakeskin feel.

"When will he—"

"Presently," said a hoary voice from the door.

Davud turned and saw a crooked man dressed in curled leather slippers and a simple black khalat. Simple for a King, that is.

Both Kaelira and Davud bowed, but King Sukru waved the formalities away.

Behind him, a girl with pigtails stuck her head in the room. "Leave us, Kaelira. Zahndrethus, you as well. And take Bela with you."

"Of course, Excellence." And they left, Zahndr guiding the girl by the shoulder and Kaelira closing the door behind her.

"Infernal girl," Sukru said under his breath. As he shuffled closer to the bed, his eyes turned on Anila. "Well, well . . . The burned one I've heard so much about."

"She wasn't burned," Davud said. "She was—"

"I know," Sukru said, his small eyes narrowing. "Drawn thin like thread from wool in your attempt at quelling the flames in Ishmantep."

Drawn thin. Like thread from wool. He'd never heard it described as such. But there was some truth to it. Her body had suffered the effects, but it was Davud's drawing on her soul that had caused it.

As Sukru reached the bedside, Anila gave no sign she'd noticed them. She stared at the ceiling, blinking every so often. The King picked up one hand, examined her fingernails carefully. "She eats?"

"Yes," Davud replied, feeling awkward standing so close to a King.

"Does she soil herself?" Setting her hand down, Sukru drew a short knife from inside his left sleeve, the sort cooks used to pare apples and the like, then tugged back the bandaged covering Anila's shoulder.

"No. She uses the pot we bring for her."

Sukru lifted his head and scowled at Davud. "But she does not speak?" He returned to his examination of her shoulder. After bringing his eyes close and squinting, he brought the blade close and scraped it along Anila's scaly skin. He did so lightly at first, then in stronger, longer waves. Anila's eyes pinched. Then they began to redden. She winced with every stroke of the blade.

"Please, my Lord King," Davud said, "there's no need for that."

He turned his beady eyes on Davud. "I asked you a question."

"No. She hasn't spoken since the incident."

"Incident . . ." A low rumble of a laugh escaped Sukru. "Tell me about it, boy. This *incident*."

Davud told Sukru everything. The voyage to Ishmantep after escaping the Moonless Host, the fire along Ishmantep's docks, how Anila had offered her blood and Davud had accepted. King Sukru watched most intently when Davud spoke of using the power of Anila's blood, how he'd caught the flame and smothered it, and how in doing so he'd burned Anila through their bond.

He'd recounted this tale a dozen times since returning to Sharakhai. He'd even told it in this very room, but he'd never done so in front of Anila. It made the story feel weighty in a way it never had before, as if he now stood before a tribunal, and the King was preparing to render judgment for his crimes. He supposed, looking at this immortal man who stood proxy for the other Kings, it wasn't too far from the truth.

"I didn't know this would happen," he said at last, glancing uncomfortably toward Anila. "I'd been swept away by the fire, but the sheer power in her blood . . ."

"Yes, yes." Sukru waved his hand, brushing Davud's words away like a platter of honeyed sweets. "When did she last speak?"

"Ishmantep."

Did we finish it? she'd asked as they stood beside the still-smoking ship. She'd meant the men within the royal clipper, had she and Davud saved them . . .

We did, he'd whispered to her. *We saved them all.*

That's good, she replied, her words soft as gossamer. *That's good.*

The King was staring at Anila uncharitably, the way one might at a thoroughbred that had developed a limp. He was weighing a decision he wouldn't give a second thought to once it was made—he wasn't called the Reaping King for no reason. Davud was trying to formulate the right words, to divert the King's thoughts from Anila and her fate, when Sukru reached into the folds of his robes and drew out a small book, the very one Hamzakiir had penned for Davud.

"Hamzakiir gave you this?"

"He did."

Sukru thumbed through it as if it were nothing more than a curiosity. "You are a learned young man."

Davud stammered his reply. "You honor me, my King."

Closing the book with a snap, Sukru frowned, his uneven gaze boring deeply. "Do you wish to join the service of the Kings? To help us balance the scales of justice?"

"I don't understand, your Excellence."

Sukru's small eyes sharpened, giving him a ratlike look. "Will you serve me as we hunt for Hamzakiir and drive the scarabs from the desert?"

"I only thought . . ." He motioned to the book in Sukru's hands. "I thought the use of blood magic was forbidden."

"The Kings decide what is forbidden."

"Of course, your Excellence."

At this, he withdrew a vial from his right sleeve. The vial was made of translucent green glass tipped with a silver cap, to which was affixed a needle. Within the vial was a dark liquid that sloshed as he flicked his fingers to Davud's left arm.

"My King?"

"I require assurances from those who enter into my service." He flicked his fingers again. "Given your nature, I'm sure you understand."

He wanted Davud's blood. He suddenly wished he were anywhere but here, but what was there to do now? He held out his arm, and Sukru grabbed his wrist and pierced his skin near the elbow. He collected the blood, then swirled it around, stoppered it, and slipped it back inside his sleeve.

To Davud's surprise, and growing horror, he withdrew another vial and repeated the ritual with Anila. When he was done, her red blood spread from the wound, stark against the white bandages over her indigo skin.

"But she's no mage," Davud said, powerless to stop him.

"But she is," he said while swirling Anila's blood, "a rather unique specimen." Davud didn't like that word, *specimen*, nor the way he'd said it. Away the vial went, into King Sukru's sleeve with the other. "Five nights hence, you will accompany me to the blooming fields."

The King waited with a curious look on his face. He looked rather like one of the masters in the collegia after they'd posed a particularly tricky riddle to his students. The answer came to Davud a moment later.

"Beht Zha'ir is five nights hence."

Sukru's flat expression made it clear he'd expected more.

Gods, Davud had never been close to the blooming fields. Their legend was fearful enough, but it was the asirim themselves that made Davud's knees quake. "If you'll forgive my presumption, my Lord King, what are we to do there?"

"Some of the adichara have been withering and are close to death. You'll investigate." Sukru tossed the book to Davud, who caught it, confused. "You'll find more sigils in those pages," he said. "Master them before we depart."

Gods, he means blood magic. "I cannot, my King."

"Ah, but you can." He strode for the door. "Your King demands it."

He left, letting the door swing open behind him. When his footsteps had faded, Davud thumbed through the book, horrified at what Sukru was asking him to do. This was what had led to Anila's disfigurement. He'd foresworn the practice entirely, except for that which kept him from pain as the change within him continued to settle. He soon found the pages to which Sukru had referred. Written in a scratchy hand—so different from Hamzakiir's tall, elegant penmanship—were two additional sigils: one for *flora* and another for *poison* or *decay*, the text below wasn't quite clear.

Suddenly the hungry look on Sukru's face when he'd questioned Davud about his use of blood magic made sense. It had been jealousy, not simple curiosity. That, coupled with the fact that he'd asked Davud to join him, implied two important things: first, that there was some puzzle Sukru desperately wanted to solve, and second, that he wasn't gifted enough to do it alone.

Davud felt sick. He hadn't wanted the curse of magic when Hamzakiir told him of it, and he didn't want it now. He'd give it up in the beat of a butterfly's wings if he could. But he couldn't. It was foolish to pretend otherwise.

Turning the pages, he found an overlaid sigil, penned in three different inks. It combined the two earlier sigils with a third: the one for *binding* or *mastery* that appeared earlier in the book. What the King meant him to do with it he wasn't certain.

He turned back toward Anila, and shivered. She was no longer staring at the ceiling. She still lay on the bed, but her neck was bent awkwardly as she stared at the book in Davud's hands. She said nothing, her face held no expression whatsoever, and yet he felt a rush of shame.

Anila either didn't notice or didn't care as her gaze slid from the book to the doorway. She watched it for a time, her eyes calculating, hungry, as they'd been when she'd questioned him, day after day, about his magic out in the desert.

"Anila?"

She didn't respond, didn't so much as look at him.

"Anila, *please* speak to me."

Her only reply was to give the book one last glance, then return her gaze to the ceiling, wincing from the movement. Her look of hunger faded, and then she was back to the same Anila he'd known these past many weeks.

He was about to plead again when a shadow flitting behind the curtains caught his eye. He moved toward the window. There was a firefinch in the ornamental fig tree outside, a bird with a vivid yellow breast that burned its way up toward the bright orange feathers along its head. He wouldn't have given it a second thought if it hadn't been acting so strangely. Most such birds would flit about, hop from branch to branch. They would blink, take in their surroundings, flutter about and little more. Firefinches were *nervous* birds.

But not this one. It rested stock still, and seemed to watch Davud as he came to the patio doors and opened them. It turned its head once as he walked over the brick toward the tree.

"What are you about, then?" he asked.

It remained perfectly motionless, for all the world one of the preserved birds the traveling shows sometimes brought to the city. It was on the lower branches, close enough to touch. Only when Davud took one more step toward the tree and reached for it did the bird take wing. In moments it had flitted up beyond the walls of the small patio and was gone.

Chapter 5

ÇEDA STARED INTO KING ONUR'S EYES. She was doing her best to control her fear but felt exposed and helpless without her ebon blade. Onur snapped his fingers at Beril of Tribe Salmük, who threw River's Daughter to him. He caught Çeda's sword and pulled the blade free of the lacquered wooden scabbard. It looked tiny in his massive hands as he inspected the design near the crossguard: a heron wading along a reedy riverbank. An expression of curiosity overcame him, and then a look of understanding, as if the sword's identity had told him all he needed to know about Çeda and how she'd come to be there.

"Well, well." He lifted his eyes and stared at her, his stony face smiling in that grimy, lecherous way of his. "A Maiden lost from her flock."

Beril and the others shared a glance. One placed a hand on the grip of her sword.

Onur waved her away. "She's harmless enough." Then he turned and trudged toward the nearby tent with his characteristic limp. "Come, Çedamihn."

Far out in the desert, Kerim pleaded with her. *Flee! Flee! You must flee!*

His terror for her was so strong she nearly complied. Part of her wanted nothing more than to run, but she knew Onur's presence here represented a shift in power in the desert, and she'd be a fool to let this chance go, danger or not, so she followed Onur into the tent, watching him carefully for signs of aggression, wary as well of the four women standing beside the wooden throne near the back of the tent. The women, all with shamshirs at their side, were dressed much like Blade Maidens. From the battle skirts to the boots to the bracers and the boiled leather sewn into the fabric. Except the cloth wasn't black; it was the sandy color of the desert, and their turbans were red, a sign of war in the desert, and their veils were pulled over their faces, hiding all but their eyes.

Onur practically fell into his throne, as if it pained him to remain standing. "You've come a long way," he said in his deep baritone.

"As have you." She nearly added *my Lord King,* and was glad she hadn't.

"How is it that you, that bitch Sümeya's lap dog, has ended up here in the desert wastes?"

Sümeya was Çeda's former commander in the Blade Maidens, their First Warden. Çeda had hoped the news of the battle hadn't made it this far into the desert, but stories like these, ones that shift the very sands of the desert, traveled as fast as ships could carry them. He might already know some of her reasons for fleeing Sharakhai, which left her with a choice. Should she speak the truth and hope to gain some small amount of trust, or gamble that he didn't know all of it, and that he wouldn't learn the truth before Çeda escaped the *protection* of his tribe?

She wasn't sure. It all depended on why Onur had left Sharakhai.

Knowing the halls of the House of Kings as she did, she could make some guesses. Onur was slovenly. He was brash. He took only his own counsel, and offered his with neither hesitation nor invitation. He was barely tolerated by the other Kings. Had that changed? Had something made the other Kings exile him, or had Onur left on his own? The former seemed unlikely. Onur was stubborn and belligerent—he would have defended his throne to the death if challenged.

But what if he'd simply grown weary of his life in Sharakhai, of ruling the city with eleven other Kings? Could a man like Onur not return to the desert and rule whatever tribe he wished?

"Come, child," Onur snapped, "tell your tale."

His reaction to her hesitation, the pinched look on his face, made her decision for her. Revealing more than she needed to Onur, who rarely repaid the trust others placed in him, would be the height of foolishness. "All I may say is that I'm on a mission from King Yusam."

Onur laughed deeply, genuinely, though on him it seemed a sort of vulgar foreplay that would lead to violent acts. "*May* say. You are here in *my* tribe. You've entered *my* domain. And you'll share what *I* will. Now, why are you here in the desert?"

"I was on Tribe Masal's lands."

"They can no longer make claim to those lands."

"They've ceded them to you?"

"I've *taken* them, as I will take the entire eastern reach of the desert." His brow furrowed; his eyes darkened. "Now out with it. If you force me to ask again, I'll have these women quarter you alive, then man and god alike will see that you're made of naught but flesh and blood and bone."

"Yusam sent me into the desert the day after the battle. He shared little with me, but I believe he foresaw this meeting in his mere. My only question is how it fits within his grand vision."

"Your only question?"

"Yes." Çeda had tried her best to sound confident, but there was a note of irritation in Onur's voice that worried her.

"From where I sit there are more relevant questions. Such as how you escaped the Night of Endless Swords, with Cahil and Mesut in tow. How you survived while Mesut died and Cahil was almost sent to the tomb that awaits him beneath his palace. Or what, as some have whispered, you had to do with the Wandering King's death."

Onur stood and immediately his women flanked Çeda. As Onur strode forward, his intentions clear, she dropped into a fighting stance and felt for their heartbeats. She managed to find the women's, but Onur, as strong as his should have been, eluded her completely.

"Most curious to me is why the gods have seen fit to place you in my waiting palm like a glittering jewel when all I've ever done is spit upon them and their *gift* to the Kings of Sharakhai." He swung one meaty fist at Çeda, a blow she easily avoided. "It's a sign as sure as the moons in the night sky."

He swung again, and this time Çeda stepped in and drove one fist deep into his belly. She only just escaped his grasping hand, but was kicked forward by the tribeswoman behind her. Onur charged with a speed that belied his bulk and grabbed her left wrist. Her right she drove into his neck. It struck hard, with all her weight behind it, but Onur took it with little more than a cough.

She tried to send the heel of her palm up and into his nose, but he snatched her hand and drew her toward him. She had only a split second to turn away before his forehead crashed into her cheek. She saw stars, and took another blow to the left side of her head. One more thudding blow came in from her right and then she was tipping down and rolling blindly along the carpets.

She stumbled while trying to regain her feet, to the amusement of Onur, who stood over her, a cut on his forehead dripping blood down into his left eye and along his sweaty cheek. He grabbed the front of her dress and pulled her up until they were eye-to-eye. "Do you know what tipped your hand?" Before she could answer, another strong blow came in from his right fist, driving her down to the carpet.

The world began to spin away, as Onur spoke one last time. "Yusam, the only man I halfway respected in that entire stinking city, died the night of the battle."

And then the darkness claimed her.

Çeda woke to the sound of scratching. Her head felt like a smith had been using it for an anvil.

Not a smith, she thought. *Onur.*

Memories of her fight with the Feasting King swam before her. Gods, how fast he'd moved. It wasn't right for an ox to move so quickly. Yet another thing the gods would one day answer for.

For all the pain in her head, her limbs felt strangely numb, as if she'd been thrown in an ice bath. Her hands were bound behind her, tied to what felt like an iron spike driven into the unforgiving stone beneath her. She tried to get her fingers around the spike, see if she might pull it loose, but the smallest movements made her head pound so badly she abandoned the exercise.

The scratching sounds continued. She was both curious and annoyed to realized there were two sorts. One was soft, a *scritching* sound, like a reed pen on papyrus. The other was harsher. Metallic. Both made the roof of her mouth itch and opening her eyes brought sharp pain from the bright light. She closed them and only after waiting a good long while for the pain to pass did she pry them open once more. She was in a tent. A small one layered in bright, patterned carpets.

Two women were in the tent with her. One sat cross-legged in the corner, writing in a book, dipping a pen into the nearby well before writing with quick, precise strokes. She gave Çeda a sour glance but then went back to her task.

The other woman sat on a stool, a sword across her lap. She was scratching something into the blade with an awl. The steel blade was dark, Çeda realized. An ebon blade. Dear gods, it was River's Daughter. Years ago Çeda would have laughed at the thought of caring about a sword, but she and that blade had been through much together—too much to allow some girl from the desert to carve things into its dark steel.

"Leave that—" Çeda squinted against the piercing agony that speech brought. She waited for it to subside, again sensing a strange numbness in her frame, then tried again. "You will lay that sword down, now, before I use it to carve things into *your* skin."

The woman looked up. She was several years older than Çeda. Blue tattoos marked her forehead and framed her eyes, trailing along her cheeks and down her chin, making it look as though she were wearing a demon mask. "Speak again you'll wish our Lord had led you to the farther fields."

"I said lay that sword aside."

The two women exchanged a look. The one who was writing, the older of the two, nodded, and the other took Çeda's sword up and stood. She used the flat of the blade to strike Çeda's hip. "You will remain *silent*."

Çeda felt for her own heartbeat. Even as battered as she was, she became attuned to it as never before. It calmed her. Gave her confidence. The numbness she'd felt earlier had become a prickling beneath her skin. "You're not worthy to touch that blade."

This time the woman aimed for Çeda's face. She put no great force behind it, but she was quick.

Çeda was ready, though. She'd felt the woman's intent before her arm moved. She twisted aside as River's Daughter whirred past her face and struck the carpets. Rolling back onto her shoulders, Çeda kicked upward. Her heel caught the young woman's jaw, but that was only part of her purpose. Even as she reeled away, Çeda locked her legs around her sword arm. She pulled down, twisting her hips and legs as she went. The sword spun free, and the woman stumbled into the wall of the tent.

The other woman was caught by surprise. She threw aside her book and pen and lurched to her feet.

Çeda felt her own fear and anger coursing through her. Her right hand was hot as windblown embers, as it had been before she'd fallen on Yndris in Sharakhai and beaten her bloody. Then it had been the asir, Havva, working *through* Çeda. Havva was dead . . . but Kerim was not. This power was his; he was giving her what aid he could.

There was something odd about his emotions, though. Regret? Sorrow? She couldn't tell, and there was no time to figure it out.

She pulled hard on the rope restraining her wrists. It held, but her hand and wrist burned the hotter for it. She tried again, and the rope snapped just as the other woman charged forward, a curving kenshar held in her right hand. She'd not taken two steps before Çeda *pressed* on her heart, making her cough. Her eyes widened as she stumbled, creating an opening so large Çeda could have ridden a horse through it. Çeda stepped in, blocked the sloppy stab of her knife, and brought her fist so hard across the woman's face her eyes glazed even before she'd struck the carpets.

The younger woman was on her feet again, but she was disoriented from Çeda's kick. She was pushing herself up off the tent wall, ungainly as a waking infant, and then Çeda was on her, a punch to the throat to keep her from crying out and then slipping behind her and snaking one arm around her neck.

She grasped desperately at Çeda, trying to free herself, but she seemed to know it was a lost cause, which was perhaps why she desperately flung one foot out to catch a small table holding a host of copper bowls. They clattered across the tent, surely alerting the entire camp that something was amiss. Indeed, as the woman went slack, Çeda heard a cry of alarm. Through the tent flaps she glimpsed Onur's trunk-like legs plodding toward her. He was dragging something behind him. She picked up River's Daughter and charged toward the opposite wall. Slicing down, she cut through the tough fabric with ease.

Çeda sprinted toward the edges of the camp, looking for something—a horse, a skiff—she could use to escape. She'd not gone ten strides, however when she heard a booming voice behind her. "Çedamihn Ahyanesh'ala!"

Onur had sensed her flight. Why else would he have been heading toward her tent so shortly after her attack had begun? But she could still escape into the desert. There were horses tied to a stake behind a sleek caravel. She would take one, find Kerim, and return to the desert—

"Flee if you wish," Onur thundered, "but if you do, the one you're bonded with dies."

Çeda slowed, then stopped in her tracks.

Kerim. *He'd* been the cause of her numbness. Onur had been stifling his presence and Kerim had still somehow lent her strength so that she might escape, knowing full well he would remain under Onur's control.

She hadn't considered how completely the Kings could dominate the asirim—a terrible, foolish mistake on her part. She should have sent Kerim far away the moment she saw Onur.

She turned to find Onur stalking across the sand, dragging Kerim by his rags as if he weighed no more than a gutted lamb. The asirim had always seemed so godlike, almost otherworldly—she'd never considered that they might succumb to trauma as mortal man did. Yet here Kerim was, his limbs dragging, his head swinging awkwardly, his eyes were drunken and half-lidded.

With one hand, Onur heaved Kerim, tossing him to the sand at his feet. In his other hand he held a great spear, its broad head etched with ancient sigils. He lifted it to one shoulder, the tip pointed vaguely at Kerim's chest. "How very tender-hearted you are. I'd half thought you were bonded to this pathetic soul against your will and would be glad to be rid of him." The spear's tip slowly pierced Kerim's skin. Black blood oozed. Kerim did no more than moan and twist gently away.

"Leave him!"

Onur raised his eyebrows. "Drop your blade."

There was fear in Çeda, strong and building, that Onur would kill Kerim no matter what she did, but what else could she do? She couldn't stand by and let Onur kill him, a soul who had done so much to protect her.

She threw River's Daughter to the sand.

Onur's amused expression deepened across his flabby face. "I'd rather hoped we would cross blades. I haven't slaked my thirst on the blood of a Maiden in many long years." He shrugged and motioned to the men and women by his side to take Çeda. "Another day, then." When Çeda's hands were bound once more, he turned and plodded away.

Chapter 6

THE CAMP MOVED ON the day after Çeda gave herself up to Onur. She was forced to help tear down the tents and pack them onto the waiting ships, and then she was chained to the hull in the hold of their largest galleon. She hadn't been told where they were going, but she'd gleaned several clues as the ships were being made ready: the dour looks on everyone's faces, their worried glances toward Onur and, while Çeda was carrying things aboard the ship, she'd seen men and women training with shield and spear on the sand. Onur had led them, shouting commands, the ranks of desert soldiers moving in disciplined order. Beyond them, archers fired into dummies made of hay-stuffed canvas. Even the ballistas were being fired, some releasing grapnels, others long bolts, others clay pots that, while not alight now, would be filled with oil and lit before being launched on the enemy.

Tribe Salmük was preparing for battle. The question was: battle with whom?

The Kings? Çeda mused.

It seemed unlikely. The tribe, given enough ships, could take down a royal ship, but only if they managed to catch it, and the royal clippers and yachts, unless caught off guard by ill winds, were too fast for all but the swiftest vessels in the tribe's small fleet.

They might be turning to piracy, as many tribes did from time to time. It was conceivable a caravan was headed their way, and that Onur's plan was to sack it, but base piracy felt out of character for Onur. There was a third possibility. That Onur had set his sights on another tribe. *That* Çeda could believe. He'd established his power in the desert very quickly, and he'd surely not rest at ruling a single tribe. He'd force more—whether through reason, gold, might, or some combination of all three—to join him.

Which tribe, though? The ships are headed north. And north means Red Wind territory. The land of Tribe Masal.

Over the course of the night and the following day, Çeda tried to reach out to Kerim. She could feel him, just out of reach, like the light from a bonfire over the horizon. Onur's will was smothering him, which made her wonder how in the great wide desert Kerim had managed to overcome Mesut's will and bond with her. She refused to believe Onur was stronger. Mesut's resolve had not only been strong, it had been precise and righteous, things Onur might match but not exceed.

Mesut had spent centuries lording it over the asirim, though. Could Kerim have learned his weaknesses and exploited them to break from Mesut and bond with Çeda? Even if he had, Kerim was now as distant from her as the shores of the Austral Sea. Days passed. Her world became marked by simple meals of water and flatbread, shitting and pissing in the pot they'd provided, and the unceasing motion of the ship as it maneuvered the ever-changing dunes.

Three days into their sail, Beril, the woman who'd first found Çeda in the desert, came for her. She was unchained from the hold and led in shackles to the captain's cabin. Onur sat within. He waved Beril away, and Çeda was alone with him.

Or so she'd thought. She'd been so fixated by Onur that the form hanging from the hull to her right hadn't registered. As the door thudded closed, however, she gasped and stepped back. Kerim hung there, limp, his hands and feet fixed to the hull with massive iron spikes, making him look like a puppet waiting to be taken up for its next show.

"Breath of the desert . . ."

She hadn't meant to speak, especially not in front of Onur, but she couldn't help it. How frail Kerim looked. The asirim were so often hunched, moving with menace, and a power that spoke of the desert's elder days. To see Kerim reduced to an object of Onur's sick amusement shook her.

"Release him!" she commanded.

Onur was sitting on the same wooden throne he'd used in the desert tent. He eased his bulk from it and waddled around the desk. "Soon enough." He stood before Kerim, all but ignoring Çeda. "Curious creatures. Their chests may rise and fall, but they don't *need* breath." He glanced back, his porcine eyes spearing her. "You can take it from them. It sends them into fits of terror if you bury them away from the adichara. You can bleed them as well. Bleed them until there's nothing left. It comes back after a few weeks if you leave them be, and you can do it all over again."

Çeda felt sick. He'd been torturing Kerim, and he wanted her to know it. But why hadn't she felt it? It was yet more proof of his dominion over the asirim.

It was then that she noticed the object around Onur's fat wrist. She'd been so shocked by the sight of Kerim she hadn't noticed that he wore Mesut's bracelet.

Onur noted her surprise, raised his arm, and examined it. "I must admit, I had doubts when I heard Mesut had been killed, and more when the rumors said *you* were responsible. But now . . ." He lowered his arm and took her in from head to toe. She suppressed a shiver. His lecherous gaze felt not only foul, but fervent, as if he wished to own her as he owned Kerim.

"They're calling that great battle in the harbor Beht Savaş. The Night of Endless Swords. I left that very night, and do you know why?" He paused, perhaps wondering how much she knew, but in this she had no idea. She shrugged, if only to keep him talking.

"I found a traitor amongst our ranks. A coward who'd been playing the Kings against each other in a bid to rule Sharakhai on his own—or at least with fewer other Kings to contend with. King Azad, or should I say King Azad's *daughter*, stood by his side. She gave me this." He pulled up the sleeve of his thawb and showed her a puckered scar. "And this." Another just below his collarbone. "And a handful more."

"A pity Nayyan's knife didn't slice higher," Çeda said.

With Kerim's pitiful twitching, her anger was threatening to boil over, but the fact that Onur had chosen to reveal some key information wasn't lost on her. Çeda had long since guessed that her mother had killed King Azad, and that the Kings had chosen to replace him, through wizardry of some sort, with his daughter Nayyan. It was deeply pleasing to learn she'd been right, but it left one burning question: Why would Onur share this with her?

Onur shrugged his massive shoulders. "Nayyan was skilled, but she fell like a sack of turnips when I struck her. She did, however, manage to spill Yusam's blood all over the floors of Ihsan's pretty palace." Though Onur's mouth drooped into a frown, his eyes twinkled. It was a look Çeda was beginning to associate with genuine amusement from this, the most unpleasant of Kings. "Whatever the fates decided that night," Onur went on, "you've touched on an important point. Nayyan was one of the finest wardens the Maidens have ever seen. She is not just a fine warrior, but a leader. Those trained in the arts of war are rare. Those gifted at it even rarer. As young as you are, I see much of her in you." A pause. "There is a thirst in you, is there not, to kill more of the Kings?"

Next to her, Kerim squirmed, and Çeda's insides with him. "Just get on with it."

A flash of annoyance marred Onur's features as he considered her. "You have the same fire as your mother. She wished for the downfall of the Kings, yes? And she was not wholly unsuccessful. She took Azad's life before she died." He leaned back, his fingers interlacing over the roundness of his belly. "And now comes her daughter, searching for vengeance."

Çeda felt her face drain of blood. Onur of course knew that Ahya had assassinated Azad—all the Kings knew—but until now only Ihsan had pieced together the clues that tied Ahya to Çeda. Did the other Kings know as well? Likely so, but in the end she supposed it mattered little. More important for now was the fact that Onur was dangling the information before her like bait in a snare. Could it be? Had Ahya pretended to love *him* in order to have Çeda?

Had Çeda a handful of sand, she would have lifted it to her lips right then and there and sifted it through her fingers. *Please, Nalamae, if there was ever a thing you would grant me, grant me this.*

"Do you know who my father is?" she asked, afraid of the answer but refusing to hide from it.

"I do," he replied, letting the words sit between them like a golden chest, waiting to be opened.

"Who is he, then?"

His rumbling chuckle filled the cabin. "That's too valuable to give up for so little from you."

"Then send me back to the hold. I tire of your stench, and I would sooner die than stand by your side as you lay ruin upon the desert."

"I've heard rashness is your greatest weakness. Don't let it be your downfall." He cast his gaze toward the hull, beyond which lay the bulk of the tribe's ships. "Train these savages how to swing a sword. Prepare them to march on Sharakhai. Help me knock the Kings from their merry perches atop Tauriyat and watch them fall like coneys struck through with arrows."

"I want *you* to fall as well."

His face turned sour. "If you truly wish to avenge your mother's death, set that aside. Come with me, and command an army. Come with me, and watch Kings take their last breath. The coward, Cahil. The snake, Ihsan. The mighty King of Swords. Even Kiral, King of Kings."

"And if I decide to take a sword to your throat first?"

"Then it will be a day for the ages, will it not? A day all the gods of the desert will come to observe." She was shocked to see a grudging respect in his gaze. "There would be no shame in dying that way, for either of us."

"But why would the tribes follow *you*, a King they've loathed all their lives?"

"Because I'm giving them what they want: revenge, the strongest motivator of man. The desert people may loathe me, but only as a vague notion of King. Their hatred for Sharakhai lives in their *bones*. They're forced to abide by the city's rule, and so the Amber Jewel has become a symbol of all they hate. Permanence. The influence of foreign powers. The tainting of the ways of the desert and the raping of its resources. They hate that *far* more than they hate any one King. And if I can promise them the city will fall then what does it matter that I once ruled it?"

"Why?" Çeda asked. "Why share all this with me? Why not tell the other Kings how Ihsan and Azad have betrayed them and watch them fight from within?"

"I never said the other was Ihsan."

"No. But it was?"

As he worked his tongue across his yellow teeth, Onur considered her more carefully. "You discovered much in your time as a Maiden."

"Answer me. Why not tell the other Kings?"

"Because I want them at full strength when I tear them apart. The Kings crushed the desert tribes four centuries ago. Let us see what happens when I set that conflict alight once more." A knock came at the cabin door, but Onur ignored it. "Say that you will stand by my side. Tear down the walls of Sharakhai with me. Avenge your mother."

Gods help her, Çeda actually considered it. Onur was building an army. She might free Kerim and use Onur even as he hoped to use her. She could still do all she hoped to do, but for once from a position of power instead of weakness.

"You'll even have your asir back."

An echo of what she'd been thinking, and yet the words were like cold water to her face.

She turned to look at Kerim, whose head was turned to one side, lifting slightly, as if he were trying to look at Çeda but couldn't summon the strength to do so.

"You would give me my asir . . ."

"And more if you wish. Only tell me how many you can safely bond with."

More of them . . . As if the asirim were his. His playthings to distribute as he saw fit. As the knock at the door came again, more urgently, Çeda moved to the wall. The chains of her fetters clanking, she took Kerim's head in her hands, and lifted him up until she was gazing into his eyes. His eyes were clouded but seemed to focus on her.

"Blood of my blood," she whispered.

Kerim's eyes closed. Fluttered, opened again. Words were on his lips, but nothing came. It didn't matter, though.

"Forgive me for what I'm about to do," she whispered, then turned and spat on the deck between her and Onur. "You are a coward. An enemy of my people. And I would never fight for you."

Onur's face went red. His features screwed up in anger. He stepped forward, grabbed for Çeda's chains. She backed away, but he kept coming, and there was nowhere for her to go. He backhanded her, then followed her down to the floor, raining blows down with his meaty fists.

A third time the knock came, someone spoke in a rush. "My Lord King, sails have been spotted on the horizon."

Onur's movements slowed. His breath came heavy as he stared at her, spittle rolling from his mouth. "You'll see things differently when I have more of his kind in my power."

Çeda said nothing as he dragged her to a stand in one great heave and shoved her out onto the deck of the ship. Her ankles still shackled, she spilled across it, falling near Beril's feet.

"Put her back in the hold," Onur spat, then lumbered past her, surveying the way ahead, where the sails from several dozen ships made a sawtooth pattern over an otherwise smooth horizon.

"Come," Beril said in a low voice. She pulled Çeda, not so roughly as Çeda might have expected, and led her belowdecks.

Chapter 7

ÇEDA WAS CHAINED BELOWDECKS, alone in the hold as Onur's battle against Tribe Masal neared. Through the deck above she heard orders being called more crisply. The nervousness in their voices was plain. The tribes were no strangers to battle, but this was something altogether different: not a raid to steal horses or ships or cargo, but war, and it had been generations since such a conflict had wracked the desert.

Onur wanted to subjugate the Red Wind of Tribe Masal. If he was successful—and with a surprise attack and overwhelming numbers, Çeda had no reason to think he wouldn't be—he would move on quickly to the Burning Hands of Tribe Kadri, the Standing Stones of Tribe Ebros, or the Rushing Waters of Tribe Kenan.

Just another cruel desert overlord.

As she had over the past several days, she reached out to Kerim, but she still felt little save his pain which, while bright, was like peering at a burning brand through a shroud of canvas.

I'm sorry, she said. *I wish you hadn't been found.*

She heard no reply.

Feet pounded over the deck as a new flurry of orders came from above.

The ship tilted sharply as it adjusted course, and heeled so far to the starboard side she thought it would tip over, but a moment later it was thrown the other direction, and Çeda was slammed back against the hull.

The battle began a short while later. The ballista and catapult crews shouted as they identified targets or reloaded. The sound of breaking pottery was followed by a whoosh of fire. Drops of fiery liquid dripped down from the deck, landing on Çeda's shoulder. She shifted away and smothered the fire as shouts of pain came from all about. Thankfully blue sand drifted gently down—a dousing agent for the fire.

The battle continued, the ship heeling this way, then that. The thud of arrows came and more breaking pots, followed by people shouting to douse the flames. Çeda felt like a bean in a rattle. She'd grown accustomed to sailing as a Maiden, but she'd never been through anything like this. The inability to anticipate the ship's movements was making her sick.

Suddenly the ship slowed, and she was thrown forward. The chains securing her went tight and she slapped against the hull.

They'd either dropped the rake—a device sometimes used to slow enemy ships after grapnels had been thrown across their rigging—or the same had been done to *this* ship. Whatever the case, a battle was soon raging across the deck above. Clomping footsteps resounded and swords rang out, followed by a symphony of pain and anger and desperation. Sometimes it came louder, the combat happening directly above her, at other times it dwindled, but it was clear the ship was in a fight for its life.

Several times she heard Onur rage, almost growl, as he fought.

"Onur is here!" she heard above the clash of the battle. "Onur is—"

The voice was cut off with a gurgle.

On the far side of the hold, the hatch was thrown back. Two soldiers, both women, dropped down with swords in hand, but it was so dark Çeda couldn't tell whether they were of Tribe Salmük or Tribe Masal, whom Onur was here to conquer.

"Who are you?" Çeda asked, hating that fear had bled into her voice.

"Be quiet," said the nearer of the two. "If we're found, all three of us will be killed."

It was Beril, Çeda realized. *But why would she—*

"Is it true?" Beril went on, almost breathless. "Are you the White Wolf? Did you kill the Kings as Onur said?"

"What? Why are you asking—?"

"Is it *true*?"

There was no reason to hide it. "Yes, it's true."

"Külaşan and Mesut and Cahil?"

"No, not Cahil. He escaped."

"But you fought him?"

"And wounded him."

Beril and the other woman shared a look, after which Beril nodded. When the other woman did too, Beril took up the chain that secured Çeda to the hull. "Help us," she said. "We need to make it look like you escaped on your own."

As Beril gripped the chains, the other woman—the one Çeda had knocked unconscious before cutting a hole in the tent—slipped around Çeda to her left and took the chain in both hands as well. Confused but seeing no reason to deny them, Çeda helped as they began pulling on the chain. It took some doing. The three of them strained mightily, but then the bolt finally gave and all three of them flew backward.

"Now," Beril said, taking a key and unlocking the manacles, "head southwest. In two days' walk, you'll find a hill with an old abandoned tower and a well beneath it." From around her waist she unbuckled a sword belt. She was wearing two, Çeda realized. And one held River's Daughter.

Çeda buckled it on, realizing how very good it felt to have her sword back. "Why are you doing this?"

Beril took a skin of water and slipped it over Çeda's neck. "A skiff will come for you bearing a blue pennant. It will take you to the Moonless Host."

Çeda gripped her wrists. "*Why* are you doing this?"

Beril's eyes were filled with sudden passion. "Because you are blood of my blood."

The words struck Çeda like a hammer. Blood of my blood. Beril was one of the thirteenth tribe. It explained her actions, but more than this, it made Çeda feel connected to the desert tribes more than she ever had before.

"I'm sorry I couldn't free you before you reached Onur. Had I known . . ."

Çeda shook her head. "You couldn't have known." She gripped Beril's hands and said, "Thank you."

"Thank me by fulfilling your vow to kill the Kings of Sharakhai. Now come." She motioned to the hatch that led down into the bowels of the ship where, surely, she meant for Çeda to leave through the access hatch along the bottom of the ship's hull.

But Çeda refused to follow. "I can't leave without Kerim."

"He is lost to you."

"No he isn't, and he's leaving with me."

Beril looked to the other woman, who merely shrugged. "Very well, but take this." She unwrapped her turban and quickly wrapped it around Çeda's head in the Salmük style. Then they were off, Beril leading the way up the ladder, to the deck. Çeda followed, her heart beating fiercely in case they were seen. But the ship was nearly empty. Four crewmen stood on the foredeck, throwing sand on a fire still raging over the deck. One man stood on the vulture's nest atop the mainmast. When he saw Beril and Çeda heading for the captain's cabin, Çeda thought they'd been found out, but the man merely nodded.

They entered the cabin and found Kerim, still nailed to the hull. They rummaged through Onur's desk until they found an old sextant, which they used to pry the nails free. Çeda tried to be careful with Kerim's skin, but there was simply no way to avoid harming him, so she pulled harder.

"I'm sorry," she said as she laid Kerim down, the black blood oozing from his wounds staining the bright golden carpet. Kerim, eyelids heavy, his breath terribly weak, made no reply. She wasn't even sure he could.

Leaving him there, she returned to the desk and hunted through the lower drawers, then the nearby shelves. "Beril, I need the bracelet as well. The one with the onyx stone."

The two of them tore through the cabin as quickly as they could, opening the chest in the corner, looking through the drawers in the desk and beneath the bunk. But it wasn't there.

"He must have taken it into battle with him," Beril said.

She'd no sooner spoken than Çeda looked up. She could *feel* something—small and dark and angry, like a secret door to an oubliette. She felt along the cabin's roof, moving the boards. The closer she came to it, the more certain she was of its location. One of the boards popped loose, revealing a hidden compartment. Within was a bag with coins, a woman's ring, and the bracelet.

"How . . . ?" Beril asked, but then shook her head. "Never mind. We must hurry."

Çeda stuffed the bag inside her dress and rushed to Kerim's side. She lifted him up and carried him to the shuttered windows at the rear of the cabin. He hardly moved. After setting him on the sill, she gave his weight over to Beril, then climbed out of the window and leapt to the ground. Beril lowered him down, and Çeda caught him as best she could, the two of them collapsing to the sand.

"When you see Ishaq," Beril said, "tell him Onur was hunting for something in our tribe. He never told me what, but I believe he hopes to find it among the treasures of Tribe Masal."

"Very well," Çeda said, wondering what it might be. As quickly as she could, she bore Kerim away from the conflict, praying to Nalamae for the darkness and the blowing sand to hide her. "Hold on, Kerim. We're nearly safe."

It was a horrible lie—they were anything but safe—but soon enough they were beyond the next dune. And soon after that, the sun had fallen. She headed southwest, walking as far as she could manage before laying Kerim down in the trough between two dunes.

As the stars brightened on a moonless night, Çeda held Kerim as he shivered.

Çeda took the stairs down into the earth, unwinding her turban and wrapping it around her shoulders. The earth's chill embraced her like a lost love, welcoming after so long in the desert. It was quiet beneath the tower Beril had described. Lonely. It felt as if she were walking into a catacomb to find her own tomb.

The stairs led to a natural cavern, utterly black save for the stairwell's faded smudge of ash-gray behind and above her. She moved slowly, warding her way forward, then heard it. The drip of water. It came rhythmically, oddly timed to her every third footfall, as if a lost god were weaving a spell to draw her near. When her boots splashed into water, she crouched and reached out, finding a shallow pool, cold to the touch. She took a small mouthful. It tasted of minerals and sulfur but was drinkable all the same. With her knees in the water, she drank deeply, then cupped the water and splashed her face over and over, cooling her skin and washing away the dirt and grime of the desert.

Stepping deeper into the pool, she lay in the water, rolled over, soaked her dress in it before simply floating, arms out, staring into the darkness. It felt like the passage to the farther fields to simply sit here and pretend she was not a part of the world above. But then the dripping seemed to come louder. It was only a trick of the mind, as if the lost god had grown bored with her presence, and was telling her to return to the sun, to leave this place or suffer his wrath. As much as Çeda might wish to sever her ties to the troubles of the world, she had no choice. She was woven into the desert's story as much as Onur, as King Ihsan, as Macide and Queen Meryam and Kiral, the King of Kings.

And Kerim and the other asirim.

She stayed a long while, but thoughts of Kerim, who waited for her above, alone and in pain, sobered her, and she made ready to return to him. She drank more water, filled her water skin, then made the climb back up to the surface, where she found him lying exactly where she'd left him, in one corner of the tower's square interior. He was facing her, but his eyes wouldn't focus. Nor did he move as she knelt by his side and placed a hand on his shoulder.

She knew better than to offer him water. The asirim neither ate nor drank. *Except when forced to by the Kings.*

"My mother used to go to the blooming fields," she said, if only to take her mind from the grisly curse the desert gods had lain across the shoulders of the asirim. "She'd bring back the blooms and press them in a book." A book Çeda had lost when she'd fled Sharakhai.

"How I miss it. The heft of it was so like the weight of my mother's hand in mine." Çeda reminisced, flashes of memories playing in her mind's eye— holding her mother's hand as they went to the well, or watching as she bartered for salt and lemons from Seyhan, or shivering by her side in their shared bed, trying to fall asleep while the asirim howled their way closer to Sharakhai. "But it's gone now. Given back to the desert."

She stroked Kerim's bald head. His eyes were slits, the pain within him great.

"Still," she went on, hoping to draw his mind away from memories of his torture at the hands of Onur, "that book held three of the riddles the gods gave to the Kings on Tauriyat the night of Beht Ihman. I found them years after my mother died, and they led me to Sehid-Alaz. Led me to the asirim."

She took a drink and wiped her mouth with the back of her hand. Glancing through the gutted window on her left, she wondered if the Moonless Host really would arrive tonight as Beril had promised. She had no great desire to delay her return to Sharakhai, but she had to admit that the chance to speak to Ishaq, her grandfather, was strong. And taking a bit of time to gather some support, *any* support, would be welcome.

"After pressing the petals, my mother would store them in a necklace." She slipped the necklace over her head. It was silver. A bit tarnished, but not terribly so, and shaped like a candle's flame, with an intricate desert design etched onto its surface. "This very one." She opened the locket and breathed in the scent of the adichara blooms. "There are no petals left, but you can still smell them."

She held it to the twin slits of Kerim's narrow, desiccated nostrils. His eyes closed. He breathed deeply, like one might a bouquet of flowers after having being lost for years in the desert. When he opened his eyes once more, they seemed to have gained a bit of clarity.

"My mother carved." His wheezing, rattling whisper reminded Çeda of a sandstorm—the shriek of it, the rattle of the sand. *"She carved wood. But later, stone. Trinkets to sell in the bazaar or far out in the desert during our pilgrimages."*

"What did she like to carve?"

"Buhrr—" Kerim swallowed. Tried again. *"Birds. Amberlarks. Finches. Blazing blues. Herons wading in the Haddah, like your sword. And other animals. Word spread, and she was commissioned by those from Goldenhill. She was asked to create a bronze sculpture of Beşir for a fountain in the merchant's quarter, near Hanging Gardens."*

"I know the one," Çeda said.

"She made it"—Çeda could hear the pride in his voice—*"and it was glorious. Perfect. Beşir claimed it had not captured his likeness well enough and refused to pay. Two months of work gone, and debts stacked high after borrowing against what she was promised by the House of Kings, and still they put the statue up, removing her sign from the base so that no one would know it was her work."* Kerim's eyes were intense, angry. *"When trouble began to brew with the desert tribes, there were rumors that our tribe would bear the brunt of the battle. My*

mother harbored a naïve belief that our family might be saved, that we might ask one small favor of Beşir to protect our family."

He went silent. They both knew the folly of such a hope.

"Does she yet live?"

"No, but you met her before she died. She was killed by Sehid-Alaz when he was nearly driven mad by Mesut."

Dear gods. Çeda remembered. An asir, who had been a woman once, had taken Çeda into the strange cavern beneath Sharakhai, where the glowing stone had been. Sehid-Alaz had been there and, in his grief and near madness from Mesut's torture, had killed that asir, beaten her head in against the glowing stone, then come for Çeda and nearly killed her too.

"What was her name?"

"Her name was Verahd, and she was kind until the last."

"She *was* kind," Çeda echoed, taking one of Kerim's emaciated hands in hers. She kissed his fingers as a tear rolled down Kerim's cheek. "Oh, Kerim, I owe her my life."

He swallowed hard. Shook his head. *"Fighting the will of the gods is no easy thing."*

He meant the urge to return to the blooming fields, to join the others hidden beneath the adichara. "I will find a way to free you." It felt right the moment she'd said it, like it was something she'd been avoiding for years, though in truth she'd learned the true nature of the asirim only a year ago. "I will find a way to free you all."

Kerim was shaking his head. *"I warn you, through us, the Kings can reach you."*

She already knew it was so. Kerim was right. She had to be careful. But the asirim had to be her priority. If Sharakhai were to be freed, the Kings' greatest weapon must be taken from them. Sensing movement, she turned and saw the white knife of a sail cutting along the horizon. Standing, she saw a blue pennant twisting in the breeze atop the skiff's lone mast. It looked like a snake, freshly pierced by a spear.

The scene was so striking, and her relief so palpable, it felt as if this moment had been preordained, a vision in one of Saliah's hanging glass prisms.

"Don't worry, Kerim. Help has come."

Chapter 8

THE TWIN MOONS WERE BRIGHT scythes in a star-filled sky as Emre waited beneath an archway, the crumbling entrance to an old boneyard. He watched the way ahead for the signal Macide said would come when the moons were high, but he was spending nearly as much time watching the ranks of crumbling pillars behind him for telltale signs of the dead rising from their graves. He would have waited elsewhere, but the truth was that most in Sharakhai were as leery of the dead rising from their graves as he was, and these days it paid for a scarab of the Moonless Host to be in places where other people were not.

Things had only grown worse in the days following Galliu's betrayal. At least a dozen scarabs had been found murdered. More had been taken. The Kings had been finding their safe houses with such frightening frequency that Emre feared there were more traitors in their midst. Some believed Hamzakiir's honeyed words, believed that he would lead them where Ishaq had not been able to. Was the Night of Endless Swords not proof? Many thought so, ignoring all the work Ishaq had done to build a coalition among dozens of warring factions. A surprising number had already thrown their lot in with Hamzakiir, but those pockets still loyal to the old guard were vulnerable to spying, treachery, and assassination.

A hulking wagon with bars across its windows trundled past. A hunched, angry-looking man sat atop it, whipping the horses. It looked like a slaver's wagon heading for the blocks, and Emre feared the driver was his contact. For a moment he was sure the wagon would stop and the driver would bark at Emre to jump in the back, but thankfully the man never turned, the wagon was soon gone, and Emre was back to glancing at the boneyard for unexpected company.

Nearly an hour passed while the moons marched westward. Occasionally, small groups of men would file into the oud parlor up the street—laborers from the quarry, most like. A few stumbled out, often singing in slurred verses, an old woman yelling from the building across the street whenever they did. Finally, as a pair of cats began hissing on a rooftop, a man with a cap sitting at a jaunty angle came strutting down the street. He paused as a cluster of dirty gutter wrens flocked past—he warded them away from his purse with a hand on his knife—and then headed toward Emre.

He was Emre's age, a touch over twenty summers, and handsome. His clothes weren't what one would call finery—he was no east-end lord—but they were rich for this part of the city. Still, he wasn't the usual sort Osman—who owned and ran the most popular of Sharakhai's fighting pits—would hire to shade information across the city. He was about to tell the young man so, give him a ribbing and see what he was about, when he recognized him. Suddenly all the words Emre had at the ready flew up and away like a flock of blazing blues.

"By the stars above, if it isn't Tariq Esad'ava." He said it in the tone of a mother who hadn't seen her son in years.

Tariq's face screwed up in annoyance as he glanced to the darkened windows along the street. "Announce it to the whole fucking city, Emre."

He kept it up, running his hands over Tariq's clothes as if he couldn't help himself. "It's only, I haven't seen you in *ages*. And now you show up at my doorstep."

Tariq slapped his hands away.

"Has Osman demoted you?" Emre went on. "Sent you back to shading?"

"No, I'm not bloody back to *shading*. I've got my own crew. I'm practically running the pits now. But your . . . *employers* are paying a pretty pile of rahl for this, so he thought it best I come." He paused. "Wipe that ruddy look off your face. This is serious."

Emre sniffed, pretended to wipe a tear from his eyes. "My baby, all grown up." When Tariq shoved him back into the boneyard, Emre smiled all the more. "Never could take a joke."

"And you never knew when it was time to stand up and act like a man."

Emre shrugged off Tariq's annoyance. It did his heart good to be with someone, anyone, from his days before the Moonless Host. He wished they could sit awhile, talk of things other than Kings and killings and the cruel realities of life in the city, especially since he was about to leave Sharakhai, perhaps for good. But he guessed it wasn't meant to be. Tariq may have felt the same—he knew Emre was about to leave as well—but if he did, he said nothing and the awkward look on his face was soon gone.

"You've got the name of the ship, then?" Emre asked.

In answer, Tariq handed over a folded piece of papyrus with a wax seal on one side. It looked like a rearing Malasani lion. The note would contain the name and location of the ship that would smuggle many of the remaining scarabs in Sharakhai to the desert. Emre was desperate to read it, but Macide was the one who would break the seal.

It was a desperate step they were taking, but these were desperate times. Those trying to hide were dying by the dozens while those who tried to escape aboard ships had been found by the Kings' warships, or by the Silver Spears before the ships set sail. It didn't seem to matter if they posed as crewmen, paid for a cabin, or stowed away belowdecks. Even skiffs were being hunted down with cruel efficiency, leading to more and more hangings at the foot of Tauriyat.

"When?"

"Dawn, but be there an hour before. No later, or you'll not be allowed on." As he spoke, Tariq reached up and tapped his cheek with two fingers. It was a signal shademen used to indicate that they were being watched, and to act normal. They'd used it years ago, primarily when the Silver Spears were near but hadn't caught on to whatever it was they were up to: a drop, a pickup, whatever Osman had asked them to do.

"Very well," Emre replied. He turned and nodded toward the oud parlor.

"You want to get a drink? For old times?" He'd scanned the street, marking the alleys, trying to spot anyone who might be watching, but if anyone was there it'd take better eyes than his to spot them.

Tariq paused, unsure how to voice his thoughts, but then he shook his head. "You know," he said, his voice so low Emre could barely hear it, "Osman's always looking for good men. Might be you could still find a life here in Sharakhai."

He was suggesting that Emre abandon the Moonless Host and remain in Sharakhai. Emre had heard it often enough from friends from his old life and dismissed it out of hand. But to hear Tariq say it only moments after a signal that they were being watched . . .

"What would I do?" Emre asked, just as softly.

"A man like you would need to lie low for a while. It's dangerous these days, *especially* around the harbors. But we'd find a place for you."

As a fucking shademan, Emre thought, work he'd done when he was fifteen. Those had been simpler times but ultimately empty. He'd been reborn when he'd joined hands with the Moonless Host, and he wasn't ready to give it up, certainly not to become an errand boy for Osman.

"Take care of yourself, Tariq."

Tariq seemed disappointed, more than Emre would have guessed, but then he nodded. "You as well, Emre." And then he was gone, back to some rich place near the pits.

Hopefully somewhere safe in the arms of a woman he loves, Emre thought as he strolled past the oud parlor. He recognized his thoughts for the foolishness they were. There was no such thing as a safe place in Sharakhai. Not anymore. Not for the Host, nor Osman and his crew. Even the innocent men and women who walked the streets each day were as likely to get bloodied as anyone else.

Emre wandered the west end, making sure he wasn't being followed. Only when he was sure it was safe did he head for the back of a weaver's shop, stepping into the small yard from the back alley. A pair of women holding bows crouched on the roof, watching, waiting.

Frail Lemi's tall form lifted from behind a pile of crates. "You get it, Emre?"

"I got it."

Even in the darkness Emre could see Frail Lemi's wide grin. "We'll be leaving soon, right?"

"That's right. Just need to talk to Macide about it."

"Right." He balled his fists, released them. "Right. Best you do that, Emre. It's important. Real important."

"I know, Lem."

Inside, twenty looms were spread across a mostly open space. Several men and women slept on the floor along one side, but on the other, near the door to an office, was Hamid's stocky figure. He waved Emre over.

When Emre reached the small office he was surprised to find a man he recognized, though not from his dealings with the Host. The thin man was sitting at the desk in voluminous purple robes and a beaten pakol the color of the desert sunrise atop his head. This was Adzin, the old soothsayer. Scattered over the desktop before him were more than a dozen scarabs. They crawled, constantly moving, skittering toward the edges of the desk. Whenever one came close, Adzin would reach over, pluck it up, and set it back in the center of the desk.

Macide stood by the desk. Darius was there as well, plus several other men and women, elders of the Moonless Host. They all watched Adzin, transfixed.

When Emre came closer to the table, Macide looked his way. "Emre," he said with a note of relief. Gods, he looked terrible. Sunken eyes. Stooped posture. And on his face a look of worry and weariness that seemed wrong on a man who projected confidence at all times, and whose reserves of energy had always seemed bottomless. "We thought you might have been taken."

"No idle chitchat," Adzin said, picking up another scarab and setting it practically on top of another. "Now is the time for haste."

When Macide glanced Adzin's way, it was clear that, for now at least, worry was winning the war against weariness. "Come," he waved to Emre, "tell Adzin your tale."

"Tariq came to the boneyard—"

"From the beginning," Adzin snapped. "In detail."

Macide nodded. "Start from your walk to the oud parlor."

Emre launched into the events of the evening, from his walk north through the city, to the people who went in and out of the oud parlor, to his uneventful watch from the boneyard's archway.

"Was there a sign above the oud parlor?" Adzin asked, his arms moving like a juggler's, keeping all the scarabs in play. They had become more animated, moving with more speed, but Adzin kept pace with ease.

"Yes," Emre answered.

"The device upon it?"

"A rearing goat."

With those words, Adzin picked up one of the beetles, but instead of setting it down in some other place atop the desk, he popped it into his mouth and began to chew like it was a honey-coated almond from the spice market.

Gods, the crunching sounds. Emre couldn't help but grimace. He'd eaten a scarab once. On a dare. Çeda had told him she'd eat one if he did. When he said no, she'd raised her stakes to two as long as he ate his first. He still refused, but when she upped her bid to three, with Hamid and Tariq both watching, he'd finally agreed rather than lose face. He'd managed to get the squirming thing down, but only after retching a half-dozen times. He'd thought Çeda would stand and run, make it a big joke, but she hadn't. Her face screwed up as she summoned her courage, she'd picked all three up and shoved them in her mouth. Her eyes had watered, but she'd chewed as if she were on a mission to save the world.

Afterward, she'd opened her mouth after to prove she'd eaten every last bit. Emre was already queasy, and the sight had pushed his stomach over the edge. He'd thrown up right there on the dusty street, to the laughter of all his friends, none louder than Çeda's.

Emre stared in horror as Adzin continued to chew, until Macide made a hurrying motion with his hands. Emre told them about the sober men marching in, the drunks stumbling out.

"The songs being sung?" Adzin asked when he mentioned the music coming from the oud parlor.

Emre had to think. "'The Trollop and the Tinker.' 'The Beggar King of Ashdankaat.'"

Another scarab popped into Adzin's mouth like a Savadi treat. "The sorts of graves?" he asked when Emre came to the boneyard.

"Old. Tightly packed. Crumbling pillars."

Another beetle, the crunching sound making Emre's teeth itch.

And so it went, Emre talking, Adzin downing more of the beetles until only three were left. Adzin inspected them very carefully, moving closer until they were mere inches from his face. "How long did the two of you speak?"

At this Emre paused. If he told the truth, Macide might wonder why they'd chatted so long, whereas a lie might doom the entire undertaking. "A quarter turn, perhaps."

Macide turned to Emre, his gaze becoming more intent, but he remained silent.

"So long?" Adzin pressed.

"We grew up together," Emre said.

Adzin shrugged, then picked up both remaining scarabs, one in each hand. "Lastly, the appointed time you were told to meet the ship."

"An hour before sunrise."

The scarabs crawled over Adzin's fingers, and he flipped his hands back and forth like a Mirean teacup dancer. "And so we arrive at your two choices," he said to Macide. "Do you take the offered ship or do you steal a ship of your own?"

Macide watched Adzin and the scarabs intently. "That's why we've come to you!"

He held his hands out to Macide. "That is for you to choose. But know this: Lives will be lost either way, and on one of the paths, *yours* is lost."

Macide blinked. He licked his lips. Emre had never seen him look so haggard. "If I die, will more live?"

Adzin pulled his gaze up from the scarabs to stare deeply into Macide's eyes. "If I delve too deeply, Macide Ishaq'ava, it will foul everything. I've given you all I can give."

Macide closed his eyes, took a deep breath. As he released it, he opened his eyes, plucked the scarab from Adzin's right hand, and stuffed it into his mouth. As he chewed and swallowed, Adzin studied the one remaining scarab. "The decision is made," he said. "Take the ship that was offered."

Macide looked to the rest of those gathered. "We'll rest for a time, then head to the harbor. Hamid and Emre, come with me."

The three of them took the stairs up to the roof. The two archers Emre had spotted earlier bowed their heads to Macide, but at a wave from him they cleared the roof.

Hamid began speaking as soon as they were gone. "I still think we should—"

But at Macide's raised his hand, Hamid's words trailed off and his expression turned to one of sullen silence.

"Do you know why we chose Adzin for this?" Macide asked Hamid.

"Because he can see the future," came Hamid's sharp reply.

"There is that"—Macide shrugged, the weariness in him showing even in that one small gesture—"but Adzin cannot know all. His divinations have been known to fail, or only proved accurate using the narrowest of interpretations."

"Then why use him at all?" Hamid pressed.

"Because we are nearly done here. With Hamzakiir's spies and the King of Whispers hounding us, we won't last long. There's no shame in retreat, my young falcons, as long as the fight is kept alive. We must make sure of it, the three of us. Now."

"What can we do?"

He motioned downward, indicating the room below. "We've spoken now. Despite all our preparations, the King of Whispers may have heard us, or the Jade-eyed King may have seen it, perhaps written of it before he died. We cannot know. But we must get as many safely out of Sharakhai as we can. So I ask that you two stage an attack on a ship as planned. Take the ship if you can, retreat on skiffs if not, then meet us in the desert."

He didn't say where the Host were gathering; he'd shown them the name three days ago then burned the paper: Faramosh, a large oasis beyond the caravanserai of Tiazet in the far eastern corner of the Shangazi. It was where most of the higher ranking members of the host were headed, Macide among them. Others were headed elsewhere, returning to life among the desert tribes where they could act as spies or garner support. At the least, they'd help stem the flow of blood that Hamzakiir was exacting from the Moonless Host.

It was hard to remember what a tremendous victory they'd achieved on the Night of Endless Swords, especially knowing how few had remained loyal to Macide and his father, Ishaq. But the greater the victory, the more desperate the enemy. They'd always known a terrible storm would descend; now that it had come, they had to weather it as best they could.

"Take another man each," Macide told them, and before they could protest: "It's all we can afford." Then he left them to talk and to plan.

Two others, Emre thought. Gods, there were few enough in Sharakhai left, and he knew this was only a feint to throw the Kings off their scent, but this was suicide.

"Let's go," Hamid said sharply, his voice, at least, still full of fire.

They went down to ground level and chose Frail Lemi and Darius to join them. Darius seemed appropriately afraid when they told him. Frail Lemi, however, looked as though it were nothing more than stealing a pile of copper khet from a lone, blind beggar. "Which ship?" he asked, stretching his neck as if he were about to fight.

"Doesn't much matter," Hamid replied, and off they went, heading for the southern harbor by way of the Corona, the street that hugged the outskirts of the city.

"Which one, though?" Lemi called from behind them, confused.

"I'll show you when we get there," Emre replied. "Strange how Tariq was acting tonight," he said to Hamid, who jogged by his side. "Offered me a place with Osman if I stayed."

Hamid glanced his way with a self-satisfied grin. "For as much hot air as came out that jackass mouth of his, he was always soft."

Emre shrugged. Tariq had always felt like a brother to him, more so than Hamid. Tariq had gotten Emre out of plenty of scrapes; little matter that he'd gotten him into half of them. It made Tariq's offer all the more curious.

Frail Lemi caught up to them, looking like he had something important to say. "I know Tariq." They ignored him, hoping he wouldn't launch into a litany of the times he'd seen him. It was a thing Frail Lemi did often, as if it showed how good his memory was. "Gets around, Tariq does."

Hamid and Darius remained silent, their pace steady, but Emre began to slow, and when he stopped, Frail Lemi did too.

"What did you say?" he asked Lemi.

"Tariq. He gets around."

Darius and Hamid had started walking back. Hamid glowered at both of them. "This is no time for your nonsense!"

Emre raised a hand, focusing squarely on Frail Lemi. "What are you talking about, Lem?"

"He came by Adzin's ship when Darius and I were watching it."

All eyes turned to Darius.

"That true?" Hamid asked.

Darius shook his head. "No."

"Sure," Lemi countered. "When you were off taking a piss."

A stunned silence fell over their group.

Darius looked aghast. "Nalamae's teats, Lemi, why didn't you *say* something?"

Emre and Hamid shared a look.

"We've got to find him," Emre said.

"We have *orders*," Hamid shot back.

"Not anymore we don't." Emre was running toward the Well, where Osman's pits were situated. "I smell a rat, Hamid. Best we find it before it leads the Kings right to us!"

"Gods damn you, Emre," Hamid rasped, "come back!"

But Emre kept running, and the others soon followed.

Chapter 9

RAMAHD WALKED ALONG a busy street in the Shallows with Amaryllis by his side. Cicio led the way, fixing anyone who came near with that dead-eye stare of his, daring them to challenge him. Vrago, his long hair pulled into a ponytail, brought up the rear, his peacock strut on full display.

Amaryllis tipped her head to an alley on their right. "Right there."

Without slowing, Ramahd shot a glance down the alley. A dozen paces up, three toughs squatted in the dirt, playing bones. One whipped the dice against the wall, then grinned as he took half the coins from the pile of copper near his feet. The other two hung their heads and groaned.

"They're the ones who stopped you?" Ramahd asked. The day before, Amaryllis, Cicio, and Vrago had come on Ramahd's orders to get Tiron, but they'd been stopped by the toughs who ran the drug den.

Amaryllis nodded. "Those three and one more. He's probably inside, tending the addicts."

A year ago he would have walked right up to them and demanded to know where Tiron was, but this business with King Kiral had made him nervous. The last thing he and Meryam needed were rumors that Qaimir was starting trouble in the streets. "There's another entrance?"

Amaryllis pointed up the street. "Around the back."

They continued to the choked intersection, the crowd squeezing past an open area where tourists and fools were tossing money at a con artist sliding chipped ivory bowls over the dusty street. Ramahd and the others pushed past, then continued until they'd reached a small courtyard selling incense and scarves and vests. They got dirty looks from the vendor and her husband as they pushed through the stall and headed for a gap between the buildings. A boy wearing a dusty woolen cap was leaning against the wall, whittling a stick into the form of a snake. The vendor's son, perhaps, but he was blocking their way.

"Best move on," Ramahd said.

Wide-eyed, the boy made way, and Ramahd, Amaryllis, Cicio, and Vrago squeezed themselves into an alley barely wide enough for them to sidle along. They reached a window with boards nailed haphazardly across it. Ramahd took out his stout knife and pried the lower boards off. Ducking low, he angled himself in, knife at the ready as his eyes adjusted to the darkness.

The smell in the room was thick. A haze of lotus smoke hung below the ceiling like a rare winter fog passing over the city. All about the ramshackle room, dozens of men and women, a few children as well, lay sprawled across the dirt floor in varying states of delirious repose. Some leaned against walls or corners. Others sat cross-legged or with one leg stretched out, heads lolling as they rode the dark waves of the lotus. Most simply lay on the floor, eyelids heavy as they stared at the ceiling. Their limbs occasionally twitched.

A few paces from Ramahd, close to a broken set of stairs leading up, sat a massive shisha with eight tubes snaking out from it. Six were occupied. A woman sat near it, a beaten tin cup sitting forgotten between her legs. Her eyes were the most alert of those lying about the room. Even so, when she turned to Ramahd it took several long seconds before her gaze drifted down to his knife.

The whites of her eyes shone as she snatched up her tin cup and began to rise. She stopped, however, when Ramahd put a hand on her shoulder. Words of alarm died on her lips as Ramahd tapped the blade of his knife against his lips and made a long shushing sound. The woman dragged her gaze to Amaryllis, then to Cicio, who had folded himself practically in two to slip through the window. After a pointed stare toward the front door where, just outside, the three toughs were still playing at bones, she lowered herself back down.

The four of them moved quickly after that, searching for Tiron in the choked rooms along the ground floor. Then Ramahd pointed upstairs and motioned for Amaryllis to follow. Cicio and Vrago remained at the foot of the stairs, fighting knives drawn.

The stairs groaned as Amaryllis and Ramahd headed up. Near the top, another tough with a shaved head met them.

"Hey!" he shouted, reaching for the long knife at his side. "Hey!"

Ramahd charged, grabbed his sword arm, and punched him hard in the throat. The tough coughed and tried to snatch Ramahd's shirt, but he'd lost his leverage. Ramahd shoved him hard against the wall, one forearm pressed against his throat while holding the knife to the man's stubbly cheek. The tip came to rest along his twitching eyelid.

Amaryllis checked the four adjoining rooms for Tiron. "He's not here!"

"Was this one here yesterday?" Ramahd asked her in Qaimiri, indicating the tough he was holding.

"I wasn't—" the man began.

"I asked the lady."

"He wasn't here," Amaryllis replied.

"You're sure?"

"Yes, I'm sure," she snapped, annoyed.

"Down," Ramahd said in Sharakhan. The young tough looked petrified, but he didn't move a muscle. Ramahd hooked his ankle and threw him to the floor. He fell with a thud, grunting, but remained silent.

Amaryllis gagged him, then tied his hands and ankles together behind his back and bowed down close to his ear. "Quiet now, wouldn't want you to lose your tongue."

They stole down the stairs and headed for the front door, collecting Cicio and Vrago along the way. The four of them filed into they alleyway, where the sounds of the Shallows, muted in that boarded-up cave, lifted suddenly around them. Ramahd walked to the nearest of the men playing bones and sent a crushing punch across his face. Sweet Alu's grace, it felt good. The man looked more surprised than angry as he tried to catch his balance. His arms windmilled, eyes blinked rapidly, and he thumped hard against the dirt.

Vrago, smiling, held the tip of his sword to the man's throat to keep him where he was. The other two remained on their knees when Cicio motioned them down using his sword.

Ramahd addressed the shirtless one with a long row of earrings on each ear and tattoos along his temples and forehead. "What's your name?"

"Pony."

For a moment, the words died on Ramahd's lips. "Why Pony?" he asked.

Cicio laughed and looked to Vrago. "Pony! Like a little boy, ah?"

Vrago's smile widened, revealing a perfect set of teeth.

Pony's eyes moved quickly between Ramahd and Cicio and Vrago. He was trying not to let his fear show, but he was young and it was plain to see. When his gaze landed on Amaryllis, his brow knitted for a moment. Recognition coming and going in the span of a heartbeat.

"Yesterday, *Pony*, the beautiful woman standing behind me came to find my brother, but you and your little lambs refused to let her take him. Why?"

The man licked his lips and gathered some small amount of courage. "None of your business."

"Of all the answers you could have chosen," Ramahd told him calmly, "that was likely the worst."

Amaryllis was already striding forward, her fists raised. When Pony realized she wasn't going to stop, he raised his fists as well. He managed to make it to his feet. He even managed a swing at her, but it was clumsy and oafish. Amaryllis ducked the blow and sent a left hook to his kidney. Pony grunted and tried to land an uppercut, but Amaryllis juked around it. Her next punch was a vicious right hook to his opposite kidney; it struck so hard, so perfectly, that a cringe-inducing *slap* rose above the din of the nearby crowds. Pain contorted his features as he fell to his knees. For long moments he simply groaned while his body curled around the punch.

Ramahd crouched until the two of them were eye to eye. "She's in a good mood today, Pony. Do you know how I can tell?" Glancing up at Amaryllis, the man shook his head. "Because she let you off easy. But I wouldn't test her again if I were you. Now why don't you tell me why you refused to let her take Tiron?"

He coughed, but otherwise remained silent.

"Very well." Ramahd stood, and Amaryllis strode forward again.

Pony's hands were waving in the air before him. "It was the Widow!"

Ramahd put a hand on Amaryllis's arm. "Come again?"

"The Widow told us to keep him here, make sure no one took him."

"And who is the Widow?"

Pony stared at him as if he were an idiot. "She *owns* the place, and a dozen more just like it."

Ramahd and Amaryllis shared a look. She nodded to Ramahd's unspoken request, more than ready to find out more. Ramahd lifted the man up by one arm. "You're coming with us. It's time the Widow and I have a chat."

Just past high sun, Ramahd stood with the others beneath a bridge that spanned the Haddah's dry bed. He was studying a three-story mansion that the man called Pony had identified as the Widow's home. Some passersby had spotted them, but none had taken much note, especially when Cicio had shown them the keen edge of his knife.

"She's there now?" Ramahd asked.

Pony nodded from the safety of the deeper shadows. "She drinks wine on the top floor near midday."

Unlike most of the nearby buildings the mansion was made of cut red stone, and was well kept, a ruby hemmed in by a fistful of common stones. "Even today?" It was Salahndi, a day of rest in the desert.

Pony shuffled his feet, kicking up dust from the dry riverbed. "Most like."

He was nervous. He'd hardly looked at the Widow's mansion. Ramahd knew little about her, but Pony had talked on the way there, impressing upon them that she was a woman who repaid betrayal with blood.

Ramahd nodded to Amaryllis, who used her knife to cut his bonds. "Run back to your little friends," she said, then kicked him away. He stumbled and fell, then got up and sprinted along the riverbed, keeping his head low.

With him gone, Ramahd, Amaryllis, Cicio, and Vrago climbed the bank and made for the entrance as fast as they could. They wanted to give the Widow as little time as possible to prepare. The front door was closed, but there were windows open, a breeze blowing soft white curtains inward. Ramahd was just about to start taking the stairs when the front door opened and out stepped three guards: two women, shamshirs already drawn, and a bull of a man holding a studded club easily in one hand. Behind them, Ramahd saw a boy he recognized: the one with the woolen cap who'd been whittling the wooden snake.

I should have bloody known, Ramahd thought, feeling foolish. He should have waited, watched the place more carefully, but he'd been too worried about Tiron to delay.

"I'm here to see the Widow," Ramahd said, coming to a halt at the foot of the stairs.

"You can meet her," the barrel of a man said in perfect Qaimiran, "but only you, and I'll have your weapons before you go in."

Ramahd stopped and took the man in anew. He had the copper skin of the desert, but a bit of the heavy brow that indicated Qaimiran blood. "What's going on?"

Slinging the club over one shoulder, he held out his hand. "You'll have to ask the lady."

Ramahd considered, then pulled his sword and knife and handed them over.

"Take him," the man called over his shoulder as he accepted the weapons.

The boy nodded, then waited as Ramahd stepped inside the house. The building was moderately impressive, especially in comparison to its neighbors, but on the inside . . . Mighty Alu, it looked as expensive as any of the homes in the Hanging Gardens in Sharakhai's rich east end. Bronze statues on pedestals. Paintings on the walls. Frescoes on the ceilings and in grottos spaced throughout the blocky architecture. They reached a central stairwell and took it up two stories. From there the boy led him through a set of open doors onto a patio, where a woman sat wearing a dowdy dress and a black shawl over her head. She was old, Ramahd realized. Very old. With wrinkled skin and sunken cheeks that lent her a hound-like appearance. Her eyes were sharp, though, and her mouth downturned, as if she were angry and not concerned that it be known.

She waved toward the opposite chair.

Ramahd took it, a wicker chair, a thing found commonly in Qaimir, though rarely in the desert. "I must admit you have me at a disadvantage."

He'd spoken in Sharakhan, but the Widow responded in perfect Qaimiran.

"Seems to me I have both your balls in one hand. The question is whether I ought to squeeze." Her eyes moved to the thick, flame-shaped bottle between them. "Pour us some, won't you?"

Ramahd did, pouring what looked to be Qaimiri brandy into two heavy glasses. As he did, he noticed the maker's mark on the bottom. This particular brandy from Qaimir's southern coast was highly sought after here in Sharakhai, so it wasn't so strange to see it, but when added with everything else it did feel odd. Ramahd had been brewing toward a battle with some local drug lord, but now it felt as if he were sharing cordials with a fellow noble along the shores of the Austral Sea. All that was missing was the cool breeze and the briny smell.

"Who *are* you?" Ramahd asked.

"Well, I am the *Widow*." She motioned to the brandy, then picked up her own glass, which was shaped more like the wooden cups given to Qaimiri children than a glass meant for proper drinking. After tasting the apple-sweet liquor, she said, "The more pertinent question is who *you* are, and why you're asking after Tiron."

Ramahd sat back in the chair and drank. He savored the strong taste, the caramel notes, before speaking again. "Where is he?"

"You didn't answer my question," she said, her words more biting than a moment ago.

"I'm a man who cares about Tiron."

She stared into his eyes, measuring him. "Tiron came to my home of his own free will."

Ramahd laughed. "Is that what you call that rat-infested den? A *home*?"

"The shelter it provides, as you well know, is not of the material sort."

"I could argue it doesn't offer shelter of *any* sort. But that's beside the point. I care about Tiron. No more, no less. He may at first have come of his own free will, but not any longer. I doubt he knows who he is most of the time. I wish to take him home."

"He is a paying customer, and he'll be allowed to stay as long as he wishes."

"Is it about money, then? If I pay you, you'll give him to me?"

"Who is he to you?"

"Who is he to *you*?" Ramahd shot back. "What do you care as long as you get paid?" He pulled the leather purse from his belt and upended it. "Twenty rahl and twelve sylval. More than enough for a man to smoke of the lotus in a den like yours for weeks on end." *More than enough to kill a man,* Ramahd thought.

"Tiron is a special guest."

"Of yours?"

The Widow stared, her face set in stone.

"If not yours, then whose?"

"I would never share such things." Her chin jutted as she tightened her hold on the brandy glass. "Now tell me who you are and your purpose with Tiron."

"I am Ramahd Amansir, Lord of Viaroza, brother by marriage to Queen Meryam shan Aldouan."

The Widow stared, her eyes turning uncertain. "Lord Amansir . . ." Her brows pinched in a look of confusion, as if her life depended on solving the puzzle that had just been set before her. "My Lord Amansir," she finally said, "I'm afraid you'll have to speak to the queen about Tiron."

"Mighty Alu, why?" But he was already beginning to understand.

A moment later, as the widow set her glass down with a thump, his fears were confirmed. "It was the queen herself who asked me to keep Tiron."

Chapter 10

THE PATIO OUTSIDE DAVUD'S apartments was an oddity created when a new wing had been added to King Sukru's palace centuries ago. It was a triangular space surrounded by tall walls on all three sides, which prevented him from seeing any more of the palace than the top of a minaret and one rough shoulder-like projection, where Sukru's apartments were situated. For many nights since his return to Sharakhai, Davud had enjoyed sitting on the patio, listening to the palace as it settled down to slumber. The night sky, the chittering insects, the cool breezes had all comforted him, but now they served only to mock, for they marked the end of another day of failures.

It was the day before Beht Zha'ir. He was sitting with a glass of the finest rice wine he'd ever tasted, hunched over the patio table while poring over Hamzakiir's book of sigils, the one Sukru had embellished. Zahndr, his personal guard, had thankfully, finally, been given other duties. Davud still saw him from time to time, especially with Anila, but he'd given Davud time to work in peace.

Leaning back in his chair, Davud released a pent-up breath of frustration and took a much larger swallow of wine than he was accustomed to. The journey to the blooming fields was tomorrow, and he'd been trying unsuccessfully to master the sigils King Sukru had added. There was one particular sigil. He thought he'd missed something, but now he wasn't so sure. He'd tried it dozens of times and had yet to feel any sort of spark from it. Hamzakiir's sigils had all been flawless and worked for him almost immediately. Sukru's were . . . less so. Perhaps they'd been copied imperfectly. Or perhaps the originals, whatever tome or scroll or table they'd been copied from, had been wrong.

Still, what could he do but try? Over and over he'd attempted to use the combined sigil on the nearby ornamental fig tree—the sigil that used *flora* as its base with *decay* and *mastery* layered upon it—and felt nothing. Would it be different out in the desert? Were the adichara so different from fig trees that the sigil would work there though it had failed miserably here?

He doubted it. That Sukru seemed outright vengeful wasn't helping matters, but he resolved to keep trying until he'd run out of time. After piercing the skin of his hand with the blooding ring Sukru had given him, he drew the sigil on his palm while cradling the three related concepts together in his mind. Standing, he stretched his hand out toward the tree, hoping to sense its true nature, as Sukru seemed to want him to do with the adichara.

As before, he felt a vague sense that the tree existed, that it was bound to him as long as he concentrated on the sigil. But after long minutes of trying, he gave up, knowing he'd get no further this way. Golden Rhia climbed further in the sky, and he wondered how angry Sukru would be with him. Many in the city described him as an opportunist, a vulture among Kings. But to Davud he'd always seemed more like a wounded animal, a man as likely to attack his own as his enemies, perhaps for the mere spite of it.

It was then that Davud realized he wasn't alone. There was a small figure in the branches of the tree. The firefinch had returned. As before, it remained oddly still. "Why do you keep coming back, my little friend?" He thought of approaching it, but what would be the point? It would only fly away again. Besides, it was a wonderfully cool night. It smelled of early spring, of the Haddah beginning to swell. And the wine, of which he rarely partook and had probably drunk too much, was doing much to lift his mood.

To his amazement, the finch flew down and landed on the mosaic tabletop. Pinched in its beak was a small twig, which it set down on the table. "A present?" Davud asked, amused.

The finch returned to the tree, then came back with another twig, which it laid down beside the first so that they were more or less in line.

Davud laughed. "*Two* presents!"

By the time the third twig was laid, Davud was starting to understand what the finch was doing, but still couldn't believe it. As he'd suspected, the finch returned with a fourth twig, then a fifth and sixth. It lay each beside the others, taking care to place it just so. Like this, flying into the tree, returning with a twig or leaf, or even a small stick, the firefinch was forming a shape.

A sigil, Davud realized with growing wonder, for it looked somewhat like the sigil he'd been studying these past many nights. It wasn't the same, though; there were many similarities, but the new sigil was also different in notable ways. Slowly it became clear. Within it Davud saw *flora.* He saw *mastery.* But not *decay.* A new sigil had replaced it—easy to distinguish, for it was rendered using leaves instead of twigs or branches.

"And what is this?" Davud wondered.

He flipped to an empty page in Hamzakiir's book. He drew the new sigil on its own first, then the combined sigil on the following page. He gave it no name, not knowing its nature, but he repeated the ritual he'd tried earlier, first wiping away the blood on his palm, then drawing the new sigil with a fresh tap of blood.

When he reached out to the fig tree again, he felt something different. Something more. Much more. He saw the tree's seed as it was planted in a nursery, saw it grow until it was knee-high, saw it uprooted with intense discomfort, before being replanted here on the patio and surrounded by decorative stone coping. The tree grew. Days became weeks became seasons. The passage of time felt like waves of heat and cold, of darkness and light. Of the very breath of life, for he felt not only the tree itself, but also the living mites and beetles and caterpillars that crawled along its length, the birds nesting in its branches, the chicks hatching, the nestlings flying from the nest, far away from this lonely patio.

Time slowed, and Davud realized he was nearing the end of his journey. He woke, and took a deep breath so deep it felt as if he could inhale the entirety of the desert. Rhia, he realized, had spanned the night sky. It was preparing to set in the west.

He blinked away his disorientation. *What in the name of the gods just happened?*

Disorientation, he realized, *not lethargy.* He was more energized than he'd been since those moments in Ishmantep when he'd commanded the fire away from the burning ship.

Gods, Davud thought. *I was that tree!*

With his own thoughts and memories returning to him, he looked around for the firefinch and saw that it was gone. He looked up into the tree, but saw no birds of any kind. As he was heading back toward the table, he started. Two figures stood in the doorway leading into the apartments.

Anila with Bela, the granddaughter of Sukru's head chef, who was himself a distant relative of Sukru's. They were quite a pair: Bela young, inquisitive, and bright-eyed; Anila with her glistening black skin, the thread-of-gold head scarf she used to hide her baldness, and eyes that seemed to weigh everything they came across. Anila was peering into the branches, but then her attention swiveled to the table where the sigil was still formed by the branches, where the book was still open to the freshly inked pages.

Davud closed the book, then swept away the twigs and leaves. They tumbled to the patio stones. Holding the book, feeling his face burning red, Davud faced Anila. "How are you feeling?"

Anila's eyes bored into his, unforgiving, questioning him more effectively than words ever could. Bela, sensing the tension, fidgeted, as if waiting for Anila to say something.

"Do you need anything?" Davud asked.

Anila stared a moment longer. Wincing, she turned and limped awkwardly away. After sharing a quizzical look with Davud, Bela followed her.

Davud took a moment to scatter the twigs even more—as if afraid the wind might push them back into the sigil's shape. Then he gathered his things and went inside.

The following day, Davud wandered the palace. He strolled through the central gardens, climbed the library tower, and made his way to the great hall, which was filled with rare art: beautiful paintings, fine vases, golden plates.

He lingered, enjoying himself, but kept an eye out for one particularly precocious girl.

After a long and fruitless search, he found her by pure chance. He had given up and was heading back toward his room when he heard the sound of splashing. Of course. There was a small wading pool nearby. He walked through a scalloped archway and came to it, a large, oval pool filled with the clearest water Davud had ever laid eyes on. Painted ceramic tiles lined the pool. Around it were flagstones made of pretty blue slate.

In the pool, a handmaid was tending to a flock of children, who ranged in age from toddlers, barely old enough to walk, to Bela and a wide-eyed, black-haired boy, who seemed roughly the same age. All wore simple white tunics, which clung to their skin as they splashed and kicked the water about.

Davud waved to the young handmaid, who smiled back, but quickly went after one of the young ones, who was trying to go into the deeper water.

"Hello, Bela." Davud crouched near the edge of the pool. The ceramic bed was sloped so that the waves lapped softly at his feet. He went in until his leather sandals got wet, then leapt back, wrapping his arms around himself as he shivered from head to foot.

Bela laughed.

He tried again, teeth chattering, making a show of touching one toe to the water. "Why, it's cold as snow! How can you stand being in there?"

Bela laughed harder. "It's warm, silly! You're just pretending!"

Davud stepped back in carefully, closing his eyes and sighing loudly, as if the water were now warming his frigid feet. "Anila *told* me this pool was magic but I didn't believe her."

"She didn't, either!"

"She did!" Davud paused, as if he were debating on sharing a secret. He glanced at the handmaid, then stepped closer to Bela and crouched down. "Anila is magic, too, you know."

Bela nodded. "She was burned by the fire, but she used her magic to make it out alive."

Davud decided not to correct her. "Do the two of you speak often?"

She nodded again, this time so hard her pigtails shook. "Almost every day."

"What about?"

Bela shrugged. "My horse. I'm going to race her one day. Memma said I could."

"Does she ever talk about me?"

She lifted her foot high and stomped the water, making a *plunk* sound. The water flew high, splashing her and Davud, both.

"Bela, does she ever talk about me?"

"No."

"Does she ever say what *she* wants to do?"

Bela waded through the water, arms wide, kicking it up into the air ahead of her, a parade of diamonds before a striding princess. "She wants to learn."

"Learn what?"

Bela jumped in up to her neck then came up dripping. "Learn like she did in the collegia. She misses it."

I do too, Anila, Davud thought.

"Bela?" The handmaid was waving her over. "Come dry yourself. It's time to eat."

Without another word, Bela turned and splashed hard through the deepest part of the pool to rejoin the other children. As Davud watched them go, he thought, *how can a girl who's only just met Anila know more about her than I do?*

He knew the answer, of course. *She cared enough to ask.*

As the handmaid herded the children from the water, Davud smiled sadly, then turned and left.

Chapter 11

K ING IHSAN RAN HIS FINGER up the page of Yusam's journal and started the passage again.

A storm rages above Tauriyat. No mundane storm. The clouds are struck through by light, striations of blue against charred marble. Goezhen, god of chaos, walks alone, twin tails lashing in his wake. He has climbed above the palaces, intent on reaching the mount's uneven top. He waits there, surveying the city below, the desert beyond. Sharakhai is largely whole, though fires burn along the western edges and war still rages in the southern harbor and deep in the merchant's quarter, threatening the city's porous inner walls.

Tulathan follows Goezhen. Her long, silver hair flows in her wake, not unlike the swaying of Goezhen's tails. Her naked skin is tinged in blue, resplendent in the storm-bred darkness. She reaches Goezhen's side. The other gods approach. Golden Rhia. Thaash, tall and stoic. Bakhi, as intent upon the sky as Goezhen, though with little of the dark god's anger. He is accepting, somehow, and I wonder whether this is important.

Yerinde is there as well. She has fallen on the slopes, unmoving, all but forgotten by the other gods. Her body lies unnaturally, one hand clutching her throat. That she died in pain is clear. Has she betrayed them in some way? Failed them?

The gods gather. They take each others' hands. And they wait.

This is where the vision ends. I am thrown from it, as I often am, by pain, which indicates that the mere has shown me something that might be related to my own demise. Yet this differs from many previous visions. The city is not a wasteland, as the mere has shown on a number of occasions. Does this mean the steps we've taken have helped us avoid the path of destruction we walked for many years? Time will tell, but I am hopeful.

Yerinde's death and her position on the mount both concern me. Must she die? Is this what the vision has proscribed? In many previous visions she became un-characteristically aggressive, meddling in the lives of mortals, both in Sharakhai and the desert beyond. In one she even spoke directly to several of the Kings—Kiral, Husamettín, Sukru, and Cahil. All toward some greater purpose, it seemed to me. I felt certain I was coming close to finding that purpose, but now this, and I worry I'll never know.

And what of Nalamae? Again and again I am foiled in my attempts to find her, to sense her path. I have long thought she has worked actively against me. Now I'm certain of it. Since her last known rebirth two generations ago, my abil-ity to see anything about the goddess has diminished, no doubt from her slow awakening to what has come before.

Does her ability to hide affect mine to see the paths ahead? I must set aside the time to investigate further. If only there were some news of her . . .

The sound of footsteps roused Ihsan from his reading. "My Lord King." Tolovan, his tall vizir, spoke from the horseshoe archway nearby. "King Azad has arrived."

They both knew, of course, that King Azad was in fact Nayyan, but Ihsan had always been careful to keep a strict code of keeping to appearances. Nayyan was supposed to have been lost, after all, the same night Azad had been killed by Çeda's mother, Ahya.

"Send him in," Ihsan said.

Tolovan bowed and left, returning shortly with King Azad. Uncharacter-istically, Azad wore a flowing cloak over his rich robes, a Qaimiri import.

"A bit much, don't you think?" Ihsan asked as Tolovan left and Azad came to stand before the desk.

"Kiral wanted me to meet with Queen Meryam." Azad shrugged. "He asked that I humor her. I saw no reason to deny him."

"And how is she, Qaimir's new queen?"

"Well enough. It was a luncheon, though Kiral asked her to remain with him as the rest of us were dismissed." Azad took a seat, stiff-backed, on one of the upholstered stools across from him.

"Forgive me," Ihsan said, remembering himself and waving Azad to take his padded chair. Though the body before him showed no signs of it, Nayyan was carrying his child. That and Nayyan's natural form had both been transformed through the magic of the necklace she wore.

Azad stared at the chair crossly.

"Please," Ihsan said.

"I need no pampering, my Lord King."

"It isn't pampering." A half-truth. "I've asked you here so that you can read what I've found."

Azad looked unconvinced, but he stood and came to sit in the large, high-backed chair that not so long ago had belonged to King Yusam. Azad read over the passage Ihsan had been lingering over for several days now—that one and several others like it. When done, Azad pushed the journal away. "What of it? There are likely a dozen other accounts that contradict this entirely."

"You're not mistaken. There are." Ihsan paced before the wide table, his footsteps echoing. "I might have given Yusam more credit when he was alive. The things he saw would have driven me mad."

Azad paged through the journal, written over forty years before. "They *did* drive him mad."

"I don't think so." Ihsan stopped his pacing to point to the marginalia: dozens of notes penned in red or green ink, contrasting the ochre of the rest of the page. Ihsan pointed to one near the corner. "See here?"

It was a note that referenced a date—*the 208th year of the Kings' reign in Sharakhai, Twelfth of Sindra, Tavahndi*. It was a reference to a particular day, a particular vision, in yet another of Yusam's endless journals. That very journal was on the desk, already open to the relevant page. He pulled it toward himself and pointed to the entry, which spoke of a specific attempt to find Nalamae, which in turn referenced yet one more entry from a particularly strong vision Yusam had received over a hundred years before: an account of Nalamae being hunted and killed by Thaash, the god of war.

Azad read all three accounts, then leaned back in the chair, shaking his head. "It's dizzying."

"Now imagine dealing with four centuries of it. It's a wonder he remembered to take his cock out before pissing."

Azad frowned at the analogy. "And you claim he wasn't mad?"

"My point is that while Yusam may have become lost in trying to deal"—he waved to the shelves upon shelves of journals that lined the walls around them—"with all of this, he *did* remember to take his cock out before pissing." He pointed to the journal. "His memory for events was much better than I ever gave him credit for. Throughout these journals he draws upon vision after vision, tying it all together, or ruling out certain predictions that, based on evidence, could never come to pass."

"He hardly saw a thing toward the end."

"True, but I don't think that was due to madness. I think it was because he was nearing his own death." Ihsan recited Yusam's bloody verse: "See far his eyes, through cloak and guise, consumed by sight is he; yet as death nears, will grow his fears, still blinded shall he be."

Azad, who'd heard it only once before, nodded. "So his abilities were diminished as he neared his death, unable to see his path forward, or others."

"That about sums it up, yes. He was consumed by his fading power, and started to focus heavily upon it, trying to fool the gods, but lost sight of much else in the process."

"I'm sure this is all fascinating, my King, but what is your point?"

"My point is that there is much here." He waved again to the journals. "This is a grand resource I hope to use to navigate *our* way forward. Yours and mine."

"There is Yusam's heir to consider."

"Heir . . . He's a madman."

Yusam hadn't fathered a child in over eighty years. His one remaining child was presently locked in one of the towers of this very palace, a lunatic who thought himself the leader of a troupe of minstrels. When he wasn't shitting himself, he was demanding to be taken to his tent, and for the troupe's best jongleurs, his granddaughters, to be brought before him. That he had no sons or daughters, much less granddaughters, didn't seem to bother him.

"Mad he may be, but there are already those who seek to use him to gain a seat at the table."

"No one, least of all Kiral, will stand for it. They've all had enough, begging your pardon, of petulant children demanding to sit at the head table."

Any time such things were brought up during council, it understandably rubbed Azad the wrong way. The young King Alaşan, on the other hand, Külaşan's son, was another matter entirely. He'd been given the Wandering King's crown and his title, and now he was pressing for a say in matters of state. The young man had nearly lost himself his head the last time council had met, arguing with Kiral over the right to more of the city's coffers.

"Hungry children or not," Azad went on, "trouble will come of it sooner or later."

Yusam's situation was the most easily dealt with. They couldn't allow his son, a barking basset of a man, to take his father's place. His descendants in Goldenhill would balk at it, trying to position themselves for more, or at least not *less* than what they'd become accustomed to, but in the end, Yusam's throne would remain empty.

Onur's seat was a different matter. Here they had the opposite problem. The man had too *many* children, few of them legitimate, and many of *those* had been formally disowned. Onur was a jealous man and had seized on any insult to withhold the inheritance of those he'd sired. Fortunately for Ihsan, Onur was so spiteful he often had his children stand before him as their proclamations of forfeiture were read. Those very same proclamations now provided Ihsan and the others all the leverage they needed to keep many of the claimants at bay. At the very least, he would ensure that their claims to Onur's crown would take years to sort out.

It helped, certainly, that Onur had fled, which had given Ihsan time to craft and plant stories about his betrayal of Sharakhai and its rightful rulers. It helped as well that Onur was active in the desert. It created fear and uncertainty in any wishing to sit the throne of the Feasting King.

"We'll deal with them easily enough," Ihsan said.

"We cannot afford to have more lords withholding their taxes from us."

"Is it Beşir, the King of Coin, who sits before me, or Azad, who has more to worry about than filling the city's coffers?"

Azad frowned, and spoke carefully. "I think you're underestimating just how dry the tinder is in Sharakhai. We've been pushing too hard for too long. The city is ready to rise against us."

"Then we'll put it to good use, but only when the time is right. In the meantime"—Ihsan motioned to the journal before him—"there are riddles to be answered."

"Nalamae?"

"She's set to rise once more."

"What of it? The desert gods will likely kill her once more."

"That's exactly what troubles me. They've taken her life a dozen times since Beht Ihman, perhaps more. Why?"

"Because she betrayed them. She didn't heed Tulathan's call. She chose to remain away from the city while all the other gods met on Tauriyat."

"Yes, and why was *that*?"

Azad shrugged, looking over the account he'd read a moment ago only with more interest. "You have thoughts?"

"Nothing worth mentioning now. But this is why it's vital to take a true accounting of Yusam's writings."

"And what will you do that Yusam could not?"

"Apply a fresh eye. You're right that he was less reliable near the end. It may have led him to tie the wrong events together, or overlook some simple connections."

Azad stood and shrugged. "It seems a waste of time."

"No matter what we do with Sharakhai, we would be unwise to forget the desert's true masters."

Tolovan ducked his head inside the room. "My Lord Kings, a message has arrived. King Zeheb wishes to see you both at his palace."

"Impertinent," Azad said. "Could he not have made the journey here?"

Tolovan shook the rolled letter he held in his knuckly right hand. "The letter indicates it's to do with the men taken to his palace."

Prisoners. Men of the Moonless Host, Ihsan knew, captured recently. "Have the coach prepared, Tolovan."

Chapter 12

IN THE DARK OF THE NIGHT, with the moons casting long shadows over the city, Emre waited not far from the fighting pits. As dark as it was, he wasn't watching so much as listening, but he could see the open window of Tariq's home three stories up. He heard the crash of a door being kicked in. Heard a woman scream. Heard a scuffle and the scream being cut off.

Muffled words filtered into the night, Hamid giving orders to Darius and Frail Lemi. They were quiet enough, but they'd moved beyond stealth, and Emre could hear them, searching the small home.

Lemi had said he'd seen Tariq pay a visit to Adzin's ship. Why? Many thought the old soothsayer a quack, a swindler. The fortunes he gave were often not well received; the man was too truthful for most. But Emre believed in his power. He'd seen it at work with his own eyes. Others in the Host had as well, and Macide had grudgingly come to trust him.

But that did nothing to explain Tariq on Adzin's ship. Osman was well known for despising such men. *Even if he* can *tell the future,* he'd once told Emre, *why would a man want it? Everyone knows the fates come calling for those who try to escape them, and when they do, it goes much worse than if they'd left well enough alone.*

Tariq and Osman's role in this was simply to organize a ship, so why would Tariq have visited Adzin's sloop? For Osman's sake? Or his own? Perhaps, but the timing of his visit with Moonless Host's departure from the city was suspicious. Emre had to know the truth, and he was sure he could get it even if Tariq tried to lie—the two of them knew one another too well to hide much from the other for long.

Emre caught movement along the rooftop. The silhouette of a slender man moving with speed. Limned in moonlight, he looked like Tulathan's servant, a thief sent to Sharakhai to do her bidding. Emre was supposed to warn the others if he saw Tariq leaving, but he remained silent as Tariq glided onward, picking up speed as he neared the gap between his building and the next. He leapt from the roof's edge, spanning the alley before landing on a brick balcony with an acrobat's grace. Then he was climbing down, the darkness swallowing him as he was lost to the moonlight.

Emre's old instincts kicked in as he padded toward him. He moved with liquid ease. And yet Tariq still sensed him. He'd always been the best of them at sensing danger. No sooner had his head swung toward Emre's position than he was leaping the last story and a half, dropping and rolling, and coming up in a dead sprint.

Emre was ready, though. He was running hard to intercept. Tariq tried to change tack. He stopped and went for his sword, but Emre closed the gap too quickly. He caught Tariq around the waist and brought him down like an oryx being felled by a black laugher.

Tariq grunted, rolling with the tackle, trying to throw Emre off. Emre caught an elbow across the jaw in the midst of it, but held tight. "Stop fighting, Tariq. I only want to talk."

Tariq still struggled to get away so Emre levered his weight over him, being careful to not let Tariq's shamshir clear its scabbard. Then he struck Tariq across the face. "I said *stop fighting*. I'll release you, but you have to answer some questions."

"I'd sooner lick my own sack."

"That can be arranged." Emre lifted him, then drove him back down with everything he had. "Hamid's on your trail too. And believe me, if *he* finds you, what happens next is out of my hands."

Silence followed. Tariq finally relaxed. "I'm supposed to believe you're my bloody savior, then?"

"I'm the one who decides whether you live to see the sunrise, Tariq. Now tell me why you betrayed the Host."

"I don't know what—"

Emre punched Tariq hard in the mouth. "By now they'll be coming down the stairs, Tariq."

Tariq squirmed, reeling from the pain. "I didn't betray the Host." Emre pulled back his arm to strike him again, and Tariq blurted, "It was Pelam!"

Pelam was Osman's second, who ran the pits on a day-to-day basis. "Go on."

"They took Osman, Emre. Five of those bloody Maidens walked right into his home in the dead of night and took him. A man came to the pits the next day, told Pelam that Osman would be returned and his businesses left intact as long as Pelam did what they said."

"When was this?"

"A week ago."

"Don't lie, Tariq."

"I'm not lying. It was a week ago today."

"I said don't *lie*. A week ago we hadn't even contacted Osman."

"They knew everything. They said you'd come, that you'd be desperate, that you'd ask for a way out of the city. They even said I had to deliver the message and that you'd be the one to meet me."

A sliver of ice formed and grew inside of Emre. "Me?"

"They said my oldest friend would meet me."

"But how?"

"How else? It must be the Jade-eyed King!"

"But he's dead. Everyone's saying so."

"You believe everything you hear on the streets now?"

Was it true, then? Did Yusam live? Or was this something he'd passed on before he'd died? *What does it matter?* Emre thought. *We're in for it now.* Emre heard Hamid calling for him.

"It's a trap?" Emre whispered.

"They'll take every last person who shows up at that ship."

Gods. Fucking gods. Macide and the rest, they're all going to die.

"I meant what I said, Emre. You could lie low awhile. We can get past this."

Emre heard the others approaching. He pulled Tariq up to his feet. "*You're* the one who needs to lie low awhile."

"I'm not afraid of Hamid."

"You should be. He's as savage as the Confessor King when his blood's up. And it *will* be when he hears this."

"Emre, you can't help them anymore."

"I need to try. Now hit me, quick."

Tariq just stood there. His eyes saucers in the darkness.

"Do it, Tariq."

And then he did. He punched Emre across the right eye. It was a hard hit, but not as hard as it might've been. Emre fell—only an act, but he had to make it look good for the others. Tariq was gone in a flash, sprinting down a darkened alley as Hamid, Darius, and Frail Lemi came running around the corner.

"Where *were* you?" Darius asked.

"I saw him escaping."

"You were supposed to call," Frail Lemi said, punching one hand into the other.

"If I'd called, he would've escaped."

"He *did* escape!" Hamid spat.

Emre sent an ineffectual wave in the direction Tariq had run. "I thought I had the drop on him."

"You were supposed to call," Frail Lemi repeated. It was dark, but Emre could still see the great furrow in his brow, the one that came when he couldn't piece things together.

"He let Tariq go, Lem," Hamid said before Emre could reply. "Gods curse you, Emre, I *knew* I shouldn't have left you alone."

"*Me?*" Emre cried. "I was the one who spotted him! I took him down while the three of you were holding your cocks upstairs."

Hamid strode forward and shoved Emre back so hard he fell to the street. Hamid's knife was out the next moment. "You decided to let your old friend go. The only thing I'm not sure about is why."

"Hold on!" Emre shouted, scrabbling away. "Hold on! I know what to do!" He knew no such thing, but Hamid had that look in his eye. *Why did I let Tariq go?*

"Wait, Hamid," Darius said, grabbing Hamid's sleeve.

Hamid ripped his sleeve free. "Don't think to deny *me*, Darius." He pointed the knife at Frail Lemi as well, who was walking forward with arms raised in a placating gesture, as if he hadn't seen Hamid fly into a murderous rage like this a half-dozen times before. Hamid shoved the knife at Emre. "He *betrayed* us."

"I betrayed no one!"

"He said he knew what to do," Frail Lemi said.

Hamid made a show of flourishing to Emre. "Well then do go on, Emre! Tell us this *brilliant* plan of yours."

Frail Lemi shuffled his feet and wrung his hands. He always became this way when his friends fought. "Go on, Emre."

Emre had no earthly idea what to do. How could he possibly navigate the Host to safety when the Kings had stacked so much against them?

"You see?" Hamid said, pointing at Emre with his knife.

And then it came to him in a flash. But sunrise was near . . . Gods, the horizon was already beginning to brighten.

"All of you, follow me." He tried to run wide around Hamid but Hamid imposed himself.

"Where are you going?"

"Adzin. We're going to Adzin. He's the one who betrayed us." When Hamid remained still as a statue, Emre clasped his hands and shook them, pleading, "*Quickly*, Hamid. While we argue, the night is wasting away."

It took Hamid a moment. He looked to the others, then back at Emre. Then he slammed his knife into its sheath. "Better be right, Emre."

And then they were off, running for the western harbor.

From the darkness of a tavern pergola, Emre, Hamid, Darius, and Frail Lemi watched as the crew of a ramshackle sloop prepared to tow back from the pier and into the harbor. Lanterns cast a meager golden glow over the rigging and deck of a ship that was in such disrepair it looked about to take its final voyage. Five crewmen worked the tow ropes. At a call from a giant of a man, a dark-skinned Kundhuni standing on the pier near the prow, the crew pulled the ropes taut and heaved while the Kundhuni held the gunwale and used his legs to power the ship back along the pier.

Tariq had come here to Adzin, perhaps to offer him a bribe, perhaps to coerce him under threat of harm, perhaps both. Adzin had agreed, of that much Emre was certain. The ritual he'd performed in front of Macide had likely all been for show, leading them to the answer the Kings themselves had preordained: that Macide and the rest should embark on one particular ship the Kings knew about, making it all too easy for them to intercept and either kill or capture them all.

That wasn't what Emre cared about most, though. Explanations could come later. What he needed now were Adzin's particular gifts, and this time, Adzin would either use them for real or Emre would kill the man himself.

"Now," Emre whispered.

The four of them moved quickly across the quay and rushed down the pier like a pack of wolves, making sure to keep the stern of the ship between them and the men pulling at the tow ropes. The Kundhuni straining along the gunwales heard them, but by the time he'd turned, one of Frail Lemi's studded leather gloves was already rushing toward his jaw. He fell across the gunwales and was lost in a heap on the deck.

The crew shouted. They dropped their ropes, most sprinting for the pier's ladder, a few heading toward the ropes hanging down over the stern. Emre and the others, meanwhile, rushed onto the ship and down into the open hatchway. Darius and Frail Lemi closed the hatch after them and barred it.

Ahead of Emre and Hamid, golden light spilled from a cabin doorway, bathing a passageway lined with odd, grisly assortments nailed to the walls. Braided hair, baby's sandals, strings of blackened teeth, rusted iron forks with some lumpy, brown residue coating the tines, a papyrus doll in the shape of a woman wearing a crown of thorns. Emre rushed past it all just as the cabin door ahead began to close. He charged and struck it like a battering ram. A thump and a high-pitched scream came from the opposite side just before he burst into the cabin.

Adzin lay on the carpeted floor, wincing and tenderly probing his forehead, where a gash was starting to well and drip a river of crimson. He stared at the blood on his fingers, then took in the looming forms of Emre and Hamid, with confusion and anger and something else. Resignation?

"Have I not given the Host enough?" he said.

"You know," Emre said as he grabbed two fistfuls of Adzin's robe and hauled him to his feet. "You'd think he would have seen this coming." And then he punched Adzin in the stomach.

Adzin doubled over, his breath wheezing from him in one long whoosh. For several long seconds, the sound of his aborted attempts at breathing filled the cabin. After one long, wet breath he started coughing like a man in a losing battle against consumption. "Who says I didn't?" he managed.

The crew had reached the hatch door. There were shouts, and something hard crashed against it.

"No," Emre said. "You wouldn't have gone to all this trouble, setting up the Moonless Host only to have us track you down, if you'd known."

"That depends, doesn't it?"

"On what?"

"On the other choices, you bloody fool. On the other choices."

Hamid's face turned to stone, an indicator he'd heard more than enough. He grabbed Adzin and shoved him into the passageway, making a dozen things fall and clatter against the warped floorboards. Hamid pressed Adzin's face onto the nails until Adzin began screaming from it.

Hamid yelled in his ear. "Order your men to help us or I'm going to gut you like a desert coney!"

The pounding against the hatch came louder, and something gave.

"Enough!" Adzin cried. "Okzan. Cenk. Let us be awhile!"

The pounding at the hatchway door stopped. "Adzin?"

"I said let us be!"

"Good," Emre said, then motioned to the low table in the cabin. "Bring him in here."

Hamid did, shoving Adzin so hard he tumbled over the pillows and struck his head against the hull.

As Adzin righted himself and straightened his robes, Emre knelt and stared him in the eye. "Here's what happens next. We're taking your ship,

Adzin, and then you and your crew are going to help us free Macide and the others."

Adzin swallowed, again with that strange look of his. This time Emre recognized it for what it was. There was resignation, but it wasn't anger or confusion that mixed with it. It was sorrow.

Chapter 13

"**I** REMEMBER MEETING YOU when I was young," Çeda said to Salsanna, the woman who'd come in the skiff to rescue Çeda and Kerim from the tower.

A glimmer of recognition had plagued Çeda since they'd started their journey, but she'd only just remembered where they'd met that morning, when Salsanna had woken early and practiced sword forms along the top of a dune. She was a tall woman with rust-colored hair. She was muscular, the small scars she sported somehow complementing the blue tattoos on her chin and cheeks and forehead. She was beautiful in the way ebon blades were beautiful, in the way the curve of a perfectly balanced spear was beautiful.

Salsanna, choosing not to reply, adjusted the tiller to take a steep rise along a dune more easily. They were sailing west, and had been for three days now. Ahead, tall and imposing, were the Taloran Mountains. The ground had become steadily more treacherous as they'd neared the foothills, which loomed not so far ahead. Rocky surfaces were becoming difficult to avoid, forcing them to occasionally sail over them, and the small red boulders that littered the ground had become massive and much more numerous.

Çeda grew annoyed by Salsanna's silence. "You watched me while my mother spoke with Leorah." Çeda didn't know it when they'd first met, but Leorah was Çeda's great-grandmother, the mother of Ishaq, leader of the Moonless Host.

"Watched you fumble your way around your sword more like." She said it with a humorless smile, glancing at River's Daughter with a look like she'd caught something unpleasant between her teeth. She'd been doing so over the course of their journey, and always with a similar look of distrust, even of anger.

"I was six." Çeda still remembered how intimidated she'd been. Then, as now, Salsanna had projected an intensity no one could fail to recognize.

Salsanna shrugged. "It was clear how well you would take to the sword."

"Oh, this?" Çeda put her hand on the pommel of River's Daughter. "Would you like to see it?"

"Why would I wish to see a blade that has tasted the blood of my people?"

"Because you seem to be spellbound by it. Perhaps it will help you understand that I was trained in the House of Maidens, that while I obeyed some of the Kings orders, I also sought to bring them down."

"Did you?" She pulled the skiff easily around a standing stone. "Seek to bring them down?"

"Two Kings have fallen to this blade."

Salsanna sneered.

"You doubt me?"

"The Wandering King died when he succumbed to adichara blooms. Hardly a wondrous victory. And the Jackal King Mesut died on the Night of Endless Swords. Who's to say you had a hand in it? Especially since you fled."

"The Confessor King witnessed Mesut's death. As did the gods themselves."

Salsanna snorted. "As you say."

Çeda grinned while nestling herself into the prow, her arms resting along the gunwales. "If you wish to test my skill, you need but ask."

Salsanna eyed River's Daughter again, then Mesut's golden band on her wrist. She looked about to speak, but was interrupted by Kerim, who lay in the skiff's bottom. He stirred, and Salsanna looked at him with naked revulsion.

Çeda ignored her and knelt beside Kerim. "Are you well?"

Kerim managed with great effort to lift his gaze and look at her. *Onur's presence is lifting at last.*

Her head jerked back involuntarily. Kerim hadn't spoken to her in this way since she'd left with Beril to join Tribe Salmük. Indeed, she could feel his anger once more, his misery, the love for his mother whose memory had been rekindled as Çeda had talked about her own. *Rest,* she bade him. *Soon we'll be in the mountains.*

To her surprise, his heart lifted.

Have you ever been? she asked him.

Never. His eyes blinked. Tears slipped from them. And then he said aloud, *"I'd always hoped to."*

Salsanna started, ready to draw her blade at the mere hint of movement from Kerim. She stared at him with annoyance but said nothing as they sailed on. Soon they were crossing patches of stone regularly. The scraping sound of the skis made Çeda wince. It reminded her of her mother, Ahya, who'd had much the same reaction when Çeda had scuffed the skis. It reminded her of Djaga as well, her old mentor in the pits, from whom Çeda had borrowed skiffs from time to time, fouling them more often than she'd meant to. Djaga was furious when she did, but she always let Çeda take a skiff when she needed it.

The way opened up after hours of Salsanna's careful navigation. The rocks became fewer, and then suddenly they were on open sand once more. It was a natural place for the Host to hide, Çeda reckoned. Most larger ships would grind to a halt before they reached this area of open sand, and their hulls and masts would be masked by the standing stones. Near nightfall they came to a grotto, where Salsanna anchored, and Çeda carried Kerim to a good place to build a fire. She'd no sooner set Kerim down, however, than she found Salsanna with her sword out, the tip wavering beneath Çeda's chin.

"What are you doing?" Çeda asked.

"I've thought on it, and I *do* wish to test your mettle."

"You're acting like a child."

"On the contrary. I take great care over the welfare of the Moonless Host, and in you, I sense only lies."

"You are your people's judge, then? You'll know the truth of my words at the very crossing of our blades?"

"I'll know if you've told the truth about your skill with a sword, and that alone will tell me much about you."

Çeda's hand was hurting, she realized, the poisoned wound on her thumb flaring up. She rubbed it, feeling the familiar pain. Feeling her anger rise as well. When Salsanna took one more step and slashed with the speed and force of a woman who meant to draw blood, Çeda drew River's Daughter in one swift motion and blocked the blow.

This was no *crossing of blades*, as they'd done when she was young. This was a pissing match, plain and simple, but she'd had enough of Salsanna's smug looks, her questioning stares. When they were young, Salsanna had taught her about anger and not letting it get away from you. It was time for Çeda to return the favor.

She went on the offensive and the two of them flew over the sand, their breath rising. Salsanna blocked blow after blow, riposting with an eagerness that reminded Çeda of Kameyl—though Salsanna was nowhere near Kameyl's match. And Kameyl had taught Çeda well. So had Sümeya and Melis and Zaïde.

Çeda felt Salsanna reaching for her heart as Blade Maidens did. Salsanna had some skill, but after all of Çeda's training with Zaïde, and the months of practice using the ways of the heart as a servant of the Kings, it was child's play to sidestep Salsanna's attempts at gaining an advantage. It angered Salsanna. She pressed with a dangerous fervor. Her lips drew back to reveal clamped teeth. Her eyes widened and her swings turned wild. Çeda blocked everything Salsanna threw at her, planning to simply let her fury expend itself. When it finally had, Çeda would disarm her and this foolishness would come to an end. Only a few breaths later, however, a dark form galloped in from her left.

"Kerim, no!"

Çeda tried to intercept him, but it was too late. Kerim was on Salsanna in a blur of dark movement before she could raise her defenses against him. She was thrown sideways, the sand spraying where the two of them fell. Kerim's arms rose and fell, long nails slashing. Salsanna screamed in pain as she tried but failed to ward off his powerful blows.

Çeda tried to pull him away, but he was too strong.

Stop it! Kerim, you're going to kill her!

It wasn't until she felt *his* heart beating—with a pace like the swells of a ship on a windswept voyage—that his movements began to slow. "Return to me," she urged, daring to grip his arms once more. The pain in her right hand flared terribly, but she ignored it, slowing her breath, bringing herself in sync with Kerim's rhythm. "There's no sense in this. She is blood of our blood."

Finally, Kerim obeyed. He stood above Salsanna, chest heaving, eyes filled with rage. But he allowed himself to be pulled away. With a long, warbling howl, he loped into the desert.

Çeda dropped to Salsanna's side.

"Leave me!" Salsanna shouted, but Çeda ignored her, quickly tearing away her sleeves to survey the damage. There were a dozen deep gashes along her arms and shoulders. Lighter ones along her face and chest.

"Set aside your pride," Çeda said as Salsanna tried to push her away. "If we don't get these stitched, you're going to bleed to death."

After several deep swallows, Salsanna allowed herself to be led to the fire. Çeda bound the worst of the wounds with torn strips of cloth from Salsanna's sleeves, then raided the supplies in the skiff. After giving Salsanna a small ball of fermented black lotus to put between her cheek and gum, she stoked the fire, boiled thread in red wine, and stitched the worst of the wounds. When done, she bound the wounds in fresh bandages. Stoic through it all, Salsanna never cried out, never so much as whimpered. Instead she stared at Çeda with a look of regret that was mixed with a certain arrogance that kept her, perhaps, from voicing what both of them knew: that their duel had been beyond foolishness.

"Why does he follow you?" Salsanna asked, her eyelids growing heavy from the effects of the lotus.

Çeda laid out blankets for Salsanna to sleep on. "Because he knows I'm ready to help his people."

"Our people," Salsanna said as Çeda laid her gently down.

"Yes, but you can hardly compare what you and I have gone through with what *they* have, he and his brothers and sisters. Beht Ihman is a burden we will never understand."

As Çeda sat cross-legged on the sand opposite the fire, Salsanna met her eyes. For a long while Salsanna said nothing but then nodded. "You're right." She stared up at the cascade of stars spilling across the indigo sky. "I was born in Tribe Rafik, one of the Biting Shields. I fought the asirim, and the asirim fought us, hounded us, took down several of our ships. For *infringements of royal decree*, our shaikh was later told. The Maidens killed my father for refusing to bend his knee when one of our ships was stopped, then one of the asirim killed two of my cousins who were enraged by my father's death." She fell silent, and Çeda thought she'd fallen asleep, but a while later she went on drowsily. "I learned to hate them well before I knew about the lost tribe. Forgive me."

She wasn't sure whether that last was for her or for Kerim.

Then Salsanna slept, leaving Çeda to listen to the snap of the fire and the occasional wail from Kerim in the distance.

Chapter 14

ÇEDA WOKE to the sounds of shushing. She'd been unable to sleep long into the night, worrying over Salsanna's wounds, worrying over whether she'd be able to stop Kerim from attacking her again. She'd managed to fall asleep only after the moons had set.

The shushing sounds came closer, and she realized dully that they were footsteps. Fearful that Onur had found her, she rolled over to find an old man with six young male warriors behind him, each with swords at their sides, bucklers hanging from their belts, and bows across their backs.

Çeda stood immediately, but left River's Daughter where it lay, half hidden by her blanket. A few hundred paces beyond the men were a dozen ships with women, men, and children disembarking, unloading tents and crates. In the distance, the razored teeth of the dark Taloran Mountains were framed by a pale honey sky.

Gods, how could I have slept through all this? To her wakeful ears they were loud and raucous, while only moments ago they'd been a muted part of her dreams.

The old man's eyes glittered in the morning sun. "Look at the lost doves we've found."

Smiling as he was, he looked like a desert lynx who'd stumbled upon a succulent scorpion. He had a long gray beard with twin streaks of black running through it. He wore simple desert garb: a sandy thawb with yellow embroidery, a wide belt made of sea green silk, a kenshar and a shamshir with simple leather sheaths. He looked like many who lived in the Shangazi and traveled ceaselessly along her hidden paths, but Çeda knew this was Ishaq Kirhan'ava, the leader of the Moonless Host. Çeda's own grandfather. She recognized him from his visit to her mother, Ahya, in Sharakhai. He had the same intense expression, the sharp features, the golden rings in his nose and the blue tattoos around his eyes and cheeks and chin.

And there was the vicious scar that ran down his neck, lost beneath the collar of his thawb. She'd seen it. She'd asked him about it long ago, and remembered the wicked gleam in his eyes as he'd opened his thawb and showed it to her. "You think *you* could live after getting cut like this?"

He'd said it with pride, but it had scared her witless. She'd shaken her head, too terrified to say a word.

"No, I don't think so either," he'd replied, thankfully covering up the scar. "So be careful, little one. Always be careful."

Ahya had walked in a moment later, a disgusted look on her face. At the time Çeda thought her mother was simply protecting her. But through the eyes of adulthood Çeda could see it wasn't true at all. Or at least, wasn't the whole truth. She'd taken great pains to hide her own past from Çeda; she'd not wanted Çeda to know that the man was her grandfather.

Had Ishaq wanted to hide the truth as well? She wasn't sure. But if so, why?

Ishaq's gaze moved to Salsanna, who lay on the opposite side of the cold fire pit. Her eyes were barely open. With great effort, she pulled herself up into a sitting position. "You're early."

Arms folded across his chest, he jutted his chin toward Çeda. "I suppose I shouldn't be surprised Leorah sent you to fetch her."

Salsanna squinted at the rising sun, took in the warriors fanning out behind Ishaq, then met Ishaq's disappointed eyes. "Is that why you came running to meet her?"

"Watch your tongue," Ishaq said with anger. "You have much to answer for."

Çeda didn't understand everything, but she knew enough to know that

Leorah had somehow intercepted Beril's plea for help, and that she'd sent Salsanna there before Ishaq could find out about it. She suddenly felt like a prize that Leorah and Ishaq were fighting to win, and she didn't like it one bit.

Salsanna made her way slowly to her feet, grimacing all the while. "You'd rather I left Çeda there?"

"I'd rather I was told before you left."

"Your mother sends her apologies, but time was of the essence."

Ishaq made a noncommittal grunt and stared at the rust-stained bandages on her arms. "So you fetched her. Then what? A bloody ehrekh attacked you?"

Salsanna remained silent. When Ishaq looked to Çeda, though, Salsanna finally spoke. "We sparred. I took my eye from her asir for a moment, and it attacked me."

"*Your* asir?" Ishaq took Çeda in anew, suddenly viewing her as a threat. "It *attacked* Salsanna?"

"*He,*" Çeda corrected. "His name is Kerim, and he attacked Salsanna to protect me."

A wail sounded in the distance. Kerim, hidden among the standing stones. *Be silent,* Çeda urged him, *and leave, at least until this is done.* Kerim refused to move away but thankfully came no closer.

Ishaq's frown deepened, making him look like a wolverine, and the men behind him bristled. Çeda was just about to reach for River's Daughter when Salsanna said, "It was my fault."

Ishaq's bushy eyebrows rose. "Yours?"

Salsanna glanced sidelong at Çeda. "We had a minor disagreement. The beast was only trying to protect her."

"He is no beast," Çeda said flatly. "He is blood of our blood."

Ishaq seemed to have trouble grasping those words. He glanced at Salsanna's wounds, then regarded Çeda with the same sort of distaste Salsanna had shown the day before. Surely he knew the truth, though. Surely he knew the asirim's history, perhaps better than Çeda did. But perhaps he believed the asirim were forever lost on the night of Beht Ihman.

"Can you bring it to heel?" Ishaq asked her.

"When needed."

"Good." He drew his shamshir. "Then do so now, and we can be rid of it."

Çedas rocked back in surprise. "I told you, he is blood of our blood."

"No. *Our* blood was taken from it long ago. His veins now run with the blood of the Kings."

"He is loyal to me."

"Today, perhaps. But what about tomorrow? What about the day after?" He waved to Salsanna. "What about when he feels the need to defend you once again. Who will he attack then, our elders, our children?" Before Çeda could speak, he went on. "My heart rejoices that you're safe in our care, Çeda, but I will not allow such a creature near us. As surely as the sun does rise, it will be sniffed out by the Kings or the Blade Maidens, and through it they will discover us."

"We've avoided the Kings for weeks. Kerim is mine, I am his, and I will die to protect him."

Ishaq considered this, his face long, as if he were saddened by what he was about to do. With a flick of one hand to the men behind him, he said, "Go. Kill it if you can, drive it away if you can't."

Çeda stood, regarding them all. "You'll face my blade first."

The men pulled the bows from around their shoulders and strung them easily. The one closest to Çeda drew his sword, quite rightly wary of her.

Diving and rolling over her blanket, she came up holding River's Daughter.

The lead man charged toward her. She blocked two blows, then performed a reverse spin, bringing her heel neatly across the back of his head. He fell limp to the sand, but the others were abandoning their bows and drawing their swords, fanning out to flank her.

"Çedamihn Ahyanesh'ala," Ishaq roared, "stop this madness!"

But she was no child to be cowed by his presence, nor a callow girl impressed by the power he wielded. She was a Blade Maiden, and that meant much.

As the men advanced, Çeda retreated to the nearest of the standing stones. They tried to cut her off, but she used their haste against them. She took the nearest with a flying kick to the face while blocking his slow attempt to cut across her midsection. The next she felled with a sweep of her legs. The other three came at her from the opposite side of the stone, swords blurring. They tried to pen her in, pressing her toward the tall red stone. Çeda blocked a series of blows, then ran up the stone, kicking up and away and flying over their heads.

The nearest followed her movements, hoping to take her as she landed, but he was overeager. He brought his sword down like a headsman. It was a simple matter of dodging that downward swing and hammering the crown of his head with the pommel of her shamshir. He fell backward, eyelids fluttering, while Çeda turned and blocked a tentative slash from the other warrior. She lifted her shin to block his kick, then snapped the toe of her boot into his jaw. Spinning the other way, she sent him flying with a back kick to the chest.

The men and women of Ishaq's ragtag tribe were leaving the business of unloading their ships and skiffs, drawing swords, and rushing to aid their fallen brothers.

Salsanna, closer than the others, limped toward Çeda, sword in hand, but instead of attacking Çeda, she stood beside her, protecting her.

"Leave her alone!" Salsanna shouted. "Her *and* the asir!"

Ishaq had twenty more warriors behind him, ready to do as he wished. "I'm sorry, Salsanna. I will not—"

A bell rang over the desert. From the east came a ship, a small yacht Çeda recognized from childhood, from the time she'd first met Salsanna. Tulathan's bright smile, this was *Leorah's* ship. As the bell continued to ring, all eyes turned toward it. It sailed in at near full speed, heading straight toward Çeda and Salsanna. As the crew—four women wearing wheat-colored dresses— pulled in the sails, an iron grate with hooks was thrown from the back. The hooks bit into the sand and dirt, throwing up furrows as the yacht slowed sharply.

As it came to a halt, a gangway was lowered. Along this, an old, heavyset woman holding a warped cane made her way down to the sand. Her simple yellow dress, which flowed easily in the stiff wind, made her look like a flame dancing over the desert. Small grimaces might have accompanied each uneven step, but she held her head high, seeming to will herself forward.

A host of memories welled up inside Çeda. This was Leorah, the woman Ahya had taken Çeda to see so that they might gain her counsel. She was Ishaq's mother, and Çeda's great-grandmother.

Most in the crowd bowed their heads. Some did not, however—among them was Ishaq, who seemed both unsurprised and displeased by Leorah's sudden arrival.

Leorah tugged her scarf down, revealing deep crags along the skin of her face. Tattoos of birds taking wing and crescent moons were faded and misshapen with age, but there was what looked to be a fresh tattoo of an acacia, the top of which was inked across her chin, the trunk and roots lost to the sagging skin of her neck. The most striking thing about her, however, was the bright amethyst ring she wore on her right hand, the one that gripped the cane. It sparkled beneath the sun, drawing the eye like a sundog in the sky.

"What is this?" she called in a strong if tremulous voice.

"Your servant returned with your prize," Ishaq replied. "She's brought one of the asirim, a creature even you will agree must die before the Kings are alerted to our presence."

Leorah's tongue ran along the inside of her cheek as if she were trying to dislodge something stringy. She stared at Çeda as if she wished to peel away her skin and lay her secrets bare. "Or we might abandon them here. Or drive them both away under threat of death."

Ishaq closed his eyes for a moment, as if he recognized the sort of battle that was brewing. "Is that what you wish? To send them away?"

"It is a possibility."

"Clearly that isn't what you wish, so get to your point, old woman."

"Another possibility," she said as if she hadn't heard her son's words, "is to send the asir away to live out its life in the desert or return to the Kings as it wishes. Or, before doing anything else, we might speak to it and learn what it knows."

"The asir must die," Ishaq said loudly.

"Çeda has been in the desert for some time now. Weeks. One presumes that the asir has been with her the entire time. One also presumes that the Kings very dearly wish to speak to her. Yet she has not been found. So I wonder what rush there is to kill the asir when there might be very much gained by letting it live."

"Have you not seen what it has done already? Salsanna was attacked by that creature, and Çeda was right there." He turned to Salsanna. "Is it not so?"

But before Salsanna could say a word, Leorah went on, "Are we so scared of a little blood that we would kill the innocent?"

"It attacked one of our own!"

"And you ordered your men to attack your *own granddaughter* to get at a creature who cowers from you. Look beyond this day, my son." She spread her arms wide and turned in a circle, taking in all who had gathered. She looked triumphant, oblivious to her own infirmity, a goddess in her own right. "I ask you all to look beyond this day. Our daughter has returned to us, and she has brought one of those who was forced to hunt us for centuries. They have been merciless. They've killed many of our number. But I ask you, whose fault is that? They've been caught in the spell of the gods and given to the Kings to do with as they will. But now! Now one comes to us unshackled. Freed. That you could *think* of spilling its blood without learning more shames me!" She turned her gaze on Ishaq. "Have I not told you? The Night of Endless Swords was a turning point. This is but more evidence. We will not take the life of one who has come to us in need of shelter, one weakened by centuries of enslavement, ground down by four hundred years of duty forced on them by the gods themselves. Look what Çedamihn Ahyanesh'ala has done! Thank her for the gift she has brought before us, for in the hated asirim there is *knowledge*. We must only be brave enough to unlock it!"

Ishaq looked ready to say more, but the words died on his lips when another of Kerim's wails filled the cool morning air. It trailed off into a strange, sorrow-filled barking. Gods, he was *crying*. Çeda didn't understand why at first, but after a moment, she thought she understood. The asirim were compelled to protect the Kings, and here was Ishaq Kirhan'ava, their sworn enemy. There was a powerful urge in him to attack, just as he had Salsanna. He *wanted* to do it. Kill Ishaq and Leorah and Salsanna and more.

And yet, he and those gathered were all of the same blood. Kerim felt the same sort of loyalty toward Ishaq that he did toward his brothers and sisters of the asirim.

The internal struggle was tearing him in two.

Go to the desert, Çeda said to him. *I'll find you when we're preparing to leave.*

To her surprise, she felt not only assent, but relief. Ishaq's will to see Kerim dead had ebbed; more importantly, his willingness to hurt Çeda in order to do it had weakened as well, giving Kerim the space he needed to obey.

As Leorah's words faded, all eyes turned to Ishaq. If he was embarrassed at his own mother's defense of the asirim, he didn't show it. He waved to those nearest. "Go. Unload the ships. Prepare the tents. We have much to do before others arrive." Then he turned and walked away, toward the nearest of the ships beyond Leorah's yacht. His men followed, leaving Çeda and Salsanna alone with Leorah.

Leorah followed Ishaq's retreating form. "Come," she said over her shoulder, "unless you wish to be left in the dark once again."

Chapter 15

DAVUD STOOD ON the foredeck of a royal yacht, watching the setting sun throw shadows against the dunes. The desert ahead looked like the skin of a slumbering beast, a dragon waiting to rise and consume the world.

Beht Zha'ir, night of the asirim, had returned to the desert. Tulathan, a bright silver coin against a sky of autumn leaves, had already risen. Golden Rhia would soon follow. Somewhere ahead of the ship, a long, low moan came. It rose above the rainfall sound of the ship's skis, but then was lost, as if the dunes had swallowed it. Another came a moment later, this one closer, and Davud's skin prickled. Back near the pilot, Sukru's man, Zahndr, leaned against the gunwales, arms crossed over his broad chest, his long, dark hair tied back into a tail. He looked not merely bored, but irritated at having been asked to accompany Sukru on this voyage. Amidships, Sukru himself stood crookedly, watching the way ahead with one hand on the mainmast to steady himself.

Davud didn't understand how the reaping could commence in Sharakhai with Sukru here aboard the ship. Sukru was the Reaping King, who was supposed to guide the asirim to their tributes in the city, but here he was visiting the blooming fields while the asirim stirred and began their nightlong journey. Perhaps he'd already marked those who would be taken. Or maybe he'd whispered the names of the chosen to the asirim on a previous journey. Davud didn't know, and he daren't ask. Sukru made Davud's gut churn just to look at him. It seemed wrong that a man should live so long as the eldest of the Kings had.

Davud wondered what *he* would do were he given four centuries more— or rather, what those four centuries would do to *him*. Would he turn as sour as Sukru. Would the decades eat at him, rotting his insides until he yearned for the farther fields?

What a curse, to live so long. And yet, not so long ago, he'd thought how magnificent it must be to be a King of Sharakhai. *The foolish thoughts of a boy.*

The sun's light faded and the moons continued their rise. Ahead, the blooming fields were nearer; pinpoints of light among the greater darkness, pale blue stars reflected in pools of black ink. But they weren't stars. They were the adichara blooms, opening to take in the full light of the twin moons.

"Prepare to anchor!" the pilot called.

"Preparing to anchor!" echoed the crew.

The ship slowed and eventually came to a rest a short walk from the expanse of stony ground that surrounded the blooming fields. A long gangplank was laid out for Sukru, who took it cautiously down to the sand. "Come, boy!"

Davud obeyed, and together the two of them approached the nearest cluster of trees. Following them at a respectful distance were Zahndr, wearing his black leather armor, and a Silver Spear in his white hauberk and chainmail. Shortly before Davud and Sukru reached the edge of the trees, a wailing sound rose up, so close it made the hair along the back of Davud's neck stand up. He halted reflexively, while Sukru took a whip from his belt and sent it cracking over the tops of the nearby trees. It sounded like thunder rolling slowly over the broken landscape. The wailing stopped immediately, replaced by the sound of movement. The adichara branches parted, and out loped an angular figure. Dropping to all fours, it galloped north toward Sharakhai.

"Come," Sukru said, and made for a gap between the trees. "They're often found within the groves."

They followed a winding path through the trees. The smell here was fragrant, and so floral it made Davud's nose itch. At times they passed through archways where the branches reached like grasping hands. When Sukru came nearer, branches shied away like penitent children, clearing the way. Davud watched carefully for any stray branches; his whole body curled inward as they moved deeper into the grove.

"There." Sukru stopped and motioned to a particularly gnarled mass of thorny branches.

At first Davud had no idea why he'd chosen it, for it seemed no different than the others. But he soon saw that its movements were markedly different. The way its branches swayed made the grove look like an overturned insect, legs wriggling as it neared death. The moonlit blooms, which gave off a faint glow of their own, had a different hue, a pale amaranth purple instead of the washed out blue of the trees surrounding it. And the smell . . . The fragrance of the blooms was still present, but so too were the scents of rot and decay.

Sukru was bent over, staring intently at the base. "I found the first of these years ago. I thought it a simple aberration and had it destroyed. But I found another months later, then more after that. They litter the killing fields."

"What happened to them?"

Sukru glanced back at him. "That is what you're here to find out." He faced Davud. Even by the light of the twin moons, Davud could tell he was being measured. "What I tell you now is between us."

"Of course, my Lord King."

"I believe you are true to the cause of the rightful Kings of the Great Shangazi. If I did not, I would have ended your life by now. There are few with talent like yours in the House of Kings, and I trust none of them, but Kaelira has judged your soul worthy, as has Zahndr, and the masters who taught you at the collegia, and the people of Roseridge and the bazaar, whom we spoke to at length. They've convinced me that we can work together to solve this riddle."

"My Lord King, you honor me. I would be happy to help in any way—"

"Lend your ears, not your mouth." He motioned to the writhing adichara. "For generations, the asirim have protected our city. I won't insult your intelligence by reminding you that every last one embraces their role as protector. But their burden is heavy, and not every man and woman, even with power bestowed by the gods themselves, can shoulder it. Some bend. Others break. So it is that some few have defied the Kings. They have fought our will. Some have attacked us, even killed Maidens before they were put down.

"Mesut had been at great pains to learn why. He never did for certain, but now I wonder, might the asirim have been infected in some way? Might the adichara have tainted them? This is, after all, where they lie when not called upon by the Kings. I wonder if the earth itself has been poisoned." Sukru motioned to the writhing trees. "Most are unaware, but the souls who are taken in tribute each night of Beht Zha'ir are returned here. Their blood sustains the twisted trees, and the trees in turn sustain the asirim. Blood, boy. It's all to do with blood."

Davud thought a moment. "You're suggesting that the blood of those brought here is tainting the adichara?"

"I've pondered the notion. Perhaps that's why the trees writhe so. Or perhaps the trees themselves have begun to die. Or it might be that some other magic is at work. We must learn more." As the branches all around them continued to wave softly beneath the moons, Sukru spread his arms, as if to encompass the whole of the blooming field. "And so you will bind yourself to the trees. You will learn what you can and share it with me."

"Shall we begin now?" Davud asked.

"You'll need blood," Sukru said.

Davud paused. "Am . . . Am I to use *your* blood?"

Sukru's laughter was biting. "You think I would give you *my* blood? You take me for a fool, Davud Mahzun'ava!"

Davud thought of the blood Sukru had taken from him and Anila, stored in vials somewhere for purposes Davud could only guess at. "I'm happy to use mine, though the effects will be diminished—"

"You'll not take my blood *or* your own." He waved to the tree. "We are here tonight so you can take the blood of the dying as they are fed to the adichara."

"My King?" He knew exactly what Sukru meant, but the thought of being here when it happened . . .

"The asir will return within an hour. Best you begin your preparations now."

"I . . . Of course, my Lord King."

Dear gods, he was going to force Davud to watch. He prayed the unfortunate soul who'd been marked by Sukru would be dead by the time he arrived, but something told him he wouldn't be. Given the eagerness with which Sukru was watching him, and the trouble he'd gone to to prepare for this night, Davud was sure the King would require fresh blood. *Alive*, as the saying went.

As Sukru had bade, Davud knelt in the sand. He drew the sigil from memory—not the one the firefinch had drawn with twigs and leaves, but the one Sukru had copied into Davud's book. He did it for Sukru's benefit, but it was also calming. He wanted to focus on something, anything, besides the sacrifice that would soon come.

When he finished, he wiped it away and began anew, but soon slowed his movements. His stomach had begun burning from the moment he realized what lay ahead, but the feeling of the sand beneath his fingertip reminded him of his childhood, when he would draw pictures in the dunes with his older sister, Tehla. Slowly, he was able to push away his fears and stand to face Sukru. "My Lord King, you needn't take a life," he said confidently. "I can do this with my own blood."

Sukru, stretching one shoulder as if it pained him, sized Davud up as if he had just spat in his food. "If you suppose that *your* blood will be equal to a tribute whose blood will mix with the very roots of the adichara, then you are a fool. Wait, boy. Be patient. Use the blood I've called here for this purpose."

There was sense in his words. And whoever was brought here would have died anyway. *Coward. You simply don't wish to bloody your hands.*

He tried to tell himself that being chosen was a high honor, but he found reassurance impossible when the wail of an asir sounded over the desert. It came again soon after, higher than before, more pained, as if it grieved over Sharakhai.

Davud saw it approaching through the thorny branches. It was heading for a different cluster of adichara, but when Sukru's whip cracked overhead, the asir changed course and headed straight for them. It trudged along the pathway Sukru had forged earlier, dragging an old man by his ankle. When it came near, Davud stepped back in horror. Sukru, however, merely gestured toward the afflicted adichara. Immediately the asir lifted the man as if he were made of cloth and hay and threw him into the tree. The poor soul woke screaming. The branches of the adichara wrapped around him and *squeezed*, ever tighter, while the nearby trees moved with the verve and violence of a riot.

Thankfully the man's voice was choked off a moment later as a vine wrapped around his throat. Davud clutched his hands to his own throat. He felt a fool for doing so—a little boy who'd lost his memma—but he couldn't help it. He'd stood before the dead, but he'd never *seen* someone die before. And to see it like *this*, a tree tearing a man apart, made his gut feel like a nest of roiling termites.

A long, gurgling rasp escaped the man's throat as he was pulled deeper and deeper into the tree, the branches squeezing until his final breath was pressed from him at last.

The blood slicking his clothes and skin was turned silver and black by the light of the twin moons. Only the barest hint of crimson remained. *It looks like poison,* Davud thought, *poison from the adichara, leaking from his skin, as if he too has been tainted.*

"Find your nerve, boy," Sukru said. "It's time."

Davud glanced at the King and nodded, yet it took him the span of one deep breath to take a step forward, to kneel, to carefully reach between the quivering branches and touch his finger to the blood that had gathered near the base of the tree. *Merciful Bakhi, it's still hot.*

Of course it was. The man had just died. But it felt as though he were stealing a part of his soul by doing this. It was a thing that would surely displease Bakhi, who would even now be leading the man to the farther fields.

Earlier Davud had drawn the sigil Sukru had given him. Wasn't the first rule of creating an illusion to show the audience what you wanted them to see? This time, he drew the firefinch's sigil. He projected self-assurance, as a cheap confidence man would, and kept his hand tilted away, just enough that Sukru wouldn't be able to see the sigil clearly but not so much that he'd suspect Davud of trying to hide something. As he worked, he built the sigil in his mind and reached out to the adichara—just as he had with the fig tree.

Little happened at first, but then, like the coming sun burning brighter along the horizon, a feeling grew within him, a sense that there was more around him than sand and stone and spilling moonlight. Çeda had once told him she could sense the asirim, and although Davud couldn't feel *them*, he certainly felt the trees. Collectively they felt like a vast body of water, with him standing at its very edge. He tried to take a step into it, but could not.

It was too strange, too unknowable. When he tried harder, he felt the waters retreating before him.

"No!" he said, heedless of what King Sukru might think. Yet even though he tried harder, the waters still fell until it seemed as though they were being drawn into the desert and would be forever unreachable.

With a calm born of an instinct to learn, a skill he'd honed in his years studying in the collegia, he said, "No," once more, and pressed the sigil against the blood-soaked sand.

The waters came rushing back. They splashed against him and the tree, rising up along his body. They swallowed him whole. And suddenly he felt the trees all around him, and *this* tree especially. He felt the soul within its arms fading, fading, going to gray. He felt the tree's slow death as the desert's dry heat clawed at it. Felt its renewal as more lives were given to it by the asirim on the night of the twin moons.

Soon he realized that the night of Beht Zha'ir was when these visions—memories, if trees could be said to have such—were brightest. While Rhia and Tulathan stared down, he felt the souls being given, sometimes to this very tree, sometimes to others in the grove, sometimes to others in the vast chain of blooming fields that surrounded the city. On and on it went, one holy night after the next, reaching back through time slowly but surely toward Beht Ihman.

And then he saw a vision so clear it felt like a blow to the head. He stood, staggered back from it like a man struck by the grandeur of the desert for the first time.

The very land he stands upon lies bare. He sees sand. A shelf of stone. The stars shine as though the sun has been shattered, a diaspora of broken glass. And in the distance, coming nearer, a figure of palest blue. She comes naked, limned in silver light, her gossamer hair trailing in the wind. Her arms are spread to the heavens as though beckoning the stars to attend her. And where she treads, green shoots lift from the stone. On she walks, the twisting branches of nascent trees sprouting like a broadening green carpet behind her.

She is walking toward Davud. Gone is Sukru. Gone are the asirim. Gone are the tortured trees. There is only the bright goddess and Davud. Until now she has walked across the landscape as if she were alone, but as she nears Davud she stops and smiles a leopard's smile, perhaps over some secret she hides, or from simple surprise at finding Davud here.

Her nakedness bothers him not at all. It seems only right, for the desert is hers to command. "Why have you done all this?" When she doesn't answer, he asks, "What's happened to the adichara?"

She seems to stare at him as she passes, but says nothing, making him wonder if she truly saw him. She continues to walk toward the horizon, her path slowly curving until she is gone, leaving Davud alone with the wind, the gently blowing sand, and the trees that have already grown as high as his knees.

When the vision faded Davud was unsure how much time had passed. One moment he was watching Tulathan's wake, the next he was facing the eastern horizon as the morning sun rose above the adichara. The trees themselves were still, their blooms closed. It was so disorienting he staggered back, then realized his sleeve was caught. Immediately he stopped, remembering he was among killing plants, deadly if their thorns were to pierce his skin. Slowly, he pulled the fabric free, making a mental note to burn these clothes on his return to the Sun Palace.

The asir was gone, which was hardly a surprise, but Sukru was gone as well. As he left the grove, he found Zahndr a short distance away, pissing into to the trees. He finished his business, tied his trousers, and trudged toward Davud.

"I . . . I think I saw the goddess—"

Davud stopped speaking when Zahndr raised his hands. "I don't want to hear it. Tell your King."

Davud nodded numbly, and together they headed back toward the yacht. Sukru met them halfway, gliding over the sand with the look of a vulture hopping toward its dying prey.

As Zahndr continued on, Sukru said, "Go on, boy."

Gods, where to begin? "It worked."

Sukru was not amused. "Had it not been for the five hours you just spent staring at the same tree, I would never have guessed. Tell me what you've learned."

Davud did. All of it. From the feelings of connection to the receding water to the sacrifices going back through time. He spent the most time on Tulathan, partially because he'd been so transfixed by her, but also because Sukru kept asking for clarification: about what she'd said, her description, and her affect on the trees and the surrounding land.

"And the tree?" Sukru asked when he was done.

Davud shrugged. "I could sense the illness in it, but in truth no more than by merely staring at it, or smelling it. Whatever sense of disease there was faded entirely as I was drawn back toward Beht Ihman. I learned nothing more."

Sukru considered for a time. "Very well," he said at last, flicking his fingers for Davud to follow him toward the ship. "We'll try again soon. Until then, I'll provide you with more sigils."

As they walked side by side over the sand, Davud couldn't help but wonder: *if the blood of a tribute achieved this much, what might the blood of the asirim give me?*

He glanced sidelong at Sukru.

What might the blood of a King?

Chapter 16

ERYAM WAS IN her apartments when Ramahd returned from the
Widow's estate, but it took her nearly an hour to finish discussing
plans for Basilio's return to Qaimir. When Basilio finally left, he strode past
Ramahd with the look of a sow that had just enjoyed its fill of slop. Ramahd
would like nothing more than to wipe that smug look off his face, but he was
still so angry about Tiron he held his tongue and walked in through the
double doors leading into Meryam's apartments. He closed the doors behind
him and found Meryam sitting by the fireplace.

"How could you have let Tiron—"

He stopped, for Meryam was shaking her head and beckoning him closer.
As he stepped near, she bit the inside of her lip and touched her forefinger to it.
It came away bloody. She used it to wipe her spit and blood over Ramahd's own
lips, a precaution so that their words wouldn't carry to the King of Whispers.

It may be wise, but the delay made him feel manipulated, and it only made
him angrier. "How could you have given Tiron to a woman like the Widow?"

"Don't be such a fool, Ramahd. Tiron *volunteered*."

The words struck like a hammer blow. "Tiron—"

"Yes, he *chose* this. He was weakened after the loss of his cousin Luken and fell to the touch of the smoke. So I summoned him and gave him the choice: I would help him heal or he could give himself to this mission. He chose the mission. And now we're nearly there. Soon he'll be taken to the Tattered Prince."

"The Tattered Prince . . ." And suddenly Ramahd understood all of it. Understood Tiron's being given to the Widow, being left there until near death, and what Meryam planned to do with him now. "You're using him as bait."

If Meryam were embarrassed, it didn't show in the skeletal features of her face. "Yes. I am."

The Tattered Prince, also called the Torn Man for the scars that riddled his body, had become something of a legend in the city's west end. His real name was Brama, and he had a small but loyal group of men and women. It was said he healed those in the grips of the black lotus's lure. Some were so thankful they joined him in what Ramahd could only describe as a cult, with Brama as their enigmatic leader. More importantly for Meryam, Brama had a gemstone, a massive sapphire that housed, in all likelihood, a powerful demon. An ehrekh.

"We have enough to worry about without calling that sort of trouble down on ourselves."

"There's always danger, Ramahd, when one seeks power."

"Perhaps, but this sort of power isn't worth the risk."

"I disagree. If we succeed in this, it will all have been worth it." She seemed incredulous at his hesitance. "Can you not *feel* Guhldrathen's impatience? Time is a luxury we can no longer afford."

Guhldrathen was the ehrekh they'd bargained with in the desert to free themselves. Ramahd had promised neither his own life, nor even Meryam's, but Çeda's if they failed to deliver Hamzakiir. And he'd given his own blood to seal the bargain. In the months since, he'd felt the weight of that bargain, not only from the guilt but from a growing compulsion. It had the feel of black magic about it, the same feeling as when the ehrekh had used its magic to draw symbols around the dead body of King Aldouan. At the moment, the urge was directionless, but he knew it would soon become a *need* to do as the ehrekh wished.

"Of course I can feel it," Ramahd said, "but there's time yet. Which is why we should be spending our efforts searching for Hamzakiir."

She flicked one hand, as if chasing a fly away. "Unless you're ready to go to the desert yourself, we're doing all we can."

"Then let me go in Tiron's stead. He's been through enough."

Meryam pulled herself taller in her chair. "No. I have other plans for you. And Tiron is in too deep to change plans now."

"If you had only told me. I could have helped."

"I don't need explain to you every decision I make, Ramahd. I don't think you appreciate how aggressive the Kings have become of late. The fewer who know, the smaller the chance the King of Whispers will hear us." When he continued to stare, she closed her eyes and released a long sigh. "I didn't tell you because I knew you would act"—she sent a dismissive wave in his general direction—"like this."

"But Tiron—"

"Tiron is a *soldier*, and we have only begun taking the steps we need in order to make Qaimir safe."

"This is all for Qaimir then?"

Meryam's face reddened. "*And* for revenge! Don't tell me you've lost your will to see Macide Ishaq'ava hang! Don't tell me you'd let Hamzakiir walk for his crimes! Because I won't have it. They will pay, both of them, before this is done. And in the meantime, everything I do will make Qaimir far more powerful than the Kings would allow, more than my father ever thought to seize."

"Tiron was my man."

Meryam pushed herself off the chair in a rush, her eyes afire. She only came up to his collarbone, but she seemed well larger. "You're setting your feelings above the needs of our nation. There was a time that I admired you for it, especially when you were my sister's husband. But I tell you now it has become an obstacle. Years past, you and I would joke. I'll have your head if you don't fetch me tea, I'll have your head if you don't rub my shoulders." She stepped closer, the fire in her heart reflected in her eyes, making her look crazed. "Hear my words. Those days are gone. I *will* have that gem, and you will help me to get it, not on your terms, but on mine."

Ramahd couldn't deny that Meryam had done much. And he was certain she had Qaimir's interests at heart. The only question was whether she placed her own thirst for power above them. "Forgive me, my queen," he said at last.

"I've been too easy with our relationship, treating it as it once was. When I press, it is for Qaimir, always."

The stiffness in Meryam's frail body softened, and a hint of relief showed in her eyes. "I don't blame you for it. But there is always more going on than I can share. Question me, but by the gods, heed me when I have spoken."

"Of course. What would you have me do?"

"Brama must offer to heal Tiron. The trouble is he no longer heals everyone. When the two of us inveigled our way into Tariq's mind, we stumbled across a sapphire. The soul we felt within it, the ehrekh . . . Her name is Rümayesh, and she is an almost mythical being among the halls of Golden-hill. She once collected souls as I collect Mirean ivory. She chose her victims for how interesting their lives had been. Lately, Brama has been choosing to heal those with rather storied pasts, a marked difference from months ago when he would heal nearly anyone, no matter their history. I believe Rümayesh is the reason for his change."

It took Ramahd a moment to understand. "You chose Tiron because of what happened to us in Eventide." The satisfaction in Meryam's sallow eyes gave him his answer. "It's dangerous. There's no telling what Rümayesh or Brama might do with the information. It could implicate *you*."

"We're beyond danger. We have been for some time. I need that gem, Ramahd. I need it to find and defeat Hamzakiir and save us from Guhldrathen." Meryam took Ramahd's hand and squeezed it, a rare show of emotion. "Make them take notice of Tiron. The story he tells them will do the rest."

Ramahd nodded slowly. "I know what to do."

Two days later, shortly after dawn, Ramahd found himself in the west end once more. He was waiting in the shadows of the same bridge, studying the Widow's bulky estate. This time, he knew exactly where Tiron was. Before he'd left the embassy house, Meryam had given him some of Tiron's blood mixed in wine. She'd bid him drink half of it, then dripped more into his ears, whispering words to bind him to the earth, to the very world around him, in ways Ramahd would never fully comprehend. It left behind a keen ringing, which had increased as he walked across the city toward the west end, and led him to Tiron.

It was strong enough now that Ramahd could not only *hear* Tiron's presence, but *feel* it as well, as it moved from the rear of the estate to the front entrance. Tiron left on his own, heading north as the city came alive, and looked a proper wreck, holding one arm tight to his body, shambling as if every step pained him. And his eyes . . . Mighty Alu, how empty they looked, how focused on one thing and one thing only: finding more black lotus.

Ramahd ran ahead, taking a parallel route on the dry river bank's opposite side. He lost sight of Tiron as the Haddah's path curved, and Ramahd headed into the Shallows proper. The two of them were now headed toward the same place: the Knot, the Tattered Prince's domain. Soon Ramahd spotted Cicio leaning against the wall of a bakery, tearing apart a still-steaming hunk of bread and popping it into his mouth. The two of them didn't acknowledge one another, but as Ramahd passed Cicio fell into step and together they neared the southern entrance to the Knot.

They stopped on the near side of a cross-section of streets where the morning crowd grew thick. The ringing sound rose in both pitch and intensity moments before Tiron appeared, limping along as if it were all he could do to keep himself from curling into a ball right there in the middle of the street. He entered the Knot through an arch of sorts formed by the mudbrick houses on either side and the oddly angled structure that had been built across their shoulders. It announced the character of the neighborhood every bit as effectively as the bronze-capped pillars that stood at the borders of Goldenhill.

Tiron made his way deeper into the Knot, then came to the dead-end street where the Tattered Prince's territory formally began. As he turned to head along it, Tiron, on queue, glanced back, then played his part perfectly. He stumbled. His eyes went wide. He began moving faster.

As he rushed up the street and was lost from view, Ramahd moved faster, but not *too* fast. He turned onto the street, and Cicio trailed him. Ahead, Tiron glanced back again. And then Ramahd saw the first of them. A woman wearing simple flaxen robes, flanked by a taller man with the look of an enforcer. The woman gave Ramahd more pause, however. The palm of her hand, which she'd raised to Tiron, was scarred in the shape of a starburst. Ramahd had heard about these, the sign of those most loyal to Brama, but not about the gem embedded there. Like a blue eye, a sapphire gleamed at the center of the scars on her palm.

She spoke to Tiron, halting him just as Amaryllis exited a small home where she'd had her fortune read—a ruse to ensure she would be along this street at this precise moment.

She turned as Ramahd drew his sword and headed for Tiron with more speed. Amaryllis gasped loudly, then backed away while pointing at Ramahd. "On your guard!"

Ramahd moved faster. "Traitor!" he shouted at Tiron.

Ramahd knew Brama's followers kept the peace here, but he hadn't expected them to rush toward him so aggressively. And he certainly hadn't expected a burst of light to blaze from the gemstone buried in the woman's hand.

But that's exactly what happened. As Tiron backed away, shouting, "Please help!" the woman strode past him, holding her ruined palm toward Ramahd as if it were a lantern and he a demon in the night.

A blue light flashed. Ramahd blinked, trying to clear it away, but it wouldn't. It burned like the sun wherever he looked.

His world tilted.

He heard Amaryllis shouting something. Heard Cicio raging until his voice was cut short. Heard the scrape of sandals over the sandy street and saw a scarred hand poised above him. A wave of nausea took him until her palm lowered and touched his forehead.

A rush of memories came unbidden—of Qaimir, of sailing the desert, of wandering the endless streets of Sharakhai. The memories came faster, a cavalcade of sounds, sights, sensations followed by a flood of emotions. He could relate to all of them and none of them. Soon it became too much, and he became lost.

Chapter 17

ZEHEB, THE KING OF WHISPERS, met Kings Ihsan and Azad just inside his palace doors.

"Well met," Ihsan said, giving Zeheb a bow, as did Azad.

"We shall see," Zeheb replied, the rolls beneath his chin creasing as he gave a stiff nod and led them down through the palace to its cool lower reaches.

"How fares your daughter?" Ihsan asked him.

"Pharrali died this morning," Zeheb said.

He said it with as much emotion as he might speak of the weather, yet Ihsan knew how close they'd been.

Pharrali had been a Blade Maiden—one of many sent to verify his whispers, or to act on them—but her mission had gone awry. A man she'd been sent to question had a slow-acting poisoned needle secreted up his sleeve. She'd managed to subdue him and bring him back to Zeheb before being rushed to the Matrons for their curatives. For several days all had looked well, but now . . .

"My tears for your loss," Ihsan replied, genuinely shocked. "The poison took her?"

"No. She was strong. She fought it off." Zeheb was angry now. Ihsan could see it in the stiffness of his strides, the way he swung his arms, as if he wished a weapon was held in each. "It was the infection. It seemed to be under control, but then it returned, rushing in like a sandstorm. Within a day, she was gone."

Pharrali's death was yet another test of resolve for Zeheb, the sort every King was forced to contend with sooner or later. Zeheb could have used one of his small cache of the old elixirs, those made by Azad before his death; he could have healed his daughter in moments. But the Kings had long ago agreed never to share them. Ihsan had never once done so, though he had been sorely tempted several times. Some of the Kings may have made exceptions, but Ihsan doubted it. It was one of the more sacrosanct rules they'd agreed to after Beht Ihman four centuries ago, that only the Kings would use them, never others, lest their secrets be discovered. The elixirs were gifts from the gods meant only for those who were worthy. To share them would not only dishonor the gods, it would surely anger them. And, Ihsan admitted, a hoarding mindset had settled in among the Kings; start using them too much, and they wouldn't have enough for themselves.

The only exception Ihsan knew of was Nayyan, but having taken Azad's place she was like to a King, and deserved all that went with it.

They reached a guarded doorway. The Silver Spear bowed his head, unlocked the door, and pulled it wide. Zeheb swept in, leaving Ihsan and Azad to follow. Inside was a clean, unadorned room with a smelly chamber pot in one corner. Wedged into the opposite corner, chained to an iron ring, was a middle-aged man dressed in a bright Malasani kaftan, sirwal trousers, and fine, if dusty, leather sandals. He was clearly scared—eyes wide, harrowed brow—but otherwise looked unharmed, fresh from the streets.

The man's gaze moved to each of the Kings in turn, then he seemed to remember himself and shifted to a kneeling position.

"Tell them what you told me," Zeheb ordered.

The man bowed low, touching forehead to folded hands. "Of course, my Lord King. I said Macide Ishaq'ava is still in the city. And that the remains of the Moonless Host are scared of the Kings' power. They know their days are numbered. Their leader Ishaq has already fled the city, but Macide and many of his captains, Hamid the Cruel, Darius One-Arm, Shal'alara of the Three Blades, are preparing to leave the city en masse."

"And how would you know this?" Ihsan broke in.

"A number of them are hiding in my tenements." His words were so rushed Ihsan thought he might start to hyperventilate. "I've only recently stumbled across the information. I proceeded to discover all I could so I might pass it to the Silver Spears and the House of Kings." He bowed his head again. Was he *shivering*? "I was preparing to do so when I was so kindly invited here"—he bowed his head and flourished toward Zeheb—"by My Lord King's most gracious servant."

Zeheb crossed his arms over his chest. "And your offer?"

"I am more than willing to tell you where Macide and his comrades-in-arms are hiding, or how and when they plan to leave the city. You need only release me for a day, and you'll have them, my Kings, on my word as a loyal citizen of Sharakhai, my word as a child of the desert. There is no need for you to hold or involve my brother or his wife. They are innocent lambs, both."

Well, that certainly explains why the man is in such pristine condition. If he were to leave and go hunting for information about the Host looking like he'd fallen down a mountain face-first, it would make the Host suspicious, as would an extended absence from his daily routine, which made it likely that Zeheb had brought him here no more than a day ago.

"Let me understand," Ihsan said. "You wish to be released so that you might serve us Macide Ishaq'ava on a platter."

The man's eyes lit up. "You have the right of it, my Lord King!"

Ihsan turned to Zeheb. "I've heard enough."

Zeheb glanced at Azad, but he only frowned and left the room. Zeheb followed, but Ihsan tarried for a moment. "Your tenements, do they include the one where a man burst through a brick wall and crushed a Maiden's head with an iron pot to escape?"

For a moment the man didn't seem to know how to answer, but then he nodded tentatively. "Indeed, your Grace, that's one of mine."

Ihsan clasped his hands behind his back and followed Zeheb, the pieces falling into place. The slum lord was a traitor to the Moonless Host—how could he provide Macide's whereabouts otherwise?—but his betrayal signaled more. An irreconcilable rift had formed in the Host, with Ishaq and his son Macide on one side of it and Hamzakiir on the other. Since his return to the desert, Hamzakiir had been peeling away more and more of Ishaq's support in the host; the slumlord was but more proof of it.

If this man was Hamzakiir's, then Zeheb's caution made sense. Acting now would weaken Macide's hold on the city, thereby making Hamzakiir's position stronger. It had taken Ihsan years of careful cultivation to gain the trust of the right people—Zeheb and Azad included—and to begin funneling resources and information to Ishaq so that the Moonless Host could better work against the interests of the Kings. Not so long ago, Zeheb wouldn't have thought twice about trying to turn this situation to the advantage of their alliance, but now he hesitated, and Ihsan had to wonder why.

"Are you losing heart, my Lord King?" Ihsan said to Zeheb as the three of them walked down the hall.

Zeheb said nothing until they'd taken one set of stairs up to an empty landing, then he spun and jabbed his finger at Ihsan. "I am not *losing heart*. You've no idea how close Kiral is to finding us out."

Azad was clearly confused. "What in the wide great desert are the two of you on about?"

"Zeheb is concerned that if we don't fall in line with Kiral and the rest, we'll be sniffed out and strung up like thieves before the gates."

Azad motioned to the stairs behind them. "And what did our prisoner have to do with any of that?"

"He is a sacrificial lamb," Ihsan began, "almost certainly set up for us by Kiral, who for some unfathomable reason has decided to back Hamzakiir in the Moonless Host's internal war. This leaves us with a difficult choice: use our lamb to betray the Host's old order, Ishaq and Macide, thereby ruining our years of careful work. Or we can use him to find Hamzakiir and go against the implicit wishes of Kiral, perhaps exposing ourselves in the process."

Zeheb faced Azad. "The choice is not so complicated as that. We have a chance to cripple the Host. What does it matter if Hamzakiir helps? If we fail to seize this opportunity, there's no telling what could happen. Ishaq and Hamzakiir could come to an accord *tomorrow*. Let us strike while the opening presents itself."

"And Kiral?" Azad asked.

"I agree with Ihsan," Zeheb said. "Kiral is more worried than ever about betrayal. Let's toss him a bone and let our slumlord betray the Moonless Host, or he may start sniffing in places that would best be left alone."

Azad considered. "Have you heard whispers from Eventide? Elsewhere?"

"That Kiral has evidence of our treason? No. But believe me when I tell you he's wary of everyone, especially after Onur's sudden departure and the stories we've crafted to explain it away." Zeheb drew breath, his nostrils flaring. "Let me put this plainly. Kiral, in no uncertain terms, is demanding we step in line. If we don't, the things we've done, our aiding of the Moonless Host, will not survive his scrutiny. We're not prepared to oppose him. We must bide our time, especially since we've failed to re-create the elixirs."

Ihsan had decided there was no reason to tell Zeheb that Azad had managed to perfect a new version of the life-giving elixirs, not leastwise because of the likelihood that Zeheb *would* lose heart. Ihsan had wondered what he'd do if the day came where Zeheb decided that their pact was no longer in his best interests. He'd never found a satisfactory answer, largely because it would depend on how the pieces lay on the aban board when that happened.

"You play a short game," Ihsan said. "If we cede ground to Hamzakiir, we may be handing the keys to the House of Kings to *him* instead taking them for ourselves."

"This is no short game. What we do pits the two factions of the Moonless Host against one another. It will weaken Hamzakiir as well, with little harm to Sharakhai. Hamzakiir is dangerous, but he is a threat we can deal with in due time."

Ihsan was tempted to try and persuade Zeheb, to lure him back to their side. But there was danger in it. He might very well convince Zeheb to remain bold, but Ihsan could sense how uncertain he was. Zeheb might change his mind again. If he did, if he thought *Ihsan* wouldn't bend to his request to align themselves with Kiral, he might very well offer them up as sacrifices, or worse, send his assassins to present them with a kiss of steel. For now, being seen as pliable was more important than pushing for advantages that may or may not bear fruit.

Rock will break, Ihsan's father had often told him. *But water goes where it will.*

Besides, Zeheb was right about one thing. They weren't prepared to oppose Kiral directly. Not yet. And the old guard of the Moonless Host, while a useful tool, could be replaced in time. So instead of using his god-given powers to convince Zeheb to remain resilient, he used them for another purpose. "I see the wisdom in your words," he said while giving the slightest tug on Zeheb's heart. "Better to cut the head from the snake before worrying about its nest."

He'd learned over the years just how much he could draw upon Tulathan's gift without being discovered. He did so now with the care of a master craftsman, using words and expression and tone, even the set of his body, in conjunction with his power, creating a symphony that masked the use of his power.

Bowing his head, Ihsan tugged again. "Hamzakiir will keep, and there's no telling what Macide might do once he leaves the city." He turned to Azad. "Wouldn't you agree?"

Azad considered for just the right amount of time, as if he too saw the wisdom in Zeheb's words. "Very well."

Zeheb looked at them both as if he'd been prepared for more of a fight and, now that it was over, wasn't sure what to say. "Well and good, then!"

Azad's apathy played in stark contrast to Zeheb's relief. "Are we done here, my good Kings?"

"Yes!" Zeheb was most affable, almost giddy.

He led them back upstairs, where Ihsan and Azad returned to their coach. As it trundled away, Azad regarded Ihsan levelly, annoyance now marking his features. "I don't know that the use of your gift was necessary."

For the first time in years, Ihsan was caught flat-footed. "You *felt* that?"

Azad touched his stomach. "I feel much from you since . . ." He left the rest unsaid. The child Nayyan carried inside her was hidden by the disguise she now wore, but the babe was there. Had some of his power been passed to her along with his seed? He laughed. In all his years, he would never have even considered the notion.

"Wondrous!" he said, a genuine laugh filling the cabin, warring with the sound of clopping hooves. "But it *was* necessary. For Zeheb to renege is no small thing. He is an honest man. It took much for him to consider abandoning our plans."

"Honest or not, if he's gone this far, he's considered betraying us."

"Which is precisely why I had to use more than words to convince him."

Azad bowed his head with a hungry look that put Ihsan on edge. "We must prepare for the worst."

Ihsan wasn't sure whether to be nervous or proud.

Both, he decided. Nayyan was more impulsive than he liked, and more bloodthirsty, but those very qualities would see them to the end of his long-laid plans. "Indeed," Ihsan replied, acknowledging that Zeheb may soon have to join Yusam, Külaşan, Mesut, and Nayyan's father, the true King Azad, all of whom now lay in their crypts beneath their palaces, their chances to rule the desert lost with their lives.

Chapter 18

THE *GRAY GULL*, Adzin's rickety sloop, left the city's western harbor under cover of darkness. They needed to reach the northern harbor by dawn, but with the wind against them, they had to head northwest until they could tack and set a path around the city's rocky northeastern shoulder. Adding to Emre's distress, this was a day when every second mattered, but the wind was meager. Less than meager. Were the wind to find a friendly breeze to join it, *then* it might be considered meager.

Lissome Rhia, Emre prayed silently, *I would dream beyond this day. Please, lend the weather more ambition than this!*

The soothsayer, Adzin, sat cross-legged on the foredeck, doing his best to hold a wriggling, black terror of a creature with both hands. Another flapped violently in a metal cage beside him. The horrific beasts, ifins, were the size of a small dog, and had two sets of saurian wings and smooth, scaled necks that tapered to eyeless heads. They had no jaws, but instead funnel-shaped mouths with row upon row of needle-sharp teeth. Adzin curled over the one he held as it squirmed. He spoke gibberish to it like the Malasani witches who whispered to their cats before sending them off to perform some errand.

"Take it," Adzin said to Emre.

Gods, Emre thought, *the only thing worse than watching it is holding it.*

The infernal thing twisted as Emre grabbed it. Its twin sets of wings flapped madly. Its head snaked around to snap at his hands and wrists. It managed to latch onto the protective gloves he wore several times, and once bit *through* the thick leather. In a moment of panic, Emre slapped the head away, which made it wriggle all the more. Hissing from the pain, Emre held its neck more securely, wondering if he'd just made a grave error by letting it blood him. There was no telling what one of Goezhen's children might do to him. Track him for days, maybe, perhaps even months or years, then return one moonless night and suck his blood dry.

Darius, Hamid, and Frail Lemi stood on the edge of the foredeck, eyeing the *Gull's* crew. Adzin had promised he would see them through the day, but even so, things were tense. Unsurprising when Emre and the others had effectively stolen the ship and threatened to kill their captain unless they obeyed. For now, they were complying with Adzin's orders. Emre consoled himself with the knowledge that he only needed their loyalty a short while longer.

The ifin flapped its bat-like wings again, scratching Emre's face. He held it at arm's length until it had calmed. "When can I release this fucking thing?"

Adzin took out the second of the ifins. "It won't be much longer." His words, like his actions, were tranquility itself, which was more than strange considering the position he and his men were in. *The man is a soothsayer,* Emre reminded himself for the dozenth time. *He might know every move he has to make to get through this day with his skin intact.*

As if he'd heard Emre's thoughts, Adzin turned and smiled his calming smile, then ducked his head and spoke softly to the second ifin, the words as nonsensical as before.

The ship rattled and shook, slowing momentarily as it crossed the dry bed of the Haddah. They were now rounding the northwestern shoulder of Sharakhai and sailed east-northeast, but gods it was taking a long while to get anywhere. Every moment they spent sailing toward the harbor endangered another of the Host.

Thaash, lend this tepid wind your anger!

As if he'd heard Emre's prayer, Adzin suddenly lifted the writhing demon and flung it into the air like a sacred dove. The ifin flapped its wings, sounding like the clouds of bats that plagued the banks of the Haddah in late spring, and headed straight for the entrance to the northern harbor, where a pair of lighthouses stood sentinel, twin brands that mirrored the light of the coming dawn.

"Quickly," Adzin said, holding his hands out to Emre.

Emre gladly handed the ifin over. It wriggled, managed to clamp its teeth on the leather gloves again, but then lost hold as Adzin cradled it.

As the *Gray Gull* slid over the sand, the mood grew darker and the eastern horizon brightened. They could see two of the Kings' patrol ships several leagues north and a small yacht stationed at the entrance to the northern harbor. Across the harbor's entrance, strung between the two lighthouses and held up by posts driven into the sand, was a stout chain meant to stop any ships not approved by the Kings' agents.

"Track the ifin closely," Adzin shouted to the pilot.

"Aye." The pilot, a rangy woman with a scar that ran down one cheek and along her neck before being lost beneath her roughspun shirt, adjusted their heading, making sure the sloop's course and the ifin's matched.

As they came closer to the harbor entrance, however, it became clear that the ifin was flying a path that would lead them over a raised section of rock.

"Here's where it gets interesting," Emre said.

"Here's where it gets interesting," Frail Lemi echoed, his eyes brimming with childlike anticipation.

The swath of stone, harbor, and the city beyond looked unreal, a painting on canvas. Ochres and purples and rust dominated the landscape in the early morning light. The stone was mostly flat, with pools of sand contained within its topography, though there were outcroppings of rock as well. No captain in their right mind would run their ship across such terrain. Not unless they were desperate or mad. It could cripple the ship, especially if they struck one of the larger stones.

Adzin seemed neither desperate *nor* mad. Once he'd resigned himself to finding a way to save Macide and the others, he'd set about it with surprising zeal. It was as if he now viewed this mission as a test, perhaps one he'd never faced before, or ever would again, and had taken it as a personal challenge.

If there was one saving grace, it was that the wind had finally picked up. The ship was now moving with proper speed, enough that Emre thought they might actually make it to the harbor.

The ship lurched as it struck stone. Emre held tight to a shroud lest he be sent sprawling to the deck. The ifin flapped and twisted, guiding the ship over several of the larger pools of sand, narrowly bypassing large rocks that would cause serious damage. The ride was rough, and the sudden adjustments made the twin masts sway alarmingly. Ahead, however, was the worst obstacle yet, a ridge that was simply unavoidable.

"All hold!" roared the pilot.

Everyone held tight, even Adzin. The sloop's nose bucked as they crossed the ridge. So steep was the angle that Emre was sure the struts were going to give way when they landed. The ship came down hard, the hull groaning. Everything rattled, including Emre's teeth. Something cracked as the ship's ass end tilted up from the rudder catching the same ridge. Then finally, blessedly, they were past it and into the harbor proper.

Off the port side, a bell started ringing on the King's yacht, and the crew rushed to pursue them, their warning being picked up along the quays.

"Now!" Adzin called. "Sail along the piers until the ifin finds them!"

"Aye!"

The pilot adjusted course starboard toward the docked ships while the ifin flew well ahead, angling between masts and rigging. It twisted this way and that, looking more like a buzzing fly than the demon Adzin had somehow found and tamed. It was searching for the ship where Macide and the others hid. It circled and searched, and as they came ever closer to the end of the line of ships, Emre began to worry that the ifin wouldn't find them. Then it finally began to flip and dive around the mainmast of a caravel.

"That's it," Emre said, and began looking for any signs of the Host, both on the deck of the ship and along the sand below.

He'd hardly begun when he heard footsteps thumping over the deck behind him. The towering Kundhuni was barreling toward him, a slim knife in his hand that was already speeding toward Emre's neck. Emre jerked backward, and felt a burning sensation run in a line across his neck. From the corner of his eye he could see the other crewmen rushing the foredeck. They'd been relieved of their weapons earlier, but they'd found makeshift clubs or belaying pins to fight with.

"Stop!" Adzin shouted, throwing the second ifin into the air. "All of you, stop immediately!" The Kundhuni stayed his next swing, staring at Adzin in wide-eyed disbelief. The rest of the crew did the same.

"We've taken a commission," Adzin went on, "and we will fulfill it. Back to your stations!"

The crew frowned, visibly reluctant.

"Man this ship!" Adzin shouted.

Only then did they obey, albeit slowly. Okzan, the mountainous Kundhuni, glared at Emre, daring him to attack, but then slipped the knife up his sleeve. Emre grimaced as he touched his hand to the shallow cut he'd taken from Okzan's knife. As he pressed his sleeve to it, the others returned to the work of guiding the ship around the harbor's curving interior. Adzin, meanwhile, watched as the second ifin wheeled higher into the gauzy yellow sky, as if he had no doubt the mythical beast would lead him and his crew to safety.

"There they are," Darius said, pointing toward the caravel.

Emre spotted them beneath the pier: a dozen men and women in thawbs, dresses, and leather armor were emerging from the caravel's lower hatch. Macide was at their head, his twin shamshirs hanging from his belt. In that same moment, the first ifin released a piercing screech and flew west, its mission fulfilled.

"Slow the ship!" Hamid called.

Adzin's crew was ready at the *Gull*'s stern, lowering the iron-toothed rake. It thumped into the sand, digging deep furrows, slowing the ship, and throwing everyone forward.

Macide's confusion was plain.

"Quickly!" Hamid called. "We've been betrayed!"

A black arrow thudded into the back of the woman standing behind Macide. Another arrow took the man beside her in the thigh. And then suddenly the air was thick with them.

Emre ducked behind the gunwales as arrows streaked in against the *Gray Gull*. Beyond the quay, fifteen Blade Maidens, wearing turbans and black fighting dresses, and a score of Silver Spears in conical helms and lapping chainmail hauberks surged forth from a warehouse. Many held bows and had stopped to launch volleys, but five of the Blade Maidens were sprinting ahead, ebon blades drawn. Emre wondered if Çeda was among them, but he had no time to look more closely. Darius was handing him a bow.

While Macide ushered those following him toward the *Gray Gull*, Emre loosed arrow after arrow into the sprinting Blade Maidens. Emre had deadly aim, but the Maidens were amazingly quick and seemed to know exactly where he was aiming. Each time he released an arrow, they would dodge out of the way, hardly slowing in the process. So it was that with the first six shots, he managed only one grazing wound.

The Maidens hurtled along the pier and dropped to the sand as the *Gray Gull* approached those fleeing the caravel.

"Port side!" Emre shouted, waving frantically to them. "Move to the port side of the ship!"

They took his meaning. Many flew across the sand and beyond the *Gull*'s prow, where they grabbed at the ladders and ropes that Frail Lemi had lowered for them. Others turned and confronted the Maidens rather than be cut down from behind. Swords clashed as the scarabs of the Moonless Host met the line of Blade Maidens. At first, the Maidens were severely outnumbered. Two dozen scarabs stood against their five, but the Maidens worked in effortless concert, moving easily with one another as if they were a single five-headed, black-skinned beast—a demon not unlike the ifin that had led the *Gray Gull* to dockside.

Arrows continued to rain down, but now the *Gull*'s crew joined in the counterattack. All knew the grisly fate that awaited them if they didn't escape this harbor. So they accepted the bows Hamid handed them and pulled arrows from the quivers stationed around the ship, loosing them with a zeal that matched Emre's.

Adzin was pointing madly to the second ifin, spinning in a tight circle near the mouth of the harbor. "Quickly! Pull up the rake!"

The crew did, though one of them took an arrow in the arm for the trouble. Another arrow came screaming in and took the pilot straight through the neck. The woman grabbed it, trying to pull it free, but the moment she succeeded a torrent of blood gushed from the wound, and she fell writhing to the deck. Okzan grabbed the wheel, steering them back on a heading even with the ifin's path while the rest of the crew set the boom for the coming change in wind.

Emre and Hamid rushed to the stern to get a better view of the battle, to help if they could. Several scarabs fought around Macide, but two had already fallen. A third had his legs cut from underneath him as the Maiden he was fighting ducked and delivered a vicious two-handed strike across his knees. A heavy thud sounded to Emre's right as the ballista fired. The bolt struck low, creating a burst of sand in front of the two Blade Maidens sprinting past Macide toward the *Gray Gull*. The sudden spray of sand slowed them, but not by much. If even one of them gained the ship, they could easily cripple it.

Emre turned as Cenk, Adzin's second mate, began cranking the ballista's windlass again. By his side were more of the larger bolts, but also a grapnel and a coil of rope. It was usually launched across rigging to cripple enemy ships but the sight of it gave Emre a flash of inspiration.

"Give me a turn," Emre said.

Cenk grudgingly allowed him to lay the grapnel and rope into the bolt groove.

Emre aimed high and fired. As the grapnel flew and the coil unfurled behind it, Emre whistled sharply twice.

Macide glanced back, then redoubled his efforts against the two Blade Maidens, his twin shamshirs flying. The grapnel flew by him, and would have caught the Maiden on his right across the head had she not somehow sensed it and ducked in time.

The rope pulled taut and the grapnel raked the sand. It tripped the Maiden, who cried out as one of the grapnel's sharp hooks tore through her foot, boot and all, and dropped her to the sand. It pulled her along as she reached for it, trying vainly to release herself.

Macide gave one last flurry of sweeping blows from his shamshirs, then turned and sprinted for the Maiden being dragged ever faster by the ship. Sheathing one of his swords with practiced ease, he ran *onto* the Maiden, using her as a platform to launch himself forward. Grabbing the rope with his free hand, he sliced it clean through so that the Maiden was freed, and *he* was now being pulled along the sand.

Emre and Hamid worked together, hauling Macide closer and closer to the ship as the remaining Maiden gave chase. Darius fired arrow after arrow at her, forcing her to alter her path, but it still wasn't enough. She lifted her sword, preparing to leap and chop her blade down against Macide when another thud from the second ballista sounded and a bolt caught her straight through the chest. The blow was so powerful it knocked her backward and pinned her against the sand.

Hamid and Emre were both beginning to tire, but luckily Frail Lemi rushed in to relieve them. Alone, he pulled the rope with his cordwood arms, drawing Macide closer to the ship with more speed than Emre and Hamid had managed together.

Finally, Macide was up and over the edge of the gunwales, breathing hard, his legs bloody where sand and stone had torn through his clothes.

Another of Adzin's crew was felled by an arrow, but the *Gray Gull* was building speed now and heading toward open sand. The royal yacht guarding the harbor's entrance had set its sails and was gliding toward the rocky area where the *Gull* had entered the harbor. They clearly thought to cut off their escape.

"Where's the ifin?" Emre snapped.

Okzan, at the pilot's wheel, squinted at the sand ahead, the sky above. "It was just there," he said in a thick Kundhunese accent, "I swear it!"

Before he'd even finished the words, Emre heard urgent flapping to his left. He turned and saw the ifin arcing toward them. It fluttered around Macide, then *landed* on one of his swords. It gripped the scabbard, its head twisting this way and that, as if it were confused.

"Go!" Hamid shouted, waving his hands at it, but it only fluttered away and landed on the sword again.

Only when Macide drew the sword did it fly, turning in a tight circle, and soar ahead of the ship directly for the center of the long chain spanning the mouth of the harbor.

"What's it want, Emre?" Frail Lemi asked.

Hamid frowned at Frail Lemi and headed to the foredeck while staring at the ifin. "Does the thing expect us to just run past the chain? It'll shatter the struts!"

Emre watched the odd patterns of the ifin's flight as Hamid grabbed

Adzin by the front of his robes and shook him. "What does that ruddy thing want?"

Adzin, practically ignoring Hamid, was staring every bit as intently as Emre. "I don't know."

"It's *your* bloody beast!" Hamid pressed.

Adzin turned to him and replied as if he were speaking to a child. "I have no special insight into their minds! Once given a scent they follow it, trusting wholly to the winds of fate. How they reveal it is up to them and is for us to interpret."

"It wants us to break the chain," Emre said.

"What?" Macide asked, stepping alongside them.

"Look at it. It wants us to break the chain."

The ifin was darting down toward one particular spot in the long, black chain, swooping up, then doing the same. Over and over it repeated the maneuver, a thing not unlike a sword cutting across it.

Emre turned to Macide. "Give me your sword."

Hamid barked a laugh. "You're mad!"

But Macide had no humor in his eyes as he glanced between the ifin and his shamshir, which he still held in his right hand. It was a fine weapon, every bit as beautifully crafted as the Maiden's ebon blades. It was darker than normal steel, the materials that went into forging ebon steel perhaps a part of its alchemycal making.

The ship was getting closer and closer to the chain. The sound of the skis over the sand came like a hiss now that they were picking up good speed.

Cenk, Adzin's man, had come near. He was staring in awe at the ifin. "Best bloody do it if you're going to."

Hamid looked incensed, but Macide nodded and handed the weapon to Emre, who headed for the prow, where he hopped up to the bowsprit. Navigating the foot of the jib, then the flying jib, he made it to the very fore of the beam and held himself in place with a stay line. He crouched and waited as the *Gull* approached the chain. Gods, how fast the ship was moving now, the waves of sand below accentuated by shadows from the sunrise.

The ifin was still swooping, but as the *Gray Gull* came near, it flew beneath the ship like an arrow.

Emre took a deep breath. Exhaled sharply.

And leapt.

Taking the sword in both hands, he brought it down with all his might against the black length of chain. He heard a metallic shearing. Felt the chain give way and the sword bite into the sand below.

And then the ship loomed above him. The forward struts struck the chain. Chips of wood flew as the chain's two halves were whipped to either side of the ship. But the struts held and the *Gull* sailed on.

Emre knew what the ifin wanted him to do. The rudder was flying toward him with alarming speed. He tried his best to soften the blow as he threw himself across it, but it still drove mercilessly into his ribs. He heard something snap, and saw stars as he held tight to the ski.

He was horrified to realize he'd lost Macide's sword. It lay in the sand, falling away as the ship headed past the lighthouses. He nearly let himself slip off the rudder—he might be able to grab the sword and run back to the ship if they slowed for him. But he may as well wish to be King of Sharakhai. The pain in his ribs was already beginning to soar.

Soon the access hatch on the bottom of the ship was being opened, and Emre was making his way slowly, gingerly toward it, using the handholds in the stout wood of the strut. He was practically yanked through the opening by Frail Lemi.

"Careful, Lemi!" Blackness began to close in around him. "Broken ribs!"

Frail Lemi hardly seemed to notice, smiling broadly, though he thankfully took more care after that, helping Emre up along two ladders and back to the deck. Everyone on deck was smiling. Even Adzin. *Especially* Adzin, though the man must know the hour of his reckoning was near.

They sailed throughout the day, still following the ifin, whose job—with a capital ship, a clipper, having joined the royal yacht in chasing them—was not yet done. Over and over it led them across rocky terrain, but chose the safest path possible, necessitating that the yacht and clipper slow down or risk running aground. Over the course of the day they fell further and further behind, and were finally lost altogether.

The *Gray Gull* sailed on through the night, the ifin still flying close enough that they could see it by moonlight, and when the moons set they followed the sound of its flapping wings.

When morning came it flapped up and away, and Macide called for a halt. He ordered that Adzin and the five remaining members of his crew be brought before him on the sand. They were lined up, surrounded by the Host's survivors, Adzin standing two steps ahead of them.

"I've heard the whole tale," Macide said simply. "You betrayed the Moonless Host."

"One might look at it that way," Adzin replied. His words were deadened in the cold morning air.

"There's no other way to look at it," Hamid broke in.

Macide raised his hand to him. "Is there another way?"

Adzin spread his hands and bowed his head, a supplicant before a mighty king. "To truly know, you'd have to see all the other possible paths of fate."

Hamid frowned. "And you saw them, these other paths?"

Adzin gave him a placid smile. "For you and those gathered here, there were few enough to see."

"You knew it would come to this," Hamid said. He was gripping the hilt of his shamshir. The deep-seated rage in him was clear, but Macide seemed to discount it; he merely raised one hand to forestall Hamid, keeping his eyes on Adzin.

Adzin, meanwhile, nodded. "The other paths were less agreeable than this one."

In that moment, Hamid gripped his sword and drew, closing the distance between him and Adzin as he did. Macide moved to intercept, but his hand reached for his favored shamshir, the one that was now lost because of Emre. Hamid roared as he brought his blade, flashing in the sun, against Adzin's throat.

Blood flew. For a moment, everyone stared. Adzin fell to his knees, gripping the wound, his eyes wide, disbelieving at last. He collapsed quivering to the sand, his lifeblood spilling crimson down the slope of the amber dune.

"You bloody fucking goat!" Macide yelled at Hamid, who hadn't yet taken his eyes off of Adzin. "Go!" Macide yelled again, shoving him into motion. "Go!"

Craning his head back, Hamid spit at Adzin's twitching form, then marched over the sand, sheathing his sword as he went. Adzin's crew stared on with shock or barely suppressed rage. Okzan, the quiet giant, looked as if he were ready to explode in fury.

Macide's jaw jutted as he struggled to recover himself. He looked to each of the crewmen in turn, offering no apology but saying instead, "Your lives are worthless in Sharakhai. We'll give you our skiff and enough food and water to reach a caravanserai, then you can see where your fortunes take you."

A beetle's wings rattled in the distance. Okzan stood tall, meeting Macide's stare with an expression of stony hatred. "The Host is a plague upon the desert."

For several long moments no one spoke. Emre was certain violence would erupt again, but then Cenk moved to stand in front of Okzan. He had no less hatred on his face, but his words were more politic. "We'll take the skiff."

Macide nodded then turned to Emre. "See that it's done."

Emre did, loading enough provisions for seven days' sail, a map, and instruments to sail by. Adzin's crew, meanwhile, were allowed to bury Adzin's body in the sand. On the ship, meanwhile, a hellacious shouting match played out in the captain's cabin of the *Gull*—Macide and Hamid coming to terms.

Soon, Adzin's five surviving crewmen were sailing away. As the sun rose in the east and the *Gray Gull* set sail for the eastern desert, the skiff was lost beyond the horizon.

Chapter 19

A WEEK AFTER VENTURING to the blooming fields with Sukru, Davud sat on his patio after dusk, penning a letter to his sister, Tehla, by lamplight. The day after his visit to the blooming fields, the palace steward had told him he could write a handful of letters. He was certain they'd be read before delivery, but he'd still be glad to get news to Tehla and his family—any news since his return from Ishmantep. So far, all Sukru had allowed was a messenger to say he'd survived and was a guest of the Kings. He hoped that, if he continued to please the King, his family would be allowed to visit him. Or maybe he'd be able to visit *them*. Tulathan's bright smile, how he'd love to spend a day baking bread with Tehla. He'd thought it tedious when he was young, but he could do with a bit of tedium now.

He stopped his writing as the nearby lamp shed light on a familiar bright-breasted finch flitting about the branches of the fig tree. As he set the vulture quill into the inkwell, he realized the bird had something in its beak. It wasn't a bit of twig this time, nor a leaf; it was a small, perfect triangle. He beckoned and said, "Come, come, there's no need to be shy," and the bird flew down onto the mosaic tabletop and dropped the triangle near his wineglass. As it hopped away, Davud picked up the golden device and was stunned by how heavy it was.

The finch spun, then tapped its beak on the tabletop. Then again, and a third time. Davud, brow furrowing, set one point of the triangle on the tabletop. The bird tapped and spun, tapped and spun.

Curious, Davud gave the thing a spin.

It spun and wobbled, looking ready to topple, but it didn't. It continued to spin, a whisper above the table's surface, glinting in the lamplight as it turned faster and faster like a child's top. Slowly, it lifted into the air until it was nearly eye level.

Davud shivered as the thing began to speak in a soft voice.

"So we meet at last."

The voice had a strange vibrato. Was the spinning causing it? He wasn't sure, but it made it impossible to determine whether the speaker was man or woman. After glancing about for signs of Anila or Zahndr or *anyone* else watching, he turned back to the spinning triangle. It felt strange to speak to it, but what else was there to do? "Who *are* you?"

"You may call me the Sparrow." With the speed of it increased, the vibrato had somehow lessened.

"Very well. But who are you really?"

"It's too soon for such talk. Let me instead tell you what I know about *you*." As the voice spoke, the triangle sped up and slowed down—faster when the voice was strongest, slower during lulls or when the voice had fallen silent. He decided the voice sounded male. "You are one of two scholars known to have survived the massacre on the collegia grounds. You either escaped or were spared in Ishmantep. The same is true of the woman, Anila, who shares your room in the Reaping King's palace. You were awakened to the red ways in the desert, and I can only assume it was Hamzakiir himself who gave you that spark."

"You make it your business to know those awakened to the red ways?" Davud felt more watched than ever, and wanted to get the Sparrow talking about himself.

"I do." A warbling chuckle came from the spinning device. "I do, indeed. I consider it my calling. What else can you surmise?"

Davud remembered what Hamzakiir had told him out in the desert, that he should find a mage to learn from before one found him. "I can only guess that you're hoping to train me. Or at least determine if I'm dangerous to you." Davud checked the door and the windows again. When he spoke this time, it was in a low voice. "But I have to wonder why you would risk Sukru's wrath on a gamble such as this."

"I no longer fear Sukru. You, however, have plenty of reason to fear the Reaping King. He preys on young magi, and I fear he will one day prey on you."

"That's ridiculous." Though the words came out less confidently than Davud had intended. "Sukru has been helping me since I arrived. He's helping me to learn the red ways!"

"Now, yes. But Sukru, as you surely know by now, yearns for the sort of power you already wield. He has some small amount of it himself, but not nearly enough to satisfy his desires. As you grow in your abilities, so will his jealousy grow. No doubt he's taken your blood already? Likely Anila's as well?"

Davud tried to swallow the lump in his throat, as the sinking feeling inside him accelerated.

The Sparrow laughed. "Your silence is answer enough. He's one to be careful of, Davud. He has the patience of a butterfly and the anger of a bull."

"How do you know all this?"

"Because I was once in your position." The spinning device continued to hum. "Know that there is a place for you here, should you wish it, out from under the watchful gaze of the House of Kings."

"I . . . How do I know I can trust you?"

"How do you know?" The voice was incredulous, affronted, though also affected—the sort of voice actors use. "At great risk to myself, I gave you a sigil that in all likelihood saved your life in the blooming fields. Is it not so?"

Davud couldn't deny it, but this was all so strange. And he wasn't at all sure that the Sparrow's story was the real one. And there was Anila to consider. If he left, it would mean something terrible for Anila. "I thank you for your offer, truly, but I think it's best if I remain here."

The spinning triangle went silent. It hummed in the air for so long that Davud reached up to touch it. When he did, the finch hopped forward and pecked his hand.

"Very well," the voice said as Davud sucked on his knuckle, "but let us speak again, yes? Keep the device secret. It works under starlight. Simply give it a spin, and I shall be there."

As the words faded, the triangle lowered toward the table. Davud caught it in his hands as the firefinch flew into the night. The triad's edges and angles were warm as melted candle wax. Part of him wanted to throw it over the nearby wall so he'd never find it again. But another part wanted to keep it safe, a talisman against a coming storm. The two warred for a time, but then Davud stuffed it away inside his thawb and returned to the palace, feeling watched and vulnerable. His earlier thoughts of having his family visit him vanished like summer rain.

The following day, Davud entered his room to find the patio doors open. Anila was sitting at a table, hunched over as she often was while eating. Except she *wasn't* eating. She was bent over a book. And not just any book, but an ancient text on blood magic, a source that had broadened Davud's understanding of its use, the sigils that guided the magic, and even a bit of history of those who had used it in the service of the Kings of Sharakhai.

Since returning from Ishmantep he had never seen Anila read. She'd done no more than eat, sleep, and suffer through what had surely become a miserable grind of an existence. But now Davud glimpsed a bit of the old Anila, the woman who was curious and always ready with answers for the collegia masters, or pointed questions that showed a strong mastery of the subject at hand. Davud had thought her thirst for knowledge burned out of her for good, but here she was, reading as intently as ever, though the subject of study sent a chill down Davud's spine.

He tried to close the door silently but wasn't careful enough. It clicked, and Anila's head lifted. He thought she'd heard him, but realized a moment later he'd been wrong. She was staring at the fig tree on the patio, and he was certain he knew why.

He stepped closer, ducked down, and peered through the nearby window. There was the firefinch, and Davud was suddenly and inexplicably concerned that Anila had overheard his conversation with the triangle. The finch was perfectly still. As Anila stood and stepped toward it, it flapped its wings and flew down to a lower branch. It flitted higher, then lower again, then higher once more. It looked frantic, a bird caught in a cage as the cat approaches.

Anila looked fascinated, as if it were the first time she'd seen a bird in her life. The closer she came to the tree, the more the finch's movements slowed. As she reached out to grab it, Davud walked quickly onto the patio.

Anila turned, eyes wide, shivering like a gutter wren caught stealing bread. The bird fluttered up and away, and was soon lost beyond one of the palace's minarets.

"What were you doing?" Davud asked.

Lowering her arm, Anila visibly calmed herself, shuffled past him, and sat at the table, ignoring Davud as she resumed her study.

He stood opposite her, but she kept her gaze down. The sunlight reflected off her reptilian skin.

"Anila, what were you doing with that bird?"

She folded her hands, studiously *not* looking at Davud. And then she shocked him. She *spoke*.

"The next time you wish to know something, Davud, ask *me*. Not Bela." Her words were slurred, drunken from the pain and the damage she'd endured.

For a moment, Davud could think of nothing to say. These were the first words she'd said to him since Ishmantep. "Very well," he managed, wanting to say so much more.

She glanced down at the book as if it were her chosen reading for a pleasant Savadi afternoon. She touched one corner and shifted it ever so slightly. "Have you learned anything from the sigils?"

"What? No. I mean, yes, I have, but nothing to help with . . ." He motioned ineffectually to her form. Gods, how he wished he could sweep her pain away and bring the old Anila back.

"I don't mean . . ." She closed her eyes, swallowed once, then tried again. "I only wish to know what Sukru is teaching you."

Confused, Davud shook his head. "Why?"

"Sukru wouldn't suffer your existence, or mine, if he didn't think he would get something out of it." She used that tone of hers, the one that condescended, still stubbornly refusing to look at him. "So you must ask yourself: What does he want?"

"I don't care about Sukru. And I don't care about the book. I only care that you—" He stopped, for she'd raised one hand and closed her eyes as if she couldn't bear to hear it. "I'm sorry, Anila."

"Stop it."

Davud pulled the chair out and sat down. "We must speak of what *happened*." He reached his hand out to take hers, but she pulled away, clearly pained by the sudden movement.

"No."

"Why?"

"Because it doesn't matter."

"Of course it matters!"

"It's *history*, Davud!" Her words echoed off the cold walls of the patio. She spoke slowly at first, but the more she went on, the more her confidence and pace increased. "We were taken by Hamzakiir, nearly turned into those mindless . . . things. Those shamblers. But by the grace of the gods, you saved us both. You tried to deliver us back to Sharakhai. You nearly did, until *I* forced you to go to Ishmantep, forced you beyond your skills, forced you to use your power before you were ready." Her eyes were red and watery as she looked at him at last. There was a well of pain there, a small glimpse into what she had lived through. "This happened because of *my* presumption. This is the punishment the gods have given me for my lack of charity, for ushering you into danger."

"Dear Anila." He found tears coming to his own eyes. He would have taken her hand were it not sure to cause her pain. "You're wrong. I am a man grown. I could have denied you any time I wished. I wanted those things as much as you did."

She stared at him, lost in her sorrow. She blinked away her tears, diamonds over fields of coal. "Dear Davud." She smiled, then laughed, a bitter echo of their days at the collegia. "Do you not remember those days? You could no more have said no to me than a hyena could sing."

Davud wanted to laugh, but he didn't have it in him. "You were no force of nature, Anila."

"Perhaps not, but you were no man. Not then, not yet." Teeth gritted, she lifted her bandaged arm and ran the back of her fingers along his cheek. "But you've changed."

"We've both changed."

She nodded. "We may both be forces of nature yet."

Davud didn't like the way she'd said that, as if she'd stop at nothing for revenge.

"So," she said, motioning to the book again, "what have you found?"

"I . . . Anila, I don't think sharing this is a good idea."

The small glimmer of hope in her face vanished. "Why not?"

"The King shared this with me so that I could help him, but if he knew you were reading it—"

"He gave it to you knowing full well we're sharing this room."

He stepped over, picked up the book, and held it to his chest. "Concentrate on getting better, Anila. On the day you can return to your family."

"I don't *want* to. I want to bring Hamzakiir to justice."

As he stepped away, she stood. From the look of pain and concentration on her face, it was clear how much that small movement cost her.

"Sukru has summoned me. I'll send for Kaelira to tend to your wounds today."

"I want to *help*," she said. It was a command, from a woman of Goldenhill accustomed to being obeyed.

"I can't allow it," he said, walking through the patio doors, back into the room. "I won't."

"You won't *allow* it?" she cried as he reached their chamber door. "You owe me this, Davud! You owe it to me!"

I owe you much, Davud thought as he opened the door and left, *but not this*.

Chapter 20

Çeda sat with Ishaq and Leorah inside a pavilion. The floor was layered with a host of riotously colored carpets. The smell of cook fires filled the space as the entrance's flaps blew lazily in the warm desert wind. Ishaq sat opposite her. Leorah's bent form was cradled in a nest of pillows to Çeda's left. On the low wooden table between them was one glass of araq each and a shisha with four tubes snaking out from it. Only Leorah was drawing from her tube, producing swirls of smoke that twisted their way up toward the vent. With it came the scents of sunburnt stone, aging leather, and fragrant rosewood.

Ishaq raised his drink high. Leorah did the same, followed by Çeda, and the three of them downed a healthy swallow of the sweet, biting araq.

He then motioned to the empty place on his left. "Would that your mother could have joined us," he said to Çeda. "Four generations sitting side by side is a rare thing indeed."

Çeda didn't know what to say. It would have been sweet, but had Ahya still been alive, the four of them would almost certainly not be here in the desert, drinking araq in a pavilion. Still, she raised her glass to the empty place and took another swallow.

"Let us speak plainly," Ishaq said. "Our tribe is in dire straights. Onur has fled to the desert to raise an army of his own. Hamzakiir is peeling away support among the Twelve Tribes. Malasan prepares to march west and cross the mountains to the desert. Qaimir and Mirea have both been biding their time, but their queens will not sit idly by, especially if Malasan allows a single one of their soldiers to set foot in the desert. The Kings have been wounded but are prepared to bring war to the desert unless we are given up to them. If we don't take care, it will be a culling like we've not seen since Beht Ihman."

Like a northern mountain dragon, Leorah breathed smoke into the air between them. "You would speak of war and murder before we've had the chance to hear Çeda's tale?"

"It is part and parcel of Çeda's tale, and *hers* is but one piece of the grand tapestry we all weave." Ishaq regarded Çeda with a seriousness that reminded her of Kiral, the King of Kings. "I've been told much about you and Sharakhai, but I would hear it from you. I would know how you became a Maiden and how you slew King Külaşan."

Çeda was deathly tired of being questioned by men like her grandfather and being given so little in return. So it had been with Osman. Then with the Kings—especially King Yusam. And again with Onur here in the desert only days before. She'd be damned before she let it happen again.

"Tell me where Emre is first."

Ishaq stared at her, his brow pinching. For long moments words failed him. "Great things are afoot, and you would ask me of the *boy* you grew up with?"

Çeda took an olive from the platter set between them and chewed. A low rumbling sound filled the pavilion. Ishaq, his face turning red, gave Leorah an indignant stare. Leorah was oblivious, however, her body heaving as a cascade of throaty, rolling laughs escaped her.

"Goezhen's sweet kiss," he said, "what are you laughing at?"

The sound built even higher. It was loud and sonorous and infectious. "Oh, my dear son—" It took a moment more for her laughs to subside, and even then, her shoulders continued to shake. "And you thought you were free of Ahya's stubbornness when she left for Sharakhai."

She laughed again, louder than before. Çeda did as well. She wasn't even sure why. After a moment, Ishaq's stormy look faded, then a smile cracked his features, and then he too was laughing, though it sounded more rueful than Leorah's full-throated, tent-filling mirth.

"If the gods are kind," Ishaq began with a regal bow of his head toward Çeda, "Emre is on his way here along with the few who remained in Sharakhai."

Now this was surprising news. "You're abandoning the city?"

She thought Ishaq might deny it, but he shrugged, as if admitting it was something he would never have considered years before. "The Host is patient . . . The Kings have thrown their lot in with Hamzakiir. Better to leave and see what the Kings will do with a man who wishes to rule Sharakhai alone."

"And if they let Hamzakiir take up his father's crown?"

"It would be like inviting an adder into their midst. Sooner or later he'll try to sink his fangs into them. And if Hamzakiir does take up his father Külaşan's crown, he will have forfeited his support in the desert to us. None of those aiding him now would openly support a King of Sharakhai."

"You're assuming he hasn't ensorcelled them in some way."

"He may have," Ishaq said, "but it cannot last. Such power fades over time, and would leave the tribes even more eager for revenge. Either way, their power will be returned to us. And if he continues his fight against the Kings, they will have no choice but to focus on him, which will allow us to heal in the desert."

"Will Macide and the others arrive soon?"

Ishaq nodded. "In a few days. No more than a week."

Please deliver Emre safely, Çeda prayed. "And what then?"

Ishaq knocked back the last of his drink, then poured for all three of them. "That depends greatly on what we learn from them"—he paused before setting the green bottle down with a thump—"and you."

Çeda tipped her head, an acknowledgment that it was time to tell her tale. She covered it in broad strokes at first, from the kiss Sehid-Alaz had given her in the canal when she'd gone to save Emre, to the poems hidden in her mother's book and her visit with Saliah in the desert, to the fight with the Blade Maiden in the fields after the adichara had pierced her thumb. She told them of Dardzada delivering her to the House of Maidens, how Zaïde had saved her, how she'd felt the asirim in the blooming fields on the night she'd killed Külaşan the Wandering King. Ishaq and Leorah both interrupted at times, looking for clarifications or a deepening of their knowledge, so it was some time before she finished, up to and including the harrowing events on the Night of Endless Swords, her flight into the desert, and her time in Onur's camp.

Ishaq seemed to peer through the far wall of the pavilion. "You can truly feel the asir?"

Kerim was far out in the desert, cowering, listening to this conversation as if he were a part of it, as if he could speak and his voice might be heard. *I am your voice,* she told him. He was too embarrassed to reply—he felt as if he'd been caught with his hand in her purse—but she could feel the gratitude within him as well.

"His name is Kerim," she said, "and yes, I can."

With his drink, Ishaq motioned to Çeda's left wrist, where Mesut's bracelet lay. "There as well?"

She ran her fingers over the polished onyx stone. "Yes, but only distantly, as if we're parted by a thick curtain."

"And now you've come here," Leorah said, a smile crinkling the corners of her eyes.

"Yes"—she took a deep breath, preparing to voice the thought she'd been wrestling with—"but I can't stay long." She faced Ishaq squarely. "I would return to Sharakhai, grandfather, and I could use help when I arrive. I need people I can trust, for food, weapons, or places to hide as I make plans."

"What plans?"

"First, there are those in the House of Maidens I would speak to."

"Zaïde?"

"Among others. I wish to see if any will join our cause."

A bark of a laugh filled the pavilion, but a moment later, when he realized she was serious, he sobered. "The *Maidens?* Çeda, we have some few spies like Zaïde, but you'll find no more allies there."

"I disagree. I think I can turn one of the women from my hand."

"Who?"

"Melis."

"Melis Yusam'ava? She's *fiercely* loyal to the Kings."

"She is, but she tires of the struggle. Sümeya does as well."

Ishaq reeled, an angry look distorting his rough features. He turned to Leorah. "Are you listening to her?" Then to Çeda, "Sümeya is *First Warden!*"

"Yes. But you don't know these women like I do. At the very least, I'll be able to sow doubt among them. And I would look further into the silver trove."

Ishaq made a chopping motion with his hand. "Who told you about that? Your mother? It's nothing but a wild tale, Çeda."

"Perhaps, and perhaps not. I would learn the truth either way. And lastly, the asirim are there. I must know if there is a way to free them. Zaïde may help. Melis or Sümeya may too. Perhaps even our lost King, Sehid-Alaz."

The hint of a frown that seemed always to be present on his lips deepened. "Even bone crushers learn to eat their kills one bite at a time, girl."

"I'm no girl."

He paused, his dark eyes assessing her anew. "No, you're not. You've done much to sing about. Which makes your words all the more bitter. With you safe at last I thought you would join us."

"I may still, but all roads lead to Sharakhai. The asirim are there. The Maidens are there. The Kings are there."

"The desert is in turmoil. Tribe Masal has fallen to Onur. Word came only yesterday that Tribe Kadri have sent emissaries to *him*. Their shaikh, Mihir Halim'ava al Kadri, the new Lord of the Burning Hands, has little love for the Kings of Sharakhai and sees this as an opportunity for revenge for his mother's death at the hands of King Ihsan. Onur may soon have the strength of three tribes at his command. And when word spreads, a fourth may follow, then a fifth. If we're not careful, he may unite all the desert tribes."

"Doubtful," Çeda said. "Tribes Ebros, Okan, and Kenan are loyal to the Kings. The rest have no reason to take up sword and spear to stand against Sharakhai, certainly not standing beneath *Onur's* banner."

"You are a child of Sharakhai," he replied in lofty tones, "so you cannot understand how ready the tribes are to see the Kings fall. Few will say it openly, and many will not be easily convinced it can be done, but there is a long-burning hatred in every tribe. Onur, though a King himself, need only to throw oil on that flame it for it to be rekindled." He paused. "Perhaps, after due thought, *we'll* be the oil that spreads the fire. This is why we've taken such a risk in calling the tribe together. We're ready to decide how *our* tribe, Tribe Khiyanat, will proceed. Which is why I'm glad you've come. You have much to offer. You can share what you know of the Kings. You can train those who need it."

When Çeda said nothing, Ishaq stated it flatly. "Join us, Çeda. For those of our tribe, the roads of Sharakhai have too often led to the farther fields. We need everyone we can, here in the desert."

She couldn't do it. Not now, in any case. Accept, and she would formally become a part of the tribe. Accept, and she would need to obey his commands just like everyone else in the tribe did. "I will return to Sharakhai."

"Even though Melis may betray you at her first opportunity? Even though the silver trove may be a mirage? Even though it may take years to undo the chains that bind the asirim?"

"Yes. Who am I to you anyway but one more warrior to add to your ranks?"

"You are my granddaughter."

"Then give your granddaughter the freedom she needs."

Ishaq was red-faced. There were words on his lips—a command for Çeda to remain, no doubt—but just then a bell began to ring, a call to the midday meal. Leorah spoke quickly. "Help an old woman to food by a fire with those she loves." And she held out her arm for Ishaq to take.

After a moment's hesitation, he did. "We are not done discussing this," he said to Çeda, "not by a league." Then he helped Leorah toward the exit.

As Çeda rose to follow, Leorah turned and winked at her.

Chapter 21

THE SUN WAS SETTING OVER THE SHANGAZI.

Çeda sat on the sand near a spitting fire while dozens of small children gabbled and groused and giggled around her. They were in the space between the tribe's ships, and it was abustle with the ends of the midday meal. The heat of the day was easing, and the air was filled with stories, mirth, and no small number of friendly arguments.

The day had flown by. After a meal with the tribe, Çeda and Leorah had taken a long walk together—her constitutional, Leorah called it—then sat on the deck of her yacht and talked. Leorah seemed to be taking great pains to keep the conversation light. She spoke of inconsequential things. The foods Çeda liked. The ones she hated, particularly those Ahya might have forced her to eat. She laughed when Çeda confessed to despising eggplant, a thing her mother insisted on making at least once a week.

"That was my recipe," Leorah said, then laughed at Çeda's embarrassment.

"I liked it a bit," Çeda said, trying to recover.

But Leorah waved her worries away. "There's no telling the appetites of babes. I never liked it much myself. We rarely had it—few enough caravans carried eggplant in those days—but when we did, Ahya always took a stack of flatbread and devoured half the bowl herself. I suspect it became a piece of home after she'd left the desert."

They spoke further of the sights, sounds, and smells of the city. They spoke of music, of plays, of jongleurs and storytellers, and the confidence men of Sharakhai who preyed on those who came to the city with purses full of gold and eyes full of wonder. Occasionally Çeda would ask Leorah of life here in the desert. She would gladly answer, but always in such a way that allowed her to steer the conversation back to the desert's Amber Jewel.

She's fascinated by it, Çeda realized. *Perhaps because Ahya went there and she never saw her daughter again. Or because she'd never been. Or both.*

From then on, Çeda went on at length on any topic Leorah chose. There would be time soon enough to talk about growing up in the Great Shangazi.

When the evening meal came, Çeda decided to sit with a group of the children. She missed their laughs, the sounds of them playing along the streets of Roseridge. A young girl with brown hair hanging like a curtain over her face looked over to Çeda and gestured at her bowl. "Do you like it?"

Çeda smiled. "It's joyous."

The girl's grin was wide as the sunset. She'd helped to make the stew—as she'd made a point of telling Çeda and everyone else before they'd sat to eat. The food was simple but mouthwatering. Spit-roasted goat in a broth of tomatoes and onions and pine nuts over puffy brown rice. Lemon-salted flatbread dipped into a mouth-watering yoghurt laced with garlic and goat cheese and a fresh herb collected from the nearby mountainside that tasted like fire-kissed cumin. They drank clear, natural well water laced with cucumber and mint. And araq the likes of which she'd never tasted. It had a nose of rich leather and hints of smoke, tasted like currant and fire berry jam mixed with fresh honey, and finished with a pleasant coppery burn.

"My own!" said an old, thin man one fire over when he saw how much she appreciated it.

He was raising his glass, and Çeda raised hers in reply. "An elixir Bakhi himself must lust after."

He smiled more broadly, revealing a landscape of missing teeth, then both of them took another healthy swallow.

The twin moons rose in the eastern sky—Tulathan a silver sickle, Rhia a beaten golden coin. There was music and dancing and song. When true night fell, Kerim released a long wail that fell across the celebration like a burst of rain. The music stopped. All, even Ishaq, looked around nervously. They were used to this, Çeda realized—the threat from the Kings always hounding them, always hanging over their heads.

"Please," she said, standing and raising her glass. "All is well." She motioned for the music to continue, then took the hand of the girl who'd sat by her side. She'd been dancing with her brother, and Çeda motioned them both to dance with her. They did, the three of them twirling with one another as the song resumed. The mood of merriment returned, if slightly more subdued than before.

"May I have this dance?" a voice asked as a new song began.

She knew the voice well but was still surprised to find him standing before her when she turned. "Dardzada."

The old apothecary bowed his head to her, his hand raised.

"When did you arrive?" she asked as she accepted his hand and the two of them began to dance over the carpets.

"Only a short while ago."

Çeda looked over his shoulder toward the ships, where others were trudging toward the gathering, some carrying huge bunches of fresh dates over their shoulders.

"Is Emre with you?"

"No." Dardzada smiled sadly. "I thought he'd be here by now."

They danced for a while, the two of them silent. It felt strange. Their history still stood between them—him raising her for a time after her mother died, the harsh way he'd treated her—but she couldn't deny it felt good.

"Do you plan to stay with the tribe?" Çeda asked. "Find yourself a wife?"

This time when Dardzada smiled, it was genuine. "I fear it's too late for me. I am married to our cause."

Çeda laughed. "I daresay you could be married to the cause and still share warmth beneath a blanket."

"You may be right. Perhaps I'll be struck by Yerinde's curse yet."

Continuing to dance, Çeda took in the night around her. The ships, the songs, the dancing, the children running around their parents or spinning until they fell laughing to the carpets on the sand.

"What are we doing out here, Dardzada?"

"Rebuilding," Dardzada said as the song began to pick up its pace.

"It's hard to believe, isn't it? That we're finally coming together?"

"It is," he replied softly, "and it's dangerous as well."

She looked to Ishaq, who was sitting with several older men and women, each drawing from a shisha tube and talking low with one another. For a moment, Çeda saw them in their youth, not so different from how she, Emre, Tariq, and Hamid once were.

"You don't approve?" she asked Dardzada.

"Who am I to approve or disapprove of what Ishaq is doing?"

"The danger may be great," Çeda said, "but it was always going to be, no matter when it happened. Perhaps it will give everyone heart. Perhaps it will bolster support for us among the other tribes. Perhaps it will sway those in Sharakhai as well. It could even lead to revolt in the city."

"Perhaps, but there is no doubt it will soon attract the attention of the Kings. Sooner or later they will come for us."

"Then we'll have to be ready for them, won't we?" In that moment, Çeda wished she was already on the way to Sharakhai. She closed her eyes as Dardzada lifted her hand and she twirled. The music, the conversation, the laughter . . . It filled her. She hadn't realized how much she needed this, a reminder of all she'd been fighting for. "If we accomplish nothing else, we will have revealed the truth. The Kings will have to admit what happened to our tribe."

"Oh, Çeda." Dardzada stopped dancing, though he still held her hands. "Even before I left, the Kings were starting rumors, spreading more propaganda, saying the Moonless Host are pretenders who are fabricating stories of a lost tribe for their own benefit. It's laughable, they're saying. The traitor Ishaq's last gamble as the Host lose faith in him. The lords and ladies in the House of Kings and Goldenhill are eating it up, spreading it wide. Those who live off the teat of the Kings believe it, or say that they do, prompting others to repeat the same story. Only in the west end do they speak openly of denying the Kings' stories, and when have they ever mattered in the grand scheme of Sharakhai's workings?"

"The truth will spread," Çeda said, releasing Dardzada's hands. "It must!"

Dardzada shrugged, as if this meant little more to him the price of figs.

"Only the gods can know, but already the war of ideas has resumed. Death comes for those who speak openly of the thirteenth tribe while those who take the Kings' word are favored."

When will it end? Çeda wondered. But she already knew the answer.

When the Kings lay dead, their bodies burned, their bones buried in the sand.

She glanced east, where Kerim was hidden by the night. *No,* she vowed. *The truth will come. I will* make *them believe.*

Kerim's wail lifted above the celebration. It was lonelier this time, an echo of Çeda's feelings. The celebration quieted, but Ishaq nodded to the musicians, who hardly missed a beat.

Free us, Kerim pleaded. Gods, the ache in him. She could feel it smoldering in her chest.

Soon, she replied. *Trust me.*

"Çeda?" a voice called from across the nearby fire.

Leorah was beckoning Çeda to follow her, a solemn expression on her tattooed face. For a moment, the amethyst on her left hand seemed to glow in the firelight before her. Çeda blinked, realizing just how much araq she'd drunk, and the strange effect was gone.

"I am called away," she said to Dardzada.

Dardzada waved one meaty hand. "Go. We can speak tomorrow."

Çeda followed Leorah, who led Çeda toward her yacht. Her limp was noticeably better. She walked more upright, as if the years no longer weighed on her so heavily. *Probably the araq,* Çeda thought, though she couldn't remember seeing Leorah drink any.

Inside the yacht they moved to Leorah's cabin, which was small but had more than enough room for both of them to sit—Leorah on her bed, Çeda on a small padded stool near the desk built against the opposite wall. Colorful scarfs and sun catchers were arrayed like the petals of a blooming flower across the ceiling. A lantern hanging from a hook at the center set the petals to dancing. *Pleasant,* Çeda thought, *something uniquely Leorah's.*

"I've something to show you," Leorah said as she rummaged in a small chest by her feet. She took out a piece of papyrus, upon which was an impressive charcoal sketch of a tattoo laid across a woman's back.

My back, Çeda realized.

Dardzada's oval-shaped tattoo—the ancient calligraphic sigil he'd forced on her when she'd turned thirteen—was in the center. Above it Leorah had sketched Tauriyat, and added lyrical words that captured the battle, the death of King Mesut, and the role she'd played in both. More of her tale, including small pictographs, were added along her shoulder blades, so that together it all looked like a spread-wing falcon across her upper back and neck, with the tips of the feathers brushing her shoulders and arms.

"It's beautiful," Çeda said.

"I'm glad you think so," Leorah replied. She motioned to a set of inks and bowls and various bamboo tattooing needles. "Shall we begin?"

"Now?"

"What better time? You'll be leaving for Sharakhai soon."

"Not if Ishaq has anything to say about it."

Leorah's smile was confident. "Ishaq will come around."

Çeda stared at the drawing, taking in all of the words, all of the images, and how they seemed to be consuming Dardzada's old tattoo. *No, not consuming it. Adding to it. Creating a larger tale.* Suddenly tears were falling down her cheeks. She wiped them away and nodded to Leorah.

After shifting the stool, she shrugged her arms out of her thawb and gathered the cloth around her waist. Leorah poured blue inks into a well, then wiped Çeda's skin with an araq-soaked rag. Then she set to, tapping away with a striking stick, the needle biting into the nape of Çeda's neck.

"I hope you'll remain long enough for me to finish it."

Her speech seemed to have a different cadence than earlier in the day. Çeda might not have noticed had they not talked so much after the discussion with Ishaq. It wasn't something she could attribute to liquor. If anything, Leorah was talking *more* steadily than before. *You're being foolish,* Çeda thought. Leorah had vanished for some time as the sun was setting. She might have simply taken a nap.

"Of course I will," Çeda said.

"You remind me of Ahya, you know. You're direct. You stand your ground. You're loyal to those you love. But Ahya was always headstrong. Too much so in the end."

"She killed a King."

"One, when her goal was to kill them all." As she continued to strike the needle, Çeda's body rose to meet the pain, and it became something wider, deeper—something more grand, as if the pain itself were telling part of Çe-da's tale. "Ishaq isn't like Onur, you know. He isn't a King, and doesn't pre-tend to be."

Çeda stiffened. "He wants to control me."

"Mmm, yes and no. He wants control over his burgeoning tribe, a thing I can hardly blame him for. He's navigated the sands well enough since taking the reins of power so many years ago. But that isn't the only reason he asked you. He doesn't want to lose you as he lost Ahya. And when he looks at you, he can't help but be reminded of her."

It made perfect sense, but for some reason the realization made her un-comfortable. "Was it difficult for him when he learned of her death?"

As Leorah leaned back to stretch, the sound of whooping and laughter drifted in from outside. "Of course," she said, resuming her work. "That isn't quite what I meant, though. Ishaq lost Ahya *ten years* before she died at the hands of the Kings. He never wanted her to go to Sharakhai. He was fearful from the beginning over what might happen to her." Leorah paused her nee-dle. "Sit still."

Çeda realized she'd started to shake. *You're skittish as a lost kitten, Çedamihn.* She wasn't even sure why, until she voiced her next question. "Did he know why Ahya went to Sharakhai?"

Leorah took a moment to respond. "Say what you mean."

"Did he know she intended to have a child from one of the Kings?"

Leorah laughed a deep rumble of a laugh. "I suspect there's another ques-tion hiding behind that one, but as you wish. I'll answer them as they come. Yes, he knew, which is perhaps why he resisted for so long. But I am a per-sistent woman, as was your mother. Eventually, reluctantly, he came to see it as a wish cast into the wind."

"A wish that could cost his daughter her life."

"Indeed! A wish that was *likely* to cost her life."

"Then why did he agree? Why did she want a child from one of the Kings?"

"Tulathan's poems. We found one part, the end, we believe, that spoke of a scion who would play a part in the downfall of the Kings. But Ahya, like many of us who believe that Tulathan recited poems on Beht Ihman, grew frustrated the more she learned. Four centuries had already passed. How long did the people of the lost tribe have to wait? She believed that by going to Sharakhai, by having you, she would force the hand of the fates."

Çeda turned on her stool. "I'm no messiah."

Leorah returned Çeda's shoulders to the proper position. "No one said you were. You are one who may help lead us to our freedom, one of dozens, hundreds, who've worked toward this end over generations."

The way Leorah spoke of both Ahya and Çeda made Çeda feel like a means to an end, nothing more, and it showed, perhaps, why Ishaq would sacrifice his own daughter.

The talk had lit a fire in Çeda's heart, one she was careful not to blow upon lest it grow and burn her. "You know who my father is, don't you?"

"Now *there's* the question that was hiding earlier."

Çeda felt the heat rising in her cheeks. She felt like a child all over again. "A woman deserves to know who her father is."

"Most do, yes, but in your case it might do more harm than good."

"How could it?"

"You've said you have a mission to complete. To kill the Kings of Sharakhai. Would you complete it if you knew who your father was?"

"Of course I would."

"Oh? Even if he had nothing to do with your mother's death?"

"The Kings deserve to die. No man should rule the desert for so long."

"That may be true, but will it matter when you're standing before him with blade in hand? How many have been lost to matters of the heart when reason has told them otherwise? They are numerous as the stars, Çeda, and I won't let you become another."

Çeda turned, forcing Leorah to lift her needle and striking stick. "Who is my father?"

Leorah laughed her rumbling laugh. "Raising your voice won't help with *me*, girl. We have much to do, and I won't have your mind clouded by the knowledge." Before Çeda could speak again, Leorah raised her hand and began wiping away the excess ink from her back. "There's something else that's long overdue, Çeda, if you'll allow me to get to it."

Çeda stilled her tongue before she said something she'd regret. "What?"

She finished wiping, then applied a salve. "You said Dardzada had given you a key." When Çeda nodded, she went on. "May I see it?"

Çeda reached into the small purse at her belt and held it up. Leorah nodded with a melancholy smile and reached her bulk past Çeda to pull open one of the lower desk drawers. She rummaged inside and retrieved a lacquered wooden box with beautiful ivory inlay over the surface of its lid. It was hinged, and had a lock built into its front face.

As Leorah went to sit on the bed, Çeda's fingers and toes began to tingle and a high-pitched tone rang in her ears.

Leorah held the box lovingly for a moment. "Ahya made this when she was about your age." She held it out to Çeda. "I know withholding your father's identity hurts, but perhaps this will dull the sting."

The key in her hand felt suddenly red-hot. "What is it?"

"I don't know. Ahya gave it to me the last time I saw her. I think she knew what lay ahead and worried over you. She told me to keep it safe until you found me at last. I asked her what I should do if you never came. She told me you would."

Çeda accepted the box with trembling hands, at which point Leorah grunted and pushed herself to a stand, then ran one hand down Çeda's hair, tugging at her ear before taking her cane and sidling along the passageway. Alone in the cabin, with the sounds of revelry coming from outside the yacht, Çeda ran her fingertips over the smooth lacquer. She admired the handiwork, the rich grain of the wood, the perfect seams of the inlay.

"What are you afraid of?" she asked herself, gripping the key tightly.

Swallowing hard, her hands trembling, she put the key into the lock and turned it. The hinge creaked as she lifted the lid. Inside were two things. The first was a folded piece of papyrus with a wax seal on it. The seal was a curving, ancient sign that meant *wedge* or, more accurately, *tip of the spear*. It was often used in ancient texts to indicate an event that led to many more changes, a catalyst of sorts.

The second thing was a silver vial with a cap that screwed off. She was nervous about the letter, so she picked up the vial first. It was etched with an intricate design along its cylindrical length and the cap was decorated with tiny ornamental ivy leaves. She shook it and heard something rattle inside. She unscrewed the cap and tipped the vial over her hand. Out rolled a single oblong seed no larger than the nail of her pinky. It was ebony colored, but on the tip was a bit of yellow crust that looked like she could scrape it away.

After slipping it back in the vial and screwing the cap back on, she took up the letter.

For Çeda,

Contained herein is a treasure stolen from the House of Kings, the seed of an acacia.

Years ago, shortly before I made up my mind to go to Sharakhai, I went to see Saliah. She had me stand before her own acacia, the one in her garden. No doubt by now you know the importance of that tree and the shards of glass that hang from its branches. She asked that I make the tree chime for her, in whatever way I chose. I grabbed a single branch and pulled it down, which somehow made the entire tree shake. I was swept up by the light that played through the branches, that in turn was caught and twisted by the surfaces of the glass. I was granted many visions. Glimpses, I believed, of the future. Or perhaps of the past. It was impossible to tell, and Saliah refused to answer my questions.

One of the visions I saw was of a seed pod falling to the ground. It fell from an acacia in a vale in the mountains. Which mountains, I cannot say. There were many other trees in that vale, pine and larch and spruce, and there was a small stream, near which the acacia stood tall and vibrant. Footsteps came. A man's hand reached down. Faded orange tattoos covered his palm. A golden ring with a bright emerald stone graced one finger. The hand picked up the pod and turned it over, inspecting it, I suppose, and then the vision faded.

It was replaced by another, a view of the same place, at dusk, though clearly it was many years later. The tree was there, but it was barren, the branches withered. A black form with cloven hooves and twin tails walked over the landscape, stopping where the pod had fallen. Black claws scratched at the ground, gouging it. A head with a crown of thorns dipped to that place. Nostrils flared as it breathed in the scent. It huffed, then roared to the dying sun, and stomped one foot on the spot where the dark earth had been revealed.

As this second vision faded, I wondered if the creature was an ehrekh. I've searched long and hard since and believe instead it was their

maker, Goezhen himself, though the reason he'd been searching for that
fallen pod is lost to me.

A third vision came, of another acacia in a garden in the middle of
the desert. The very tree where I'd stood before. But the tree was dying,
and Saliah's homestead was a crumbling ruin.

Time passed, and I heard word of a treasure. An acacia seed hidden
in the House of Kings. I knew I must find it before I struck against the
Kings. It took me nearly a decade, but I found it, hidden in one of the
vaults beneath King Yusam's palace. How it came to him, I do not
know, nor do I know the meaning of the visions or the acacia seed. But I
know they are of great import. To me. To you. To our cause.

I give it to you now because soon I go to the mount. It is a journey
that I hope will uncover more treasures, but there is danger there, and
whatever I might find, I know the struggle for freedom is a long one. It
may be that you will find the seed's place in the world. Or someone close
to you will. I trust the goddess will guide you.

Take care, Çeda. Listen to Leorah and Devorah, for they both see
beyond the horizon.

Ahyanesh

For a long while, Çeda stared at the letter, her chin quivering. To come so
far, to come so *close* to speaking with her mother one last time, and have her
speak as if Çeda were a servant, a soldier to be commanded. It felt so very familiar—she'd used that tone with Çeda while growing up—and yet, before
Çeda had opened the box, she'd still hoped there would be something special
from her mother inside, for *her* and her alone. A token of her love, a remembrance of a moment only they shared, like seeing the vivid little bluebirds, the
blazing blues, in the great salt flat. But of course there wasn't. This was all about
Ahya and her grand quest, and about Çeda being swept into it once more.

All at once, the frustration of moving from place to place in Sharakhai, of
never growing roots, never knowing who she was, the distance she'd always
felt from her mother, the desire to feel something more from her, all of it
came surging up. Before she knew it she stood and threw the wooden box
into the corner of the cabin, shattering it.

That was when she realized she wasn't alone.

She turned to find a man standing in the passageway, wearing dusty desert clothes, his turban wrapped loosely around his shoulders like a scarf. Breath of the desert, it was Emre. He stared at her, then the shattered remains of the box, then her again.

Çeda opened her mouth, but she had no idea what to say. Too many memories were flooding through her. Too many emotions. So she folded him in her arms instead. He immediately grunted, and she saw that he was in pain. She felt the bandages that wrapped his chest beneath his sweat-stained shirt.

"Ribs," he said. "It's nothing." He took her back in his arms, held her and, bless him, said no more.

Time was lost to her as the two of them became little more than their breathing bodies, their beating hearts. Çeda cried against his shoulder, while Emre rubbed one hand along her back. Outside, a song played. A yelp of surprise lifted above it, followed by peals of laughter and calls for the man to do it again.

Eventually she pulled away, and Emre stared into her eyes, a soft smile on his lips. "I made it," he said.

She kissed him deeply, passionately, before wiping her tears, and taking a proper look at him. "I noticed."

Smiles broke across both their faces. They started laughing, a spontaneous thing, like an amberlark taking flight.

"I tell you true," Emre began, "we nearly died a dozen times." But he stopped when Çeda held up a hand.

"Wait," she said, and jutted her chin toward the sounds outside. "There's a celebration. Let's enjoy it, like we always said we would. A fire in the desert. With bread and olives and wine. You can tell me your story there."

With a grimace, Emre sketched a short bow, looking more like the Emre of old. It did her heart good to be reminded of their days with one another. He held out his arm to her. "My lady?"

She stuffed the letter and the silver vial into her purse, along with the key, and took his arm. "Why thank you, kind sir."

And then the two of them headed down the passageway, up the ladder, and into the crisp desert air.

Chapter 22

RAMAHD WOKE TO DARKNESS and chill air seeping into his bones. He was chained to a wall, his shoulders screaming from the abuse. He managed to pull himself to his feet only to find that his legs were chained as well.

Filtering down a set of stairs to his left was the barest amount of light. It was nearly silent, but he thought he could hear breathing. Someone sleeping, perhaps. "Tiron? Cicio?" Nothing. "Amaryllis?"

"No." The voice was deep, resonant in this confined space. "But thank you. It's good to know their names."

Ramahd remembered that voice. He'd heard it once through the magic of Meryam's spells. "You're Brama."

"And *you* are in a difficult spot."

"Where are we?"

"Don't waste your breath on questions. You're going to need all the strength you can muster."

"For what?"

The sound of creaking wood interrupted the cool stillness. Footfalls came nearer, as did a dim blue glow floating in the darkness. The sapphire, Ramahd realized, hanging around Brama's neck. The cerulean light grew, casting shadows across the landscape of scars on Brama's neck and face, making him look like a wight, freshly risen from the grave and driven by thoughts of revenge. "It was you, wasn't it, who stole into my mind those weeks ago?"

Ramahd tried to mask his surprise, but Brama merely smiled, a grimacing crevice across his ruin of a face.

"Was it *just* you, I wonder?" He held up a ring with a sharp protrusion on one side. A blooding ring. *Ramahd's* ring. "Do you walk the red ways alone?" His eyes flamed blue as he stared intently at the ring as if it, not Ramahd, might answer. "Or was there another?"

He took another step forward until he was only an arm's-reach away. Ramahd could see the cloth of his simple robe, his curly hair, all bathed in blue. "Would you care to tell me, or would you rather I took it from you?" He slipped the ring onto his thumb so that the claw extended beyond his thumbnail. "It matters little to me." Gripping Ramahd's right shoulder he used the ring to press the point into Ramahd's chest. "But it will save you much pain."

He pressed deeper, piercing skin. Ramahd's breath was forced through gritted teeth as he tried to ignore the pain. "Who are you?" Brama asked.

"I'm no one," Ramahd said.

"No one . . ." Brama pulled the ring away, then made a face that revealed how young he was. "*No one* is an interesting answer. We are all *some*one, are we not? Take me. I'm a thief who came to a rather tragic end and was reborn. A simple enough story, though they were days filled with leagues of pain. Now *you* try."

Ramahd had assumed Tiron had been taken, perhaps Amaryllis and Cicio too, but if he was asking such simple questions, the assumption didn't make sense. "I come from the sea."

Brama waggled his head from side to side, as if this were a reasonable response. "And now that you're here in Sharakhai? Where do you spend your time?"

"In your mother's bedchamber."

Brama gave a pitiless smile. "Very well." There was no malice in the way he said it, which made it all the more chilling. Reaching out, he took Ramahd's head in his hands; the warmth in them was inhuman. He could smell the fennel and garlic on his breath. The point of his own ring was now pressed against his left eye. Ramahd was sure Brama was going to use the ring to put his eye out, but he didn't. He gripped Ramahd's head tighter and sent him crashing into the stone wall, once, twice, a third time.

A sea of lights swam in the darkness before him. He could feel himself blacking out, but he breathed deeply, fighting it.

"Your name," Brama tried again.

"Tiny," Ramahd replied. "Like your cock."

I tire of this, came a voice. It was ephemeral and distant, as if spoken from the depths of a dark forest. *Give him to me.*

A silence followed, and then Brama said, "Very well."

The sensations of this place—the grit on the floor, the dampness in the cool air, the sounds of the city floating down from above—were replaced by the presence of another mind. It felt so similar to joining his mind with Meryam's that for a moment he thought it *was* Meryam.

But it wasn't. This was a more ancient soul. Wilder. More violent. It felt as if the desert itself had come to pick Ramahd apart and examine him, bit by bit.

Rümayesh . . . It must be Rümayesh.

But the knowledge gave him no comfort. It was all he could do to fight down his fear.

He's Qaimiri, the ehrekh said.

Even that small piece of information felt like a violation, as if it were a gateway that would lead to the loss of everything else. Ramahd tried to raise a defense, tried to sap the power from this spell as he'd done against Hamzakiir in the desert, but he was weak and he was wounded, and in the end stood no chance against the cruel advance of Rümayesh's will.

The ehrekh's presence enshrouded him, picked at the edges of his mind like a swarm of wood wasps. His terror grew as he tried to think of something, anything, that might save him. He didn't wish to die like this, in darkness away from those he loved, his mind lost.

"You might be freed!" Ramahd shouted desperately, and incredibly, Rümayesh's unrelenting advance slowed, then halted.

I might be freed? Rümayesh cooed. *And who would free me? You?*

"Yes."

Brama laughed, though it was Rümayesh who controlled him.

"Are you so kind?" she asked with his mouth, "to free one such as me?"

Brama's hand trailed down Ramahd's cheek, to his neck, and along his naked chest. "Is your heart so charitable?"

Ramahd swallowed. He wished he hadn't. "Wouldn't it be better than where you are?"

To his surprise, he felt a pang of doubt. And it was coming from *Brama*. This was a fear that plagued him in the darkest moments of his days, the thought of losing the sapphire, and Rümayesh with it.

The thought was hardly there before it vanished.

"That depends on your perspective," Rümayesh said. "Were I you, a man whose life is gone in the blink of an eye, I might agree. But imagine you had more days to your name. Imagine your dark father, Goezhen, granting you undying life. Might you not want to experience more?" Rümayesh pressed the sharpened point of Ramahd's ring into the skin just over his madly beating heart. "Things you might never have thought of?"

"I would never accept being imprisoned."

"Imprisoned?" she scoffed. "Who speaks of prisons? I ride a river. To what end, I do not know, but I know that it has led me to places I would never have found otherwise. A life of meager means along the flood-prone banks of the Haddah. A host of lives who intersect with Brama's in devastating ways, showing life's cruelty with an honesty I'd never known before. There is beauty in that chaos." Brama's smile widened. "Take you, for example." Brama's fingers trailed up Ramahd's skin, raked through his hair, as a lover might. "I wonder where the stream of your mind will take us."

Brama's bright green eyes, so intent, stared deeply into Ramahd's. The swarm of wasps had returned. Louder than before, they stung. They delved into his mind.

"Perhaps to Macide Ishaq'ava," Rümayesh said easily, "who slew your wife and child?"

They bore deeper, the pain intensifying.

"To Çedamihn Ahyanesh'ala, the White Wolf?"

The sound was deafening. The buzzing. The chittering.

"To your queen, Meryam shan Aldouan?"

Mighty Alu, lend me strength. Ramahd pushed harder against her. He was somehow managing to keep her at bay, but for how long? The din of the insects was maddening!

"Come," Rümayesh said. "Allow me in of your own free will? I'm afraid the alternative might leave you a bit . . . tattered."

Ramahd's fear was so great he nearly gave in, but in that moment the memory of a room in a distant tower came to him. Not his own memory, but Brama's. He saw Rümayesh in her true form: hooved feet, taurine legs, a forked tail that swished this way then that, a crown of thorns and two horns sweeping back from her forehead. Worst were her depthless eyes and the dark humor in them—for all she'd done to Brama, for what she was about to do.

The memory dimmed as Brama mastered his emotions, though Rümayesh seemed pleased, amused, not only by Ramahd's fear but Brama's. She was delighted that even after all the time they'd spent together, Brama still viewed those days with unbridled terror.

"You are a wicked demon," Ramahd said through gritted teeth.

"Perhaps. But I get what I want."

The pressure on Ramahd's mind intensified, becoming a gale of wind and sand and biting stone. The insects consuming flesh, bone, and blood. As he had with Hamzakiir months ago, Ramahd tried to resist, tried to snuff the ehrekh's power before it became too great, but it was impossible. He was too fatigued. And how could he, a mortal man, stand against a creature forged by the hand of Goezhen?

His walls fell altogether, but in that moment something brightened deep within his mind, as if it had been waiting for him to reach his lowest point. This new presence stormed forth, grabbing Rümayesh, lashing at Brama, bulling forward as they tried to raise their defenses against this new threat. An anguished cry escaped Brama's throat, though whether it was from Brama or Rümayesh or both of them, Ramahd wasn't sure.

Brama fell. He scrambled away as the light in the sapphire went out, plunging the room into darkness.

Ramahd heard something scraping across the cell floor. Heard Brama's panicked breathing. He felt Brama's terror as Meryam—Ramahd was certain it was her—clawed through his mind. She had to reach Brama, Ramahd realized, and through him she would reach Rümayesh. Rümayesh may have realized this as well, for even though she was fearful of Meryam's power, she acted with a calculated calm, pressing on Brama's mind as well, squeezing him from both sides.

She was trying to stop Meryam from reaching her. Meryam knew it, and she tried to bolster Brama's defenses, to keep him awake long enough for her to take both Brama *and* Rümayesh while they were so intent on Ramahd. Ramahd tried to help as well, but what could he do? He was but a locust caught in a terrible storm.

In the end, Rümayesh pushed too hard, and Brama succumbed to the weight of the onslaught. He fell limp, and in that moment a brightness blasted Ramahd's mind so quickly, so forcefully, there was nothing he could do to prevent it. Then the brilliance was gone, and Ramahd was falling into darkness.

Ramahd woke feeling as though his arms were being ripped from their sockets. He was still chained to the wall of the cellar. The same bare light filtered in from the stairs to his left. Brama was now a vague, man-shaped smudge in the darkness of the dirt floor. *How long have I been under?* Not long, he thought. Surely Brama's army would have checked on him at some point.

Ramahd pulled himself tall. Feeling along the wall behind him, he touched the iron hoop where the chain looped through it and around his wrists. Feeling with his bare feet, he found a second hoop. His fingertips touched the iron spike in the wall, which had been driven into the mortar between the stones. Secure enough if the mortar was fresh, but this was an old home with old foundations.

Wrapping the chain around both hands, he yanked it down. It held. Taking a deep breath, he tried again, pulling his legs up until those chains pulled tight as well. Like the string of a bow drawing the ends closer, he drew on the chains, pulling with all his might. They didn't budge.

Moments later, he heard a door creak and footsteps walking across the floor above him. His fear over what they would do when they found Brama unconscious sent his fear soaring. He pulled again, heedless of how bright the pain in his joints was, of how deeply it cut into the skin of his ankles.

Brama moaned in the darkness.

A wheezing grunt escaped Ramahd as he heaved against the chain. He became a part of it, as unyielding as steel.

At the top of the stairs came a knock.

"Brama?"

A woman's voice, muted behind the closed door.

Ramahd pulled harder and finally something gave. With a sound like shearing steel, he fell hard to the floor and the chains clanked down loudly around him. He reached into the darkness. Felt Brama's ankle. He dragged him closer, once, then again. He patted along Brama's waist, and found a leather belt. A ring of keys.

The door creaked open. Candlelight flooded the stairwell, pushing back the darkness. "Brama?"

Ramahd pulled the ring free and felt each of the three keys, trying to judge which might unlock the chains. But as the footsteps came nearer, he simply tried the first one on his ankle. It was wrong, but the second one fit, and when he turned it, he felt the sweet release of the mechanism.

"Stop!" he heard the woman call.

The light wavered wildly as he unlocked the second shackle. He threw the chains off and rolled backward and onto his feet just as her lithe form swept forward in the gloom.

He was just able to avoid the sweep of her knife. He backed away as she swiped again, warding away the knife with the chain he now held between his hands. As she came in a third time, he flicked the chain around her wrist, trapped it, and pulled her close. She tried to recover, to adjust the blade and slash him across his right arm, but he was able to control her movement by tightening the chain. He head-butted her, slipped a foot behind her ankle, and sent her spilling to the ground. From there, it was simple to wrap an arm around her neck, still keeping the knife secure, and choke her until she lost consciousness.

He moved quickly after that.

The keys were where he'd dropped them. After unlocking the chains around his wrists, he retrieved the woman's candle from the stairs where she'd left it and brought it near Brama, scanning for the sapphire.

It wasn't around Brama's neck but had been thrust away as he'd fallen back. He could hardly believe it. He picked it up and found it was heavy, like lead instead of crystal. It was wrapped in leather cord, covered in something sticky, sooty. But for all that, as simple as it appeared, he could tell he was holding a thing of power.

He became so transfixed he lost track of time until he realized minutes had passed.

Shaking his head, he remembered the fierce battle that had sent Rümayesh into hiding. He had no idea what had happened to Meryam, but he had to get back to her.

But what to do with Brama?

He took up the knife of the woman who'd tried to kill him, then approached Brama carefully. By the gods, his mouth was working. His head lolled from side to side, but he didn't open his eyes, not even when the light from the candle came near.

Ramahd stood over him. Meryam might have use for him, but given how many zealots had decided to throw their lot in with him, he had power, and that power made him dangerous. He stared at the scars that crisscrossed Brama's face, his neck, the skin of his hands. He had no idea what had happened to the man, but it was likely a mercy to do what he did now, which was to run the knife across Brama's throat.

Blood ran in gouts as he turned to the woman. She was young. She could still make a life for herself. She might rally those loyal to Brama, but given their nature—men and women who not so long ago had been addicted to black lotus—he doubted they would stay with her for long, not without their savior.

In the end, Ramahd let her be. He moved upstairs, found his boots and sword on a table in the simple home, and left.

Chapter 23

AVUD TRUDGED TOWARD the blooming fields. King Sukru was by his side, walking like an old hyena: crook-backed, bald pate, and hungry, piercing eyes, the sort of creature a pack might devour rather than be slowed down. As had been true the last time they'd come, both Zahndr and a Silver Spear accompanied them, but unlike last time they were dragging between them a bound and gagged man—one of the few scarabs who had survived the Night of Endless Swords.

Ahead, the blooming fields sketched an imperfect line toward the horizon. The thorny adichara branches were motionless. The air was still, as if the trees were rapt, waiting to see what the King and Davud were preparing to do.

"My Lord King," Davud began, "might we speak of the man we've brought?"

"The *scarab*," Sukru spat as he led them through a gap in the trees.

Within was a sizable clearing. Along the far side of it lay a swath of trees that looked different from the rest. Healthy adichara were large thorny bushes that choked the space around their thick, gnarled base. Their branches were brown, with tinges of green near the ends that matched the small, spade-shaped leaves. The famed blooms were encased in indigo buds. The trees

Sukru led him toward were blackened, with few leaves and fewer buds. Unlike on Beht Zha'ir, when Sukru had brought him to a lone tree, here was a
wide swath of disease that went deeper into the grove—a dozen trees clustered together like children lost in the desert, huddled, crying, dying.

"All I ask, my Lord King," Davud went on, "is that you allow *me* to apply
the knife."

Ignoring Davud, Sukru motioned the Silver Spear to bring the prisoner
before him. The Spear complied, forcing the man to his knees, while Sukru
swung his withering gaze to Davud. "Why?"

Zahndr, standing behind Sukru, was shaking his head—a warning for
Davud to go no farther, but Davud had made up his mind. The prisoner was
hardly more than a boy. He was thin and malnourished with a haggard expression that gave some hint to the horrors he'd seen as a prisoner of the Kings.
He was trying to put on a brave face—one last defiant act before he died,
perhaps—but his eyes betrayed him. They shifted nervously between Sukru
and Davud. He no more wished to die than he wanted to kiss Sukru's feet.

"When we last came here, I suspect I could have learned more had the
tribute not died. If I might be allowed to take some of his blood while he lives,
perhaps we can go further than we did that night." Davud thought no such
thing, but satisfying Sukru's curiosity over the dying adichara wasn't worth a
life. Growing up in Roseridge, Davud had known many like this young scarab.
He might not agree that the path to peace was through war, but that didn't
mean he couldn't save a life when there was no need for it to be taken.

"There was no mention of this in the book I gave you," Sukru said, "nor
the one Hamzakiir left you."

"No," Davud replied, hoping he didn't sound too eager. "It was something Hamzakiir said when he confessed his nature, and my own. He said the
ehrekh hunger not for blood alone, but the blood of the living. I would try
this with a living soul."

For long moments Sukru's eyes searched Davud's. Then he looked to the
scarab as if he'd pissed on Sukru's curl-toed shoes.

"His lifeblood can still be spilled if I'm wrong, my Lord King." He hadn't
wanted to say it, but everything about Sukru spoke to the desire to end this
man's life. *He's been anticipating it since Sharakhai,* Davud realized. *I should
have spoken sooner.* But there had been precious little time. He'd only seen

him for a moment as he boarded Sukru's yacht, and the King had immediately hidden himself away in the rear cabin.

From the sheath at his belt Sukru pulled a broad-bladed kenshar. From the sour look on his face Davud thought he was going to run it across the scarab's throat just to spite him and his pet theory. But after a moment, he held it out, hilt first. "The gods forbid we end the life of a filthy *scarab*."

Davud tried his best to hide his relief but was unsure how successful he'd been given how churlishly Sukru was watching him. He ignored it as he flicked his fingers for the young man to move closer to the diseased adichara.

When he refused, the Silver Spear took him roughly by the arms and dragged him there.

"Give me your hand," Davud said.

The man's breath came faster now. "Please! Not my soul!"

Zahndr backhanded him. When he still refused, the Silver Spear grabbed him by the neck and choked him until his face turned red.

"Please, don't!" Davud cried.

The Spear didn't listen, and then Zahndr was wrenching his arm away from his body, preparing it for Davud.

Bakhi, please don't let this end in death.

As Davud brought the knife near, the scarab's face turned hard. "No!" he shouted, and leaned back and kicked Davud in the face.

Davud reeled as pain blossomed across his cheek and nose. He thumped against the sand, falling just short of having his face raked on an adichara's thorns. He rose to the sound of Sukru laughing. It was a low rumble, like thunder in the distance, but it grew the longer Sukru stared. Soon the King was gripping his knees. "Would you spare him now?"

Davud tenderly touched his nose to see if it was bleeding. Thankfully it wasn't. He could only imagine Sukru's laughter if it had been. With the pain subsiding, he moved more carefully toward the young man. "I only need a bit of your blood."

The scarab was shaking his head furiously. "I would die before I give it to you."

"Well then . . ."

Before Davud realized what was happening, Sukru snatched a thin knife from Zahndr's belt.

". . . your wish is granted!"

"No!" Davud shouted.

But it was too late. Sukru drew the knife sharply across the young man's throat and threw him against the diseased adichara. The scarab—Davud realized he'd never learned his name—clutched at his throat. His legs kicked, scoring deep furrows in the sand.

"Not another word, boy," Sukru said as he handed the knife back to Zahndr, who accepted it with a grim, accusatory look at Davud, as if *Davud* had been the killer. "Now get on with it."

Davud was petrified by Sukru's cruelty, and angry with himself for not finding some way through it. The scarab stared at Davud, blinking, fingers clutching, and then slowly he went still. In that moment, he couldn't help but think of Çeda and her plight, the secrets she was trying to uncover, the cruelty she hoped to end. And here he was, a willing participant in that same cruelty. He wanted Hamzakiir to pay for all he'd done, but first Davud had to learn more about his abilities and the cruel realities of this ancient conflict.

I advise you to find another mage when you return to Sharakhai, Hamzakiir had told him in Ishmantep. *It won't be easy, and I suspect before long one will find you, one you mightn't like to have as your master, so work quickly.* Davud *did* have a master now, and he wasn't at all sure he liked him.

Sukru's stare became more intense. "I'll not ask you again."

"Of course, my Lord King." Davud knelt on the ground beside the young man. *May Bakhi deliver you swiftly to the farther fields.* Then he touched his fingers to the blood that oozed from the slit in the young man's throat. He used it to draw sigils on his palms. The first combined *subsume* with the sigil the firefinch had given him, a sigil he'd come to call *delve* for the feelings of burrowing and deepening it seemed to bring about. The other encompassed several from the book Sukru had given him: sigils for *graft* and *grow*.

In Sukru's book, Davud had learned of blood magi who used multiple sigils at the same time. The mage would, as the author had put it, *grip* the sigils, which would in turn summon the desired effect. He hoped this combination would allow him to delve more deeply than he had the last time so that he could learn why some of the adichara trees were beginning to wither and die.

That done, he retrieved an ampule from the pouch at his belt, filled it carefully with blood, and downed it in one swallow. He was no longer new to the taste of blood, but the raw potency of it still awed him. Just as it had when he'd snuffed the flames in Ishmantep, it offered him enough power to do whatever he wished.

He forced it into the earth, trailing after the blood that had seeped below the surface. He felt the roots combine, felt them merge and merge again to form the trunk, felt them divide and divide again as the branches fought for space with its brethren. As his awareness grew, he willed them to tell their story, limiting himself to the ones that were diseased. The dozen trees before him were strong in his mind, a life like his, and yet unlike it. These trees had lived through the ages, since their quickening at Tulathan's hand.

Suddenly a vision swept him up. A woman, tall with plaited blonde hair, carried a gnarled wooden staff, the head of which looked like a cobra spreading its hood. The woman had seen forty summers, perhaps. She was broad-shouldered, with a broad, handsome face to match, not unlike the first men and women depicted in the frescoes of Yerinde's temple.

The desert's harsh sun drove down, creating stark shadows against the sand as she walked. As she approached the blooming fields, the branches leaned away as if she were aflame, unbearable to be near. Upon reaching a clearing, she knelt before an adichara and put her staff down. For a time she breathed, eyes closed, arms to her side, palms outward, as if she were feeling the rhythms of the grove. The sun stretched toward sunset. At the precise moment it kissed the horizon, she leaned forward and *blew* upon the base of the adichara before her. Sand and stone lifted like dust, revealing ever more of the knobbly trunk as it dug deeper into the earth. Again she blew, and a third time, until the mosslike roots were revealed.

Her hand scraped the rough bark. Her fingers clutched the roots. The moment was dizzying, for Davud felt himself at the same time, kneeling beside a similar tree while a King named Sukru stood near and a dead man lay close enough to touch. *Who are you?* he wanted to ask, but his courage was failing him. Then he was drawn down, down, down into the earth, and he couldn't tell which of them it was happening to.

Both, you fool.

Deep into the earth he went, the roots creeping through stone, along tunnels, through gaps, into caverns large and small. The roots filled cracks and crevices, wriggling ever deeper, a great coalescing as they fused with one another to form a trunk.

All of them, Davud realized. *All them. As if the individual trees are nothing more than the leaves of a grand arboreal organism growing beneath the bedrock of Sharakhai itself.* But if that were so, why were some of the branches dying?

The roots met in a cavern. They coated the walls, reached up to the very center of the cavern's high roof, where they braided into a thick clump that grew thinner, thinner, until only one small tendril was left. From that distal thread, moisture dripped, pattering against a stone that lay below.

And the stone . . . It glowed violet, like a heavenly body being fed and nurtured within the womb of that very cavern. Davud didn't know the nature of it, but he was certain the adichara had created it. Their roots been guided here by unseen hands so that their essence might feed this stone. But what *was* that essence? It wasn't water. And it certainly wasn't blood.

Before Davud could think further, he was swept back to the desert. The woman lifted her head, suddenly wary and afraid. She turned the way she'd come, then stood, picking up her staff.

Her brow furrowed in concentration as the dying light of dusk lit the desert red. From beyond the line of trees there came a snuffing sound. A huffing. Lumbering toward her were a pair of dark forms, animals with ridged backs and heads held low. They had thick fur with long black spines along the shoulders and back. Desert hyenas. Black laughers. Bone crushers. Except these two were much larger than those that typically roamed the desert.

They sniffed along the stone where the woman had entered the blooming field—a path now blocked by the poisonous branches of the adichara. Still, they tried, growling as they pushed their massive heads into the undergrowth. When the woman moved in the other direction, the trees parted, and the black laughers sensed it. One backed away from the adichara, yipping. The other laughed its chilling laugh. Then both tipped their heads back and howled to the darkling sky.

The woman reached the sand, but already she could hear more of the black laughers on this side of the adichara. There were three. No, four. Sprinting toward her while tails of sand kicked up behind them. She held her ground, ready for battle. When the nearest came close, she swung her staff, caught the beast across the jaw, and sent it flying, its massive head lolling. It struck the sand and lay still.

The others fanned out, refusing to come in range of her staff. She sprinted forward, so fast that the largest of the beasts had no time to back away, and caught it on the top of its skull. It was driven down, but the others were darting in now, and more laughers were approaching.

Jaws snapped and throats growled. Those farther away yowled. One bit her leg. Another lunged and clamped its jaws around her wrist before she managed to tear it away.

With a grand wave of her staff, the adichara came alive. The branches reached out, grabbing the fetlocks of the nearest laugher. A second was grabbed by its neck. Then a third by its snout, the thorns refusing to let go no matter how much it snapped and struggled. More branches wrapped around their legs and barrel chests, then drew the laughers into the groves, where thicker branches wrapped them and squeezed. They whimpered and whined as the trees tore them apart.

Then the adicharas went still. The remaining bone crushers backed away, then laughed louder, longer, higher than before. A smell pervaded the deepening night, a scent like myrrh and loam and burning pitch. Fear lit the woman's features as she turned toward the bright horizon.

Silhouetted by the sun's dying light was a massive figure. Black skin, a crown of thorns, legs like a bull's. Two tails lashed the air behind it. It was Goezhen, who traveled with a pack of bone crushers, the elders of those that plagued the desert. He held a javelin loosely in one hand and was approaching at a walk, but then he seemed to recognize the woman, for he smiled and began to lope forward.

She lifted her staff high, gripping it with both hands. Putting her whole body into one savage movement, she speared the tip into the ground between her feet. It sunk a foot into the stone. Eyes closed, she whispered to the head of the staff. From the point where the staff entered the ground, the earth split. A crack formed and shot forward like lightning, running toward Goezhen in a jagged line, then cutting beneath him. The gap widened, earth fell away, and Goezhen had to scramble, stabbing his javelin into the wall of the crevice that had formed. He tried to climb out, but the earth came snapping back, trapping him from the waist down.

Goezhen roared as the shaking of the earth began to quell and the stone pressed ever inward. It was crushing him, but Goezhen was not done. He pressed his arms against the ground and with a roar lifted one leg free of the earth. The ground beneath him tore as he climbed out. The woman—surely she was Nalamae; who else would oppose Goezhen?—was whispering again. Goezhen, however, seemed ready. He lifted his javelin, took two long strides, and sent it flying through the air.

It flew true and struck Nalamae in the chest. She shattered, breaking into pieces as if she were made stone. Indeed, her skin and clothes had dulled, turned an amber color. She fell apart like a statue at the strike of an iron maul.

Goezhen neared, crouched low, lips pulled back in shock and anger. His jaundiced eyes narrowed. He leaned to one side, sniffing, scrutinizing. Nothing happened, however, until he took another step. The stones burst, exploding with a sound that shook the earth. Goezhen reared back as a sound like chittering insects filled the air. Chunks of stone and scree fell to the ground. As the sound died away, a great cloud of dust was borne on the breeze.

Goezhen pulled a thick shard of stone from the meat of his thigh where it had been driven by the explosion. He pulled more from his chest and arms. Black blood flowed, slicking the fur along the joints of his taurine legs. He stared, hands balled into fists at his sides, his face and chest and arms bleeding from a dozen wounds. His entire body tensed and the god of chaos released a bellow of rage.

As it rang through the dusk, Davud was returned to himself though the sound still echoed in his mind. But Goezhen was gone. Gone were the black laughers. Gone the brilliant sunset. Instead, Davud found himself staring at the trunk of the adichara before him. By his side, the dead scarab lay, flies crawling on his eyes and lips, slipping inside his open mouth. Zahndr stood nearby and seemed surprised when Davud lifted himself up off the ground and came to a stand.

Davud ignored him. He couldn't shake the feeling that there were black laughers near, that Goezhen was coming. Had Nalamae been *here?* But no.

"How long?" Davud asked.

"Six hours," Zahndr replied, eyeing Davud as if he expected him to sprout reptilian legs and crawl into the sand. He held out a skin of water. Davud accepted it gratefully, drank deeply, then wiped his mouth with the back of his hand.

"There were black laughers. In the dream, I mean . . ."

He stopped, for Zahndr was shaking his head grimly. "This story isn't for my ears." He motioned Davud to the way back. "Best get on. The King's been anxious for you to wake."

Soon Davud was back on the yacht, sitting in Sukru's cabin as the deck tilted easily with the slope of the dunes. He shared his vision. Most of it in any case. He withheld the part about Nalamae and Goezhen. He wanted more time to think, to speak with someone he trusted. *If only his old collegia master, Amalos, were still alive . . .*

Sukru's eyes stared past Davud as if Sukru had just learned he was dying. "The cavern—what sort of stone?" he barked after a time.

Davud shrugged. "It looked like crystal, but not faceted. It was smooth, and violet light glowed from within." He paused, waiting for Sukru to ask more. When he didn't, Davud asked, "Is there any such cavern?"

Sukru's mouth worked. He seemed restless, worried. His eyes flitted to and fro, as if he were lost in some grand equation he couldn't quite solve. "Leave me."

"Of course, my Lord King."

"And Davud?" Sukru said when he was halfway through the door. "You will speak of this to no one."

"Never, my Lord King."

The way Sukru had said it . . . Davud already knew he shouldn't tell anyone. Sukru had given that order before they'd taken their first voyage to the blooming fields. The very fact that Sukru had said it again, with such a malevolent look on his face, made Davud realize just how dangerous it was to be party to this information.

That made two things perfectly clear. First, Sukru hadn't known about the cavern. And second, now that he *did* know, he was worried. *The patience of a butterfly and the anger of a bull,* the Sparrow had said of Sukru. Although Davud believed those words, he hadn't felt their weight. Not until now.

He spent the return voyage wondering if Sukru would storm in and run a knife across Davud's throat, as he'd done to the scarab.

Chapter 24

SEVERAL DAYS PASSED after unexpectedly finding Emre in Leorah's yacht. They were busy days. Çeda met what felt like a thousand people. She heard tales. She helped to unload food and water and firewood from the ships for a feast held over the course of the day. She learned how to make a sour flatbread that had a thin, crispy, almost burnt shell and a soft, airy interior. Coupled with a rich tagine of lamb, potato, tomato, eggplant, and rosemary, it was divine. She tasted a dozen other dishes as well. Buttery saffron rice in the morning. A simple meal of pears and cheese near midday. The bread and tagine as the sun was lowering.

Leorah finished Çeda's tattoo. Staring at the finished image in a mirror, Çeda felt proud. To have her own story inked indelibly into her skin by the hand of her own great-grandmother was a thing she couldn't have imagined a year ago. The image and its making bridged the distance between their generations, a weave that encompassed not only the two of them, but Ahya, Ishaq, and Macide as well.

After two days of celebration, the mood of the tribe sobered. They had a purpose here, and the dangers mounted the longer they remained. Ishaq held council for long hours of each day. Most of those attending—Macide,

Dardzada, Darius, Hamid the Cruel (as he'd come to be called), a broad-faced woman named Shal'alara who was said to have more lives than a cat, and more—had been leaders in the Moonless Host. The lines between the Host and the tribe had become so blurred that they were all now de facto tribe elders.

Only once was Çeda summoned, and then only to recount her story for the elders to hear for themselves. She answered a few questions, but it was clear they already knew most of her tale. She'd hoped to speak to Ishaq about her plans to return to Sharakhai, to make her case clearly and calmly, but she was dismissed before she had a chance.

She had gone to Ishaq several times after, hoping they might come to some accord, but he'd rebuffed her each time, making it clear to Çeda how poorly she'd handled herself the other day. She shouldn't have been so impolitic, especially at their first meeting. She'd created a rift between them and now was having trouble finding a way to mend it. Wait, and he might assume she'd decided to join the tribe and cede her will to his, but push too hard or too quickly and it would cement his impression of her as an immature girl filled with fire and brimstone and little else.

On her fifth day at camp, several ships prepared to sail. They didn't want to risk the whole tribe being together for so long. Not just yet. So they ordered those ships carrying the tribe's eldest and the mothers and the youngest of the children to sail for one of the safe havens the Moonless Host had used over the years. The rest would take to the sands the next day, following one final council.

The ships eventually departed. Çeda thought Ishaq might come to bid the ships farewell, but he didn't, and when sunset neared, Çeda began to worry that he now assumed Çeda was a part of the tribe. He might not give her a chance to speak after all. The council still hadn't broken, and the morning would be consumed as the rest of the tribe prepared to leave. Swallowing an urge to walk into the pavilion and demand that Ishaq speak with her, she went to Leorah's yacht, hoping to ask for her advice. Salsanna was there, sitting on one of the runners. Çeda made to head up the gangway, but Salsanna rose to her impressive, full height and stepped in Çeda's path. "Leorah will be along soon."

The way she'd said it, so matter-of-factly, reminded Çeda of her mother's manner, which in turn reminded her of the strange way she'd closed her letter. "Who is Devorah?" she asked Salsanna.

Salsanna brushed the sand from the back of her blue skirt with the sort of absent care that made it clear just how much she was surprised by the question. "How do you know that name?"

"It was in a letter my mother left to me. She said to trust Leorah and Devorah, for they both see beyond the horizon."

"Devorah was Leorah's twin sister. She died when they were young. Your age, in fact."

"Died how?"

Salsanna glanced at the gangway leading down from the ship, perhaps nervous that Leorah might hear her. "Years ago the shaikh of Tribe Rafik sheltered Leorah and Devorah, but Sukru somehow found them and demanded Leorah as his bride. On the morning Leorah was to depart for Sharakhai, Devorah went to Sukru's ship. She posed as Leorah and told him before the crew and the entire tribe, that she would never consent, nor would any other woman from the tribe. She would die first, or if forced to go to Sharakhai, then she would kill him as he slept." She glanced at the ship again, and lowered her voice before continuing. "It's said she drew a knife right there and then and tried to cut Sukru's neck. Sukru seemed to know she would try. He took the knife from her and drove it into her belly, dragged her to the edge of the deck, and threw her down to the sand. With Devorah dying below, Sukru stared out over the tribe. None had known what Devorah planned, and they were shocked, but they now stared defiantly at Sukru, as though each and every woman there was ready to treat Devorah's threat as her own.

"After spitting onto Devorah's lifeless body, Sukru returned to Sharakhai. Many considered it a victory, but it had left Leorah without her sister. As the King's galleon sailed away, she lay on the sand by Devorah's side. She took the amethyst ring from her, the one she wears to this day, as a remembrance of the sacrifice her sister had made."

Out in the desert, Kerim wailed. It sent shivers down Çeda's spine. She knew the sort of man Sukru was. Gods, the very thought of being married to him made her blood run cold. "I don't doubt your tale, but why would my mother ask me to listen to them both, as if Devorah were still alive?"

Salsanna shrugged. "Leorah won't admit it, but she talks to the ring. She's said now and again that *both she and Devorah* agreed on this or that. I think something broke in her the day Devorah died. When it did, she placed the broken pieces into that ring, along with her love for her sister."

A hollow thumping sound came from the yacht, and Leorah emerged. "Are you telling stories about me again?" She stood bent to one side, her cane helping to support her.

Salsanna helped her down the gangway. "Would you rather I didn't?"

Leorah smiled slyly. "Depends on which story."

"Only the good ones," Salsanna replied.

"Well then," Leorah said, winking at Çeda, "tell all you like."

Behind them, the elders of the tribe were stepping out of the pavilion. Another long wail fell across the sand, and many turned to look, including Ishaq—Çeda could see his silhouette, standing just outside the entrance, back-lit in gold.

Leorah's story had sparked something in Kerim. Çeda could feel his hatred for Sukru, as well as a burning desire to obey him. She felt the same conflicted feelings from him toward Ishaq as on the morning they'd met several days before: a familial bond coupled with a deep-seated yearning to end his life.

Suddenly all of Çeda's worries over what to do with Ishaq vanished like winter fog. "Can you wait here a moment?" she asked Salsanna and Leorah.

Confused, they both nodded.

Çeda ran toward the pavilion. The elders turned to look at her, Macide, Hamid, Shal'alara and the rest, but Çeda ignored them, focusing squarely on Ishaq. "There's something I would show you, my shaikh," she said breath-lessly. "Please."

Ishaq looked to the others. "Very well, but it will have to wait until the morning."

"Tomorrow will be too late," Çeda said. "It must be now." She motioned to Leorah and Salsanna, both burning orange under the brilliance of the western sky. "Please."

Ishaq paused, working his mouth, as he often seemed to do when he was annoyed. "Very well."

Çeda led him away from the others, feeling their stares at her back. She ignored them, and brought Ishaq toward the skiff resting near the stern of Leorah's ship. She motioned to Leorah and Salsanna as she went. "Come."

Soon all four of them had boarded the skiff and were sailing out to the edge of the standing stones. When they stopped, most of the stones were behind them, leaving the desert to sprawl ahead of them.

Çeda could not see Kerim, but she could feel him, sitting out there, cloaked in the gathering darkness. *I know your mind, child of Ahyanesh. Do not ask it of me. I cannot.*

We have no choice, she said to him. *Fates willing, I'll be leaving soon, and I cannot take you with me.*

A stab of fear. A spark of sadness. *You would abandon me?*

Never. I will return, but I must leave you with the children of those who survived Beht Ihman. Come, Kerim, take Salsanna's hand. Take the hand of the one you blooded.

Using the same tone—calm but forceful—Çeda turned to Salsanna and said, "I've brought you here to bond with Kerim."

There was no hiding the look of repulsion and shock on Salsanna's scarred face. Leorah, however, seemed suddenly eager, and Ishaq was unreadable.

"Bond?" The note of fear in Salsanna's voice was plain. "I will not bond with it."

"Do not call him *it* in my hearing again," Çeda said. "And yes. You must bond with him that he may know you, and through you, the others in our tribe."

Salsanna looked between Leorah and Ishaq, waiting for either to object. When neither did, she said, "You cannot *leave* him."

"I cannot take him with me." Çeda met Ishaq's gaze. "If I am to go, by your leave, and with your help, then Kerim must remain here. You were right the other day. His presence anywhere near Sharakhai will alert them to my presence. And it's long past time that we learn more about the asirim, and the asirim us."

Salsanna looked as if she was about to speak, but she fell silent as Leorah gripped her wrist.

Ishaq's gaze drifted from Çeda to Leorah to Salsanna. His only response was to give one sharp nod, an acknowledgment that Çeda may try, and that Salsanna should as well.

"Go on," Leorah said, "draw him near."

Salsanna seemed unsure, even scared, while in the desert, Kerim's anger flared. *Nalamae's grace,* he said, *I bled for you.*

I bled for you as well. And would do so again gladly if my pain would set you free.

Doubt grew inside him like a cancer. *I will die for your sake if you but take me back to Sharakhai.*

It's too dangerous, Kerim, for both of us.

His wail broke the still silence of the desert, driving a spear of ice through her heart. *Please don't leave me*, he begged.

She knew he would feel betrayed by her demand, but she hadn't understood the depths of it until now. After centuries with the other asirim, souls who'd suffered the same fate, he was terrified of being alone.

Don't you see? she said to him. *You won't be* alone.

But Kerim wasn't listening. He was drowning in his own emotions. She had to finish this quickly, before he lost faith in her. She had to make him wake and *see* the others, or she'd be condemning him to death.

She faced Salsanna now. She might be willing to try for Ishaq's sake, maybe even Leorah's, but that wasn't enough. She had to believe, or this would never work. "He can protect you," Çeda said to her, "even as you protect *him*. For the first time since Beht Ihman, he can *heal*."

Çeda reached out Kerim, giving him the love for the family she'd never known but had dreamed about since she was young. *Come to me, child of Deniz, cousin to Sehid-Alaz. These people are your blood. Our tribe is reborn.*

Reborn, Kerim scoffed. *Our tribe will be reborn only when the asirim are freed and the Kings have paid for their misdeeds.*

Then let me go, Çeda replied. *Let me do just that.*

Her next words she spoke aloud, for they were meant for all of them: Kerim, Salsanna, Leorah, and Ishaq. "It won't be chains you forge this day, but bonds to one another's hearts. It will make us *all* stronger." She took Salsanna's hands in hers. Salsanna, to Çeda's great relief, did nothing to stop her. "Let him heal. Let him see what life is like in *your* desert, the one so different from the one he's known. Let him hear the laugh of a child. Let him hear the songs written when he walked the earth a man, and those that have been written since. Let him remember his *own* joys, his *own* loves, even as you revel in yours."

Kerim didn't want to return to Sharakhai. Not truly. He was only scared of Çeda's leaving. And Salsanna, for her part, was a woman who deeply revered the thirteenth tribe; she simply had yet to recognize Kerim as part of it. Both of them seemed to understand these things, for in that moment Salsanna's grip softened, and Kerim's reluctance began to melt.

Çeda's heart sang to see it, but they were not yet done. She held out her hand to Leorah, motioning to the locket around her neck. "A petal, Leorah, if you please."

Leorah's eyes flitted to Salsanna as her hands went to her throat and opened the locket. From it she retrieved a petal, which glowed blue-white in the last light of sunset. She handed it to Çeda, and Çeda stood before Salsanna. "Open your mouth."

Salsanna did, and Çeda placed the petal beneath her tongue.

Çeda's awareness of Salsanna blossomed, as it no doubt did for Kerim as well. Kerim crept closer as Çeda, Leorah, and Ishaq stepped away, leaving Salsanna to wait alone as Kerim crawled from the darkness. His breath came in broken fragments. His body tilted sideways, as if he were moving against some unseen current.

Tears streamed down Salsanna's face as she fell to her knees and held out her hand. Kerim came nearer, but it seemed a bridge too far to take her hand. Like a man lost and weary after days in the desert, he collapsed against the sand and clutched himself. Salsanna touched his shoulder, then knelt by his side and pulled him up until she was embracing him. For all the world she looked like a mother consoling a child who'd grown fearful of the night.

Çeda felt her own bond with Kerim slipping away. His thoughts became muted. His emotions dimmed. Soon he was little more than a distant presence, a figure in the fog.

Taking both Leorah's and Ishaq's hands, Çeda moved farther away, leaving the two of them in peace. When they reached the skiff, Çeda turned to Ishaq. "You let my mother go when it was her will to journey to Sharakhai and carry out a mission she believed in. I am the result of that decision. Your decision, grandfather. Everything your daughter did led to me, to this day. Everything she did is pointing me back toward Sharakhai. I would go, but I would have your blessing before I do."

To her surprise, Ishaq, this legend of the desert, a man who seemed made of stone, seemed unsure of himself. He swallowed. He looked to Leorah, and then the scene that was playing out between Salsanna and Kerim.

"We've only just met." There were *tears* in his eyes.

"I know," Çeda said. "And we'll meet again." She took his hands in hers and kissed both his cheeks. "If the fates are kind, we'll meet again."

He looked at her as though she were a lovable fool. "The fates are not kind."

"No, but they cannot be *this* cruel."

Lifting his hands and gripping her head, Ishaq kissed *her* cheeks. "Go to Sharakhai, granddaughter. See if the asirim can be freed. See if the Maidens can be turned. Find the truth of my daughter's journey the night before she died. You'll do this for me?"

"I will." Çeda's tears flowed freely now. She released Ishaq's hands and took a deep breath, wiping her eyes with the palms of her hands. "I have one last request." She removed Mesut's bracelet from her left hand and held it out to Leorah. "Take this. Become its guardian until I return. Learn whatever you can about it, for there are more here we must care for."

Leorah looked scared to touch it, but then she reached out both hands and took it in hers. Slipping the bracelet over her wrist, she looked at Çeda with wonder in her eyes. "By Nalamae's grace, child."

"What?" Çeda said, feeling suddenly uncomfortable.

"When Ahya left for Sharakhai, she went to make a child with one of the Kings. We dreamed of that child becoming a weapon, being their ruin. But if Ahya could see you now, she would see you are no weapon, but a mirror through which we can see our very soul."

"I'm no such thing."

"Ah . . ." Leorah waddled forward and took Çeda into an embrace. "But that's the thing about mirrors. They're unable to witness their own reflections."

Chapter 25

THE FOLLOWING MORNING, many of the Khiyanat ships were taking to the wind. All flew new pennants atop their mainmasts, a white mountain on a blue field.

"Tauriyat?" Çeda asked Dardzada, though the shape of the mountain wasn't quite right.

"No," he replied gruffly. "It's Arasal."

"Why Mount Arasal?"

Arasal was the source of the aqueduct that fed Sharakhai's reservoirs, and so was viewed as a giver of life in the city. Knowing Ishaq, however, a man who prized symbolism, there would be more to it than that.

"After Beht Ihman, the surviving members of our tribe fled to a valley beneath that peak. They used to meet there in the depths of summer. For a time they thought themselves safe, but days later they were set upon by the asirim." Dardzada's perpetual frown deepened. "Few escaped the slaughter."

Çeda stared at the pennants as the ships sailed farther away, feeling renewed anger at the Kings but also a rekindling of pride. How fragile those days must have been, and yet some few escaped to carry their story through the pages of time.

As the ships dwindled in the distance, Çeda marveled at what Ishaq had managed to accomplish. Even as the Kings had stepped up their attacks in Sharakhai, Ishaq had faced a coup from within. Hamzakiir, using guile or blood magic or both, had siphoned off support from those who'd provided Ishaq not only with the coin he needed to wage his war against the Kings, but also the supplies, skill, and labor. But Ishaq had not been idle in the years leading up to that struggle. He'd foreseen trouble, even if he hadn't known what form it would take. He'd secreted away dozens of ships in desert caches, each of which had been loaded with essential supplies. Those ships were now being used to draw the tribe together and sustain them as more came out of hiding. Slowly but surely, the tribe was finding its footing.

Later in the day, Çeda was preparing the skiff Salsanna had used to rescue her and Kerim from the tower. She'd said her farewells to Ishaq, Macide, Leorah, and Salsanna. She had yet to visit Emre, however. Or Dardzada.

But lo and behold, as she hoisted the last jug of water over the side, she saw Dardzada approaching with a bag over his shoulder. The sand shifted beneath his feet, giving him an odd gait. He looked like a bloody heron out of water. In a strange bit of timing, Emre emerged from Ishaq's tent and began following him. And right behind Emre came the huge man they called Frail Lemi, who had a vaguely worried, almost puppy-like look on his face. When Emre noticed him he stopped and raised his hands. Çeda couldn't hear what he was saying, but when he was done Frail Lemi nodded and remained where he was, watching as Emre quickened his pace, so that by the time Dardzada reached the skiff, Emre was right there beside him.

For a moment the three of them were awkward as mismatched teacups. Emre and Dardzada simply stared at Çeda, or more to the point, were pointedly *not* staring at one another. Last night, after agreeing to her request, Ishaq had promised to send someone with her. She knew she needed the help, but . . .

"Goezhen's pendulous balls, you're not *both* coming with me, are you?"

Emre looked sidelong at Dardzada.

Dardzada laughed that deep, biting laugh of his, the one Emre used to hate so much. If the look on Emre's face was any indicator, time had done nothing to temper the feeling. "You think Ishaq would let someone like *Emre* accompany you?"

Çeda stared at him. "So *you're* to join me?"

"Does that present a problem?"

"I . . ." Çeda shifted uncomfortably. "I don't—"

"Breath of the desert, girl, spit it out."

"The journey will be taxing," Çeda said. "Wouldn't you rather—?"

"Don't waste your breath," Dardzada broke in. "Believe me, I'd let you go on this fool mission alone, but Ishaq has ordered it, so I'm going." With that, he hoisted the bag over the side of the skiff and stared at her, as if he expected her to set sail and leave on the spot.

He'll be a chain around my ankles. But what could she do about it now? She should have pressed Ishaq last night. She might have argued against Dardzada then, but not now, not with the entire camp already packing up to sail.

She turned to Emre. "And you?"

He waved at a distant cutter. "I'm leaving today on the mission to Tribe Kadri. To see if we can stop Shaikh Mihir from joining hands with Onur."

"Time grows short," Dardzada said, his hand on the gunwale.

"No, it doesn't," Çeda snapped. "Wait." She led Emre away with Dardzada watching her and Frail Lemi watching Emre. She couldn't help it. If felt so awkward that a laugh burst from her.

"Stop it, Çeda." He looked hurt. "These are dangerous days."

"Yes, but for the first time since my mother died, I feel *hopeful*, Emre."

He seemed to lighten at that. "Hopeful . . ." He said it with furrowed brow, then gave her that unbalanced smile of his. "I just hope the Blade Maidens don't string you up too high."

"I hope Onur doesn't crush you like a rattlewing."

"He'll have to catch me first. By the time he's lumbered after me, I'll have stuck him three times on that fat arse of his with his own spear."

Çeda laughed as she stepped in and embraced him, taking care not to put pressure on his still-tender ribs. "Take care, Emre."

"And you."

As he headed back toward camp she kicked a massive spray of sand over his back. He turned, mouth agape as he shook the sand from his hair and his clothes. He laughed and kicked sand back at her. But Çeda was already skipping away and escaped the confrontation unscathed. Both chuckling, they went their separate ways. Near the skiff, Dardzada rolled his eyes.

"Ishaq said you hope to find the sliver trove," Dardzada said the first night of their voyage. He was sitting on a stone, paring the skin off a juicy cactus leaf. The yellow-green peelings fell to the sand between his feet.

"Or at least, learn more about it." Çeda sat across from him, a fire crackling softly between them. "I think your instincts were right. I think my mother believed in the trove, and I think she went to find it."

Dardzada shrugged. "My instincts also tell me it was a trap. Are you going to believe that part too?"

"I'm not discounting it. But I want know more about what happened to her that night. I want to retrace her steps before going to the House of Maidens."

"You don't know where her path led her."

"I think I do." She pulled Ahya's letter from her pouch, and handed it to Dardzada. As he read it by the firelight, she continued, "When I came to you in your apothecary, you said she'd found a mirage."

Finishing the letter, Dardzada stared into the fire, perhaps lost in memories. "She told me she'd gone to *find it in the whispers*, but that she found only a mirage."

She motioned to the letter. "And there it says she was preparing to go to the mount, and that she hoped to uncover more treasures. I think the silver trove might not be silver at all. I think it might be the poems recited on Tauriyat. The silver might refer to Tulathan herself."

Dardzada's body drew inward while his face soured. It was what he did while worrying at a problem. "Tulathan . . ."

"Yes. And if it's true, then I want to begin my search there, at the site of the ritual."

"*If* it's true . . ."

"Yes, *if*, but it makes sense. It would explain why my mother risked so much to go there. It might also explain why she returned as she did, perhaps under the command of King Ihsan." She paused a moment. "I want to go there on Beht Zha'ir."

To her surprise, Dardzada didn't immediately try to deny her. "Why not the night before, as your mother did?"

"It's likely I won't have this chance again, and whatever the Kings are trying to hide is because of Beht Zha'ir, so I think it's best if go then, don't you?"

He slid the knife over the cactus with a practiced hand. As a peel flew into the fire and sizzled, he shrugged his stocky shoulders. "I suppose if it *was* a trap it's likely been sprung. I can't imagine the Kings will be sitting there every night, waiting for someone to show up. But you're forgetting one rather important thing."

"What?"

"You don't know where the ritual was held."

"I *do* know. I've seen it, Dardzada. That day in your apothecary, when I fought Macide, I was overwhelmed by the asir, Havva, and I saw the gods standing on a plateau near the very top of the mountain."

He could hardly hold her gaze. When he spoke again, his words were tentative but caring, the sort a parent might use after finally deciding to give a child more freedom. "You'll be able to find it by moonlight?"

"I'm certain of it."

Dardzada became fixated by the fire. "You'll take care?"

"Of course. As much as I'm able."

He blinked and drew breath sharply through his nostrils. "Very well, then."

Çeda's lips curled into a smile as she set about the business of boiling water for rice. "Dardzada, did you just *agree* with me?"

He shrugged as another peel flew. "It's important, what you're doing. I see no reason not to find out, one way or another, if you're right." He rushed on before she could say anything to embarrass him. "What about the asirim?"

"That's a bit trickier. Unless the Kings work actively against me, I'm certain I can bond with several asirim, perhaps as many as five or six. I might even be able to draw them into the desert. The pressure on Kerim diminished the further he got from the blooming fields."

Dardzada lifted his head, his knife held steady. "You could maintain such a bond for months?"

"Perhaps."

"Even so, the *pressure* on Kerim, as you call it, was hardly minimal."

"Granted. It will likely prevent us from unleashing them against Sharakhai directly, but it may be enough to keep them by our side far out in the desert. They could help to protect us as we rebuild, and we could learn, hopefully find a way to free them."

"Still, five or six . . ." He picked up another cactus leaf, the last for their meal, and set to peeling it. "It's hardly inspiring."

"I know. The permanent solution may only be found when the Kings are dead, but there might be another way. Sehid-Alaz. I think there is a bond between him and the other asirim."

Dardzada considered. "You mean *all* the other asirim."

"Yes."

"You think he's still alive?"

"I'm certain of it. Through Kerim, I felt him, though the link to him was thin as spider silk. It's another reason I want to speak with more of the asirim. If we can learn more, and if we can find Sehid-Alaz and take him with us, speak to him, we may find a way."

"It's a lot to do, Çeda." Done peeling, he began cutting long, thick slices off the white, edible cactus leaf. He handed one to Çeda. She took a large bite. The mildly sweet meat crunched in her mouth like a juicy melon.

Beht Zha'ir was less than a week away. She would try to find the trove that night and on her way out steal into the House of Maidens to speak to Melis. If all went well, she and Dardzada might be able to travel to the blooming fields and bond with some of the asirim. It would be a good night to do it, she reckoned. Their anger was upon them then, and they might be better able to use it to throw off their yokes.

"Don't worry," she told Dardzada. "I'm not setting my sights too high. My only hope for Sehid-Alaz is to locate him. We can make plans to return another time and free him."

As they ate their simple meal, passing a water skin back and forth, Dardzada frowned. He opened his mouth, stopped, and then said, "How will you get into the House of Kings?"

She had the impression that wasn't what he'd been about to say, but she let it go. "Through the tunnels."

Dardzada nodded, lost in thought.

"Is there an apothecary in the city we can trust?" she asked, partly to gauge his reaction.

He turned sharply toward her, his face a mixture of feigned and genuine shock. "What am I, minced goat?"

Çeda laughed. "Components, Dardzada. We need components so you can make me something. Is there someone you trust?"

The firelight played over his round features as he considered. "Make you something? What does that mean?"

She began to catalog what she would need to get into the House of Maidens—and out again as well, especially if things turned bad. But she could tell that Dardzada was only half listening.

She stopped halfway through and waited for him to take notice of her. "What is it you're not saying?"

"Sehid-Alaz . . . You seem to think that freeing him will somehow free the other asirim."

"I said that it could *lead* to freeing them."

"Yes. Well, you also said that you thought the asirim might not be freed until the Kings lay dead."

"Yes . . ."

"Have you not considered that for the asirim to be freed, Sehid-Alaz himself might have to die?"

She wanted to laugh, but the dead serious look on his face prevented it. Her mind wandered to all she knew about the King of the thirteenth tribe. He was taken like the other asirim, but there had been a power in him unlike the others. Over the centuries he'd found a way around the spell of silence the gods placed on him. He'd spoken to those with blood of the thirteenth tribe, hoping that one of them might find a way to kill King Mesut. He'd stood against the Kings on the Night of Endless Swords. He'd *disobeyed* their commands. Any other asirim would have been killed. Why not Sehid-Alaz? Why would the Kings show restraint? Why not kill him and be done with the problems he presented?

Çeda's bowl lowered into her lap as a terrible shiver ran down her frame. "Oh, gods . . ."

The poem. The one she'd heard from Sehid-Alaz's own mouth. How could she have forgotten?

Rest will he,
'Neath twisted tree,
'Til death by scion's hand.
By Nalamae's tears,
And godly fears,
Shall kindred reach dark land.

She recited it aloud. Dardzada remained silent after, his eyes sparkling in the firelight, his body still as stone. The realization was beginning to settle in him, the same as it had for her—the realization that after all the King of the thirteenth tribe had done for her, she may have to kill him to free the rest.

Chapter 26

EMRE WATCHED THE SKIFF SAIL AWAY—Dardzada sitting at the tiller, Çeda working the sail.

"You like her, Emre?" Frail Lemi asked as he trudged up behind him.

"Sure I like her."

Frail Lemi pursed his lips as he considered the skiff's dwindling form. "Should've told her, then."

"You're probably right."

"I *know* I'm right. She'd be good for you."

"Doesn't mean I'd be good for her."

"Nah, you would." With a nod, as if he'd never been more sure of anything in his life, he pulled Emre in and kissed the top of his head, much like Frail Lemi's waif of a mother did to her massive son each time he left her home. "You would."

A whistle made them both turn. Beyond many of the largest standing stones, Hamid was waving to them from the deck of a small cutter. Macide stood behind him, barking orders as the ship prepared to set sail.

"Time to go, Lem."

"Time to go."

Soon they were off, a small delegation sailing east on the cutter, *Drifting Sun*. They passed beyond the standing stones and over open sand as the bulk of the tribe's ships turned south.

Several times a day Macide's nephew, a skinny boy with closely shorn hair and big ears, would send up a falcon, a gorgeous bird of mottled brown with a tan belly and auburn markings behind its eyes.

"Looks like it's painted for war," Emre said jokingly to him one day.

"It is," the boy shot back, his face stone serious. He caught Emre's wry smile, and went on. "Thaash himself kissed the egg that hatched him."

When Emre laughed, the boy glowered and launched the falcon into the air. The bird ranged far ahead, traveling in a vast arc ahead of the ship. When it returned hours later, it would alight on the boy's outstretched arm, which was protected by a double-thick glove. The falcon would get a vole for its trouble, and no small amount of petting along its crest feathers, before a leather hood was placed back on its head, and it was returned to its wicker cage near the pilot's wheel.

On the fourth day, as the falcon was flying a few points off the starboard bow, it began to circle.

"Ships ho!" the boy called, pointing to the falcon.

Macide ordered the ships to adjust course. As the *Sun* sailed closer, the falcon's lazy circles brought it progressively lower, until it executed a pinwheel turn and dove straight for their ship. One moment it was flying like a spear toward his handler, and the next its wings were wide and its talons were extended. It landed on the boy's arm, triumphant, where it received not one vole, but two, and was allowed to rest in its cage for a time without its hood.

"Come," Macide called a short while later, waving Emre and Hamid toward the foredeck. The three of them joined Shal'alara, who stood at the bow. Soon enough they spotted the masts of several dozen ships.

Macide, the wind tugging at the twin tails of his pepper-flecked beard, placed one sandaled foot on the gunwales and stretched. "Onur has two tribes under his yoke already, and unless we can convince Tribe Kadri otherwise, he'll soon have another." He pointed to the ships ahead. "We will speak with their shaikh, Mihir Halim'ava, who sent one of his tribe's elders to treat with Onur. He hopes that in approaching Onur, he'll be able to ensure a favored place for his tribe in the fight against Sharakhai."

Shal'alara hawked and spat over the side of the ship. "Blood traitors," she said, "Mihir included." Her turban, a rich eggplant color with flecks of gold, was wrapped in the desert's western style: unbalanced and low enough on one side that it covered her right ear. Combined with the tattoo of a ram's skull that spanned her forehead, it deepened an already rakish look. Emre guessed she was younger than Macide by five years, and perhaps ten years Emre's senior, but her attitude and the way she looked at Emre from time to time—as if she'd make a meal of him given half the chance—made her seem younger.

"That remains to be seen," Macide said. "Until we know more, leave such thoughts unspoken."

The wind made the sleeves and skirt of Shal'alara's white abaya ripple like windblown silk. "The man would clasp hands with a King!"

"Mihir has no love for the Kings. He lost his mother to their cruelty and saw his father pass to the farther fields while kneeling to them."

"And now *he* would do the same. Better to die with sword in hand than kiss the feet of your enemy."

"He's practical," Macide replied easily. "He sees Onur as a tool he might use to stab at the heart of Sharakhai."

"And if Onur's quest to conquer Sharakhai is lost?"

"Then Mihir still wins. The Kings are weakened and he slips back into the desert with his tribe."

Hamid sat easily on the gunwales opposite Macide. Since their terrible row after Adzin's death, Hamid had been quiet around Macide, but now he seemed anxious, almost angry. "What in the great wide desert are we doing? He's not going to change his mind. He's already reached out to Onur!"

Macide shrugged. "Mihir wants two things. Revenge for his mother and father, and to protect his people. If we can give him both those things, and show that Onur can't, he'll join us."

"And if he doesn't?" Emre asked.

Macide smiled, a broad thing that revealed how confident he was of the coming meeting. "Then we remind him of his heritage."

He would explain no further, and soon they were nearing the Kadri ships, which had formed a large circular enclosure across the dunes. A sand-colored pennant was hoisted atop the *Drifting Sun*'s mainmast, a signal for truce and parley. As the *Drifting Sun*'s skis sighed to a halt, several dozen warriors wearing orange and yellow thawbs and brown turbans and veils met them.

Macide headed for the gangway. "Shal'alara and Emre, with me. Hamid, ensure the safety of the ship. If things turn bad you'll take word to my father, so keep her ready to sail."

Hamid, who had begun to follow Macide, came to a stuttering halt. He stared at Macide's back, then at Emre with that stony, nearly emotionless look of his. Emre had seen it a dozen times before, the sort of cold calculation that came from being slighted, which Hamid would stew over for days, even months, before his anger came back in one violent rush.

Emre shrugged. "I can watch the ship, Macide."

"You already have orders, young falcon," Macide shot over his shoulder.

And so Emre left, trailing after Macide and Shal'alara through the gap in the line of warriors who watched them warily, though thankfully with no great enmity. They were led to a ship on the far edge of the circle, where a pavilion and several tents had been erected. A young man no older than Emre came out to meet them. His hands were raised, his palms toward them, revealing the complex orange tattoos there. It was a sign of peace, a gesture Macide returned, and the two of them embraced.

"Well met, Mihir," Macide said, slapping his back affectionately.

"And you," Mihir replied, doing the same. He was a handsome man with dark skin and dark eyes and a wide smile, all of which accented his rust-colored thawb and thread-of-gold turban. "And you've brought friends!" He clasped his hands and bowed to Emre and Shal'alara. "You're welcome to share our fires and our bread."

"As long as we've brought a bit of araq?" Macide asked, pulling an oval-shaped bottle from the bag at his side.

"It certainly doesn't hurt!" Mihir said, accepting it. "Bakhi's bright smile, you've brought me a bottle of Tulogal!"

Macide laughed. "Though the Great Mother was parched and tried to drink of it many times, yes."

"In that case, we'll all partake." He swung the bottle in a beckoning motion, a simple but welcoming gesture that somehow encapsulated Macide, Emre, and Shal'alara. "Please. Honor me."

"The honor is ours."

Mihir led them to the pavilion, which sat in the lee of the largest and sleekest of the ships. A dozen older children, guided by a doddering matron, were busying themselves, bringing pillows to lay about the carpeted floor, laying out dates and olives and cups of water, plus empty blue glasses for the rare araq. Mihir introduced his wife and his brother, and many more besides, the elders of Tribe Kadri, but Emre's eyes kept drifting to one particular woman, a Malasani who was conspicuous among the desert folk. She wore silk trousers so baggy they could easily be confused with a skirt, an embroidered white shirt made of some rich, supple fabric, and a red-brocaded waistcoat. The necklace of a thousand coins around her neck accented her headdress, which was large and ornate and had many more tiny coins and chains hanging from it. They glinted in the sun sneaking through the pavilion's thin cloth roof. And yet none of that was what made her stand out. It was her eyes. They were dark. Demanding. She was royalty of some sort, Emre had no doubt, the sort who confused covetous thoughts with ownership.

Three steps behind her was a man as rotund as Emre had ever seen. He was shorter than Emre, but probably outweighed Frail Lemi by three stone. He had hulking arms crossed over his broad chest and by his side carried a huge curving scimitar with metal rings worked in along the blunt edge. They made a *shink* sound as he shifted to face Emre. The way he stared—a stonelike scowl while the sun shone off his bald pate—was so comical Emre nearly laughed.

Mihir waved to the pillows and most sat. Emre, however, remained standing. He scanned the desert beyond the ring of Kadri ships, and spotted another beyond its edge. A Malasani dhow.

"I see no need for a Malasani spy to sit with us."

The conversation, which had been lively up to this point, came to a complete and immediate halt. Macide, who'd already sat on Emre's right, gave him a look, but Emre didn't care. He'd be damned before he sat with a Malasani, especially with the future of the thirteenth tribe hanging in the balance.

"I am Haddad," she said before anyone else could reply. "A caravan master. An ally to Tribe Kadri. I could be an ally to Tribe Khiyanat as well."

"You are an interloper," Emre shot back, "not worthy of a seat at this council."

Unperturbed, she sat cross-legged on one of the pillows nearest to Mihir, took a clutch of grapes from a nearby bowl, plucked one, and crunched on it loudly.

"She is an honored guest," said Mihir, who had remained standing. "As were you, until now. Sit, young one, before you embarrass your lord further."

When Macide motioned for Shal'alara to sit, she took her seat with same sort of leisure as Haddad. Macide took Emre by the elbow and whispered, "*Control yourself.* Why do you think *you* are here and not Hamid?" He waved to the space on his left with a look that made it clear Emre would be playing with fire if he disobeyed the order.

Doing his best to ignore Haddad's satisfied smile, Emre complied. Macide's words had been like a bucket of cold water. Hamid had a terrible cruel streak in him, a thing Emre had always been somewhat afraid of. Was that how he, Emre, now seemed to Macide? To Mihir?

They ate for a time and spoke of sailing in the desert, of hunting in the mountain reaches. A song, one of Tribe Kadri's oldest, was sung by a young girl with a magical voice. As promised, Mihir shared the araq with everyone gathered. Emre was sure it was exquisite, but it tasted sour on his tongue.

At last they came to business. "I've come at my father's behest," Macide said. "We've come to ask that you join us as we raise our spears against the Kings."

The implication was clear. *Onur* was a King, not to mention a growing threat in the eastern reaches of the Great Shangazi.

"Your ships are few," Mihir said, "as are your spears."

"We have enough," Macide said, "and our numbers continue to grow as more heed our call."

"You have enough to stand against Sharakhai? Enough to stop the Silver Spears? Their Maidens? The asirim?"

"My good shaikh, there is but one King who stands before us."

Mihir set his glass down on the low table between them with a clack. "Fine, then. You think you can stop *Onur*?"

"Not on our own. But if we stand together, yes."

Haddad laughed, the coins on her headdress clinking. "Did I not tell you? I said they would come begging favors while foolish tales spill from their mouths."

Mihir raised a hand. "Onur wishes to pit himself against Sharakhai. We'd be fools not to allow it. If we fight him now we only weaken ourselves. Join *us*, Macide. Join us, that we might tear down the walls of Sharakhai!"

"You don't know what you're asking. For four hundred years have we been hunted. For four hundred years have we hidden in the cracks of the desert—"

"Like cowards," Haddad interjected.

At this Macide stopped. He swiveled his head to Haddad. "Mihir, Shaikh of Tribe Kadri, you have allowed this woman to sit beside us. You said her counsel has value. And I'll not deny you any of that, but if she speaks ill of my tribe again, I'll cut her tongue from her mouth and throw it at your feet."

The hulk of a swordsman behind Haddad lumbered forward, his trunk of an arm reaching for his sword. The rings along the top of his scimitar sounded like rattling chains as he made to draw it, but when Haddad raised her hand he stopped in his tracks.

The rest of Tribe Kadri bristled, until Mihir raised both hands high, showing his tattoos once more. "Peace," he said. "Peace." And slowly, those assembled went silent. "I have a duty to my tribe," he went on, focusing intently on Macide, "to protect them, to see them safe through the storm."

"Then fight! We'll gather more to our cause before the Kings come." He waved to Haddad. "And before Malasan can cross our borders like hungry wolves. Join *us*, and we will cut from the desert the cancer that is Onur before it grows."

When Mihir spoke again, his voice held some measure of regret. "I'm afraid it's too late. The emissary I sent to Onur returned last night. The King has agreed to my terms."

"An agreement with the King of Sloth means nothing," Macide shot back. "Have you not heard of his atrocities—his appetites are obscene. He *feasts* upon the flesh of man!"

"These," Haddad said, leaning toward Mihir, "are but stories, nothing more, shaikh."

Mihir nodded. "They do seem far-fetched."

"Nothing is too cruel for the Kings of Sharakhai."

"You speak of cruelty. Of course they are cruel, but I would use that cruelty *against* them." Mihir paused, as if debating how much to share. "I have made overtures to the other shaikhs. For years! But everywhere I was denied. If *all* came together, some said, then perhaps."

"This is precisely my point," Macide said. "Join *us* and together we will convince them!"

When Mihir threw his head back and laughed, Emre saw Macide's calm exterior crack for the first time. His face reddened slightly, and his jaw worked for a moment before he calmed himself.

"You have only just begun to gather," Mihir said. "When the Kings learn of it—and surely they already have—they will order the shaikhs to put a stop to it. You'll lose the support you need, there will be nowhere in the desert for you to hide. And then the Kings will come for you while the blood mage Hamzakiir picks at your bones." He stared at Macide sadly. "Come, you know this to be true."

"The thirteenth tribe will stand against any who would deny us our right to live."

Mihir pressed his hands together and touched them to his lips in prayer. "I beg you. Open your eyes and see the truth. Onur is drawing the Kings' attention *away* from you, but it will not last forever." He poured a fresh glass of araq for both himself and Macide and then downed his in one throw. "Join *us*," he said, baring his teeth from the alcohol burn. "Let us use Onur. Let us drive him like a wedge between the other Kings. When the other shaikhs see what we have done, they'll rally to *our* cause. Soon the whole of the desert will come together under our banners, and then we can do as we please with the Feasting King."

Macide nodded, as if he were considering Mihir's words, and then said, "Four hundred years ago, Onur stood on the mount in Sharakhai and gave his assent to the sacrifice of my people. He watched as they were enslaved by the power of the gods. He *used* them to hunt those of us who survived, to murder for the crime of allowing our name to pass their lips. He tried to wipe us from the face of the desert. And you would sit here and ask me to *fight* for him?"

Like a candle in rain, the hope in Mihir's eyes faded. "I had hoped we could do great things together."

Macide nodded grimly. "As had I."

"Well"—with a sudden inhalation, Mihir took in the camp and ships around him—"there are preparations to make before we sail."

"I have one last request. We have no right to ask, but there are some few of our tribe hidden in Onur's camp. We've not heard from them in some time. My father would consider himself in your debt if you would allow two of our number to join you to learn of their fate."

Mihir looked ready to deny the request, but then he paused and looked at Emre, then Shal'alara, then the *Drifting Sun* behind them. His look turned to one of grudging sympathy. "Give us one of the skiffs from your ship. Two may come, as long as they promise to abide by my wishes, and leave as soon as the fate of your brothers and sisters is learned."

Macide refilled Mihir's glass, then took up his own. The two of them raised their glasses, then downed the lot. They stood and hugged, a gesture marked by much less enthusiasm than their earlier embrace, and the camp began breaking down around them.

Macide led them back toward their ships. As the crew were lowering one of the skiffs, he pulled Emre aside. He reached into his thawb and pulled out an ornate kenshar. "I have another task for you," he said, and held the kenshar for Emre to take.

Emre accepted it. "What's this?"

"The knife of Mihir's brother, Anish."

"Oh?" Emre tipped his head back toward the Kadri ships. "I assume there's a reason you didn't give it to him just now?"

"There is," Macide said. "Here's what I need you to do . . ."

Chapter 27

DAVUD HAD NO CONTACT with Sukru in the days following his vision in the blooming fields. He couldn't shake the feeling that the strange cavern was a secret the Kings wouldn't have chosen to share. But what could he do?

He filled his days with reading, but never in his apartments, so as to avoid Anila. He'd asked for and been granted another room to read in. It was high in one of the palace's towers, with a stunning view through the lone window that overlooked the green estates of Sharakhai's rich east end. The texts Sukru supplied him with were mostly useless with respect to Davud's current needs. Nearly all had been written by historians of a sort, or masters from the collegia who'd collected stories about blood magi over the ages. The most useful book was the very first one Sukru had given him. He realized when he came back to it a few days later, however, that a page was missing.

He couldn't recall what it contained, but he remembered how intensely Anila had been studying the book, so he returned to their shared room to speak to her. When he arrived, however, Anila's things were gone.

The spindly young chambermaid, the one who'd been at the wading pool with Bela, was sweeping the floor around Anila's bed. She was crying, Davud realized. "Whatever is the matter?" he asked, wondering if something had happened to Anila.

"I'm sorry, my lord. It's little Bela." She waved toward the door, her other hand to her mouth while tears streamed from her eyes.

"What happened to her?"

"She was sliding down the banisters from the great hall when she slipped and struck her head on the floor." The maid shrugged, as if to say, *it is the will of the fates.* "Zahndr found her this morning. Already gone."

"Gods . . . My tears for your loss." She looked so forlorn that he embraced her. "Truly. She was a bright child."

She cried, and Davud let her until she pulled away, sniffing loudly and wiping her tears with the backs of her fingers.

"Forgive my ill manners," Davud said, "but I need to speak with Anila. Do you know where she's gone?"

"She was given another room in the palace, my lord."

"Where?"

"Just this morning."

"I said *where.*"

She shook her head, as if clearing it of cobwebs. "Forgive me, my lord, I'm no good today. I can take you there, if you please."

Davud nodded, waving her toward the door. He felt hard-hearted for doing so, but talking to Anila couldn't wait. She led him to another wing of the palace, where they came to a door with an iron knocker. As she bowed and walked away, Davud knocked. From within the room he heard a fluttering sound, like the pages of a book being flipped through quickly. When there was no answer he tried again, and heard shuffling footsteps soon after.

Anila opened the door wearing a flowing purple dress. She'd tied a red scarf around her head to cover her baldness. There were still bandages around her hands and wrists, and one on her right foot, but those around her face and neck had been removed. Her black skin shone, the patterns within it vivid in some places, muted in others.

Anila made no move to invite him in. "What do you want?"

"I . . . I didn't know you were leaving."

"Well, you certainly knew I would leave *one* day."

"Yes, but I came back, and you were just gone."

"It was time, Davud." She was stiff as a deck board, her face emotionless. Davud had rarely felt so awkward.

"Have you heard the news? About Bela?"

For the first time her hard expression softened, but not as much as Davud would have guessed, especially given how close she and Bela had been. "Yes, I heard."

"Might I come in?" he asked.

"Perhaps another time."

Davud waved down the hall, toward their old room. "It's only, there's a page missing from the book Sukru gave me."

He paused, waiting for her to admit that she'd taken it, but Anila only shook her head. "I don't know anything about that."

"It was in the book you were looking at."

She gave him a shrug, the sort children gave their parents when they were tired of being asked questions. "Ask the maids."

Beyond Anila was a large table, and on its surface, beside a number of open books, a bird cage. "What's that?"

"Davud, I'm really quite busy."

The sound Davud had heard earlier—it had been wings flapping, he realized, not the pages of a book. He pushed his way past her and entered the room. As he came closer to the table, he saw the firefinch lying lifeless on the cage's floor. "What *happened*?"

Anila closed the door and approached with a distinct limp. "It died."

"That's the bird that came to my patio." The one that brought the golden triangle, and with it the mage known as the Sparrow, but he couldn't tell Anila that. "The one you were staring at so intently."

"And?"

He rounded on her. "Why is it *here*?"

She shrugged. "I liked it. They're not so difficult to catch."

"But it's dead now." Gods, the heat from the nearby fireplace was stifling.

Anila smiled. Then she reached across the table, picked up the cage, and set it before Davud. "No it isn't."

To his surprise the finch was now standing on the floor among the shit and wood shavings, blinking, its wings shivering as if it were clearing sand from its back. It took wing and alighted on a branch in the upper reaches of the cage. Unlike the times he'd seen it on the patio, it now looked and acted quite like a normal bird. It blinked, taking in its surroundings with quick swivels of its head, and as Davud moved his hand closer, it chirped excitedly, flitting about the cage.

"But it was just lying there," he said, lowering his hand. "Not moving."

"Perhaps the heat was too much for it," Anila said easily. "Now if you please, I have work to do."

"What work?" He motioned to the books. "Did King Sukru give you these?"

"Well, who *else* would have?"

"But *why*? Are you conducting experiments on that finch?"

Her expression turned grim. "What if I am?"

He reached for the handle of the cage. She tried to stop him, but her movements were dulled and pain-filled and he snatched it away. "Experiments of what sort?" he asked, holding the cage up before him to examine the finch.

"I seem to remember you making it perfectly clear I was not to interfere in *your* work. I couldn't ask a question without you lording your power over me. You've no right to pry into *my* business. Now if you please"—she motioned to the cage—"set that down and leave."

He couldn't. The finch tied him to the Sparrow. He wasn't sure if Anila knew about the link, but he couldn't leave it to chance. He made for the door, cage in hand.

"Davud!"

He kept walking, closing the door with a clatter behind him. Back in his room, he rushed to the patio and opened the cage. The bird fluttered up to the fig tree. Davud chased after it, waving his arms like a fool.

"Don't return," he whispered to it. "Not when she's near, do you hear me?"

A moment later, the finch was gone, and a terrible chill went down Davud's spine. He'd just remembered the missing page from the book.

It had contained the sigil for *death*.

Two days later, Davud was summoned to join King Sukru in a short journey down the mountain to the Sun Palace. He went to the grand entrance, where two covered arabas waited in the carriage circle. He was just climbing the stairs into the cabin of the first carriage when he realized it wasn't empty. Anila was sitting on one of the benches, a blue scarf around her head matching her long, patterned dress and strapped leather sandals.

She looked defiant, not toward him, but the world. A part of him was pleased to see her again, but given where they were about to go . . .

"Did Sukru ask you to come?" Davud asked.

"And a good day to you as well."

Davud shook his head, embarrassed. "I'm sorry. It's only, I was surprised to see you." When she said nothing, he went on. "Did he, Anila? Summon you?"

She released a pent-up breath. "Breath of the desert, you're exasperating, Davud . . ."

She looked as if she was about to say more when her attention was caught by something outside the window. Davud turned and saw four Kings walking down the palace steps toward the second wagon: Sukru, bent and aged; Cahil, who looked nearly as young as Davud; Husamettín, the King of Swords; and the imposing form of Kiral, King of Kings.

Gods, Davud thought, *four of them.* Clearly the vision he'd stumbled upon of the strange cavern was much more important than he'd guessed.

"Has it ever occurred to you," Anila went on, "that Sukru *values* my opinion? You've a brilliant mind, and you would be a valuable asset, a keen advisor in any King's court. It's a pity you don't think the same of me."

The carriage lurched into motion, the Kings having entered behind them. Around the carriage circle they went. When they'd passed beyond the palace walls, the amber sand met a sky of hazy blue. With a steep drop-off on their left, they followed King's Road, the whole of Sharakhai sprawled below them.

"I *do* think the same of you," Davud said. "You know that."

Jaw jutting, Anila stared out her window. "How I tire of men who speak with words and never deeds."

She had bandages around her wrists and ankles. Her elbows were ashen gray and flaking, as were the spots along her neck below her ears, but otherwise she looked as whole as she would ever be. Davud could see how much it still pained her, though. Even small movements on the bench made her grimace. Anila had never been one to admit or show weakness, and the tendency had intensified since Ishmantep—the indefatigable courage in her eyes was sharper, on display more often. He wanted to tell her all this, but she'd nearly died because of him. He had no doubt she would prove to be a valuable advisor to *any* of the Kings, but he couldn't willingly aide her desire to follow in his path.

"I don't need your ruddy permission," she spat at him, guessing his mind, "nor your approval. I'll find my way to power with or without you." When he made no reply, she made a disgusted sound and leaned heavily into her seat, refusing to look at him.

The ride passed in cold silence. The araba went lower along the mountain, coming nearer and nearer to their destination, the Sun Palace.

"Anila . . ." Davud pinched the bridge of his nose. Why was this so difficult? With Amalos gone, hadn't he said how much he wanted someone he could confide in? "When the gods saw fit to put us together on that ship, when Hamzakiir finally granted me my plea, and we ended up together, I . . . I thought it meant something."

Davud could see Anila chewing the inside of her lip, something she did when she was nervous. "What did you think it meant?"

"That we were supposed to be together. It's why I was so hurt when you paid more attention to Tayyar than me."

"I told you, that was because—"

"I know, to gain his trust." Tayyar was the man tasked with ensuring their return to Sharakhai. She had gained his trust and later used it to lure him into the desert and drive a ruddy great stone against his skull. "I don't blame you for it. And when we escaped and reached Ishmantep, I was sure the gods were ready to reward us. But they stole it all away. Stole your life from you. Your future. Stole *our* future together."

For a long while Anila was silent. Higher on Tauriyat, the bells of the dawning sun began to ring. "Our future doesn't have to be lost."

She was right. Of course she was right. "I had a vision," he blurted, picking at his fingernails. He couldn't seem to look at her.

He felt more than saw Anila shift in her seat. "What?"

"It's what I've been doing for Sukru. He found diseased adichara in the blooming fields and asked me to accompany him, to try to learn more." He lifted his head and found her staring at him in wonder, silent, as if she didn't want to break the spell. He answered her unspoken question. "I found something. Something big, I think, though I don't yet understand it."

"What?" she asked again.

"I felt the disease within those trees, but I felt their history as well. I saw them being born at Tulathan's touch. I saw Nalamae come to them and then fight with Goezhen for her life. Most disconcerting, though, was their very nature."

"What do you mean?"

"The adichara are not separate, Anila. I felt the roots connecting, coming together like the tributaries of a vast river system. They're all one being, and they meet below the city." Fingers still picking at his nail, he shot a glance through the window toward the Sun Palace. "I suspect that's where we're going today. They want to see it with their own eyes."

Anila's eyes went distant. "The adichara . . ."

"Yes." The coach rattled as they passed over the short bridge leading to the Sun Palace. The sun was blocked as they entered through the barbican. "What is it, Anila?"

She shook her head.

"What did Sukru tell you?"

"Only that I was to come and observe."

"Yes, but to what purpose?"

Before Anila could explain, the coach rattled to a stop and the footman arrived at the door. The Kings disembarked first, and then Anila, Davud, Zahndr, and several Silver Spears. They went into the palace and down seven levels deep before arriving at a sculpted archway. A natural cavern lay beyond. The Spears held lanterns, lighting their way, but it was Sukru who guided them, telling the Spears which way to turn.

Ever downward they went, moving closer, Davud was sure, to the cavern he'd seen in his vision. Sure enough, nearly an hour into their journey through the underbelly of Sharakhai, they came to a tunnel choked with thin tendrils. The roots of the adichara trees and the tunnel led to the massive cavern Davud had seen in his vision.

All who'd come, even the Kings, stared in wonder. The vast space. The roots. The narrowing braid at the top of the cavern. And the glowing crystal beneath it. They walked carefully over the spongy surface of the roots, occasionally hearing the patter of softly glowing liquid dropping onto the crystal.

King Cahil began walking around the cavern, taking it in step by step while Sukru stared intently at the crystal, his face mere inches from it. King Husamettín spoke in low tones to Zahndr while sending dark glances toward the crystal, Davud, and Anila.

King Kiral turned to Davud. "You saw this in the blooming fields?" He had a deep voice, resonant, but it sounded deadened in this place, as if it were the last place in the world and everything else had gone.

"I did, my Lord King."

"Do you know its purpose?"

"I do not," Davud replied. "Only that the roots of all of the adichara end up here."

Behind Kiral, Sukru held his fingers flat and pressed them near the crystal. He was careful not to touch the surface, however. There was something about it. Davud could feel it, even several paces away. It was *cold*, the sort that chilled one's very soul.

"You'll try your spell again," Sukru said without even looking at Davud. He pointed to a spot a few paces away. "Prepare yourself."

"Of course, my Lord King," Davud replied.

"You." Sukru snapped his fingers at his guardsman, Zahndr. "Give him what he needs."

The Kings stepped away and they chatted softly with one another. Davud knelt on the roots, and Zahndr sat cross-legged before him. Zahndr had always struck him as a brave sort, a man accustomed to battle, but the muscles along his neck were tight and his eyes focused squarely on Davud's, as if he feared to look anywhere else.

"I won't take much," Davud said softly.

"You'll take all you need!" Sukru cut in. "He is willing to die for Sharakhai. And you," he snapped at Anila. "Watch. Learn."

"Take all you need," Zahndr echoed, holding his knife out.

Embarrassed over speaking loudly enough for the King to hear, Davud took the knife, doing his best to ignore Anila. "Very well." He used the point of the knife to pierce Zahndr's wrist. With the blood that welled, he drew the same sigils he'd used in the desert, first on his left palm, then on his right.

As he touched Zahndr's blood once more, ready to lift it to his tongue, he felt his mouth go suddenly dry. The hairs on his arms and the back of his neck stood up. He felt as though something or some*one* was standing at his back, ready to touch him. When he flinched and turned he saw only the Kings and the Silver Spears standing in a meandering line, but the troubled looks on their faces, even the Kings', only heightened the sense that something was very, very wrong.

He and Zahndr both stood. Davud felt a growing desire to flee, but he stifled the urge as he felt a soft breeze pick up and circulate through the cavern. Motes of dust flew about, scintillant in the crystal's soft glow. As one, the Kings and Spears turned toward a tunnel on the cavern's far side. Davud felt it as well, a presence nearing, powerful as the Great Shangazi. It was vast and deep, but it felt strange, as if it didn't belong below the earth but soaring through the sky like one of Thaash's great eagles, or roaming the towering mountains that ringed the desert like Bakhi's fabled ram.

In ones and twos, moths with iridescent red wings exited the tunnel. More came, and then more, until a stream of them spilled into the cavern, circling in the same direction as the glowing dust. In their wake strode a woman. She was tall, like the first men and women. She towered above even Kiral and Husamettín. Her lustrous black hair was held in place with an ebony comb carved to look like the spread wings of an amberlark. Her olive skin glistened.

Hot tears slid down Davud's cheeks. Emotions welled up from deep inside him, growing with every step she took and swirling in a way that somehow mirrored the cloud of moths. Her face was so comely, so serene, he felt inadequate to look upon her. Clusters of the crimson moths adorned her frame, their wings beating like hearts. As she moved, some lifted into the air, momentarily exposing a breast, her thighs, her stomach, her sex. Fine blue sandals adorned her feet, the moths lifting and landing with every footfall.

She was a goddess, Davud was sure—not Tulathan, nor Rhia, for it was said their skin glowed silver and golden, but Yerinde, goddess of love, goddess of ambition, who had stolen Tulathan from the sky until she'd been rescued by Rhia.

As she approached, the Kings knelt. As did the Silver Spears and Zahndr. Davud, however, forgot himself. He stared openly until Anila stepped beside him, tugged on his wrist, and knelt before the goddess. Even then, Davud only took one knee. He couldn't take his eyes from her. He knew it to be blasphemous, knew she could strike him down for the affront, but he could no more take his eyes from her than he could rip his heart from his chest.

She stared at him, drinking in his form as if he were a curiosity, an orchid growing in the desert. Her eyes were violet. They shone brightly in the light of the nearby crystal, deep and knowing, as if they'd witnessed the making of the world. He felt naked before her, defenseless, not in body but in mind. He was a babe before a demon.

At last she turned her gaze on the Kings, and Davud felt a release inside him, an unshackling. Her lips were sealed, but Davud heard her command resonate within his mind.

Rise.

As one, the Kings stood, while all others remained on bended knee.

Yerinde motioned to the crystal. Moths fluttered and returned to her. *Thou hast come to see what the adichara hath wrought?*

It was Kiral who answered. "We have come, Lady of Love, because the adichara have shown signs of weakness. As have the asirim."

Are the asirim not bound to the adichara? Does their death not breathe sickness upon bough and branch?

Kiral paused.

Davud dared look up. "It may be as you say."

Dost thou doubt my word?

"Never. But we had reason to believe that this"—he motioned to the glowing crystal—"was the cause, not the asirim."

What reason?

"This young man was granted visions of the roots leading here. We thought . . ." Even the mighty King Kiral seemed cowed by Yerinde's presence. "We had need to know the truth."

Truth. Dimples formed in Yerinde's cheeks as she smiled. *A word with many meanings.*

Her gaze slid past Kiral to rest on Davud. She approached him. The moths flying about her frame filled the air with a soft fluttering sound that perfectly matched the feelings inside Davud's stomach. She smelled of vetiver and sweetgrass.

Visions, she said.

"Yes," Davud replied.

Wouldst thou give them to me?

Davud swallowed, clearing his mouth of spit. "If you will it."

Yerinde's smile widened, revealing perfect teeth. *Oh, but I do.* And with that she touched a finger to his forehead. With that touch came an excitement and a fear and a love so deep Davud's heart could hardly contain it. He relived the visions, from Tulathan giving life to the blooming fields, to Nalamae kneeling before them, to Goezhen and the black laughers attacking her as she tried to flee.

Nalamae, came Yerinde's voice. *She who meddles in the will of the Kings of the desert, the will of the gods.*

"Yes," Davud said.

"Yes," Kiral echoed a moment later, and Yerinde turned to him.

A plague has she been on thy rule.

"Yes," Kiral said again, though with less conviction than a moment before.

She approached Kiral and the other three Kings, looking at each of them in turn as she had Davud, as if deciding which one to devour. *Thy wish is for thy reign to continue? For the adichara to thrive? For the asirim to remain thy loyal servants?*

Kiral glanced to Sukru on his left, Cahil on his right. "We do, my Lady Goddess."

Then bring me her head.

The Kings seemed shocked.

"Her head?" Kiral said.

The head of she who has wronged thee.

"Nalamae?"

Yerinde smiled.

Kiral swallowed. A man so powerful, now cowed, unsure of himself. "Of course, my Lady." He pulled himself taller, then worked his jaw before speaking again. "So it shall be."

Yerinde looked to Sukru, who nodded, then Cahil, who nodded as well. And finally Husamettín, who took much longer but in the end fell in line with his brother Kings.

Very well, Yerinde said, then turned and strode away. She paused near the crystal, regarding it as if admiring her own handiwork. Whether she was pleased or not Davud couldn't say. She left the cavern, more and more flowing red moths trailing in her wake until they too were gone, and the Kings and Spears and Davud and Anila were alone once more.

For long moments no one said a word. Cahil stared at the tunnel where Yerinde had walked. Sukru looked at the crystal as if his curiosity had been piqued and he desperately wished to examine it further. King Kiral saw, however, and shook his head. "You will cease your investigations into the adichara immediately."

Sukru's pinched face looked crestfallen. His mouth worked, as if he were trying to find the right words to convince Kiral otherwise, but before he could, Kiral turned and strode back the way they'd come, leaving the rest to follow or risk his wrath.

Sukru glared at Davud as if *he'd* been the one to deny him his prize. "You heard your King," he snapped, then followed Kiral from the cavern.

Soon they were walking back through the tunnels, up toward the Sun Palace, the weight of their bargain, to kill a god, resting heavily on all their shoulders.

Chapter 28

EEP IN THE DESERT, in a tower made of stone, a boy named Brama lies naked on a cold slab of rock. A bloody kenshar rests on his stomach, its obscene weight rising and falling with every breath. Marking the skin along his ribs are wounds that no longer bleed openly, but they weep. A normal man's wounds might become infected, but not Brama's, for his mistress will not allow him to die. Not so easily as this.

His entire body wants to coil like sunburned leather when he hears her approach. Her hooves clap against the stone stairs. Her forked tail whips and slaps against the spiraling stairwell in rhythms that speak of chaos and pain. As her tall form ducks through the archway on the far side of the room, Brama cringes but does not move; his mistress has forbidden it. She comes closer, her smiling face revealed. Her ebony skin, her crown of thorns, her sweeping ram's horns, all ruddy in the light from the banked coals of the brazier in the corner.

"And here we are again," she says in a voice as deep as a vale. She trails her ebony claws across his fresh wounds, eliciting a wince. "Though I wonder, have you learned your lesson?"

He swallows, ignoring the pain of that simple movement, ignoring the fact that he should be incensed that it *does* cause him pain. "I have, mistress."

She paces around the slab, her rust-colored eyes never leaving his. "We shall see. Sit up. Take the knife."

He feels a release. His limbs are his own once more. As is his will. He can obey or disobey as he chooses. He could run from the room. He could try, as he has many other times, to fling himself from the nearby window. But he knows the ways of his mistress's mind. How he prayed in the early days that Bakhi would come for him. How he wished the god of final sunsets would show mercy and usher him to the farther fields. He'd run for that window in the past, to meet Bakhi and to pass beyond these shores, but each time Rümayesh stopped him, forced him to crash into the walls, to batter his body until he'd collapsed from the pain.

Months passed before he attempted it again. Only a week ago, he'd tried, thinking he'd finally caught her off her guard. He learned that he hadn't only *after* she'd allowed him his leap. Through the window he'd flown, joyous, triumphant, his arms spread like the wings of a swan as he rushed toward courtyard below and his own demise. When his body met the flagstones, he was not granted the mercy of blacking out. He felt every moment of it—each broken bone, each tear in his flesh. Moments later, in a swirl of sand and sighing wind, Rümayesh joined him. He stared up at her, feeling the warmth of his blood as it leaked from a dozen wounds, praying he'd soon be freed.

She had watched with mirth in her eyes, content in the knowledge that he'd not escape her this way. As the painful reality of it dawned on him, his body began to mend. His bones realigned themselves loudly, with intense pain. His joints popped into place. His skin moved in strange and sudden increments, creating a maddening itch all over his body as if a host of scarabs had been sewn up inside him. Tears mingled with the blood on the stone beneath him. *Leave me be,* he pleaded. *Leave me be.*

All the while Rümayesh stared, her inhuman eyes brimming with satisfaction.

As she had so many times before—and in so many different ways—she'd tricked him. She'd crafted the illusion that if he could reach the window, he'd be allowed to die. And when the illusion had been made perfect, she let him leap, knowing full well he would remain by her side for as long as she wished.

Lying on the slab, he wonders why she enjoys it so. Had her cruelty been passed to her by her maker, Goezhen? Was it an inseparable part of the alchemy used in her making? Or is it simple fascination, a way for her to measure the stuff of mortals, who to a creature such as her were little different than the rattlewings that infest the oases?

"Do you disobey?" Rümayesh asks him.

"No," he replies immediately. "Never."

As he takes the knife from his belly and rises, his mind scratches at the question that's been hounding him since he fell into her hands: *What will it take for me to die?* He wants it so, but the very thought of angering her makes his soul quake.

Rümayesh stares deeply into his eyes, saying nothing.

He swallows, wanting to remain silent, knowing that he mustn't. "What is your desire, my mistress?"

"Why, whatever it is *you* desire, Brama." And then she waits, savoring the disquiet in his mind, his growing fear of the torture to come. This is the game. She wants enough of his pain to be sated, but asks *him* to choose how much. Give too little and she'd take the rest and more. Give too much and he'll have tortured himself for nothing.

This is what she enjoys the most, not merely the pain itself, but the indecision, the weighing up of misery to square a ledger he knows nothing—and *can* know nothing—about. It is a cup from which she drinks deeply, like a lord of Goldenhill on the finest araq.

If I could turn the tables . . . If I could stand where you stand now . . .

The moment the treacherous thoughts come, he smothers them. Were she to hear them . . .

"Tell me, Brama," she coos, "what is your desire?"

To die. To leave the desert behind. To walk amongst the green grasses of the farther fields.

But he cannot say such things. Voicing them would anger her. Worse, however, would be to give in to the temptation. That is what she desires most: to give him hope of being free that she might take it from him.

Tears slip down his cheeks. "I wish to make you happy."

"Oh? And how will you do that?"

His tears make him feel weak, which allows him to grip the knife harder and drive it into his thigh. A tremulous exhalation of pain pours from his throat as the knife sinks deep. He keeps as much of it in as he can. It is an offering of sorts, for he knows how much she enjoys it, him facing his pain bravely despite the suffering that lies ahead.

Her eyes brighten. She smiles a jackal smile, then leans close and runs her tongue along his thigh, lapping at the blood he's shed. She kneels before him, a shiver running through her, then whispers, "Yes." She grips his knees, spreads his legs further apart until her head is between his thighs. "Yes." She licks again.

When he drives the knife into his other leg, her head arches back. "Yes!" She bares her neck to him, daring him to run the blade across her throat.

But he doesn't. He can't.

How could he?

The things she would do to him if he tried . . .

So he grits his teeth and goes on, stabbing deeper, offering more of his lifeblood to the demon licking his skin like a lustful wife. Stabbing again, he prays that when enough has been spilled, she'll allow him to fall unconscious.

⊢—●—⊣

"Brama?"

Somewhere, not too far away, Brama heard soft scraping sounds. A chair over dirt. Shoes over stone.

It came nearer, louder, and then, "Dear gods, no! Brama!"

Someone gripped his shoulders and shook him. A sunrise of pain blossomed along the horizon of his mind. Then hands pressed against his cheeks, the fingers cradling his neck. "Please, Brama, wake!"

Brama forced his eyes open and found Jax kneeling over him. For some reason, her dirty face registered before her terrified expression. Her eyes were wide as teacups. For him, he assumed, though he couldn't understand why.

He did a moment later, as Jax stood and shouted for help. Lighting the small cellar was the thin yellow light of a candle that sat halfway up the nearby stairwell. It lit the stain of muddy red that spread like a fan from where Brama lay. From his prone vantage it looked like a kicking mule.

My blood, Brama realized. *That's all my blood.* A vision of Rümayesh laughing danced before his eyes.

"Brama!"

Gods, he'd fallen asleep again. How very difficult it was to remain awake. If only he might sleep awhile; forcing his eyes open was like lifting a ten-stone.

"Brama, please!" She was shaking him again. "Wake up!"

I'm well, he wanted to say, though he was anything but. He tried to speak, but all that came out was a strange, wet gurgle.

That, finally, was what spurred him to movement. He sounded like a bellows doused in yoghurt. He was going to die unless he got help.

Gingerly, he probed his neck. Like a beacon fire being lit, a terrible burning sensation rose up all along his throat. Pain he could handle. It was the depth of the cut that scared him. Would he lose his voice? Each time he probed further, his fingers came away sticky. The wound went all along the front of his neck, he realized, a cut that should have ended his life, but hadn't.

"Listen to me." Tears were streaming down Jax's cheeks. "I'm here. We're going to go home, the two of us. But I have to get help first."

She began to rise, but Brama grabbed her wrist. He flicked his gaze meaningfully to the wall where the Qaimiri had been chained.

Jax looked back, her jaw jutting in anger or shock or both. "He's gone."

Of course he was. He'd slit Brama's throat and left. Brama knew he should feel angry. But he didn't. In truth he wasn't sure *how* to feel. Grateful to be alive? Despondent over being kept once more from the farther fields? Filled with a desire for revenge on the Qaimiri for trying to kill him?

He stared at Jax, wondering why the Qaimiri hadn't run a knife across *her* throat. There was a nasty bruise along her neck—a wound sustained as the Qaimiri tried to escape? He was grateful, he decided. Jax was still alive. She didn't deserve death for his fool actions.

He tried sitting up, but Jax pushed him down. "You bloody fool, I'm going to get help. Just rest until I return."

He held his hand up to forestall her, then felt for his necklace and the sapphire. The falcon's egg gemstone had been his constant companion for years. It was the source of his power, the home of his enemy. He crawled over the floor, running his hands wildly over the packed earth. The emptiness inside him told him it was gone, but it didn't feel *possible.*

Jax helped him search, but it was half-hearted. She knew as well as he that the Qaimiri had taken it. Jax stared at him with an expression of terror or worry, perhaps both. As painful as Brama's life had been, the gem meant much to them both. They'd used it to forge a life here in Sharakhai. Likely she was already wondering what life would be like if they no longer had it.

There was a fury inside Brama for having the gem stolen from him, but a part of him, the part that had been subjected to months of torture at the hands of Rümayesh, felt relieved. No longer was it needling him every waking moment. No longer would he have to face the one who'd been so cruel to him, no matter that they'd come to an accord years ago, no matter that Brama was now the master and Rümayesh the prisoner.

His neck itched terribly. Instead of scratching it, he looked down and began dusting off his bloody clothes. Why he bothered he wasn't sure—they were hopelessly soiled and caked in dried and still-drying blood. Not knowing what else to do, he headed for the stairs, and promptly fell over.

"Oh, gods!" Jax helped him back up, then wrapped his arm across her shoulders and helped him climb the stairs.

Under a cloak of starlight, they trudged along the dead-end street in the Knot the two of them called home. These were Brama's buildings, all purchased as part of his growing empire, fueled by his use of the sapphire. Few of his chosen were up at this hour, but those who were stared at him in horror. There was an unmistakable note of wonder in their eyes as well. They'd thought Brama untouchable—he'd never wished for it, but he'd become their idol, and now the pillar upon which they'd placed him was beginning to crumble.

As they reached home, Jax and several others helped remove his filthy clothes. They cleaned him and stitched his wounds and gave him fresh robes. They guided him up to his room on the topmost floor, looking as though they were ready to die in his place, asking what they might do for him. But he had no answers. He was no hero, no savior. He was a thief who'd stumbled across a bauble that had granted him indescribable power. None of it had ever been his. Not really. It had always been ephemeral, ready to slip through his fingers like so much sand. And now that it had, he felt strangely free, as if it had always been a prison but it had taken this for him to realize it.

He waved away their questions, then took Jax's hand and led her to their bed. As he held her, he pretended that he was some *other* man—a proper man with a proper wife, a man who got up and went about his day in the Amber City like any other. A locksmith, perhaps. He almost laughed at the thought.

"What?" Jax whispered.

As Brama shook his head, she looked at the bandages around his neck and laid her head back down. He stroked her hair, falling into that very dream. He and Jax, living a normal life.

Holding that dream to him like a talisman, he slept, blissfully free of the nightmares that so often plagued him.

When morning broke, Brama rose from bed, probing his neck to feel how well the cut had healed. It was coming along well. Only a dull pain remained. Another few days and it would be just another scar to add to the rest.

He went to the nearby window and stared down over the courtyard—which in truth was nothing more than a dead end in the most convoluted and densely packed section of the city. His acolytes were there, the servants of a false god, speaking to those who'd come for healing. They came with bread in hand, a bit of watered wine. Some even had real money. They gave it over to Twarro, the rangy Kundhuni with the wild eyes, a man who'd remained here even after his brother had been killed in Brama's service, or Shei, the young Mirean woman who'd arrived shaking so badly from the call of the lotus Brama had doubted he could save her.

A knock came at the door.

"Come," he said in a harsh rasp. Speaking brought on a sharp burn along his throat, but it was manageable.

Jax entered and joined him by the window. She considered the courtyard, as Brama was doing, but given how troubled she looked, Brama very much doubted she was having the same thoughts.

"Already they come," she said, jutting her chin toward the end of the street, where a young man wearing only threadbare trousers was walking toward Shei, shaking as bad as a newborn lamb.

"So we help him," he whispered.

"And how will we do that?"

"A bed to sleep in. Lotus tea to ease the pain, a bit of food to help with the cramps."

Jax nodded as if she agreed, but he could tell she was working up to something. He had a very good idea what it was.

"We may ease his pain," she said. "We may provide succor to the others. But how long will they continue to come when they learn you've lost your power? How long can we afford to buy lotus tea when fewer come with coin? Or provide beds, for that matter, and those to attend them?"

"We have money set aside."

"And how long will that last?"

They both knew it would last only a few months, less if their donations began to dwindle. He might have had more, but he'd been focused on buying all the buildings along this dead-end street, and it had become more expensive the closer he'd come to getting them all, the last few slumlords holding out for higher prices. Brama had hardly haggled with them. At the time it felt important to gain the whole street so he could better secure it.

Now he felt the fool, but he hadn't expected to lose Rümayesh. He'd always thought he'd have trouble from the Silver Spears or the House of Kings—a question of diplomacy and graft, not blades—before he'd face a challenge from the streets.

"We'll sell a few of the buildings. We'll ration—" Brama swallowed reflexively, wincing from the pain it brought on. "We'll ration the supplies, stretch them further."

"That will only further the rumors that the Tattered Prince has lost his power. And you're mad if you think you'll get even a quarter of what you paid for these hovels, especially when those greedy bastards get wind of what's happening in their old territory."

She was right. About all of it. He swallowed again. "We'll find a way, Jax."

"You're going to let him go, then? Let that Qaimiri worm take everything from us?"

Brama regarded her levelly as he took her by the shoulders. "You don't understand. He's *freed* me from her."

"Brama, I know what you've been through with Rümayesh, but you must see it. The Qaimiri has set a plague of termites beneath our home. Mark my words, they will eat away at the foundation of all we've built, and sooner than you think." She waved to the window. "They're already talking about what happened."

"Losing her was always a possibility."

Jax's mouth fell open. "That man tried to *kill* you."

"And I was prepared to kill *him* to get what I wanted."

"He must pay for it."

She was right, of course. It was dangerous, especially here in the Shallows, to let challenges go unanswered. The sapphire had been stolen from him—taken forcibly, his throat slit for good measure. Part of him wanted to stave the Qaimiri's head in for doing it. But another part of him felt free in a way that he hadn't since having the misfortune of stumbling into Rümayesh's path. He'd told himself nearly every day since that he was keeping the sapphire, keeping *Rümayesh*, for good reasons—to keep the ehrekh's power from those who would use it for ill purposes, and so that *he* could use it to heal those who needed it most—but deep down he'd known that Rümayesh had been doing it only on a whim. She didn't care about him. Not truly. Nor did she care about those they'd healed, those they'd helped in the Knot and beyond. For her, it was merely a way to satisfy her curiosity. What was this enslavement to her in any case? She had centuries to live. So why shouldn't he, Brama, now live his life as he chose? Why should he care if some Qaimiri had stolen her away?

"Haven't you had your fill of revenge?" Brama asked. "Have you forgotten where it leads?"

Jax had lost her brother to his thirst for revenge. He had been the rightful heir in Malasan and had his title stolen out from under him when a pair of conspiring lords had killed his mother and father. He and Jax had fled to Sharakhai, chased by assassins. Her brother hadn't been able to relinquish his thirst for revenge, and had lost his life because of it. Jax had been different. She'd reconciled herself with her fate, and had stood by Brama's side ever since.

"Don't dredge up the past and lay it before me as if you remember it better than I do." She threw her hands up in the air, indicating the house they stood in, the courtyard beyond, the buildings that surrounded it, all filled with those recovering from their addictions or those who had decided to stay after being healed. "We *built* this, Brama. It's something to be proud of. I won't just let it go."

"Proud," Brama scoffed. "It's a haven for those with one foot in the grave."

She stared at him aghast. "You don't believe that."

"Do you know how many return after we've healed them?"

Jax's jaw was set grimly, her eyes flat.

"Perhaps you haven't seen, or perhaps you haven't *cared* to, but for every five that leave, four return. We deliver them back to their lives, but be it soon or late, the lotus resumes its siren song."

"And the one that makes it out? I thought those were the ones you were fighting for, and the others, to give them a chance."

He rubbed his temples absently. A terrible headache was coming on. "We still can."

Jax shook her fists in the air. "Make up your mind, Brama Junayd'ava! Do you want to help them or have you given up?"

"I don't know!"

"Well, you'd better sort it out before the decision is made for you." She left, slamming the door behind her.

Brama's headache raged throughout the morning, continued as a dull ache throughout the day, echoing the defeated looks of those who stared at him. Without fail, their eyes wandered to his neck, to the thick bandage, the place where his necklace and its massive sapphire had once rested. He nearly left that very day to procure another, a fake that could pass for the old one. But he knew it would deceive no one, least of all him. It would make him a fool, an idiot dancing on the back of a pony, calling himself a knight.

That night he heard the news. Two of his disciples had left, slipped away without saying a word to anyone, taking nearly all their black lotus tea with them when they left.

When he fell asleep at last, it was fitful. The dreams filled with torture and mirthful demon eyes had returned.

Chapter 29

ÇEDA LISTENED CAREFULLY, her ear pressed against the surface of a hidden door in the pitch-black tunnel. Hearing nothing, she pulled the handles she'd become familiar with while at the House of Maidens and slid the door aside. Beyond was the savaşam where Zaïde had trained her. It was empty, though she could hear voices beyond the rice paper doors on the far side of the room. Being careful to avoid the boards that creaked, she stepped onto the wooden floor, then slid the door shut behind her, cringing at the dull thud.

She moved to the doors opposite and listened. As the voices faded, she slid through the door, then glided along the hallway like a ghost. At the far side of the Matrons building, she heard the sound she remembered; that boom whenever the Hall of Records' entranceway was closed. She went up two stories to the rarely used office of Sayabim, her old sword mistress. Dust coated scrolls and papers that littered every flat space along the shelves and desk. For a woman so fastidious about swordplay, it was surprising how untidy Sayabim left her room. It was perfect for Çeda, though, as it overlooked the House of Maidens' interior wall. Peering through the window, Çeda saw it, only a short leap down. Beyond, the whole of Tauriyat's southeastern face was revealed. The sun had set, but the thin white clouds in the slate-colored sky were lit a brilliant orange. They made it look as if the sky were afire, ready to fall upon the palaces of the Kings above.

Çeda unwound the length of rope she'd tied around her waist, secured one end to the stout curtain hook above the window, then tested it for strength. The other end she coiled below the window with all the care of a boatswain with the rigging lines. Then, from one of the pouches at her belt, she pulled out a spool of dark gray thread with an already-threaded needle sticking out of it, which she used to string the thread through one end of the rope.

Then she sat and waited. As the brightness along the western horizon extinguished, she tugged her mother's locket out. The locket was once again filled with petals: gifts from Leorah before she'd left. She left them hidden away—the asirim might sense her; it would be the height of foolishness to take them when all depended on her presence in the House of Kings remaining secret—but she *did* rub the locket while whispering to her mother.

"Guide me this night. Lead me to the answers I need."

Silver Tulathan rose over the desert. Rhia's golden disc was not far behind. She heard the first of the asirim soon after, a long, lonely wail that set her skin prickling. Another wail came shortly after, softer, more distant, then a third, this one closer. She might have heard the crack of Sukru's whip, but it was so soft she couldn't be sure.

She gripped her right hand, feeling the burn from the old wound. She'd become adept at recognizing when it was flaring, and she had started to master suppressing the pain and the anger that often came with it. They were reflections of the asirim, their anger, their sorrow. There was a time when it would have overwhelmed her. But she'd learned how to distance herself from them. She did so now, closing herself off to the asirim, especially to those nearing the city.

As another wail came, she used it to mask the soft creak of the right shutter as she pulled it back. After making sure there were no Maidens along this section of the wall, she launched the spool of thread through the window. It arced into the chill air, easily clearing the wall.

Then it was Çeda's turn. She crouched on the sill, pulled the shutter nearly closed, and leapt down to the parapet. Gathering slack from the spool below, she lay the string carefully so that it hugged the surface of the stone walkway, ran at a right angle up to a crenelation, and then to the battlement's outer edge. Satisfied that no one would easily spot it, she slithered through the crenel and dropped to the ground, absorbing the impact with a perfectly timed roll.

Choosing a path among the scrub bushes that would hide her movements, she moved fast and low away from the wall. Then she stood and began jogging up the slope toward the top of Tauriyat. The darkened city sprawled below her as she skirted the palaces along the slope. She heard crashing sounds coming from the north, then screams, which were quickly cut short. She could feel the hunger of the asirim who'd come to feast, but was grateful she felt it only distantly. Had she not closed herself off to them, she would feel not only their unfiltered glee as they murdered the living, but the self-loathing that always followed.

On she went, passing palace after palace—Külaşan's, Ihsan's, Yusam's. Eventually she was higher than even Eventide, King Kiral's palace. As the moons approached their zenith, the slope began to ease, and she reached level ground. The city below was now a mottled black blanket, the desert beyond a roll of unfurled silk.

A rocky promontory, the very peak of Tauriyat, lay only a few hundred paces away. Nearer, larger rocks surrounded a clearing. She approached it with care, nervous, though she knew not why. She thought she heard someone speaking in the distance. She peered into the gloom, moved to one side to get a better look around one large stone, but found the clearing empty.

She glanced up at the bright moons, and realized the sounds were coming from above, as if the goddesses were holding a conversation in secret. She tried to pick out the words, but it was a like a leaf tumbling in the wind—one long susurrus, the words indistinguishable. When she took a step closer to the clearing between the stones, however, the whispers grew tantalizingly close. She heard a word. *Fields.* Then, *wither.*

It reminded her of nothing so much as Sehid-Alaz. When they'd met in the night-darkened streets of Sharakhai, he'd been standing close enough to touch, reciting part of a poem. *Unmade,* he'd said, then *betrayed* and *fallen* and, the clearest of them all, *rest will he 'neath twisted tree.* She recalled the pain and wonder she'd seen in his face. The curse laid upon him by the gods forbade him from speaking of such things, and yet he'd found the strength to do it.

This, Çeda realized. *The whispers are what my mother came for. The silver trove.* She took another stepped forward, more curious, more eager, than she'd been in years.

"I'm afraid I can't allow you to go any farther." A dark figure resolved from the stones to her left.

Çeda took a step back and drew River's Daughter.

"That won't be necessary."

She knew that voice, that lilting tone. "King Ihsan."

As he stepped closer, she recognized his slight build, the way he clasped his hands before him when he walked. The thread of gold in his dark clothing reflected the moonlight. The gemstone in his turban sparkled. "Before we go any farther, Çedamihn"—he waved toward River's Daughter—"sheathe your sword."

There was power in the timbre of his words, and with it came a desire to obey. She resisted, but it led to an indescribable discomfort inside her. Like stones being stacked on a pane of glass, the tension grew, threatening to break her from within. And when she became desperate and thought to lift the sword to stop him, the pain became bright as the burning sun. Only when she'd slid her blade home did it ease.

His smile shone in the moonlight. "I wondered when you'd come. I must say, I thought it would have been before now. Now back away. The two of us should have a chat, but free of the whispers."

Again came the feeling of power, and the desire to obey. She saw no reason to refuse him, and wondered if that was part of his power, to make her *think* it was her idea to begin with, or at least to make it unobjectionable. She backed away until the feeling of tension eased.

Ihsan followed calmly, as if he'd expected nothing less. "You've been a particularly sharp thorn in the side of the Kings. Two dead by your hand. Another nearly taken by a poisoned arrow. The same King nearly felled by your own blade some months later."

"Don't tell me you're surprised. You knew, and allowed me to remain in the House of Maidens. You had Zaïde train and advise me."

In the moonlight Ihsan's smile looked beatific. He waved back the way

Çeda had come. "You'd have enjoyed the fury in the House of Maidens when they learned of your treachery. Melis was angry, though no more than one would expect. Kameyl was murderous. Sümeya, however, was inconsolable, which was rather surprising given how even-handed a commander she's been. It makes me wonder what you meant to her."

Çeda's mind flashed to the night she'd lain on the sand with Sümeya, the two of them kissing, their skin hot on that cold winter night.

"She launched an inquisition," Ihsan went on. "Every single Blade Maiden was questioned. Their past inspected carefully. Zeheb was in attendance for many of them, in hopes of ferreting out untruths. They managed, in fact, to uncover one who had been feeding information to Malasan for years. Sümeya flayed her personally in the Maidens' courtyard for all to see, though I rather think she wished it were you being lashed beneath her whip. And then there was Yndris."

Bakhi's bright hammer . . .

"Yes," Ihsan said, perhaps noticing her reaction. "Yndris recovered. She was gleeful to be proven right about you. She's still not fully healed, especially in her mind. She was always a cruel child, but now she's twisted. So twisted Sümeya almost refused to take her back."

Çeda had no idea why he was telling her this, but at the moment she didn't much care. "How did you know I would come?"

Ihsan waggled his finger at her like a scolding father. "No, no, oh White Wolf. The night is already half past, and there are things I must learn from you, such as where you've been since leaving Sharakhai."

"Then let's trade for it. There are things I would know as well, things that would help me to take down Onur, a thing I suspect you'd very much like to see happen."

"What do you know?" he asked sharply.

She was compelled, but it was no great hardship for her to share how she'd left Sharakhai, how she'd been taken by Onur. Much of it he would already know. But she spent a good amount of time telling him how angry Onur had been, how eager he seemed for revenge against all the Kings, but especially Ihsan.

Ihsan considered this. "We'll come back to Onur. There are things I need to know about the riot at the southern harbor first. Just before you quelled the riot, you said you went to the ship to free the blazing blues. I believe your excuse was that you saw one escaping the hold. When told of a woman with plaited blonde hair walking unobstructed through the crowd, you reported that you hadn't seen her. But you *did* see her, didn't you?"

"Yes."

"Who was she?"

"The goddess Nalamae."

Ihsan paused, a thoughtful smile on his lips. "Well, well. The goddess incarnate, walking along the quays of the southern harbor. You spoke to her, did you not?"

"No," Çeda said. "She walked toward the ship, knowing I would see her. I knew in that moment that there would be something in that ship for me to find, something to help quell the riot. I wanted to speak with her, but by the time I made it to the hold she was nowhere to be found."

"The riot wasn't the first time you'd seen Nalamae, was it?"

"No," she said. "I saw her when I was young." It felt a like a terrible betrayal. "My mother took me to see her several times, and once she showed me visions in her tree."

"It's quite the riddle, isn't it? Nalamae, of all the gods"—he waved toward the clearing—"missing from this very place that night so long ago. She refused to come when all the other gods did. And what has she done since? She's been hounded. Reborn. Made anew over the course of centuries." Ihsan paused, staring at her as if he could hear her thoughts whispering like the voices in the clearing behind him. "Tell me about the visions."

"There were many. I saw them in the glass that hung from the acacia in her garden. I saw the Night of Endless Swords. I saw River's Daughter being handed to me by Husamettín. I saw my mother giving birth, alone and ashamed. I only knew the goddess as Saliah, then, and I think that's how she saw herself as well. When I told her about my visions, she seemed as shocked as I was. I think she was using me to—"

Çeda felt like she'd been struck by lightning.

Ihsan frowned. "Go on."

"It's why she sent my mother away . . ."

"What do you mean?"

"She was using me to find herself," Çeda said, as confident about this as anything she'd ever learned about Nalamae. "I think what she saw led her to a choice. On the surface it was to take me in at my mother's request or refuse. In truth, though, I think she was finding her way, stumbling forward like the blind woman she was."

Ihsan remained silent as he searched her face, but for the moment Çeda didn't care what he thought. She could still see the look of shock on her mother's face when Saliah told her to return to Sharakhai. She remembered the cold calculation, the resignation. "That was the morning after she came here to find the silver trove. That was the night she met you, wasn't it?"

Ihsan nodded, transfixed by what Çeda was telling him.

"I thought you might have lured her here with lies." Çeda waved to the clearing beyond Ihsan. "But now I know they're true." She considered Ihsan's presence, and more pieces fell into place. "You come here to guard them. To make sure no one can hear Tulathan's words."

Ihsan remained perfectly still. "In a manner of speaking."

Çeda's mind was afire, pulling together the clues, picturing everything that had happened during those two fateful days. "When she came, you stopped her before she came near enough to hear the whispers. She learned they were Tulathan's poems, and you worried my mother had learned too much, so you compelled her to return to the House of Kings the following night."

For the first time, Ihsan seemed surprised by her assertions. His expression had shifted. He seemed wary, perhaps wondering just how much she knew. A wiser woman might have stopped there, but Çeda refused to. She'd come this far, and she wanted to know more. She *needed* to know more. She'd never have this chance again. "You sent her to kill Azad."

The wariness in Ihsan's face turned feral. He displayed a hunger that would look more natural on a man disposed to violence, like King Sukru or Cahil. "I did," he said simply, as if here and now, just this once, he could admit it.

For so long Çeda had thought herself a piece on an aban board, with moves being made by the likes of Ihsan and Macide and Hamzakiir. She'd thought she might rise to make moves of her own, but after all she and Ihsan had discussed she felt as if the Kings were pieces as well. How could she rise above her station when it was the gods themselves playing the game?

In the city, an asir howled. On and on it went, sounding very much like a woman crying.

"Why have you come here?" Çeda asked, suddenly and keenly interested in the answer.

Ihsan seemed confused by the question. "My reasons are my own."

"I doubt you've been sent by the other Kings." She looked past Ihsan to the clearing, all but ignoring him. "You must want to come. I wouldn't be surprised if you come most holy nights. But why would a King scratch at a wound so?" She looked to him. "Does shame force your hand?"

And then she saw something most amazing. Shock in the eyes of the Honey-tongued King. Shock. Which meant she was right. He *did* feel shame. About it all. Beht Ihman. The asirim. All that had happened since.

"Is that why you wish to remove the other Kings from this mountain? To help you forget your own shame?"

"Be quiet."

"It won't work," she said, stepping past him.

"Stop!" he roared.

She felt the physical need to obey, but in that moment the asirim in the city felt so near that she went against her earlier promise. She drew upon their sorrow, their unending anger, heedless of whichever Kings might sense her presence. Her right hand flared with bright pain. She drove forward, and the power of Ihsan's words grew. As did the pain.

A deep ache seared her joints and muscles. Her skin lit afire, and she came closer to hearing more of Tulathan's poems, enough that she heard more from the spectral whispers—*weep and desert deep*.

But when Ihsan shouted, "Cease!" her body obeyed. She willed herself to move, focused on listening to the whispers, but it was impossible. Her body was screaming in pain. There was pity in the asir, but bitter amusement as well. *What did you expect, favored of Sehid-Alaz?*

Ihsan's footsteps neared. He entered her field of vision, his face a mask of fury. "Step back, child."

She did. The whispers faded.

"Take the kenshar from your belt."

She tried to deny him. Her right hand was afire with the effort. And still she drew the curving knife and held it before her, as if she were offering it to him.

"Now hold the tip to your breast. That's it. Very good, child. Now draw it toward you."

With both hands holding the point of the kenshar to her chest, she pulled, using ever more force. The knife forced its way through the boiled leather of her fighting dress, then pierced the skin between her breasts. Her breath came rabbit quick. The pinpoint of pain was surrounded by a growing sense of warmth as blood seeped from the wound.

"Enough," Ihsan said, and she complied, keeping the point of the knife where it was. "You are not without your usefulness, Çedamihn, but I will hurry your departure to the farther fields should you disobey me again."

Sweat rolled down her face, chill in the cold night breeze.

"You said it yourself. We both work toward Onur's death. So let us make a bargain, you and I. I'll give you his bloody verse. Then you will return to the desert and take his head. Return to me with it, and I'll tell you a thing you've been most eager to learn."

Çeda hardly dared speak. "And what is that?"

"Why, the name of your father."

With sudden clarity she felt the wind across her face, felt it tug at the tail of her turban. She felt the vastness of the desert open up around her, though instead of feeling like something small, she felt powerful in a way she never had before.

"Give me Onur's weakness."

Ihsan smiled, a fox before the vole. "Our good King was given a terrible, unending hunger for flesh of many sorts, but foremost among them the flesh of man. In order to feast, he changes shape, most often into a panther with skin as black as night. It is a thing you should be wary of when approaching him, for he is terrible in that form. But once he gives in to his temptation and feasts, he is weakened, often for days. Find him then, and he will be yours."

He took her head in his hands and kissed her on the lips, stared deeply into her eyes, and she felt a deep *will* to please him.

"Go," he said, releasing her. "Fulfill your duty and return to me."

She stepped away. Turning, she slipped her kenshar into its sheath with familiar ease, then jogged back down Tauriyat. She never looked back, not once. She was still filled with the fire of Ihsan's command.

But there was also a growing awareness along the edge of her consciousness. An asir, a broken woman with shriveled black skin, was now limping toward the blooming fields under the crack of Sukru's whip. A host of nightmares, memories of things the asir herself had committed, haunted her. They haunted Çeda as well, sobered her, made her aware of what she was doing in a way she might never have been otherwise.

We are slaves to the same master, you and I, the asir said to her.

No, we are not, Çeda said as she jogged along the moonlit path. *You grant me the wisdom to see my plight, and the strength to disobey, and for that I am in your debt.*

She felt a sour sort of satisfaction from the asir. *Go then, child. Go, and see our people freed.*

Chapter 30

CEDA CREPT EVER CLOSER to the House of Maidens' interior wall. She took great pains to move soundlessly, but knew she couldn't tarry. The Moons had set, and the only light to speak of was the occasional brazier spaced along the walls, but dawn was not far off.

After watching two Maidens pass the wall on their rounds, she rushed to the silk thread she'd left behind where it hung down from the wall above. She pulled on it, which drew the coiled rope out from the window of Sayabim's office. She climbed the rope hand over hand, gained the parapet, and swung over to the Hall of Records. Instead of climbing up to the window, however, she dropped to the ground. She couldn't leave the House of Maidens. Not yet. She had one final task to perform before she returned to the tunnels in the savaşam.

She was glad for the cloak of darkness around her as she padded along the wall and the paved path to the barracks. When she reached the large courtyard that separated the Hall of Records from the barracks she pulled her veil from her face and allowed it to hang down. Maidens didn't wear veils unless they were on duty, so, while it felt as if she were announcing her presence to every Maiden and Matron within these walls, she let it be and walked with her head held high. She was sure at least one of the Maidens on the western wall saw her, but no cry of alarm was raised as she entered the building that had been her home for nearly a year.

When she reached the fourth floor, the topmost story, she pulled out a pair of woolen socks and slipped them over her boots. Silently, she slipped through the archway that led to her old apartments. Just inside was a communal sitting room, and an area with a central hearth that doubled as a cooking space. A table with chairs sat in one corner.

She made her way slowly but steadily down the lefthand hallway, which led to Sümeya's, Kameyl's, and Melis's rooms. All three were light sleepers, but Çeda took care to make no sound and, fortunately, Melis's room was first. She peered through the beaded curtain. It was too dark to see her, but Çeda could hear Melis's soft breathing. Light snoring came from the next room, Kameyl's. She heard nothing from the doorway at the end of the hall. It was too far to hear Sümeya's breathing, but that worked in both directions. Sümeya was the lightest sleeper of them all.

With movements slow as the dunes, Çeda parted the beaded curtain. The beads clacked softly as she inched into the room. Once she was past them, she listened to Melis's breathing with one hand on River's Daughter, ready to draw it if need be. She heard no change, however, as she took out the folded note she'd prepared before coming to the city. With the utmost care, she slipped it into the small leather bag halfway up the shelf near the window. It was the one that kept Melis's toiletries: her scented soap, her pumice stone, the sheaf of frayed twigs she used to clean her teeth. It was the safest place Çeda could think of and there was no other reasonable way to speak to Melis in private and share what she knew. Of all the Maidens, Melis was the likeliest to believe her. The very thought of Melis doing as Çeda asked seemed preposterous now that she was here, but what was there to do about it anymore?

After tucking the note away, she reversed her steps, parted the curtain, and slipped back toward the entrance. Only when she'd reached the doorway did she begin to breathe easier. She'd just pulled the woolen socks from her boots and stepped out from the apartments when she came face to face with another Maiden.

Sümeya.

Çeda was already in motion. She used her foot and forward momentum not to debilitate, but to shove Sümeya as hard as she could. Sümeya expelled a breathy whoosh as she was propelled backward. She gasped for air as Çeda sprinted in the opposite direction.

"Assassin!" Sümeya bellowed, then whistled the call to bring the barracks to arms.

Çeda heard Sümeya give chase, but she dared not look back. Soon she reached the end of the covered walkway. There, she launched herself up to the mudbrick railing and through the air toward the opposite barracks. She bounded against the rough exterior, leaping back toward the building she'd just leapt from. She nearly missed the lip of the roof, but once she had it, she slipped over the top. Below, she heard Sümeya's grunt as she leapt from the same railing.

Çeda had not gone five strides before Sümeya landed on the roof behind her. She sprinted hard after Çeda, giving another piercing whistle. *Enemy. Moving west.*

Çeda sprinted to the corner of the roof and leapt for another building. Below, she spotted three dark shapes rushing for the curtain wall that separated the House of Maidens from the city.

As she ran, Çeda spread her awareness. On the wall to her left, more Maidens ran toward her position, hoping to cut her off. To her right, one Maiden had stopped, a bowstring drawn to her ear. Çeda felt for the Maiden's heartbeat, felt her outward breath, and ducked and rolled as the arrow was released. The arrow whizzed overhead, biting into the roof on Çeda's left.

Çeda was up again in a flash, but Sümeya was close now, and Çeda could feel her searching for Çeda's heart, hoping to make her stumble, or at the very least distract her. But she'd been caught off guard by Çeda's sudden appearance, and Çeda had been prepared for this. It was child's play to elude Sümeya.

As Çeda neared the edge of the barracks, five Maidens were converging on the curtain wall as the Maiden on the wall drew another arrow. She aimed, waiting for Çeda to land.

Çeda withdrew a packet from inside her dress, one she had prepared herself under Dardzada's strict guidance. She squeezed it hard, heard the crunch as the glass vial within broke and released its liquid contents into the powder surrounding it. Fixing the placement of the wall and battlements in her mind, Çeda threw it for all she was worth, then leapt from the barracks. The packet struck, and the area around it was consumed in a billowing black cloud.

Çeda flew through open air and was swallowed by it. She landed. Felt something bite into her shin. Heard the arrow skitter somewhere off to her left. Gritting her teeth against the pain, she felt her way into a crenelation and leapt blindly.

She knew these buildings well. She'd walked them many times on guard duty. She knew the pattern of streets and buildings that lay ahead, some of the oldest in Sharakhai. So she landed easily on the nearest of the buildings and rolled away, finally emerging from the dense black fog created by the packet. She threw another. The smoke billowed as two sets of footsteps thumped along the rooftop behind her.

"Blood traitor! You'll not escape! Not this time!"

Gods, it was Kameyl. Çeda glanced back and saw her arm snap forward. A throwing knife spun through the air, glinting in the moonlight. Çeda tried to dodge, but it bit deeply, piercing her shoulder through the armor of her dress. The knife clattered against the clay tiles as she entered the second cloud.

Making as little noise as possible, she dropped from the edge of the roof. She landed hard, tweaking her ankle as she rolled. Gritting her teeth against the pain, she headed toward an alley that led in drunken fashion toward the temple district.

As the bells in the House of Maidens continued to ring, she heard someone drop behind her. Heard the flutter of cloth as someone flew through the air and landed on the building above her as well. Sümeya and Kameyl, one running high, the other low. Çeda ran for all she was worth, but Kameyl was catching up.

She drew River's Daughter, knowing she couldn't outrun her. Kameyl was too strong, too fast. Çeda had just reached the end of the alley, where it emptied onto Raven Road. She'd decided on this escape path days ago; thankfully, she was still on it. She waited until the last possible moment, then spun and met Kameyl's shamshir with her own. The two of them traded several blinding blows, each searching for a quick advantage over the other. Çeda felt Kameyl reaching for her heart, but this had never been Kameyl's gift. Çeda thwarted her, turned the advantage against Kameyl and *pressed* on her heart, but

Kameyl was so strong she powered through it, sending blow after blow against Çeda's defenses.

The tide was turning against her, and now Çeda heard someone drop to the ground behind her. Sümeya. Çeda quickly retreated, ducking a blow from Sümeya, rolling away and coming up while blocking a downward chop from Kameyl.

She maneuvered over the cobblestone street, trying to keep one of them between her and the other, but they were so used to working with one another, they foiled her at every turn.

She tried to turn the tables on them, to take the offense, but they gave her no chance. It was all she could do to fend off their blades.

Behind Kameyl and Sümeya, more Blade Maidens were dropping to the street. And then Çeda heard heavy footsteps pounding along the street behind her. Much heavier than any Maiden would make, and the heartbeat was loud and strong, almost ox-like.

Sümeya broke away, raising her free hand to the newcomer. "Halt, by order of the Kings!"

Kameyl, meanwhile, unleashed a series of moves that were too fast and powerful for Çeda to match. "For murdering Mesut, my father—" Kameyl called.

Çeda's sword was driven aside as Kameyl's foot came up in a swift round-house kick that took Çeda on the side of her head.

"—you will die a thousand deaths—"

Çeda stumbled, barely defending against a hammer-like blow.

"—and I swear I'll be there to witness them all."

The heavy footsteps were close. Çeda turned to see a bulky form wrapped in a voluminous thawb throw something at Kameyl.

Kameyl warded her free arm before her. Something struck her hand in a burst of bright light. A series of small explosions pounded the air and the street brightened. Çeda felt them all. They shook her insides. They rattled her bones.

She was supposed to have closed her eyes, but she'd forgotten, and now she was dizzy and blinded. She scrabbled away, finding it hard to find her balance. Dardzada's strong hands lifted her, helped her to stumble onward.

The world kept tilting in odd ways, making her nauseous. Dardzada kept her upright, though, kept her moving steadily away from the Maidens.

When they had run several streets, Çeda heard Sümeya call, "There! Down there! Find them!"

That was when Dardzada led her down a set of stairs to a cellar door. He opened it soundlessly, led Çeda inside, then closed and barred the door. After picking up a loaded crossbow leaning against the wall and pointing it toward the door, he waited, listening for sounds of pursuit.

Çeda vomited on the cellar floor.

"Be quiet!" Dardzada hissed.

The sound of footsteps grew stronger. Then a hushed conversation. Finally, thank the gods, the sounds faded.

Dardzada led her to the rear of the cellar, where a set of stairs led up. Instead of taking them, however, he went beneath them, where a false wall led to a small room stocked with food and water, enough to last for days. Two pallets lay ready at the far side of the small space.

"We're going to get to know this room well, aren't we?"

Dardzada pointed to the door with the crossbow. "It's that or take our chances out there."

"This will do nicely."

Chapter 31

K ING IHSAN LEAFED THROUGH the journal he'd been reading these past
many days. It was Yusam's, and almost a decade old. Like so many of
his entries, there were notes from more recent times, visions that Yusam
cross-referenced and embellished, or sometimes thoughts that had occurred
to him years later.

The Moonless Host, trapped in the city, this entry read. *Dozens. Macide
Ishaq'ava among them. Perhaps his father as well. Several hands of Maidens give
chase along the quay or perhaps on the sand of the Northern Harbor—the vision
was unclear here. They capture or kill all but Macide and a young scarab, handsome with striking eyes and a black beard. The two of them escape on a skiff.*

Beside it was a diamond shape, which indicated that this entry was a re-
currence. Below that was written: *Seen again, yet this time they are borne from
the city on the wings of an old gray gull.* Each note had numbers, cross-
referencing the year, volume number, and page where the full entries to the
related visions could be found.

Ihsan shoved the journal away. "You were nothing if not organized," he
said softly.

Perhaps that was what drove him to distraction, and would have driven him mad if he'd lived. Ihsan had seen it in him in recent years, how flighty he'd become, how difficult it was for him to concentrate on anything for more than a few minutes. As useful as the notes and cross-references were, maybe if he'd relaxed his vision a bit and let the larger, more important things come to him, he'd still be alive.

After downing a healthy swallow of cucumber-infused water, he pulled the journal closer and again worked his way forward. The vision of the skirmish in the northern harbor had been mentioned in another entry about a battle in the desert, which had leapt to another, a particularly vivid vision from the mere. Yusam always noted these sorts of visions, those he felt were of the greatest import to the Kings and Sharakhai, with a mark beside the entries, and then duplicated them in special journals. Most of his journals were backed with mundane leather, but these were robin's egg blue, and so had come to be known as the Blue Journals.

This particular vision was of a Blade Maiden who stood in a mountain fastness. Many were held up in that fortress. An army, too large to defend against, despite the fortress's stout walls, approached along the valley. The Maiden—and here Yusam noted that the woman may only have been *dressed* as a Maiden, then further clarified in the margins that perhaps she had *once been* a Maiden, along with a cross-reference to yet another journal. This possible Maiden spoke with a tall woman with plaited blonde hair holding a yew staff. *Nalamae?* was scribbled below it.

"Save us," the Maiden said.

"If I do, all we've done may fade into the desert."

"We have need now," the Maiden replied. "Too many will die if we do not act."

And here Yusam did something rare. He was often clinical in his descriptions, but there were times when he felt something—emotions, even memories—from those in the visions. He wrote that the woman had experienced deep sorrow, even fear. She was desperate, as if she knew her fate and would meet it to protect those she loved.

A thing that feels familiar, Yusam had written in the margins, and put a mark beside it with yet another cross-reference. What it was that felt familiar he never said. The simple feeling of desperation? The cross-reference, a journal written only months ago, was one Ihsan had yet to read.

He jotted the date down on the slip of paper he kept, noting all the journals he needed to retrieve from Yusam's palace. It was enough, he decided. He had nearly twenty more journals to find and bring back with him. He ordered his vizir, Tolovan, to prepare his carriage and was soon trundling over King's Road to the hall of records below Yusam's palace. An hour later he reached the anteroom outside the archives, where shelf upon shelf of ancient texts and manuscripts were kept. Sitting at the desk, looking a bit haggard, was Yusam's daughter, Lienn, who'd been indispensable in teaching Ihsan Yusam's idiosyncrasies and helping to find related visions that he *hadn't* cross-referenced. Lienn had read every journal, most more than once, and many a dozen times or more, especially the Blue Journals.

"Are you well?" Ihsan asked her.

"Yes, Excellence. It's—" She smiled, visibly calming herself. "How may I serve?"

He slid the paper across the desk. "Here's what I'll need today."

Lienn's gray-green eyes narrowed as she squinted through her narrow spectacles. She began to frown as her finger trailed down the list; the lower her finger went, the deeper the frown became. "My apologies, my Lord King, but I cannot bring these to you."

"Oh?"

Lienn was neither young nor easily cowed, but she looked now like a woman who'd been brought before the Kings for the first time. "They've already been taken."

Ihsan was irritated, but a growing sense of dread quickly replaced it. There were only a handful of reasons why Lienn would be acting this way. "Who took them?"

When she spoke, she gave him the very answer he feared. "The King of Kings," she said. "He arrived an hour ago, and his Spears took them away."

"These journals?" Ihsan said, pointing to the list.

"These and a hundred more."

"A *hundred*?"

Lienn looked chagrined. "And *all* of the Blue Journals."

For a moment Ihsan was speechless. Part of him was furious, but another part actually admired Kiral's boldness. It was exactly what Ihsan would have done in his place. "Kiral came for them himself?"

Her eyes wandered to the archway behind Ihsan. "He did."

Ihsan turned to see Kiral's square frame approaching from the archives. Behind him, several servants were wheeling a cart with dozens of leather-bound journals similar to the ones Ihsan had been reading these past many weeks. Their spines were stamped with Yusam's seal: the sun rising above the horizon, rays of sunlight spreading over the sky.

Curse you for a fool, Ihsan. If Kiral has come himself then he's stumbled onto something, a trail similar to my own. Perhaps the very same one.

He nearly laughed at the irony of it all. He'd thought of doing exactly what Kiral was doing now—order a goodly portion of the archive to be brought to his palace—but he hadn't wanted to draw attention to his activities. That was why he'd informed the other Kings he was reading the journals; hiding it would only make them wonder what was so important, but admit it to their faces and they'd think nothing of it. It had worked, too. He'd had weeks of unrestricted access thus far, and little reason to think it wouldn't continue. Until today. He'd been a fool to think he was the only one hoping to mine Yusam's visions for glimpses of the future.

"Ihsan," Kiral said.

"Kiral." He motioned to the retreating carts. "I didn't take you for a man who enjoyed such fanciful narratives. I warn you, the story wanders, and the characters seem a bit shallow."

Kiral looked like he was teasing a canker inside his cheek. "You have more of Yusam's journals at your palace?"

Always to the point. It was his most grating aspect. "One or two."

"Twenty-seven," Kiral shot back.

Lienn must have told him.

"I had hoped to learn more from them than I have." Behind Kiral, another cart trundled out from the archives and headed for the exit.

"What have you learned so far?"

"That I would have gone mad had I been gifted with a mere."

Kiral sucked his teeth. "This has always been the trouble with you. The jackals could be storming the walls, and you would rain quips down upon them."

"What is life without humor?"

"You may have missed your calling, Ihsan. I hear they're in need of jongleurs in the playhouses along the Trough."

"You as well. I hear the city is suffering through a great dearth of undertakers."

"I might even consider it if the pay wasn't such shit."

Ihsan smiled. The joke might have been low hanging fruit, but humor from Kiral was rare as summer rain. "As you know, I've been looking into Nalamae."

Here something most interesting happened. Kiral blinked. His nostrils flared. His *cheeks* actually flushed. It was a momentary thing, there one moment and gone the next, but Ihsan had seen it. Kiral had looked *nervous*. He must be interested in Nalamae as well.

But why? Something must have precipitated it.

Ihsan decided to share the truth, to see how Kiral would react. "Based on the visions he recorded, I suspect she will return soon. I could learn more if my access was unfettered."

For a moment Kiral seemed to consider it. He was on the verge of agreeing, but then his look of indecision vanished. "Detail all that you've found and send it to me tomorrow, along with the journals."

"Of course, my Lord King. Forgive me for asking, but why the sudden interest? Has something happened?"

When a third cart left, pushed by a stocky Spear with a bulbous nose, Kiral turned to follow him. "Yusam once told me of the fall of Ishaq and the Moonless Host. It's high time I found out more."

A lie. Or at least, not the whole truth. "And when you're done?"

Kiral didn't stop. "It may take some time, Ihsan," he said, and swept from the room.

Some time, Ihsan thought. *He means they'll never be available.*

It smacked of something other than Kiral imposing his will simply to show that he could. Whatever had happened, had been recent.

Secrets, Ihsan thought, *and me without my King of Whispers.*

Which gave Ihsan his next destination. He made his way to Zeheb's palace, and was forced to wait for nearly an hour before the two of them could speak. Eventually he was led by Drogan, Zeheb's clever young vizir, to the throne room. Using the brass knocker in the shape of a grinning demon, Drogan knocked thrice and then moved to a table beside the gilded doors. On it were a dozen lamps. Drogan chose one of the smallest, lit it, then opened the rightmost door and led Ihsan into the dark, cavernous room. Even though the sound was strangely deadened, Drogan clicked the door shut behind him, taking pains to ensure the door did not clatter.

It was daytime, and yet the throne room was dark as night. The only source of illumination was Drogan's tiny lamp, which revealed precious little save the patterns on the carpets. This space had been bright once—centuries ago, a grand vaulted room with high windows. Now it was perpetually dark. Heavy curtains were draped over the windows and along the walls as well, hiding the stone completely. The floor was covered from one end to the other in layers of carpets. Only in the vaulting recesses above could any stone be seen, and even those were obscured by bolts of orange and yellow cloth.

"I feel like I've been swallowed whole," Ihsan said to Drogan, but it was a voice ahead in the darkness that answered.

"Yes, yes. It's dark. Like a dragon's cave. Do you have to mention it every time you come?"

As they approached, a man sitting cross-legged on the carpets appeared from the darkness: Zeheb, sitting on a mound of pillows before a low table. His eyes were closed. His hands were on his knees, his palms upturned like an ascetic in the mountains of Mirea.

Ihsan laughed. "Goezhen could craft demons in here and no one would stir. An army could do battle and not a soul would come to investigate."

Drogan set the lamp on the table before Zeheb, then strode away, his footsteps silent as fog. Zeheb finally opened his eyes. "It's also quiet enough that if I strangled you, no one would hear it."

"You're sure?" The place *was* deadly quiet. "Have you ever tested it?"

Zeheb's reply was humorless. "I'm willing to try if you are."

Ihsan lowered himself into the pillows opposite Zeheb. "Another time, perhaps." Taking up the bottle of araq sitting there, he poured two helpings and slid one toward Zeheb.

Zeheb didn't take it at first, but then his posture relaxed, he sank deeper into the pillows and took the glass. He downed it in one gulp, then poured himself another. "I'm surprised you're here." Words seemed to be warring within him. But then he seemed to come to some decision. "What do you want, Ihsan?"

A rather curious reaction. "There are a few things I wonder if the King of

Whispers has got wind of." He sipped his araq, a silvery liquid thick with the taste of pear and lychee and freshly churned butter that finished with strong notes of tabbaq. "I've been reading Yusam's journals, hoping to learn when Nalamae might reappear. Today, however, Kiral forbade me from reading them."

Zeheb frowned. "Denied you outright?"

"Not in so many words. He took many of the journals I wanted and asked that I deliver those in my palace to him, further implying that access to them will be severely restricted."

"Well, we both know that when Kiral's eye lands on some new bauble, he doesn't rest until he has it."

"In this case, however," Ihsan replied, "it's something that concerns us all. He's looking for something in particular. I'm certain of it. And likely to do with Nalamae."

"What is your point?"

"My point, my good King, is that something has happened recently to cause Kiral to do this."

"And?"

"*And* I would think the King of Whispers would want to know something about it."

There was a look of sour disappointment in Zeheb's eyes, even disgust. "We agreed that we would no longer work against Kiral."

"We did, but this is important. We deserve to know what he thinks will happen to us, and to Sharakhai."

"Ah, so if *you* had learned of it, you would have shared it with the others?"

Ihsan paused and chose his next words with care. "That would depend on the nature of the information."

"Which is, you must admit, precisely Kiral's point of view."

"Meaning that it's *your* point of view as well."

"Perhaps it is," he said flatly. "Which brings me to another order of business. You agreed that we would bide our time. You agreed to step in line with Kiral's wishes. *There is wisdom in your words,* I believe you said. Your visit here, would you call it *wise* given the dangers we face from within our own house?"

"Can two Kings not talk?"

Zeheb snorted. "You may have played Yusam for a fool, Ihsan. You may even have done so with me for a time. But that ends today."

He made a hand sign, the sort the Blade Maidens used to communicate with one another. Ihsan had never made a study of them, but he knew the sign for *attack* when he saw it.

With the floor carpeted as it was, and the gloom that filled the cavernous space, he neither saw nor heard the Kestrel until she was practically on top of him. She wore a rust-colored dress, a matching turban with a veil covering all but her eyes. Emerging from the darkness, she looked like a freshly made wound that grew by the moment.

"Halt!" he shouted, imbuing his voice with power.

But the Kestrel kept coming. She held no weapon, but her hands were protected by fingerless gloves. Ihsan pulled his gods' gift, his triple-bladed dagger, from its sheath by his side. She came to a halt as he swung the blade in a broad arc—a warning, for all the good it would do.

"I command you to stop!"

But the Kestrel didn't. She stepped forward as Ihsan gave himself over to another violent swing, and then she was on him, snatching his wrist as quick as her namesake while kicking one leg into the air. Then her body was up, twisting, her thighs locking around his neck. Her momentum carried her, and she used her hold around his neck to draw him forward and down, his body whipping past her so that he fell hard on the carpet.

As the pain was just beginning to register, she rolled off him, twisting his hand as she went. His wrist and arm were torqued so ferociously his knife dropped to the carpet beside him. She immediately kicked it away, just out of reach. If he were able to crawl, only a tiny bit, he might reach it, but it may as well have been lying on the other side of the desert. His wrist and shoulder were in such agony he could make no move toward it, and even if he could stifle the pain it would be child's play for the Kestrel to break his wrist or dislocate his shoulder.

"Release me!"

A pitiful appeal, made through a veil of pain.

The Kestrel was indifferent to the power of his voice. She grabbed a fistful of hair, sent a knee into his lower back, and pressed him into the carpets.

Zeheb had made his way around the low table. When he came near, he took one knee and turned his head to the side so that Ihsan could see him clearly. "She's deaf," he said. "I had her hearing taken from her years ago, in case I ever needed to move against you. She won't hesitate to cut a smile across your throat should I give the sign. If you say but one word of command against me, I'll be able to resist long enough to signal her."

"I am a King!"

Zeheb's face screwed up in disgust. "I see no *King*. I see a man who lives or dies at my whim!" His angry eyes bored into Ihsan's. "When you talked of ruling Sharakhai together, years ago, I doubted you. I not only came to believe you were sincere, I'm nearly certain you never once used your power on me. Am I wrong?"

Ihsan's neck was pressed so hard the simple act of drawing breath caused pain. Speaking was worse. "Why would I have needed it? You wanted to believe my words as much as I did."

"I may have been blinded years ago, but now I know the truth. Your eyes see only enemies. Even Nayyan will one day wither in your regard."

"Please, Zeheb. I was in error, but I would still do as we've long planned—"

Zeheb nodded to the Kestrel, who arched Ihsan's head back so hard he feared his neck would break.

"For once, be quiet, Ihsan." Zeheb leaned closer, leering. "Know that there are others like her. Know that I can and will call upon them if the need arises, and that there's nothing you can do to stop them once they've been given your scent. Know that they have standing orders if you command me to kill myself or I die in some mysterious manner. Lastly, know that it won't be you who's taken first, but Nayyan. Nayyan and the child you thought to hide from us all."

Despite all that had happened in this room, something cold slipped between Ihsan's ribs, crept ever deeper toward his heart. He knew it well, the fear of losing a child, the anguish of knowing you might have helped but failed.

"You will not come to me like this again. If I have need, *I* will summon *you*. Do you understand me, Ihsan?"

In the darkness, a vision of his daughter swam before him: Ferah, lying on a throne, her wrists slit. The Kestrel wrenched his head back farther, eliciting a scream that echoed those he'd shed for Ferah when he'd entered his throne room and found her dead.

"I understand," he managed, pounding the carpet with one hand.

Zeheb studied his eyes a moment longer, then made a new sign to the Kestrel. She released him, then melded back into the darkness.

Taking up the small lamp, Zeheb began walking toward the back of the throne room. "You can see yourself out."

Zeheb walked silently away and was gone, the light diminishing with him.

Chapter 32

DAVUD COULDN'T SLEEP after returning from the cavern with the Kings. The dreams were haunting. Visions of the Kings swam before him. Kiral, Cahil, and Husamettín standing in the background, grim-faced, while Sukru demanded to know why Davud had done nothing to stop Yerinde. Every time Sukru spoke her name, the face of the goddess came to him, piercing him over and over with those violet eyes.

Her head. Bring me her head. Bring me her head.

The words built in intensity until he woke sweating, wondering why a god would ask for the head of one of their own.

Can the gods not squabble?

Certainly, he reasoned, but why not take her head themselves? He recalled his vision of Goezhen running after Nalamae. How she'd denied him, left him bleeding near the blooming fields. *What can the Kings do where the gods have failed?* But then he remembered all of Çeda's research below the collegia. He'd read everything she'd asked him to bring, partly to ensure it was something she'd want, but also to satisfy his own curiosity. He'd seen in those texts the number of times the gods had hunted Nalamae down only to have her reappear years later. Was this some new attempt on their part to finish the job once and for all?

Sukru had been prominent in his dreams as well. He would swoop down like a vulture and thrust a knife into the center of Davud's chest. Face sweaty, eyes like a rat in the night, he snarled, "What good have you been to me, fool boy?"

As dawn approached, he gave up on sleep and went for a walk around the palace. It was calming, the grounds dreamlike under Tulathan's silver light. He wandered the gravel walks, the topiary, the small ponds filled with exotic fish. He even wandered the hedge maze for a time, breathing deeply of its piney scent, which did wonders to dispel his dreams.

He was heading back to his room when he saw a dark form walking through the archway that led to the boneyard. A woman, surely one of those who tended to the graves and crypts.

No. It was Anila. Standing as he was behind the statue of a spread-winged crane, she didn't see him and continued deeper into the large yard. He was just about to call out to her when he saw Zahndr trailing behind her. He stopped at the entrance and turned round, blocking the path.

Guarding it, Davud realized, *but why?*

He was tempted to ask, but there was something strange going on here. The way Anila had acted in the coach the day before, as if she were ashamed of something. Sukru was encouraging her to do something. He just wasn't sure what.

Using the sharpened point on his ring, Davud pierced his left wrist. He let the blood pool for a moment, then drew a sigil upon his palm, combining *drift*, *descry*, and *obsess*. Using that same hand, he scooped sand from the pathway and blew it into the cool morning air.

It wafted toward Zahndr, scintillant as it drove against the prevailing wind, it became so thin Davud could hardly detect it. As it passed the boneyard's entrance, Zahndr blinked, then he shook his head and blinked again. The moment he turned away, Davud walked along the gravel path toward him. The crunch of his own footsteps made Davud cringe. Zahndr would surely have heard them, yet his gaze remained fixed on a tall minaret in the middle distance and remained there as Davud slipped past him and into the boneyard.

The yard itself wasn't terribly large but was so packed with grave markers, sepulchers, and entrances to underground crypts that one could easily get lost. Davud walked as silently as he could, looking for Anila. When he caught movement ahead, he pulled up short and hid behind a large grave-stone.

Along the wall of the massive wing of the palace that held Sukru's resi-dence were several dozen stone sepulchers, all with open entryways. Anila stood within one of these, her dark head scarf, skin, and dress making her look like a shadow within that enclosed space. She stood before a white sar-cophagus, staring intently at the marble lid, which looked bright and new.

Bela's grave?

Anila had cared for the girl, but this visit felt like something more than paying respects to the dead. He was proven right moments later, when Anila reached out and touched one finger to the sarcophagus lid. She moved her finger in a rough circle, then drew a line through it, followed by more embel-lishments, until it was clear she was drawing a sigil.

What good will it do, though? He could see no blood.

He thought back to the finch in the bird cage, how he'd thought it dead, but it had awoken while he'd been talking with Anila. He'd known she was doing something arcane, but he hadn't pressed her. He should have, he real-ized now.

A thin mist lifted from the sigil and spread like fog. It drifted down from the lid in thin rivulets before the dry desert air swallowed it. Both of Anila's palms were held motionless above the sigil, as if she were warming them over a fire. When she tilted her head, Davud felt something deep inside him shift. Akin to what he felt while summoning magic.

A chill ran through him as more fog crept out from the crack beneath the lid.

Gods, it's coming from inside the sarcophagus.

It drifted down and spread along the floor, swallowing Anila's feet and ankles. And then Davud saw something he'd hoped never to see again. The fog . . . It was rolling down *Anila's* form as well, just as it had when she lay on the ground in Ishmantep after Davud's clumsy use of magic had burned her. Except this time she didn't appear to be in pain. Her skin wasn't broken and bleeding, as it had been then.

Davud could take it no longer. "Stop!" he cried as he strode forward. "Stop it!"

Anila turned, her eyes wide with surprise. "Davud!"

He grabbed her hands to pull her away from the sarcophagus and snatched them back a moment later. Her skin was so cold it burned.

"Leave me!" she hissed.

"This isn't right!"

He'd just motioned to the sarcophagus when a thud came from beneath the lid. Anila froze and Davud prayed it had merely been a shifting of the lid caused by the cold. But it came again a moment later. A thud that struck the underside of the lid. The next one came so hard it made him shiver.

Breath of the desert. The girl . . .

As Anila turned to the sarcophagus, a boom came from beneath the lid, so hard the slab *shifted*. Anila began to whisper as a scratching, scrabbling sound came from within. She touched the surface of the marble, drawing another sigil. Crystals of ice trailed behind her finger, melting and evaporating as Anila complicated the sigil.

A moaning came from within, growing more desperate by the moment, followed by screaming, pounding, and scratching. Faster and more frenzied, as if the girl inside was fighting for her life. Visions of her came, a precocious thing running about the palace, her long hair loose and trailing behind her. Now she was trapped inside a sarcophagus, something *other* than what she'd been.

Anila continued to whisper, continued to draw lines of frost. Like a quieting sea, the sounds from within quelled.

After long moments, all was silence once more.

"Why?" Davud asked. "Why would you do this to Bela?"

Anila turned to him, her eyes downcast. "I had to know if I had enough power."

Davud thought of the firefinch. "But to do it to a *child*!"

"If she could help find Hamzakiir, yes."

Across the boneyard, Zahndr, his longsword drawn, was running toward them. In that moment, a terrible thought occurred to Davud. "Did you have a hand in killing Bela?"

The shock in her eyes made it clear that he'd crossed a line, but even if

Anila hadn't killed her, she was no longer innocent. The longer he thought on it, the more things fell into place: Zahndr guarding the entrance to the bone-yard, Anila being given access to Bela's tomb. "Sukru asked you to do it."

Anila turned angry. "Of course he did, and stop looking at me like that. You know how he craves magic. That's why *you're* here, and that's why he let me remain when he found out about"—she stared down at her hands—"this."

When Davud had spoken to the mage using the triangle, he'd been told much the same thing about Sukru's hunger for power. But to sacrifice a child . . . "What does he want you to do?"

"Say nothing more to him!" Zahndr said as he reached the crypt. His face screwed up in annoyance, he reached forward and took Davud by the arm.

Davud raised the palm of his right hand and drew a sigil for *obfuscate* and *bind* and *fauna*. And then a thing most strange happened. One moment, he felt the spell consuming Zahndr—it wrapped around him like gossamer—but then it was shunted into marble beneath their feet, lost like so much water on parched earth.

"Sukru would likely never forgive me if I take his latest sorcerer from him." Zahndr brandished his sword while gripping Davud's arm to the point of pain. "But I won't shed a tear if you force me to spill your blood over all this pretty marble."

"I . . ."

"We're leaving now," Zahndr said.

When Anila said nothing, Davud allowed himself to be taken away. As Zahndr led him forcibly along the boneyard's well-tended paths, he looked back only once to find Anila standing in the sepulcher, watching the sarcoph-agus with an expression he could only interpret as satisfaction or hunger.

Or both, Davud thought.

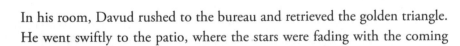

In his room, Davud rushed to the bureau and retrieved the golden triangle. He went swiftly to the patio, where the stars were fading with the coming dawn. *Don't fail me,* he said to the glittering field, *I have need of you.*

Sitting at the small table, he gave the triangle a spin. It fluttered like a dying moth, then fell to the mosaic tabletop with a jingle.

"Please," Davud whispered, and gave it another spin.

This time, it twisted in the air, bobbled, and remained spinning above the table's colorful surface. It lifted reluctantly until it was eye level. For long moments he heard nothing but its whirring.

"Hello?" Davud said.

"I'll admit," came the Sparrow's voice, "I never thought to hear from you again. I'm pleased. Have you had the wisdom to heed my warnings?"

"In a manner of speaking, yes. You said I could come to you. That you would protect me."

"And I meant it."

"Could you protect Anila as well?"

"Your friend from the collegia?"

"Yes. She has power, like me. And Sukru is using her."

"For what purpose?

"I don't know. I was hoping you might be able to tell me."

"I do not meddle directly in Sukru's affairs if I can avoid it. He has little talent in the red ways, but he has devices and artifacts he hoards like a desert wyrm, that I would have no wish to run afoul of. But," he said before Davud could reply, "I've learned that she has power, and that it is distinctly different from yours."

Davud stared at the spinning triangle, haunted by the sound of Bela fighting to escape her tomb. If Anila were willing to do that to a child, what else might she do? "She is not gifted in the red ways as we are. Her arts are dark as the night." He told the Sparrow about the missing page from Sukru's book, the one that dealt with death. Then described what had happened with the finch, finishing with Bela's story.

"Your Anila is a disciple of Bakhi," the Sparrow said. "A necromancer. There have been rumors that the high priest of Bakhi's temple is one himself, albeit weak, but there has not been another for generations. It is said that those who've stepped into the gateway to the farther fields and returned to our world gain such powers. And that the more time they spent in that state so near to death, the more powerful they become. How long was Anila so?"

A vision came of Anila, lying on the sand in Ishmantep, a cold fog rolling off her in waves. "A long while."

"It's dangerous," the Sparrow went on. "The more they draw upon the ties that bind this world to the next, the closer they come to the farther fields. Most die within a year."

Within a year . . . "She could stop, though, and she would live?"

"Perhaps, but you must know that they are drawn toward death like moths to flame. The call of the farther fields is strong. No doubt this is true for Anila as well. No doubt there's some great desire keeping her from giving into it as well. There always is."

Davud thought on it. "She wants Hamzakiir's head."

"If even half the stories I've heard of what he did to the collegia scholars are true, I've no doubt you're right. It might drive anyone to do what she's doing now."

"Is that what Sukru wants then? Hamzakiir's death?"

"Who can say? Sukru may align himself with Kiral, but he has other purposes."

"Such as?"

"As I said, I steer well wide of Sukru and his interests. Now, we have little time left." Indeed, the triangle was slowing, a top ready to topple.

"Will you shelter her?" Davud asked again. He heard the sounds of the palace's drawbridge being lowered, the rattle of chain, followed by a boom.

The triangle faltered. He thought it would fail altogether, cutting off the Sparrow's answer, but then . . . "It's more dangerous, but yes, I could manage it. I would enjoy speaking with her."

"How?" Davud rushed, relief tingling along his limbs. "How can I do it?"

"Summon the sigil for *passage* and *doorway* and cast it on the triangle."

"Only when the stars are bright?"

But it was too late. The triangle spun and clattered against the table, in dawn's light a perfect, bright triangle against the oddly shaped tesserae beneath.

Chapter 33

IGNORING THE PERSISTENT PAIN in his ankles and knees, King Onur tread over the rocky ground. Dust demons swirled over the flat, slowly rising landscape. The sun was lowering, casting dark shadows beneath the scrub brush as he headed steadily closer to the rusty face of a grand escarpment. It ran like a ribbon into the distance, and separated the near portion of the desert from a plateau above, a place choked with yew trees. Little grew along the ground below. Bushes fought for life beneath the harsh desert sun. Iron-weed and desert thistle grew in the gullies. The differences were so stark it looked as though the elder gods had granted fertile soil above while ceding the land below to the hunger of the desert.

A crack ran down the escarpment's stone face. High above it was thin and difficult to see, but the lower it went, the wider the gap became, creating a natural cavern at ground level. Onur couldn't yet discern the size of it—the scale of this place made it difficult considering how far away he was—but as his heavy footsteps bore him closer, he realized how massive it was. A bloody cathedral could fit inside of it. And who knew how far back it went? Its depths were lost to darkness.

He stared into the shadows as he came closer, clutching a large fire opal in his left hand. It was the most important of the prizes he'd won in his battle against Tribe Masal, a legendary artifact of Tribe Salmük, his familial tribe. He'd heard stories of it from his grandfather when he was young. He'd asked about it the one and only time he'd been taken by his father to visit his tribe in the desert. Most had refused to speak of it, but a waif of a girl had admitted to seeing it with her own eyes.

"Then why won't they admit it?" Onur, ten summers or so at the time, had asked her.

"Because you're from the city."

That one admission had done more to wake him to the realities of tribal life versus life in the city than anything in the hundreds of years since.

He'd hoped to find the gem hidden away when he'd come from Sharakhai to take up his role as shaikh. That he hadn't found it was no great surprise. He was only pleased that they were relatively certain who'd stolen it away: Tribe Masal, which was precisely why he'd chosen them as the first of his conquests.

When he judged he'd come close enough to the gap in the stone, he stopped and held the opal before him. It had been a long while since he'd been afraid. Truly afraid. It felt good. Made him feel alive. Fear would make his triumph here, and all that followed, feel that much more satisfying.

The sun's rays threw orange and red and ochre against the stone's surface. It was a pretty thing—even he would admit that—but it was so much more than a simple jewel. It was one of the greatest treasures ever offered up by the Great Mother.

"I call upon you, Yerinde. Goddess of love. Crucible of desire. Heed my words, for your servant has need."

It grated to name himself a *servant*, but he recognized it for what it was: a sign of how long he'd been a King of Sharakhai. Give any man all he might wish for for centuries, and he would see the world the same way as Onur did: as though everything he laid his eyes on was his to command. It was an attitude that served him well when he'd reached the camp of Tribe Salmük, and again when he'd spoken to the survivors of his battle with Tribe Masal. Project an air of inevitability, of invincibility, and soon enough everyone falls into line.

He was no fool, though. With the gods he must take care. They *were* invincible, where he only pretended to be.

"I call upon you, Yerinde." He held the stone higher. "Too long has it been since we spoke."

The desert wind soughed through the dried bushes. Sand picked up, swirling in graceful curves before distending and fading altogether.

"I call upon you," he said a third time, and threw the stone far ahead.

It landed in a patch of sand and lay there, unmoving, the desert around it uncaring. But then the wind picked up. The sand around the stone lifted. For the span of a breath it twisted in the air, a thing alive, and then it fell, the sand billowing outward. In the center of the cloud now stood a woman. She was naked, but as Onur watched, black insects the size of children's teeth scuttled up from the sand. They lifted into the air, creating a new sort of cloud, this one dark, iridescent, growing ever tighter around her frame. The insects landed on her skin, covering her arms, her legs, her chest and stomach. It looked as though she were wearing a dress that moved like a plague of termites.

Her loose black hair became wind-tossed, obscuring her face for a moment, but as the wind died, it fell in long waves down her back. She stared with violet eyes at the stone, which was now pinched between her thumb and forefinger. It looked small in her hands, which in turn made Onur feel small. He didn't like the feeling.

She turned the opal this way and that, the sunlight continuing to play across its surface. *Many years has it been since I've seen the eye of dragons.*

"I've found it that I might use it to further your glory."

Yerinde lifted her gaze to stare at Onur. *My glory? Not thine own?*

"I have no wish for glory."

The goddess stepped closer, the winged insects lifting, littering the air around her, then settling once more. *What is it then that fills your heart?*

"The journey toward justice."

Justice? Yerinde's smile was like mulled wine, like golden honey freshly poured. *And when has the King of Spears sought for justice save for himself?*

"Others will be served if I succeed. What matter that *I* might be served as well?"

Her head swiveled until she was staring at the flame-filled jewel between her fingers. *And this will give it to you?*

"It will be a start."

She turned to him, stepped nearer. Onur could smell something on the wind. Something floral and ancient, redolent of the elder gods. Or perhaps the farther fields. *What would be thy wish were I to grant thee the whole of the desert?*

A quip was there on his lips, but the words died on his tongue. Those eyes. They were deep and knowing, and yet aroused him to the point that he could hardly think. In four hundred years they hadn't changed in the least. And now they demanded truth from him.

He found it, buried deep inside him, a thing he'd hardly admitted to himself since well before leaving Sharakhai for the desert. "I would wipe away all that you've done," he said at last, "you and the other gods."

Her violet eyes twinkled. *And then?*

"And then I would give myself back to the desert."

Yerinde reared her head back and laughed. It was a sound that filled the desert, that played off the face of the cliff in the distance, returning to him changed, mingling with the fresh peals that shook her frame. When at last her laughter faded, Yerinde blinked, and a tear fell from her eye. Golden and glinting it fell on the fire opal. With it came a sense of something ancient awakening, a thing that had been hidden from the world but now returned, a titan the elder gods had thought dead before they'd departed these shores.

Very well, Yerinde said, then held the opal out for him to take.

For a moment, he couldn't move. He almost laughed. He'd lived for more than four centuries, well longer than any man had a right to live. He stood before a god who was offering him all he sought, and yet he wondered, as he had those many years ago on Tauriyat, why? Why did the gods enjoy their games so much? What was it they sought in the end?

He wanted to ask her a question of his own. *What would be your wish were you granted the whole of the world?* But as he stared at the jewel, he decided he didn't much care what her answer would be. He took it from her open hand, feeling a warmth that hadn't been there before.

The wind kicked up, blowing dust and sand into his face. When he'd blinked it away, Yerinde was gone, the desert clear for leagues around.

Holding the jewel tight, he continued toward the cavern. The same thing he'd felt before was there, deep in the shadows.

Come, he willed. *Come, and let the light of the desert shine on you once more.*

As he came within several hundred paces, he felt a rumbling in the earth beneath his feet. Dust coughed from the entrance.

No, smoke. A dense cloud of smoke.

Shadows shifted. And he saw within the deeper darkness two glinting slits. Eyes that opened wide, spying him, their centers a complex weave of colors that were very much like the oranges and yellows of the opal.

Relishing the fear now coursing through his veins, as well as the sheer potential of what he was about to do, Onur continued toward it, the pain in his knees and ankles all but forgotten.

———————— ⟨—●—⟩ ————————

Later, as Onur the King of Sloth left the cavern, a woman watched. She stood in the open wearing simple, roughspun clothes that blended well with the hard landscape. She was distant enough that it would be difficult for the King of Spears to discern her form. The few times his eyes scanned the desert in her direction, a gust of sand would lift, obscuring her further until he'd looked away.

She held a weathered staff with a gnarled head. The staff's butt against the sand, she pressed the head to her ear and listened to the rhythms of the world. They'd been altered by the events that had just taken place, and now it was up to her to discern them.

She felt a deeper power in the cavern Onur had just exited. She felt the eyes of the desert gods on it as well, which prevented her from going there to learn more. She sensed satisfaction in Onur's heavy tread. Smelled the faint scents of vetiver and sweetgrass and burning amber, all telltale signs of Yerinde. The breathing of the beast Onur had awakened rumbled in her chest. She felt an echo of each breath.

As Onur regained his skiff and began sailing away, the sour feeling in her gut intensified. It was her own indecision, she knew. That and the impossible choices that lay ahead. There was danger along any path she chose, so which was the right one?

The skiff grew smaller and smaller as she watched Onur chart a course not only for himself but for the Great Mother as well. She knew she must do the same.

As the skiff was lost to the horizon, the woman's form turned to sand, a crumbling column the wind soon ravaged and flung across the land.

Chapter 34

WHEN RAMAHD RETURNED to the Qaimiri embassy house, he expected Meryam would be there, poring over the sigils he'd gathered over the past few days. He'd spent the morning collecting the last of them by going along the city's outer wall and making charcoal rubbings from those foundation stones containing sigils. There were forty-seven in all, an attempt on the part of the Kings to protect their city from the ehrekh and other strange children of Goezhen.

Meryam had wanted to study the full set in detail before moving on to the next part of their plan to find Hamzakiir, but she wasn't there. "Gone to speak with the King of Kings," Basilio informed him when he asked of her whereabouts.

Without me, Ramahd thought. "Why wasn't I informed?"

Basilio sniffed and tugged his silk kaftan tighter against his ample frame. "Well, I'm sure I don't know."

"What did she say?" The oh-so-smug expression on Basilio's face, recognition of Ramahd's fallen position with Meryam, was enough to make Ramahd step forward, grab his kaftan, and send him crashing him into the wall. "What did she *say?*"

Basilio was completely flustered. "Un*hand* me, sir!"

He knew he should. He knew he'd crossed a line that would be nearly impossible to walk back from. But all the rage that had been building inside him over having to run about the city like a common servant came pouring out in one big rush. He pulled Basilio back and shoved him back, harder than before. "I asked you a question."

It was in that rage-filled moment that Ramahd realized what was really driving his anger. Guhldrathen. *The ehrekh has been calling to me ever since I gave it my blood. Since I offered Çeda's in payment for Hamzakiir's. And now it grows stronger.*

Mighty Alu, if Meryam didn't do something soon, the ehrekh would have him, no matter that the sigils, the very ones he'd been collecting for Meryam these past many days, protected him while he was within the city walls.

He released Basilio.

Basilio shoved Ramahd away, then tugged his kaftan down, trying to smooth out the wrinkles. His face was beet red as he lifted a finger to Ramahd. "If you ever touch me again in such a way—"

"Don't say anything you'll regret."

Ramahd and Basilio both turned to find Meryam standing in the doorway. "My queen," they said together, both bowing their heads.

"Yes, yes." She stepped into the room with a slight limp but with an energy in her eyes that made it clear she was pleased despite what she'd just witnessed.

Amaryllis followed, her long curly hair pulled into a horsetail that jutted from the top of her head. As Meryam stopped and faced them, Amaryllis continued into the next room and closed the doors behind her.

"Ramahd has given insult." Meryam waved to the place on the wall where she'd just found the two of them. "This and others, I'm sure. Suffice it to say that given what's happened in recent weeks, there is good reason for Ramahd to be . . . overly protective of me. It doesn't excuse it," she went on, interrupting Basilio, "but it will be forgiven this once."

"He *struck* me," Basilio said.

"Then strike him back and be done with it."

"You cannot keep such a man around, my queen."

"Your advice is noted. Now either take your measure of his hide or don't, but either way, be done with it and leave."

Ramahd stood there with words of apology on his lips. But he couldn't voice them, not with Basilio staring at him as if he was owed it. Basilio shook with anger, but didn't lift a hand. "You will rue this day." He walked past Ramahd and closed the doors behind him.

Ramahd was ready to spill his words of apology to Meryam, but before he could she spun on her heels and walked into the room where Amaryllis had gone, so he kept them to himself and followed.

Amaryllis was already sitting beside a small table. Meryam took the chair next to her, then waved Ramahd to take the third. On the table was a simple lead box with no adornments save for the arcane symbols marked into the sides, lid, and bottom. Around it, strapped crosswise, were two leather belts, a measure to keep the lid securely on.

Next to the box were several implements: long-nosed pliers, as jewelers might use; iron scissors, freshly sharpened; a brass censer that hung from a tripod; a lit candle beneath that filled the air with a scent like burning sage; several simple white rags; and a jar of rendered goat fat. The last Meryam had prepared herself, first slaying and skinning the goat when the moons were dark, then rendering the fat in a pot set over a fire of white myrrh.

"Are you sure we're ready?" Ramahd asked.

"We'll never be sure."

Ramahd paused, wondering at the suddenness of the ritual after all the care they'd taken with the sapphire that now sat within the confines of the lead box. "What happened with Kiral?"

"Later, Ramahd." She turned the talon ring on her thumb and made a beckoning motion to Amaryllis.

As Amaryllis offered her arm to Meryam, Ramahd reached out and snatched her wrist. "What *happened* with Kiral?"

Amaryllis tried to free herself, but Ramahd refused to let go. Meryam's eyes flared, but she seemed as in control of herself as Ramahd was volatile. "You'll get no answers that way, Ramahd. Now release her."

When Ramahd didn't, his palm lit with pain. He tried to fight it, but it was too much. He released Amaryllis, but the pain continued, a burning that made his skin feel as though it were on fire.

"Amaryllis, leave us."

Rubbing her wrist, Amaryllis rose. "Yes, my queen." She left the room, but not before giving Ramahd a murderous glare.

When the doors had closed behind her, Meryam regarded Ramahd with placid eyes. His hand still shook with pain. It was now spreading to his wrist, and Meryam gave no sign that she was ready to release him.

"It's is my fault, really," she said. "I knew Guhldrathen would place a compulsion on you sooner or later. I've been meaning to ask your about it for some time, but . . . Well, we've had much to attend to."

Ramahd swallowed hard. A sweat had broken out all over his body, and he'd started to feel chill everywhere except his burning arm.

"You've done well with the sigils. We'll look at them soon. All of them. And we'll find a way to draw Guhldrathen to the city." She motioned to the lead box. "Soon we'll have power we've only dreamed about."

Though the pain was making it nearly impossible to think, Ramahd suddenly understood what Meryam meant to do, and why her meeting with Kiral meant so much to her.

"You've found Hamzakiir," Ramahd forced out through his gritted teeth. "Kiral gave you his location."

As suddenly as the pain had come, it was gone. Left in its wake was a deep itching sensation. As Ramahd began to viciously scratch his arm and chest and neck, Meryam nodded. "The end is near, Ramahd. With the power of the sapphire you've stolen, we'll break the city's seals. And then we'll draw Guhldrathen near and deliver what we've promised. He'll have Hamzakiir. And we'll have gained Kiral's undying loyalty."

"Where is he?"

"It isn't where Hamzakiir is now. It's where he will *be*. Kiral will meet him to discuss how the two of them would share power in the desert."

The itching had faded to a prickling sensation. "Why didn't you tell me?"

Meryam's skeletal face softened ever so slightly. "I value you, Ramahd, but for the good of the kingdom, I cannot allow myself to *need* you. You understand?"

It had been difficult to let go of who they'd once been. Too often he still thought of himself as Qaimir's ambassador, and Meryam his aide. "Forgive me," he said. "I wish to see us free from Guhldrathen's shadow." He motioned to the lead box on the table. "I'll help, if you'll still have me."

Meryam looked him over, eyes narrowing. Was there regret in her eyes? Ramahd couldn't tell. "Very well," she said, and they called Amaryllis back in.

She strode across the room, all but ignoring Ramahd, but when she sat once more her look dared him to seize her arm again.

"Don't think too harshly of him," Meryam said. "Had you the compulsion of an ehrekh upon you, I don't know that you'd fare as well." She sent an offhanded wave toward the lead box. "And now we have another to contend with."

Amaryllis's shoulders softened and her hands unclenched, but she said nothing to Ramahd. "You said it would be best to do it near high sun."

"So I did," Meryam replied. "Go ahead, Ramahd."

Ramahd nodded and undid the leather belts holding the lid closed and laid them down over the table.

Meryam stiffened. Amaryllis swallowed and licked her lips. Ramahd felt as if he were standing on the edge of a precipice.

"Go on," Meryam said. "Remove the lid. It will be weak for some time yet."

Ramahd did, revealing the sapphire he'd stolen from Brama. It lay on a bed of black velvet, and was wrapped, weblike, in old, dirty leather cord. It was one of the largest gems Ramahd had ever seen, even in the halls of Santrión, the royal palace of Qaimir. It was easily the size of a falcon's egg. The facets were hopelessly occluded with grime, all but the front face, which was not clear, exactly, nor as bad as the others.

"It acts as a doorway," Meryam had told him when they'd placed the gem into the box the first time, "a way for the ehrekh to see the world."

As then, Ramahd felt his gut twist just to look at it. Judging from the wary expression on Amaryllis's face, she felt the same. Meryam, however, stared not with the hunger she'd displayed days ago, nor with any sort of fear. She was intent, a blade poised to strike. It was the same sort of look she'd had in Viaroza as she'd tried day after day to break Hamzakiir's will, except now she seemed even more grim. It bordered on dispassion, which only went to show how determined she was to succeed. Her battles with Hamzakiir had tempered her, hardening a woman already harder than steel.

Meryam held out her hand to Amaryllis, who promptly offered her wrist to her queen. Meryam pierced Amaryllis's skin with her thumb ring and quickly sucked the blood that came from the wound. After several long moments, Meryam released her, and Amaryllis coiled a waiting bandage around her wrist.

Meryam had taken care to eat well these past few days so that she would be ready. She was not weakened as when she plied the red ways too often. Still, the change in her was remarkable. Her skin flushed. Her breathing lengthened. Her nostrils flared and her eyes became so dilated she looked inhuman. More than physical traits, however, was the sheer potency Ramahd could sense within her. Most, even the powerful, were but gusts of wind in their fleeting lives. Meryam was a gathering storm, ready to strike.

And she would need to be. What they were about to do was infinitely more dangerous than toying with Hamzakiir in the dungeon of Viaroza. Ramahd shuddered to think what the ehrekh might do if it managed to break free.

Death would be a mercy.

After steadying herself, Meryam used her ring to pierce her own wrist and Amaryllis picked up the long-nosed pliers. As Meryam held the dripping wound over the brass censer, she stared soberly at them both. "Quickly now. And whatever you do, do *not* touch the stone."

Ramahd and Amaryllis shared a look. They both nodded as Meryam's blood sizzled on the censer's hot surface. When Ramahd opened the lid, Amaryllis reached in with the pliers, pinched the jaws around the sapphire, and lifted it with the care of a jeweler preparing to tip molten silver into a mold. Ramahd lay two of the clean rags on his open palm, and Amaryllis set the sapphire there. Ramahd then grabbed the scissors and immediately set to work, snipping the leather cords around the sapphire one by one. They were stiff with age and smelled foul.

Soon the gemstone was free, and Ramahd rubbed the soot and grime from its faceted surfaces. It began to shine dully as he worked. Then it gleamed like no other stone he'd seen. It was perfect, a stone Alu himself might have shed in his tears during the making of the world.

Beyond its physical appearance was a presence he'd felt twice before, once when he and Meryam had used Brama, secreting themselves within his mind to find the caches of the Kings' life-giving elixirs, and again with Brama in the cellar.

It made Ramahd's stomach turn to feel its malevolence toward him, toward Meryam, but the ehrekh was weak. Something in the nature of lead was anathema to them. So there was no difficulty as he used another rag to rub the yellow goat salve over the sapphire, nor as he suspended it over the censer. Trails of Meryam's burning blood curled upward, slowly coating the facets, occluding them, trapping the ehrekh within.

Many had been killed when they'd attempted to steal this gem from Brama, making this ritual necessary. Meryam needed to make it subservient to *her*, not Brama or anyone else.

When all the facets were clouded, Meryam took a thick steel chain from around her neck. It had an oval-shaped locket, a device made to Meryam's exacting specifications with two inner filigreed doors that allowed one to see the sapphire, and two more solid doors that could be closed to conceal it. The exterior was a bright, polished silver. The interior, however, was a dull gray—lead, Ramahd knew. The ehrekh were devious. Every precaution was needed to keep Rümayesh confined.

Ramahd held the pliers over the opened locket and set the sapphire carefully within it. With a strange sort of tenderness, Meryam used a fresh rag to wipe away the gem's large, central facet. Then she clipped the inner doors closed, trapping the sapphire within, and replaced the small pin that would kept them secure.

The sapphire gleamed within the locket, a blue so deep it reminded him of the Austral Sea, sailing and staring down into water so welcoming he yearned to dive in. He blinked, trying to clear the vision from his eyes, but he couldn't. He leapt from the edge of the ship and dove into the sea. The chill of the water embraced him, dragged him down, down, until he went rigid from it.

He stared up at the sunlight spearing through the water. He stared below into the yawning darkness. *Come,* it beckoned. *Your daughter awaits. As does your wife.*

He blinked once more, and found himself staring into a different sort of darkness. He was on a blasted plain, standing on dark, glass-like rock. He'd returned to the desert, delivered here by Hamzakiir as an offering to one of Goezhen's children.

"Ramahd . . ."

The ehrekh had come. It had devoured King Aldouan here, in this very place. Later, Meryam had leaned over her father's dead form, touched her forehead to his. *I'm sorry,* she'd whispered. *I'm sorry, I'm sorry, I'm sorry.*

"Ramahd."

They'd left after Ramahd had promised Çeda to the ehrekh if they didn't deliver Hamzakiir. They'd headed into the desert, making their way toward Sharakhai. They swam in an oasis pool, the water warm as bathwater. *I've done a terrible thing, Ramahd.* She'd fallen into his arms, sobbing. They'd held one another. Made love beneath the stars.

"Ramahd!"

He heard a metallic click, and realized Meryam was snapping her fingers before his eyes. Slowly, the vision of the desert faded—*I've done a terrible thing*—and the room in the Qaimiri embassy house resolved from the fog. Left in its wake was a manic fear. Some small remnant of the ehrekh's desperation, Ramahd knew.

"Do you see now?" Meryam said, gripping the locket so tightly her knuckles had turned white. The outer doors were closed, cutting off the power of the gem. "Every step from this point forward must be taken with the greatest care."

"Of course." Ramahd shook his head, though whether it was to emphasize his point or clear his head, he wasn't sure. "Of course you're right. Forgive me." When Ramahd had returned with the gem two weeks before, Rümayesh had been greatly weakened by Meryam's attack. She would return to power soon if left untouched, but time surrounded by lead would be sufficient to render the ehrekh all but powerless. They'd both agreed to keep Rümayesh in the box for two weeks anyway. But Mighty Alu, the sheer power in that creature. "I never realized how easy it would be to fall into her trap."

"Fear not. Her anger is lending her strength, but it will soon burn itself out. We've done well this day."

"And now?" Amaryllis asked.

"Now?" Meryam lifted the locket and let it swing before her eyes. "Now comes the first test of the ehrekh's power."

Chapter 35

"RIDE ABOARD HER SHIP," Shal'alara told Emre as Tribe Kadri prepared to sail for Onur's camp.

"What?" Emre shot a look toward the Malasani dhow, where Haddad was seeing to her crew's preparations, while her hulk of a guardsman, Zakkar, stood beside the mainmast, still as stone. *"Why?"*

"Yerinde's honeyed lips, Emre, you can't tell me you haven't seen her looks." When Emre continued to stare, confused, Shal'alara's knowing smile turned to one of surprise that bordered on outrage. "She can't take her eyes off you."

Emre tried to recover himself by remaining silent. *Can't take her eyes off me?*

"Men," Shal'alara said, and shoved him toward Haddad's dhow, *Calamity's Reign*. "Go. Find out more about her king's plans. It's something Macide will want to know. And if things have to happen between the sheets before she talks"—she winked—"I won't be the one to tell."

"I wouldn't—"

But Shal'alara was already walking away.

Emre felt the fool as Shal'alara's biting laugh cut above the sounds of ships preparing to sail, and twice the fool as he turned and realized Haddad had seen the whole exchange. She turned away quickly but, gods curse him, he'd seen her hiding a smile. He just hoped Shal'alara hadn't been speaking loud enough for her to hear.

"You look like you've been sentenced to hang," Haddad called down from the deck when he drew near.

He felt his face redden. "Yes, well . . . I wonder if there might be room for one more."

Haddad looked as if she were about to say something biting, but then her look softened, and she shrugged. "Why not?"

After a moment's pause, Emre headed up *Calamity*'s gangplank. Haddad largely ignored him. The crew, however, sent him furtive looks, and Zakkar watched him like he wanted to draw his scimitar and see how far he could make Emre's head sail.

Soon they were headed east. Emre was standing amidships when Haddad broke away from her duties and joined him. "Is it true you saved Macide and the others?"

Emre shrugged. "I had a hand in it."

She laughed loudly, head tilted back like a hyena. "More than a hand if even half of what I've heard is true."

"Forgive me, but could you tell that stone-faced idiot to stop staring at me before I cut him a new smile?"

Haddad turned, confused. Zakkar was still watching from his spot at the mainmast, where he'd been standing since Emre had first spotted him. "Ah. Zakkar does forget his manners at times. Go below," she told the big man.

Zakkar obeyed. His footsteps thudded against the deck and, by the gods, Emre *felt* it beneath his feet.

When he was gone, Haddad said, "Better?"

"Better. Now, what was it *they* were saying about me?"

"Your own lord said that twice you sniffed out betrayal before it happened. Shal'alara said you stole Macide's sword and shattered the chains across the harbor so you could all escape. Frail Lemi said you fought a dozen Maidens before fleeing on one of the Kings' own ships to meet Macide in the desert and return his sword to him."

And now it was Emre's turn to laugh. "And you believe them?"

"Of course not. But the truth lies in there somewhere, no?"

Emre waggled his head. "Some small amount, I suppose. What of you? I've heard tell you saved your Mad King from a terrible decision several years ago."

He'd said Mad King to provoke, but Haddad merely raised one eyebrow. "Mad is it?"

"As an old, drunken goat."

She tilted her head, as if granting him the point, but with an expression that made it clear he'd sparked a painful memory. "The tale has grown in the telling."

"You prevented a war was how I heard it." After her reaction, Emre was suddenly eager to talk about something other than the Mad King of Malasan, but he pressed anyway. If the thirteenth tribe was to survive, they needed to know more about their neighbors.

Apparently Haddad's own caravan had delivered a shipment of dates to King Surrahdi's palace, and he'd taken offense to the quality. He'd gotten it into his head that the purveyor had meant it as an insult to Surrahdi himself. That very day he'd summoned a thousand of his best cavalry and ridden well into Sharakhai's territory, to the caravanserai of Ashdankaat. Haddad, knowing well what Sharakhai's response would be should her king attack, had sailed back there herself and managed to talk Surrahdi down before blood was shed.

"Everyone in the east is sure the king will march once more," Emre continued. "All it will take is for him to stumble across a patch of sand to remind him that he still wants to conquer the Great Shangazi."

"I'll share with you a secret, Emre Aykan'ava. Few yet know it, but the Mad King of Malasan is dead. He passed only weeks ago. His son, Emir, now sits the throne in Samaril."

News, indeed, Emre thought. "How did he die?"

"Rumors are flying that Emir killed him, though if so, it wouldn't have been for his own sake. Surrahdi was in terrible pain these past many years. Killing him would have been a mercy. I think those rumors are just rumors, though. Emir would never have done that to his own father. I suspect it was his ill humors that finally took him."

"The dunes do shift," Emre said.

"Grinding bones until all has been forgotten. Isn't that what they say?"

"It is." Emre watched as two crewmen began oiling the deck nearby. "What now? Does King Emir covet the desert as his father once did?"

"How could he?" she asked with a wry smile. "In the desert, none can oppose the will of the Sharakhani Kings. All know this."

Not the Malasani, Emre thought, *whose kings are nothing if not bold.*

The tribe sailed on and days passed. Emre didn't always remain on *Calamity's Reign*, but he found himself sailing on it more often than he would have thought. He'd been right about Haddad. She was a conniving woman, but after hearing her tales of navigating favor among the desert tribes, and the auction blocks of caravanserais, he developed a grudging respect for her. One didn't become a caravan master without the ability to bargain shrewdly. That her king had turned that to his advantage was no real surprise.

On their twelfth day out from the meeting with Macide, Mihir's young cousin, Aríz, sent up their falcon, and this time it began circling in the distance. By evening, they saw the masts of Onur's tribe on the horizon, and by sunset they were drawing near. They stopped well short of the large camp, which was gathered around a set of oases. A dozen small water holes were revealed with trees and desert ferns huddled close around them. Beyond the pools, Onur's ships and tents were set in a defensive ring. All flew a pennant depicting Onur's new sign: a black spear over a field of amber. There were also other pennants flying on various ships and tents. The red design of Tribe Masal were the most common, but there were a few sporting the river design of Tribe Kenan and even one showing the white tree of Tribe Halarijan.

From the Black Spear tents, a dozen warriors, men and women both, came to meet the Kadri ships. Mihir spoke with Onur's vizira, a hardened woman named Sibyl, and soon learned that Onur was not in camp.

"Where has he gone?" Mihir asked.

"He will return in a day, perhaps two. We have much to do before then, in any case."

"I didn't ask when he would return," Mihir pressed. "I asked where he's gone."

Sibyl sniffed and swept her gaze over the entire Kadri assemblage, as if the words she was about to speak were not only for Mihir, but all of them. "Onur goes where he will."

Now that Tribe Masal had bowed to Onur's will, she said, their fleet was preparing to attack the nearby caravanserai of Tiazet, and much of the camp's activities were dedicated to it. The crews trained relentlessly, launching grapnels, firing ballistae, some practicing ship-to-ship raids. Others drilled with spears and swords and shields, units moving in well-oiled concert. Tribe Kadri was expected to play its part. Sybil began by demanding that Mihir break his ships into three groups, that they might drill with others.

"As soon as I speak to Onur."

"You're already speaking to him," Sibyl replied easily. "Until our lord returns, *I* am his voice."

"My ships are my own," Mihir replied, "and they will drill together."

"Your ships are *Onur's* and you will drill with those you'll fight beside." Sibyl paused, regarding Mihir as she might a molding lemon that threatened to ruin the bushel. "Are you with us, Mihir Halim'ava of the Burning Hands, or are you not?"

Emre hoped Mihir would say no, that he would leave and join hands with the thirteenth tribe, but he already knew Mihir wouldn't. He had committed himself, and there was little to be done until Onur returned.

"Tribe Kadri is with you," Mihir replied to Sibyl.

Emre nearly took out the knife Macide had given him—it was hidden inside his thawb—but Macide had been very clear that he should wait for the perfect time, when Mihir would be most open to it. If Sibyl's tyrannical behavior was any indication of how the Burning Hands would be treated under Onur's rule, waiting would only help Emre's cause.

The days that followed were strange. Tribe Kadri, her ships and her people, were ordered to remain well away from the center of the camp. Onur's tribe, Salmük, was camped around the watering holes, which no one outside Tribe Salmük was allowed to visit. Water was always brought *to* the Kadri ships.

Every night, screaming came from Onur's camp, making life more difficult. "Tribe Masal was taken by force," Sibyl told them when Mihir asked of it. "There were bound to be those who refused to recognize Onur as their shaikh. But do not worry. Those who resist are fewer each day, and soon we will sail united."

On their third night, Shal'alara returned to Mihir's ship with a grim expression. "Beril is dead," she said when they were safely in the hold.

Mihir's expressive eyes filled with worry. "How?"

"Some knew she was blood of our blood. After Çedamihn escaped, Onur suspected Beril of treachery. One night, a few weeks before we arrived, she and nine others were bound and taken away."

"Taken where?" Emre asked.

"No one knows." Shal'alara turned to Mihir. "But who can doubt they were given the knife? Or worse, given to Onur to feed his monstrous appetites."

"Someone must know the truth," Mihir said.

"Of course, but they'll never tell *me*. Nor you. Nor anyone from Tribe Kadri. I was lucky to learn this much. Sibyl saw me returning from their camp after I'd heard the news. Gave me a look with those dead eyes of hers." Shal'alara was no wilting flower, and yet a violent shiver rattled up her frame. "She chills me to the bone, that one. She considers herself one of Onur's *daughters*, as they're being called now. Part vizira, part shaikh, part Blade Maiden."

Emre couldn't take it any longer. "Will you not reconsider, Shaikh Mihir? The gods have shined upon you. You still have command of your people. Onur is missing. We might yet leave without suffering his wrath."

For a moment, Emre thought he'd won him over, but Mihir hardened and refused to listen to reason. "Tribe Kadri does not run from conflict. I will speak with Onur." When Emre made to speak again, Mihir spoke over him. "Do not press me. I've allowed you here as a favor to your lord, but I will brook no challenge to my commands."

On their fourth day at the oasis, Sibyl came to their camp with a dozen warriors in her wake. They would make for Tiazet in the morning.

"Not a single sail of Tribe Kadri will be hoisted before I've spoken with Shaikh Onur," Mihir protested.

"He will speak to you after the battle," Sibyl replied, and strode away.

Mihir was left with an impossible choice. Shout at Sibyl's retreating form and be seen as a man not worth listening to, or say nothing and be seen by his own tribe as weak. With grim determination he strode toward her, but stopped when the warriors flanking her drew the bows on their backs and nocked arrows. They hadn't drawn the strings, but they didn't need to.

"None of my ships will sail for Tiazet before I speak to Onur."

At this, Sibyl turned. She was a tall woman. A grim woman. But at Mihir's words, a wide smile broke across her face. "Some say we all dig our own graves. There's truth in those words, I think, but I hope you won't dig yours so soon, Mihir. We need you. And if what your herald told us is true, *you* need *us*. Assuming, that is, you still wish to—how did your emissary put it?—drive a knife through the black heart of Sharakhai."

Without waiting for a response, she left. Her warriors backed away, bows at the ready, and then turned to follow. Mihir looked ready to protest, but just then a horn sounded from the far side of the camp.

In moments, the entire mood of the camp changed. There was little enough joy to be found here, but now, men, women, children, all became tight, their eyes nervous as they glanced eastward, where a skiff was now approaching.

It's now or never, Emre said to himself. Approaching Mihir, he pulled out the kenshar Macide had given him and held it out, hilt first. Mihir stared down at the knife, confusion plain in his eyes. As he accepted the knife from Emre, however, his face lit in a mixture of wonder and confusion and surprise, even a bit of anger.

Haddad, standing nearby, pointed at the knife. "What is this?"

"It is my brother's knife," Mihir said breathlessly. "But how did you come by it?"

"Macide tells me Anish was a good man. Loyal to his last," Emre replied.

"He's dead?"

Emre nodded and chose his next words carefully. "You've heard, no doubt, of the abduction of the collegia scholars over winter. It was a terrible blow to the Kings, and after it, as a show of power, they gathered up many sacrificial lambs. Anish was one of those taken."

Haddad's eyes flitted between Emre and Mihir. "I don't understand."

"Anish left for Sharakhai after my mother died." Mihir pulled the kenshar from its sheath and examined the blade with a look Emre could only describe as reverent. "He refused to listen to my father, who urged us to live in peace with the Kings of Sharakhai. He took up with the Moonless Host in the city. I'd thought him dead many times, but news always came that he was still alive."

"He was chosen at random," Emre said. "Locked in a cage like an animal. His eyes put out. Laurel leaves stuffed in his eyes and mouth. His hands were lashed to the bars of a cage to keep him propped up, as if begging for release. He was paraded through all of Sharakhai, then brought to the southern harbor where he and the others were hung from a tower, the leaves fluttering down like plucked feathers." Emre pointed at the knife, allowing any sense of mercy to leech from his voice. "Anish did not die in battle. He did not die fighting the Kings. He died because the Kings wanted to make an example of him. He was as subject to their cruelties as you will be should you clasp hands with Onur."

Mihir's eyes were for the kenshar alone. Near the center of the camp, among the many ships anchored there, the skiff had stopped. A giant of a man was now climbing over the side. Onur. Emre had only seen him a few times before, and always from a distance. He'd never realized how massive the man was.

"You see Onur as an opportunity," Emre pressed on. "I don't blame you, but it is a mirage. You cannot be blinded by his promises. Nor can you listen to a Malasani king, who sends his servant to the desert with sweet promises even as she gathers information about you and the rest of the eastern tribes." Haddad's eyes widened in anger, but Emre ignored her. "Join the Al'Afwa Khadar. Together we can settle an injustice that is centuries overdue."

"My shaikh," Haddad said. "What has the Moonless Host ever done for you? They took your brother. They failed to protect him when the Kings came for him. And now, in recompense, they give you his *kenshar*? I may be new to the ways of the desert, but that seems a poor bargain to me. The Kings are cruel, yes, but you reached out to Onur for a reason." She waved dramatically behind her toward her ship. "Tell me it isn't so. Tell me you no longer wish to ally yourself with Onur, and I will board the *Calamity* now and sail for Malasan. But we both know you can *use* Onur. You can pit him against Sharakhai, and the desert will be better for it."

"Better for Malasan, you mean," Emre said.

Haddad shrugged. "Is it so wrong for us to want better men to deal with in Sharakhai? We have no designs on the desert. We only want peace."

Emre laughed. "And you're willing to pay for it with the blood of Mihir's tribe!"

"You'd rather we invade?"

"Enough," Mihir said. He turned coolly to Emre and lifted the point of the knife to Emre's chin.

Emre felt its bite, but he didn't shy from the pain.

"Why would you have kept this from me until now?"

Emre told him the truth. "Macide wanted you to have it before you spoke with Onur."

Mihir gripped the hair at the back of Emre's head and shook him roughly. *"Why?"*

"So you would see him for what he truly is. He *chose* your brother, Shaikh Mihir. Dozens and dozens were gathered up by the Silver Spears, but Onur chose whose throats would be slit, whose mouths would be stuffed doll-like with leaves before being strapped inside cages and paraded about the city. He chose those who were hung from a tower like so many crows."

Emre thought Mihir would slit his throat and be done with it—such was the anger in his eyes—but when he shoved Emre away and turned to look upon Onur, Emre knew he'd taken the bait.

Haddad saw it, too. "Mihir—" she began.

He ignored her and strode forward, backed by a dozen warriors from his tribe. Onur lumbered over the sand to meet him, Sibyl and the rest of Onur's retinue following. Onur came to a halt several paces away. Gods the man was big. He towered over Mihir, staring down at him with a hungry sort of look. He lifted one hand and cracked a knuckle. In his other hand he gripped something. A stone, perhaps. It glinted and had a bright orange surface.

"Well met," Onur said in a deep, gravelly voice that sounded anything but pleased.

Mihir lifted the knife. "This is the knife of my brother, Anish Halim'ava al Kadri, a son of the Burning Hands. He was taken by the Spears in Sharakhai and was paraded, naked, before the entire city."

Onur looked Mihir up and down in a way he hadn't when he'd first arrived. He did not look beyond Mihir to the people of Tribe Kadri, but Emre had the sense he was now more aware of them than he had been a moment ago. "What of it?"

"You chose those who were slaughtered."

"Is this why you've brought your entire tribe? To ask me senseless questions?"

"Did you choose them?"

"Who told you this story?"

Mihir gripped the knife so hard his arm shook. "Did you *choose* them?"

Onur all but ignored Mihir as he looked to the warriors behind Mihir. He took in Haddad, Shal'alara, and Emre. His gaze dropped until his eyes were lingering on Emre's hands. They had no orange tattoos, as tribe Kadri did. He took in Shal'alara's hands as well, then lifted his gaze and sneered at Mihir. "Would you expect anything different? Would you not punish those who killed the children of your tribe?"

"Anish was not part of the attack on the collegia."

"Even so."

Mihir took a step forward, still gripping the knife as if it were his last link to sanity. "You've not answered my question."

Onur spat on the sand between them. "I not only chose them, I chose the example to be made as well. Sharakhai needed to learn what it means to test the might of the Kings. It's a lesson they still need, a lesson I'll administer when I sit the throne, the one throne, of Sharakhai. I stood before those my Spears had gathered up, the scum of the west end, the dross from the forgotten harbor. I selected each. I selected the method of their death. I selected the route they would take through the city. I even killed a few myself. Perhaps your brother was one of them."

For a moment, all was silence. Eyes shifted between Mihir and Onur. Mihir swallowed, the muscles along his neck taut, the shade from the sun casting them in stark relief.

And then he was flying over the sand toward Onur.

Chapter 36

ÇEDA CROUCHED LOW within the blooming fields, three leagues north of Sharakhai. Concealed by the thorny branches of the adichara trees, she was little more than a darker patch of black beneath the shade of the twisted trees. The dunes rolled southward before her under the heat of a relentless sun. Over those dunes, a horse and rider approached. For a long while, the wavering heat concealed all details, but as the rider came steadily nearer, she resolved into a Blade Maiden riding a tall akhala with a brass coat and fetlocks the color of wrought iron. Çeda recognized Melis.

Seven days had passed since Beht Ihman and Çeda's escape from the House of Kings. Dardzada thought this meeting a fool's errand, but Çeda would not be swayed. He didn't know Melis as Çeda did. She was loyal to the Kings, but her heart tired of the conflict. She wanted a way out of the endless war. She'd said as much to Çeda. If Melis wouldn't accept the truth, no one would.

Focusing on the trees around her, Çeda flexed her right hand. Pain came with the movement, and with it a rapidly expanding awareness of the adichara and the creatures that slept among their roots. *Come, brothers and sisters.* Many of the asirim were too deep in slumber to heed her call. Others were awake but savage as wounded animals. She felt pity for them, but had no use for them here; she needed a soul who could share her story. So she flexed her hand again and reached farther, searching carefully for one that was aware, that understood the asirim's plight.

The wind picked up, making the thorny branches rattle. To her right, a black snake with bright yellow stripes slid away and was lost to the deeper shadows. *Come,* she called, calming her mind. *Today could change all our lives.*

Still there were none, and Melis was riding closer.

She considered taking an adichara petal, but quickly rejected the idea. Patience was needed here, not force or desperation. At last she felt a child. A huddled, angry soul. Children were rare among the asirim, and Çeda had never spoken with one, so she took care as she reached for the girl. *Will you tell me your tale?*

She seemed fearful, perhaps of Çeda. Perhaps of Melis. But something like grudging assent came from her.

Then gather your courage and listen as I speak with this woman.

No woman, the child corrected. *A Blade Maiden.*

A woman, like me.

When Melis was several hundred yards from where Çeda hid, she pulled on her reins and slipped down to the sand. She walked lazily, shading her eyes, peering into the adichara as she went. Çeda waited, watching the horizon closely for signs of other Maidens or Silver Spears.

Coming to a stop some distance from Çeda, Melis whistled the Maiden's call for *attend me.* Ignoring her for the moment, Çeda crept along a path in the blooming fields to its outer edge, where she scanned the horizon for signs of anyone hoping to catch her unawares. This was a tricky gamble. The very nature of the blooming fields, which were set in a great ring around the city, meant she couldn't watch every angle of approach. But she'd chosen a time near enough to nightfall that if she sensed anything amiss, she could hide in the groves until the sun had set and then make her escape in her skiff, which was hidden a half-league deeper into the desert.

Dardzada had wanted to join her here. In fact, after a terrible quarrel, he'd insisted on it, which was precisely why she'd left a note and slipped away in the dark of the night. She'd made a vow to Melis that she would come alone. Everything depended on her believing she could trust Çeda.

Seeing nothing amiss beyond the grove, she returned to the inner ring, stepped out from the shelter of the twisted trees, and headed over the stony ground toward Melis.

Melis turned and walked toward her, her horse plodding behind.

"That's far enough," Çeda said when she was ten paces away.

Melis came to a halt and dropped the reins. Countless nicks could be seen in the leather of her Maiden's dress. She wore her turban, but the veil hung down along her front, revealing her broad, freckled face. She betrayed no emotion as she scanned the adichara behind Çeda.

"I'm alone," Çeda said.

Melis ignored her, continuing to peer through the trees until she was satisfied. Then she looked Çeda up and down. "They're turning the city upside down trying to find you."

"I know."

"You've done me no favors. I'll be killed if the Kings learn of this meeting."

"I know."

"Then know this as well, Çedamihn Ahyanesh'ala. I've come not for you. I've come because you claimed you know a way for us to move beyond the constant bloodshed."

"Melis, I—" Çeda began. She'd practiced this speech a hundred times, yet no matter how she arranged the words, they always sounded leaden and unconvincing. There was nothing for it now, though. "The asirim are not holy warriors, as the Kings would have you believe. They are the remains of the thirteenth tribe, sacrificed for the Kings. Beht Ihman was a tragedy, an event that took my people"—she waved toward the adichara—"and turned them into slaves."

"You admit it, then? That you are part of the Moonless Host?"

"No. I'm a member of the thirteenth tribe."

"There is no such thing as the thirteenth tribe. Only a band of fanatics hoping to overthrow the Kings."

"No. The tribe is real. Many would proudly declare themselves scarabs, but many others only want peace and to have their birthright restored."

Melis seemed to compose herself. "Çeda, I know the west end tells such stories to their children. The thirteenth tribe is at best a fanciful tale to justify bloodthirsty acts. At worst, it's a cynical lie they use to fill their ranks."

"No. It's the Kings who have been lying. They've hidden what they've done from the beginning."

Melis's face had turned to one of sufferance, as if she were saddened by Çeda's naiveté. "If what you're saying is true, why has it only now come to light? Why wouldn't the truth have been handed down for generations?"

"Because the Kings suppressed it! They won the war, Melis. They had the power of the gods behind them."

"Because their cause was just."

"Because the gods are cruel and bloodthirsty!"

"If you're only here to repeat the Moonless Host's propaganda—"

"It isn't propaganda, Melis. It's *true*. The lost tribe lives."

"Çeda—"

"No"—Çeda clasped her hands before her and shook them—"*please* listen to me. I can *prove* it. I've felt the truth from the asirim themselves. I've felt their stories through our bond."

Melis frowned. "What do you mean?"

"They still yearn for the lives they once led. They still dream. They want freedom for their descendants, me and the rest of the thirteenth tribe."

"I've been bonding with them for well over a decade, and I've felt no *dreams*. I've felt nothing save anger for the enemies of the Kings."

"Of course there's anger, but it's anger over their imprisonment. Anger over what's happened to them." Before Melis could say more, Çeda went on. "That's why I've asked you here. Let me *show* you, Melis. Let me share their dreams with you."

"I told you, I've felt nothing from them."

"Of course not. They're forbidden from sharing them with you, but not with me." She walked forward until the two of them were near, then held her right hand out for Melis to take. When she didn't, Çeda took another step.

Melis stood like stone, almost fearful of taking Çeda's hand. "This is blasphemy."

"Don't you want to know the truth?"

"I *know* the truth."

But they both heard the uncertainty in her voice. Melis's gaze swept over the adichara, though it seemed to Çeda as if she were staring inwardly, searching for guidance. In the end, she steeled herself and gripped Çeda's hand.

The moment she did, Çeda reached out to the asir she'd touched earlier and felt the same reticence as earlier. *All is well,* Çeda said. *Share your tale, and through me, show the Maidens what became of the thirteenth tribe.*

Çeda felt the desert dissolve away until she was standing beside a girl with long curly hair. She stood upon a wall with thousands of others, soldiers, craftsmen, children, many wounded and bloodied, their eyes filled with worry. As one, they looked out over the desert, where hundreds of ships had gathered, where the might of the desert tribes was amassed for war. They stood innumerable, the soldiers of the desert tribes, a veil of spears before the might of the city and its Kings.

The girl's terror was unbearable. She cried as she looked out over the gathered host, wondering if today was the day they would take the city. Only last night they'd broken through the walls in two places. The valor of the city's guard had pushed them back, but all knew it wouldn't last much longer. They couldn't hope to stand against so many.

The fear within the girl ebbed as Kiral, King of Kings, strode from the city's gates over the paved road beyond. He wore a shining helm, bright scale armor, and a white, knee-length surcoat beneath. Five from his personal guard accompanied him. When they came to a stop, the front line of the host parted and a man marched forward. Suad. The Scourge of Sharakhai. The shaikh who had somehow united all twelve tribes.

Unlike Kiral, Suad came alone, a bold statement: *Not one of us fears you.*

Suad's host was utterly silent. The people of the city standing along the wall watched breathlessly as Kiral and Suad spoke. The sun shifted in the sky by the time Kiral broke away in anger and marched toward the city gates. Suad remained, watching Kiral and his guardsmen retreat, hands clasped behind his back as if eminently pleased. Only when the gates had boomed shut did the shaikh turn and stride back to the gathered host.

Suad said something as the soldiers made way for him. A great roar picked up around him, then spread, moving farther and farther along the line, the desert warriors thrust their spears skyward and ululated until the sound of it shook the foundations of the city. It continued for hours, ebbing at times, then returning in a rush. Only when the sun set did silence return, but that made it worse, as if the lord of all things was preparing to break down the city gates himself, the gathered host ready to sweep in behind him.

The scene faded. The girl now stood on a plateau high above the city. Sharakhai lay below. Fires were sprinkled throughout the city. The roar of battle still echoed through the streets, sounding distant and dreamlike from the mount of Tauriyat.

She stood now with many others, from all twelve tribes. Only a short distance away, the Kings were arrayed before six numinous figures. The gods themselves had come at the behest of the Kings. Tulathan, her silver skin resplendent in the moonlit night. Rhia, surveying all who had gathered. Mischievous Bakhi and dour Thaash and winsome Yerinde. And Goezhen, his twin tails lashing as he stalked over the earth behind the other gods. Their very presence meant they believed in Sharakhai. They would save it.

Pride swelled inside the girl. To have been born here, to have lived in the city the gods themselves claimed as their own. It drove away the fear that had been building since the tribes had arrived; it made her wish there was a way she might help.

The sounds of battle diminished, and then vanished altogether. The Kings spoke with the gods for a long while. They granted the Kings their wondrous gifts. Kiral an immaculate sword, Sukru a black whip, Mesut a golden band with a beautiful stone of jet. Each came with a kiss from Tulathan herself. And then they called for volunteers.

The girl's father went first. Her brother next. She was not far behind. She followed in their footsteps, knowing she would be helping to save the city, knowing she and the rest would drive the gathered soldiers away from Sharakhai and back into the desert where they would be hounded for their offenses. She went gladly, her heart singing, and when Goezhen himself kissed her on the lips, and she felt the change coming over her, she rejoiced.

She was changed. She became one with the desert, a holy warrior, a blade the Kings themselves would wield until the final days of the world. She went from the mount, bounding down the slope with glee in her heart. Dozens, hundreds, of others ran by her side, howling the pride that could not be kept within them. To the walls they went, then through the city gates like birds from a cage.

Ahead, the desert soldiers stood, spears arrayed. She could already taste their fear. She could feel their growing knowledge that the tide had turned against them. They were many, but that would not save them.

She bayed like a jackal as she leapt among the enemy. Then all around her was madness.

Çeda lay against the sand. She started, confused by the wall of soldiers marching toward her. A moment later she realized it was only the adichara trees, their branches slowly churning as they did on Beht Zha'ir. It was so strange she hardly knew what to think. Not once had she seen them move in sunlight.

She turned, the emptiness of the desert striking her. She had returned from the asir's vision. Except . . .

"It's wrong," she said.

Melis, who was on her hands and knees a few paces away, lifted her head and regarded Çeda with an angry look. "Not wrong. It was the truth, seen with your own eyes."

"No," Çeda said, coming to a stand. "There's something wrong. That wasn't how it happened."

Melis stood as well. "It was, Çeda. It was exactly this way." She drew her sword. "The only question is whether you knew it."

Melis's eyes looked over Çeda's shoulder. Çeda turned and saw warriors in black dresses walking through the gaps in the adichara. Sümeya first, followed by Kameyl. Yndris came last, walking with a noticeable limp. Çeda was struggling to understand what had happened. Melis had betrayed her. That much was clear.

But the asir . . . How could she have remembered the story in that way? It wasn't right. It couldn't be right.

A man followed the women through the gap in the trees, and a knot formed in Çeda's throat. King Husamettín, tall and imposing, wore a striped blue keffiyeh and a golden agal across his brow. A black aba, a sleeveless cloak, covered a white tunic and wide cloth belt. In his right hand he held his two-handed shamshir, Night's Kiss. Like the Maidens' shamshirs, the length of the blade was made from ebon steel, but it drew light in, making it look like a piece of the night sky hungry to devour the day.

Çeda heard Dardzada's words. *Folly. Folly. This was all folly.*

They fanned out before her. Yndris had several ragged scars across her lips and chin that marred her otherwise pretty face. Kameyl's face showed pockmarks from the acid the shamblers had sprayed over her in Ishmantep. As the Maidens moved to circle behind Çeda, cutting off any hope of escape,

Husamettín came to a stop a few paces from her. His eyes were dark and forbidding, his posture ready for anything.

"Give me your sword," he said.

In reply, Çeda drew River's Daughter. The Maidens all drew their ebon blades in response. Yndris, standing to Çeda's right, was the only one who advanced.

"No!" Husamettín's voice boomed.

Yndris kept her eyes on Çeda, but she lowered her sword and took a half step back.

Çeda thought of charging Husamettín now, hoping to take him down before the others could react, but she sensed he was hoping for it, so she remained, rooted where she was.

Husamettín feinted with his sword, testing her reactions. It buzzed in the dry desert air. "The gods as my witness I thought you would cower in the desert, protected by your newfound allies. I said as much to the other Kings, but Cahil had the right of it. He said that ere spring returned to the Shangazi you would return to the city to spread your lies. However much a traitor you might be, I said you were wiser than that." His sword swayed, thrumming low. "But here you are to prove me wrong."

"I came to show everyone the shame you brought upon yourself and the city when you agreed to sacrifice us."

"Shut your foul mouth," Yndris said, advancing.

But again Husamettín forestalled her and focused on Çeda. "Your claims are sad echoes of the lies aped endlessly by the Moonless Host. I suppose I shouldn't be surprised, but I would have thought you, one who's seen the truth with her own eyes, would have changed your mind by now."

Çeda could sense the asirim all around her. She'd never felt them like this: *muted*, muffled somehow, including the girl who had given Çeda and Melis such a powerful vision of the past.

"*You* did it," Çeda realized. "You were the author of that girl's tale." She turned to Melis. "Don't you see? He forced that story on the asir so you would believe their lies."

"What she saw," Husamettín said before Melis could respond, "was the cold, simple truth, a truth that all in the Moonless Host have willfully ignored for generations in their quest for power."

"I tell you," Çeda said to them all, "I've seen their stories. I've *felt* them. The asir Yndris beheaded. And Havva, the one who so enraged me that I attacked Yndris in revenge." Yndris's face turned red, but she remained silent. "Kerim, who came with us to Ishmantep. Sehid-Alaz, their King!"

Çeda turned to them all, even Yndris, praying they would hear her words. But to a woman they stared back with faces of stone, while Husamettín looked on with a chilling mix of satisfaction and joy, pleasure at yet another avenue of truth having crumbled. "One day the desert will see your shame," Çeda said.

Husamettín advanced, Night's Kiss held at the ready. "There is much in my life to be ashamed of, Çedamihn Ahyanesh'ala, but not this."

Çeda met his first swing with River's Daughter. She controlled her swings, controlled her breathing, controlled her heart. She had long since felt Husamettín's heartbeat, as well as the Maidens', but the moment she tried to use it against him, he sidestepped her. Again and again she tried, but he was like a silverscale slipping through water. He seemed content not to press that advantage against her, though.

For aching minutes, the sound of their swordplay filled the air. They moved easily over the sand, the Maidens retreating to give them space to fight, but always keeping themselves between Çeda and the adichara trees, cutting off any possible escape.

She rained blow after blow on Husamettín's defenses, but he blocked them all, moving with the power, speed, and agility she'd grown accustomed to seeing from him during morning prayers in the House of Maidens. Then he unleashed a blinding series of moves, each of which struck River's Daughter harder. The last left him with an opening that he used to bring his blade flat against the side of her head.

She remembered tilting sideways, her turban flying free. She remembered trying to right herself, her body refusing to comply. Then she struck the sand, and the desert went dark.

Chapter 37

ÇEDA WOKE TO DARKNESS and the smell of mold. She lay on cold stone. Somewhere, water dripped. It tapped like rainwater from a roof long after the storm had passed. Her limbs numb and tingling, she rolled over and saw a dim circle of light, little more than a puff of stardust against the utter blackness. Along the floor was a thin line of similar light. *A door,* she realized, with light shining through a window and a gap below.

She wanted to investigate, but oh how her body ached, especially her head, which felt like a quarry stone being hammered to pieces, blow after merciless blow.

Husamettín. The desert.

It all returned in a rush, along with a conviction that Melis would never believe her. Nor Sümeya nor Kameyl nor any other Maiden. All the tales the asirim had shared with her would now be seen as lies.

A short while later, Çeda felt more than heard a presence. She tried to reach out for a heartbeat, but the pain in her head spiked so badly that for a while she could do nothing but lie there and hold her head to keep it from bursting. When the pain had passed, she lifted her head and stared at the round window. There were two stripes of black where the bars would surely be. Was it darker than before? She couldn't tell.

"Hello?" she called weakly.

There was no reply, and soon she was sure she'd been mistaken.

More time passed, and then a clink sounded in the darkness. She heard a scuffing outside the cell door, and then a soft glow flooded the hallway outside, coming from the left. A jingling of keys came nearer. As did heavy footsteps. The yellow light grew, then stabbed harshly through the window. Keys clinked, the door swung open, and light came crashing into the room, bringing with it pain and an unwelcome image of molten glass being doused in water.

"Leave us," came a deep voice. Husamettín's.

The gaoler's footsteps shuffled away. When Çeda cracked her eyes open she saw Husamettín sitting on a bench along the far wall near the door. The lantern was near his feet. It seemed strange to her that the door remained open.

Husamettín was staring at her as if she were an oddity, a new prisoner he hadn't realized was here. From somewhere inside his black khalat he retrieved a flask wrapped in leather. He unscrewed the cap and held it out to her. "It will help with your pain." When she made no move to take it, he shrugged and tipped his head back, the liquor gurgling as it poured from the flask's mouth into his. He bared his teeth while swallowing it.

"I considered ending your life in the desert," he said, screwing the cap back on and stuffing the flask inside his clothes.

"Why—" Çeda paused as a new wave of pain and nausea overcame her. She spoke more softly. "Why didn't you?"

"Because there are things I wish to know. And because, once I'm satisfied, there is the matter of justice to consider."

Çeda pushed herself onto her hands and knees, refusing to lie before this man any longer. But gods, the pain. Spittle flew through her clenched teeth as she fought to control it, but how could she? It was lancing through her body in a dozen places, none worse than her head. "Justice?" She managed to roll back until she was leaning against the wall opposite Husamettín. Finally the pain began to subside. "For what? Killing men who accepted gifts from the gods and used them to murder an entire people? If you wish to deliver justice for that, I'll gladly accept it."

"You admit it then?" Husamettín's hands were on his knees, his back stiff. He stared at her like Bakhi incarnate, weighing her before leading her to the farther fields. "That you took the lives of Mesut and Külaşan?"

"With joy pouring from my heart."

He looked at her with mild surprise—perhaps he'd been expecting a different answer—but there was also a low-burning anger there as well. "You had help, and I want their names. Those in the Al'Afwa Khadar and any others hidden within the House of Maidens."

"I acted alone."

Husamettín shook his head. "Come. A child would realize that you had help. Share their names, and I can guarantee that you'll be treated with no undue cruelty. Do not, and I'll hand you over to Cahil."

Çeda debated whether she should tell Husamettín about Zaïde and Ihsan, how the two of them had been working against the interests of the others. Might it create a rift between the Kings that would help tear them down, no matter what it meant for her? Perhaps. But Husamettín would not stop with only two names. He'd want more. Dardzada. Emre. Macide. Even old Yanca in Çeda's old neighborhood of Roseridge would suffer if they learned of her, and the chances of that increased the more Çeda said.

"Was Melis involved?" Husamettín asked. "Was Sümeya?"

"You have so little confidence in my sister Maidens?"

"Sister Maidens," Husamettín sneered.

Çeda shrugged. "They were once."

"No one is above suspicion. So I ask again, did any of the Maidens in your hand know?"

She found it strange that he would ask of Sümeya, his own daughter. She was First Warden of the Blade Maidens and was fiercely loyal to the House of Kings.

"I acted alone. None of the Maidens knew my purpose. They mistrusted me from the beginning, but when Yusam vouched for me—"

"And me." The King's face was so placid she couldn't tell how much anger he was harboring behind it.

"And you . . . After that, they fell in line. They tested my loyalty now and again, but little more than that."

"And yet the very same night you killed Külaşan, a group of scarabs stole into the catacombs of his palace and stole Hamzakiir away. You would have me believe that was a chance encounter?"

"It was, though I won't deny it helped to distract King Külaşan."

The muscles along his jaw worked, only for a moment, but for a man like Husamettín it was an admission of rage. He turned his head toward the door and whistled sharply, a sound that drove waves of pain through Çeda. "There's more I might have asked," he said with a calm that gave her chills, "but I see you're in no mood to be forthright."

Somewhere far away a door opened. Footsteps neared. Chains clanked. *There are two approaching,* she realized. One set of footsteps was crisp upon the stone. The other shuffled along. She heard a wheezing breath as well and knew long before the gaoler entered the cell that an asir was being led to her, and yet she couldn't sense it.

The asir crawled by the stocky man's side like an obedient hound, a collar around its neck. A chain trailed from the collar to the gaoler's hand, but the gaoler hardly seemed to need it. The most sickening thing wasn't that the asir remained close to the gaoler; it was that it seemed uncomfortable unless it was near him. It had none of the irrepressible anger Çeda had grown accustomed to feeling from the asirim—not for the gaoler or Husamettín, in any case. Its attitude toward Çeda was completely different.

As it sat with its hands between its legs, its eyes roamed her body. The look was akin to what men did from time to time, except the asir didn't want sex. It wanted her flesh. It wanted to *devour* her.

But it seemed to be waiting for something. Just what it was waiting for Çeda wasn't sure until Husamettín crouched by the asir's side, touched his hand to the wrinkled landscape of its bald head, and said, "Break her."

The asir leaned forward, its eyes locked on Çeda's. Its lips pulled back, revealing a ruin of teeth. A terrible presence grew. Like a flash flood, pressure built quickly in her mind. She was already in pain, but now it was a pure agony. She put her hands to her forehead, hoping to press away the pain, but it did nothing. She pounded the stones with her hands, harder, harder, writhing as the asir tore its way deeper inside her mind.

Stop! she called. *Blood of my blood, please stop!*

It didn't. And then, through the pain, she had a vision of her mother. Ahya was leading Çeda by the hand into Dardzada's apothecary. It was the night she'd left Çeda there and gone to the House of Kings.

The asir, she realized. It was searching for memories as Husamettín had bid him.

No! Çeda cried. *I beg of you, don't take these from me!*

But it cared nothing for her protests. She couldn't even feel it, not as she could feel nearly every asir she'd come across so far. This one was more like a beast. Single-minded. Driven by the hand that fed it. How long might it have suffered? Decades? A century? Had this poor creature been Husamettín's ever since Beht Ihman?

Another vision came, of Çeda accepting a mission, a *shade*, from Osman. She saw Emre joining her. The two of them trading secrets when Tariq gave them their separate destinations.

Stop!

Crouched on her rooftop, she waits for Emre's return.

She knows he won't, so she takes a petal, lifting it from her mother's locket and placing it under her tongue. How it fills her with power. With pain. With worry. The memories mix with reality as the asir digs ever deeper.

She runs the streets on Beht Zha'ir. The city lies quiet, a mighty beast in slumber. She finds Emre in the canals, wounded. They maneuver up the old tree and back to the streets. Emre falls unconscious.

And she sees it. An asir. She'd hoped in those days never to see one, never thought to stand before one. She waits, petrified, as it nears and whispers long-forgotten words into her ear. *Rest will he 'neath twisted tree.*

The asir takes her head in its dry hands and places a kiss on her forehead, its lips so warm it repulses her.

There is another presence nearby. She feels herself, Husamettín's hound, and one more. But where? She turns and looks around the street, which now stands empty.

She blinks.

She was back in Husamettín's dungeon.

But the presence . . . It was still there and growing. She recognized it and wondered if her memory had somehow summoned him. Sehid-Alaz.

He was near, though exactly where, Çeda couldn't say. He seemed to be all around her, attacking the asir, Husamettín's hound.

Çeda's breath came in great gasps. Sweat gathered along her brow, on her palms and the backs of her arms. Only a short distance away, close enough to touch, Husamettín's asir rolled across the cell as she'd done only a short while ago. It scraped at the stones with fingers raw and bleeding. Streaks of black blood were left across the floor in strange, sickening patterns.

And then the asir stopped and lay still, its eyes staring into Çeda's.

I'm sorry, Çeda said.

The asir did not reply. Dark blood dripped from its nose. Its mouth worked as if it were trying to speak. She hadn't realized how young it was. This was a child whose whole life had been stolen from it.

"Well, well," Husamettín said. He'd turned to look at the wall to Çeda's right.

Sehid-Alaz is there, Çeda thought, *so close I could call to him, and he would hear.*

The King of Swords seemed ill-pleased that Çeda had noticed what he was doing. He stared down at her. "Gather your strength, Çedamihn Ahyanesh'ala. We'll continue your questioning soon."

And with that he swept from the room, while the gaoler took up the lantern and used the chain around the asir's neck to drag it from the room, shutting the door behind him with a heavy clatter.

Soon the sounds of their departure had dwindled to nothing, leaving Çeda alone in the darkness with the dripping sound in the distance.

When Çeda woke again her mind was muddy. It took her a long while to remember Husamettín and the asir.

Sehid-Alaz had come to her in her dreams. Indeed, the dream itself had been an echo of their first meeting. It had seemed true to the events as they'd happened, but then the differences had begun to grow. It was due to her growing awareness of Sehid-Alaz, she understood, that she'd been able to sense them at all. She now understood his purpose as well: he'd been working to hide certain memories from the asir.

She pushed herself up off the floor and scraped back along the stones until she could lean against the wall and cradle her aching head in her hands.

Her heart ached for that creature. The lives of the asirim might be poor, but at least they remembered themselves somewhat. That one had been so robbed of its humanity that it had become loyal to Husamettín.

It led her to a problem she hadn't anticipated. The King of Swords was more adept at controlling the asirim than she'd given him credit for. He'd proven it in the desert when she'd wanted to enlighten Melis, and he'd concealed the young asir's memories and replaced them with his own. And again, here in the dungeon. She'd assumed the Kings would be at a disadvantage with Mesut gone, but she'd clearly been mistaken.

She massaged her forehead slowly. It hurt terribly, but not as badly as with the asir. *When had that been? Yesterday?* She'd lost track of time in this place.

She searched and found a water cup she'd caught a glimpse of earlier. After downing all of it, she gripped her right hand. Felt the old wound come to life. It had been quiet, almost numb, but the more she squeezed, the more the effects of the poison spread. She'd become accustomed to it now, knowing how much she could push, and how quickly, before it overwhelmed her. She took just enough, and reached out carefully for some sense of Sehid-Alaz.

Where are you, my King?

She was nearly ready to give up when she felt the barest glint of light on the edges of her mind.

Is that you?

She reached further, knowing that whatever kept Sehid-Alaz enthralled did so still. She was aware that Husamettín might be watching, that other Kings might be as well, but she didn't care. She had to take this chance while she could.

What happened? she asked.

At last Sehid-Alaz spoke. *I thought you safe, my child. You should not have returned.*

Çeda's heart rejoiced to hear him. *There is too much to do. Sharakhai cannot be ignored.*

No, but now you are back in their grasp.

Yet all is not lost, my King. Our tribe forms once more in the desert. They lift their swords in honor of Ishaq Kirhan'ava and in honor of you. More will come, and the Kings now know it.

She said it so that Sehid-Alaz would take heart, knowing his efforts had not been in vain. Indeed, it seemed to spark a memory in him. She saw her King riding at the prow of a ship, a line of mountains in the distance. She saw the tribe celebrating in a valley with steep walls covered in evergreens and a lake so clear even the deepest folds of its bed were laid bare.

Yes, Çeda said, reveling in the memory with him.

The reminder of her presence drew his thoughts to darker times. To the call of Tulathan, to the transformation he'd gone through on a different mountain, this one in the center of a vast desert city. Through him, she heard the cackle of Sukru and the crack of his whip as he reveled in the pain of those who'd been given to the gods.

Sehid-Alaz had watched as the other Kings bade his people to throw themselves against the army of the desert tribes. "Do not go!" he managed to say. "Do not heed their call!" They'd not listened. The call of the gods was already upon them. In ones and twos, their shriveled forms had hunched. They'd loped forward, and oh, how they howled as they ran. It sent shivers of regret through Sehid-Alaz. They had become a terrible host, and were now preparing to storm the lines of the gathered tribes and break the siege of the city.

For a long while all Çeda could think of was her conversation with Dardzada in the desert. *Have you not considered that it's Sehid-Alaz himself who must be led to the farther fields in order for the asirim to be freed?*

But what was there to do about that now? *Come, my King,* she said to him. *For now, let us look to the future, not the past.*

Sehid-Alaz was silent and still, suddenly fearful for himself, for Çeda. He'd sensed another near them, and now Çeda did too, someone listening like a thief in the shadows. She remembered the telltale scuff of feet when she'd awakened. She pushed herself up, shambled to the door, and held the iron bars of the window. She pressed her face into the gap and called, "You needn't fear. I'm locked in a cage."

There was no reply. She tried again to feel for whoever was hiding there, but felt nothing. They were either too distant or too skilled at masking their presence. Sitting back down, she tried once more to reach out to Sehid-Alaz, but he was gone as well.

Alone in the darkness, Çeda gave up and fell into a fitful sleep.

Chapter 38

WHEN IHSAN RETURNED TO HIS PALACE, the bright fury he'd felt in Zeheb's throne room had diminished to a burning crimson flame, one of many that lit him with purpose, that fueled him when it felt like the road he traveled was too dangerous or too long or too ambitious. If he had been the only one threatened by Zeheb, he might have overlooked it. He was a patient man and could afford to be more patient because of the elixir Nayyan had perfected to carry him through the decades that lay ahead.

But Zeheb *hadn't* been satisfied with threatening only Ihsan. He'd threatened Nayyan. And worse, Ihsan's unborn child. There was nothing he wouldn't do to protect her.

You have grossly underestimated me, my good King.

"Something's happened," Nayyan said to him a few nights later. "What is it?"

He'd told her nothing about Zeheb, nor would he for now. "Kiral. I can't wipe his smug face from my mind."

He'd ordered his scribes to copy every single one of Yusam's journals before delivering the originals to Kiral. He'd tried reading the duplicates in the days since, but he'd got nowhere. He couldn't concentrate on the complexities of Yusam's visions.

He hadn't lied to Nayyan. He *was* annoyed by Kiral. But he was *consumed* by how helpless he'd felt in the darkness of Zeheb's throne room, how inconsequential in the face of Zeheb's bloody henchman, the Kestrel, who held him down like some base criminal. An afterthought. A piece of dross. And Zeheb! Cloaking himself in righteous indignation as if Ihsan was in the wrong.

You've made a terrible error, my good King. You've no idea what I could do to you.

Nayyan, naked in bed next to him, shoved him. "You're brooding again."

"I know," he said, "I'll stop."

"Good."

"But perhaps only *after* I walk into Kiral's palace and command his men to deliver the journals here. Perhaps I'll have Kiral hand me his crown while I'm at it."

Nayyan shrugged. "Be prepared to meet Sunshearer if you do."

"I might tell him to run it through his own gut, like Husamettín does with that bloody black sword of his."

Ihsan smiled, picturing it, but Nayyan became suddenly serious and propped herself up on one elbow. "Do you think he would?"

He pulled her back down, ran his fingers through her hair. "It was only a jest."

"I know," she replied, taking his hand and kissing it several times. She shifted closer, lifted one leg and lay it across his. "But if it came to that"—she moved closer, ran her fingertips through the hair on his chest—"would he?"

As her fingers moved steadily lower along his stomach, he stared at the grand ceiling above. He felt the warmth of her sex as she began grinding slowly against his hip. "In truth, I'd give even chances between him complying and my head being lopped off in the moments he was able to resist."

She scratched the hair between his legs, her hand brushing unsubtly against his rapidly hardening cock. Using one finger, she touched his helm, as she called it, and ran soft circles around it. Pleasure swelled as she gripped his shaft and slid the skin down until it could go no further. She held it for two beats of his heart, kissing him warmly on the neck, then began to stroke him in long, slow movements. "May it never come to that."

He ran his hand down her back, admiring her by touch alone. She pulled the sheet and blanket back, exposing him to the knees, then moved herself steadily downward, using the drape of her hair to tickle his shoulders, his chest, his stomach, all while continuing to stroke him. He twisted in the bed and moved his head between her thighs, kissing, licking, taking her in his mouth as she did the same with him. For a time, the two of them lost themselves in one another, moving like the hot currents of air that eddied around Tauriyat in the height of summer, twining, moving *through* one another, until they crested, each shuddering rhythmically, Nayyan first, then Ihsan. They descended like the waning sun and lay side by side, languid as the end of day.

Her head cradled against his chest, one of her legs draped over his, she spoke softly. "I tell you true, if Tulathan came this very night and said if I would lose a hand, I could walk in the open with you, I would do it." She looked up at him. "Wouldn't you?"

He made a show of considering it. "Would it have to be *my* hand?"

Insult and injury somehow accentuated the sultry look in her eyes as she formed the perfect smile. "You'd rather I give one of mine?"

Squeezing her right breast with one hand, a smooth cheek of her buttocks with the other, he said, "I need both of mine."

"And I don't?"

He took her hand and placed it on his softening cock. "One will do."

She gripped him and squeezed hard. When he ground his hips into the motion and released a ridiculously exaggerated moan of pleasure, she bit his nipple until he shouted for her to stop.

Laughing, they fell into silence and stillness once more.

His mind lingered, though. He *would* walk with her in the light of day. They couldn't hide her pregnancy forever. And he didn't know that he wanted to. Because no one knew the effect the transformation might be having on the child as it grew within her, they'd taken to using the necklace less and less. Nayyan declined the vast majority of official functions. And those where King Azad *did* make an appearance, it was kept as short as possible. The other Kings had noticed, and had questioned it in their last council meeting before

Beht Zha'ir. In her disguise as Azad, Nayyan had given them prepared excuses, most related to the threat of the Moonless Host in Sharakhai.

With the danger of the Host all but extinguished, however, Ihsan would need to find another excuse.

"Is it time for Nayyan to step forward as Queen?" he wondered aloud.

She looked up at him, considering, perhaps weighing his earnestness. "Not yet."

She was right, of course. But how he wished for it. "Soon," he said, the same useless, grating refrain he'd been spouting for years.

From beyond the scalloped archway leading to his sitting room, a bell rang. As he slipped from the bed and pulled on a silk robe, it rang again.

"My Lord King?" came a hoary voice.

It was Tolovan, but he sounded excited, a quality no one would typically associate with that placid man.

Ihsan moved quickly to the small greeting room, where heavy green curtains were draped across the entry to his apartments. "Come," he said.

Tolovan's tall form pushed through the curtains. His face was flushed with worry. "Excellence," he said in an undertone, "word has come. Çeda has been captured."

Ihsan felt a tingling sensation run along his spine and went to his dressing room. Tolovan followed. "Where is she being kept?" Ihsan called over his shoulder.

"Husamettín's palace."

Husamettín, Ihsan thought. *He's nearly as bad as Cahil and Kiral.* He was so bloody inflexible. "Tell me what you know."

"She was apparently taken near the blooming fields by Husamettín himself and the Blade Maidens in Çeda's old hand."

"Has she been questioned?"

"I wasn't told, my Lord King."

"Send a messenger now. Inform them I'll be arriving shortly, and request that they wait for my arrival before doing anything further."

When Tolovan had left, Nayyan said, "I'll join you," already half dressed in King Azad's raiment.

"We can't both appear interested. Return to your palace. I'll send word once it's done."

Nayyan was clearly eager to join him. "I told you she was dangerous."

"I've never disagreed."

"But you've still not cut her loose. You should have, months ago."

"Not now, Nayyan."

She looked like she wanted to say more, but she held her tongue and left.

When Ihsan reached Husamettín's palace, he heard shouting well before he reached the throne room. Husamettín's vizira, a woman who could easily be mistaken for the King's twin, showed him inside, where he found Husamettín with three other Kings—Kiral, Sukru, and Cahil.

They looked as if they were in the streets outside an oud parlor, a brawl about to begin. Kiral and Sukru stood to one side, watching Cahil practically scream at Husamettín. And Husamettín, their King of Swords, Lord of the Blade Maidens, was standing at the foot of the daïs before his throne, arms crossed, his face serene as a block of bloody granite. His sword, Night's Kiss, hung by his side, as much a part of the stoic King as his broad shoulders, his closely shorn hair or his dark, trim beard. It was, Ihsan decided, as delicious a scene as he could remember in the halls of Tauriyat.

"She *attacked* me," Cahil railed. "She killed two of your brother Kings. She nearly killed Yndris, my *daughter*, who is still in pain every waking moment from her injuries!"

"Be that as it may," Husamettín said, his dark eyes unimpressed by Cahil's argument. "I found her in the desert. If she is a prize then she is mine to do with as I please."

"A *prize?*" Spittle flew from Cahil's mouth. "She is a traitor!"

"And will be treated as such," Husamettín said evenly.

"I have the right to question her. I demand it!"

When Husamettín remained unswayed, Cahil turned to Kiral, for all the world an angry boy appealing to his baba.

Kiral stared at him a moment, the pockmarks on his face standing out in the light thrown by the braziers along the walls. "Our Confessor King has a point," he said, lifting his eyes to Husamettín.

"I have not asked you here," Husamettín said, "to discuss how Çedamihn will be treated, nor where, nor by whom. I informed you out of courtesy, and to seek your council. I used one of my hounds on her, to unlock her secrets, but Sehid-Alaz came to her aid. I might try again, but I fear he may break his bonds, and then—"

"Enough!" Cahil broke in. "I am not requesting permission. I have come for the traitor, and I will have her—"

"My good Kings," Ihsan said before Husamettín could respond.

But Cahil went on. "I have the right to question her. If Husamettín has doubts about how far I'll go to protect that right"—both hands moved to his weapons, his right to a gleaming war hammer, his left to a long, curved fighting knife—"he may say so now."

Ihsan came to a stop several paces away, but turned as the throne room doors were opened behind him. Zeheb had joined them. He stared, clearly confused. Sukru eyed Husamettín as if he were ready to uncoil his whip and stand beside Cahil. Kiral was raising his hands, ready to play the role of diplomat, but Husamettín spoke before he could.

"I do not wish for this to come to blows, Cahil Thariis'ala. But know that if it does, it will not end until one of us lies dead." He'd not moved an inch toward the pommel of his sword, but Ihsan could see how ready he was.

Cahil was incensed. His callow face reddened, enraged, he drew his knife and pointed it at Husamettín's head. "I will have that girl."

"You will not," came Husamettín's easy reply.

"Enough!" Kiral shouted, raising his hands in a sign of peace.

But Husamettín was already on the move. He drew Night's Kiss, a razor-sharp length of glimmering ebon steel. Before it had even cleared its scabbard, Cahil charged, drawing and swinging his bright war hammer in a downward blow. Husamettín sidestepped and used the draw of his sword to slash for Cahil's exposed side.

Cahil blocked with his fighting knife while swinging the hammer's sharp point for Husamettín's sword arm. He actually caught him, the point tearing the sleeve of Husamettín's khalat and drawing blood, but then Night's Kiss was blurring through the air. Cahil was immediately driven back. The ring of their weapons filled the audience hall. Sukru looked on with wild eyes, Kiral with horror.

Ihsan actually considered letting them fight. He would shed no tears for Cahil. And if Husamettín were killed, well, he might have lost a potential ally, but the man was a rigid obstacle Ihsan would have to contend with one day anyway; what better way than for their *King of Truth*, Cahil, to have done it for him? Ihsan might even press for Cahil to lose a hand for what he'd done;

he was an imbecile who, much like his pretty, boyish face, never seemed to mature. His fall from grace could only serve to help Ihsan.

Kiral ordered them both to stop, and they ignored him.

Night's Kiss blurred. It hummed like a rattlewing, darkness billowing in its wake. Cahil tried to mount an offensive, but Husamettín was quick as his blade. He foiled every attempt Cahil made to strike, taking not so much as another scratch, while Night's Kiss delivered a cut along Cahil's thigh, another to his shoulder, a third that cost Cahil his fighting knife as Husamettín's sword cut viciously across his guard.

Ihsan waited, knowing that to act too soon would turn too much attention on *him*, but when Sukru, a staunch ally of Cahil's, uncoiled his whip, and Kiral warded him away with a wave of his long arm, he knew it was time. As Husamettín's sword described a blinding, buzzing flurry of blows, Ihsan put up his hands and roared, "Stop!"

Tulathan's power flowed as his voice stormed through the room. The walls could hardly contain it. He felt it reach out and seize Husamettín and Cahil.

In truth Ihsan didn't know what the effect would be. He'd used it so rarely on the Kings, and never on these two. They were both so headstrong, he thought perhaps they would shrug it off—Husamettín at least, if not Cahil—but neither did. Both halted, lowered their weapons, and turned toward Ihsan as if awaiting orders.

"Please," Ihsan said, drawing less of Tulathan's power. "We cannot fight over one prisoner, traitor or not." He took a step toward them, his hands to his sides in an open, placating gesture. "Your battle does the work of our enemies for them. There must be some arrangement we can make. Husamettín mentioned Sehid-Alaz. We cannot risk him commanding more of the asirim against us, nor can we risk his death." Ihsan motioned carefully toward Sukru. "Why not give Çedamihn to a neutral party? Sukru has a young mage in his house who might work to unlock her secrets."

"The mage *knows* her," Husamettín said slowly, as if he was just risen from a very long slumber. "They were childhood friends in Roseridge." His eyes were angry, and a touch confused. No doubt part of him wished to separate Cahil's head from his shoulders. Much like Zeheb after he'd recovered from the effects of Ihsan's power, Husamettín would be angry about what Ihsan had done. But Ihsan had appealed to the part of him that searched for tranquility. Husamettín was a man more accustomed to the grip of a sword than anyone else in the Great Shangazi, yet he also valued accord and the gains that could be made in times of peace.

"What of it?" Ihsan said. "Sukru can oversee the proceedings. We can all be there to watch. Once we have what we want, we can decide who will take charge of our errant Maiden."

For long moments no one spoke. Sukru looked pleased, though it was difficult to tell on his perpetually sour face. Zeheb watched Ihsan warily. Husamettín and Cahil stared at one another, the air between them charged. Cahil, wisely, slipped his hammer back into its steel ring on his belt. "Very well," he said, keeping his eyes on Husamettín.

"Very well," Ihsan echoed, turning to Husamettín. "Might it not be best to separate Çeda from Sehid-Alaz in any case?"

Husamettín was still eyeing Cahil intently. He glanced at Ihsan, but then nodded once to Kiral, sheathing Night's Kiss.

"We are agreed," Ihsan said. "Let Sukru take Çeda to his palace, where we'll meet on the morrow's afternoon. And then we shall see what we shall see."

Ihsan used none of his power now. He couldn't risk any more than he already had, and he was already certain they would agree to his request.

Kiral, ever the statesman, nodded first, then the others, at which point Ihsan nodded back to them all with a calculated smile. "Very good. I'm sure you'll have arrangements to make."

And with that he gave a quick bow of his head while backing away. When he turned to head for the exit, he ignored Zeheb completely. As he closed the door behind him, he heard Husamettín say something, but he could spare no more thought for them. He had a very short window of time if the other part of this harried plan was to work.

It took all the patience he had to keep his pace steady as he walked to his heavy coach and waited as its four horses pulled out from the courtyard and began winding down the mountain toward his palace. When the path met King's Road, he called for the driver to stop.

"Unbuckle the lead horse," he said, stepping out of the coach.

"Yes, Excellence."

When he'd done that, Ihsan leapt up to the back of the horse, gripping the akhala's silvery mane. "Wait for me below my palace, on the hidden bend. Speak of this to no one."

Gripped in Ihsan's power, the driver nodded numbly, climbed up to the bench, and gave the reins a sharp snap. Then Ihsan was off, riding hard for Sukru's palace.

The gates were open, and Ihsan rode through. Several Silver Spears watched from the walls and from the gatehouse. A footman approached, with more servants standing at the entrance to the palace. Ihsan had used his power sparingly over the years, for many reasons. But this was no time for half measures.

"Attend me!" he shouted, opening the floodgates.

His power flowed through the courtyard. Drove its way through doors and windows. All those who heard came and stood before him. It felt good to let the full effect of Tulathan's gift course through him. It was a heady thing, vibrant, nearly as strong as the moment the goddess had spoken his bloody verse, thereby granting him his second voice.

A score of men and woman came to him, arranging themselves in a ragged circle, attentive, eager to please.

"You have a young man named Davud in your care," Ihsan said.

"We do," they spoke in unison.

"Take me to him."

Chapter 39

"He's here, my Lord King," Davud heard from the hallway outside his room.

"Forget what you've seen this night," said a soft voice. "Forget what you've heard. This has been a night like any other."

"Quite right, your Excellence. It has."

Davud sat up in bed, confused. *My Lord King,* the voice had said, but the voice wasn't Sukru's.

"Go now," commanded the anonymous King.

A sound of shuffling footsteps lifted and faded—the servant complying with the King's request—and then Davud's door creaked lightly open. Honey-colored light spilled into the room as a man stepped inside, his features hidden behind a lantern. Davud could tell he was of medium height and build; when he came closer and the lantern's light reflected off the bedcovers, he could see more: the King's rich raiment, amber accented in blue and thread-of-gold, his handsome face with its impeccably manicured beard.

"You are Davud."

"I am, Excellence."

"You and I have a lot to talk about." Davud was terribly confused and nervous, but when the King smiled, it chased away all the worries that had been building inside. "I've been most curious about your story, your time with Hamzakiir. You and I could probably spend a night and a day talking about it, but our time is limited."

As the King sat at the foot of the bed, Davud finally recognized him. This was Ihsan, the Honey-tongued King. He was certain this should worry him, but just then he couldn't put his finger on the reason. "Of course, your Excellence."

"You've been here for some time now. Tell me what Sukru has been teaching you."

"Nothing," Davud said in all honesty.

The King seemed more than a little surprised.

"If anything, *I've* been teaching *him*." He would never had spoken it so plainly before anyone else, but Ihsan seemed an eminently trustworthy soul.

"He's not provided you instruction to broaden the use of your magic?"

"He's given me books. I've broadened my own knowledge. As has Anila."

It felt strange to talk about Anila, but he was eager to please the King. Indeed, when Ihsan smiled quizzically, as if Davud had both surprised and impressed him, his heart swelled.

"Anila," he said.

"She was the only other survivor of the attack on the collegia's graduation ceremony."

"She was burned in Ishmantep?" Ihsan asked. When Davud nodded, he went on. "I'd thought her dead."

"Her survival is a miracle, to be sure. She's been here since our return, healing, but lately she's been learning how to commune with the dead."

Ihsan's eyes narrowed to slits. "I beg your pardon?"

Gods, he was angry, or disappointed. It was a secret Davud should probably have kept hidden, but sharing anything with Ihsan gave him a thrill.

"She isn't dangerous!" he said quickly. "But she can bring the dead back from the abyss. At least for a time." Davud told him all of it, how she'd raised Bela from the dead. "She's a good woman at heart. She just wants to use her power to destroy Hamzakiir."

"And Sukru," Ihsan said pensively. "You said *you* were teaching *him*. Teaching him what?"

"He asked for my help to determine the cause of the sickness in the adichara. He thought it might be related to the growing madness in the asirim."

"And were you successful?"

"Yes, until Yerinde came."

If Ihsan had seemed disappointed before, he seemed utterly shocked now. "What did you just say?"

"Yerinde came to us in the caverns below Tauriyat, my Lord King." He proceeded to tell him all of it, the shift in mood, the goddess striding in, those depthless eyes. *Bring me her head,* she'd commanded the Kings. *The head of she who has wronged thee.*

"*Yerinde* said this?"

"She did, Excellence."

"And then she left . . ."

"Yes."

"And who was in attendance?"

"Myself and Anila. Sukru's man, Zahndrethus—"

"Which *Kings,* Davud?"

"Kings Sukru, Kiral, Cahil, and Husamettín."

Ihsan was lost in thought, his face heavy in shadows from the light cast by the lantern. Suddenly he breathed sharply, as if returning to himself. "There's something I wish you to do for me, Davud."

"Anything."

"You know a woman named Çedamihn, I believe."

This struck something deep within Davud. Love. Friendship. Loyalty. "I do."

"She will be brought here tonight to be interrogated by you. You will find a way to free her, by any means necessary. She cannot remain here under the power of King Sukru."

Çeda? Brought here? "But she fled the city."

"She foolishly returned, Davud, and she's been captured. Here's what you will do."

The King leaned closer, took Davud by the back of the neck, and gazed into his eyes in a way that was not so different from what Yerinde had done in the cavern. Ihsan spoke, but Davud could no longer understand the words.

He caught one here. *Escape*. Another there. *Blood*. But so much was lost, the sound was akin to the snap of a bonfire, as mesmerizing as the flames.

All too soon Ihsan was standing. "Do you understand all I've told you?"

"Of course, my Lord King."

"Very well," Ihsan said, moving like a memory toward the door.

The moment it thudded home, Davud was up and washing his face. He had much to prepare for, but he started only a short while later, suddenly aware of a new presence in the room. "My King?"

He expected to find Ihsan, but it wasn't him. It was another.

"You will forget my face," came a voice so soft it was nearly a whisper, "and you will forget that I was here."

Just like that, the form blurred, becoming like a shadow. "Of course," Davud said.

"There is one last request your King has for you, Davud. The most important of all."

"Anything."

"When you've done all Ihsan has asked of you, you will take Çedamihn's life, and then you will take your own."

"I . . ." It seemed an odd request. "Excellence, are you certain that is what you wish?"

"I'm certain."

Davud nodded. "Then it will be done."

"Very good, Davud." And the door clicked shut.

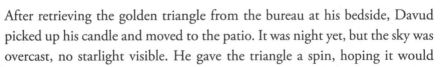

After retrieving the golden triangle from the bureau at his bedside, Davud picked up his candle and moved to the patio. It was night yet, but the sky was overcast, no starlight visible. He gave the triangle a spin, hoping it would work anyway, but it fell, tinkling against the mosaic tabletop.

Perhaps it only needs time. As he held it in his palm, hoping the night sky would grant it the power it needed, he rubbed his temples, trying to clear a bit of the pain. He'd had a terrible headache since waking and setting about the tasks he'd been set by . . .

Now that was strange. He couldn't recall who. *I'm tired. I can worry about that when the sun rises.*

He spun the triangle again, and again it rattled against the tabletop. He tried a third time, and a fourth. *Gods, no!* He *needed* this to work.

The Sparrow's words played in his mind. *You need but summon the sigil for passage and doorway,* he'd said. The moment he'd spoken those words, Davud had felt wary. He'd said it pleasantly. With kindness, it seemed. But this whole situation—Sukru and the hunger in his close-set eyes, Anila and her growing power, the sudden appearance of the Sparrow and his stories of Sukru—it all had Davud on edge.

He mightn't have done it now, not if it was for him alone, but this was to save Çeda. She was here at least in part because of him. He'd been the one to show her the tunnel to the collegia tower. He'd helped her uncover the Kings' secrets. *Thaash's bright blade, who was it that told me Çeda was captured? Sukru?*

The triangle glinted in the candlelight. He picked it up. Felt the sharp edge of one of the corners, carefully considering what he was about to do. *Such a treacherous path.* In that brief moment of indecision, his headache became markedly stronger, and he decided it was worth the risk. He pressed the triangle into his thumb, piercing skin, and worked the flesh until blood welled. He drew the sigil the Sparrow had described on his palm, then placed the triangle there and gripped it.

Immediately he felt a hollow sensation building in his stomach. It came on so swiftly he threw the triangle from him. It turned in the air and wobbled like a top. But then it started to rotate more smoothly, and *grew.* The sides expanded, becoming larger and larger until each was nearly as long as Davud was tall. What shocked him more was that the triad's center now revealed not the trunk of the fig tree behind it but another place entirely.

Davud approached carefully. Within the triangle's borders was a room with sandstone walls. A clutch of candles held in an iron sconce lit the room in pale light. On the far wall stood a shelf of books and scrolls of all sizes, plus a host of clay tablets in wooden trays. There was a rocking chair on a rug. A hearth beside it. Dominating the left side of the room was a table of thick wood, like a butcher's block. All about the space were cages both large and small, some on desks, others on pedestals, others still hanging from the walls and ceiling. Within were dozens, hundreds of small birds. There were many firefinches, like the one the Sparrow had sent to spy on Davud and to deliver him the triangle, and many others besides. Berrypeckers and tailrunners. Saddlebacks and thornbills. A dozen more Davud had no name for.

"Hello?" Davud called softly. "Sparrow?"

The birds chirped softly, some fluttering in their cages before settling once more.

"Hello?" he called again.

Taking a deep breath, he screwed up his courage, hiked up his robes, and stepped through. He moved swiftly lest the thing return to its previous size and chop him in two. The triangle, however, continued to spin.

"Hello, it's Davud. I've come to speak to you."

The fire was low in the hearth, but the room was quite warm. Davud peered into the darkness beyond the open door, fearful of leaving the triangle lest it close and trap him here. There was nothing for it, though. He was committed. As he took a step toward the open door, he noticed a book in the rocking chair. A journal, perhaps. He was reaching for it when a voice spoke from the darkened hallway.

"So cometh the young mage." At the sudden sound, the birds flapped noisily about their cages, then settled like windblown leaves.

"I've just . . . I've just come from Sukru's palace."

"I'd be surprised if you'd come from another."

He thought he'd known who he was speaking to, but now he wasn't so sure. The voice sounded deeper, more hoarse. "I'm here to see the Sparrow?"

The shadow shifted, and Davud could just make out the silhouette of a smallish man. "Mmmm," the voice said noncommittally. "I'm pleased you've come. I'd begun to wonder if you'd ever take up my offer."

"I haven't come to take up your offer, exactly. Not yet, in any case."

"Not yet?"

"I need your help. There's someone who will need shelter. She must be hidden from the Kings and then seen safely into the desert."

An uncomfortable silence followed. "Would the Kings be wroth to learn of her departure?"

"Yes."

"Mmmm." The birds flapped noisily for a moment. "Who is she to you that you would risk so much?"

"A friend."

"A friend," the Sparrow echoed. "Who is she to the Kings, then?"

Davud didn't wish to reveal Çeda's identity, but he supposed there would be no hiding it in the end. Better to let the Sparrow know now than discover it when he needed his help the most. "When we first spoke, you said you would do much to anger Sukru."

"And it was the truth."

"The woman is known as the White Wolf. She took up an ebon blade but has since been named a traitor. She killed two of the Kings, if the stories are true."

Davud felt certain he'd erred in sharing this, but then a deep chuckle issued forth from the darkness. "You wish to steal Çedamihn the White Wolf from beneath their very noses?"

"Just so."

The chuckle built into a rumbling laugh. When he spoke again, his satisfaction was plain. "Very well, Davud. Very well. I will help. Under one condition."

"Which is?"

"You'll need a place to shelter. A place to hide until the storm has passed. If I help with your White Wolf, I ask only that you remain here with me. You'll share what you've learned, and perhaps I can teach you a bit of what *I* know."

Davud had expected this, but still felt uncomfortable about it. It felt as if he were freeing himself from one man only to give himself to another. "Before I give my answer, I would know who you are. Show me your face."

"What good would that do you?"

"It would show your trust in *me*, which would tell me much about you."

"I am but an old man, forgotten by the world."

"I will see your face or find another way."

Another deep chuckle came from the darkness. "If I but walk in the light, you would join me?"

"Let us see," Davud said, growing more nervous by the moment.

A pause. Then the figure began moving toward the room. The urge to turn and run became so strong, Davud felt his feet shifting on the carpet beneath him.

But then the Sparrow paused. "No. I think not." He sniffed, then hawked to clear his throat. "Not yet. I'll share more when you return. *If* you return." When Davud didn't respond, he continued, his tone indignant. "Have I given you reason to doubt me? Have I not helped you when you needed it? Suffice it to say that Sukru wronged me many years ago, and I've since made it my business to see that he does it to no one else. To those who walk the red paths, in any case. I can't be expected to save all that Sukru sets his cruel eyes on." The Sparrow's silhouette shifted. Davud saw the glint of his eyes. "What say you, Davud Mahzun'ava? I'll have your answer now that you've come to *know* me so well."

Davud felt ill at ease, but he had no cards to play. "Very well, but I'll need your help first. A sigil—"

Davud stopped. He'd heard footsteps behind him. He turned and peered through the edges of the slowly turning triangle to find Anila stepping onto his patio. "Davud?"

Davud turned back to the Sparrow, unsure what to do.

"Best you go now, boy," the Sparrow said. "I've seen those entering and leaving the palace. I've heard the tales flitting over Tauriyat like a flock of blazing blues. I know the sort of sigil you'll need."

"Very well," Davud said. "Be prepared for us, later today."

Without waiting for a response, he stepped through the triangle and released the trickle of power he'd been using to sustain the portal. The triangle slowly shrank to its original size and he snatched it from the air just as it was beginning to fall, then turned to face Anila. For a moment she looked like the Anila of old—a brash young student always pushing herself to outstrip her peers, always pressing the collegia masters to understand a thing inside and out.

She pointed to the place where the triangle had been spinning. "Would Sukru be pleased to learn of this?"

"No, he would not."

The nerves from a few moments ago faded as Davud settled into a decision that felt right. He had planned to tell Anila about this anyway, but it felt good to share with her, like they used to.

"Anila, I have something to tell you."

"Is it to do with the Maiden, Çeda?"

"I . . . But how?"

"She was brought to the palace a short while ago. I thought you'd want to know."

The feeling inside him felt impossible to contain. It felt as if he were being pulled in a thousand different directions. As succinctly as he could, he told Anila about the Sparrow. "I'm going to be leaving the palace. Today." With the admission, the feeling inside him began to ease. "Come with me, Anila."

Her brows pinched. "Why?" She looked over her shoulder, toward the door to his apartment. "To save *her*?"

She meant Çeda, of course, but why was she so angry? "Yes. I owe her this. But I would leave with *you*."

"You don't owe her anything. She's a traitor to the Kings!"

Davud's headache had receded, but now it was storming back, stronger than ever. His heart felt like it was going to gallop right out of his chest. "I'm going to save her," he said through the growing pain. "And then I'm leaving Sukru's service."

"To do what?"

"Find Hamzakiir and punish him."

"And you don't think that would be easier in the service of the Kings?"

"The Kings seem to be doing a rather poor job of it, Anila. Haven't you wondered just how interested they are in finding him?"

Anila shrugged. "I'd be lying if I said no, but we're in a better position to achieve our aims if we remain here."

"I don't *trust* Sukru."

"You would trust a man you don't even know more than a King who's sheltered you, who's given you access to texts you would never have had otherwise?"

"Sukru has twisted pleasures. Tastes I suspect will be turned on us sooner or later."

Davud was sure Anila was going to rail against him, call him a liar or a fool for believing what others have told him about Sukru, but instead she shrugged. She seemed truly off-balance for the first time in this conversation. "I've heard stories as well, but you know how truth is distorted over time."

"The man I've been speaking to. The Sparrow. He's promised to shelter us."

"Shelter us or you?"

This time, *Davud* felt off-balance. "I'm sure he'll keep you as well."

Anila laughed. "A woman he's never met, who he would have every reason to believe might tell Sukru what he's about?" When he tried to speak again, she raised her hand. "Enough, Davud. I'm not going with you. I think you're making a terrible mistake, but I'll not stop you if you're set on it."

It was a silent plea for him to remain. He could see it in her eyes, the way she was holding her hands before her. Davud wanted to go to her. Wanted to take her in his arms and plead with her to join him, but he could tell it was a fool's errand.

"Very well," he finally said.

"Very well." And with that she turned and strode stiffly away, moving faster as she neared the door.

The moment the door clicked shut behind her, a firefinch flew down and landed near Davud's feet. It had a twig in its beak. After setting it down, it flew up and grabbed another. And another.

Ignoring his feelings of disappointment—in himself, in Anila, perhaps both—he ran to his room to retrieve a quill, ink, and his growing book of sigils.

Chapter 40

"WE DON'T NEED TO TRAVEL THIS WAY," Ramahd told Meryam as he pushed her in her padded wheelchair along the halls of the embassy house. The wheels rattled over the terra-cotta tiles, then bumped over the threshold that led to a courtyard. A small, stone-lined pool sat at the courtyard's center, and near it a lantern hung from a hook. The lantern swung easily in the crisp evening air, sending the shadows of the nearby bushes to swaying.

"Preserve your strength," Ramahd went on. "Let me call for a coach to take us into the city. *Then* we can begin."

Ramahd thought Meryam might be considering it, but then he realized she'd merely nodded off. She woke shivering as he was turning the wheelchair around.

"It must be done tonight, Ramahd."

"Which is why you should save your strength for the stones."

For the past week she'd been studying the sigils Ramahd had collected for her, the ones from the city walls. Tonight the plan was to return to certain ones and alter them, a process that would accomplish two things: lure the ehrekh, Guhldrathen, to the city, and weaken the protections the sigils provided so that the ehrekh could pass beyond them. She'd also been spending time mastering the sapphire, pushing herself at all hours, calling for blood from Amaryllis, Ramahd, even Cicio.

Both tasks required the utmost care. It was not only dangerous work, but mentally and physically draining as well. It had sapped Meryam of all the vitality she'd shown during the ritual on the sapphire, so much so that she was nearing the point of exhaustion. Ramahd hadn't seen the like since Viaroza, when Meryam was trying to break Hamzakiir's will.

Meryam motioned to the pool. "I must test Rümayesh's strength before we reach the sigils."

"You've tested her strength."

"Not like this. And besides, this night of all nights, I wish for no one outside these walls to know of our comings and goings." She reached over one shoulder and patted his hand, then motioned to the pool again. "Come."

Knowing that to argue would only make her dig in, Ramahd spun her chair back around and pushed her onward. The night sky was moonless, the air brisk. The lantern by the pool shed pale light over the shrubs, the paved walkways, the lilies in the water. It would have been pleasant were it not for the business at hand.

Once Ramahd had wheeled the chair to the edge of the pool, he turned her to face him and held out his wrist. He felt the familiar prick of her blooding ring against his skin, felt the warmth of her lips as they pressed against the wound.

Weeks ago, Meryam's posture would have straightened, as if a great weight had been lifted from her. Her eyes would have sharpened, fatigue vanishing before his eyes. Now, all she could manage was to lift her head a bit. She blinked as if clearing sleep from her eyes, and drank more.

When done, she gave him back his wrist and pushed herself unevenly to a stand. Rümayesh's lead-lined amulet swung wildly from her neck. She looked as though she were ready to tip back into her chair, but she steadied herself, strictly avoiding Ramahd's gaze. She'd always detested revealing weakness of any sort, but she'd become especially sensitive to it around Ramahd.

When she'd recovered, she looked up into Ramahd's eyes. A rare, shy smile came to her lips. "I was certain you'd fight me harder."

"I only wish there was more I could do."

For a moment she looked at him as she had in the desert, when they'd traveled together after leaving her father's dead body. "There are days when this wears on me so." She looked at him as if he could fix it, make the pain and sorrow go away. And then, as soon as it had come, the look was gone. She swallowed hard and stared into the black depths of the pool, Qaimir's queen once more. "Let's begin."

She took the amulet and opened its outer doors, revealing the sapphire within. It shone dull blue in the lantern's light. Lifting it before her, she stared into the central facet, the one least covered by soot. Her expression was determined at first, but the more she stared into the sapphire, the more that look faded, replaced by a look of wonder, as if she were staring into another world.

"Meryam?" Ramahd asked, worried she'd been ensorcelled by Rümayesh, as *he* had been the first time. "Meryam!"

He was just about to reach for the amulet, to clasp the doors shut, when she shook her head. "I'm fine, Ramahd." Without taking her eyes from the gemstone, she motioned to the water. "Step in. I'll follow."

He knew what was coming, and yet it still felt strange to step into a pool with water as high as his ankles and fall headlong into it. Water rushed up around him. Enveloped him. It pressed along his back, the sound of it suddenly raucous. He steadied himself in the current, for he was no longer in a pool, but a river: the Haddah, swelled with spring rains, its flow trying hard to bear him downstream.

The city's stout outer wall was only a short distance away. Darkened homes greeted him all around. The river gurgled along its banks, but beyond this the night was silent, the city asleep. The only lanterns were those twinkling within the towers spaced along the curtain wall.

He turned to face the flow and swept his arms through the water, waiting for Meryam to appear. He felt her a moment later, and pulled her upright, steadied her as she began to cough.

"Breathe deep," he said, rubbing her back.

She coughed harder, and he worried they might be spotted, but no one called out from the wall. No one seemed to be watching from the shoreline, either. As the current tried constantly to knock them off balance, Ramahd guided Meryam to the southern shore. To their left, barely visible, were the thick iron grates that ran beneath a wide arch built into the wall. Years ago the grates, just like the rest of the city entrances, were left open, allowing free traffic along the river in the short rainy season or passage along the riverbed in the dry months. But the troubles with the Moonless Host had forced the Kings to close them to control movement in and out of the city.

It was one of the reasons Meryam had felt it necessary to travel here in such a strange manner—they couldn't risk the city guard learning what they were doing—which made Meryam's terrible coughing fit all the more alarming.

As soon as Ramahd had led her out of the water, he took out a chunk of licorice root from the bag at his belt. It was wet but would still work well enough. "Quickly, Meryam, it'll help with your cough."

She waved him away. "They won't hear us, Ramahd."

Indeed, he looked up and saw two Silver Spears walking side by side with the sort of ease that came with boredom. Neither gave any sign that they'd heard Meryam's coughing. Even so, he guided her quickly to the foot of the wall.

"Hold my neck," he told her.

She did, and he carried her to the first of the stones, some two hundred paces away. He set her down gently and she dropped to her knees. Her right palm had already begun to glow with a dull orange light. She used it to reveal deep, chiseled lines in the stone's surface—a sigil, one of dozens that protected the city from the desert's more dangerous creatures. Using confident, practiced strokes, she brushed the stone with an outstretched finger. The stone melted where she touched, leaving behind a gouge that looked little different than the original. With waves of her hand, other places were filled in, masking the previous lines. Her movements reminded Ramahd of nothing so much as the Mirean women who painted calligraphy in confident, graceful strokes.

In little time she was done, and a new sigil now graced the stone. Ramahd knew what he was looking for, and still it appeared as though the new sigil had been there from the very beginning. More importantly, he could feel its effect—an easing of the pressure that had been with him since his return from the desert.

"Help me up," Meryam said.

Ramahd did, and they moved to the second sigil stone, then the third, Meryam altering each one just so.

"It's working." Ramahd felt nauseous. "I feel him coming closer."

"Good." She closed her fist, and the orange light was snuffed. "Now help me up."

He did, and carried her back the way they'd come. He felt as though a race had just begun, and that for every stride they took, Guhldrathen was taking three. *How soon before it catches us?* Meryam had said the ceremony with Kiral was set for the morning. It seemed preposterous that Guhldrathen would wait that long.

When they reached the banks of the Haddah and began wading into the water, his feelings of helplessness intensified. The water was trying to press the life from him. The sounds of the gurgling flow were the ehrekh's infernal laughs.

Mighty Alu, protect your servant.

But the laughs only grew stronger.

Chapter 41

BRAMA SAT AT THE EDGE of his bed holding a steel nail in one hand, ignoring the ever-present sense of unease that had been with him since he lost the sapphire. He pulled back the sleeve of his nightshirt and examined the small round wounds along his arm. There were seven, one for each day since that night in the cellar.

When your throat was slit.

The highest crime had not been the theft of the necklace, but the attempt on Brama's life. That Brama had lived was inconsequential; the neck wound would have killed a normal man in moments. Jax's words followed him like a hungry gutter wren—*the Qaimiri must pay, the Qaimiri must pay*—but he'd had enough violence in the past few years to last him lifetimes. What did he care if some Lord of Qaimir had stolen the ehrekh away?

Good riddance. I'm glad to be rid of her.

Still, he had no idea how long the effects she'd granted him would last.

He ran a finger over the line of puckered wounds like a harpist strumming notes. The oldest was a week old. He'd given it to himself the day after waking to find his own blood spilled across the cellar floor. He felt nothing from it now. Indeed, it looked like a ten-year-old wound. He felt nothing from the next either, or the next three after that. The sixth was different. He'd given it to himself two days ago. He felt only the smallest amount of pain from it, as if it were a fortnight old and nearly healed.

The seventh, though he'd driven the nail deep into the muscle only yesterday, felt merely sore. The ability was still with him, then, despite Rümayesh's absence. Was it permanent, then, or would it be lost with Rümayesh's death? He was embarrassed to admit he didn't know. He'd only discovered it years ago after falling headfirst down the stairs after healing a lotus addict who was so obese Jax had advised him not to heal her. He'd done it anyway, taking both her addiction and the lotus into himself with the help of Rümayesh. Afterward, with his mind addled by so much of the reek, he'd tumbled headfirst down a flight of stairs. He'd managed a broken forearm, several cracked ribs, and a hit to the head that had knocked him out for hours. But by the next day, the breaks had partially healed and the bruises had vanished. By the day after that, his bones felt as good as they ever had.

He had stood before the beaten brass mirror in his room that night. For a long while he saw only his own ruined face, but as he continued to stare at the imperfect reflection, Rümayesh's features slowly replaced his: skin black as night, eyes the color of a rusty blade, horns sweeping like sickles up from her forehead and back behind her ears. Long spikes replaced his mop of curly brown hair.

"What is it you wish, my master?" Rümayesh had said with an easy smile.

"You know what I wish," he said, ignoring the way she'd addressed him. She only called him *master* when she wished to annoy him. "Why did you do it?"

"Why, whatever do you mean?" Rümayesh had replied with an easy smile.

"Why did you heal me?"

The face in the mirror had laughed. "Did you think I would leave you so vulnerable, to be taken down by yellow fever or dysentery or typhus or, my Lord Goezhen forbid, a fall down a bloody flight of stairs?"

"I didn't *ask* you to do it!"

She'd stared for a moment, her expression hovering somewhere between amusement and shock. "And why ever would you care?"

He paused. Men would kill for such a gift, *had* killed for it, so why *did* he care? The answer was uncomfortable, but he couldn't lie to her; she would sense it before he even opened his mouth. "It makes me *beholden* to you. It makes you a permanent *part* of me."

"The notion disgusts you?"

"How could it not?"

Rümayesh had given him the scars that riddled his skin. She'd tortured him for months, stopping only when Çeda had captured her soul within the gemstone.

"Do you wish me to take it away, then?" Rümayesh had asked. "Make it vanish as if it had never been?"

"Yes!"

She'd paused. "Surely you jest."

"I do not."

They both knew it was true, and her smile had turned sad. "Very well . . ."

He'd felt relieved, but even in those few moments afterward he'd begun to doubt his decision. *What have I given up?*

The thought had gnawed at him for months, until a scuffle had broken out. A man half crazed on reek had taken out a knife as they'd tried to help him. Brama had tackled him from behind, but took a nasty cut in the process. The slice along his forearm had healed by the time he'd made it to bed that night. Coward that he was, he'd never brought it up with Rümayesh. Despite all his bluster, he'd been *relieved* to find the power still in him.

Will I live forever? he'd wondered. *Will I reach the end of days with Rümayesh still by my side?* Now, as he sat in his room holding the nail, he asked himself the same question, unsure what he wanted the answer to be.

He took the nail and pressed it deep into the meat of his forearm. It punctured his skin, drove into the muscle. His body felt pain like any man's, but his lessons at ignoring such things had been interminable, and he was no longer afraid to admit that he'd learned those lessons well. Driving a nail into his own flesh wasn't a pleasant experience, but neither was it unpleasant. It simply was. Finished, he pulled it out quickly, the skin distending like a single-poled tent. And then it was free.

Blood welled. It ran in a warm trickle down his arm and dripped from his elbow onto the bandage he'd lain across his leg. He pressed the bandage to the wound, but could already see how well it was closing. He stared at it, a thousand thoughts plaguing his mind. *Does it mean she yet lives? Are they torturing her? Do I care if they are? Do I want them to torture her?*

He cleaned the wound and stood before the brass mirror, the same one he'd used to speak to Rümayesh so many times. He saw only the twisted features of a tortured man. How he'd wished to die while in Rümayesh's care. She'd kept him alive so she could bury him in pain and dig him up just to bury him all over again. He'd asked himself *why* in those early days, but it wasn't so difficult a puzzle. Part of her enjoyed inflicting pain. Another part blamed him for losing Çeda, the woman she'd coveted. And part of her wanted to please Goezhen, her maker, a god who reveled in such things.

As the hum of life in the Shallows filtered in through the nearby window, a worm turned inside him. How could he feel so empty? He still had much. He could go on and continue what he and Jax had started.

But there was a constant feeling of . . .

He stifled the thought, pressed it deep down lest it take root within his mind.

He left the room in a rush, taking the stairs down and heading to the largest of the three houses that acted as their infirmaries. He threw himself into his work. Helping those who'd come for succor.

"Give it to me," he said to Shei, who was preparing a bottle of poppy milk for a woman strapped to one of the beds.

Shei smiled her pleasant smile and nodded, bowing as she handed the bottle and spoon over. After three shuffling steps backward, she spun and left him in peace.

The afflicted woman's daughter sat in a chair, watching him, staring at his scars. He did his best to ignore the scrutiny, concentrating on the patient instead. She might have been pretty once. Now she was gaunt, with sallow eyes and ashen skin. As her head lolled and her throat convulsed, Brama poured a spoonful of the thick white milk from the bottle. The woman had been tugging at the restraints as if caught in a terrible dream, but when the spoon touched her lips, she stopped and sipped.

Brama had taken care not to pour too much, but seeing how little he'd used, the daughter leaned forward. "Could you not give her more, my lord?"

I'm no lord, and we have little enough milk to go around. Not to mention a dwindling supply of money with which to buy more. "It will be enough to ease her pain."

The girl tried to smile. She'd brought her mother in yesterday, desperate to see her healed. She'd come with all the money she had, a sad collection of copper khet and a handful of six-pieces. It had broken Brama's heart to tell her he couldn't heal her, not as she'd hoped. It would take long, painful days. Days in which her mother would likely leave to find more reek rather than suffer.

"I could find more." Her eyes had been so hopeless, Brama had nearly wept.

"It isn't the money."

"I'll find more," she pressed, staring at his scar-torn face. "Just heal her and I promise we'll return with twice this."

"I don't know what you've heard—"

"That you heal with but a kiss to the crown of the head." Her eyes went wide, as though a brilliant idea had just occurred to her. "I know you choose carefully, my lord, but she's pretty, is she not? She could stay with you, or others that come with more money."

"This is no brothel," Brama had said, "and this *isn't* about the money. We don't do what you think. Not anymore. It's beyond us. But we'll give her a bed. We'll help her through this."

A betrayed and lost look settling over her, she'd merely sat in the chair by her mother's side and fed her water from the misshapen mug Jax had brought for them. Now the look of betrayal was gone, replaced by worry for her mother and fear for her own future.

"Is it true what they say? That you've displeased the gods? That you've lost your power?"

Brama stoppered the bottle as he stood. "We'll take the restraints off tonight. You can sleep here if you like, or you can leave and return in the morning. Either way, she'll have to leave tomorrow."

"But she needs more time, doesn't she?"

"We need the bed." Being unable to heal as quickly meant the beds had filled up faster than they were used to. "I'll give you a small vial of the poppy to take home."

"It was all a lie, wasn't it?" she said to his back. "The Tattered Prince was a lie!"

Yes, Brama thought as he walked away. *He was always a lie.*

Nearby, a stocky woman was struggling to rise from her bed. "Heal me!" she screamed at him. Her eyes were manic, her lips pulled back in the pain of withdrawal. "I need it. Please, I'll be good this time. I promise."

Brama had healed the woman three weeks earlier, and a few months before that. Neither had stuck. She'd returned yesterday, demanding to see Brama, and when he'd finally come and told her the truth she'd refused to believe it. Only when they'd given her an extra dose of milk of the poppy had she given up and gone to sleep.

"I'll give you more milk, but that's all I can offer."

"No! You will *heal me!*"

"This is all I can offer." Brama nodded to two of the nearby men, who swooped in and guided her back to bed. She went, but she was shaking so badly Brama had to abandon the spoon, grip her jaw, and try to force some of the milk down her throat through her clenched teeth. Even then, she spat it out.

"Stop it!" Brama shouted at her. "I'm trying to help you!"

He wasted nearly a quarter bottle trying to feed her, but it wasn't until she managed to lift a leg and kick Brama in the groin that he became enraged. He backed away, nursing his flaring balls, then released a pent-up roar and threw the bottle against the wall. The bottle smashed, shards and milk spraying everywhere.

The men stared at the thick serum slipping down the wall. That half-bottle had been worth more than either man had ever owned. The woman seemed pleased somehow, but also worried over what Brama would do next.

But Brama hardly knew she was there. His breath came heavy. His arms hung at his sides as if he were ready to fight. Gods, where was all this anger coming from? He was *free* of her.

"Send her out," Brama said.

Now the woman seemed unsure of herself. "No, please," she shouted at him. "I'll be good! I won't be a bother to anyone!"

"Out!" Brama roared.

The men complied, pulling her forcibly from the bed and dragging her screaming to the door, where they shoved her out into the street as she pleaded to remain. "I'll take the milk!"

The milk . . . Brama walked to the wall where the plaster still glistened. He could smell it. Not the fragrance of the milk, but a burning smell. It was the smell of the brazier in Rümayesh's tower in the desert. It was the smell of his own skin burning. And by the gods, he *missed* it.

The rage that had been bubbling up inside him over the last week boiled over. He punched the wall in the center of the glistening stain. The plaster cracked and pieces of it fell away, pattering to the floor.

He punched it again. And again. Over and over, his fists worked like the arms of a loom, driving with more speed and power, impelled by the rage and confusion warring within him.

How can I miss her? How can I miss the torture?

The plaster crumbled further, revealing the wooden slats beneath. The rain of rubble collected in piles and still he went on, releasing a primal scream. Only when the brick gave way behind the slats, creating a small hole in the wall to the building's exterior, did he stop and stare at the ruin he'd made of his hands. They shook as the pain slowly registered. The backs of his hands were rough landscapes of blood and torn skin. He'd broken fingers. But what did that matter? They'd heal. He'd be whole in another day.

The room had gone utterly silent. Everyone stared at him. Those who cared for the afflicted, those who knew him, watched him with a confusion and wariness he'd never seen in them before, but even that was merely a pale imitation of the sick, who stared with naked horror.

"Brama?"

He turned and saw Jax standing in the doorway, the cut of her newly shorn hair and her slight build making her look like a waif. Her eyes drifted not toward the hole Brama had made in the wall, nor to his bleeding hands; her gaze steadily held his, a calming influence over the storm raging inside him.

"You'd better come with me."

At first he thought it was because of the way he was acting, a measure meant to protect everyone else, but he realized a moment later it wasn't. Or at least, it wasn't *wholly* because of that. By the gods who breathe, there was something new. He could tell from the way she'd said it, as though this was something the others shouldn't hear, not yet.

Dropping his hands to his side, he nodded and lumbered toward her. Blood tickled its way down his fingers, pattered against the weathered gray planks of the floor.

After accepting two bandages from Shei, Jax wrapped his blood-soaked hands as she walked with him to the next building, where their most violent patients were taken. Inside the long, narrow room were ten beds. A small crowd of his followers dressed in simple linen thawbs and dresses were clustered around one bed. A woman named Arna was lying there, her face screwed up in pain.

Arna had been one of his chosen. One of *Rümayesh's* chosen. She'd been one of eight who had been given small sapphire chips embedded in the palms of their scarred hands, allowing Brama to see through them, to keep watch over his small empire. That sight had been robbed from him when the sapphire was taken. Brama felt small when he'd realized the truth of it after waking in the cellar, but that was nothing compared to what he felt as he stared at Arna's hand.

The center of Arna's palm was red and puffy, infected. They might have to chop off her hand to save her. And the stone . . . It was missing. Twarro, who towered over Brama, held his own hand out flat so Brama could see the sapphire there. Bits of drying blood covered it, and spots of puss.

"It just came out," Arna told him.

"How long has it been like this?"

"Three days." Her blue eyes avoided his now.

"Why didn't you tell me?"

She swallowed, color flushing through her freckled cheeks. "You've had enough to deal with."

Brama took in the rest of the eight chosen, who were all there: kind Mualla, intense Rezan, patient Sabriye. Koro'kahn, Viah, and Ishalla. They all held their right hands out to him. All had reddened skin around the embedded sapphires.

He looked to each of them in turn, and was struck by how unfair it was to all of them. They'd pinned their hopes on a charlatan, a man who could heal any wound, and they'd been infected by mere association with him. "Why didn't you *tell* me?"

To a person, they remained silent, but more than one flicked their eyes toward Jax.

"I told them not to," Jax said.

He turned to her. As he stared into her fair features, he found only defiance staring back at him. *"Why?"*

"I came to see you were right. We have much still to do here."

There was no denying Jax's words. There *was* much good they could do. He'd said as much himself only days ago. But things had changed since then. Still, Brama waited, knowing there was more to come. She was doing that thing she did, avoiding his gaze when she had something to hide.

Jax swallowed hard, as if words were getting caught in her throat. "I did it because I knew when you learned of it, you'd go after the Qaimiri."

He lifted his hands, stared at the blood-soaked bandages. As he flexed his fingers, it brought terrible pain. He could already feel the bones starting to knit, though. The skin starting to heal. Beyond the facade of that simple, bodily pain was an ache that was only going to get worse. Was it the promise of the sapphire calling to him? Or a spell Rïimayesh had laid on him when she'd granted him the ability to heal? Or was it both?

It doesn't matter, he decided.

"Stay," he said to Jax, then took in the rest of them. "All of you, stay." Then he turned and strode from the room.

Jax caught up with him in the dusty street and tugged on his arm until he stopped and faced her. The people in the street gave them a wide berth.

"You can't do this," she said.

He gripped his hands, reveling in the memories the pain summoned. "Her hooks are *inside* me, Jax. They're pulling at me even now, and it's getting worse by the day."

"But surely it's like the call of the lotus?" Jax looked so very desperate, so very small. Part of him wanted to take her into his arms, but his feet stayed firmly rooted. "It will pass," she said in firmer tones. "You have to be strong enough until it does. Isn't that what you tell those you've healed?"

"But I don't *want* to, Jax. Whether I like it or not, she is a part of me. Perhaps I'm part of her as well. I am not whole without her."

"You can't let her do this to you. It's a spell she cast to protect herself should her prison ever be stolen from you."

"I know! I *know!*" He stared at his body. "I hate her! She *ruined* me." At the mere thought of voicing the deeper truth, his heart began to pound so quickly that fainting was a real possibility. He voiced it anyway. "I can't live without her."

Jax swallowed. Tears welled in her eyes, but no words came, not until he began walking away. "Whether you find that gem or not, it's going to kill you."

Good, Brama said to himself.

"Brama!"

He ignored her, and lost himself in the throngs of the city.

Chapter 42

WHEN THE GAOLER OPENED Çeda's cell door, it wasn't the Silver Spears who came to accompany her. It was her old hand—Sümeya, Melis, Kameyl, and Yndris in their black Maiden's dresses, with ebon swords and fighting knives hanging from their belts. Sümeya and Kameyl's eyes were hard. Melis had a blank expression Çeda couldn't read. Yndris, however, studied her with naked glee.

Çeda hadn't eaten in two days. She'd been given little water. Her dark hair hung in ragged clumps. She *smelled*. "It takes four of you?" she asked, if only to wipe the looks from their faces.

"Speak another word," Sümeya said, "and I'll have Yndris gag you, using whatever she cares to use."

Part of Çeda wanted to force her to do it, if only to get in a shot or two at Yndris, but she held her arms out, and the gaoler put her in irons. The cold metal bit into her wrists and ankles, and the chains clanked as she walked. With Kameyl and Yndris ahead, Melis and Sümeya behind, Çeda was led through the palace. She saw no servants as she walked along the halls, only Silver Spears, who stood at attention and eyed her nervously, as if she were about to break her chains and kill them all.

She was thrown in a wagon. *To the gallows?* she wondered. *To die like my mother?*

Not to the gallows, she soon learned, but to another palace—Sukru's. She was led to a large room occupied by the Kings and some few of their most trusted advisors. She'd expected Husamettín and Sukru. She hadn't expected the rest to be there as well.

Çeda was led to a stout chair, positioned near Sukru's. As Sümeya and Kameyl strapped her in, the Reaping King watched with a look of hunger that made her insides squirm. Husamettín sat across from him with a detached expression. Beyond them were Ihsan the Honey-tongued King, Zeheb the King of Whispers, Azad the King of Thorns, Beşir the King of Coin, and Cahil the Confessor King. Lastly, sitting at the head of the long table, was Kiral the King of Kings.

Only Cahil sat away from the table. He was leaning his chair against the wall in the far corner of the room, looking like he wanted to plunge his knife into Çeda's chest. It was an unabashed desire that had, perhaps, earned him his distant position beyond the head of the table.

As a group, the Kings seemed strangely tense. That, along with the fact that she hadn't been passed directly to Cahil for interrogation, made her wonder. There had clearly been some sort of struggle over her, but which Kings were on which side she couldn't tell.

Servants poured wine for each of the Kings. Husamettín immediately pushed his away. "Where is our interrogator?" he asked brusquely.

In answer, Sukru nodded to a man in the corner behind Çeda who looked more like a sell-sword than a King's guard. He was stocky, with piercing blue eyes, and had seen the greater portion of forty summers, she guessed. He had the look of a man who could take care of himself, the sort Çeda always took more seriously when she'd fought in the pits. After an overly familiar bow to his King, the man left the room and returned a short while later with a handsome young man in tow.

The newcomer was tall, with a narrow frame, wearing simple scholar's robes. His dirty blond hair was kept from his eyes by way of a braided leather circlet.

Çeda's mouth fell open: it was Davud. She'd known the Kings would either monitor him, deciding when and how to use his newfound abilities, or kill him outright.

"Might I sit, my good Kings?" Davud asked, motioning to the chair between Sukru and Çeda.

When Sukru nodded sharply, Davud sat down with a strange sort of ease. This was not the impressionable young man she'd once known, nor the more confident version who'd graduated from the collegia. As strange as it was to admit, he had the air of a man who would be comfortable as the world fell apart around him.

He had a rolled leather case, which he presently untied and unfurled across the tabletop before him. Within were a series of needles, glass vials, and instruments that looked rather like painter's knives.

Çeda watched, the worry in her growing as he took several of them out, preparing, apparently, to question Çeda through use of blood. He went about his business methodically, heedless of everyone in the room, be they King, prisoner, or Blade Maiden. When he finally lifted his gaze to look at her, he hardly seemed to recognize her.

Like an insect he was readying to dissect. What happened to you, Davud?

He took her hand, and she felt a prick of pain as he pressed one of the needles into her palm. He did the same to his own hand. Blood welled in both, and he quickly used the two to draw a sign.

Only then did Çeda understand what Davud was about to do. She'd heard the tales of Hamzakiir dominating others' minds, finding their secrets. Davud was about to do the same *to her* for the Kings. She didn't know what secrets he wanted, but she knew she couldn't allow it.

She gripped her hand tightly, smearing the design. Davud merely used the needle to make another wound on her forehead.

"No!" Çeda said as he began drawing the design anew. "Davud, don't!"

As she struggled against her restraints he ignored her and turned calmly to King Sukru. "You or one of the others may wish to join me, to witness the questioning. I give you fair warning, however, it is disorienting and may be stressful to the body."

"I'll do it," Cahil immediately said, then seemed to catch himself and bowed his head to Sukru. "With my good King's permission, of course."

As this was Sukru's palace, it was his prerogative to deny. After a moment he flicked his fingers with an air that spoke of wanting to speed things along.

"Very well," Davud said, motioning Cahil to the empty chair across from him. "If you please, my Lord King."

After downing a healthy swallow of wine, Cahil sat and held his arm out to Davud. Davud used the blood in his palm, now mixed with Çeda's, to draw a symbol on Cahil's palm, though Çeda noticed it was subtly different to his own.

"Now take my hand," Davud said.

Cahil stared at Davud as if he were about to bite him. He'd done this so that he might peer into Çeda's mind, but that didn't mean he trusted Davud. "Is it necessary?"

"If you wish to see what I see, yes," Davud replied easily. "It will be best if you grip my hand tightly."

Cahil did, but there was worry in his eyes.

"Davud," Çeda said softly. But what was there to say? "You can't do this. This is bigger than you or me."

For the first time, Davud showed emotion. He swallowed once, hard, but then he closed his eyes and gripped Çeda's wrist firmly. Immediately she felt a small but rapidly growing presence: Davud, with Cahil but a dim torch in the distance.

"What is it you wish to know, my Kings?" Davud asked.

Çeda thought Cahil might say something, but his face had gone pale, and he was breathing hard, as if it was all he could do to keep hold of Davud's hand.

"Her allies in the House of Maidens," Husamettín said. "Name them and the help they provided."

Davud turned to Çeda. *Gods, his eyes. Cold as winter steel.* How could he have changed so much?

Davud's presence brightened in her mind, but strangely, although his eyes remained fixed on her, she felt him *pressing* on Cahil. Cahil's brow and upper lip started to sweat. His breath came so fast he sounded like a saw cutting green wood. And then, with no preamble whatsoever, his eyes closed and he slumped onto the table.

He slid slowly off and would have fallen to the floor had Sümeya not rushed to catch him. A servant pulled his chair out and laid him on the floor while another rushed to summon a physic. Sukru hovered around them as the physic arrived and tended to Cahil. "Is a delay in order?"

"He seems only to have fainted." Kiral waved a hand toward Davud. "Continue. This is too important to wait."

Davud seemed to be concentrating, his breath coming rapidly as Cahil's had, and yet she felt no assault against her mind. *He isn't trying,* Çeda realized. A moment later, she understood why.

"She had no help from within the House of Maidens," Davud said, regret and conviction coloring the tones of his voice.

It was all she could do to keep the relief from showing on her face. Davud was lying for her. She had no idea why, but she played her part. She jerked her head from side to side, struggled against her restraints, tightened the muscles along her neck, and bore down hard to make her face redden, feigning being trapped in Davud's spell.

"She had allies," Husamettín insisted. "Find them."

Davud nodded. He licked his lips and his eyes flicked to the far end of the table where Kings Azad, Zeheb, and Ihsan were sitting, but then he pulled his gaze back to the King of Swords as if he were afraid to look anywhere else. "I have, my King."

"Then out with it!" Sukru snapped.

"I'm afraid . . ." Davud shifted uncomfortably. "I'm afraid she had the help of a King."

For a moment no one moved. The Kings looked surprised, angry, even contemptuous. Zeheb set his goblet down on the table with a loud thump. The wine splashed over the edge and soaked into the fine needlepoint runner.

Sukru stood. "Clear the room! Now! You as well, Zahndr. Leave no one in the hall."

The man named Zahndr bowed and left. The servants followed, including those tending to Cahil, which left the Confessor King awake but slumped in his chair, groggy and holding his head tightly in his hands. The Maidens went last, Sümeya sparing one last glance for Çeda that was nearly impossible to interpret. Pity? Anger?

When they'd gone, Çeda watched Ihsan surreptitiously. Did Davud know of the Honey-tonged King's involvement? Was he going to expose Ihsan?

"Now speak," Husamettín said to Davud. "Tell us what you saw."

"I saw messages exchanged between Çedamihn and a King. Clandestine talks explaining how to defeat Külaşan, and then Mesut. And more. Had she not been unveiled, she would have gone for Onur next, for the King shared his *bloody verse*, as he called it."

"Prove it," Cahil spat. His skin was pale as snow, but the hunger to see someone burn had returned. "Speak the verse."

Doubt and worry were clear on Davud's face. To speak such a thing—indeed, merely *knowing* that the bloody verses existed—was enough to get him killed. It likely would, unless the Kings found him indispensable, and what were the chances of that?

> *"His reign began,*
> *As taken man,*
> *A King with loosened tongue;*
> *With but a sigh,*
> *Near Bakhi's scythe,*
> *His form is drawn and wrung.*
>
> *When Gods of sky,*
> *Do close their eyes;*
> *Dread hunger burns, enflamed;*
> *Though horror grows,*
> *Like budding rose,*
> *That craved, remade his bane."*

The Kings shared stoney looks but no one said a word against Davud or claimed the verse was false.

Çeda's gaze was drawn to Ihsan. The verse was a reminder of the bargain they'd made on Tauriyat, that if Çeda took Onur's life, he would disclose her father's name. But when Ihsan finally caught her eye, he had the look of a man who was cutting his losses—understandable given how closely the Kings were watching each other. But it made Çeda's heart go cold.

He'd done this, she realized. All of it. Arranging for Çeda to be moved. Gathering the Kings together. Feeding the information to Davud to reveal here. So she knew that when Davud gave a name, it would be anyone but Ihsan.

"Who helped her?" Husamettín asked.

Davud swung his gaze to Zeheb's stocky form. "The King of Whispers."

All eyes swung to Zeheb. Çeda had been so fixated on the other Kings, she'd hardly noticed him. He was staring at the tabletop with a look of confusion, blinking as if he'd just stepped into the sun after days spent hiding in his palace. She doubted he'd even heard Husamettín's question, nor Davud's reply.

"Zeheb?" Husamettín snapped.

Zeheb swung his gaze to his left, the rolls of his neck shifting over his collar as he did so. "What?"

"Did you speak with her?"

Zeheb looked to him, confused. "With whom?"

Husamettín stood, his chair scraping back noisily. "Did you give Çeda Külaşan's bloody verse? And Mesut's and Onur's?"

Zeheb shook his head. "No," he said gently, as if Husamettín had just offered him more wine. What in the wide great desert was wrong with the man?

Husamettín swung his gaze to Çeda. "Was it King Zeheb? Did he aid you in your mission?"

And here it was. Ihsan had somehow set up the pieces to implicate Zeheb. The question now was, should she?

But what choice was there? If it worked, it would topple another King from the heights of Sharakhai. And she would still have her deal with Ihsan.

With a look of defiance, she said, "What of it?"

The room exploded with voices. Some cast doubt on Çeda's admission. Others, Ihsan among them, pleaded with Zeheb to tell them what he knew, ostensible allies searching for some reasonable explanation. Azad and Husamettín, however, demanded Zeheb defend himself.

All the while, Zeheb stared as if he hardly recognized them, confusion in his eyes. Doubt. Worry.

"Let him speak!" Kiral shouted, and finally the voices quelled, all eyes on Zeheb.

"Did you plot against your brother Kings?" Kiral asked, his voice calm as winter's dawn.

Zeheb fumbled for words. "I . . . I don't believe so. I wouldn't . . ."

The room was deadly quiet as understanding seemed to finally dawn on Zeheb. His eyes shed their lethargy, becoming wild as the madmen along the Trough. "I would never!"

"Take them away," Kiral said to Sukru, waving darkly toward Davud and Çeda.

Sümeya and Kameyl were summoned to lead Çeda and Davud from the room, as Zeheb cried, "Kiral, tell me what's happening!"

Sounds of a struggle erupted behind them. Çeda thought they were killing him, but a moment later, Kiral's voice boomed, "Tie him to the chair." The sounds from the room died away as they strode down the palace halls, until all that was left were the muffled sounds of Zeheb's rantings. Davud kept glancing back, though, the worry clear on his face.

Çeda looked back as well and saw that Zahndr, Sukru's guardsman, had peeled away from the wall and was following them.

"Are you well?" Çeda asked Davud under her breath.

"Yes," he replied. He was rubbing his forehead with the look of a man working up to something.

Yndris clouted Davud's ear. "No talking!"

Davud shook his head, looking confused. "If I could just speak to Çeda for a moment."

"You may not!" Yndris said, and shoved him hard against the wall. She held him there, one forearm pressed against his throat.

Davud clamped his hand with the bloody sigil over Yndris's forehead.

Her eyes bulged and her mouth opened in a silent scream. Davud had hardly touched her, yet she reeled backward as if she'd been kicked by a mule.

Melis and Kameyl pulled Çeda back.

Sümeya charged Davud, who pressed his palms together, then spread his hands out as if warning Sümeya not to come near.

Zahndr was chanting something behind Çeda. He was staring intently at Davud, his hands moving before him in strange ways, as if he were shaping clay. Çeda was still in chains, but Zahndr was close enough that she could duck her shoulder and drive it hard into his chest.

Zahndr was thrown backward. He twisted awkwardly as he fell, trying to keep his feet but managing only to increase his pace as he tumbled to the immaculate marble floor.

A terrible wind howled through the halls, almost knocking Çeda off her feet, but then it quelled as it swirled around her like a dust devil. The Maidens and Zahndr, however, were blown back like leaves in a gale. The five of them, including Yndris's unconscious form, were sent sliding, spinning, crashing into pedestals and potted plants, coming to a rest twenty paces down the hall.

"Davud, what in the gods' names are you doing?" Çeda asked.

He was staring at her with a look of deep regret. "I'm sorry, Çeda."

He pressed his hands toward one another, and a flame formed between them. It was not so different from what Hamzakiir had done, sending balls of flame after Husamettín when they'd fought along the top of the aqueduct. As Davud turned his hands toward her, the flame was released like an arrow from a bow. She tried to dodge it but she was too near, the flame moving too fast.

Suddenly it split in two, the twin ropes of fire spilling against the floor to her right and the wall on her left. As the flames licked upward, Davud turned to see Zahndr sprinting along the hallway.

Davud tried to create another ball of flame, but Zahndr moved his hands in arcane rhythms, somehow working against the spell. A candle flame was born between Davud's hands, but it grew no larger. Again he tried to release it at Çeda. It became thin and tenuous as it moved toward her, twisting like a sidewinder, then fell across Çeda's thighs and lit her clothes afire.

Zahndr was there immediately, putting it out, then pulling her away from the fire, which was coughing smoke and burning like spilled lamp oil on the marble floor.

In that moment, Çeda saw Davud staring at her with a look like he had no idea what was happening to him. He turned and flung something to the floor, something that glinted like gold—an amulet, perhaps, or a large earring. The thing grew, spinning just above the floor. And inside it . . . Breath of the desert, she saw not the marble flooring of Sukru's palace, but somewhere else entirely. A dark room. A hearth fire.

Something flew from Zahndr's hand and struck Davud across the back of his head, sending him reeling. He tipped forward . . . and fell through the hole.

"No!" Zahndr shouted, diving for Davud's ankle.

But Davud was already through and the strange device was shrinking, ever smaller. When it was the size of small melon a brightly colored bird flew through the opening, and then, when it was once again the size of an earring, it fell and chimed against the floor. As they watched, the bird picked it up in its beak and flew away, leaving a stunned silence in the halls of Sukru's palace.

Chapter 43

DAVUD FELL HARD onto a matted woven rug. He was in the center of a stiflingly hot room, a space filled with a myriad of cages and the sounds of chirping birds.

Gods, my head.

Beside him he found the knife Zahndr had thrown at him. How could something that small make him feel like someone had taken a hammer to the back of his skull? His fingers probed. Pain flared around the site of the wound. The hair all around it was matted with blood. The cut didn't feel terribly large, but the pain was adding to the splitting headache that had been building since he'd awoken early that morning. He hadn't been able to shake it since he'd spoken with—

"Well, hello," the Sparrow's voice called from the darkened hallway.

For a moment, the chirping sounds abated, but they picked up a moment later as Davud stood, confused. It felt as if a bag had been placed over his head. For the life of him he couldn't remember what he'd just been thinking about. A brightly colored hallway? A twisting ribbon of flame? He put his palms to his eyes and tried to press away the pain, but it felt as if the blasted birds had escaped their cages and were determined to peck their way inside his head.

Then it all came back in a rush. The sigil the firefinch had given him. Practicing it for hours along with the others he knew he'd need. Conducting Çeda's questioning and uncovering Zeheb's treachery.

Çeda . . . He should have brought her here, but he hadn't, had he? He'd been knocked through the spinning triangle.

Nalamae's sweet tears, I attacked her.

He remembered how *hungry* he'd been for her death. But what had made him do it? For the life of him he couldn't remember.

"You seem to be missing some few of your promised friends."

The footsteps shuffled closer. The door swung wide, and the Sparrow was revealed at last.

Davud felt the blood drain from his face. By the gods, it was Sukru.

After Anila had left Davud's room, she headed back toward hers but stopped in her tracks when she saw Zahndr ahead, leaning against the wall. He'd known she would come here, which made her wonder if he'd overheard anything.

"You don't have to follow me everywhere I go," she said as she brushed past him.

He fell into step beside her. "Were Sukru to give you an express order, would you consider disobeying it?"

She thought he had some further point to make, but when he remained silent she realized he expected an answer, which made her wary.

"No," she said carefully, "unless there was new information Sukru wasn't aware of."

Zahndr tipped his head cordially. "A reasonable reply were we not speaking of the Kings of Sharakhai. And you should know that Sukru is the least forgiving of them. When he gives an order, I follow it. And so will you."

"I wasn't told not to speak to Davud."

"You were told to leave him alone."

"I didn't realize that meant avoid him *entirely*. We are friends, after all."

"You're a smart girl, Anila." Zahndr grabbed her by the elbow and began leading her back toward her room. "You should've bloody well figured it out."

"Unhand me!"

"Why, *certainly*, my lady."

He kept his hand where it was, though, forcing her to keep up or be dragged. His grip was not rough, yet on her altered skin it felt like a snake bite. It also gave her some surprising insights into Zahndr. Before Ishmantep, she was like anyone else. She saw *life* when she gazed upon people or animals or desert flora. She often marveled at how any of them could master the Great Shangazi and thrive.

Now she saw death, decay, and disease, however subtle their shading. Zahndr's skin, which to anyone else would appear a light shade of copper but to her looked dark, seemed almost rotted in places, especially where blood flowed the strongest. Some sort of affliction was eating its way out of him. She could smell it on his breath, the scent of rot, which she could smell on many, including, strangely enough, King Sukru. In Zahndr, however, it was more pronounced, the difference between smelling a midden from the back alleys of Sharakhai and rolling around in one. She was unsure of the nature of the affliction—she'd hardly studied such things at the collegia—but she was sure it was nearing the point where he would succumb to it.

When they reached her room, Zahndr shoved her inside. "Stay here, lest Bela's fate befall you."

Anila felt as if he'd physically struck her. "What?" When he tried closing the door, she put her hand to it and held it open. "What did you say about Bela?"

Zahndr sneered. "Perhaps you're not half as smart as you thought." With that, he shoved her away and slammed the door. A moment later she heard the metallic clink of the lock engaging.

She tried to force it open, but it wouldn't budge. "Tell me what you meant about Bela!"

His reply was the sound of dwindling footsteps.

Bela, he'd said. *Bela's fate . . .* Everyone had said it was an accident when Zahndr found her at the bottom of the stairs.

As she stood before the stout door, a dark fury grew inside her, threatening to boil over. A year ago she might have let it, but if Ishmantep had taught her anything, it was that her worst emotions must be bottled, not to be ignored but to be employed with care and precision.

She who allows her emotions to run wild becomes a tool of the fates. Control them, however, and your fate becomes your own.

Kneeling before the door, she placed her hand over the lock. Just as she could feel decay in living things, she could feel it in materials as well. From the lock itself, the metal, she felt nothing. It was like the void of a moonless night to her new senses. The door was different. The wood was stout and lustrous, well maintained, and she felt some echo of the life it once had. But she also felt its slow decay. She concentrated on it, accentuating its hunger. Like an apple going to rot, once it began, it spread quickly, until the wood was dark and soft all around the lock. All it took was a quick tug and it sprung free. Bits of black, moldy wood crumbled from around the handle and lock and fell to the floor as she swung it wide.

The urge to run was strong, but it would bring unwanted attention so she kept her pace steady, her head down, and returned the cordial bows of the servants as she wove through the palace toward the boneyard. She hadn't been there since trying to speak to Bela. She'd been too afraid. What Davud had said made sense—she'd been toying with the domain of the gods—but she would ignore her power no longer.

She walked to Bela's family crypt, where the scent of decay had been strong but was now overpowering. Anila buried her nose in the fabric of her sleeve, collecting herself before continuing. She stood before Bela's sarcophagus and laid her hands on the marble's cool surface. She could feel Bela lying within, not her body, but the wisp of her soul. It was so faint she wondered whether she could summon her, but what was there to do but try?

She drew the sigil on the marble, combining the signs for *death* and *summon*. Frost trailed in her finger's wake, creating a kaleidoscope of tiny patterns that dissipated, devoured by the warmth. She drew it again and again, and each time the sigil persisted a little longer.

"Come, Bela. There are things I must know."

She felt nothing like before. Bela was much more distant, so removed from her own death it was difficult to know if she would *ever* come.

"Zahndr said it was an accident," Anila said, louder than before. "Is it true, Bela? Or did he lie to everyone?"

Still nothing.

"Would you see him go unpunished? Your true death forever unknown, even to your father?"

There was a stirring like a candle in a storm, snuffed before it could take. But it was something.

Anila crouched and whispered to the crack below the lid. "How your fa-ther misses you, Bela." It was an unspoken promise. Bela belonged to the farther fields, but if she could return, even for a short while, she might be warmed by love. It was a lie, and Anila felt craven for voicing it, but she needed Bela. Davud needed her.

Bela's soul brightened. Anila felt that weightless thing fill the space be-neath the heavy marble lid.

"Lift it," Anila bid her. "Let me see you."

The lid shifted. Small hands wrapped in white gauze pushed the lid down toward the foot of the sarcophagus.

"Enough," Anila said. "Sit."

And Bela did. She was covered in funereal wrap—the white linen around her hands had been wrapped around her again and again until she was com-pletely obscured by it. With tender movements, Anila pulled them away, revealing her eyes, her face. Her black hair was woven into a single braid. Her face was necrotic, peeling in some places, and her eyes were milky. They re-garded Anila coldly, her face utterly still.

Anila swallowed hard, momentarily at a loss for words. "My tears were a river when I heard . . ." She stopped. Those words were more for her than they were for Bela. "I'm sorry for your return to this poor world," she began again, "but I must ask you some questions."

Bela took in the crypt around her as if she were in a deep, dreamlike haze. Her brows pinched as she turned back to Anila.

"How did you die, love?"

Her mouth worked. Her frown deepened. She drew one long breath that sounded like leaves being raked, then spoke in a scratchy whisper, "I went to see the man in the east tower."

The east tower was forbidden. "King Sukru?"

"No." She smiled, a piteous thing on her ruin of a face. "The bird man who looks like him."

A rush of fear tingled in Anila's fingers and toes. She glanced through the crypt door, feeling eyes on her, but found the boneyard blessedly empty. "Tell me about the bird man."

"King Sukru's brother. He sends birds all over Sharakhai, all over the palace, to spy for him."

"How do you know?"

"I've seen them. The birds. Firefinches and thornbills and saddlebacks and more. They always fly to one window in the east tower. I asked memma why and she told me to shush."

"But there are guards posted there. How can you know?"

"I watched them." Bela's lungs rasped. "They saw me and told me to leave, but then I started hiding. They talk a lot, and sometimes step away from the door. When they did, I snuck in."

The whimsy in Bela's features faded, replaced by a growing sense of dread. "What happened, Bela?"

"I went up the stairs, and I saw him. He calls himself the Sparrow. He told me before . . . Before he . . ."

"Did he strike you, Bela?"

A viscous green substance leaked from Bela's eyes. It crept like honey down her cheek, the slow pace somehow intensifying the hopeless look on her face. "Yes."

Anila heard running footsteps and a moment later, Zahndr loomed in the crypt's entryway. He stared at Bela, his face a mixture of shock and rage. "You dare!"

Anila took several steps back. "You have much to answer for. Her death to begin with."

Zahndr's brow furrowed, and he shook his head. "*I* didn't kill her!"

"You played your part. You let her mother and father think she died from a fall."

Bela was staring at them both, confused, but Zahndr spoke as if he hardly knew she was there. "Sukru is a cruel master. More cruel than you will ever know."

"A coward's words."

"Then I am a coward." He stepped toward her, regret plain on his face as he drew his knife. "I'm sorry, Anila."

Before he could take another step, she drew upon his sickness, putting all of herself into it, knowing that half-measures now would cost her her life.

Zahndr coughed. His eyes turned bloodshot and started to tear. He seemed to master himself, his whole face going red. He made a fist and lifted his gaze until it rested on her. The look of regret was gone. Now there was only anger.

She tried harder. As she backed into the corner of the crypt, she tried to deepen the sickness running through him, to make him go to rot, just like the door. She guided it to his heart, to his mind. He stumbled as he came for her. His lips drew back like a feral dog, revealing clenched teeth and spittle. He was somehow fighting her power, and she was losing the battle.

And then he was on her. He blocked her blows and snatched her throat. She tried kicking him, but he hooked one of her ankles and twisted her down to the stone floor. Her head struck stone, and her world became stars. She couldn't breathe. She saw only Zahndr's face, shivering, eyes maniacally wide as he used both hands to choke her. A keen ringing sound filled the air, then grew and grew and grew, a sound the dead must hear as they rushed toward the farther shores.

Among the near-deafening ringing, she heard a crack. A crumbling. A wheezing grunt.

The hold on her neck eased. "No!" Zahndr cried.

Through the twinkling gauze of a thousand flecks of light, she saw Zahndr raise his hands. Saw a bronze statue arc through the air and sweep through Zahndr's defenses to strike him across the head, driving Zahndr from Anila's field of vision in a mass of flesh and blood and bone. It was as if Thaash himself had struck Zahndr down.

Anila coughed. She rolled over, holding her throat as she fought to regain her breath.

She lifted her head and saw Bela standing there, still holding the bronze statue of a winged goddess, now covered in blood. As anger and fear and confusion warred on Bela's face, Anila stood and took the statue from her. When Bela let it go, it was so heavy it practically fell to the floor. The anger was fading from Bela as she stared at Zahndr, her hands covering her mouth. Zahndr lay twitching, the crown of his head a mottled, broken mess.

"Quickly," Anila said, leading her from the crypt. "We may already be too late."

Davud stared, mouth agape, as Sukru shuffled into the room. "By the gods. You're . . . My Lord King!" He bowed, which made the pain in his head intensify.

"Rise," the Sparrow said. "I am no King of Sharakhai, though only by dint of being born second."

Understanding dawned. "You are his twin."

He didn't require the Sparrow's nod to tell him the truth of it. His lank hair. His bald pate. His hooked nose and rat-like eyes. The two looked so similar the Sparrow could easily pass for Sukru.

"But how . . . ?"

Just then a firefinch flew through the open doorway to land on the Sparrow's shoulder, the triangle pinched in its beak. But how could it be here so quickly? The Sparrow took the golden device, then carried the bird on an extended finger and put him in a nearby cage filled with a dozen other firefinches.

"You wish to know how I ended up here." The Sparrow tied the triangle to a leather cord, then wore it like an amulet. "How I came to peck at the corpse of my brother's rule."

Davud could only nod.

"Let's return to that in a moment." As he came nearer, he stared intently at Davud's head. "For now, there's something that needs fixing."

He lifted one enfeebled hand to Davud's forehead, closed his eyes and whispered words too soft for Davud to make out.

When Davud was young, a snake charmer had come to the bazaar. He used no flute, like all the rest did. He didn't sit before a basket and tease the snake out. Instead, he would wrap the cobra over one arm, then run his hand along the back of its black-and-yellow hood, whispering to it. As he stroked the cobra's skin, the snake would stiffen. It became like a length of wood that the charmer would then place on the tip of one finger and balance in the air. He'd do this for as long as coins were dropped into the snake's woven basket, and then he would nod to the boys and girls in the audience, whom he'd prepped before the show had begun. His assistants would clap their hands loudly, and the snake would wake, forcing the charmer to grab its tail before it fell to the ground.

That was how Davud felt, like a snake being charmed. He knew he could move, he knew that to remain immobile was perhaps dangerous, and yet he was in perfect thrall to the simple touch of the Sparrow's finger on his forehead.

"Well, well," the Sparrow said, smiling. "There is a taint upon you, boy. Laid by none other than the Honey-tongued King." His smile widened. "Won't my brother be pleased to hear it?"

The Honey-tongued King? A taint? "How—"

But before he could even form the question, memories returned. Ihsan coming to him in the morning's darkest hour. Spelling out his role. And when Ihsan had left someone else had given commands. To kill Çeda, and then himself.

To kill Çeda.

And then himself.

The urge was so strong that Davud was startled from the spell that had been laid upon him. He slapped the Sparrow's hand away, ran to Zahndr's knife.

He'd just taken it up when the Sparrow shouted, "No! You must deny him!"

Davud's hand was stayed. The urge was still in him, but now it warred with the truth, that this was not his own decision. It took long minutes of the Sparrow's whispering for him to deny the order from the mystery man who'd come to visit him, but gradually the urge became less like a need and more like a memory, still present but easily ignored.

Breathing heavily, Davud realized the headache that had worn on him throughout the day was gone. It brought with it a sense of elation that was so strong he laughed from it, long and hard. It felt strange and wonderful to be himself once more, or nearly so.

But then a disconcerting thought made his laughter vanish like rare winter snow. He stared straight into the Sparrow's small, narrow-set eyes and said with certainty, "If you're Sukru's twin, then you've been alive since Beht Ihman."

"Very good, Davud," said the Sparrow and placed his palm on Davud's forehead.

His legs buckled, and the world shimmered before him.

———— ⟵—●—⟶ ————

He woke lying on a bed, a blanket draped over him. The Sparrow was sitting by his side on a stool. The disorientation made him feel dizzy, as if not a single moment had passed between the time the Sparrow had placed his palm on Davud's forehead and now.

He tried to sit up, but realized he couldn't move. He couldn't even feel his body. Only his face. "What's happening?"

"I'm glad you've returned," the Sparrow said. "It's a sign of your strength." He pursed his lips, as if chewing on a thought. "I often think those who come into my care would like to see the end of their days rather than wonder what happened when they reach the farther fields."

Davud couldn't understand a word of what he was saying. "What are you doing?"

The Sparrow turned to him. "I am preparing to *consume my winnings*, as they used to say in the betting parlors."

Davud shook his head. "You said you were going to help me. To shelter and train me. You said it was a rebuke against Sukru."

"It *is* a rebuke. Sukru deserves this for stealing the last several from me."

"Stolen . . ." At last, Davud managed to turn his head and see what it was the Sparrow held in his hands. A needle with a small channel along the top leading to a reservoir for blood. He was cleaning the metal with a cloth, making it shine. "You said Sukru wronged you."

"He did! He took my son from me. A long, long time ago now. He was a promising young mage. He would have been more powerful than I have ever been."

"You said you would save me."

The Sparrow turned sharply, his pinched face annoyed. "Of course I did, boy. You would hardly have come if I'd told you the truth!"

A hard lump had formed in Davud's throat. He couldn't seem to get rid of it. "And what is the truth?"

Done with the polishing, the Sparrow laid the cloth on his lap, held Davud's arm, and pressed the strange needle into it. Blood welled, flowed along the channel, and began to collect in the reservoir. It stung, but it was nothing compared to the feeling of helplessness before this mage, the brother of a King of Sharakhai.

Staring at the needle, the Sparrow said, "I discovered my son was a mage shortly before the tribes came for Sharakhai. I offered myself and my son to the Kings before Beht Ihman, but they refused, seeing our power as too little to turn the tide of battle. It was true enough, I suppose, but the real reason was they didn't *trust* the red ways. After Beht Ihman, they decided blood magi were a threat and less than a year after the tribes were turned back, they came for me and my son. My son was lost, but Sukru saved me, pretending I had been killed."

"How have you lived so long?"

The Sparrow smiled, a grisly thing filled with misshapen teeth. "The favor of the gods did not shine on my brother alone."

"And your son? You forgave Sukru for his loss?"

"Jabrar was taken from me, but it wasn't in Sukru's power to stop. Not truly. I will never forgive my brother for his part in it, but we have since come to an accord."

The reservoir full, he pulled the needle from Davud's arm and, like a master vintner testing last year's harvest, upended the crimson liquid into his mouth. He closed his eyes as a shiver overtook him, the picture of a man who'd taken a long pull from a shisha filled with black lotus.

"Do you know, I think you might be as strong as Hamzakiir." He caught Davud's look. "Yes, I knew him. He was one of the few who knew of my existence here."

"But why am *I* here?"

"Magi, from time to time, are found in Sharakhai or the desert beyond and given over to Sukru. They are not trusted, exactly, but the Kings are no fools." He tipped the reservoir once more, swallowing the last of the blood. Another, more violent shiver ran through him. He arched his neck back, as if in the throes of pleasure. "They don't flinch at making use of them so long as Sukru believes they're no threat."

"But why pretend to be someone you're not to lure me?"

"I do not pretend. I *am* the Sparrow. And this is a game Sukru and I play. I attempt to make the mage to come to me willingly, while he tries to prevent it, without either of us revealing the truth. If he keeps the magi for two seasons, they are his, and if I win . . . Well, you're about to see what happens then." He stood and set the needle down on a nearby shelf, and took up a slim steel knife with a razor-keen edge. "Sukru has won the last several times we've played our little game. But what I've lost in quantity I've now gained in quality."

Davud tried to struggle again, but it was no use. He was trapped in his own body, and would be forced to watch as the Sparrow drained his blood from him, or cut out his heart, or whatever it was he was about to do.

But Davud had power in him yet. He'd taken Çeda's blood before questioning her. It was still in him, and that was no small thing. He'd never cast a spell without a sigil before, but they were only a framework, weren't they? A way to focus the mind? Did he truly need them?

As the Sparrow used the knife to cut away Davud's robes, Davud searched for a spell to use against him. *Flame*, unfocused, might burn Davud instead of his intended target, or harm the Sparrow but not stop him. *Cold* and *wind* were of no use. In his desperation, he concentrated on the sigils for *harden* and *shatter*. If the Sparrow sensed it he could stop it, but Davud could think of nothing else.

Concentrating on the knife drawing near, he laid one sigil over the other and drew the combined image over and over in his mind's eye. His fear was running wild. His breath wheezed through his nostrils, but he never took his eyes from the knife's bright edge.

It isn't working! It isn't working!

But then, just as the knife sliced into his sternum, the blade shattered. The Sparrow's hand shot up like he'd been stung, and the knife's hilt, now bladeless, clattered to the floor. He stared at Davud's chest, where a constellation of blood was forming from the myriad shards of metal that had cut his skin. For the first time, the Sparrow seemed consumed by emotion. He took one long stride back forward and backhanded Davud across the mouth. "That won't *help* you," he spat.

Davud cringed, expecting another blow, but the Sparrow stalked from the small room into the larger one beyond, with the birds. A knocking came, then a pounding. Then an almighty crash of wood, some of which flew into Davud's field of vision.

He could see the Sparrow, his eyes lit with anger and a raw potency derived from Davud's own blood.

"Zahndr?" the Sparrow called. "Zahndr, stay where you are!" He lifted both hands. A darkness was forming within each, a void Davud could feel thrumming in his chest. "I command you to stop, Zahndr!"

As the Sparrow backed away, Zahndr lumbered into view. He walked steadily as the darkness in the Sparrow's hands deepened and buzzed like a rattlewing. And then a rope of darkness was released. Like chain lightning it flew across the floor, up to the ceiling, covering a wide expanse in tendrils of dark power. Where it touched Zahndr it singed his clothes, blackened his skin. His right arm, near the shoulder, shriveled, dissolving like clumps of sugar in steaming tea, and then the lower part of his arm fell bloodless to the floor.

Another arc of dark lightning came, cutting across Zahndr's waist and thighs. It melted so much skin his organs came spilling out and exposed his thighs to the bone. But Zahndr was close to the Sparrow now, and the Sparrow could retreat no farther; he was already backed up against the wall near the hearth.

Zahndr, no longer able to walk, *leaned* forward, brought his remaining arm down like a sledge, and struck the Sparrow across his greasy, balding head. As the Sparrow fell, his eyes going slack, one last arc of lightning was released. It cut Zahndr in two.

As the two of them lay on the floor, motionless, another form rushed into view.

"Anila," Davud breathed.

She hurried to his side. After stripping a bit of cloth from his robes, she licked it and rubbed at his forehead. A sigil upon his skin, he realized, confirmed a moment later when he felt movement returning to his arms and legs.

As she helped him walk into the next room, he heard shuffling steps from beyond the now-shattered doorway. Another form plodded forward. "Gods, Anila, no."

It was Bela. She walked over the carpet, over the broken remains of the door, over Zahndr's remains, toward the Sparrow's stirring form.

"Quiet, Davud. She deserves this."

The Sparrow opened his eyes as Bela neared, and he blinked up at her, his eyes going wide. "No!"

Bela didn't listen. She knelt beside him, picked up a wedge of wood.

With all the innocent curiosity of a child crushing a beetle beneath her thumb, she drove it into his neck. Blood flew and the Sparrow fell slack to the floor. The very moment his eyes went glassy, Bela tipped over and fell on top of him, unmoving, as if she'd followed him to the farther fields to haunt him there as well.

For long moments Davud and Anila stared at the carnage. The smell was terrible. Rot and burning and something acrid. The birds in their cages had been aflutter, but now they settled, another part of the eerie silence.

"We have to go," Anila said numbly. Her eyes were aghast, as if she hadn't realized it would go this far. "Sukru. The Spears. They'll be coming."

Davud looked around the room. Took in the birds. He crouched and unwound the leather necklace from around the Sparrow's head. He untied the triangle from it, then pierced his skin with one corner, giving him the power he would need. He then went to one of the cages, the ones filled with the firefinches. After flipping the tiny latch and swinging the wire door open, he retrieved a finch from within.

"Take it," he urged, using a simple spell of *fulfill* and *bind*. The bird did, eyes blinking as it ruffled its wings. "Go," Davud said, "anywhere but the House of Kings."

The bird fluttered noisily away, taking the triangle with it. Somewhere, the sounds of men approaching could be heard. They grew louder and louder until Davud was sure they were only a floor or two below.

"Davud?" Anila asked, her nervousness clear.

"One moment," he replied.

His sense of the triangle, formed when he'd used it earlier, dwindled as the bird flew deeper into Sharakhai. Only when the first of the Silver Spears arrived at the end of the dark hall did he call upon that link and summon the sigils for *passage* and *doorway*. A spinning, triangular space opened up before him, a window that revealed a sloping hill, rows of planted crops, and a vast reservoir of water beyond.

Three tall Silver Spears ran forward. "Halt!" the lead soldier called as Anila stepped through. Davud followed, and the triangle closed behind him.

Chapter 44

EMRE WATCHED as Mihir sprinted over the sand, his long, swift strides kicking up a tail of sand as he flew toward Onur.

Onur waited, a feral grin on his face, his massive arms spread like a dirt dog in the pits. His left hand was empty. In his right, he still held the fist-sized fire opal.

When the two warriors engaged, Onur met Mihir's onslaught like a bear before a snapping wolf. His movements looked ungainly, and yet, for all his mass, he moved with deceptive ease. He was nearly as fast as his smaller opponent, dodging Mihir's kenshar, swinging his fists like bludgeons to keep Mihir at a safe distance. Onur had that same black laugher grin on his face the whole time. It enraged Mihir, whose movements became wilder, overeager, and when he stepped just a bit too close, Onur backhanded him so hard he spun and fell to the sand. Onur's personal guard closed in, but stopped when Onur held out one meaty hand.

"Leave him," Onur said as he pounded forward.

Mihir, recovered somewhat, rolled away from a great stomp of Onur's leg. He slashed at Onur's leg as he came up, but Onur's armor warded the blow and gave him another opening, which Onur used to deliver a crushing kick that sent Mihir falling and scrambling away.

Onur loomed over him. "You should have kept that fool mouth of yours shut."

With a quick roll backward, Mihir was back on his feet, but Onur was already on him. He pummeled Mihir, who had finally regained his senses. Mihir retreated, dodging when he needed to, rolling gracefully over one shoulder, sand spraying, to come up at the ready. Over and over Onur tried to bring his tankard-sized fists to bear, but Mihir took only glancing blows. And in return he used his brother's knife to deliver a cut to Onur's forearm. Then another to Onur's opposite hand.

Onur's massive fists became coated in blood. His skin and leather bracers glinted red in the bright sun. Onur was becoming angry, his eyes lit with anger, his teeth bared. He bulled forward, faster than before, but Mihir was always quicker. Soon Mihir had scored another cut, then two more. Mihir *smiled* as he fought, eyes bright as he wove an intricate pattern over the sand that was much more careful and considered than his initial violent rush. He was a mongoose now, not some clumsy hyena.

Onur's breath came in great rasps. Like a wounded bull he chased Mihir, but again and again the smaller man was too swift. When Onur stumbled, an opening presented itself. Mihir ducked a clumsy sweep of Onur's arm, drove his shoulder into Onur's chest, and stabbed his brother's kenshar into Onur's side. The knife was buried to the hilt. But in that moment Onur grabbed Mihir's wrist with his left hand. His right, the one holding the stone, came down like a sledge against the top of Mihir's head.

Emre heard a dull crack, the sound of wet wood being split by an axe. Mihir went stiff. His right hand released the knife while his arms trembled, a thing that grew worse with every passing moment.

Onur lifted the bright orange stone and brought it down on Mihir's skull again. The knife was still sticking out of Onur's side as Mihir tipped like a tent pole to the sand. Onur pulled the knife free, tossed it aside, and dropped to one knee by Mihir's side. With a crazed expression, he grabbed a hunk of Mihir's hair and brought the round stone against the crown of Mihir's head over and over.

Only when Mihir's body had gone still and the upper part of his head was a pulpy mess of hair and skin and bone and blood did Onur stop. His chest heaving, he turned to Tribe Kadri and held the stone high. "You see what comes from defying your King?" He levered himself to his feet, favoring his left side where the knife wound bled freely. He gestured toward them, and his personal guard, and the dozens of soldiers standing behind them, charged. As one, Tribe Kadri drew their shamshirs and roared as they met the advancing line of Onur's warriors—a mixture of the Black Veils and the Red Wind. Onur didn't move. He merely watched while holding the orange stone high. His lips moved, but the roar of the ranks of charging soldiers was too loud for Emre to hear.

Beyond the looming battle, beyond the pools of the oasis and the vast cluster of ships, Emre heard a groaning sound. On and on it went, becoming more intense, rising in pitch until it sounded like a trumpet blast from the herald of Thaash, lord of battle.

The sound shook the desert floor. All around, the soldiers stopped, their battle momentarily forgotten. All eyes turned to look back beyond the camp where a great tail lifted into the blue sky. Frills with long spikes running through the translucent skin spread to either side of the lashing tail. The skin and spikes were a mottled landscape of stone and sand and rust.

As the tail dropped, a reptilian head lifted and a gasp fell over the warriors. They could see the sheer size of it now. It was longer than a ship, as broad as ten men. Long horns fanned back from the back of its wedge-shaped head. Even from this distance Emre could see the orange of its eyes, a near perfect match for the stone in Onur's hand. Its body leaned to one side, then the other, neck craning as it surveyed the scene before it.

It was not a sand drake, which could not fly, nor was it one of the smaller wyverns of the desert's southern reaches. This was a wyrm, one of the great dragons of legend. Longer frills ran along its back. Translucent skin stretched between them, the sun shining through it in hypnotic patterns. Midway along its length, the frills grew longer, into wings. The thin skin of its wings extended unbroken from its neck all the way down its length until just short of the tail, which had a second, smaller, leaf-shaped set of frills attached.

With a terrible roar the beast launched itself into the sky. Every man, woman, and child went into a half-crouch, arms over their heads, as if the creature was about to attack them. It didn't matter if they were loyal to Onur or not. All were terrified.

A whooshing sound accompanied each sinuous beat of the wyrm's elongated wings. Its body moved like a Mirean kite, twisting through the sky as its wavelike movements brought it higher and higher, while the rolling rhythm of its frills were more like a millipede's crawl.

"Burning Hands!" one of the women from Tribe Kadri called. She was near the front of the line and had turned to face the bulk of the warriors, one hand high, her tattooed palm facing them. "We must take Onur!" When she lifted her shamshir high, the Burning Hands lifted swords and spears and shouted, "For Mihir!"

As they renewed their battle, warriors on both sides woke from their daze. Battle cries grew like a coming storm.

Emre, however, paused.

Onur *wanted* this battle, perhaps as a way to test his mastery over the wyrm. He'd gone out into the desert alone to find it, and now he wished to use it. How else to ensure it would work in other, larger battles to come?

How it had all come to pass, Emre couldn't begin to guess, but he was sure they couldn't stay here. If they did, they'd all be killed.

Emre gripped Shal'alara's arm and pointed to the Kadri ships, where some of the crews were preparing them to sail, but not enough. Not nearly enough. "We must make them see sense! They must return to their ships! Get them ready to sail. I'll bring as many as I can."

Shal'alara nodded, as if she'd been thinking the same thing, and made for the largest cluster of Kadri ships. "Try," she called over her shoulder, "but follow if they refuse to listen."

Emre drew his sword and sprinted in the other direction. Dozens of Kadri warriors were now engaged. The clash of steel rang out, mixing with the cry of battle and a renewed roar from the wyrm above. Onur lumbered forward, looking as though each step pained him. There was no sign of the stone. Instead he held a great, broad-headed spear, which he used to run the nearest Kadri warrior through. In one great show of strength, he lifted the warrior up and over his head, throwing him like a cut of meat onto an open fire, and then he waded deeper into battle, eyes filled with glee, laughing all the while.

Haddad was nearby, stout Zakkar by her side.

"We must retreat!" Emre said.

Haddad said nothing. She couldn't take her eyes from the wyrm, which moved closer with every rolling beat of its great wings.

Emre took her arm and shook her. "By the gods, *help me!* Those who remain will die or be enslaved by Onur, including you and your crew."

She nodded numbly, as if her mind were only now lifting from the ruin Onur had made of her plans when he bashed Mihir's head in. "Come," she snapped at her bodyguard, Zakkar.

Together, the three of them stood before a second wave of Kadri warriors running from the ships, hands high, gesturing wildly. "The tribe!" Emre called, looking up to the wyrm. "We must save those we can!"

Many paid him no heed, but a few, and then more, paused, paralyzed with fear as the wyrm reached an apex and dropped into a dive. Its wings pulled tight to its body as it speared toward the nearest of the Kadri ships. When it came close, it curled its body in, legs forward, wings snapping outward while its tail twisted sharply to adjust the angle of its landing. It crashed between the ship's masts, snapping rigging as it fell upon the crew.

Its tail lashed as its jaws came in reach of any man or woman who hoped to stand against it. The ship's crew had spears, swords, and bows, but they didn't stand a chance. Its jaws snapped at bodies, crushing them before throwing them wide. Its claws rent flesh and bone and wood alike. From the aft of the ship it slipped down to the sand, tail whipping behind, delivering terrible cuts from the sharp spines, only to climb back on the foredeck and begin its assault anew.

More of Onur's soldiers approached the battle. Many swung their swords over their heads, rejoicing at this demonstration of Onur's power.

"Now!" Emre commanded Mihir's tribe. "We go now!"

"With me," Haddad said, motioning to her ship. "Convince as many as you can to follow."

"I'll fight with you," Emre told the dozen nearest him. "The rest will get the ships moving. We retreat only when they're on the move!"

As Haddad led most of them toward the ships, Emre ran with those he'd chosen, his heart pounding with fear as they joined the battle.

Shouts of anguish and moaning mingled with cries of rage and desperation. The sound of steel on steel was all around him, as was the crack of wooden shields being struck or sundered. The roars of the wyrm felt as though they were coming from just behind him. Several times he looked over his shoulder and saw that it had laid the first ship to waste and had fallen upon a second.

He nearly lost his head as a Masal warrior attacked him with a feverish energy. Emre was no master swordsman like Macide, but he held the warrior off, retreating while shouting for those nearest to prepare to retreat. Thankfully, several of the Kadri ships were beginning to glide over the sand. A horn blew, signaling the warriors that the fleet was nearly ready. No sooner had it sounded, though, than the wyrm landed on that very ship. The woman blowing the horn was lost and the sound cut short as the wyrm's jaws clamped over her. It lifted her up, thrusting its neck like a stork swallowing a fish, devouring her whole.

More ships began to move.

"Now!" Emre cried. "Retreat!"

But Onur's warriors had started to surround them. They'd curled around their flanks like a crescent moon. There was now only a narrow gap through which to retreat, a gap that was quickly closing.

Onur, Emre realized. Onur was still nearby. If he could wound the King, it would distract his warriors and give Tribe Kadri the diversion they needed. Emre released a primal scream, putting all of himself into wild swings against the two men before him, preparing to push through a gap and charge for Onur when a stout figure began wading through the battle.

It was Zakkar. Haddad's bodyguard.

He had the same scowl he always wore. The warriors before him were unable to stand against his powerful strides. He moved across fallen bodies, through men and women locked in battle, heedless of everything and everyone but Onur.

He wielded his massive scimitar to devastating effect, but he took cut after cut from swords all around him. One bit into his shoulder. Another sunk deep into the top of his bald head. But strangely, the cuts didn't bleed, nor did they go as far as they ought. It was as if Zakkar were made of earth and stone, not skin and bone.

A shout alerted Onur to Zakkar's advance. He turned just in time to meet a downward chop from Zakkar's scimitar. Onur blocked it to the side, then did so a second time. On the third swing he blocked it wide and struck Zakkar across the jaw with the butt of his spear. It struck with such force that Zakkar's entire jaw flew wide from his face and spun over the heads of the nearby warriors. Even Onur stared in horror at the place Zakkar's jaw had once been.

What remained was a misshapen gap made of what looked to be red clay. *A golem,* Emre understood suddenly, *just as the stories of Malasan told.*

Zakkar hardly seemed to care. He drove his sword so hard against Onur's side that even though Onur blocked it he was thrown backward several steps. All those around Onur converged on Zakkar, but Zakkar's dead eyes were fixed on Onur alone.

"Tribe Kadri!" Emre called, knowing they would never have a better chance. "We go now that we may fight another day!"

En masse, the Kadri warriors roared and delivered a flurry of blows before disengaging. They ran, but Onur's soldiers were ready. Emre was nearly cut down from behind, but an old man with a long white beard threw himself at the Salmük warriors chasing him. He fought bravely, but was cut down a moment later.

Emre and the others flocked toward the ships. Their sails were raised, billowing as they gathered the hot desert winds. Emre made for Haddad's ship, his throat and lungs burning. The muscles of his legs nearly gave out, but he managed to gain the ship with Haddad's help as a rain of arrows began to fall, biting into the hull and deck of the dhow.

As the crews answered with their own rain of arrows, Emre helped more up to the deck. One slipped, her eyes wide when an arrow struck the meat of her calf. Emre held on and managed to hold her tight to the ship. One of Haddad's crew dropped to the deck by his side, grabbed a fistful of her thawb, and hauled her up, the woman screaming the whole while.

Behind the ship, the wyrm lifted into the sky. It circled once, twice, then dove straight for Haddad's ship. A crewman was at the rear ballista, a heavy bolt in the channel, ready to fly, but just as he was aiming it, an arrow took him in the neck. Blood spurted as he grabbed for it. He jerked on the arrow shaft reflexively, and actually managed to pull it free, but the moment he did, a spray of crimson flew from the wound, staining the ballista, the bulwarks, and the deck beneath him.

An indescribable terror frothed up inside Emre, threatening to overwhelm him, but he quashed it while dashing for the ballista, knowing he only had moments before it was on them. The wyrm swooped low and began its strange, undulating flight toward Emre's ship. Its shadow swept across the ground below, a dark companion as the wyrm's shape loomed ever larger.

When Emre reached the ballista, every fiber of his being urged him to squeeze the lever that would release the bolt, but he couldn't risk a miss.

The wyrm came closer and closer. It dipped and pulled sharply up and stretched its clawed feet forward and opened its great maw to reveal razor teeth and a barbed tongue.

Emre squeezed the lever. The bolt flew with a great thud.

The wyrm's neck came forward, and a black cloud issued from its mouth, which flew toward the ship in one great stream, as if the wyrm hoped to spray the entire ship, stem to stern, from the top of the mainmast down to the decks.

But then the bolt pierced the wyrm's wing just above its right shoulder, puncturing the skin. Immediately it curled to the right, the inky cloud trailing off along with it.

"Take cover!" Emre shouted, and ducked under the ballista.

Where the black spray had struck, it ate through the sails. It burned the wood. The crew screamed in pain. And then it hit Emre too. Black droplets burned through his shirt and along his shoulders and back. Wherever it touched, his skin sizzled and bubbled. Emre found himself sucking air through gritted teeth. He tore off his shirt and used it to wipe himself wherever he could reach. It may have helped, but did nothing to ease the pain, which grew worse, until he was crying out with the rest of the crew.

The mizzen sail was eaten through so badly it looked as though it had lain moth-eaten for a hundred years. The remnants at the head flapped in the wind. The mainmast was better, but was beginning to tear from the sizable holes near the top. The foresails, thank the gods, were largely intact.

Looking back, Emre saw that perhaps two dozen ships had manage to sail away. Another twenty were still at the site of the battle.

The victors, Onur's warriors, raised their swords to the sky and gave ululating calls. The wyrm, praise be to Bakhi for his kindness, had dropped to the ground and was nursing the hole in its wing. Its tongue lapped at the blood running along its skin.

As their forms dwindled into the distance, Emre's relief became anger. Bakhi may have shown them some small kindness, but the gods had given Onur more than he already had. Long life. Terrible strength and speed. And now a bloody great wyrm. *How can we fight him when the gods are his allies?*

With no answers likely to arrive soon, Emre turned away and went to help the wounded.

Chapter 45

DEEP BENEATH SUKRU'S PALACE, Ihsan walked down a darkened passageway. The gaoler accompanied him, holding a lantern to light their way, though the combination of his noticeable limp and unsteady hand made the light swing so wildly it made Ihsan sick.

"If you please," Ihsan said, holding his hand out for the lantern. "It's enough to make a mule vomit."

The man handed it over but not without a sullen look.

"Hello?" came a booming voice from the passageway ahead. "Can you hear me? Tell the King of Kings I would speak with him alone!"

It was Zeheb's voice. Ihsan never thought he'd see the day. He sounded completely terrified.

"I will speak with Kiral! *I am King Zeheb, and I will speak with Kiral!*"

"Enough you bloody crow," the gaoler groused. "Do that again and you'll get dog bones and piss water for a week!"

To Ihsan's utter astonishment, Zeheb fell silent.

"You do know you're speaking to a King, don't you?" Ihsan asked the gaoler.

The gaoler's sullen look turned darker. "I know my lord Sukru gave a prisoner over to me and that he's as loud as the end of days."

"Still," Ihsan said, allowing a touch of power to leech into his voice. "You'll not speak ill of him again."

The gaoler said nothing, but his face was now scrunched up so badly he looked like a prune. They reached a door shortly after, and the gaoler used his jingle of keys to open the door.

Zeheb's voice called tentatively from the darkness. "Kiral?"

"No," Ihsan said. "Not Kiral." There was no reply as he stepped inside and held his hand out to the gaoler. "The keys."

The gaoler's mismatched eyes stared at the keys for a moment, then at the open doorway.

"Now," Ihsan said.

"Of course, my Lord King," he said contritely as he handed the keys over. "Now wait for me above."

And off he bobbed, into the darkness, leaving Ihsan alone with the King of Whispers.

When he was sure the man was far enough that he wouldn't hear the conversation, Ihsan entered the cell. He held the lantern in his left hand, his triple-bladed knife in his right. The cell was large, meant for several at once, which was perhaps why Zeheb looked so small, huddled in one corner as he was.

"Are you well?" Ihsan asked easily. "Have you been fed? Would you like water?"

Zeheb gaped in pure befuddlement. "Ihsan, there's been a terrible mistake."

"Undoubtedly, but it will be corrected soon enough."

Zeheb shook his head as if Ihsan hadn't just threatened him. "Can you call for Kiral? I didn't know what I was saying, but I'm better now. I can explain everything."

"That won't be necessary."

"I'm so confused, Ihsan. I didn't do those things. *You* did."

"Yes, of course."

Ihsan didn't bother telling him about the tincture that had been slipped into his wine during Davud's interrogation of Çeda. What would be the point other than to gloat? The drug was a Kundhuni import and very rare. Its original name was difficult to translate, but meant, more or less, "wanderlust," and in this case was the perfect solution. It caused confusion for a time, and often docility. Like this, the victim was unable to piece together his thoughts, unable to recall his memories. Under the right circumstances, it could make a man seem as if he were hiding things, which was exactly how Zeheb had seemed and exactly what Ihsan had wanted.

It also made him suggestible. The drug was wearing off, but there was still enough running through Zeheb's veins that he wouldn't be able to resist Ihsan's voice, nor deny him answers.

"Have you been listening to Kiral?" Ihsan asked, allowing power to flow through his words.

Zeheb shook his head. "I would never."

"I need the truth, Zeheb, or I'll never be able to help you."

"I haven't! The chances of him sensing it were too great!"

"Have you been taken beneath his wing, then? Are you his man?"

Zeheb swallowed hard. "Yes."

Interesting. "When?"

"Not long before you came to my palace."

"When you had me attacked?"

It took Zeheb some time to nod. "Yes."

Ihsan nodded. He'd suspected as much. "And yet, if you're half the man I remember, you would still keep an eye on him."

Zeheb had always been good at hiding his emotions, but affected by the drug, his old instincts were apparently lost to him. It was almost comical seeing how transparently guilty the man looked. "I've listened to some whispers. But not Kiral's! I swear it! Only those around him."

"And what did they say?"

"Kiral and Hamzakiir are in league. They've made arrangements for the burgeoning thirteenth tribe to be destroyed."

Ihsan started piecing the puzzle together. "They're going to help Onur."

Zeheb nodded. "At least insomuch as they can quell the knowledge of the tribe before it threatens the natural order of things."

Ihsan nearly laughed. *Natural order . . . The natural order would have seen us dead four centuries ago.* "And I suppose Hamzakiir, if this is successful, will suddenly find himself with a seat at Sharakhai's table."

When the lantern's light guttered for a moment, Zeheb stared at it, his brows pinching, as if within that lonely glow he'd found some small amount of hope. "Yes."

"And who suggested this arrangement?"

"Hamzakiir."

This time, Ihsan *did* laugh. "Now let me guess the price for this bargain: half of our elixirs of long life; the very elixirs that Hamzakiir managed to steal from your palace."

Zeheb's eyes widened like a little boy who'd just been shown his first magic trick. "Just so."

In the end, the arrangement wasn't surprising, but it did make Ihsan wonder just how far Kiral planned to take this. How much of Sharakhai was he willing to surrender to Hamzakiir? And conversely, how much was Hamzakiir willing to settle for?

"Who else knows?"

Zeheb was quivering. He was trying to resist, and Ihsan could tell it was becoming easier for him. There was little time left, then.

"Who else knows of the bargain, Zeheb?"

"Sukru and Cahil."

"What of Husamettín and Beşir?"

"I've heard no whispers of import coming from their halls."

It made sense. Both Husamettín and Beşir would likely balk at such an arrangement. "Very well," Ihsan said. When he stood, taking up the lantern, Zeheb looked relieved.

"We were allies once, Ihsan. Will you speak with Kiral? Convince him that this has all been a mistake?"

"No. But I do have one last request of you, after which you will be free to do as you will." He paused. "Are you ready?"

"I am. I'll do anything."

Ihsan smiled widely. "I don't blame you for threatening Nayyan. I was angry over it, but I can understand why you would do it. But you should *never* have threatened my unborn child."

"I know." In the span of a heartbeat, much of the hope in Zeheb's eyes vanished. "I swear to you, I'll never do so again."

"You're right. Because what I want you to do, Zeheb, is listen to the whispers."

Zeheb's face brightened. "Of course. Which ones?"

Never before had Ihsan put so much of himself into his power. "*All* of them."

Zeheb couldn't disobey. Not this. His chin quivered. The worry in his eyes intensified even as they lost their focus. He was now staring *through* Ihsan, as if he could see the whole of the desert. His breath came faster. His hands pressed flat against the stone beneath him. His jowls shook. The long moan that escaped him reminded Ihsan of a wounded black laugher he'd seen on a hunt once. As the hunters had closed in, long wheezing breaths had overcome it. It had tried to struggle, tried to fight, to no effect in the end.

Zeheb was that doomed beast, a man who recognized his fate as more and more of the whispers came to him. From this palace. From the House of Kings. From the city beyond. Soon they would reach even to the desert, for his ability to control it, his *desire* to control it, had been stolen from him with Ihsan's command.

Ihsan left the cell and calmly locked the door behind him. The first of Zeheb's screams chased him down the dark hallway. By the time Ihsan had reached the gaoler's room, they'd become so maniacal there was hardly a pause for breath from one to the next.

Ihsan handed the gaoler the keys. "You'll forget that I was here. And you'll ignore the King's screaming. When he falls silent, you'll inspect his cell and then tell King Sukru what you've found."

"Of course, my Lord King."

Ihsan took the stairs, wondering how long it would be before Zeheb drove himself perfectly, utterly mad.

Chapter 46

CEDA WAS CHAINED to the bed of an enclosed wagon. Sunlight slanted in through the lone, barred window at the rear, sometimes playing against the wagon's dark interior, at other times lost as they navigated the many switchbacks along King's Road. It was the end of a miserably hot day. Sweat tickled along her skin, made her scalp itch. The cramped space inside the wagon was hot as a bloody oven.

After nearly an hour of waiting, the wagon began to move. It rocked, creaked, and leaned awkwardly as it navigated the stones and potholes of King's Road. The rattle of the wheels mixed with the jingle of tack and the clop of hooves. The distant sound of temple bells honored the setting sun. It made her wonder if Davud, wherever he was now, could hear them too.

She was still so shaken by the look on his face, his intensity as he sought to kill her. She'd seen that look before, but only on men like Hamid. Cold-blooded killers. Davud, a peaceful dove above all else, was anything but. So why had he done it? She'd been able to come up with only one answer: *Ihsan*.

Why *else* would Davud have done such a thing? She supposed it was possible Sukru had threatened him, but the way Sukru had stared so hawkishly at every move Davud made, as if in awe of Davud's powers, made her think it wasn't so.

Ihsan had been a different story. He'd seemed intrigued, then surprised, then shocked at all the right moments. A good performance, but Çeda felt certain it had been just that. A performance.

When Davud had shared Onur's bloody verse, she'd thought Ihsan might have been subtly nodding to her about the pact they'd made on Tauriyat—that he would reveal the name of her father if she brought him Onur's head—but she realized what a mistake that had been. After her capture, Ihsan had likely seen how ill-advised their compact had been and decided to tie off that thread before it unraveled all his careful planning. He'd only given Davud Onur's bloody verse because Onur was now an enemy. It would prove Davud a trustworthy source, and if it also reminded the Kings that Onur was still a threat to them, so much the better.

It struck her how brilliantly Ihsan had orchestrated Zeheb's implication. He must have pulled dozens of strings just so, including the ones that tied him to Zeheb. When he'd been accused, the King of Whispers had sat there, dumbfounded, as if waking from a dream. Had Ihsan whispered in *his* ear as well?

After Davud's peculiar escape from the palace, the Kings had come to inspect the damage. They'd questioned Sümeya and Zahndr. Allowing only a cursory explanation, Husamettín had halted the interrogation and ordered Sümeya to return Çeda to his palace.

"She is in my care," Sukru had spat, with King Cahil standing just beyond him. "She is now *mine* to question."

Husamettín had stared at him with a look of such intensity Çeda thought he might draw his sword and cleave Sukru in two, but he'd merely kept his eyes fixed on Sukru and repeated his order for Sümeya to lead Çeda away, which she'd done a moment later. Melis, Kameyl, and Yndris had accompanied them to the palace, where the wagon and horses had been waiting for them. It was strange that Sümeya had ordered the driver down from the bench and taken the reins herself.

Gods, what happens now?

Perhaps Husamettín would give her over to the dark asir again. Perhaps he'd threaten Sehid-Alaz's life unless he got his answers. Perhaps she'd have her day on the gallows after all.

After a time Sümeya called, "Woah, woah!" and the wagon creaked to a halt. The clopping of the horses behind the wagon, the ones carrying Kameyl, Yndris, and Melis, came to a halt as well.

"Kameyl and Yndris," Sümeya's voice called from the driver's bench, "continue on to the House of Maidens. Inform the Matrons that we'll return when we're able."

"Don't you think it best that we *all* accompany you to the palace?" Yndris's voice, grating and impertinent.

"Do as I've ordered, Maiden," Sümeya replied easily. "Go, and we'll speak in the morning."

"Come, girl," Kameyl said. "The First Warden has spoken."

One of the horses exhaled noisily. "Call me girl again"—hooves thudded against packed earth—"and we'll have more than words."

Çeda heard a snort from Kameyl. She could picture her sneer, a thing she'd seen a thousand times while practicing their swordcraft. Soon two horses were trotting away. When the sound of their retreat had dwindled, the wagon lurched back into motion, heading downhill for a time, then uphill, surely along the spur of King's Road that led to Husamettín's palace. It was a goodly distance away, and yet a short while later the wagon came to a halt.

Çeda thought they were waiting for other horses to pass, perhaps another wagon, but she heard nothing save the lonely call of an amberlark.

"I have to piss," Çeda said as the silence continued to lengthen. "I'd rather do it in the bushes than in the back of a wagon."

The window at the front of the wagon snapped open, and Sümeya's face appeared there. "If ever there was a time for silence, Çedamihn, it is now." She slid the door shut with a loud clack.

Çeda was tempted to goad her again, but there was something in the way she'd spoken, as if she were on the cusp of changing her mind about something.

Through the window at the rear, Çeda saw sunlight fade. Stars began to glint through an apricot sky, and the heat in the wagon, thank the gods, began to abate.

"She should be here by now," Çeda heard Melis whisper.

"There's time yet."

"I'm still not sure this is wise," Melis said, her voice soft but urgent.

Sümeya's reply was calm reassurance. "We no longer have a choice."

A choice in what, Çeda thought, *killing me?* But if that were so, why wait? Why not slit her throat and be done with it?

"There she is," Sümeya said a short while later.

Soon Çeda heard a lone horse coming toward them.

The wagon rocked; a sharp crunch of stones followed, Sümeya leaping down from the driver's bench. Soon there came the clank of the bar at the back of the wagon being lifted. The hinges groaned as the door swung wide. Sümeya was there, Melis behind her, and beyond them, a Matron rode toward them. Her identity was obscured by the darkness, but Çeda quickly recognized her.

By the gods. Zaïde.

As Zaïde pulled up, Sümeya met her and held the reins of her horse. Çeda realized she'd been wrong about their location on Tauriyat. They weren't along the road to Husamettín's palace, but in a small vale lower down the mountain. It was used as a festival grounds to honor the rites of spring and autumn. More importantly, it was largely hidden from view.

"Is all prepared?" Sümeya asked.

"Yes," Zaïde replied, who untied a sack from her saddle. Zaïde may have seen the better part of seventy summers, but she carried herself like a woman decades younger. "Have you told her?"

"No," Sümeya said, turning back to Çeda. Zaïde, holding the small sack, approached. Melis flanked her. All three stared soberly at Çeda.

"What's happening?" Çeda asked.

Sümeya took a deep breath before speaking again. "When we found you in the desert, you shared the tale of an asir with Melis."

"No, what I shared was a story concocted by Husamettín. There was no truth in it."

Sümeya tilted her head noncommittally. "That has yet to be determined."

Çeda waved to the wagon, to the vale around them. "Then why all this?"

"Because I will have my *own* answers, not those of my father, nor those of his brother Kings."

Çeda thought back to her dungeon cell. The sounds of footsteps coming from the darkened hall. "That was you in Husamettín's dungeon."

Sümeya's silence was answer enough.

"You know Sehid-Alaz is there, then. You know the truth."

"Sehid-Alaz is there," Sümeya replied, "but I learned nothing from him. The chains my father placed on him have robbed him of his ability to bond or even speak."

"Then we must go to him. I'll show you what he's said is true."

Sümeya shook her head. "The paths to his cell are guarded too closely."

"Then what do you propose?"

Zaïde pulled a black Maiden's dress from the bag. "We go to the blooming fields, and you will prove your story, free of any influence from the Kings."

Çeda stared at the three of them. Zaïde already knew the truth, of course. It was Sümeya and Melis who had to be convinced. "If you were fooled once," she said to them both, "what difference will it make now? I could manufacture a story as your father did."

"What Husamettín did felt true at the time," Melis said, "but in the days that followed it felt hollow. A play performed for our benefit."

"Now that we know the signs of the asirim being manipulated," Sümeya echoed, "we'll sense if you're lying or if another is affecting them unduly."

"And if we go," Çeda said, "if I show you the truth, what then? You risk your lives. At best you'll be expelled from the House of Maidens. At worst you'll be tortured and hung as traitors."

Sümeya's look of regret made it clear she was not at all sure she'd made the right decision. "You'd rather I return you to your cell?"

"I have no way of knowing what you'll do when you learn the truth. For all I know, this is a way for the Kings to learn more about the asirim or the thirteenth tribe."

For the first time, Sümeya's veneer cracked. The First Warden of the Blade Maidens was just a woman with the weight of the desert on her shoulders. "I was born to the House of Kings. I was raised to become a Blade Maiden. It is a role I have relished from the moment I took my ebon blade from my father's hands. I revere all that we have fought for, for it is our strength that protects Sharakhai from her enemies. No matter what we find in the memories of the asirim, what the Maidens have done is not nothing. Sharakhai would have fallen long ago had we not been there to protect her. Yet still I would not have the House of Maidens built on a foundation of lies. The truth may shatter all I've known, but I would still learn it, for only in truth can justice be served."

In Sümeya's bright brown eyes there was a bit of the forlornness she'd shown on their journey to Ishmantep and back. It was a look that spoke of love. It made Çeda uncomfortable, not because she didn't share some of those same feelings, but because she was aware of the influence it might have had in delivering Sümeya here. But there was so much more to this than love, and Çeda took measure of it. She weighed Sümeya's words, her sincerity, her resolve, and found that she believed her. Sümeya would do as she'd promised and grant Çeda a chance to prove herself. And that, Çeda decided, was all she could ask.

As she reached for the Maiden's dress in Zaïde's arms, Sümeya seized Çeda's wrist.

"And if I was wrong to trust you." Sümeya's look had hardened; she was First Warden once more. "If I find you're lying, then I'll confess my sins and deliver my sword to my father, but only *after* I've used it to take your head from your shoulders. Zaïde's as well. Your blood will feed the twisted trees and the sand will swallow your bones."

Çeda nodded, and Sümeya released her.

As Çeda accepted the dress from Zaïde, the two of them shared a look. Zaïde had much to answer for, foremost among them the death of Amalos, the master at the collegium who had mentored Davud. But now was not the time. Zaïde had done much in bringing Melis and Sümeya to this moment.

After giving Çeda a chance to don her dress, they were off, riding down King's Road—three Maidens and a Matron, all of them veiled. They came to level ground and headed west toward the House of Maidens. As they rode through, they went unchallenged, both as they entered the inner gates and as they rode out and into the city. Those on guard, Çeda was sure, had been handpicked by Sümeya.

When they came to the Wheel, they turned north and rode hard to the northern harbor, then headed down one of the ramps that led to the sand. Four Silver Spears forced them to a halt at the chains across the mouth of the harbor. When Sümeya ordered them to lower the barricade, they quickly complied, and the four of them were off again.

As the lights of the city began to dim, Çeda kept glancing over her shoulder, listening for the sounds of alarm from the harbor or from the palaces on their dark hill. She could see them on Tauriyat, huddling like a murder of magpies, a thousand eyes aflame. But no alarm was raised, no one gave chase, and soon they were into the desert proper. They reached the blooming fields just as Rhia was rising in the east. They dropped from their horses and walked into one of the groves. The trees were silent around them, their blooms closed. Under Rhia's light they looked as if they'd been dipped in gold, preserved until the end of days.

"Here," Çeda said.

They knelt in a circle on sandswept stone, Çeda across from Zaïde, Sümeya across from Melis. They clasped hands and their breathing fell into sync with one another. When Çeda had calmed herself, she reached out for the asir. They were deep in their slumber. Deeper, in fact, than at any time Çeda could remember. There had always been *some* like this in the blooming fields—the weak; the wounded; those who'd recently feasted on the blood of the living—but their number had always been few. This night, *all* of them were so.

Husamettín's doing, Çeda knew.

It was a fear that had been building since leaving Sharakhai. Husamettín would likely sense her presence when she tried to waken them. He may even work to hide the truth as he had before, but she couldn't allow it. Not this time. She would need to be ready to work against him.

Wake, my brothers and sisters. Wake, for I would listen to your tales.

Some few stirred at her call, yet they remained hidden, their minds cloaked. She tried harder, and yet they remained as they were, minds dulled, their bodies inert.

"Calm yourself," Sümeya said.

Çeda realized she'd lost her balance. She took a deep breath, felt the circle of their clasped hands, and tried again.

Merely bonding with the asirim was a crude act, akin to chaining an unruly hound. The ability to *commune* with them, as she was attempting now, was something else entirely. She was sure it was tied to her heritage as a child of the thirteenth tribe. That in turn made her wonder about Husamettín. Did he have blood of the thirteenth tribe running through his veins? Had his mother or father, or a more distant ancestor, been born in the tents of

Sehid-Alaz's people? Perhaps. Perhaps it had been true of Mesut as well. Was that why these two Kings were stronger with the asirim? She refused to believe it was merely the gods granting them power; if so all the Kings would be equally strong.

She felt Melis stir by her side. She felt Zaïde's waning hope, Sümeya's rising disappointment. She might have been rattled once, but there was something about being here with these three women—women she did not fully trust, nor who fully trusted her, but who had given her a chance.

She spread her awareness farther. Became attuned to those beneath the sands. She felt the wound on the meat of her thumb flare and for once did nothing to either quell the pain or intensify it. She merely felt the familiar ache, felt it spread along her hand, her fingers, her wrist and up her tattooed arm. It made her aware of the adichara as much as the asirim, which felt truer, somehow. More complete.

Come, now, she called to the asirim, *it's time that your voices were heard.*

Her voice seemed to stir the asirim. She felt their dreams turn toward her. One, only a short distance away, began clawing at the sand. It squirmed and rose up from the roots of the adichara like a rattlewing from its chrysalis. A fleshy frame was limned in golden moonlight. Lanky hair. Sagging breasts. A woman once. Wounds were visible—a gash along her ribs, more on her shoulders and arms, all half-healed, suppurating, revealing rotted flesh.

The adichara made a path for her. The limbs of the twisted trees cracked like the joints of the aged, as if they could not suffer the asir's touch. Once free, the asir stood at odd angles, an ungainly doll propped up by children's hands. She stared at Çeda, intense, her eyes bits of broken diamonds.

"What is your name?" Çeda asked.

The asir's breath rattled in her throat. She flexed her fingers, worked her lower jaw, which seemed askew, as if broken.

More dark forms rose up behind her: two then five then ten then twenty. Çeda understood with sudden and fierce clarity that they followed the first, their unlikely matriarch. Çeda knew that they retained some sense of who they'd been before Beht Ihman, that they still deferred to their King, Sehid-Alaz. She even knew they hoped that he might one day save them. She'd had no idea that they still retained any sense of *tribe* beyond that, yet here were dozens who deferred to another, a dark queen while their King was missing.

Their sickly smell grew as they surrounded the grove. Several moved along the pathways toward the clearing, effectively hemming Çeda and the others in. They had the look of the worst of Sharakhai's malnourished. Knobby joints, sticklike limbs, the space between their ribs and hips a terrible, sunken valley.

"Çeda," Sümeya called nervously.

She had every right to be nervous, for the asirim were hungry beyond reckoning, but Çeda could spare no time to assuage Sümeya's fears. She focused her attention on the matriarch.

Tell me your name, she repeated.

Silence greeted her words, but Çeda could feel the asir's intent growing. *Rend. Wreck. Devour.*

It was a compulsion. A directive that smothered all else. Her heart. Her soul. Even her memories. This was the taint Çeda must lift, or surely she and the others would die.

As the asir lumbered forward, ever faster, Çeda called, "Get back!" and sprinted forward, placing herself in the matriarch's path. She raised her hands, spread them wide in a gesture of peace. *Grandmother,* was all she said.

The asir slowed, then pulled up. Surprise and confusion warred on her corpulent features. The two of them were now close enough for the asir to grip Çeda's neck, for her chipped nails to pierce Çeda's flesh.

The other asirim had slowed their pace but continued to trudge closer, their own murderous desires feeding their queen's. The adichara branches rattled and shook as if the very trees fed off the hatred pouring from these gathered souls.

Çeda turned and saw Sümeya and Melis gripping the hilts of their shamshirs. "No!" she cried. "Leave your swords sheathed, or we will feed the adichara."

Her words seemed to anger the matriarch. One meaty arm flew out, but Çeda was ready. She snatched the asir's wrist with her left hand, twisted it before the asir's greater strength could be brought to bear. She held her right hand up, palm open, revealing her tattoos and the wound she'd received from the adichara.

"Can you sense it?" Çeda asked. "Can you sense the poison that burns within me?"

The asir's anger burned brightly, threatening to consume her, but Çeda's words had made her pause. For the time being, her curiosity was stronger than her desire to kill.

"Blood of my blood," Çeda said.

The asir shook her head, her mouth working, tears forming in her jaundiced eyes. Çeda released the asir's wrist, then used her own thumbnail to gouge her right palm, sawing, the pain rising, until she'd broken skin and blood began to flow.

She showed the wound to the asir. "Blood of my blood." She held it out, an offering, plain and simple.

For the first time since rising from the earth the asir seemed unsure of herself. Her eyes flitted between Çeda's unyielding stare and the bloody palm held before her. She reached for Çeda's hand, then took it in both of hers. Çeda had never seen a creature seem so fragile.

"The memories you feel are not your own," Çeda said softly. She could feel Husamettín's influence, distant yet strong. "They come from another, the King of Swords."

Around them, the asirim began to wail. It was soft at first, but it grew until it felt as though the desert itself was shaking from it. They were working themselves up to something. *No, they're trying to convince their matriarch to return to them.*

"Blood of my blood," Çeda said a third time, and spread her fingers wide, willing the asir to hear her words, to recognize the truth.

At last the asir's will seemed to crumble. Holding Çeda's hand tightly, she kissed Çeda's palm. Tears slipped along her blackened cheeks, two glistening rivers that met beneath the asir's chin and fell, pattering against the back of Çeda's hand.

The asir blinked, then took in the clearing anew, as if she were confused to find herself there. The others howled. They beat the ground with their fists. Their bodies twisted, as if they were being tortured by the Confessor King.

But they did not attack.

"Tell me your tale," Çeda said to the matriarch.

With this the asir straightened and the confusion faded, to be replaced with a steely resolve. She released Çeda's hand, then pressed her own nail into her right hand, as Çeda had done. Black blood welled, and she held it up before Çeda.

Çeda didn't hesitate. *Blood of my blood.* She took the asir's hand and kissed her blackened skin. She licked the blood from her own lips. It had a bitter, acetous, coppery taste, and with it came a rush of awareness. The asir became *known* to her. As did her sisters and brothers, as did the adichara that sheltered them. The knowledge expanded so quickly Çeda's head was thrown back.

As the brilliance of the night's grand canvas filled Çeda's eyes with tears, and the veil separating her from the asir was torn, she was drawn down, down, down, into a great, consuming darkness.

Chapter 47

A YOUNG WOMAN, MAVRA, hardly more than a girl, hid behind a tall bush at the edge of an oasis, spying a woman swimming naked in one of the oasis's many pools. How she wished she could slip into the water, take the woman in her arms, but the way her heart was pumping she was sure she would die.

The scene shifted and the hand of the woman Mavra loved was being wrapped in a veil, then tied to a man, the two of them now married. They kissed, and with that one act Mavra's heart was broken.

Two months later, Mavra was herself given to a man, a tent and sail maker from their sister tribe to the south. By then she'd already given up hope of ever being with her one true love. She'd finally worked up the courage to speak with her, to confess everything, but the woman had shunned her, had laughed and sent her away, forbidding her return lest the gods *take notice* and curse them both. Mavra's heart still bled at the very thought, so she buried her love and took her husband's hand.

She gave birth to twins. Sweet Trinn and incontinent Amile. How quickly they grew. The two of them were dancing on the sands of the Great Mother when they had their third, Evrim, who lit Mavra's world with every laugh.

Her husband was soon lost to war, a skirmish with the Sharakhani Kings. But she was still young and took another—a dour man, but kind enough, and favored by the shaikh.

With him she bore three more children—Lela and Gevind and Kamila, all of whom were babied by Trinn. Trinn's affection was a thing Mavra appreciated at first but eventually came to regret. Shortly after Kamila was born, her husband died from an infection, a simple cut from an old knife. On his deathbed, he said through his tears, *such a foolish thing to die over*. And then he was gone, given back to the desert.

Her third husband was a beautiful man, and attentive in his own way, but he drank too much. He gave her one boy and one girl, Mehmet and Natise, but took Evrim with him to an oasis to learn the ways of Tribe Masal, who were meeting to celebrate the summer solstice. Both died in a drunken brawl. Forever more the solstice brought Mavra sorrow, not joy.

Her fourth husband wished to take her to Sharakhai.

"And what has Sharakhai ever given us but tears?" she asked. But he was adamant. Opportunity lay in the city, he insisted. It was a place to live, to secure the lives of their children.

And so they went.

Five more children came before her fourth husband died in an honor killing. A man from their tribe had come from the desert and slit his throat as he was being handed a loaf of bread at the edge of the bustling spice market. For months after, she was deathly afraid of the same thing happening to her or her children.

She took no more husbands after that. She had many children already, and no great will to have more. Her family, however, grew. Like a rose unfolding before her very eyes, her children had children. Those who had not so long ago seemed so very young were now teaching children of their own what she had shared with them, what her own mother had shared with her. Her pride swelled beyond all reason.

But, pride or not, life in the city was hard. She thought many times of returning to the desert but, as many in her tribe had warned her, roots will grow beneath the feet of the unmoving. Something always changed her mind, so she remained in Sharakhai, finding work as a jeweler's prentice. Her children and grandchildren helped provide for their growing household in the city's west end, and if some of them stole a bit along the Trough, well, if it meant more milk, rice, and bread for the babies, she was willing to overlook it.

And then the desert shook.

War arrived on Sharakhai's doorstep. The tribes had gathered and were threatening to raze the city to the ground. All within the city feared for their lives, for the tribes' gathered might was terrible to behold. Word came that the Kings had called all thirteen tribes to attend them on Tauriyat. Little was known, but the whispers spoke of a plan to save the city from the invaders. Not all could go—the site of the gathering was not so great as that—but the jeweler bestowed a great honor upon Mavra: he asked her to join him. *Might my family come?* she asked. It was a bold request. The master was sure to deny her, but she would not go unless she could take some of her loved ones along. To her great surprise, the jeweler said they could all come.

They stood upon the slopes of Tauriyat that very night, gathering with hundreds of others. Thousands. And a wondrous thing happened. The Kings called upon the desert gods, and they came. Tulathan, whose hair was molten silver. Rhia, whose skin shone golden. Mighty Thaash and dark Goezhen. Bakhi came next, his bright smile lit by Tulathan and Rhia's light. Last was Yerinde, whose dark eyes reminded Mavra of her first love, who lived in the desert still.

Mavra quaked merely to look upon them. Many of her grandchildren cried, but they were quickly shushed. They waited, all of them wondering if the gods would listen to the pleas of their Kings.

King Kiral strode forward, the twelve Kings arrayed behind him. He was not a god himself, but Mavra would swear he looked like one of the gods' children, a man who might inherit the desert.

Mavra looked often to Sehid-Alaz, the King standing closest to her and her family. He was no shaikh, but the King of Tribe Malakhed here in Sharakhai. She had never considered him her true King—she'd spent too long in the desert to think that—but this night, she prayed for him to see them through.

Save my children, she prayed to her King. *Save them, and I will fill your coffers with all I can spare. This I promise.*

No sooner had she made her wish than the King of Kings slowed in his speech. He spread his arms wide, as if he might wrap them around the whole of Sharakhai. "Save our city," he begged the desert gods, "and what we have is yours."

Tulathan spoke, but Mavra could hardly hear the goddess's words, for Goezhen had swung his head toward her, toward her whole family. With teeth made perfect for rending, he smiled. His tails lashed. His crown of thorns glinted beneath the twin moons, full and bright in the sky above.

She forced herself to look away, to concentrate on Tulathan's words. "You shall have your city and your desert, too," she said in ringing tones, "but we require payment, a tribute of our own."

"You have but to speak it," said Kiral.

"Our price is dear," the goddess intoned.

"Nothing is too dear."

"Blood," said Tulathan.

"Blood," said golden Rhia.

"We require blood," said dark Goezhen, finally drawing his gaze from Mavra.

The King of Kings paused. He took a deep breath, as if gathering up his courage, and then he waved one hand toward Sehid-Alaz and Mavra and all the rest—all those who hailed from Tribe Malakhed. "And you will have it."

A gasp came from those gathered. Some ran. Some rushed toward Sehid-Alaz, begging for protection. Mavra, however, stood rooted to the spot. As Kiral had spoken his words of sacrifice, Goezhen had swung his gaze to her once more. He watched hungrily as the change overcame her, as madness started to dawn. She ignored him as the feeling grew, looked instead to those around her. Her family was turning to ashes before her very eyes.

Her body began to wither. Her pain began to mount. She turned back to Goezhen as the seeds of a never-ending hunger were planted within her mind, urging her to obey, to never question, to give the Kings anything they wanted.

"Go," Kiral commanded. "Fly beyond the walls of Sharakhai. Destroy those who thought to destroy us."

Mavra was compelled. It pained her to hold Goezhen's gaze, to fight the growing compulsion within her, yet fight she did. How could the Kings have done this? How could the gods have demanded it? Her most desperate hope, however, the thing she clung to like a rock in the midst of a terrible storm, was that she might still find a way to save her family. Might she plead to the Kings? Or to the gods? Might she fight them if only to save one or two?

The god of chaos stalked closer, tails lashing, the earth shaking with every step. She held her ground as he towered over her.

Goezhen's eyes glistened as he took her in. "Defiance shall not save thee."

Her body quivered as the pain built inside her, but she would not give up.

The dark god's amusement deepened. "Nor shall thy pride."

She tried—breath of the desert, how she tried—but in the end, the pain, the hunger inside her, proved too strong. Her children called to her. They howled for her to join them as they bounded down the mountain.

Forgive me, she called to them. *You are my perfect treasures, and I have failed you all.*

They only howled louder.

Unable to resist any longer, she followed them to deal death beyond the walls.

Çeda woke coughing from the vision. It took her long moments to shake the feeling of hunger within her. It was but an echo of Mavra's, the one that had driven her to hunt the desert tribes on Beht Ihman—a hunger that drove her still. It would never leave her, Çeda knew, nor her brood.

Her brood . . .

They were the other asirim. The ones who'd risen alongside her. Her children. Her grandchildren. Breath of the desert, there had been three great-grandchildren as well. Çeda saw them, crouched beneath one of the adichara, huddled together like hungry orphans. *Except what they hunger for is neither bread nor water, but the blood of the living.*

The very thought sent a deep pang of regret through her—another echo from Mavra. Mavra had felt, *still* felt, responsible. She should have protected them.

Yet none of the other asirim felt this way. Through it all, their centuries of pain, the terrible yokes the gods had lain across their shoulders, the will of the Kings and the burden of pain they'd inflicted on the children of Sharakhai, they still looked to Mavra for guidance. And Mavra, for her part, though she wished she could have done more, had somehow managed this much: to keep them all together. Were the Kings even aware that such love still existed beneath the blooming fields?

Sümeya came forward until she stood by Çeda's side. Çeda had been so swept up in Mavra's story she hadn't spared the other Maidens a thought, but the stunned look on Sümeya's face made it clear she had seen it all. She was staring at Mavra, this wrinkled, blackened thing, with naked reverence.

Çeda could see the confusion, her thoughts warring within her. Melis was much the same.

"My tears—" For a time Sümeya was lost to her own wracking cries. When she recovered, she wiped her eyes and sniffled. "My tears for your loss. No excuse can be given for this. No defense." She dropped to one knee. "My heart is sundered."

Mavra stared down at her, the confusion in her jaundiced eyes echoing the warring emotions within her. But then Çeda felt something new. A small shift in mood. Nothing more. A seed of dark emotion growing, its roots working deeper and deeper into her mind. Çeda wasn't even sure Mavra herself knew what was happening, but it was a feeling that now echoed among her children, who were growing ever more restless at this Blade Maiden, a *daughter* of the Kings, standing before their monarch.

"Sümeya, get back."

No sooner had Çeda spoken than Mavra's hand lashed out. Sümeya jerked back, but Mavra's long nails still caught her across the throat. Blood flew and Sümeya's hand went to her throat as she rolled backward.

Mavra followed her with a feral grin. She was so fixated on Sümeya she hardly reacted as Çeda stepped in and snapped a kick into her chest. Mavra was heavy, solid, but Çeda had kicked her *hard*. She fell back, arms flailing, into the thorny branches of the adichara. The asirim around them howled, louder than before. Yet they didn't attack.

Çeda was looking around for an escape route when she spied movement. A line of horses were charging hard toward their location—a dozen Blade Maidens with Husamettín at their lead, his great sword already drawn.

Zaïde rushed to help Sümeya up. Her eyes were wide. Blood flowed from beneath her fingers, making the cloth of her Maiden's dress glint in the moonlight. As Mavra's brood began to close in, Çeda drew Sümeya's ebon blade.

The passage leading to their horses was blocked. The one on the clearing's opposite side, however, the one leading away from Husamettín and the approaching horses, had only a few asirim guarding it.

She whistled a pair of signals that together meant *retreat north*, then led the way herself. Sümeya and Zaïde fell in line behind her. Melis came last, slashing her sword to ward the asirim away. The four fought their way along the passage between the trees, moving like a seasoned company of mercenaries.

The asirim seemed strangely slow. In the madness of the sudden battle it took Çeda a moment to understand why. Husamettín had given them a commandment—to stop or kill the traitors in their midst—but they were not yet wholly his. They had attained free thought through Çeda's blood and the sheer power of Mavra's will.

It was likely the only reason Çeda made it to open sand. But make it she did, with the others close behind. They moved away from the adichara as quickly as they could. But gods, the speed of the asirim! Already they were bounding past to cut off their escape. They ran in small, ragged groups, hounds hungry for the desert hare.

Melis whistled hard, a call to their horses. A short while later Çeda saw them coming. Gods, if they could just make it to their mounts, they might yet escape. Melis whistled again, a reinforcement of the previous command and a call for the horses to break through any resistance they found.

The lead horse, Sümeya's, was a terrible beast named Whiteknife. It crashed into the nearest asirim, knocking several aside in a tumble of limbs and sand. Another was trampled as it tried to outrun the horse. When another asir, the tallest of them, faced the horse with arms wide, Whiteknife reared and swiped its forehooves wildly through the air. A loud crunch came as the asir's skull was caved in. The asir tipped over, arms quivering, its body rigid. Then Whiteknife plowed forward once more while Mavra wailed in anguish as she watched her offspring crushed beneath a horse's hooves.

The two horses following Whiteknife made it through, but the trailing horse, Melis's, was caught across its foreleg with a rake of long claws, then again along one shoulder. Blood flew, dark against the gauzy night sky, and the horse screamed, falling to the sand. A half-dozen asirim descended, tearing it to pieces.

As the three horses neared, Melis and Çeda swung their swords broadly to ward away the nearest of the asirim. In that moment, Husamettín, riding his stallion, Blackmane, burst from the tree line. He and his horse fairly flew over the desert, sand kicking in tails behind Blackmane's hooves. Husamettín rode low and tight to the saddle, reins in one hand, Night's Kiss held in the other, high above his head. A dozen more Maidens on horses galloped in his wake, each calling in high, melodic tones that sent a chill down Çeda's skin. For a moment, all her childhood fears of the Blade Maidens returned.

Shaking them off, she helped Sümeya into the saddle, then swung up behind her and held her steady as Zaïde and Melis mounted the other two horses.

The asirim, meanwhile, had backed away, an unspoken command from Husamettín, perhaps.

She understood the truth a moment later. Mavra, still standing near the adichara, had lowered her bulk toward the ground. Crouching, she placed one palm against the sand. A rumbling shook the desert floor. Sand shifted. Stones skittered. Çeda could feel a *buzzing* in her teeth and in her bones.

No sooner had their horses leaned into a gallop than they began to slow inexplicably. They nickered. Their eyes rolled. Their ears flicked this way and that, as if they were being harassed by a cloud of gnats. Looking down, Çeda saw their legs sinking deep into the sand. The horses stamped their hooves, trying to stay above it, but the harder they struggled, the lower they seemed to sink.

Gods, it was slipsand summoned by Mavra, whose hunger, anger, and confusion Çeda could still feel. She wanted simultaneously to feast on Çeda's bones and deny the King of Swords that which he sought. The two desires warred within her, which gave Çeda hope.

Allowing her own desperation to drive her, she *wedged* her will between Mavra and Husamettín. She'd done the same in Ishmantep with Kerim and Kameyl, but she took no care to spare either of them this time. She wielded her will like a knife, and Mavra, already so conflicted, couldn't take it.

Her ungainly form crumpled to the sand like a sack of stones.

Immediately, the buzzing ceased. The horses, however . . . Breath of the desert, the legs of all four of them were in so deep they could hardly move.

As Mavra's brood wailed and flocked toward her, terrified their matriarch had just been killed, Melis gave a quick series of whistles.

East. Ship approaching. Danger?

Over the shallow dunes, Çeda spotted it, a skiff approaching fast. It was the one she and Dardzada had sailed here. She could just make him out sitting at the back, steering the craft. He stood and waved, beckoning her toward him. "Quickly!" he bellowed as he crested a dune and curved the ship around. "Quickly now!"

"Come," Çeda called to Zaïde and Melis. She slipped off the saddle and helped Sümeya to do the same.

Zaïde hesitated only a moment. After one last glance at Husamettín and the Blade Maidens pounding after them, she headed for the skiff. Melis came to help with Sümeya, who was still holding the bunched veil of her turban hard against the wound across her neck.

Çeda made to go, but Sümeya pressed her hand to Çeda's chest and pointed to the saddlebag. "The sword and the bag," she said, then she left with Melis, the two of them loping toward the skiff.

Çeda hadn't even realized it, but there was an ebon blade along Whiteknife's back, mostly hidden by the saddlebag and bedroll. Using Sümeya's sword to cut the ties, she grabbed both, then followed the others. She knew, as she knew the tattoos on her own two hands, that this was River's Daughter. Sümeya had brought it for her. She'd been ready to believe Çeda. Perhaps she'd even *wanted* to believe.

As Çeda ran, her feet sank into the sand like mud, but by moving quickly she was able to reach a normal swath of sand. Hooves pounded behind her, charging ever closer. They were nearing the strip of slipsand, but Husamettín gave it a wide berth, affording them a few more precious seconds to reach the skiff.

Ahead, Dardzada had pulled the skiff to a stop. He was now bent over and striking something over and over. Sparks lit in time with the frantic movements of his arm, illuminating his pillowy face and long beard. As Zaïde, Melis, and Sümeya came near, he lifted a small bow. On it was an arrow with a cloth tip that burned with a sinister green flame. What in the great wide desert he was going to do with it Çeda had no idea, but gods, she hoped it was something good.

As Zaïde fairly rolled Sümeya into the front of the skiff, Dardzada stomped down onto something affixed to the central thwart. A loud thudding sound accompanied a round pot flying into the night sky. A dark cloud trailed behind it. *Powder,* Çeda realized as it fell across her path.

The pot struck in the path of the oncoming horses and broke. Powder burst outward in a cloud. As Dardzada took aim with his bow, Zaïde climbed onto the rear thwart and took the tiller, while Melis and Çeda pushed hard against the transom.

Dardzada's burning arrow flew. It streaked through the night, a burning emerald star. When it came near the fallen pot the greenish-yellow flames flew outward as if Thaash himself had come bearing a piece of the sun. Where the powder had been borne by the wind, flames followed, but it went well beyond. The sound of it barreled unevenly along the lee of the dune like the cackle of hyenas. A moment later, a *thoom* sound filled the air.

Horses screamed and threw their heads back. Blackmane reared wildly, forehooves raking the air. Husamettín managed to keep his saddle, but when Blackmane dropped back down, he danced away from the flames, heedless of his master's wishes.

Meanwhile, the fire snaked backward. Like a bloodhound on a runaway's scent, it followed the trail of powder that had drifted down from the pot. A roiling, uneven column billowed in its wake. It came on so fast, so hard, that Çeda barely had time to turn away before it was on her.

Where the powder had touched the sleeves of her dress, it was now aflame. It lit along her wrists as well. She leapt into the skiff, and then Dardzada was on her, patting out the flames with quick, precise slaps of his meaty hands.

As the flames were snuffed, and the skiff picked up speed, heading deeper into the desert, Çeda looked back. Several of the horses and Maidens were on fire. Those that weren't were now spooked, even Blackmane. They galloped and bucked, many of them neighing and screaming. When Husamettín finally regained control, Dardzada's skiff was deep into the desert, too far to follow.

The fire burned, outlining Husamettín's silhouette as he watched from the top of a dune. Several Maidens rode to their King's side, one of them hulking above the others. Kameyl most likely. They all grew smaller and smaller as the skiff sailed on, and the immensity of what Çeda and the others had done began to wash over her. The First Warden and a sister Maiden were willingly fleeing from a King of Sharakhai with a spy, a scarab, and a traitor.

Behind, the fire shrank in on itself, sputtered and went out, and the King of Swords and his Maidens were swallowed by the night.

Chapter 48

RAMAHD RODE WITH Amaryllis in a covered araba through the temple district in one of the worst sandstorms anyone in the city could remember. They were headed toward Thaash's temple, where a shrine to the grassland god, Onondu, was being consecrated. The temple's high priest was set to meet with King Kiral, many of Sharakhai's highborn, and a large delegation from Kundhun.

Wind buffeted the carriage, its symphonic creaking mixing with the clatter of wheels and the clop of hooves. They were making their way over a narrow, cobbled street. Amaryllis craned her neck to peer through the side window to the way ahead, which was choked with carriages. Passengers at the front were disembarking and running up the temple steps to escape the wind.

"Mighty Alu," Ramahd grumbled, "a dead goat could get us there faster." When they crept forward and came to another creaking halt, he'd had enough. He knocked on the roof and bellowed through the window, "Let us out here!"

He and Amaryllis left the driver to his own fate and headed up the street, occasionally raising an arm to protect against the biting wind. Tauriyat loomed over the shoulders of the temples, but with the sand so thick, it was a featureless mound, its many palaces lost to the weather.

As they walked, Ramahd put a hand to his stomach. He yawned, trying to clear away the nausea. His attention, as it had been the whole way here, was drawn *beyond* the temples, beyond Sharakhai. Since Meryam's alterations to the sigil stones last night, Guhldrathen's presence had been growing. Ramahd hadn't slept at all. The dread inside him had grown too great. And at that time the ehrekh had still been leagues out into the sand. Not anymore. Closer and closer it had come, all throughout the morning hours, each increment twisting Ramahd's insides further. Then, several hours ago, it had halted near the city's outskirts, as if wary of entering.

It was Meryam's doing.

Using her newfound power from the trapped Rümayesh, she'd woven in a way to make Guhldrathen *aware* of the city's wards. The danger was that Guhldrathen would come anyway, and well before the summoning ritual, but so far the gods had been kind; the beast's patience was outweighing its thirst for revenge. Soon Meryam would erase all awareness of the sigils and at the same time enflame the beast's anger. Guhldrathen would come, they were both sure. The only question was: how quickly? Guhldrathen was an ancient beast. And sly. It might wait longer than they wished. Or come too quickly, its thirst for Ramahd's blood driving it to rash behavior.

Amaryllis squeezed Ramahd's arm. "Ahead, my lord. Face the way ahead, as if nothing is the matter."

"Of course." Ramahd wiped the cold sweat from his brow. It was paramount that he not let his fears give him away. He was attending the ceremony precisely *because* Guhldrathen was chasing him. The thinking was that it would focus on Hamzakiir once it caught his scent.

Hamzakiir is the key, Ramahd reminded himself. *He is the key to all of this.*

Kiral had told Meryam that he and Hamzakiir would meet in the temple after the ritual was complete. They were to discuss plans so sensitive that it could only be done face to face. Hamzakiir had also agreed to return some of the elixirs he'd stolen on the Night of Endless Swords, elixirs Kiral desperately wanted. Such a thing could never be done in the House of Kings. The ways in and out of Tauriyat were watched by too many spies beholden to the other

Kings. But a simple ceremony in the temple district? It was the sort of menial task most Kings hated. As long as Kiral did nothing to draw attention to it beforehand, the others would suspect nothing. And for Hamzakiir's part, the temple was open enough that it could be watched to ensure he wasn't betrayed.

And yet, Ramahd still wondered whether this was a fool's errand, a slow and very painful way to commit suicide. Hamzakiir might smell the trap and decide not to come. Or he might have the foresight to mask himself from detection, from Guhldrathen among others. He wouldn't know the ehrekh was coming for him—if he did he wouldn't come at all—but he might have worked a spell to hide his presence from other blood magi, a thing that might hide his presence from Guhldrathen as well.

"The way *ahead*, my lord," Amaryllis said, tugging harder on his arm.

Ramahd squeezed her hand as they neared the foot of the temple's steps. "Of course."

Steeling himself, he ignored his growing nausea and dedicated himself to studying the sizable crowd on the steps ahead of them. Making up the bulk of the crowd were tall Kundhuni men and women, perhaps three dozen in all. Several children were among them, some holding the hands of their elders, others running up and down the stairs. One dark-skinned boy was kicking a puddle of sand that had gathered along the steps. The sand sprayed when he kicked, creating a momentary cloud that was immediately thrown skyward by the prevailing wind.

Others were Sharakhani men and women wearing fine clothing. Their turbans and veils were pulled tight while the hems of their thawbs and dresses flapped fiercely. These were lords and ladies of the city, guests of Kiral and the other Kings of Sharakhai.

When Amaryllis and Ramahd reached the head of the stairs, they were greeted warmly by the high priest, a burly man with a bald head, a thick red beard, and fists that looked like they could break stone. "Good of you to come," he said to them, his deep voice carrying easily above the wind.

"Of course," Ramahd shouted. "It's too bad the weather isn't cooperating."

"This?" The priest waved around, smiling with pinched eyes and rounded cheeks. "What else should we expect? Thaash and Onondu have met. And it's glorious!" Even in those few moments, more sand and dust gathered in his beard, a man turning to stone before their very eyes. "Come!" he roared to the crowd, waving them all to follow. "Come! It's time!"

Most had already moved into the temple, but the stragglers now followed the priest into the most spartan of the city's temples. They made their way through its heart, the sound of the wind waning momentarily, and to the rear, where a great lawn with several gardens and shrines was situated. Thankfully, the wind was not so strong here.

The priest led them to the newest of the shrines, a circular arrangement of white travertine pillars topped by a ring of obsidian stone. The shrine had no roof, a nod to how Onondu has been welcomed by Thaash to the desert, as if the two of them might sit there, cross-legged, and talk beneath the stars.

In the center of the shrine was a stout pedestal of simple sandstone, and upon it, a massive piece of carved ivory—a horn, it was said, from a beast of the Kundhuni grasslands. The carving was the work of an artisan, one of Kiral's great-great-grandchildren, it was said, and depicted a tribe of grassland warriors who'd gathered with spears and shields to kill the very beast that had given up the ivory. It was made in honor of the territory Kundhun now patrolled for the Kings in the western reaches of the Great Shangazi.

The one who seemed proudest of the sculpture was also the eldest of the Kundhuni tribesmen, a man with wild hair and great golden rings in his ears and nose. He was a king of the grasslands, the very one who'd agreed to patrol the western desert for pirates. The priest was regaling him with the story of the horn and the artist who'd carved it when a new train of people exited from the rear of the temple. King Kiral was at their head, striding tall, eyes pinched as the wind and sand drove him forward. His left hand rested on the pommel of Sunshearer, his great two-handed shamshir. A hand of Blade Maidens in their dark dresses and veiled turbans followed. Trailing behind were two dozen courtiers, their bright jewelry and thread-of-gold clothing a glinting counterpoint to the amber haze in the air that tended to mute all other colors.

All bowed as Kiral stepped into the shrine. The King of Kings was introduced to the tribal king, a pleasantry filled with so little humor and warmth one might think them newly reconciled enemies. The high priest seemed to notice, and launched into his prepared speech shortly after.

It was when he began anointing the ivory horn with rosewood oil that Ramahd felt a change. His awareness of Guhldrathen increased so sharply it sent pain through his heart. A cough escaped him. His left arm went numb and tingly, as if it had fallen asleep. The same feeling started along the finger-tips of his right hand and began creeping up his arm. He worked his hands into fists, pumping the blood, hoping to ease the alarming numbness without drawing attention to himself, but even that simple act was difficult.

All thoughts bent toward survival. Even breathing had become a chore. It felt as if a thousand needles were being driven through his chest. Another cough escaped him, this time earning him stares, including a dour look from King Kiral, but what did Ramahd care? Guhldrathen had broken through the city wall and was hurtling toward them. The fear that had been slowly build-ing was no longer an insubstantial thing. It had seized him. It was as real as the shrine, or the bloody great horn the priest was rubbing with oil, or Kiral's god-given shamshir, or the storm that was scouring the city raw.

Without meaning to, Ramahd took a step back. He bumped into a Shara-khani man, who frowned deeply at him. The simple contact sent bright shards of pain running along his left arm. Someone—Amaryllis?—grabbed his hand, but it was so painful he gasped and pulled away.

Amaryllis whispered something, but her words were lost as Ramahd stared to his left beyond the wall bordering the temple grounds. He saw only tall stone buildings cloaked in amber, but he knew Guhldrathen was coming from that direction, knew that it would reach the wall in moments.

A crash of stone sounded in the distance. Sounds of alarm broke out. People screamed. Some had been staring at Ramahd, perhaps wondering what was the matter with him, but now, as one, the crowd turned toward the wall. The Blade Maidens drew their swords and two of them flanked their King. The other three advanced beyond the shrine and onto the lawn.

Several in the crowd gasped as two black horns lifted above the wall. They shouted, backed away, scooping up their children as they went. A great head rose above the wall's decorative lip. Yellow eyes peered through the dusty wind. When its black hand touched the wall, the stones cracked, then crum-bled, flaking away as if made of so much caked sand.

Guhldrathen took one long stride onto the temple grounds as the wall collapsed completely. The ehrekh's tails whipped behind it. Corded muscles spread its arms wide. It hunkered low, as if ready to do battle against Thaash himself should he appear to defend his sacred ground.

"My King," one of the Blade Maidens shouted, "to the temple!"

But the King ignored her and drew his sword. He didn't advance on the ehrekh, but neither did he retreat.

The beast was speaking, Ramahd realized. Its right hand was moving in strange ways, as if it were drawing arcane symbols in the air. Indeed, as it continued, a strange ochre light trailed behind its hands and tails.

Something *pressed* upon Ramahd's body, slowing him as he instinctively backed away. It felt as if he were moving through slipsand. Soon, he'd come to a complete halt. His body was caught in amber, a slave to the ehrekh's magic. Only his eyes could move, and even that simple movement was slowed to a crawl. The same had happened to everyone in Ramahd's field of vision. They stood rooted to the stone beneath them. Even the King.

The ehrekh approached, its forked tongue tasting the air. Sand gathered in its crown of thorns, just as it had in the priest's beard. When it shook its head, the sand sprayed outward. Like silt in the eddies of a river, the sand was caught by the same magic. It moved in odd, expressive increments, matching the lift of Guhldrathen's muscled arm, the turn of its horned head, as if even the air now obeyed Guhldrathen's will.

Guhldrathen had been heading straight for Ramahd, but as it neared the edge of the crowd, it slowed. Its nostrils flared while its head tilted to one side. "Hamzakiir . . ." It approached a young Kundhuni woman with braids, huge silver hoop earrings, and a choker made of tiny red beads. "Where dost thou hide?" it said to her, though clearly it was meant for them all.

Guhldrathen lifted the woman off the ground. The only outward sign of her emotion was her breath, which had devolved into rapid, wheezing inhalations followed by outward huffs like moans of pain.

Guhldrathen smiled, a host of leonine teeth. "Art thou inside?"

With sickening leisure, the ehrekh used the claws on its thumbs to prize open the woman's chest, as if she were little more than a jakfruit. Blood spurted outward, coating the ehrekh's ebony skin. The woman's innards spilled like coiled rigging. The ehrekh ran its forked tongue along the ruin of her chest cavity and then, displeased, tossed her aside in one violent motion that sent her skidding over the ground like an ill-favored doll until she crashed hard against the trunk of a distant palm tree.

Guhldrathen continued forward, gripping a man Ramahd had seen earlier holding hands with the woman who'd just been torn apart. It repeated the ritual on him.

"That thou hoped to hide from my vengeance," it said as it took up a third, a young man no older than sixteen summers. "It doth please me." It tore the poor boy in two, tossing the remnants aside like trash on a midden.

As it chose its fourth victim, Ramahd remembered his time with Hamzakiir—in Viaroza, in Almadan, in the desert. Time and time again he'd been able to throw off Hamzakiir's spells. Hamzakiir had even commented on it on the deck of the ship, shortly before they'd been taken to the blasted plain and given to Guhldrathen.

Ramahd had had few enough occasions to use his gift since, but he found his sense of it growing once again. He pushed as he had in Santrión while trying to prevent Hamzakiir from taking King Aldouan. He pushed as he had in the hold of the ship before walking up on deck, ready to take Hamzakiir's life if he could. He pushed, and he found himself able to move his arms. Able to shift one foot.

His freedom was coming too slowly, however. Guhldrathen was stepping closer to Ramahd. Amaryllis stood directly in its path. Her back was to the ehrekh, but she could hear it coming closer. Her nostrils flared. A tear streamed down one cheek.

When Guhldrathen used its tail to grab a Sharakhani man around the neck and whip him aside, leaving his path to Amaryllis clear, something inside Ramahd broke. He took one agonizing step forward. Then another. As Guhldrathen reached for Amaryllis, he grabbed her arm and pulled her away. The ehrekh tried again, faster this time, but Ramahd was already dragging her backward. He tripped over someone's foot, and Amaryllis tumbled with him.

Guhldrathen towered over him. Its eyes glinted. Its mouth opened in something like a smile. "Thrice have mine eyes laid upon your form. Twice have I given thee leave to go. Not again, child of Qaimir." It took one long stride toward Ramahd as he tried in vain to scramble away. "Not again."

The claws of its reaching hand had just wrapped around Ramahd's left leg when it roared in pain. Releasing Ramahd's leg, it twisted around to face the threat. King Kiral was there, his sword, Sunshearer, at the ready. The blade was bloody, and Ramahd could see a deep gash on Guhldrathen's back.

One of Guhldrathen's tails whipped toward Kiral. The King delivered a blinding uppercut. The barbed end of Guhldrathen's tail flew into the air from the point of contact. Black blood flowed as the severed end toppled through the strangely thick air. But the second tail had flown beneath the King's guard. It stabbed deeply into the King's thigh. Blood gushed from the wound as Kiral backed away.

Guhldrathen powered forward. Kiral dodged, swinging Sunshearer in broad arcs to keep the ehrekh at bay. How he'd managed to throw off the effects of the spell Ramahd wasn't certain, but the Kings had many gifts from the gods. Could this not be one of them? Whatever the case, he was fast and powerful, and managed to strike several more deep gashes into Guhldrathen's black flesh.

It couldn't last, though. The ehrekh was simply too powerful.

When Kiral retreated beneath the shrine, Guhldrathen drove one fist into a pillar, collapsing one side of the structure. As Kiral rolled away, it picked up a massive round pillar stone and launched it at Kiral. It struck only a glancing blow, but the stone was so weighty it was still enough to send Kiral tumbling to the ground.

He came up favoring his left side, his right shoulder hanging low, the arm perhaps useless. He managed one deep cut into Guhldrathen's leg as the eh-rekh charged, but took a backhanded blow while doing so.

Kiral was down, as useless as Ramahd had been only moments ago. But something strange had happened. Whether it was from the damage Guhldrathen had sustained or something else, movement was returning to the gathered crowd. Most moved as if trapped in honey, but one man was now sprinting away, as if he'd not been affected by Guhldrathen's spell at all—the Sharakhani man who'd frowned when Ramahd had bumped into him.

Nonetheless, Guhldrathen's focus seemed to be only on King Kiral, but then the beast slowed, turned, and fixed its jaundiced eyes on the running man. One moment, it seemed confused, but then its eyes lit in recognition. It bellowed as it dropped to all fours and began pounding over the earth.

Many of the ritual-goers were crushed as Guhldrathen closed the distance. A woman who'd fallen screamed as a cloven hoof crunched down onto her leg. The fleeing man, perhaps knowing the end was near, stopped and faced Guhldrathen. That was when Ramahd saw his form change. A round, well-shaven face elongated into Hamzakiir's drawn features and pepper-gray beard. As Meryam had suspected, he'd been here all along.

As Guhldrathen came nearer, a bright ball of flame formed between Hamzakiir's outstretched hands. It grew quickly in size. Ramahd could *feel* it, an awareness of magic being coaxed threadlike from the aether.

Ramahd was hardly aware of what he did next—it was more akin to a reflexive parry than anything else. He reached outward, drew upon the threads of magic Hamzakiir relied upon for his spell, and severed them.

The flame flew from Hamzakiir's hands, breaking apart like the shards of a shattered urn. The shards flew in crazy patterns, bright but ineffective against Guhldrathen's fearsome charge.

When Hamzakiir tried again, Ramahd stopped his spell entirely, cutting him off from his power before he could even gather it. Hamzakiir's eyes then met Ramahd's. There was a split second of recognition in which the two of them shared a look of mutual hatred—and then the ehrekh was on him. Hamzakiir was forced to the ground, where Guhldrathen clamped its massive jaws over his chest. Half of it was ripped free in one explosive wrench of its great, horned head.

But in that moment, as Hamzakiir's screams mixed with the howling of the wind, Ramahd felt a spell trigger. In a blink, much faster than Ramahd could react, Hamzakiir's soul was whisked away. Like a stream of sand slipping through an hourglass, he was transported, leaving behind something poorer and dimmer, perhaps the soul of the man whose body he had stolen to attend the ceremony.

Ramahd had little more than a vague sense of direction.

South, he realized. *Hamzakiir has gone south.*

Guhldrathen sensed it too. It paused its bloody rending of Hamzakiir's former body and stared in the same direction as Ramahd.

With a bellow that sounded like a blast from the fabled horn that presaged the end of days, Guhldrathen hurtled toward the southern wall. The stone began to crack even before it came near, and when Guhldrathen lowered its head and crashed into it, it crumbled beneath the onslaught. Soon the ehrekh's form was obscured, then lost altogether, swallowed by the cloud of dust kicked up by its passage.

"Away!" called one of the Blade Maidens.

Ramahd turned to find Amaryllis kneeling beside King Kiral. She had the skirt of her dress pressed against the worst of Kiral's wounds, the one along his thigh. The Blade Maidens had imposed themselves between Guhldrathen and their King, and had only now realized that Amaryllis was there.

The nearest of the Blade Maidens, their warden, was the one who had shouted at Amaryllis. "I said *away*!" She grabbed the back of Amaryllis's ivory dress and yanked her back.

"Forgive me," Amaryllis said. "I only saw him in pain and thought to help."

Kiral's wounds were serious. The puncture to his thigh. A terrible gash along his ribs. The white cloth of his khalat glistened red all along his left side. Amaryllis's ivory dress, likewise, now shone with the King's blood.

The warden dropped to her knees to help the King herself, while the other four Maidens from her hand, their ebon blades at the ready, pushed Amaryllis and everyone else back.

Some rushed to help the rest of the wounded. Others stood dumbstruck, their expressions a mixture of relief and shock and concern. Most of all, though, they looked wary, as if worried Guhldrathen might return at any moment.

And well they might. Ramahd could still sense Guhldrathen moving away, but who was to say he wouldn't return if Hamzakiir escaped?

Soon all had been moved into the temple, the King included. Shortly after, the King was whisked away in a carriage. Everyone else was questioned, first by the Maidens and later by a host of interrogators from the Silver Spears. The ehrekh had come for him, they said, and he'd been seen fighting Hamzakiir. When they called Ramahd for questioning, they pressed him hard, asking him what he knew of Guhldrathen's attack, of Hamzakiir's presence in the crowd. Ramahd, however, told them he knew nothing, that he was only trying to protect himself, and later, when he'd spotted Hamzakiir, to bring the villain to justice.

They seemed unconvinced, and intimated that they would soon take him and Amaryllis, perhaps even Queen Meryam, to the garrison for further questioning—a process they would not enjoy, Ramahd was assured. But miraculously, word came from Eventide. They were to be allowed to leave immediately, and Kiral himself would speak to them when he had recovered sufficiently. Upon receiving the news, the captain of the Spears stared at Ramahd, his discontent plain to see, but he grudgingly accepted the order and allowed both Ramahd and Amaryllis to go.

As the sun was setting, they were back in their araba, heading for the embassy house and to Meryam. Amaryllis was quiet. Ramahd too. He couldn't stop staring at the dark stain on her dress, blood from the King of Kings.

Chapter 49

SAILING AT NIGHT was dangerous business, but it was necessary if Çeda and the others were to have any hope of escaping Husamettín and the Blade Maidens. No doubt they'd mounted a search and as fast as some of the navy ships were, they'd have to be careful in the days ahead to keep their skiff on the move.

Sümeya's neck wound was bad. Despite the danger of being seen, they lit a small lantern so that Dardzada could tend to her while Melis took the tiller. The wound was deep and caused pain when she tried to speak, forcing Sümeya to whisper if she spoke at all. After cleaning the wound thoroughly, adding a dozen stitches, and applying a salve to fight off infection, Dardzada had declared it sufficient. "Don't strain it, or you'll sound like a talking lizard for the rest of your life."

"I'll be fine," Sümeya said in a rasp.

Dardzada's only response was to put his finger to his lips and let out a long "Shhhhhh . . ."

He'd given the order to Sümeya, but everyone, including Çeda, obeyed it. They sailed in silence, and the sun eventually rose. The events of the previous night washed over them in different ways. They spoke only rarely—to pass food or water, to change the dressing on Sümeya's wound, to discuss their heading or to pass the bucket they used to piss and shit in, rather than halt the skiff.

Dardzada plotted their course over the desert. They all knew they were heading to join the thirteenth tribe, and no one balked. At least not outwardly, not until sundown.

"We've given up every dram of power we once had," Sümeya whispered, wincing as she spoke.

"You would return for it?" Melis asked, though it hardly seemed she cared. Her voice was devoid of emotion. She was staring at the setting sun, her broad face unreadable. She'd unwrapped her turban so that it hung like a cowl around her shoulders, leaving the wind to tug at her curls of hair. It was a strangely intimate thing, as if, with that simple alteration to her uniform, she'd given up her status as a Blade Maiden, allowing all to see her as she was: a woman with a kind face full of freckles that spoke of younger years in the sun. She was quick to smile, though she rarely made jokes of her own. She was also quick to bite if she felt you'd been unjust. She was as fair a woman as Çeda had ever found in the House of Maidens, and now the very thing she'd believed in since she was old enough to talk had been proven a lie.

"If I could but speak to Kameyl—" Sümeya said.

Melis barked a laugh. "Kameyl? She would as soon kiss a cobra as speak to any of us!"

"No, she would listen." Sümeya's words were sharp, as if the one she was trying to convince was herself. "If I could get her away from the others, she would listen."

"And there's the rub," Zaïde said. "The Kings will be watching her as closely as they will Yndris. As closely as they will Sayabim. They'll do the same to everyone we knew. They're likely to give some over to Cahil for questioning after last night."

Sümeya blinked, her brown eyes bright in the light of the lowering sun. She looked lost. Utterly lost. As if the ramifications were only beginning to hit her. "They'll question my mother. My sister and her husband. Their *children* will be watched."

"At least they're alive to be watched," Dardzada said, echoing Çeda's own thoughts.

Sümeya stared at him, her eyes going straight through him.

Çeda thought about telling them stories from her childhood, stories of the Kings' cruelties, stories they would now see in a different light. But tell them while they were in a state of shock, and it would be for her own benefit, not theirs, a way for Çeda to exorcise the hatred that had been building since her mother's death. Sümeya and Melis needed time to work through everything and to see the centuries of pain caused by the Kings.

It had taken a lot of courage for them to trust her, especially Sümeya, First Warden of the Blade Maidens. Çeda would never have guessed she would listen to the story of the thirteenth tribe, but she had. She'd *wanted* to know the truth, and she would have questions. Many questions. Until then, Çeda would let her be.

"Ship!" Dardzada called.

They all turned south and saw a ship in the distance.

It didn't look like a navy ship, but they'd all agreed that no ships, even caravan ships, would be allowed to see them if it could be avoided. The chance of word getting back to the Kings was simply too great. Çeda lifted the tiller, braking their skiff into a trough between the dunes. Melis and Zaïde pulled down the sail, then lifted the mast and laid it across the prow.

They watched and waited as another ship came into view. Then another. And another. Fourteen in all flowed across the sand. It took nearly two hours until they'd all passed by and slipped from sight. Çeda fretted the whole time, staring back the way they'd come, toward Sharakhai, wondering how many of the Kings' ships were looking for them.

Sümeya turned to Melis just as they were setting sail once more. "They'll claim we're part of the Host." Her voice was rough as quarry stone. "That we've *always* been part of the Host."

Melis stared at her woodenly, as if she were ready to accept whatever punishment the gods saw fit to deliver. "What matter the label they give us?"

"My father will agree with them." She stared at her hands, gripping them over and over again. "He'll bow his head in shame and admit that his daughter was lured by the Moonless Host."

"What *matter* is that?" Melis repeated, angry now.

"Because this may all be for nothing. They'll *still* hide the truth. They'll mark us as traitors. Kill us if they can. But if not, they'll claim we're nothing more than mouthpieces for the Al'afwa Khadar. My father will retain his hold on the asirim. And if any question him, if they investigate the asirim, he'll simply mask the true story, as he did with us."

Melis stood in a rush of movement. "Well, of *course* he will, you bloody stupid mule! What did you *think* was going to happen?" She looked completely impotent, shivering there like that. Çeda could tell she wanted to storm away, but they were on a gods-damned skiff. Still, she went as far as she could. She stepped over the front thwart, knocking Zaïde aside as she did so, and sat at the prow, her legs dangling over the front of the skiff. "Now be quiet, as the apothecary bade you."

But it wasn't more than a few breaths before Sümeya spoke again. "We have to go back." She turned to Dardzada, who sat at the tiller, and shouted, "We have to go back!"

Çeda, resting along the bottom of the skiff, her back to the hull, said, "We can't."

Sümeya went on as if she hadn't spoken. "If we return now, we'll be able to spread word before my father can poison the House of Maidens against us."

"We *can't*," Çeda said.

"We will!" She stood and pointed at Dardzada, one hand on the hilt of her sword. "Turn this skiff around."

Dardzada stared at her with indifferent eyes, then returned to watching the way ahead.

"Turn this skiff around!" Sümeya's words came out in a long rattle.

She tried to pull out her sword, but Çeda snatched Sümeya's wrist. "We are returning to the thirteenth tribe," Çeda said, "where we will help with the effort against Onur."

Sümeya looked incensed. She tried to pull her shamshir again, more forcefully this time, but it was merely a feint. She pushed Çeda back, enough that she could lift her foot and snap a kick into Çeda's chest.

Çeda flew over the edge of the skiff, struck the sand hard, and rolled to a painful stop. As she was coming to her feet, she saw Sümeya leap over the side, drawing her blade as she went. Çeda drew River's Daughter, and the two of them met, crossing blades, as the skiff sailed on.

Sümeya spoke between wild and mighty swings of her blade, her voice little better than a wolf's growl. "The Kings must answer for what they've done! They must explain it to those they've wronged! They must free the asirim!"

"These things they will never do," Çeda said, retreating quickly, lithely, always remaining clear of Sümeya's sword.

Sümeya fought like a child new to swordplay. Her swings were born of rage and shame and the sudden shift from a position of power to one of staggering impotence. Eventually she stopped, breathing hard, and bent over. Then she arched her back and howled at the sky. For a long time she raged, and then dropped to her knees and drove the edge of her blade down into the sand over and over again. The sand splashed around her, flew in arcs above her, until finally Sümeya's energy was spent.

She lifted her eyes and regarded Çeda with a look of pure revulsion. "I rue the day you darkened our door."

"There are many wrongs to right in the desert, Sümeya"—Çeda pointed eastward—"and one lies that way. Onur is alone. Isolated from the other Kings. He is not weak, but neither does he command a force that can stop my people if we strike quickly." She stepped closer. "Surely you have no love for the King of Sloth. Let us go, you and I. Let us cut him from the roots of his power and free the tribes beneath his yoke. *Then* we can decide what to do about Sharakhai."

Sümeya still seemed lost, but at Çeda's words, one of her defining features returned—her authority, her command. She stood and looked out over the eastern reaches of the desert. "Very well," she whispered, and trudged toward the skiff, which had come to a stop some distance away.

They sailed well beyond sunset but were forced to anchor when twilight faded. They ate a cold meal of hardtack and smoked meat that was as tough and tasty as saddle leather. The desert was fiercely cold that night, and the wind was strong, but they reckoned it was still too dangerous to light a fire, so they laid out blankets in the lee of the skiff and suffered through the night.

When the sun rose, and they were ready to sail, Çeda forestalled them. "I must speak to Zaïde about Amalos before we go."

Sümeya and Melis shared a look. Dardzada frowned. Zaïde had been shaking her blanket free of sand but stopped as if she'd known this moment would come. "What good will it do to dredge up the past?"

Çeda's mouth fell open. "You would dare say that when our *own* history was nearly lost to the desert?"

"Who is Amalos?" Melis asked.

"A collegia master," Çeda said before Zaïde could speak a word. "A learned man who knew much of the city's history. He agreed to help us uncover the truth but was discovered when Yusam saw him in one of his visions."

Zaïde snapped her blanket once then rolled it tightly. "What happened to Amalos was unfortunate."

"*Unfortunate?*" Çeda could hardly believe her ears. Master Amalos had helped both Çeda and Zaïde research the Kings and their history. He'd discovered invaluable insights in the collegia's archives, and shared his wisdom with Çeda on many a long night as they'd pored over various texts, looking for clues as to how Çeda could use King Mesut's bloody verse to gain an advantage over him.

In the end, Amalos had found the very revelation, written on a beaten sheet of copper, that Çeda had used to gain mastery over the wights summoned from Mesut's onyx bracelet. His brave actions had led directly to Mesut's death, but King Yusam had seen it in his mere. A squad of Silver Spears were sent to apprehend Amalos. Amalos managed to escape by fleeing into the tunnels beneath the city, but his lifeless body was found a short while later, a knife wound to his gut. Çeda was nearly certain Zaïde had played a part in it.

"Amalos came to you for *help*—" Çeda said, reliving her anger.

"He knew the risks," Zaïde replied easily.

"He came to you for help and you *murdered* him for it. Don't deny it! King Yusam told me what he saw. A woman in a white cowl. The flash of a knife in the darkness. A dress stained red."

Zaïde looked awkwardly to Sümeya and Melis. She didn't appear shamed, exactly, but nervous to be speaking of such things before two women who would, only a few days ago, have strung her high for uttering them. "I *had* to kill him."

Çeda's heart beat madly. "What?"

Zaïde's eyes had gone distant. She looked afraid and small. "The Silver

Spears had found Amalos in his study below the archive tower. When he escaped and came to me, I brought it to Ihsan."

"*Ihsan,*" Melis broke in. "By the gods who breathe, why?"

"Ihsan has been pulling her strings for years," Çeda said. "He's been working to topple the other Kings so that he can stand upon Tauriyat alone, without answering to other men."

Zaïde held the blanket under one arm and picked at the frayed edges. She at least had the decency to look miserable while doing it. "Amalos became a scarab the moment he agreed to help you."

"To help *us,*" Çeda corrected.

For the first time, Zaïde seemed flustered. "Of course, us."

"Did Ihsan command you to do it?"

"Of course he did," Zaïde said. "If Amalos was discovered as a scarab, it would—"

"No. Did he *command* you to do it?"

She was referring to Ihsan's ability to command others. Ihsan used it sparingly, but Çeda hoped he had used it here. She hadn't wanted to believe that Zaïde would do such a callous thing of her own accord, but after hearing her speak, Çeda was nearly certain Ihsan hadn't commanded her, but simply appealed to fear.

"If Amalos had been taken by the Kings," Zaïde said, "it would have ruined everything. I would have been taken and tortured. So would you. And Ihsan . . . Can you not see? We would have lost our greatest tool."

Çeda laughed. "You call *Ihsan* a tool when *you're* the one he's been playing like a harp?"

"I gave him only enough to help him destroy the other Kings."

"And yet he managed to get you to kill an ally with but a word. Had Yusam not shown me Amalos's body, I would never have learned enough to kill Mesut."

At this, Melis stood and stared at them all—Dardzada, Çeda, Zaïde, and finally Sümeya. She shook her head as if she were about to speak, then walked away.

"Çeda," Dardzada said, "keeping Ihsan as our ally was an opportunity we couldn't allow to pass us by."

"That isn't what I'm talking about. Do you think I care that we're using

Ihsan to destroy the other Kings? I'll use any of them if it will see them wiped from the face of the desert. But *you*," she said to Zaïde, "took your *knife* to a man who came to you for help, a man who trusted you, who might have helped us further. You could have seen him to a safe house. He could have joined the tribe in the desert."

"Ihsan would have known." Tears crept down her cheeks, sometimes side-slipping along the wrinkles in her aged skin. They looked like shards of citrine in the morning sun.

Çeda spit into the sand between them. "I name you coward, Zaïde Onur'ava. You should have seen Amalos free or died trying."

Çeda had never seen her like this. Zaïde seemed lost, a woman adrift. She blinked away more tears and nodded. With a stricken look, she turned, walked to the skiff, and began lifting the mast into place. Sümeya stepped inside the hull to help her. Çeda watched them, furious that Zaïde chose not to fight her, nor to offer some sort of explanation for her actions. But what *could* Zaïde say? There was no defending what she'd done.

Strangely, Çeda felt no better after her tirade.

"Come with me," Dardzada said.

"I'm not going to listen as you try to soften what she did," she shot back. "You're not my bloody father."

"Always so fucking stubborn."

"And who taught me that?"

"Your mother did. But I thought some of it might have been drummed out of you in the House of Maidens. I see now I was foolish to think you'd learned to shut that mule mouth of yours and listen to those who are trying to help you."

"And who is that? *You*, a man who hides things from me as often as the sun shines in the desert?" She stabbed her finger toward Zaïde. "Or that one, a woman who would sacrifice anyone so long as *she* isn't found out?"

Dardzada motioned to her right hand. "That woman saved you when no one else could. She gave you those tattoos and fought to keep you in the House of Maidens when she could easily have denied my request. And then she fought to keep you there, to ensure you were given an ebon blade, to train you herself so that you would be ready for all that lay ahead. She might have handled Amalos differently. From what little I knew of him, he was a good man, and I wish he was still with us. But if it came down to a choice of either you or Amalos, I'd choose you every time."

"But it didn't have to *be* that way."

"You have no idea how it *had to be*. Zaïde has been maneuvering around the Kings for longer than you've been alive. If she thought it necessary, then I believe her."

"I won't work with her anymore, Dardzada."

"She can tell us much about Onur."

"Her own father."

"You think you know so much?"

"I know the ties of blood are strong."

"Oh? Are you're saying you'd stay your sword if you knew who your father was?"

"I . . . No."

"Did she ever share with you the tale of her mother?"

"No," Çeda admitted, her voice softer.

Dardzada maneuvered his bulk toward the skiff. "Perhaps you should ask her about it before you start strutting across the sand claiming she's wasting lives."

Chapter 50

ÇEDA AND THE OTHERS set sail shortly after, and headed east over the next several days. Fearing the Kings navy, they pushed past the first few oases and stretched their water to the limit, making for a small oasis not regularly visited. As they were nearing it, they reached a swath of desert littered with patches of stone. It was treacherous for any ship larger than a yacht but perfectly navigable for a skiff.

When they reached the oasis—little more than a gully surrounded by a burst of green vegetation—they began to breathe easier. Ten days had passed since their escape from the blooming fields. They huddled in the lee of a tall, misshapen boulder, warming themselves by a fire, the first they'd dared on their voyage. Çeda sat cross-legged on the sand, basking in the fire's warmth while oiling River's Daughter. It was strangely comforting to have the blade back, even after so short a separation.

I thought I'd lost you for good, Çeda mused as she ran the oily rag up and down the blade.

"You're giving it enough oil to drown it," Sümeya said from across the fire. She'd been resting her voice, but it still sounded terrible.

"I know," Çeda replied. "But I owe it this much."

"Well, you're not a whore from the southern docks," Melis snapped, "and that isn't a cock. Wipe it dry and be done with it."

Çeda's only reply was to rub it as if she *were* holding a cock, slow at first, then faster and faster, the hilt resting along her crotch.

Melis scowled, but Sümeya laughed. A moment later, when Çeda threw her head back and screamed in false pleasure, Melis's scowl softened, and then she was laughing louder than Sümeya. Dardzada rolled his eyes, while Zaïde ignored everyone.

"I never thanked you," Çeda said to Sümeya.

With the hint of a smile she said, "You still haven't."

Çeda laughed. She lifted the sword, pinching the blade on either side of the balance point, and lifted it to her forehead. "My life in your debt."

At this, Sümeya's smile turned genuine. Then her eyes narrowed, and she seemed to come to a decision. She stood, moved over to the skiff, and grabbed the bag Çeda had retrieved from Whiteknife's back. "In that case, you're about to owe me your next life as well."

From within the bag she took out a small, leatherbound book. Its features were lost in shadow, but when Sümeya held it out for her and the firelight struck its worn surface, Çeda saw it for what it was. Her mother's book. It was surreal accepting it from Sümeya, feeling its familiar heft, opening the pages and reading the first of the many poems within.

Tears came unbidden to her eyes. "But it was lost in the desert."

"It was found during the search for you and brought to me."

Çeda thumbed through the pages, lingering on several with marks in the gutters. Those were the pages that hid a piece of a bloody verse in plain sight. She tipped the book down so she could see better, and saw them: the places where her mother had re-inked the words with brown ink, an indicator that it was one of the words in Külaşan's poem, the one that had led to his downfall.

A tear slipped from her cheek and fell against the page. She quickly wiped it from the paper's rough surface, then dried her tears with a sleeve. "My life in your debt," she said again, this time with perfect sincerity.

While Dardzada and Zaïde began preparing food, Çeda read through the book, savoring every word. She remembered those rare, lazy days, she and her mother sitting and reading together, sipping rosewater lemonade from the roof of the latest west-end tenement to be called home. Dardzada's words from the other day returned to her, his urging her to learn more of Zaïde's past before she passed judgment. "You know of my mother," she said to Zaïde, "but I've never heard of yours."

Zaïde, sitting across the fire from her, glared at Dardzada.

He shrugged. "She deserves to know." And went back to sprinkling salt over a pair of large, skinned lizards.

Whatever small amount of annoyance Zaïde had been harboring lately faded, and her eyes drifted back to the flickering fire. "What does it matter?"

Çeda closed the book and put it into the pouch at her belt. Its weight felt right and pure. "Above all, the desert is a tale of blood, and I would hear yours."

Still Zaïde balked.

"If what they've said is true," Sümeya rasped, "we may meet your father in battle. I think it's time we all heard."

Zaïde's look of indignation spoke of a different time, when *she* had been the one in charge. But the look soon faded, and she began to speak. "Onur is and always has been a cruel, detestable man, especially to my mother. He refused to let her leave his palace. She knew she couldn't disobey him, so she began calling others to come to her, her distant family from the desert among them. I was young then, perhaps ten. It was when I first met Dardzada." She looked at him, and he nodded, allowing that she should tell the full story.

"I met many from the thirteenth tribe in those days, though I had yet to learn what it meant. I might even have met your grandfather, Ishaq," she said to Çeda, "though if so, I can no longer recall. One of my family was a seer, Imarine, my aunt, and she saw some potential in me, which she began to hone over the months and years that followed. I began to read the palms of my friends, and I generally saw in them paths that would take them to fruitful places. They were mostly the children of Goldenhill, after all. I did it, occasionally, for those who came from the desert.

"When I became more confident, I desperately wanted to read my mother's palm. Most days she was miserable, and I hoped to find happier days for her and tell her about them. She refused with a fierceness that made me realize it was fear that drove her decision, fear that ran deeper than the roots of Tauriyat. For many years I didn't dare ask again, afraid of what I might see, but then one day I heard our maids speaking in low tones. One of them was crying, the other trying to console her. I snuck into the dining hall, and the girl who was crying said that Thian, her brother, a most beautiful man who worked in the stables, had displeased the King. Onur had come to ride with a Malasani prince. Thian had ridden out to the desert with them and a dozen courtiers from Malasan and Sharakhai. They rode quickly, too fast for the horses on such a hot day and for such a long ride. Onur was so large his horse grew tired more rapidly than the others, but Onur refused to slow their pace. Soon his horse, a fine akhala, was staggering, and Thian offered Onur his own horse.

"'Why?' Onur asked. 'Mine is doing well enough.' And then Thian lied, in hopes of allowing the King to save face in front of his guests. 'A thousand apologies, my Lord King. In my haste to make the horses ready, I forgot to give him a proper ration of water before we left.' 'Nonsense,' replied Onur, his voice full of disdain. Then he looked to those gathered and spurred his horse into action. 'This akhala could deliver me to Ishmantep and back, I assure you.'

"The horse collapsed not a half-league later. Onur was thrown from his saddle, and was cut along his forehead, a mark that can still be seen today. In his anger, he drew his sword, ready to kill the beast that had failed him. But Thian shouted, 'No!' and put himself between akhala and King. 'My Lord King, this is all my fault. Please, take my horse. I'll remain here until yours recovers from this interminable heat.' It was a grave mistake, and Thian knew it from the start, but what was he to do? Onur smiled. You've met him now. You know the sort of smile I mean. Hungry. Covetous. 'Very well,' my father said to Thian. 'Bring the horse to my palace on your return. I would speak to you of how you're keeping them.'

"Thian had done as Onur asked and hadn't yet returned. And now the maids were worried. 'Surely he'll be home soon,' I said to them, coming out of my hiding place. But they shushed me and sent me away with barely concealed horror on their faces. I found out why that night. My mother had been gone the entire day, summoned to attend Onur. When she returned, I found her sitting in a chair, staring out the window. She wasn't crying, but she was haunted. I've never seen the like, as if her very soul had been taken from her."

Zaïde slowed and then stopped. She turned to face Çeda. Throughout the story, she'd spoken in a distant way, as if it were an ancient tale told a thousand times, over a thousand fires; but now, as she paused, gathering herself, her eyes flitted to and fro as if she were reliving those fearful moments. "I asked my mother what had happened, and she held out her hand to me. Her palm."

A chill settled inside Çeda, a feeling as cold as the winter sky. "What did you do?"

Zaïde's distant gaze focused on Çeda once more. "I shook my head and pleaded with her, but she was adamant. 'You will know the sort of man your father is.' In the end, I was weak. I took her hand and read her palm. It was the strongest vision I have ever had, then or since. I saw her secreting a slim blade in her shoe. I saw her going to Onur in his palace. I saw her stab him, but she managed only one strike, and then Onur had her. For all his weight, he is a powerful man, stronger even than Husamettín, and he broke her. I saw nothing after that. I begged my mother not to leave. When she refused, I tried to run from the room, but she held my wrists, gripping them so tightly her nails tore my skin. She made me stare into her eyes, eyes filled with hate and regret and so much sorrow. More than anything, though, I saw her resignation. 'You know it will be so,' she hissed at me, 'so do not fight it.'

"In the days after, I learned that she and Thian had been lovers. I knew she cared for him, but callow as I was I had no concept of a wife being unfaithful. My mother was a careful woman, more careful than I had ever given her credit for. What she shared with me next shook me to my very core. You may have heard rumors of Onur the Feasting King. That he eats his will, and that his will is great. That he feasts on the bloody flesh of horses and goats and all manner of beasts. He has other, more abhorrent tastes as well." Zaïde's lips became a thin line. "Onur had learned of my mother's misdeeds and contrived to bring Thian to him, and then summoned my mother to sup."

Çeda's hand shot to her mouth. But Zaïde seemed utterly composed, which only magnified Çeda's horror.

"Onur forced her to sit by his side, two Blade Maidens standing behind her chair, while he ate and spoke of the weather, how very hot it had been on their ride, how kind Thian had been to give up his own horse, even if he'd erred in not preparing Onur's horse properly. Never once did he mention that he knew she and Thian had been lovers. Nor did he ask her to his bed, thank the gods, or I might never have seen her again. My mother refused to eat. You can guess why. And she feared he would force her, but he merely waved his fork to the meat on her plate, asking her why she wasn't hungry.

"He left her in that room after a kiss to the back of her hand." Zaïde's chin quavered. "My mother left that night, hours after I'd read her palm. She went to Onur's palace and never returned. She was never even given a funeral. To this day I don't know where her bones are buried, if they even are."

The way she said it was so pitiful, it made Çeda's arms and shoulders curl inward. Zaïde noticed. She looked to the others, who looked stricken as well—even Dardzada, who knew the story already. She forged on, as if the simple act of acknowledging their sadness would be to give in to her own.

"I had no idea that I was one of the thirteenth tribe. I'd only heard whispers of its existence. But after learning of my mother's death, my Aunt Imarine told me all of it. Our story in the days leading up to Beht Ihman; of the massacre, of our blood being sheltered among the remaining twelve tribes, of the origins of the Moonless Host, which was born from hatred of the Kings but also of a thirst for revenge."

For long moments, it was all Çeda could do to keep the knot in her throat from getting worse. "Why did your mother never tell you of your heritage?"

"A question I've asked myself many times. There was no time to ask her then"—Zaïde shrugged—"and she would have refused to answer in any case. I suspect she hoped to protect me from it. She felt the fight was just, but one that had little to do with her. Like so many in Sharakhai, and even the desert, she was part of the silent horde. Were they to rise up, they could overthrow the Kings tomorrow, but they will not. Their fear neuters them."

Melis had grown more and more restless. "Not everyone on Goldenhill is like Onur," she said.

"Perhaps not," Zaïde replied, "but they're not the ones in power, are they?"

"They could be," Melis fired back. "The cause of the thirteenth tribe may be just, but that doesn't mean everyone on Tauriyat should be hung for the Kings' crimes."

Dardzada scowled. "You're suggesting their heirs should take their thrones?"

"Why not?" Melis replied. "They have a legitimate right to them."

Dardzada lifted the lizards he'd been roasting and turned them over. "You speak of rights. What of the new tribe forming in the desert? What of the asirim?"

Usually Çeda would stand right beside Dardzada and join in, but she was weary of fighting, and the last thing they needed was an argument, so before Melis could respond, Çeda asked Zaïde, "Ihsan shared Onur's bloody verse with me, that he's weakened after he feasts. Is it so?"

Zaïde considered it awhile, then shrugged. "He's long been known for taking days, even weeks, to hide away, allowing none near him. Perhaps that's due to his verse, but it could also be because he hates everyone he lays eyes on."

"Ihsan also said he's a skin changer?"

"I've heard rumors." Zaïde waggled her head, an expression of impotence. "I should know more. He's my father. But after my mother . . . I couldn't bear to be near him."

As Zaïde spoke, Çeda felt something strange. A sense of worry had been growing inside her, and it now felt markedly worse. She wasn't even sure why, but she felt suddenly *unsafe*.

She reached out into the night. She easily found the others around the fire: the kettledrum of Dardzada's heart, the other women's hearts playing a lighter rhythm around it. There was something else, though. A beat on the edge of perception. She thought it might be a drake hidden beneath the sand's surface.

With sudden clarity, she understood.

The heartbeat was faint because it was being concealed.

Danger, Çeda whistled as she stood, River's Daughter in her hand.

She heard a rapid patter of footsteps moments before she saw a figure resolve from the darkness. It was a woman, dressed in black, an ebon sword held in her hands, a turban and veil hiding her face.

Melis and Sümeya were already up, ebon blades at the ready. Zaïde had turned the opposite direction, perhaps sensing another. Dardzada was lumbering to his feet as Çeda moved to intercept the Blade Maiden.

"Traitors!" cried the Maiden as she came.

Gods, it was Yndris!

Çeda had no time to wonder how she'd found them. "The skiff!" Çeda said to Dardzada.

He was already on the move as Çeda's sword met Yndris's. The two of them traded blows, Çeda's fueled by desperation, Yndris's by hatred.

Yndris had been masking her heartbeat—inexpertly, or Çeda would never have sensed her—but Çeda knew that where there was one, there would be more. Beyond the drumming of her own heart Çeda felt them approaching. Four more, each trying to mask themselves.

She was about to warn the others when Sümeya whistled: *Enemies! Surrounded!*

Sümeya intercepted the first of the newcomers. Melis took another. Zaïde met a third. As the sound of clashing steel filled the night, a fifth came rushing toward the skiff.

"Dardzada!" she shouted without turning toward him.

As she swung River's Daughter up in a sweeping block, Dardzada's heavy grunt came from behind her. A moment later there was a pop and then a flash of light that was so bright it drowned the feeble campfire. A sizzling sound was followed by a muffled scream from the Blade Maiden.

Again and again, Yndris tried to slip inside Çeda's guard. She found no openings, but neither did Çeda, and she backed away. Yndris had grown in skill. She'd become stronger in the ways of the heart as well. Çeda tried to press against her heart, but was unable to pin her down. Yndris did not attack Çeda in this way, but she'd grown adept in defending against it.

From the corner of her eye, Çeda saw a Blade Maiden rolling over the sand near the skiff. She was screaming, her hands pressed tightly against her eyes. The skiff itself was just beginning to shift. A high-pitched moan accompanied the movement. It was coming from Dardzada as he leaned his bulk against the rear of the skiff and pushed backward with his legs. His heartbeat was spiking. It was pounding faster than Çeda's—he was clearly wounded, but how badly?

Yndris tried to rush toward him, but Çeda cut her off. She blocked Yndris's high swing and snapped a kick into her midsection. When Yndris dodged left, placing the fire between them, Çeda kicked the coals into her face. Embers flew up and Yndris reeled, her arms going up to protect her face as Çeda turned and ran for the skiff. It was heading down the far side of the dune, picking up speed.

Orderly retreat, Çeda whistled. *Toward me.*

Sümeya, Melis, and Zaïde moved into a rough line and began backing up toward Çeda. There would be no easy escape onto the skiff this time. Not until they'd managed to slow the Maidens.

As a mighty groan came from the skiff—Dardzada lifting the mast into place—Zaïde released a loud *kiai*, then another. She was engaged with an imposing Blade Maiden. Kameyl, Çeda realized, who towered over Zaïde. Zaïde, who had only a small buckler to defend herself, was using it with ever more desperation. Çeda knew as well as anyone how powerful Kameyl's swings were.

Çeda lost track of Zaïde as they began to retreat more quickly. As the fire was lost from view behind the dune, however, and their opponents were outlined by the firelight, Çeda heard a muffled cry. Tall Kameyl dropped to one knee then fell face first onto the sand.

Zaïde came flying toward Melis's opponent. She blocked the Maiden's ebon blade and struck two fingers blindingly fast to the Maiden's neck, then inside her thigh, shouting with each blow, so loudly that Çeda could feel them *thump* inside her chest.

The second Maiden went down, and Zaïde rushed toward the third. Çeda could feel Zaïde's heart pattering like a skin drum on Beht Revahl, and the lack of rhythm was alarming. There were long pauses then rapid, inconsistent beats.

As Zaïde charged, the next Maiden shifted her stance, preparing her defense, but Sümeya and Melis were ready. They quickly closed in and delivered two precise cuts, one to her side and one across the back of her leg.

Yndris knew she'd lost her chance. She ran to Kameyl's side shouting "Get up!" Kameyl, however, could do little more than roll her head from side to side. "Get up!"

Zaïde staggered back, breathing like an ox. Her heart was tripping over itself. Then she simply collapsed, her right hand over her chest.

In the distance, northward, a horn sounded several distinct notes. It was the sort the Kings' navy ships used to call to one another. To the south, the blast was repeated. It came a third time from the west. Çeda hadn't learned all their calls, but she knew this one: *converge.*

While Sümeya guarded against Yndris, Çeda and Melis cradled Zaïde and carried her to the skiff. They lifted her inside, but their hold was tenuous and she slipped from Çeda's grasp and collapsed to the bottom of the skiff, striking her head against the thwart. Melis leapt in and began hoisting the sail, Çeda helped Dardzada push, and Sümeya was sprinting across the sand toward them.

"Get in," Çeda said to Dardzada.

He ignored her and kept pushing, using his stout legs to move the skiff faster.

"Get bloody in!" she shouted as Sümeya reached them.

At last he relented, and soon they were sailing with speed. Yndris had given up the chase. Kameyl was only just back on her feet, her legs wobbly as a newborn foal's. They spotted the moonlit sails of three other skiffs, but Çeda and Dardzada had taken the time earlier to plot their route out from the rocky oasis. Çeda used it now, skirting sections of stone carefully to keep their speed up. They sailed swiftly, and soon had slipped free of the noose.

Zaïde and Dardzada were in a bad way, though. Zaïde's heartbeat was still a strange pitter-patter, and her breath was coming in short, quick gasps. And Dardzada . . . Gods, his shoulder was a mess. He'd been cut deeply. Blood soaked the front of his thawb, and the wound, lit by moonlight, had bits of white bone showing near the center. How he'd managed to push the ship at all was beyond her.

Sümeya and Melis lay Dardzada onto the bottom of the skiff—it was crowded, but his head fit between Zaïde's legs. Then Sümeya sat on the thwart, her legs straddling his chest. "I'll need light," she said, grabbing the small bag where she kept her stitching thread and medical salves.

It would be seen by the trailing ships, but there was nothing for it. Melis struck a light and held it so that Sümeya could see the mess the Maiden's blade had made of Dardzada's shoulder. She went to work, and Çeda guided them through the night.

Chapter 51

EMRE MADE HIS WAY to the gunwales of Tribe Kadri's capital ship, a caravel named the *Autumn Rose*. He carried his most trusted friend these past many days, a crude-looking but surprisingly powerful spyglass. For the part he'd played in the battle with Onur, Emre had been asked aboard by Tribe Kadri's new shaikh: Mihir's young cousin, Aríz, a boy of only fourteen summers. He was a handsome boy, though gangly and awkward at times. He had hazel eyes and a head of closely shorn hair except for the braided tail that hung from the back of his head. Emre was glad to be on the same ship with him. He wanted to be able to gauge the young man's mood. Aríz had not yet committed to help the thirteenth tribe, but Emre still held out hope that he would.

Lifting the spyglass to his eye, he completed the same ritual he'd conducted every hour over the past ten days: he studied the horizon, noting any malformation, any cloud of dust, any misshapen cloud. He spotted movement two points off the port bow, but realized moments later it was only a flock of low-flying birds. Blazing blues, maybe, though what portent they might be—birds of peace that hadn't deigned to fly near their fleet—he wasn't sure.

A dozen other times he'd been sure he'd spotted the hint of a sinuous body lifting high into the sky and flying toward them like an eel through water. But it had only been his nerves. He couldn't shake the image of the wyrm's cold eyes as it had flown toward the ship. Most animals lived to feed and defend their territory or their young. The look in the sand wyrm's eyes had been malicious, as if it *hungered* to inflict harm. Emre had no doubt that Onur had summoned it using the strange orange stone, the one he'd used to crush Mihir's skull. Just how much control he had beyond that, Emre wasn't sure. What he *was* sure of was that he never wished to see the thing again.

A choice now left to the gods, a voice inside him said.

"It's licking its wounds," said a woman's voice from behind him.

He turned to find Haddad leaning against the mizzenmast. She was holding a massive purple radish, and was slicing pieces of it off with a small knife and popping them into her mouth—a peasant's meal if he ever saw one. The sort a farmer in Malasan might have beside a burbling river before returning to work in the fields.

She wore a bright dress made from a patchwork of colorful cloth. The stitching was rough, the pieces misshapen. *A peasant's dress to match her meal.* And yet her many long necklaces, the silver bangles on her wrists, the large, swaying earrings, somehow made her look as rich and stylish as any of the women from Goldenhill.

"You've come to see the sun," he said to her.

"It's infernally hot down there," she said while chewing. "Why wouldn't I?"

She'd come aboard the *Rose* to be close to Aríz, but the loss of Zakkar and two more of her crew in the battle with Onur had struck her hard. She'd taken to staying in the bunk she'd been given below decks, rarely coming up to see the sun. Today, however, she seemed to have regained a bit of her old self. She had that crooked smile of hers that was equal parts chiding and endearing; and if her smile didn't quite reach her eyes, well, Emre could understand.

He motioned with the spyglass to the rolling dunes behind them. "The wyrm was hardly wounded by the ballista bolt."

"Wounded enough, it seems."

"Perhaps. But I suspect Onur is holding it back until his ships can find us. No sense sending it out alone, where it might be crippled."

Haddad shrugged. "For all we know it might be dead from infection. What good does it do to wonder over it now?"

"Because the answer might mean our lives." He waved his arm to the other ships that sailed alongside and ahead of the *Autumn Rose*. "All of our lives."

Twenty-three Kadri ships had escaped the battle; two had been abandoned due to damage sustained from the wyrm's acidic breath, leaving twenty-one ships in all, including the *Autumn Rose* and Haddad's dhow, *Calamity's Reign*. They'd been sailing ever since, hoping to stay ahead of Onur's fleet while heading for a meeting with the thirteenth tribe, should Emre convince Tribe Kadri to join them.

Haddad shrugged again. She cut off a fresh slice from the radish and held it out for Emre. He shook his head. "It tastes like lizard vomit."

She shook it at him. "They help fight night coughs."

"I'm not sick."

Again she shook it. "Not *yet*."

She sounded like Emre's mother, what little he remembered of her. Hiding his smile, he took the piece and bit into the sharp, crunchy flesh. It wasn't so bad as he'd made out, but he made a show of it anyway.

"Baby . . ." Haddad said, hiding a smile.

They sat, their backs to the mizzenmast, and finished the radish together.

After a time, Emre asked the question that had been burning inside him for days. "What was Zakkar?"

Haddad took some time before she responded. "He was my bodyguard."

"I didn't ask what he did. I asked what he *was*."

She whipped the radish's inedible stem over the side of the ship. "Ask what you really mean to ask."

"Was he a golem?"

"He was."

"Who made him?"

She turned to look him in the eye with an aggrieved expression on her face. "They aren't *made*," she said fiercely. "Life is *shared* with them."

"Can . . ." He wasn't even sure how to ask it. "Can you make another?"

Now she stood and rounded on him properly, stabbing the air between them with the knife she still held in her right hand. "Do you know *anything* about Malasan?"

Feeling suddenly edgy, he stood as well. What could he say? He knew the Malasani people were brash and cocksure. He knew they'd coveted Sharakhai and the desert for generations. He knew of a cruel man who'd murdered his brother when he was young.

"No, I cannot *make* another," Haddad went on. "It is a sacred ritual. My brother gave his own blood, his own breath. He gave a piece of his soul that Zakkar might be my protector here in the desert."

"He died to do this?"

Haddad closed her eyes and took a deep breath. She adjusted her footing as the *Rose* tipped over a dune. "No. He didn't die to give life to Zakkar. Golems are given life by those who grant it in a sacred ritual. Life is shared with them, not taken," she said again. Then she went silent. "But Harind died three months later." She shrugged, looking as lost as she had when they'd fled Onur. "I was here in the Shangazi when it happened but hoped to see him when I returned. I knew I was giving up much of my life in Malasan when I decided to treat with the tribes for my king, but I never thought I'd lose him so early. It may seem foolish to you, but Zakkar was my only remaining piece of him."

"It's not foolish," Emre said, "but Zakkar wasn't your last remaining piece of him." She looked as though she were about to argue, so he quickly went on. "We are given the flames of our mothers' love. And our fathers', for as long as we might have them. So it is with everyone we meet. In the desert we say they kindle us, and we kindle them. Our flames are exchanged." He waved a hand to her. "The woman I see before me is not merely Haddad of Malasan. She is Haddad and some small spark of her brother. And her family. And her friends. Is it not so?"

At this, she seemed to soften slightly. "That is a facile notion." Despite the words, a small portion of her smile returned. "But one I rather like."

The captain called for a northerly turn, and all over the ship, the crew made ready. Emre and Haddad shifted over to the gunwales to make way.

"The golem . . ." Emre continued. "Zakkar."

Haddad sighed. "And I was just beginning to like you."

"It's only"—he waved to the western horizon—"Onur . . . He's a grave threat, and more dangerous than I gave him credit for. I would give anything to wipe him from the face of the desert. I would give *my* blood if it would help. *My* breath."

She turned and stared into his eyes, as if trying to judge his sincerity. Then she looked away, crossing her arms beneath her breasts. "We would never share such things with a *drylander*." She paused, and when she went on, it was with a softer tone. "And even if I wished to, it's not a gift I possess."

"You could try."

"I cannot simply *try*, you stupid Sharakhani goat. It isn't will I lack, but the ability, the training. We lack the proper materials"—she waved, the simple motion somehow encompassing the whole of the desert—"out here in this bloody wasteland. Now leave it be."

He'd known it to be a desperate idea from the beginning, but these were desperate days. He was saved from saying more when the lookout in the ship ahead of them called, "Ships ahead! Two points off the starboard bow!"

More called from nearby ships, confirming the sighting. Immediately, the mood went from one of tight efficiency to unease. Everyone on these ships, including Emre, had been worried that Onur's ships would catch up to them. It seemed improbable that Onur could have raced ahead, but Emre had seen enough from Onur that he wouldn't discount it, either. He stood on the gunwale and shielded his eyes from the relentless sun. He saw nothing immediately, but as the pilot eased the ship's heading toward the starboard side, he spotted them. Dozens of ships in a cluster, their sails lowered.

"They're not Onur's!" their crewman called from the vulture's nest. "They're flying a blue pennant with a white device."

"A mountain peak?" Emre called up.

"Aye. It might be."

A great joy welled up inside him. "It's the thirteenth tribe! It's Ishaq and Macide."

Emre had underestimated just how much Tribe Kadri hoped to find the thirteenth tribe. All across the ship a cheer went up. The men and women on deck threw their hands to the sky. The cheer spread to other ships, all across their small fleet. It was so loud that their own spotter's calls were lost for a time. He was hanging like a fool from the vulture's nest atop the mainmast, waving for the captain's attention.

"Be quiet!" Emre called, dropping down to deck and waving them to silence. "Quiet!"

"Ships aft! Ships aft!" the spotter, a thin stick of a man, called, pointing wildly to the desert behind the *Autumn Rose*. Everyone turned. When the ship took a rise, they came into view: dozens of ships a bit north of their current position, sailing on an intercept course. "Ships of the White Spear!" the spotter called. "King Onur's ships!"

Shaikh Aríz moved aftward along with the captain of the ship, a man named Ali-Budrek, who had become something like Aríz's vizir. Behind them Shal'alara came as well, her face grim.

"What shall we do?" Aríz asked them all.

Before the battle, he'd been fifth in line to inherit the mantle of shaikh. After Mihir had been killed, along with two others, it had left only Aríz's father, who barely escaped with his life. His father's wounds were many, however, and became infected; they delivered him to the farther fields three days into their journey, leaving Aríz with more responsibility than he could handle.

As young as Aríz was, he was no fool. His question showed more wisdom than men twice his age might show. Onur's ships were distant yet. It was likely they hadn't spotted the thirteenth tribe, but if they continued on their present course, they surely would, which would place the whole of tribe Khiyanat in danger.

Emre looked again to the Khiyanat ships, sails down, anchored for the night. He couldn't allow Onur to catch them unaware. "Here's what we'll do."

As Emre laid out his plan, Aríz fidgeted. He looked to the stocky Ali-Budrek, but also to Shal'alara, another he'd come to trust for her shrewd opinions and, not inconsequentially, Emre suspected, the winks and lewd jokes she directed at him. Aríz seemed nervous, even scared, but by the time Emre was done, a hopefulness, almost eagerness, had displaced some of the fear. Emre was proud of him. *It will serve you well over the course of the coming day,* he thought.

Ali-Budrek nodded his agreement with Emre's plan, though not without some reservation showing on his dour face. Shal'alara did as well. Haddad remained silent, but when Aríz asked for her opinion, she gave her assent and pledged her ship to aid in the effort. In the end, Aríz agreed, and soon their ragtag fleet had begun maneuvering in a grand arc southward. All except for one. The *Widow's Scythe*—a cutter, and their fastest ship—sped in the opposite direction on full sail, making for the huddled ships of the thirteenth tribe.

Chapter 52

O N THE NIGHT following the battle at Thaash's temple, Meryam summoned Ramahd to her apartments. When he arrived she was curled crookedly in her padded chair, leaning over her desk as a fire roared nearby, fending off the cold of the night.

"My queen," he said, standing in the doorway.

"Come." She summoned him with a perfunctory wave, hardly taking her eyes from the extensive letter she was writing. Despite the fire, she shivered enough to make her hand quiver as she wrote. More concerning, however, was the fact that she was wearing the amulet again. The outer doors were open, revealing the sapphire in its gilded cage.

"You'll catch your death," Ramahd said as he headed across the room to close the windows.

"I enjoy the night breeze."

"You're not yet recovered, Meryam."

"My *queen*."

"You're not yet recovered, *my queen*."

Meryam slapped the ebony quill down on the table. Ink splattered over the papyrus and the leather blotter beneath it. "I would think after all these years you'd trust me to take care of my body, Ramahd."

"I would think after all these years you'd recognize when you're pushing yourself too far. Look at you. You're breathing hard doing nothing more than *writing*. Hamzakiir is gone. So is Guhldrathen. We're safe for a time."

"We are anything but *safe*. The moment we accepted Kiral's summons to Eventide, we entered into a silent war. It's only a matter of time before it escalates."

"All the more reason not to expend yourself too soon."

Emotions warred on her face as she stared at him. She put visible effort into stifling it, however, and picked up her quill once more. "I need you to deliver this letter to the Enclave."

The Enclave was not a place, but rather a fellowship of other magi. Meryam had long ago reached out to those in Sharakhai with abilities like hers, first and foremost so that she wouldn't be considered an enemy, but also to share in their vow of mutual protection from the Kings and other threats.

"Cicio can go."

"I've sent Cicio and Vrago to fetch supplies."

"Then I'll give it to Amaryllis."

"Given recent events, this is too important. I would have you do it, Ramahd."

"Very well. Where this time?" The locations of drops like these changed weekly, sometimes daily, following the whims of the Enclave's members.

"Hog's Hollow."

Hog's Hollow was an oud parlor on the quay of the western harbor, a favorite of the sandsmen. Most called it The Hog, others Hog Swallow, as only pigs would eat the swill that came from their kitchen. It was as distant and inconvenient a location as could have been chosen. Even on horseback he'd be gone for well over an hour, but they'd agreed to avoid using horses for such trips; they were a rarity in most quarters of the city and attracted too much attention.

When Meryam finished writing she blew on the ink, rolled the scroll up, and applied a green wax, melting it with heat from the tip of her finger. That done, she pressed the seal of Qaimir into it. The entire time, her hands trembled.

Ramahd accepted the scroll, bowing his head to her. "Anything else?"

"That's all."

"Before I go, my queen, might I ask you to close the doors of the amulet?"

A quizzical look came over her. She stared down, as if she were surprised to find it open. "I'll do as I please."

"Meryam, that gem is nothing to toy with. We agreed you'd only open it if it was important. If it was necessary."

This time, she showed no irritation at the use of her name. "So we did," she said, clipping the doors closed. "Are you pleased now?"

"I won't be pleased until that infernal device has been removed from our lives."

"This *device* is going to lift our country to heights it has never seen, Ramahd."

"I would like nothing more, but even you must admit that it could just as easily ruin us."

Meryam practically fell back into her chair, as if she couldn't pretend to be nice any longer. "Go, Ramahd. Return to me when you're done."

Basilio was waiting outside Meryam's rooms as Ramahd left. He watched Ramahd with a satisfied smirk. Ramahd stopped and turned to him. "Do you have anything to say?"

"Me?" Basilio said. "Of course not, my lord. And please"—he bowed and waved toward the door that led to the stables—"I wouldn't *dream* of keeping you."

Ramahd turned and left, leaving Basilio to his smugness. *I will take a horse*, Ramahd decided. He was still concerned over being discreet, but there was a tavern along the Trough whose owner was a Qaimiran emigre; he would put up Ramahd's horse and let him slip out the back with no questions asked. As he rode through the gates of the embassy house, however, and the pikeman in their royal livery nodded to him, he began to wonder at Meryam's attitude. Why send *him*. He wasn't above it, but she'd acted as though it were imperative that *Ramahd* be the one to go.

Add to that Basilio's self-satisfied reaction to his leaving, as well as Vrago and Cicio being conveniently away, and Ramahd soon found himself reining his horse to a stop. He turned to look back at the embassy's dark profile. It was lit strangely in the light of dusk, like a burning ember about to be extinguished.

He kicked his horse into a trot, heading back the way he'd come. He knew what he was about to do was a small betrayal, but he'd learned long ago to trust his instincts.

As one traveled along King's Road there were a smattering of smaller embassies from distant lands, each little more than a cluster of small buildings—residences, stables, a barracks for the soldiers who protect foreign dignitaries. The four primary houses, however—Qaimir's, Mirea's, Malasan's, Kundhun's—were more impressive, with surrounding walls, larger estates and stables, and barracks to house larger contingents of soldiers.

Before he came near the Qaimiri compound, Ramahd guided his horse off the road and spurred it over a low hill to reach an orchard. There was little chance of being discovered. The orchard backed up to a small manor, abandoned for over a year after the previous ambassador, a man from a tiny country east of Malasan, had been hung for bedding one of the Kings' married daughters. Ramahd continued beyond the northern border of the estate and made for a hill where an ancient watchtower stood. The tower, too, was abandoned by all but a few children who lived nearby. But it was empty now—the perfect place to keep an eye on the entrance of the Qaimiri embassy house.

Behind the compound, obscuring much of the city, loomed the curtain wall that surrounded the whole of the House of Kings. Beyond lay the southern expanse of the city, where the huge mansions and sprawling green estates of Goldenhill gave way to the progressively smaller, though still wealthy, manors of Blackfire Gate and Hanging Gardens.

He waited as the sun set, giving way to starlight and Rhia's dim crescent. He was beginning to feel embarrassed as the minutes passed, increasingly sure it had been only paranoia that had driven him here. But then a coach pulled by two horses came rumbling down King's Road from the direction of the palaces. It slowed before the Qaimiri embassy house and was let in. Through the iron gates, Ramahd could see the coach pull around the carriage circle and come to a stop before the doors. The driver dropped down. Two Maidens riding on the rear of the coach hopped off and followed. The rest was lost to darkness.

Ramahd felt a strange numbness running through him. He and Meryam had been through much. Years spent in Qaimir before the Bloody Passage.

Years more in Sharakhai, hunting Macide, the one responsible for the murder
of his wife and child and dozens of others. The months they'd spent in Viaroza and then their return to the desert as pawns of Hamzakiir. The two of
them were often at odds over this or that. But he'd never thought that
Meryam would *distrust* him.

Did she question his loyalty to Qaimir? His loyalty to *her?* Or was her
apparent distrust merely an indicator that she wanted to keep certain things
secret from as many people as possible, for as long as possible? He might have
believed the last had she not sent his most trusted men away on the same
night. Mighty Alu, the thought of Meryam trusting *Basilio* more than himself made his blood boil. He was tempted to ride through the main gate,
order anyone who saw him to look the other way—*queen's business,* he might
tell them—and confront her. But they may have received orders to stop him
should he return. And there was no telling what the Maidens might do
should he arrive uninvited.

So instead he left his horse tied to a bush behind the tower, and ran quick
and low down the hill, to head for the place where the embassy house wall
intersected with the Kings' larger curtain wall. The wall itself was made of
sandstone and had iron spikes along the top. A thick bush growing at the base
of the wall caught his clothes in its branches as he slipped past it. And there,
hidden away, was a steel door—an escape route created generations ago and
a portal to which only a select few had keys. Ramahd took his from the small
pouch at his belt and fit it into the lock. It took some doing, but the lock was
oiled several times a year and eventually turned over.

He pulled the door open slowly. The ensuing creak sounded as loud as the
great horns used to announce the Kings on festival days, and yet no cry of
alarm was raised, and he heard no signs of approach. Once inside the grounds,
he studied the darkened yard, the stables and paddock to his left, the guest
house and the servants' quarters nestled along the far wall. To his right, the
towering bulk of the mansion stared down. Various lamps from within made
it look like the head of a desert titan, its many eyes alight in anger.

He sped quietly across the carriage path leading to the front of the estate,
slipped over a low garden wall, and used a trellis to reach the second floor.
After one last climb along a drain pipe, he reached the patio outside Meryam's
apartments. He rather suspected that for a meeting such as this, Meryam

would avoid the audience room on the first floor. Indeed, as he came nearer to the patio doors he heard voices, Meryam's soft tones and Kiral's baritone, both of which were difficult to hear.

He wondered, though, why not meet in Eventide? It seemed likely Kiral was trying to hide something, but from whom? People in his own palace? The King of Whispers?

"You promised me Hamzakiir's head on a platter," Kiral was saying as Ramahd crouched near the doors.

"And you will have it."

"So you say, but our trap was sprung too soon."

Ramahd leaned closer to the door and peered between the curtains. Meryam was seated in her opulent silver chair, her back to the door so that Ramahd could see only her right arm along the armrest. Kiral sat opposite her in the chair Ramahd often took while in discussion with Meryam. The fire in the hearth threw wavering light against his rich clothes, his closely shorn hair, his stark, pockmarked face. His eyes sparked like flint, as un-amused as crumbling granite.

"The element of surprise is now lost, true, but there's little danger to us just yet. I was able to sense him as he fled east of the city and into the desert."

"Little danger?" Kiral countered. "He may have returned since then. He may be in the city now, waiting for his time to strike. To steal into Eventide to slit my throat! I would if I were him."

"There's little Hamzakiir fears, but he fears Guhldrathen greatly, and now he knows that Guhldrathen has found a way to steal into Sharakhai." Meryam's fingers scratched at a stitch in the embroidery of her chair, then brushed something invisible away. "No, I feel certain Hamzakiir will remain in the desert. He doesn't know what you've told the other Kings. His fears of the tide turning against him will have grown by the hour."

"Then what do you propose?"

"He'll move to secure power in the desert in any way he can. He has allies in the tribes, but most are too spread out for his purposes."

"Except to the east."

"Except to the east," Meryam echoed, "the very direction Hamzakiir fled. Onur has already gathered several thousand spears to his banner. More may soon follow. If Hamzakiir can come to an accord with Onur, or dominate him as he did me, he would have a base for power that Sharakhai and all Four Kingdoms should rightly fear."

Kiral considered this. "What you say seems likely, but it will cement his power, making it all the more difficult for you to kill him."

"True, but what does an ehrekh care for that? Guhldrathen is still our best chance at bringing Hamzakiir down."

"Unless you're planning to send Lord Amansir to stand by Onur's side, we no longer have a means of luring Guhldrathen to him."

"Another lure might be fashioned," Meryam said. "Have you brought Çedamihn's blood?"

Ramahd started at the mention of Çeda's name. *Breath of the desert, what does any of this have to do with her?*

"I've brought it, but how might she be used as a lure?"

"Çeda has escaped the House of Kings," Meryam replied. "Where do you think she'll go now?"

Kiral adjusted in his seat. "She'll return to her people in the desert."

"Exactly. And where do you suppose Onur will go next? Will he sail for Sharakhai to begin his improbable conquest? Or will he face the smaller threat along his flank before it becomes a larger one?"

As Kiral's jaw worked, deep shadows cascaded over his cheeks. "It would need to be coordinated so that Çeda and Hamzakiir are together when you summon the ehrekh."

"True to a degree, but no great amount of accuracy will be required. As long as the two of them are within a few leagues of one another, Guhldrathen will sense Hamzakiir and change course."

"You're certain?"

"Reasonably. But even if we've erred, Guhldrathen will drink Çedamihn's blood and you'll have rid yourself of a different problem."

"She's hardly the threat Hamzakiir is."

"No. Not yet, but we both know she'll become more powerful as time passes. She is Ishaq's granddaughter, Macide's niece, and her own legend is growing. There are many who revere her name, telling tales of how she killed two of the Sharakhani Kings, and you know how tales grow in the telling. She's smart. She's charismatic. She'll learn to use both to gather more to her cause. Before long, she may draw more to the Moonless Host's cause than Ishaq."

"That may all be true," Kiral said as he rose, "but it's a problem for another day." He pulled two glass ampules from inside his khalat, one filled with a bright red liquid, the other with a liquid so dark it looked black in the firelight. "Çeda's blood," he said, handing her the red ampule, "taken while she was unconscious in Sukru's palace. And the ehrekh's"—he handed her the second— "collected from Sunshearer, both by the hand of my master alchemyst."

Ramahd's chest went cold as Meryam held the red ampule up to the fire-light and swirled it around. It felt as if his heart were plunging into a deep, dark hole, threatening to take him with it. He'd known from the moment he'd agreed to Guhldrathen's request that he'd stepped into a raging river, but he'd never have thought *Meryam* would be the one to shove him below the surface.

"And the elixirs?" Meryam went on. "They were found in the temple's lower level, were they not?"

Kiral frowned. "They were."

"And where are they now?"

"In safekeeping. Expect no share of them until Hamzakiir and Guhl-drathen are both dead."

"The beast was not part of our bargain."

"I was forced to *attack* it to save your man. I may not know much about the ehrekh, but I know they neither forgive nor forget. This is a complication *you* must deal with before I part with any of the elixirs."

"Very well, then fifty more must be added to the tally," Meryam said in a tone that did not allow for negotiation.

They were speaking of the life-giving elixirs Ramahd had helped to destroy in Kiral's palace. Kiral's and Ihsan's primary caches had been destroyed. But the Moonless Hosts's plans for the third and final cache, the one in Zeheb's palace, had been compromised. Hamzakiir and his men had beaten them there. What they couldn't take they'd destroyed, leaving precious few in each of the Kings' personal stores. From what Ramahd had been able to piece to-gether, Kiral had been dangling a throne before Hamzakiir—that of Külaşan the Wandering King, Hamzakiir's father—in order to get some of the elixirs back. In turn, Hamzakiir had done much to destroy the power of the Moon-less Host's old guard, both in Sharakhai and in the desert.

But Kiral would not have let it go at that. He wanted immortality, or as much of it as he could get his hands around. Now, it seemed, he had secured some in the form of the elixirs. Likely he'd not told the other Kings about it, which would explain his presence here.

"Fifty," Kiral said, practically spitting the words. He motioned to the ampules. "We've received word that Onur has killed Mihir Halim'ava and taken many from Tribe Kadri prisoner. The rest are scattered to the winds. If we are to do as you've said, we must leave soon."

Meryam considered a moment. "I can leave tomorrow if you wish."

"Prepare for the morning after. A coach will be sent at daybreak."

"Very well."

Kiral glanced toward the door through which Ramahd was peering. Ramahd jerked out of view and went perfectly still, listening carefully for the sounds of approach. A moment later, Kiral's heavy footsteps thudded over the carpeted floor, diminishing as they went. "My lady queen."

"My Lord King."

As the door clicked shut, the words echoed through Ramahd's mind. *I can leave tomorrow if you wish.* It made him deadly curious what Meryam had written in her note. He cracked the seal and read it by the dim light from Meryam's room.

Written below a request for a number of rare components was a simple closing note. *I'll be leaving the city soon but will require them upon my return.*

She had known Kiral would be leaving for the desert.

He heard the doors at the front of the estate being opened. Footsteps crunched over gravel. Soon after came the clomp of horses' hooves and the rattle of wheels. He ducked low as the carriage swept through the gate and turned right, making for the Kings' palaces.

When the sounds had dwindled and the wagon was swallowed by the night, Ramahd stood and dropped the papyrus scroll on the roof. The wind rolled it away as he opened the patio door and stepped inside.

Meryam, standing near the fire, turned, her eyes wide, her hand on the amulet at her neck. As recognition came, her look of surprise faded, replaced by a low-burning anger. The sort Ramahd hadn't seen in a long while. Rather than make him nervous, it calmed him. It seemed only right, after all. It matched his own, and this reckoning had been a long time coming.

"You would use Çeda as your pawn?"

"You would rather I use you?"

"Yes."

"Well, it's no longer a choice that's up to you. Your sentimentality will get you killed one day, Ramahd."

"I deserved to know, Meryam."

"You will refer to me as *my queen* or I'll have you whipped until you remember to treat me with respect before you open that insolent mouth of yours!"

"I *deserved to know*."

"I cannot explain *all* to you. You are but part of—"

"I'm not talking about my role as a servant to the throne."

Her hollow eyes took him in anew. "What? You think because you've bedded me that I owe you more?"

"For that. For what we've meant to one another before then. For Yasmine and Rehann."

"Don't bring my sister into this! They are gone and buried. I loved them, but they do not rule Qaimir. *I* do, and I will do what I think best. I will do what's necessary to see us safely through the night."

"Safely through the night?" Ramahd wanted to laugh. "Were that true you'd have left Sharakhai for the halls of Santrión long ago. Instead I see you hurtling through the darkness as if you're being chased, heedless of what lies ahead and with little thought for what's best for Qaimir. Admit it, Meryam, this has all been for *you*." He waved toward the doors he'd just walked through. "This is because you look to Tauriyat and you see jewels lying upon a hill, baubles to be collected."

"Whosoever rules Sharakhai is a threat to our homeland"—hunger now mixed with Meryam's anger—"unless we take it for *ourselves*, Ramahd."

"The risk is too great."

"The gods favor the bold."

"And punish the foolish!"

Strangely, Ramahd's heart beat serenely. It was Meryam who was breathing fast, nostrils flaring, her eyes filling with ever more anger.

Just then Basilio opened the door. "My queen—" He paused, shocked to find Ramahd standing there. He immediately began bulling toward him but stopped when Ramahd drew his shamshir.

"You dare!" Basilio said.

Ramahd ignored him. "Take me, Meryam. Leave Çeda alone."

Meryam raised her hand, forestalling Basilio without taking her eyes from Ramahd. "What do you care if some bitch from the back streets of Sharakhai is lost to a creature like Guhldrathen?"

"Take *me* . . ."

Meryam's eyes, so emotional only moments ago, went flat, dangerous, no different than a mongoose before it struck. "Or what?"

The moment Meryam moved her hand toward her necklace, Ramahd was ready. He snatched it and yanked, snapping the chain. She cringed as the chain bit into her neck. The droplets of blood welling over her pale skin stood out like an accusation.

But Ramahd hardly noticed. He was trying to stifle the feelings of light-headedness emanating from the amulet. He could feel it calling to someone. Not him. Not Meryam, either. Someone else. Someone nearby? Without looking at it, he closed the amulet's lead-lined doors, felt them click into place. Immediately the feeling ceased.

"You think I need the *amulet*?" Meryam ran one finger over the blood on her neck, then ran it over her tongue, painting it red. "You think *you* can stop me from doing as I wish?"

Ramahd felt it coming. He tried to stop her. He thought he was prepared. But this was nothing like when he'd stopped Hamzakiir from unleashing arcane fire on Guhldrathen. That had been deliberate and careful and practiced. What came from Meryam was wild, like the great waves that sometimes struck the coast of the Austral Sea without warning and with unstoppable force.

"Meryam—"

He wanted to plead with her, but the pain came on so strong, so quickly, he was driven down by it. He collapsed to the floor. The last thing he saw was Meryam standing over him, Basilio by her side.

"Take him to the desert," Meryam said as the world began to close in around him.

"And then, my queen?"

"Bury him."

Chapter 53

BRAMA CROUCHED behind a vine-choked pergola as Lord Ramahd Amansir, the very man who'd stolen Rümayesh's sapphire and run his blade across Brama's throat for good measure, knelt on the stones of the patio only a dozen paces away. And that wasn't the strangest thing. The strangest thing was that the man appeared to be spying on his own queen. The queen was taking council with none other than the King of Kings. From what little Brama could hear, the two were discussing a slaughter in the temple district. Kiral himself had been present. As had Hamzakiir, the infamous blood mage. Most surprising, however, was a name new to Brama: Guhldrathen.

An ehrekh, Brama realized as they shared more details. *Another ehrekh, here in Sharakhai.*

It can't have been a coincidence that the battle they were discussing had taken place mere days after Rümayesh had been stolen from Brama. What the connection might be, he had no idea, but Kiral sounded displeased. There'd been a great deal of destruction, and Kiral himself had been wounded.

It must have just happened, then. Today, perhaps yesterday.

It would explain why he'd heard nothing of it. He'd been hiding in the old abandoned watchtower the past four days, watching the Qaimiri compound, noting the number of guards and other household staff, watching their comings and goings, estimating their readiness as he planned his entry. After seeing how many had been sent into the city earlier that day, Brama had decided tonight would be the night. And then, lo and behold, Ramahd Amansir himself had ridden up to the very watchtower where Brama hid and began surveilling his own bloody compound. After the King arrived, Amansir had abandoned the tower and stolen into the compound by means of a secret door, making Brama's entry simpler than he could ever have hoped.

Brama, I suffer! Trapped in the cage she's made for me. Why won't you come? Why won't you save me?

They were Rümayesh's faint pleas. She'd called to him whenever Queen Meryam was most distracted. She'd pleaded for him to storm the room and save her, but he could hardly barge in and try to seize the sapphire now, not with Kiral and his bloody great shamshir there, not with two Blade Maidens wandering somewhere inside the estate.

And yet every moment that passed brought him closer to throwing caution to the wind. Rümayesh's need was great, and it burned inside Brama too. Twice he'd found himself rising, ready to slit Amansir's throat and break into the room, logic and reason be damned. The very notion of helping Rümayesh, a creature who'd done him so much harm, nearly made him weep. His continued horror over being here, doing that very thing, was all that had allowed him to remain where he was and wait for the right moment.

The perfect moment will never come, Rümayesh cooed. *Take the amulet, Brama, and then I will be free. Take the amulet, and none of them can stop us.*

Brama grit his teeth, fighting the urge to obey.

The conversation finally ended and the King left with his Maidens in the wagon. When the sound of their departure faded, Amansir stood and walked into the room like a man made of wood. The need inside Brama finally eased as he sidled along the patio's edge. One of the doors was ajar, allowing Brama to see Amansir and his queen. The two of them were shouting.

Come, Brama. She is powerful, but she cannot suffer the kiss of a blade. Save me, and we can be together once more.

He found himself stepping forward, heedless of the scraping sound his boots made over the stone tiles. He drew his kenshar from his belt. Powerful, Rümayesh had said of Queen Meryam. Perhaps she was, but by Bakhi's bright hammer, the woman was *gaunt*. Her entire body quavered, the same sort of shaking he'd seen on malnourished children in the Shallows. He could see the sapphire, resting in an amulet around the queen's narrow neck.

It would be so simple to take it. Two flicks of his knife, one across her throat, another across Amansir's, and then he'd slip the chain over the queen's head and around his.

Where it belonged.

Yes. Yes! He could feel the eagerness in Rümayesh, a perfect mirror of his own. *They've not sensed you. Rush in! Do it now! We can flee this place and everything will be as it was.*

He was standing just outside the door now. If either of them turned their heads, they'd see him plain as day. He was just reaching for the handle of the door, ready to do as Rümayesh had commanded, when Amansir reached out and snatched the necklace from his queen's neck.

He gripped the amulet, closed its doors, and Rümayesh's presence vanished. Her sudden absence tugged on Brama's soul. He put his hand over his mouth, trying to stifle the sudden cough that overtook him, but the queen was raging against Amansir.

"You think I need the *amulet*? You think *you* can stop me from doing as I wish?"

Amansir, his face turning red, fell to his knees, then dropped to the floor, unconscious. A portly Qaimiri lord in ostentatious clothes had arrived—just when, Brama wasn't sure.

"Take him to the desert," she told the man.

"And then, my queen?"

"Bury him." The queen retrieved the amulet from Amansir's lax grip. "Do it now before Cicio and Vrago return. And take him in the back of a wagon. I'll have no one else knowing of it."

When the man bowed his head and left, the queen pulled the necklace back over her head but did not open the doors that would reveal the sapphire. Brama couldn't decide whether he was glad for it or not. He wished to bask in Rümayesh's glow, even if she was trapped, but another part of him was sickened by the very thought. He was suddenly afraid of stepping into the room. He felt as though, without Rümayesh's power, he'd be defenseless, and the queen would do to him exactly what she'd done to her own man. And the more he focused on it, the worse it became. It felt very much like the day he'd first stood before Rümayesh. Gods, the feeling of dread that had stolen over him . . .

His thoughts were broken as the portly lord returned with two men. One of the men wore mud-stained trousers and a dark shirt; the other wore a stained cook's apron. With their queen watching on with a strangely casual air, the three of them picked Amansir up and carried him from the room.

Brama nearly charged in then, but his fear got the better of him as Queen Meryam noticed the door. She moved forward and shut it with a soft clatter as Brama backed away. A moment later, a wagon pulled out from the stables and drove toward the rear of the estate.

Amansir, Brama decided. *He'll know more about the queen than anyone. And he has reason to want to be rid of the sapphire.*

Brama moved to the edge of the patio as a door opened and the fop, the cook, and the man Brama assumed was the groundsman all shuffled out. The driver was an old, crooked man wearing a floppy hat. He opened the door to the carriage while the others carried Amansir's unconscious form toward it. They grunted and manhandled him onto the floor of the cabin, shoved his legs unceremoniously inside, then kicked the door shut, trapping him within.

"Kill him now," the portly lord said.

"Here, my lord?" the cook was saying.

"He'll bleed all over the carriage," the driver complained in a low, gruff voice.

The portly lord stared between all three of them, and finally rasped, "Mighty Alu, take him away, then. Do it in the desert as your queen bade you."

Brama's mind was beginning to race. If he let them leave, there'd be no catching up. He stared at the carriage as the men continued to talk. The gate had been opened for the King and had yet to be closed.

Gods, what am I doing?

Before he could change his mind, he slipped over the railing. If he could reach the roof below, he could drop down onto the carriage.

"It will be done," one of the men said gruffly, "though I don't see why *we* have to do it. I'm not a fecking headsman."

As the driver climbed up to the bench and made way for the groundskeeper to join him, Brama moved quick as a goat along a mountainside, the sides of his soft boots tiptoeing along the narrow stone lip. He hurtled as far as he dared, then launched himself at the team of horses.

He landed on the wagon shaft between them, startling both. They bolted into a run. The driver's eyes went wide as teacups. He shouted and jerked backward in fright, losing the reins in the process. He tried to grab for them a moment later, but Brama gave them a tug and he missed. "Now, now!" Brama said. "I need those."

"Thief!" the fat lord shouted. "Thief!"

The groundskeeper had made it halfway up to the driver's bench. "Don't know who you are," he said, "but you've made yourself a terrible mistake." He finished the climb and reached for his machete in its sheath along his thigh. Brama, meanwhile, climbed onto the rear of the galloping horse, leapt for the bench, and drove his knife straight into the man's throat.

He shoved him aside and he fell off the wagon with an unceremonious thump.

"Who the bloody hell are you?" the driver asked, shifting as far away as he could on the bench.

"Haven't you heard?" Brama said, brandishing his bloody blade. "I'm the Kings' new barber! Now get off this coach before I slice you up!"

The man's hands lifted. "I want no trouble, my lord!"

"Then I imagine you know what to do!" Brama pointed his knife over the side of the carriage, which was now hurtling toward the front gates, and the man took the hint. He leapt free, and Brama heard a grunt above the jingle of tack and the raucous rattle of the wheels.

Ahead, along the top of the walls, a pair of guards were closing in toward the gates, but the coach would be past before they could swing either of them shut.

They saw it too and stopped where they were to lift something to their shoulders. Brama ducked low as he flew through the open gates. A crossbow bolt thudded into the bench beside him. Another burst through the meat of his right leg. A roar of pain managed to escape him before he bit down on the pain. He pulled left on the reins, snapping them hard against horses' flanks to keep them moving fast. As they turned, Brama sucked air through clenched teeth and glanced over his shoulder. A third crossbow bolt thunked into the roof of the cabin just behind him. He might have heard something flutter through the air above him.

By then, the bulk of the araba shielded him. But it did little to ease Brama's worries. Blood was running from the wound to his leg. The bolt was at an awkward angle, entering halfway down his thigh and exiting just behind his knee. To even touch it brought a searing pain.

In his earliest days with Rümayesh, Brama would try to hide from the pain she dealt him, but he'd found over and over again that hiding made it worse. The only way through the pain was to accept it, but not so much that he embraced it. He had learned to walk the line between awareness and fear. Only then was he unmoved by it.

As he had a thousand times before, he balanced along that knife's edge. He calmed his breathing, unclenched his jaw, and snapped the shaft of the crossbow bolt. As he pulled it through from the opposite side, he felt it tug the skin along the outside of his leg, felt the shaft scrape through muscle, felt the skin near the inside of his knee grip as the shaft came free. The pain flared, and then slowly diminished, but he treated it no differently. The pain was. He was.

More worrisome was the feeling of lightheadedness. Fall unconscious now, and it might mean both his life and Amansir's. As the horses galloped along King's Road, the flow of blood eased, and the stars in his eyes faded.

Now what, you bloody fool?

The guards he'd left behind would be after him soon enough. And ahead lay the House of Maidens, which he'd have to pass through to reach the safety of the city streets. The Maidens would never let him pass unchallenged, not with an unconscious Qaimiri lord in the cabin and his leg bleeding as though he were fleeing a battle. At the very least, they'd question him, which would give Queen Meryam's men more than enough time to catch up.

After passing several more embassy houses, he pulled the horses to a stop. There might be some clothes in the cabin or the trunk strapped to the back. He could prop Amansir up on one of the benches and pretend the man was drunk. He might even find a bit of brandy or araq hidden away to help. And he could fake a Qaimiri accent well enough. He could tell the Maidens his lord had ordered Brama to take him into the city. It happened often enough. The lords and ladies of embassies grew bored and could often be found in many of the shisha dens along the Trough, spreading their money around.

He'd just lowered himself gingerly down to the ground, convinced he could make this work when he realized there was no one in the cabin. It was empty. He looked back along the King's Road, surveying the moonlit landscape to see if the man had somehow managed to throw himself free, but there was nothing.

"Nalamae's pendulous teats, where have you gone?"

"Right here," came a hoarse voice.

Brama spun to find Amansir standing there. He was holding a knife to Brama's throat.

"You don't want to do that," Brama said, his arms held openly at his sides, his eyes glancing down toward the knife.

Amansir coughed. His brows pinched. "Don't I?"

"Wouldn't you rather"—Brama jutted his chin toward the walls and towers of the House of Maidens—"escape into Sharakhai before your queen's men recapture you? Or worse, before she comes herself rather than leave it to the incompetents who allowed *me* to rescue you?"

"*Rescue* me?"

"Just so."

"I tried to bloody kill you. Why would you—" His words trailed off as his eyes shifted to something over Brama's shoulder. Shouts were coming from the embassy house.

"If we're lucky," Brama went on, "they'll need a few moments more before they ride out to find us. If not . . ."

He left the rest unsaid, and Amansir took the hint. He looked back toward the House of Maidens. "Get inside," he said. "Quickly."

He hopped up to the driver's bench, pulled free the crossbow bolt embedded in the wood of the bench, then tossed it into the darkness. Brama did the same with the bolt on the roof, then slipped inside the cabin.

The araba began to move a moment later. "Look hurt," Amansir called back.

"That's hardly difficult, milord."

"And act drunk, but don't say a word, even if they ask you a direct question."

"And if they take a cudgel to me?"

"Keep acting like a jackanape and we're *both* going to learn what the bite of ebon steel feels like."

The same as any other blade, no doubt.

The araba soon approached the House of Maidens. When they halted at the gates, a Blade Maiden approached, her black turban and veil hiding all but her eyes. "My Lord Amansir," she said. "Late business?"

"Grim business, I'm afraid. Our physic is traipsing about in Sharakhai, and one of my men managed to take a length of steel to his thigh."

The Maiden glanced inside the cabin. Brama gripped his leg and looked appropriately grim, appropriately drunk as well, though whether the combination was working, or if he just looked like a crazed idiot, he had no idea.

The wound had nearly stopped bleeding, but the blood all over his woolen trousers was fresh and bright.

"Swordplay?" the Maiden asked.

"Mmm. My idiot marshal downed an entire bottle of Qaimir's finest and decided that trading blows with the smith's son would make for a fine bit of entertainment."

"Let me guess. The smith was also drunk?"

With a rueful smile, Amansir touched his finger to his nose.

She laughed, though the look she gave Brama held little charity. A moment later, however, her look softened, and she tipped her head to the large courtyard behind her. "The Matrons rarely tend to such things, but if it's serious, I could ask for an exception to be made."

"Ah, the House of Maidens is too kind, and I might have accepted had my queen not made it clear she wishes for Leticia and no other to tend to him."

The Maiden stared at Brama's leg. She looked as though she were about to argue, but then merely shrugged. "Very well," she said, and let them through.

Brama might have heard the pounding of hooves as they rode through the gates and into the city proper, but he couldn't be sure. And then they were off, hurtling down the Spear.

Chapter 54

I T WAS THE SEVENTH DAY after the attack in the desert, and Çeda was changing the dressing on Dardzada's wound. Sümeya had done an admirable job, and Dardzada, once conscious, had guided Çeda to the right healing salve to help speed the healing process. Still, his collarbone had been cleaved, along with much of his shoulder muscle. Çeda guessed he'd have some, perhaps complete, immobility in his left arm for the rest of his life. Dardzada seemed to agree.

"I guess you'll have to return to my side," he said one morning as he tried to slip out of his hopelessly bloody thawb. "Milk charo like you used to."

"I'd rather eat all the sand in the desert."

He'd waved over the side of the skiff. "I've heard it tastes better over rice."

Despite herself, Çeda laughed. "It would still taste better than that garbage you gave old men to make them regular."

"They may have detested it, but their wives loved me for it."

"Loved you how much?" Melis asked nonchalantly.

Dardzada tipped his head, a move he immediately regretted. "I wasn't known as the stallion of the Merchant's Quarter for nothing."

Çeda stared open-mouthed at Dardzada's boyish grin while Melis's laugh filled the warming desert air.

Zaïde had recovered somewhat. She was able to sit, eat, and drink. But any exertion beyond that sent her heart tumbling. Even the simple act of getting out of the skiff on their rare rests, or a climb to the top of a shallow dune, caused her to slow, put her hands on her knees and take measured breaths until it had passed.

"Wipe that look from your face," she said to Çeda one afternoon as they were breaking down their camp and preparing to set sail.

"You weren't even looking at me."

"I don't have to." Slowly she stood up and turned to face Çeda. "I know the signs of patronizing concern well enough." Her face soured the longer she looked at Çeda. "Just look at you." With an expression of disgust, she trudged past Çeda toward the skiff. "Put the funeral shroud away, girl. I'm not ready to be given back to the desert just yet!"

On the twelfth day following the attack—three full weeks since leaving Sharakhai—they spotted ships on the horizon. Though their location was roughly where they were to rendezvous with the thirteenth tribe, they were worried they might be Onur's ships or those of another tribe. But when they sailed close enough to see the blue pennants—although they were too distant to make out in detail—there were the telltale signs of Mount Arasal stitched in white.

Çeda felt a palpable relief. Dardzada seemed to as well. But Zaïde, Sümeya, and Melis all seemed tense. They were entering the demesne of Tribe Khiyanat, who were, for all intents and purposes, the Moonless Host. In the span of a month, Sümeya and Melis had gone from respected Blade Maidens to traitors. Even so, Ishaq might make prisoners of them—no matter what Çeda might say, he was a man of his own mind. And Zaïde had spent practically her entire life within the walls of the House of Kings. She might be an ally of the Host, but most would view her as an outsider, a Sharakhani.

Near the end of the day, as their skiff approached a circle of three dozen ships that had come to rest for the night, Çeda reached out to Kerim, whom she'd left in Salsanna's care. She hoped to learn what had happened in her absence and gauge the mood of the camp before she arrived. Except, he was distant . . . She could sense him, but he wouldn't respond to her calls. At first she thought he was slumbering as the asirim did beneath the adichara, but the closer they came to camp's edge, the more she suspected Kerim was willfully veiling his mind from her.

Or someone was doing it for him.

Salsanna had bonded with him, after all. Perhaps she'd taken to it faster than Çeda expected. Or perhaps the answer was as simple as the passage of time and their distance from Sharakhai, and the Kings, and the other asirim; perhaps even distance from the compulsion the gods had placed on them. It might have allowed Kerim to create a stronger bond with Salsanna than he had with Çeda.

After trying a while longer, with no success, Çeda gave up. It seemed there was no choice but to sail into camp with no further information.

They were met beyond the camp by Ishaq, Macide, and several other elders, including Hamid and Darius. The sun was low. Their shadows slashed against the angles in the dunes. Many stared warily, angrily, at the five of them. And why not? Blade Maidens were reviled, and here were Sümeya, Melis, and Çeda in black battle dresses, while Zaïde wore her Matron's white.

Dardzada stepped forward to offer greetings, but before he could, Çeda moved past him to stand before Ishaq. "These two Maidens freed me from the House of Kings."

Ishaq's expression was dour, Macide's wary. The tower of flesh they called Frail Lemi stared on with a confused look on his face. Hamid, however, looked incensed. "Have you fallen and cracked your skull, Çeda? Are you bloody mad? That's *Sümeya Husamettín'ava*. First Warden. Slayer of *dozens* of our number."

"You are not wrong, Hamid, but she comes here under my protection. She and Melis freed me from the House of Kings. They saved my life from Sumeya's own father when he came to take us back. They saved my life again when two Blade Maidens from their former hand surprised us in the desert."

Çeda felt indebted to Sümeya and Melis for delivering her from the House of Kings. She felt grateful when they stood with her against Husamettín. But she hadn't felt the same sisterhood they had once shared—not until now.

"They know the truth about the asirim," Çeda went on, focusing on Ishaq once more. "Through me, the veil over their eyes has been lifted. They saw what happened and they recognize our history. They could have left at any time—returned to Sharakhai, hidden away in a caravanserai, fled the desert entirely. But they came here with me because they've seen the truth, and they're ready to help."

Hamid was beside himself with rage. "I don't care what happened." He drew his sword with one violent motion. "I don't care what they've made you believe. You were with them too long to see the truth. But as sure as the desert is vast, as sure as the Kings are cruel, *those* two"—he waved the tip of his sword at Sümeya and Melis—"are ruddy fucking spies."

"I tell you they are not."

Hamid spat on the sand. "I'll not suffer their presence here."

"You will," Çeda replied easily.

Çeda watched his every move, every flick of his sleepy, cold-blooded eyes. She saw his intent in the muscles of his jaw as they tightened, in his eyes as they narrowed, and she was on the move even before he'd taken his first step.

She drew River's Daughter as Hamid burst into motion. She felt for his heartbeat and *pressed* against him as he turned and swung for her. She blocked one swing, spinning as she did so, and sent a heel to the side of his head.

He was knocked off balance but didn't fall, so she stepped inside his guard and sent a gloved fist crashing into his mouth. This time he fell to the sand, dazed. Çeda dropped to his side, used a knee to pin his sword arm to the sand, and laid River's Daughter across his neck. She leaned in until they were face to face.

"They are under *my* protection. *I* vouch for them both. If they betray us, I offer up my own life. Is that good enough for you?"

Blood and spittle flew from Hamid's mouth. It fell on his chin, mixing in with the whiskers of his light brown beard. She'd never seen him so mad. "I'm going to kill them both, Çeda. I promise you this. And then I'm going to kill you."

By Thaash's bright blade, she considered running River's Daughter across his throat. He'd always been a rabid dog, so why not let his lifeblood seep into the sands? There was too much at stake to let a killer like Hamid decide her fate, the tribe's fate, and perhaps the fate of the asirim as well. It was in that moment—as Thaash's righteous anger burned ever brighter—that she felt Kerim clearly for the first time. He was hidden somewhere among the ships, feeding off her emotions. It was an echo of the compulsions of the gods, a thing that had somehow been largely removed from Kerim's thoughts. Until now, that is. Her fear over what Hamid might do, and her own sudden bloodlust, had rekindled it.

Like water thrown over a fire, the realization did much to douse her emotions. Kerim's were extinguished a moment later, and they both felt shame for wishing the death of another, one of their own blood. Kerim's presence faded as Çeda pulled her sword away from Hamid's neck.

"Enough," came Ishaq's voice.

With a shove, Çeda released him and stood up. Hamid did as well. He gripped his sword for a time, staring at Çeda with dull, emotionless eyes. Her younger self might have been chilled by those eyes, but she'd seen enough Hamids in her life to know that sometimes you could only meet a threat with a threat.

"Hamid—" Ishaq began, but Hamid merely sheathed his sword and stalked away bumping several people out of his way until he was lost behind them.

The expression on the face of the big one, Frail Lemi, had hardened throughout the conversation. He was now staring at Melis and Sümeya, as if daring them to draw their blades. Then he too turned and followed Hamid from the gathering.

"Until I say otherwise," Ishaq began again, "No one will touch the Maidens." The tension running through the gathered crowd waned perceptibly. "Go," Ishaq said, "we all have much to do."

At this, the edges of the crowd began to dissolve.

No one—Ishaq and Macide included—greeted Çeda, Zaïde, or even Dardzada, with open arms. "Çeda," Ishaq continued, "the three of you will tell me your story and your words will be weighed against what Zaïde and Dardzada have to say and what we already know of events in Sharakhai. Only then will their fate be decided."

Çeda spoke before Dardzada or anyone else could interject. "Best if I explain what I know first then."

Ishaq considered her request, then nodded curtly.

They retired to Ishaq's tent. Ishaq, Macide, Leorah, Dardzada, and several more Çeda had never met, sat around a cook fire with carpets covering the sand and pillows beneath them. Over the course of the next several hours, Çeda told her tale. It was a lot to take in, but she couldn't leave this tent—she *wouldn't*—without reaching an understanding on Sümeya and Melis. "My tale begins and ends with the asirim," Çeda said upon reaching the end. "It is through them that more will come to believe, as Sümeya and Melis have. That's why I brought Sümeya and Melis here. That's why I've asked them to help me to free more of the asirim."

Ishaq idly scratched the only spot on his gray beard that had any color left in it. "The asirim are important, but the Kings will be wary of your return. They'll know about your asir, and be worried you'll try steal more. You may have unknowingly helped us. The Kings may have become wary of bringing the asirim into the desert for fear of what you might do in response. It may even make them hesitant to come in full force, lest we return to Sharakhai to do exactly what you've proposed."

"All the more reason to strike quickly," Çeda countered. "The Kings cannot cover the whole of the blooming fields. We should go now, *before* they can stop us."

"Perhaps, but we must always think ahead, Çeda. If the Kings are preparing to stop us at the blooming fields, we might give hint that we're ready to do just that, and then strike at another target. We might do that again and again, and only when they feel that the asirim are a ruse do we go to free them."

"The asirim have waited for four centuries!"

Ishaq waved to a young boy who was tending to the araq. As the boy moved to refill several glasses, Ishaq regarded Çeda. "Their suffering pains me, but rash action will not aid them. Wait a few more months, and we'll be more prepared."

"Months become years in the blink of an eye."

For the first time, anger showed on Ishaq's hoary face. "Then it will be years." He flung one finger toward the door of the tent. "There is a King in the desert who may be sailing for us even now. There are Maidens on your trail. The Kings' entire navy may be sailing behind them, hoping to catch us unaware. I will *not* risk the safety of our fledgling tribe because the plight of the asirim has pushed you beyond reason."

"I'm not asking you to. I will take Sümeya and Melis, some few others, and return to Sharakhai when the time is right. There we will free Sehid-Alaz, for he, I believe, is the key. With his help we can break the bonds of the others."

"You wish to return to Sharakhai," Macide replied, "with war on our doorstep?"

"No. I won't leave until Onur's fate has been decided."

"You will *leave* when I tell you to leave," Ishaq said.

Çeda stood to stare down at him, at them all. "I am not yet part of your tribe. I made vows to Sehid-Alaz, to Kerim, to his wife, Havva, and to others. I promised to free them. I came here so you will have the benefit of everything I've learned, but *I* decide my own fate. Not you."

The mood in the tent had changed from one of amused sufferance to outright hostility. A hum began to build, but quelled as Ishaq raised his hand for silence. "Do you think to start your own tribe, then?" he asked.

"Melis was a Blade Maiden who believed in the Kings. Sümeya was *first warden*! They risked *everything* to save me and to learn the truth. And when they learned it, they embraced it, even though it was painful, even though it flew in the face of all they'd ever been told. Are they not the sort of allies we've been hoping for for centuries? Are they not the sort of women who could spark a revolution?"

"You don't know their hearts."

"I know their hearts better than I know yours. I've been to battle with them. I've bled for them and they've bled for me. I saw how viciously they both fought for what they believed in. And now they believe in *us*. They *see* our story! They *see* us!" Ishaq was red-faced, but Çeda refused to stop. "I know you have the weight of our people on your shoulders," she said in a softer tone. "I recognize that burden. I know its weight. But I beg you, let us seize the opportunity that Nalamae herself has surely placed before us."

Macide, sitting by Ishaq's side, raised his hand before Ishaq could speak. "Çeda has said her piece. Perhaps it's time to listen to the Maidens."

Ishaq stared at Macide as if he'd betrayed him. He looked as if he was about to say as much, but when Leorah began to stir from her seat he held his tongue.

Leorah held out one weighty arm and waved Çeda closer. "Help an old woman up."

In that moment, Leorah's amethyst ring seemed to glow. Çeda blinked, and it was gone, leaving her to wonder if she'd imagined it. It might have been from the nearby fire, or the brilliant light of the setting sun as it played against the tent's western wall, but she could have sworn it had shone from *within*.

"Come, girl." Leorah waved her hand again. "Don't condemn me to lie here all night."

"Sorry, grandmother." Çeda helped her to her feet, then handed her her cane.

"You're leaving?" Ishaq asked.

"There are things Çeda and I must discuss," Leorah said as she hobbled with Çeda's help toward the tent flaps. "Listen to the Maidens' stories. Tell us your decision in the morning."

And just like that, they went out into the gathering dusk. Çeda glanced back and saw confusion in Ishaq's eyes. Even anger. But there was curiosity as well, an eagerness to know what Leorah was going to say.

Still feeling strange about leaving, Çeda walked Leorah toward her yacht while Sümeya was summoned to the tent. "Don't you think we should listen to what they have to say?" Çeda asked.

"Çedamihn, I love you, but you need to learn when to still that sharp tongue of yours. You challenged Ishaq in front of everyone. Do you really think he'd listen to anything Sümeya had to say with you there? Leave them be. We have other things to discuss."

Çeda's first instinct was to argue, but it would simply be proving Leorah's point. As they walked through the warm evening air, her head began to cool and a mystery began to tug at Çeda's thoughts. In the short walk from the tent, Leorah's posture had straightened. She leaned on her cane less, her steps becoming steadier. Even her breathing seemed more at ease.

As they neared the gangplank to her yacht, Çeda asked, "Grandmother, what does your ring do?"

Pretending she hadn't heard, Leorah called out for Salsanna.

"Grandmother?"

Leorah made a face. "Never you mind, child." And she motioned to Salsanna, who had climbed onto the deck as if she'd been expecting them. "There's something Salsanna wishes to share with you."

Çeda decided to set the mystery of the ring aside for now. They had enough to worry about.

The scars over Salsanna's face and neck, evidence of her battle against Kerim, stood out in the sun's copper light. When Salsanna joined them on the sand, Leorah gripped Çeda's wrist and the three of them headed beyond the line of ships. Soon it was clear they were headed toward a standing stone. In the long finger of its shadow was a figure hunkered low to the ground, nearly lost to the darkness. By the gods, it was Kerim. She hadn't felt his presence in the least. It was as if he'd been masking himself from her. Even now, she could barely feel him.

Why do you hide from me? she asked him.

A long pause. Somewhere in the desert a jackal yipped.

Kerim's refusal to speak felt like rejection, though she was sure there must be another explanation. After all they'd been through, Kerim wouldn't do that to her, would he? But when she gave it a moment's thought, the reason Salsanna led her here became obvious.

"You've bonded deeply with him," Çeda said.

"Yes," she replied. "I've come to experience his dreams, as you have. I've felt his pain firsthand."

It proved that another could successfully bond with the asirim, which was glorious news, and made Çeda hopeful that Salsanna had had luck on other fronts. She motioned to Salsanna's wrist, where Mesut's golden bracelet rested. "Have you been able to reach them?"

Salsanna stared with a defeated look into the large, oval jet, which in the dim light looked like a deep, malevolent pool. "I've tried many times. Like you, I've felt the souls within, but I cannot speak with them. Not once have I felt more than their lament, their desire for release. How Mesut released them into a living soul, I have no idea."

Çeda hid her disappointment. Salsanna had done well with Kerim, and the mystery of the bracelet was one that might never be solved. Her thoughts were interrupted as a ship's bell began to ring. Over and over it sounded, with several of the crew pointing and shouting, "Ship ho! Ship ho!"

A cutter was sailing toward them, her hull a dark smudge of coal, her billowing ivory sails aflame in the dying light of day.

On the deck, a pinpoint light began to blink in a clear sequence. Two flashes, a pause, then two more, over and over. A crewman was using a hooded lantern to send a signal to the distant ship.

"What does it mean?" Çeda said.

Salsanna's eyes had gone wide. "It's a warning." She turned and began leading Leorah back toward the yacht. "The enemy approaches."

Since it was sailing in from the east, it surely bore news of Onur. An alarm bell rang, using the same sequence as the lantern light. In minutes, with fear driving every movement, the tents were torn down and stowed on the ships. The crews of every ship made ready, dozens working to tow the ships so they faced south, a favorable position to catch the wind.

When the cutter arrived, its captain rushed to speak with Ishaq and the tribe's elders. Çeda was called to a circle a short while later.

Ishaq pointed east. "Onur has betrayed and attacked Tribe Kadri. He's now pursuing Emre, Shal'alara, and what remains of Tribe Kadri's fleet. They're leading Onur's ships away, but ask that we come in behind them and catch Onur unaware." He turned to Sümeya and Melis. "I've not yet decided what's to be done with you, but if all you've said is true, you can help your cause and fight by our side."

Sümeya considered, and then jutted her chin toward Çeda. "I will fight by your granddaughter's side."

Ishaq looked ill-pleased. "And you?" he said to Melis.

"My sword is Çeda's to command."

Hamid snorted, his eyes burning with hatred for the Blade Maidens, but Ishaq nodded. "Good enough." He looked to everyone and spread his arms wide. "We go to battle a King of Sharakhai. This isn't something I wished for so soon after coming to the desert. But the fates give what they will. It is ours to face it or flee." Ishaq drew his sword with a fluidity that surprised Çeda, and faced the gathered crowd. "Would you flee, Tribe Khiyanat?"

"*We will not!*" they answered. So sudden and powerful was the reply, it resounded through Çeda, made her yearn to release the anger that had been hidden inside her for so long.

"Our tribe's name was taken from the old tongue," Ishaq went on. "In the days of our foremothers and forefathers, it had twin meanings. One is *the forgotten*." He cast his gaze over the crowd.

Çeda had stood before the Kings of Sharakhai. She had stood before gods. And yet when Ishaq's eyes passed over her, she felt a chill run along her limbs until her fingers and toes tingled from it. She'd known Ishaq drew people to him through the sheer force of his presence. She'd seen some of it in Macide, but she'd had no idea how strong it was. Not until now.

"Shall our name be spoken alongside Tribe Kadri? Salmük? Ebros? Halarijan? Or will you suffer the desert to forget our name once more?"

"Never!" their voices roared in unison. *"Never again!"*

Ishaq seemed pleased. "The second meaning, is *the betrayed*. We took this name after Beht Ihman, for those slain in the centuries that followed, and for the children orphaned. There is no shame in admitting we were forced to hide amongst our brothers and sisters in the farther corners of the desert for fear that we'd be murdered for acknowledging our blood. But times change. The sands shift. Now we have stepped free from the shadows!"

A great shout lifted up, more emotion than words, and this time Çeda joined them.

"Would you repay the betrayal of Beht Ihman?"

"We would!"

"Will you repay that betrayal with *your* blood?"

"We will!"

"And with theirs?"

Swords lifted toward the night sky. The butts of spears were driven against the sand and the cries built into a tumult of long-suppressed anger.

"We will!"

Ishaq waved his shamshir high above his head. "Then come, brothers and sisters! The desert is hungry, and Onur has escaped it for too long. It is time we give him back!"

As he made for his ship, the loudest roar of all engulfed him.

Leorah sat on the deck of her yacht while, all around, the ships were made ready to sail. Salsanna had gone to the desert to speak with Kerim, to prepare him for the morrow, which, if all went as Leorah suspected, would see him reunited with a King for the first time since he'd been dominated by Onur.

She'd sent her own crew away. "We're prepared enough," she told them. "Go, help wherever you can."

Leorah was nervous. This was an event they had been hurtling toward for generations, and now it had arrived. She didn't know if they would survive, but what were they to do? They could not live in the cracks of the desert like mites until the end days. So while her fear was strong, so was her pride, so was her hope.

Ahead, a woman approached her yacht, lit by the lanterns set fore and aft. "Salsanna?"

The woman didn't answer. She kept walking, a staff in her hand. Three men passed only a few paces ahead of her but, remarkably, none of them turned their heads. None seemed to notice the woman at all even though she towered over them.

Finally Leorah recognized her. Nalamae.

She had hair of honey, plaited so that it ran over one shoulder and down the front of her wheat-colored dress. She walked deliberately, ignoring all that was going on around her. When she came near enough for the lanterns to light her face, Leorah gasped. She said nothing, however. She waited for the goddess to stop near the gangplank. With her gnarled staff, she thumped the sand until she heard the dull thud of wood. Then she walked up the deck and approached Leorah's chair.

"I will admit," Leorah said, "I never thought to see you again. Not in this life."

"I will never leave these shores," Nalamae replied.

"No." Leorah felt the weight of the moment press down on her. "I suppose you won't. Have you come to help us, then?"

"Yes." The goddess stared intently at the horizon, as if she could see beyond it.

"You'll join us?"

"No," she said, "but the time grows near." There was little regret in her voice or on her broad face. She seemed exhausted, as if she'd been traveling for weeks. "The morning brings great events. The fate of the desert prepares to shift, one way or another."

"It does," Leorah replied, more excited than she'd felt in a long while. By the gods who breathe, she felt *young* again. "Tell me why you've come, Nalamae."

Nalamae held her staff before her like a spear ready to be driven into the ground. "I'm here to present you with a gift."

With shaking hands, Leorah accepted it. She stared at it reverently, confused. "For what purpose?"

Nalamae smiled grimly. "To even the scales, granddaughter."

Chapter 55

ÇEDA STOOD ON THE foredeck of Ishaq's own ship, the *Amaranth*, which sailed the morning sands near the center of Tribe Khiyanat's fleet. They'd set after the Black Spear ships of Onur's fleet and continued all through the night. The wind had been strong in the starlit hours, but now it was nearly a gale, driving their ships over the sand with a speed that bordered on recklessness. They couldn't let up, though. The Black Spear ships were still a league ahead of Khiyanat's as they in turn shadowed Tribe Kadri's fleet.

Çeda could see them a half-league ahead of Onur's ships, their sails bright along the horizon. In a few short hours, the three fleets were going to converge, hopefully giving Kadri and Khiyanat the advantage over Onur as they swept in from two sides.

Now that they were close, the Khiyanat and Kadri fleets had begun coordinating their movements. The flagmen in the vulture's nests sent messages ahead and relayed answers to Ishaq.

It won't be long now, Çeda thought. Soon dozens of ships would be locked in battle. She was as nervous as she'd ever been in the fighting pits of Sharakhai before a bout. But her heart was singing. They had a chance to show not only the Kings, but the entire desert, that the thirteenth tribe would no longer be silent.

Using a spyglass, Çeda tried to spot Emre, but the Kadri ships were too far away. She swung the spyglass left instead and studied the Black Spear ships, hoping to find Onur. She examined ship after ship and took note of the sheer number of warriors Onur had managed to gather to his cause. She saw the dozens of crews as they manned the ships and prepared for battle. Of the King of Sloth, however, she saw no sign.

"Come," Çeda said to Sümeya and Melis, who stood beside Çeda along the gunwales. "We're nearing ballista range."

As the three of them headed amidships, the crew of the *Amaranth* sent wary glances their way. They were the pariahs of the tribe. Each wore her black Maiden's dress, her black turban with veil hanging loose, and her ebon blade at her side. All three were symbols of hatred among all the desert tribes, but especially among the Moonless Host, whose warriors made up most of the tribe's number.

Their presence was suffered, but only on Ishaq's orders, and no one loved him for it. Every man, woman, and child on the ship looked as though they'd like nothing more than to throw the three of them over the gunwales—everyone but Macide, who watched them approach while leaning against the mainmast.

Zaïde and Salsanna stood nearby, speaking softly. Leorah was there as well, seated on a chair, hardly able to keep her eyes open. In place of her cane she had a staff. It rolled softly beneath the chair as the deck pitched this way or that. Had her cane been lost?

Kerim lay at the base of the stairs leading to the quarterdeck. The blackened features of his frame were curled in misery. He'd still not opened himself to Çeda, but Çeda didn't blame him. Onur was close enough now that Kerim was surely already struggling against the magic that bound him to do no harm against the Kings. The coming battle loomed, and she had no doubt he could enter the fray—such was his rage—but could he finish it? She prayed that he could and that Salsanna could help him. They would need his strength in the coming battle.

Zaïde and Salsanna stopped speaking as Çeda, Sümeya, and Melis gathered round. Macide watched and listened, his arms folded across his chest, revealing the snake tattoos that ran along his forearms.

Sümeya reached into the bag at her belt and took out a small clutch of dried adichara petals. Each was pure white save for one end, which turned a dusty blue, rather like clouds giving way to a clear sky. She began by handing one to Melis, Çeda, and Zaïde. Then, in a show of solidarity, she held another out to Salsanna.

Salsanna, however, refused her. "My bond with Kerim is strong enough. I would not jeopardize the balance we've found."

Sümeya paused, perhaps wondering if it was worth convincing her otherwise. To Çeda's great surprise, she turned and offered the petal to Macide instead. "The day will be long," she said. "It might help."

Macide stared at it, then took in Sümeya anew. In the end, he waved the offer away. "I'd likely chop off my own hand."

Sümeya shrugged and placed the petal beneath her tongue. Çeda did the same, as did Melis and Zaïde. As a war horn sounded in the distance, Çeda's awareness expanded. So often she'd felt as though the petals were a tool, little different from River's Daughter. Things were different now. She knew so much more about the nature of the petals and the adichara. The twisted trees were fed by the blood of the innocent, the tributes taken from Sharakhai, and the power of the petals came from them. The tributes had been taken against their will, but through these petals they lived on, making the petals and the verve they granted feel like a gift, a thing to be cherished, a thing to be respected as well. So as the world around her became sharper, as the sounds of the skis against the sand intensified, as the baked smell of the desert filled her senses, she gave thanks to those who had died that she might be ready for the coming day.

As the verve began to settle, she felt Kerim's discomfort more keenly. She also felt the strength Salsanna lent him. Their bond was strong indeed. Çeda wondered whether *she* had shared as much with him. Perhaps not. She cared deeply for Kerim, but he'd never forgiven her for Havva, the asir King Cahil had murdered in King's Harbor, once Kerim's wife. Havva had imprinted herself on Çeda, much as Kerim had later done before the two of them had headed into the desert together. But Mesut had sensed their shared bond, and had killed Havva for it. There was no such history between Salsanna and Kerim, and Çeda saw how truly powerful a bond could become.

Again Çeda wondered about Mesut's heavy golden bracelet, wrapped around Salsanna's wrist, the jet stone glinting dully in the morning light. Çeda wondered if they might find a way to unlock its secrets together. But it would have to wait until the battle was done.

The war horns sounded again, three sharp blasts, an indicator that battle was imminent. Çeda was just turning to look for Onur on the decks of the enemy ships when a black line streaked through the air toward the *Amaranth*.

"Cat's claws!" a crewman called.

The line writhed like a snake. Two heavy balls of iron were affixed to the ends. It splashed against the sand, well short of their ships. A second came in, and a third, these aimed with more skill. One flew high and struck the ship to the *Amaranth*'s port side; it thudded hard against the hull and fell to the sand. The other caught the ship behind the *Amaranth*. The chain wrapped around the starboard strut and slipped down to where the large iron hooks affixed to the weights dug into the sand. It not only slowed the ship, it forced it sharply starboard. Cat's claws weren't meant to debilitate but to sow chaos, to prevent an enemy's force from striking all at once.

More of them flew from both lines. Two launched from the *Amaranth*'s catapults arced swiftly toward a Black Spear galleon. One caught ineffectually in the ship's shrouds. The other snapped around the galleon's rudder. The chain seemed fouled for a moment, the hooks too high, but then it dropped and the hooks dug furrows in the sand. One by one, ships began to flag and trail behind the bulk of the fleet. It happened on the far side of Onur's fleet as well, which was now divided so that it might meet the threat of Tribe Kadri's fleet.

Crewmen were dispatched below the ships to release the cat's claws, but they were targeted by archers. Many were shot before they could reach the chains. They fell, their bodies littering the sand as their ships sailed on.

Then the fire pots began to fly.

Dozens were launched into the air, their flames trailing black smoke as they arced between the ranks of ships like falling suns. One crashed onto the deck of the *Amaranth* but was quickly smothered with sand. Another hit the foredeck. A third hit the loose netting that had been deployed across much of the starboard side. Caught in the net, the pot rolled down and was thrown over the side of the ship by two young boys wearing thick leather gloves. Their gloves were set aflame by the oil, but the pot was gone, and they put the fire out by vigorously slapping their hands together.

Far ahead of the *Amaranth*, the lead ship along their line shouldered into the enemy line. The two ships shuddered as their hulls crashed together. They sailed on, their sails and rigging shaking wildly. Warriors from both sides met along the gunwales with a roar, trying to force their way onto the enemy's ship to disable them or take it outright. Swords flew as they fought along the decks while others used ropes to swing across the gap to the rigging of their enemy's ship.

"There's Onur!" Sümeya said. She had her own small spyglass.

Çeda lifted hers and saw him, a giant of a man standing on the quarter-deck of a galleon in the second line of Black Spear ships.

Movement along the line of Kadri ships caught Çeda's attention. A lateen-sailed caravel was knifing through Onur's line. It looked as if it had hoped to fly all the way to Onur's ship, but the pilot of the carrack ahead of Onur's ship must have seen its approach. The carrack heeled to starboard, moving to intercept. The two ships crashed hard into one another. The carrack's stouter struts held while the caravel's snapped and its prow dropped sharply down into the sand as the sound of their collision rose above the sound of the fires, the shouted orders, and the roar of the soldiers engaged in battle.

Macide was staring at it, wide-eyed. "The caravel—that's Emre's ship."

Çeda felt like the deck had just fallen away from underneath her. She turned her spyglass on the caravel and searched desperately for him. "You're sure?"

"That's the *Autumn Rose*," he shouted above the battle's growing din. "Their shaikh, Aríz, rides aboard it, and Emre is advising him. It was probably Emre who suggested attacking Onur's ship directly."

Dear gods.

The sound of the battle was suddenly faint. The carrack and caravel had come to a sliding halt. As they did, the Black Spear ships behind them slowed and several struck the immobile ships, creating a glut in the center of the Black Spear fleet.

It was then that more Kadri ships came bursting through the far side, many striking the Black Spear ships head on, creating utter chaos.

They're trying to immobilize Onur. To give us a chance to attack him directly.

Onur was still standing on the deck of his galleon. The pilot had managed to avoid the growing congestion, but now five more Kadri ships were headed straight for it.

"Emre's given us a chance to take Onur," she said to Sümeya and Melis. "Now we just need to reach him."

Sümeya was as intense as Çeda had ever seen her. "May the sun set with the loss of a man over whom no one will weep."

Melis took a moment, her resolve hardening. "We'll stay together until we reach his ship, and then strike for Onur any way we can."

"Agreed," Çeda said.

Nearby, Salsanna held her hand on Kerim's shoulder. The plan had been to go with both Kerim and Salsanna, but Kerim wasn't going anywhere. He was shivering like a newborn pup. He looked terrified.

"We'll follow when he's ready," Salsanna said. She was smiling beatifically. She bore many visible scars from Kerim's attack on her—along her neck, her cheeks, her arrowhead chin—and yet she seemed at peace. Whether she truly felt that way, or if it was an act for Çeda, Kerim, or even Salsanna herself, Çeda couldn't say.

"Very well," Çeda said.

Zaïde's face was a ghastly shade of white. She had her hand pressed against her chest. She looked as if she wanted nothing more than to join them, but it was clear her heart wasn't going to allow it. "Go," she said.

Melis, Sümeya, and Çeda all nodded, and then they were off. Çeda led them to the port shrouds. They climbed the ratlines to the crosstrees, gripped three of the waiting boarding ropes, and waited as the *Amaranth* neared a ship on the starboard side. Clay pots arced toward both ships. One crashed into a cluster of warriors on the *Amaranth*'s foredeck, splashing burning oil over a dozen of them.

"Now!" Çeda called.

She swung, aiming for the shrouds. The ships collided. She felt the impact as the *Amaranth*'s masts swayed violently. Her stomach dropped as she released the rope and flew weightlessly through the hot desert air. She landed hard on the opposite ship's shroud, but held.

An arrow blurred through the air below her as Melis and Sümeya landed beside her. More arrows were loosed by bowmen arrayed along the far side of the deck below. As the battle between the ships began in earnest, a Black Spear warrior pointed up at them. "Maidens!"

Çeda knew from the Night of Endless Swords how overwhelming the sheer number of heartbeats around her could be, but since then she'd learned how to home in on those she cared about. She stripped away those fighting with swords and spears below, stripped away those trying to douse the fires on the deck and in the rigging, and concentrated on the four archers.

She sensed the tightness in their arms as they pulled the strings back. Sensed the line of aim from the pair who were focused on taking her down like a falcon from the sky. When she felt the moment of their release, she leapt for a stay line that ran at an angle toward the deck. The arrows whizzed by, one tugging on the skirt of her dress as it punctured the heavy cloth.

She flew along the stay line, her leather gloves buzzing as the rope slid through them ever faster. In one fluid move, she released the rope, drew River's Daughter, and dropped onto the hatch. It felt like falling into a sea of heartbeats. She gave over to the rhythm of it, the rage and panic of those around her somehow calming her. Pain was building in her right hand—her old wound flaring to life once more. It deepened as she gripped River's Daughter and by the time she met the swordsman who had come between her and the archers, it felt as though her arm was on fire.

She gave in to it while blocking high and cutting low. The swordsman fell to the deck, screaming, and she was already past him, slashing with both hands at the archer, who stood wide-eyed with his bow before him as if it might protect him. Her ebon blade cut the bow in two. Before he could recover, she advanced, snapped a kick into his jaw, and sent him flying backward over the side of the ship.

Men and women warriors, all dressed in desert garb, charged toward her, but she gave them no chance to land a blow. She leapt to the gunwales and followed the archer, somersaulting once before hitting the sand and rolling over one shoulder. She was up in a moment, turning to find Melis flying over the side of the ship behind her. Sümeya was still amidships. She delivered two quick cuts against another of the archers, then a blinding upward blow to the nearest warrior, then leapt in a backward somersault over the side of the ship.

Çeda turned as something dark loomed on her right.

Danger, she whistled, *north!*

A Black Spear dhow was hurtling toward them, but oblivious to their presence. The dhow's hull scraped hard against the ship they'd just leapt free of. Çeda, Melis, and Sümeya hurtled past the leading ski, then dove as the rudder scythed through the sand behind them.

Then they were up and sprinting toward the great clutch of ships locked near the center of the battle. The caravel that had slipped through the Black Spear line, Emre's ship, was now engulfed in a pitched battle. The Black Spears had numbers, but more and more of Ishaq's warriors, including Macide himself, were streaming across the sand, ready to lend their support. Kadri warriors were rushing in on foot as well. But the Black Spears were not idle. They recognized the threat and were forming lines, preparing for their enemy's charge.

Çeda, Melis, and Sümeya ran ahead, spying for Onur. So many were rushing toward the caravel she thought Onur might be making his way there was well. But then Çeda spotted someone in the crowd making a desperate stand on the caravel's main deck.

Gods, it was Emre.

"There!" Çeda shouted. "We must reach the caravel!"

Melis and Sümeya ran beside her, but Sümeya pulled her to a halt. "We have a mission, Maiden."

"I know"—she thrust a finger at the ship—"but look what he's done. If we reach Onur, it will be because of the people on that ship. Let's save them, give them time until the rest of our numbers catch up. It will give us time to locate Onur, to see how he's arraying his defenses."

"But if we go now, he may not have *time* to array his defenses," Melis said.

Sümeya looked between them, clearly unsure.

The pain in Çeda's right arm had reached new heights. It felt good. It felt right. It felt as if it knew that battle was near. "I'm not leaving him," Çeda said, and ran for Emre's ship.

Pulling out the shield strapped to her belt, Çeda entered the battle. Melis and Sümeya, thankfully, had decided to join her. With them fighting by her side, they carved through the line of Black Spear soldiers who stood braced across the sand to meet them. They were many, but they were also fearful. Çeda could see it in their stances, in the way they backed away as Çeda neared. She released a high-pitched ululation as she tore deeper through their ranks, pushing ever closer to the caravel, and they slowly gave way.

Near the ship's side, Çeda let the power of the petals and the burning in her arm drive her. She leapt, grabbed the side of the ship with her shield hand, and levered herself over the gunwale while parrying a sharp downward blow from a soldier who was waiting for her. He'd badly misjudged how quickly she could gain the deck. With three quick blows the man was down, holding his chest from a deep wound River's Daughter had carved into his ribs.

Emre spotted her. He shouted something. Though his words were lost in the clash of steel and the screams of battle, he pointed toward Çeda, and immediately those around him began fighting *toward* her. The next moments were lost to the rhythmic swings of her ebon blade, the blocking of blows against her small shield.

As their two groups met, a sense of relief washed over Çeda. It was immediately broken, however, when she spotted the undulating line in the sky off to her right. It was distant still, but closing quickly. A sound, a great bellow, fell across the desert. For a moment the sounds of battle waned. Heads turned to see the brightly colored wyrm slithering eel-like through the sky. Powerful wings bore it steadily closer, the shadows created by its sinuous flight playing against the sunlight filtering through its veined magenta-and-gold skin.

Çeda, though wrapped in the blanket of the petal's warmth, felt her mouth go dry. Her stomach sank just to see it flying through the sky, making its way toward one end of the Kadri line of ships, and then descending on it like a servant of death. The Black Spear soldiers shouted triumphantly. Their enemies quaked. Both were dwarfed by the riot of sounds that arose as the wyrm crashed onto the deck of the ship. Breath of the desert, Çeda felt it in her bones. She couldn't help but wonder if any of them would escape this battle alive.

"Onur!" Emre yelled, pointing. "If we can reach Onur, we might stop it!"

There he was. Standing on the deck of the ship Çeda had spotted earlier, holding his fist to the sky. A glittering jewel was held in that hand, she realized, a thing he must be using to control the wyrm.

As the battle rose up around her, Çeda, Melis, and Sümeya tried to pierce the line, to drive toward Onur, but there were so many warriors pouring over the interlocked ships, slipping over the gunwales to stop the advance of the combined Kadri and Khiyanat lines, that they made no headway.

Onur, however, was wading toward *them*. The flame-like gem was gone as he wielded his great spear on the deck of a clipper. His own soldiers gave him a wide berth as soldier after enemy soldier fell before him. He moved with a deadly combination of fluidity and power, so much so that those who stood against him could withstand only one or two blows before falling to his spear or to a punch from his great mailed fist.

Behind Çeda, Macide had gained the deck. He swung a pair of shamshirs in blinding patterns, pushing back the Black Spear forces. Behind him were Frail Lemi and Hamid and two dozen more.

Up? Sümeya whistled.

Affirmative, Çeda whistled back. Now that Emre and the Kadri forces had help, it was time to go for Onur.

Sheathing River's Daughter, she leapt and grabbed a boarding line and climbed hand over hand as Melis and Sümeya reached the port-side shrouds.

As she was nearing the head of the mainsail, she felt *something* approaching. Something dark, vengeful, and filled with purpose. She turned and saw a black figure bounding over the sand—Kerim, wailing as he approached the edges of the fighting.

Everyone in tribe Khiyanat had been forewarned and retreated, creating a lane for Kerim. He bounded along it and bowled into the fighters there. He was lost for a moment, but it was easy to track his progress, for wherever he went, soldiers fell. His claws rent chain and leather and flesh. And when the Black Spear soldiers closed in tightly around him, halting his progress, he crouched and released a howl the likes of which Çeda had never heard. She felt the anguish that had been building inside him since Beht Ihman. It released, spread outward, caused all those nearby to fall to their knees and cringe, hands pressed tightly against their ears.

Like a drop falling against the surface of a pond, the effect spread outward. More and more men and women warriors, including those from Tribe Khiyanat, dropped and tried in vain to stop the pain pouring outward from Kerim. The effect weakened the further it went, so that those who were dozens of yards away cringed but did not fall. And when it struck Çeda as she climbed higher along the shroud, she felt it too, a pain that drew her in on herself, like regret over one's most shameful moment.

Suddenly the wailing stopped.

Onur had not been idle. He was pounding across the deck of the ship nearest to Kerim. When Onur threw his bulk down to the sand and lumbered forward, all before him backed away, leaving a clear path to Kerim.

Kerim charged.

She felt Kerim's intent—to feast on the hated King's heart before dying—but she felt Onur's as well.

"Kerim, no!" Çeda cried.

She'd climbed through the lubber's hole and sprinted along the mainsail's boom, which was pitched at an upward angle. When she reached the end, she launched herself toward the next ship.

Kerim had come to a sudden halt before Onur. Çeda could see him standing before the giant of a man as she flew toward the mainsail of the next, smaller ship. She crashed into the billowing canvas and rode it down to the foot of the sail. With a grab of the boom and a swing of her legs, she somersaulted over the soldiers below and down to the sand.

In an instant, she was sprinting toward Kerim, her sword drawn. She could feel the pain inside him as he struggled against the ancient shackles that prevented him from harming the Kings. Çeda had thought he might be able to throw them off, as Sehid-Alaz had done for a time. She'd thought, as tight as his bond was with Salsanna, that he'd be able to wound Onur, perhaps even kill him. But she should have known better. He was helpless, defenseless before the King.

Çeda heard Sümeya and Melis land behind her. Together, they began clearing the way toward Onur.

"Stop the Maidens!" Onur growled, pointing toward them without taking his eyes from Kerim.

Çeda fought harder, shouting as she blocked blows, sliced necks, and cut legs to fell those before her. She was just able to see Kerim clearly when she saw Onur lift his spear. Holding it in both hands, he drove it straight through Kerim's chest, pushed him backward, and pinned him against the sand.

"No!" Çeda screamed.

She *felt* the blow. She staggered from it, fell to her knees as her opponent rained blow after blow against her. As much as *she* felt it, however, Salsanna suffered more. Çeda could sense her on the deck of the *Amaranth*. She'd fallen as well, and was clutching her heart.

Trying desperately to recover, Çeda blocked the sword of the Black Spear swordsman before her. She took a blow to her shoulder, another to her ribs.

Back, came a Maiden's sharp whistle.

Çeda immediately rolled backward over one shoulder and regained her feet as Melis blocked several hasty blows from the men who'd been attacking Çeda. She delivered precise strikes to one leg, then an arm, cut deeply through one man's neck, then blocked, spinning as she did so to bring her sword sharply across the second warrior's helm, cleaving his head nearly in two.

"Onur," Çeda shouted. "We must reach Onur."

Together, she, Melis, and Sümeya resumed their push. They were aided by a rejuvenated line of Khiyanat soldiers, but the Black Spear line was rebuilding as well. Çeda was beginning to worry they'd never reach him in time when a woman broke through the line off to her left.

Zaïde was rushing for Onur, dressed in her Matron's white. How she'd managed to make it through the line Çeda had no idea, but she now had an unobstructed path to Onur.

"Zaïde!" Onur growled. "My own daughter. A welcome surprise!"

Push hard, Çeda whistled to Melis and Sümeya.

They did, working in silent concert. As they fought to reach Onur, Zaïde moved like the wind. Several warriors moved to intercept her, but Onur waved them back. "Leave her to me!"

He swung his spear across his body, he stabbed with the head, tried to crush her with a cross blow. But nothing worked. Zaïde was too quick. Too lithe. She had an answer for his every move, and soon she was delivering her own. She struck with two fingers into Onur's armpits, the joints of his elbows, his inner thighs, his neck. They were not strong hits. Onur did not collapse. But they were pinpoint accurate, designed to cause pain from simple movement, to debilitate or even paralyze if she could deliver enough strikes to a certain area.

Indeed, Onur's replies had been reduced to simply trying to block her blinding combinations. He was beginning to slow from the effects of Zaïde's precise blows. Zaïde was slowing as well, though. Çeda could feel her heart pounding, worse than when she was in the savaşam, worse than when they'd escaped Kameyl and Yndris in the desert. But Zaïde pushed herself anyway, harder than Çeda had ever seen her. Her face grew red, and she began shouting with each strike, a habit she'd always railed against.

Control, she'd told Çeda over and over again. *Always control.*

But Zaïde was hardly in control. She had pushed herself well past her limits.

Onur dropped to one knee and snapped the head of his spear toward Zaïde's face. Zaïde merely slipped below it, a move as easy as a cattail bowing in the wind, and then she drove in and delivered three sharp strikes, two to his neck and one to his eyes. Onur reeled, releasing a bellow of pain as he dropped his spear and grabbed his face.

Zaïde didn't stop. She struck his kidneys, then the joint above his hips, and then she took up his spear. Onur was defenseless, but Zaïde could go no further than lifting the great weapon. She pressed the butt into the ground at her feet, one hand gripping it with knuckles white as snow as she fought for breath. Her other hand was pressed to her heart.

She willed herself past the pain. Forced her body to listen. After two more deep breaths, she lifted the spear. "For my mother!"

In trying to deliver that fatal blow, however, she missed. Onur shifted on the sand, batted the spearhead aside so that it struck only his armor, not his exposed neck. She tried again, and Onur did the same. Çeda wasn't sure how he'd recovered so quickly until she saw how dark his skin was becoming. No, not his skin. Black hair was sprouting along his forearms, his neck, his face. His arms and legs were distending, bending strangely at the wrists and elbows and shoulders and hips. His body was *elongating.*

A roar of pain erupted from his throat as he clawed for Zaïde, and she stepped back, wheezing. She lifted the spear above her head, gripped it with both hands, and ran toward him.

Another roar came from Onur, but this time it sounded nothing like a human, but a great cat. Indeed, the transformation that had been whispered of, his gift from the gods, was occurring before their very eyes. He'd taken the form of a massive panther with black, silken fur that glittered beneath the sun, larger than any cat Çeda had ever seen, even the great Kundhuni lions that were paraded through Sharakhai's streets from time to time.

The panther tore its way free of Onur's armor. Teeth bared, it bounded away as Zaïde thrust the spear at its chest. However much Zaïde's two-fingered strikes had slowed Onur's movements before, the paralysis had vanished after the change. And Zaïde was much, much slower than before.

Çeda fought harder, as did Sümeya and Melis. Those who stood before them tried to slow them down, but they had fear in their eyes and gave ground before the whirring ebon blades. Çeda had only just reached open space—the way now clear to Zaïde and the transformed Onur—when the panther reared back from one last, weak thrust of the spear, and lunged for Zaïde's throat.

Faster than Çeda's eye could follow, the panther's jaws clamped down. Çeda came rushing toward it, screaming, hoping the panther would turn to face her. But the panther only jerked its head back and to one side. A tearing sound came with it. Blood spurted high from the red, bloody, gaping hole where Zaïde's throat had once been. It spattered against her white matron's dress as the panther dove back in and bit into her shoulder. It tore more of Zaïde's flesh away, and then at last seemed to recognize the threat Çeda represented.

No. It had been waiting, hoping to catch her off guard, she realized.

It turned and swiped for her, ducking in one sinewy movement as she swung River's Daughter across her guard. The panther's paw caught her leg with one reaching swipe and sent her to the ground, but Çeda was ready. She chopped down as she fell, catching the panther just above the claw.

It was on her in a moment, jaws wide in hopes of ripping out her neck as well. Çeda's only hope was to hold River's Daughter like a bar of steel. She shoved it hard into the panther's gaping maw. It cut deep, caught in the panther's teeth. Even so, the beast used its sheer weight to press down on her and tried to bite her face or neck. She could smell its fetid breath as a foaming mixture of spittle and blood dripped from its bloodstained teeth.

As its massive claws tore into her ribs and stomach, Çeda worked the blade back and forth. It chipped teeth, cut into the panther's cheeks, but the beast seemed oblivious to it. But then it jerked its great head up and roared while twisting its body to face Sümeya. Sümeya slashed her ebon blade, but the panther was too quick. It reared and leapt, twisting its body in the air as it did so and using its great paw to club Sümeya across the head. She stumbled and fell to the sand, her shamshir flying through the air like a wounded crow.

The panther would have had her had Melis not been there. She cut once, slicing the beast's shoulder, then again across its face. The panther tried to charge, to use its mass against her. But Melis was not new to the blade. She stumbled back, dodged to one side and rolled backward, to come up with her sword at the ready.

Çeda kicked herself to a stand and rushed to her aid. "Onur!" she screamed, hoping to distract him before he ripped out Melis's throat. The panther was bleeding from several deep wounds along its ribs, forelegs, and head. None of the wounds seemed mortal, however.

Onur's great spear was just before her. As Onur rushed Melis, Çeda picked it up and hefted it over her right shoulder. Her right hand burning hot, she stepped forward and launched it just as Melis was felled by a swipe of the panther's bloody claw. The spear sank deep into the panther's ribs. It howled in pain as it rolled away. Sand caked the panther's coat where its fur was matted with blood. Çeda sprinted forward, hoping to end it, but before she'd taken two strides, the panther somehow managed to regain its feet and bound away. In moments it was gone, lost behind a line of Black Spear warriors.

Suddenly the roar of the battle returned.

The fight had reached a fever pitch. Onur's warriors, who had held back on Onur's command, now charged in. Çeda wanted to go after Onur, to stop him, but he was heading for a ship that could sail away at his command.

She was swept back into the battle. Horns blew. The Black Spears were sounding the retreat. More of their forces began to pull back and their ships began peeling away.

The Khiyanat and Kadri soldiers had been hard pressed before Onur's retreat. Some were heartened now, hoping to grind the Black Spear soldiers into the desert. But others, including Macide, were calling for a halt. Hundreds of Kadri warriors were gathered around the ship the wyrm was attacking. They launched arrows at the sinewy beast and threw spears. Some who were brave or unfortunate enough to stand before it tried to pierce its scintillant skin with their swords. All to no avail. It was impervious to all but the strongest blows. Only in a few places was there blood of any kind.

The wyrm had already destroyed three ships and was now leaping onto another as the Khiyanat and Kadri forces began to disengage. Many were focused on fighting the wyrm, but as many or more were helping the old, the young, or the wounded to flee from it.

Amidst all this madness an old woman appeared. It was Leorah, holding a staff in both hands, crosswise against her body. She looked both powerful and fey as she strode forward, like one of the first women. Any who saw her felt it as well. They stepped aside, clearing a path between her and the wyrm.

Perhaps sensing her power, the wyrm halted its attack and swiveled its great head toward her. In a burst of movement it leapt from the deck of the dhow to the golden sand below.

The Black Spear soldiers were retreating. They were turning their ships and sailing away, taking the wounded Onur with them. But Çeda paid them little mind. Her mouth agape, she walked toward Leorah, transfixed by the scene playing out before her.

With only open sand before it, the wyrm slithered forward. It looked like a serpent with thorns upon its head and bright, luminous skin. It took one lithe movement, then another, each bringing it closer to Leorah, who had stopped twenty paces away. The wyrm's approach seemed more ritual than natural. Leorah seemed calm and expectant, and in complete control, as if she and the wyrm had entered into an arcane rite, the outcome of which had already been decided.

Like a songbird wary of danger, the wyrm approached. It would twist, stop, then slither forward again. It looked as if it were describing ancient sigils. Leorah's staff was moving in that same strange way. The two of them were linked in that moment. Beast and desert witch.

In that moment, the sun struck the gemstones on the staff's bulbous head, making them glint like a distant oasis. Breath of the desert, Çeda had seen that staff before, though at the time it had been held by the hand of a goddess. It was Nalamae's staff, the very one Çeda had used to strike the acacia in her garden.

When the wyrm came within several paces of Leorah, it lowered its great head, dwarfing Leorah's bent, aged form. Its opaline eyes studied her while the movements of its head mimicked the rhythms of her staff. Then, in a movement that reminded Çeda of a crane preparing to take flight, Leorah spread her arms wide, tipped her head back, and opened herself to the sky. The wyrm erupted into the air. Its long wings flapped, once, twice, thrice, each movement a wave that continued, rope-like, along its entire serpentine length.

In lazy circles it lifted, its passage describing a winding column above the battle as its form slowly diminished. As if its departure were weighing on her soul, Leorah staggered, then collapsed unceremoniously to the sand. In that same moment, the wyrm dipped, then streaked eastward, trailing after the Black Spear ships.

Chapter 56

"THEY'RE BEGINNING TO FAN OUT, my lord!"

Ramahd stirred momentarily from his slumber, but had soon slipped back into the land of dreams. He was naked, his body bruised and beaten. Meryam stood over him in a gown made of blood red silk. The fabric cascaded over her frame to fall across his body. And where it touched, pain followed. He tried to fight it, tried to move, but fighting only seemed to make the pain and his imprisonment worse.

Her eyes brimming with malice, Meryam lowered herself until she straddled his hips. "You think *you* can stop me?" She smiled and hooked his shirt with one finger. With a single, violent motion, she ripped it down the center, then pressed her thumbnail to his chest like a hunter preparing to split firewood. Her hair fell across his cheeks as she leaned down and whispered into his ear. "After everything we've been through, everything you've learned of me, you thought I would throw it all away for you?"

She drove her thumbnail deeper in his chest, piercing skin. Her eyes, meanwhile . . . Her eyes were changing, the pupils elongating, becoming more taurine. The irises brightened to a burnished gold while her skin turned black as night.

"Your father would be ashamed," he managed to say through his haggard breaths.

"My father was a coward."

"And what am I?"

Her strange eyes blinked, as if she were surprised he would even ask the question. "A besotted fool."

"I do love you. . . ."

"You see?" She leaned close and kissed him. Her lips were inhumanly warm. "A greater fool the world has never seen." She pressed her thumbnail deeper into his flesh, and he was helpless to prevent it. It slipped between his ribs until he could feel her nail with every beat of his heart.

"My lord, the Kings' ships are spreading out!"

Ramahd lurched awake. He'd been sleeping against the bulwarks of his yacht, the *Blue Heron*. They were sailing under a stiff breeze far to the east of Sharakhai. "When?" he managed after a moment.

"A few minutes ago," Cicio called from the top of the mainmast. "Best we slow until we see what they're about."

Ramahd sat up and put the heels of his hands to his eyes, hoping to clear the nightmarish images of Meryam from his mind. "Do it."

"Aye," Cicio called.

Cicio's curly hair was caught by the wind as he slipped down along the yacht's lone mast. He and Vrago set about the business of reefing the sails, while Tiron manned the wheel and guided the ship over the softly rolling dunes.

Sleep weighed on Ramahd like a millstone, but he drew himself up and breathed deeply, absently rubbing the place where dream Meryam had pierced his skin. The horizon wavered ahead, the heat of the desert distorting all, but he could see the hint of masts and sails. It was difficult to see how many there were, but it was clear the fleet was spreading out.

Amidships, Brama was leaning over the gunwales, retching. He was no sandsman—that much had been clear from the outset—but there was more to it than sand sickness. Rümayesh's presence in the fleet they were chasing, and her imprisonment at Meryam's hands, was doing much to worsen his malaise.

After Ramahd and Brama had left the House of Kings, they'd gone to

Cicio and Vrago's favorite haunts. Tiron, with a bit of good fortune, had been there as well. They'd debated for a time what to do. Where to go. But there was really no debate for Ramahd. He needed to find Çeda. He needed to warn her, tell her everything that had happened, as well as what Meryam now planned.

They'd found the *Blue Heron* guarded, but with no more than the usual pair of guardsmen. It had taken little for Cicio and Vrago to subdue them, after which they'd bound and gagged their countrymen and left them beneath the docks, then sailed by night along the arms of the great southern harbor's entrance and out to open sand.

They'd sailed east for days before stumbling across a fleet of the Kings' ships—the one that lay before them still—but they hadn't quite known the scale of it until now. The ships spread farther and farther apart, more and more of them becoming clear along the horizon. Ramahd counted at least fifty ships, and there were probably more beyond the horizon. It looked like one of the mighty caravans of old.

"Bloody gods," Brama said, staring at it from the gunwales. "They're not taking this lightly, are they?"

"The Kings," Cicio said in Sharakhan. "They no taking no more shit from the tribes."

"One tribe," Ramahd corrected. "They want to destroy the thirteenth tribe before the truth spreads."

"What truth?" Cicio asked.

Ramahd stared at him. Cicio was not the sharpest sword on the battlefield, but Ramahd had told him all of this already. "That thirteenth tribe once sailed the desert along with the other twelve. That they were sacrificed and nearly destroyed on Beht Ihman."

The sun slanted across Brama's scarred face as he shaded his eyes. "The gem is there"—he flicked his hand toward the center of the line of ships—"somewhere." Holding one hand over his gut, he slumped onto the deck and leaned hard against the bulwark.

"It's getting worse?" Ramahd asked.

"It's as bad as it has ever been."

It meant that Meryam had the doors to the amulet open. Brama could feel it when she did. He could feel Rümayesh's emotions as well—the link between them saw to that, and ensured that Brama would either fight to save her or suffer for his inaction.

"Can you tell what she's doing?"

"No. She's too far away."

Ahead, it was becoming clear the ships were forming a curving line—creating a cordon, perhaps, or trying to hem something in. Meryam had promised King Kiral she would use Çeda's blood to summon Guhldrathen when they were near enough. When the ehrekh came near, the logic went, it would sense Hamzakiir, whom she and the King both suspected would be on hand to help Onur. Had the time come? Had they found Onur's fleet?

Brama seemed to have picked up on the same thing. "Now we come to it," he said. "Have you thought about what I said?"

Ramahd nodded. "We need to warn Çeda."

"You don't even know where she is."

"I don't, no, but Meryam does." He waved to the line of ships. "If they're preparing their trap, it means that Çeda and Hamzakiir are near. Which means that we could warn her."

Brama made a face. "Well, of *course*, milord. And I'm sure the Kings themselves will sprinkle rose petals to mark the *Heron's* path."

"I didn't say we'd *sail* in."

Brama stared across the desert. "What of the other option we discussed?"

"We can't go after Meryam now. She's too well guarded."

"Perhaps, perhaps not. Either way, what good will it do to risk the Kings' cordon just to inform Çeda she's about to be murdered by one of Goezhen's children?"

"She deserves to know."

"That's your guilt talking. She can do nothing to stop Guhldrathen. We, on the other hand, can."

"That's your hunger for Rümayesh talking."

A smile tugged at one corner of Brama's scar-torn lips. "That doesn't make it less true."

Ahead, the navy ships seemed to have stopped altogether. Yet their sails were still set.

"Strange," Brama said.

An eerie chill came over Ramahd as he watched the Kings' fleet just sitting there. "Stop the ship."

"Aye," came Tiron's reply.

Vrago and Cicio were just beginning to pull in the sails when the wind began to die. One moment, it had been strong, if blustering. Then it was a breeze, hardly strong enough to power a ship. And finally it deadened, and the sound died with it. The desert was utterly silent. The atmosphere itself was strange and primal, as if something momentous were about to happen.

"A sign from the gods," Cicio said, staring warily at the sky.

Ramahd didn't disagree. Wind or no wind, perhaps he shouldn't pass up a chance to stop Meryam. As he had for days, he struggled with what it might mean for Qaimir. What he was about to do was not only treason, it could very well put his country in great danger. *But what Meryam is doing is worse.*

"Can you guide us to the right ship?" he asked Brama.

Brama shrugged. "As long as she doesn't close the locket."

Ramahd turned to Cicio, Vrago, and Tiron. "Tow the ship into a trough. We leave at nightfall."

Chapter 57

K IRAL WATCHED as the ships of the royal navy slowed and then stopped altogether. The doldrums had fallen over the eastern desert, forcing them to stop earlier than they would have liked, but it was still an impressive sight, and one he hadn't witnessed in a hundred years: the full power of Sharakhai's navy deploying across the desert. Like the last time, it was to quell an uprising, but *unlike the last time*, this was a conflict that had the very real possibility of exploding in the Kings' faces.

A century ago, Zeheb had heard whispers of an alliance that might stand against Sharakhai, if not militarily then at least economically. Four tribes had united against the Kings, with several more considering. Azad was sent to deliver the kiss of steel to the shaikhs, while Zeheb and Onur had volunteered to lead an assault so that those who succeeded the shaikhs would think twice before making any such allegiance again.

Now Azad was dead, Onur stood on the opposite side of the battle, and the whispers had driven Zeheb mad. Their grand experiment, their alliance of Kings, was beginning to unravel at the edges. It wouldn't last much longer, he suspected. Cahil and Sukru still stood by his side. Beşir would follow whomever had the strongest hand.

Ihsan was a different story. He was involved in all of this—the traitor Çedamihn, the loss of the caches of elixirs, Onur fleeing to the desert, and Yusam dying on the way to Ihsan's palace. Kiral had yet to find the evidence, but he would. And it would be the key to securing Husamettín's allegiance. Move too quickly, and Ihsan might turn Husamettín against him, a thing Kiral could ill afford. Husamettín was formidable on his own, and the Blade Maidens, whether Kiral liked it or not, were loyal to the King of Swords. Kiral couldn't risk losing him, so he would bide his time. He would uncover enough proof to have Ihsan's head. He might even give Husamettín the honor of taking it himself.

And then we will set about the business of pushing back the interlopers. Malasan and Mirea first.

"Are you ready?" came a feminine voice behind him.

And then Qaimir.

Kiral turned to find Queen Meryam gliding across the foredeck toward him. When she arrived at his side, he waved to the scene in the distance, the site of a waning battle. Dozens of ships were huddled together. More beyond had fled, most likely Onur's. "It seems the Moonless Host have survived the King of Spears' onslaught. I wonder if they could have done so if, as you say, Hamzakiir is here, helping Onur."

"Hamzakiir is but one man. And the Moonless Host are far from powerless."

"You still believe he's gone to Onur, then?"

"I'm certain of it."

"I need more than your word. I've brought a Kestrel with me. Perhaps I should send her into his camp to find the truth of it." With Zeheb unable to so much as repeat his own name, Kiral had taken charge of his Bloody Nine. Husamettín had balked, but he'd used the excuse of this very campaign to warrant it. *You'll hardly need them as you defend the city,* Kiral had told him. *But they may be paramount to our success in the desert.*

"Send a Kestrel and you risk Hamzakiir becoming skittish. He may flee as he did in Sharakhai."

"He may very well do that after today's loss."

"Which is precisely why we must summon Guhldrathen now. Don't leave his fate to chance."

He'd known this hour was coming. And yet saying the words, giving her permission, felt as if he'd swallowed a hot stone that was now trying to burn its way out of him. "You're certain it will make for Hamzakiir?"

"It already did once. It cannot help but do so again. The rage it has for him is like no other. No matter that it might be tempted by Çeda. No matter that other forces stand before it. It will find him and consume him."

"With your help, we could simply overpower him."

"Granted, but at what cost? With the asirim left to defend Sharakhai, how much damage will your fleet take? What will remain as Malasan and Mirea creep ever closer?"

"We can retreat to Sharakhai if need be."

"And give up the desert by so doing."

"No, they're not so strong as that."

"My Lord King, we both have our spies. What do they tell you about the strengths of their armies? The size of their fleets? Sharakhai would stand against any enemy for a time, but how long could the city withstand a siege without a proper fleet?"

Kiral said nothing. She was right, he knew. There were already too many risks with this battle. Choose rashly here and he might sustain enough damage to his fleet that he'd have no chance to stop Mirea or Malasan should they advance quickly. And given that their enemies would have news of this battle soon, they just might. Were the asirim fully to heel, he'd push on anyway, but from what Husamettín had told him, it was risky. The girl, Çedamihn, had managed to override the protections Husamettín had placed on the asirim. Worse, she'd *taken* an asir as her own. If she could do it once, she could do it again.

"I don't blame you for examining this from all angles," Meryam went on. "Wise men take care at momentous times. But I tell you, oh King of Kings, your reasoning was sound all along." She waved an emaciated hand toward the distant battlefield. "Whomever you choose to fight on the sand, be it Onur or the Moonless Host or both, Hamzakiir will escape if we don't summon Guhldrathen. He will not remain to defend his newly chosen King. He will flee. And he is the greatest single threat to Sharakhai."

Kiral wasn't so sure. There were many threats to Sharakhai, not the least of them Çedamihn herself. She was the daughter of Azad's assassin. She was Ishaq's own granddaughter, and a direct descendant of Sehid-Alaz. He was furious she'd managed to fool both Yusam and Husamettín and infiltrated the Blade Maidens. How many secrets had she learned? How many souls had she turned to her side? Zaïde had either been turned or been with them in the first place. But then there were the Maiden Melis and the First Warden herself, Sümeya. It was hard to believe Çeda didn't have a hand in their sudden sympathy toward the thirteenth tribe.

She killed Külaşan. She killed Mesut. She escaped on the Night of Endless Swords and had now joined her grandfather in leading not merely a rebellion, but the rebirth of the tribe Kiral had given to the gods in sacrifice.

This has to end now. In the desert. Word of the thirteenth tribe is already spreading, and while none of the shaikhs will acknowledge them openly, they are likely doing so in private. It will not be long before they seriously consider the overtures Ishaq has surely made to them, to join him in a bid to crush the Kings of Sharakhai once and for all.

"When do we begin?" he asked Meryam.

Meryam's smile was most pleased. "Why, *now*, my Lord King"—she motioned toward the ladder leading belowdecks—"though I rather think it would be best in private, don't you?"

They retired to Meryam's cabin. In the darkened, almost stifling space was the queen's servant, Amaryllis. She stood at a set of shelves built into one wall. She was tending to a beaker, which was suspended above an oil lamp whose flame was pure blue and which burned without a trace of smoke. The faint green liquid bubbling in the beaker was surely the source of the acrid smell lacing the hot, stifling air. There was something else besides. Something that smelled of decay.

"You can douse the flame," Meryam said as she moved to the far side of the table occupying the center of the room. "It needs to cool awhile."

She remained standing and motioned to the unoccupied chair across from her, but Kiral was suddenly and inexplicably nervous. "I have much to attend to."

"This won't take long."

Amaryllis broke the tension by raising two small bottles from the shelf. "Would you care for some araq, my Lord King? Or brandy? We have some of Qaimir's best."

He waved her offer away.

Meryam, meanwhile, waited with a smile he could only interpret as a challenge. He had half a mind to call her out on it, but he would not cast himself as a petrified peasant before her comely servant. He sat, and when Meryam followed suit, Amaryllis brought out a wooden case and set it before her queen, sharing a quick, flirtatious smile with Kiral as she did so.

Meryam lifted the lid to reveal a fist-sized object hidden in gauze and two ampules, both filled with a red liquid. While the liquid looked too thin to be pure blood, it was surely a tincture derived from it. One, surely, was Çeda's blood, prepared from the very ampule he'd delivered to her, but the other . . .

"Why are there two?" he asked.

Meryam shrugged. "There's always that chance that one breaks. I prefer to leave as little to chance as possible."

Amaryllis brought a ceramic plate and the beaker holding the steaming green liquid, set them next to the case and then stepped aside to let her queen work. As Meryam took up the ampule to Kiral's left and began swirling it absently, Amaryllis watched eagerly.

Too eagerly, thought Kiral. *Servants should be noticed only when their presence becomes necessary.*

With deliberate care, Meryam tipped the tincture of blood into the beaker of green liquid. Her emaciated hands quivered, but she managed to get all of it in without spilling. Then she swirled the combined mixture around until it was a uniform brown.

"You might be interested to know that I've been studying the Malasani of late, their uses for blood." She took the wrapped object from the case and began unwinding the gauze. "I find their golems intensely interesting and have endeavored to learn more about them. Much remains hidden in mystery, however. They hide their secrets well."

She continued to unwind the gauze to reveal a red clay simulacrum—of a man, given the crudely formed genitals. Setting the gauze aside, she placed the figure on the ceramic plate, face up, took up the brown mixture, and grasped the amulet that hung along her breast.

"I've no idea, for example, how they breathe life into their golems. Even with this"—she gripped the amulet tightly—"I can do no such thing." She poured a thin stream of the brown liquid onto the figure. She took great care to wet every part of it—legs, chest, arms, then head. The clay glistened. It absorbed the liquid like a sponge, Kiral saw, swelling as Meryam turned the figure over and poured more onto its back. "They're said to have intelligence of a sort, a will. It's a wondrous achievement. Still, golems are considered, at best, simplistic, vastly inferior to a soul given life in the womb. And it makes me wonder, have they simply not tried hard enough? Are they not bold enough to grant true life to such creatures? I'll admit I don't know the answer." She set the liquid down and regarded Kiral carefully. "But it's something I hope to investigate further once I sit the throne of Sharakhai."

Even before the full meaning of her words washed over him, Kiral felt his heart beat faster, louder. *She* would sit the throne? It was such an outrageous statement he thought it was said only in jest. But her eyes were all too serious.

You think to take my throne? he tried to ask, but nothing came from his mouth. He tried again, but his tongue, his lips, refused to respond. He felt made of clay, like the figure on the plate.

His breath came faster. His heart pounded so hard he could feel it pulse through his fingertips. He felt his scalp prickle as sweat began to form. He tried to stand, but abandoned the effort a moment later as impossible. He tried to move one arm instead. *Do that,* he told himself, *and it would lead to more.*

But his arm was little more than flesh around a dead man's bones.

Draw your knife, he raged. *Draw your knife and you might yet escape this cabin with your life!*

Meryam went on as if she were unaware that he was waging a silent battle within. "I have learned *some* things, however." She motioned to the wet clay figure. "How one commands flesh, for example. Even the most willful among us." Her polite smile broadened. "Even those protected by the desert gods themselves."

A trickle of sweat crept through his closely shorn hair, slipped down his temple, then his cheek. He struggled as never before. Miraculously, his right arm began to move. It slipped from the armrest, crept along his waist, inching toward the hilt of his ornamented kenshar.

Meryam's eyebrows rose. "I am impressed, my Lord King." When he managed to slip his hand around the ivory handle, she picked up the clay figure and moved its right arm. Kiral's arm mirrored the movement, returning to the armrest. "Even after all I've done, steps I was assured would subdue you utterly"—she motioned to his arm—"you've managed this. Amazing."

When Kiral managed to utter a single word, "How?" it came out in a drunkard's slur.

"Why, with your own blood, my Lord King." Meryam poured more of the liquid onto the figure. As the clay soaked it up, Kiral felt the severing of his body from his will. "Taken in the yard of Thaash's temple."

Gods, Kiral realized, *the woman. Amaryllis.*

She'd been at the temple. She'd pressed the skirt of her dress to the wounds he'd sustained when the ehrekh had attacked. She'd taken it and delivered it to her queen.

He swung his gaze up to Amaryllis, who looked on with a dispassion that made him go cold. His breath now came in terrible, wheezing gasps. When Meryam began stroking the chest of the figure, however, his breathing slowed. For all the calm on the exterior, his terror was soaring to levels he hadn't experienced since the moment he'd first seen the might of the gathered tribes four hundred years before. In that moment, he'd felt his own death. He felt the same now, a certainty that the brightness of the desert would dim from his eyes. This time the gods would not save him. They'd come to him those many years ago, only him, days before Beht Ihman, dangling immortality before his eyes. He'd taken it, vowing to himself, if not the gods, that he would compel the others to go along with him. What was one in thirteen when all of them might otherwise perish?

They'd agreed. They'd given up the haughty Sehid-Alaz and his people and gained life for so many. But nothing so momentous as that went unnoticed in the desert. He'd always known that one day the fates would come to collect their due.

Here, in the ship, or perhaps when the sun rose, the lord of all things would come for him. The only question remaining was the manner of his death. That question was answered a moment later, part of it in any case, when the cabin door behind him opened and a man stepped into view. A man with a long beard, a long face, and expressive eyes.

"It's done?" Hamzakiir asked.

"It's done." Meryam said as she motioned to Kiral. "Best we move quickly."

"Very well." Hamzakiir turned Kiral's chair so that it faced him and not the table. "If you please . . ."

Meryam took the head of the clay figure and tipped it back. Kiral's body immediately followed suit and his mouth opened of its own accord. He knew what was about to happen, and still he was startled when something sharp pierced his right wrist; and then dumbfounded when Hamzakiir held his own wounded wrist over Kiral's open mouth. Blood trickled against his lips and tongue. The bitter copper taste spread down his throat as Hamzakiir's beard tickled his wrist. He could see nothing save the wooden beams above him, the decking boards, but he felt Hamzakiir's lips as they were pressed to his own wounded wrist. The two of them were *exchanging* blood.

A warmth filled his gut, but his fingers had gone cold. The two feelings warred, the warmth within spreading outward as rivers of cold traveled backward from his fingers, along his wrists, up his arms, and across his shoulders. The two sensations were in such direct opposition, he felt as if he were being torn in two.

How long this went on he couldn't say. The moments were strung together by threads of growing horror.

"It's enough, I think," Meryam said.

"We must be sure," Hamzakiir replied, ignoring her implied command.

"It's enough," Meryam repeated.

"I'll not risk my life because—"

"Enough," Meryam said.

Hamzakiir blinked rapidly, as if he were trying to wake himself, then ran a finger over the dripping wound on his wrist. A sizzling sound filled the air. A bit of smoke lifted from his wrist. And the bleeding had stopped. He did the same to Kiral. Other than a small discoloration on his wrist, there was no evidence of the puncture. Not even a trace of blood remained.

"A few more drops won't make a difference one way or another, and we have more to do tonight."

His head lowered. Where Hamzakiir had been sitting earlier, he saw a different man. One with closely shorn hair. Stubble along a strong jaw. Pockmarked skin, one small remnant of a childhood disease that had wracked his body for months and nearly killed him.

Any who looked at him would say here stands Kiral Ranan'ala, the Sun King, the King of Kings, a white tree of Tribe Halarijan. It was so complete, even down to the way he squinted when collecting his thoughts, Kiral had to admire it.

And he, in turn, must look like Hamzakiir.

What now? he tried to ask, but whatever free will he'd managed to summon earlier was gone. He was a spectator in this play. Nothing more.

What followed felt dreamlike. Amaryllis helped Hamzakiir to exchange clothes with Kiral. They spoke softly as they worked, but their words somehow slipped past him, strangely muted, as if he had wax in his ears. When it was done, he was commanded to stand and move to the cabin window. As his body complied, he wondered how they'd orchestrated it all, and what they planned to do next. Hamzakiir would take Kiral's place in Eventide, that much was certain. From there, they could ensure that Qaimir became favored in Sharakhai. The other Kings would remain oblivious to the truth.

How long before they stood alone on Tauriyat? A month? A year?

Kiral moved to the window. Slipped through it and down to the sand. He walked east as the stars shone above. It came as no surprise that neither moon had risen; Kiral was certain the gods had abandoned him.

As he made for the ships in the distance, not a single person from their camp called out to him. Not a single soul barred his way.

The sand beneath his boots felt soft, welcoming. It felt right, this walk, proper in the grand scheme of things. He'd not thought to return to the desert as anything but a conquerer, but to go like this, alone, felt as if he were going to speak to a dear friend, long forgotten.

In that moment, as he studied the stars above the horizon, he understood the second part of their plan, their plan for *him*. They must snuff out the legend of Hamzakiir for their grand ruse to succeed. And here he was, dressed in Hamzakiir's clothing and wearing his likeness.

And to think, it was by my hand that so many moves were made in order to see Hamzakiir dead.

For the first time in a long while, he wished Ihsan was here. The man was a jongleur in King's clothing, a fool in royal livery, and Kiral hated him for it, but he would have appreciated the beauty of this grand joke.

Had he the ability to laugh, he most certainly would have, but he didn't, so he trudged on, his possessed steps carrying him ever closer to Onur's camp.

Chapter 58

THROUGH THE BLANKET that was draped over him, Brama studied the comings and goings from the galleon anchored a hundred paces distant. He'd left Amansir and his men hours ago, wending his way closer and closer to the Kings' ships. Only a short while ago, he'd seen Queen Meryam standing on the foredeck beside the King of Kings himself. They'd gone belowdecks after a brief talk—to do what, exactly, Brama wasn't sure, but he planned to find out.

For the hundredth time on his journey from Amansir's yacht, he clutched the bag at his belt and felt the round shape of the obsidian stone within it—the stone he'd procured before hiding in the old watchtower near the Qaimiri embassy house. It would be needed to name Rümayesh if he somehow managed to smash the sapphire.

He'd debated for days on the wisdom of his plan, but he saw no alternative. He'd already given in to the urge of trying to free Rümayesh, and there were really only two alternatives for doing so: somehow steal the gem away or break the sapphire. The former seemed the simplest route, and perhaps slightly less dangerous, but it would leave the sapphire intact. He'd be beholden to Rümayesh as he was before, and he'd do everything in his power to see that he didn't fall back into his old life.

No, the only way he might see himself freed was to smash the sapphire and release Rümayesh. If Queen Meryam wasn't dead by then, Rümayesh would surely take her revenge against her. But even if Meryam was dead, Brama hoped that Rümayesh would be grateful, and see to it that he be given back what remained of his life to live as he pleased.

Listen to yourself, you bloody coward. A real man would kill himself and leave Rümayesh to whatever fate awaited her.

The thoughts were his own, but they felt like Rümayesh taunting him in that tower those many years ago. He could even hear his own pitiful reply. *I never claimed to be brave.*

Beyond the galleon, several fires had been lit. Dozens of Silver Spears and Blade Maidens wandered the area, some on sentry duty, others setting their ships to rights, others still tending to the meal. Brama's mouth watered at the smell of roast lamb as the heat of late afternoon finally gave way to night. *And thank the bloody gods.* With the air so strangely deadened, his path over the burning sand had made him feel like a piece of bacon, fried and tossed aside as inedible.

The cover of night allowed him faster movement. Over the course of the next hour, he inched closer and closer to the galleon, but froze, blood draining from his cheeks, when a Blade Maiden wearing a turban and a red battle dress dropped down from the ship and began jogging over the sand.

He'd never seen one wearing a blood-red dress before. Just looking at her made his throat go tight. He was sure she was different from the other Maidens, special, but exactly *how,* he wasn't certain. *Nor do I wish to find out.*

The blanket hid him well. He'd treated it with horse glue, then caked it in sand so that it was almost impossible to pick it out in the desert, especially from a distance. Still, this woman was a *Maiden.* One had but to enter the desert to be regaled with stories of how they could sense enemies, even fight them, in pitch darkness. He was certain she'd sensed him when she cast her gaze across the horizon.

But then someone called to her—another Maiden, though this one wore black. The two of them continued on toward the next ship over, another stout galleon.

The blood slowly returned to Brama's cheeks. *I promise you, Bakhi, coins in your alms basket for a month. For a year.* Then he began moving with speed toward the galleon.

As he neared the ship, something made him pause. Until now, he'd felt Rümayesh's gem as he'd always felt it—a hollow space inside his chest. It had been an unerring guide since leaving Sharakhai with Lord Amansir. But now he felt more. It was like the disorientation of falling in a dream only to wake and find oneself lying safe in bed. Rümayesh was being made to perform magic, he knew. He had no idea what the queen might be doing, but he knew that it was strong, and that it had something to do with Kiral, the King of Kings, who had gone belowdecks with Meryam moments ago.

With the fires casting deep shadows on this side of the ship, Brama slipped out from under the blanket and moved low and fast to the starboard ski. He climbed up along the ship's hull, fingers finding purchase between the planks, and came at last to a cabin window. He watched through blinds as King Kiral pulled a fine kaftan over his well-muscled frame. In a chair, sitting across from Meryam, was a man with a long, pepper-gray beard. His eyes were dull, his movements mechanical as he put his arms through the sleeves of a dark thawb. He seemed stricken with shock, numb to all but his thoughts. Who he was, and why these two men were getting dressed, Brama had no idea.

What magic had Meryam just performed? And on which of them? Most importantly, *why* had she done it?

Brama felt another twist inside his chest—Meryam drawing on the gemstone again. The man in the chair stood. Like heat lifting from the desert floor his form began to waver, to shimmer, and then, breath of the desert, he turned transparent as glass. Brama could see him only by his barest outline.

Oh gods, he's heading for the window.

Brama dropped to the sand and waited, breathless. He heard the sound of scrabbling, of scraping, and then something landed on the sand next to him. It was the man Meryam had cloaked with her magic. Brama could see the horizon smudging like coal on paper as he walked eastward.

As the sound of his trudging footsteps faded, the windows above were shut with a creak of poorly oiled hinges and the clatter of blinds.

Kiral's deep voice resonated from inside the cabin. "Shall we begin?"

"Yes, but not here," came Meryam's voice. "Let's retire to the desert."

Whatever they were going to do, Brama was certain it was important. The sounds within the cabin soon softened, and then he heard them coming to deck and walking along the gangplank set on the port side of the ship. King Kiral and Queen Meryam came down to the sand, where a Blade Maiden met them, a warden with four other Maidens standing behind her ready to join the King.

"We will go alone," King Kiral said.

The warden bowed her head immediately. "As you wish, my Lord King." But Brama noticed the shared look of confusion between the Maidens standing behind her.

Off they went, Meryam and Kiral walking side by side, until they were lost to the darkness of the dunes. Brama waited for a time, ensuring no one was still watching the path they'd followed, then crouched and followed along their path. As he padded softly over the sand, the hollow feeling inside his chest expanded.

Brama?

That old familiar voice. The one he'd grown to despise. The one he couldn't ignore. He knew it was lunacy to speak to her with Meryam so wary of danger, but after a moment he found himself replying.

Yes, he intoned, feeling like a fish on a hook.

As I'd dreamed, you've come for me! The voice was as faint as the wind on a cool desert night, likely due as much to Meryam's lead-lined amulet as any precautions on Rümayesh's part.

I've not come for you.

Have you not? That knowing tone of hers. *Then why?*

For me, he wanted to say, but it sounded weak and foolish.

Just then, Meryam stopped. The sapphire at her neck began to glow softly, casting the sand all around them a snowy blue. She motioned Kiral to stand across from her.

Kiral did, his eyes glinting as he watched Meryam pull a stopper from an ampule of dark liquid. "Be careful," he said, "leave none of your own scent upon this summoning or the ehrekh may come for you."

Meryam, her face ghastly in the pale light, nodded and tipped the ampule over. As the liquid pattered onto the sand near her feet, Brama felt her drawing on Rümayesh's power. "I summon thee, Guhldrathen, with the blood of the one you seek."

In the silence that followed, Brama heard Rümayesh's desperate voice. *Come, Brama. Do it now!*

Brama found himself rising to a half-crouch, one hand gripping the obsidian stone in the pouch at his belt. With Meryam occupied and Kiral transfixed by the ritual unfolding before him, the urge to rise and sprint toward them was strong and growing stronger.

Meryam tipped the ampule over a second time. "I draw you near, Guhldrathen, with the blood of the one you covet."

Do you wish me to beg, Brama? Come. You will have no better chance than this!

It was true. Meryam and Kiral stood transfixed as they stared at the sand. Yet Brama remained where he was as Meryam emptied the ampule. He could smell it on the wind, a bitter copper scent.

Kneeling, Meryam placed her hand on the black spot on the sand. With her other, she gripped the sapphire at her neck.

By the dark god's smile, now! Now! Drive your knife into her back before she returns to her senses!

The urge to charge, knife drawn, was so strong he realized he'd taken a step forward only when he'd heard his footfall. He could kill them both and free himself from the constant desire, the *need*, to liberate the creature that had tortured him for months. With a force of will, he held himself still. He wasn't even sure why, not until he heard that old voice, his own, whispering to him: *She nearly has you. If you give yourself over to her now, there will be no going back.*

Ahead, Meryam's voice gained in volume and pitch until it felt as if she were screaming. "Come, Guhldrathen, that you may devour Çedamihn Ahyanesh'ala! Come, that you may consume the heart of the White Wolf! And know that when you do, you will find Hamzakiir, the one who tricked you, the one who has for so long eluded you. Thus will you satisfy your undying hunger, Guhldrathen. Thus is my debt paid. Come hither with haste, and find not one, but both."

That name . . . Çedamihn . . .

Amansir said she was in danger—a sacrifice to Guhldrathen so that Meryam might have her way in all this—but Brama hadn't really believed it until now. It had seemed too unlikely that the thread of Çeda's life would once more intertwine with his. Çeda, after all, had been the one to draw him into Rümayesh's web. She'd been the one to save him from her as well, when Rümayesh would have kept him as a pet, to torture him until she'd found someone else and tossed him aside. It was the remembrance of all Rümayesh had done to him, the pain she'd inflicted upon him—*gods, how distant it seems now*—that allowed him to drive his kenshar into its sheath, to lie down on the sand and wait.

For a long while all was silence save for the sounds coming from the line of ships. "Is it done?" Kiral asked.

Limbs trembling, Meryam lifted herself up off the sand, but she was so weak she couldn't seem to make it onto her legs. "Don't just stand there." The words were biting, but also faint, as if she had trouble voicing them.

Kiral came to her side and helped her to stand. "Is it *done*?"

"Yes. It's on the move. I can feel it."

"It won't arrive too soon, I hope."

"No," Meryam said as she dusted her hands free of the bloody sand caked on them. As the amulet began to lose its glow, she met Kiral's gaze. "It will be after noon, I suspect. The question now is whether his quarry will still be alive or not."

"He will," Kiral said flatly. "Onur has agreed to stand with the Kings, at least until the thirteenth tribe has been destroyed once and for all. I'm more worried the ehrekh will suspect our treachery."

Meryam laughed darkly. "As you should be, but it's done now. The fates will see to the rest."

As the two of them headed side by side toward the King's galleon, the amulet's light failed altogether, and their silhouettes played against the wavering light of the distant cook fires. Brama waited until they were far enough away, then he stood and ran for the deeper desert.

Chapter 59

S ALSANNA DROPPED to the sand beside Leorah, who lay unmoving after the spectacle of chasing the wyrm from the battlefield. Çeda ran toward them, but slowed her pace as a horn blew. Another followed. Then another. These were their own horns: Tribe Kadri's, Tribe Khiyanat's.

Gasps followed. People pointed along the horizon, their faces filled with fear, anger, even grim acceptance, as if they'd expected something like this all along. Çeda came to a standstill and saw what the others had already seen. Ships. Royal galleons. By Tulathan's bright eyes, there were *scores* of them headed their way.

The sound of footsteps made her turn. Sümeya was there. Melis as well. Macide and Ishaq, father and son, bloodied and bruised, were beside them, with Frail Lemi and Hamid and, thank the gods, Emre trailing behind.

"Why are they slowing?" Frail Lemi asked.

Indeed, many of the ships were coming to a halt. Their sails hardly billowed in a strangely deadened wind.

Frail Lemi motioned to Leorah. "Did *she* do it?"

"No, Lemi," Ishaq replied calmly. "The doldrums come often enough this time of year."

"That's true," Sümeya said, "but chances are it won't last long. It could lift in the night, or in the morning. When it does, the Kings will attack. Best if you ready all the ships you can and set sail when it does."

Ishaq took in the devastation, the hundreds moving to help the wounded onto ships. "Look around you. I'd be surprised if half our ships could sail by morning, and of those, some will be hobbled. The Kings have royal galleons and clippers. Half our number would be left to die here, and more would die as the Kings took our ships at their leisure."

Sümeya's stare, her very stance, was unforgiving. "Would it not be better if some lived?"

Ishaq looked at her bitterly, as if he'd expected nothing less from a Blade Maiden. He pointed Çeda toward Leorah. "Go. We'll speak after the sun has set." And then he walked with Macide toward the shade of a nearby clipper, where many of the wounded were being taken.

After a nod to Sümeya, an indicator that they would speak soon, Çeda rushed to Leorah's side. Salsanna was sprinkling water from a flask over Leorah's dress and hijab. Leorah's breathing was shallow, her skin deathly pale, but there was a contented smile on her lips. She seemed only to be sleeping, but responded neither to gentle shaking nor shouts for her to wake.

Dardzada soon arrived with his ungainly medicinals bag and began rummaging inside it. He moved slowly due to his wounded shoulder but tended to her like a dutiful son, a strange yet welcome thing coming from a man who was so often quarrelsome.

As the sun began to set, Leorah was still unsteady, so they called Frail Lemi to carry her to her yacht. Dardzada took up Nalamae's staff and went with them, leaving Çeda alone with Salsanna. Part of Çeda wanted join them—she needed to know more about the staff, how Leorah had come to possess it, but she was in no state to talk, and there was more Çeda needed to tend to, in any case.

"Will you walk with me?" Çeda asked Salsanna. "I need to find Zaïde."

Salsanna nodded, and the two of them fell into step. As their strides carried them over the grasping sand, it was clear that something was on Salsanna's mind—she knit her brow and avoided Çeda's gaze—but she remained silent as they headed toward the site of Çeda's battle with Onur.

"Is it Kerim that troubles you so?" Çeda asked.

They were nearing the place where Zaïde's body had been laid out with dozens of others. Beyond them, set apart, was Kerim. Still. Lifeless.

"Yes," Salsanna replied, "but . . ." She looked down and pulled the golden band from her wrist, then handed it to Çeda. "Keep this, won't you? Hear them. Their call is strong at the moment."

She accepted the weighty band. "I will, of course, but—"

"I need a bit of time, Çeda." She motioned to Zaïde. "You have grieving to do. We'll speak again tonight."

"Of course, but where are you going?"

"There are those I must speak with."

She looked like she'd had a revelation of some sort. Çeda wanted to demand who she wanted to speak with, and why, but Salsanna was already running toward the *Amaranth*. She seemed to have had some sort of revelation but, apparently, the mystery would have to wait.

She'd changed greatly in the weeks Çeda had been gone. She'd been so *angry* when the two of them had sailed from the old tower in the desert. She'd *wanted* to fight Çeda. It was foolish but Çeda took the bait, and the zeal with which Salsanna had fought had revealed how deeply her anger went. Yet, as unfortunate as the skirmish had been, it had brought Salsanna and Kerim together. Kerim had changed Salsanna, shown her the truth in a way that words never could. As outwardly angry as she'd been when they met, she was inwardly focused now.

As Salsanna had urged her, Çeda felt for the souls trapped within the bracelet. Salsanna was right—they were active and Çeda could feel their sorrow at the loss of Kerim—but beyond that she felt little change from the weeks she'd worn it after killing Mesut on the Night of Endless Swords.

All around her, many were tending to the wounded, others to the dead. Others worked the ships, repairing them, preparing them to sail should Ishaq send the call to flee. Çeda, meanwhile, slipped the golden band over her wrist and walked along the line of dead. The effects of the petal she'd taken before the battle had worn off, and her wounds were fully awake. They needed tending to, but not yet.

Just as she reached Zaïde's body, she hear a voice call out behind her. "Do you still think Ishaq was wise to summon your tribe from hiding?"

Çeda turned as Sümeya approached. She stopped, across from Çeda, on the other side of Zaïde's body. Her face was unreadable. Pity? Contempt? *Perhaps both.*

"I don't know," Çeda replied. "The very notion of being together fills me with joy, but this . . ." Some of the dead had been wrapped in canvas from sails or cloth scavenged from the Black Spear ships, but so many had died that not all could be covered as they deserved. Not yet, in any case. Not until the battle had been decided. "Some will die tonight, and many more tomorrow, perhaps all of us. But Ishaq was right. Had he done nothing, the Kings could have killed us at their ease. Another great purge was coming, one way or another."

"I suppose you're right." She knelt by Zaïde's side.

Çeda dropped to the sand as well and stared at Zaïde's slack features, now painted in blood. She looked different, neither at peace nor in pain, a forgotten vessel while her soul walked among the farther fields. "I'm sorry," Çeda whispered.

"For what?" Sümeya asked.

"I don't know." Çeda pulled Zaïde's cowl over her head, hiding her face and ravaged neck, then took out a thread and needle and began sewing the cowl closed. "She had a difficult life."

"We all have difficult lives. Our worth is measured by how we rise against adversity."

"How very trite."

"Not trite," Sümeya replied "True."

"It isn't so simple as that."

"It is *precisely* that simple. The gods give us choices every day. They give us children when none were looked for. They take our mothers and fathers too soon. They place obstacles before all that we want, or give us our deepest desire only to reveal it was just a mirage. We don't give up our responsibility to make the right choice because the decisions are *harder*. It's precisely the opposite, and the harder the choice, the more our souls are tempered by it."

Çeda motioned to Zaïde. "Did she choose her father?"

"No, but she was given choices in how to deal with him. She chose not to act every day in the House of Maidens, and she made a choice today when she threw herself against him."

Çeda stared at her. "And which was the better choice, do you think?"

Sümeya made a face, the one she always made when she thought Çeda was being impertinent. "If you're asking if I regret her sacrifice, of course I don't. She saved many. Dozens. Hundreds, perhaps my own life among them. My point is she always had more control than she thought she did, and today she proved it."

Çeda stared at her body. "She did more than save lives. She gave us an opportunity. If Ihsan's words are true, that Onur is weakened when he feasts on human flesh . . ."

Sümeya turned her gaze eastward, where Onur's ships could be seen in the distance. "Is that what you wish now, to attack Onur?"

Seeing Sümeya ready to bow to Çeda's will felt strange, but Çeda was grateful for it. "It is. But we should ask Ishaq if he thinks it wise first."

Sümeya stared open-mouthed at Çeda. "Çedamihn Ahyanesh'ala, are you prepared to take *counsel*?"

Çeda tried to hide her growing smile. "I am."

"By Tulathan's bright eyes . . ." The two of them fell into step as they walked toward Ishaq's caravel. Sümeya gave a toothy smile and threw an arm around Çeda's shoulders. "I never thought I'd see the day."

"Well, I thought it best to try it once."

"Once?"

"Before I die."

Sümeya laughed grimly, then loudly, and the stress of the battle, the relief of still being alive, so struck Çeda that she laughed right along with her.

As night fell, a fire was built. Macide was notably absent, but the rest of the tribe's elders gathered around it to speak. Their scouts had counted seventy-three royal navy ships, and Onur had escaped with thirty-five. An emissary had been sent to request parlay with the Kings, but he'd been shot with a half-dozen arrows upon voicing the request.

The Kings were here to crush the thirteenth tribe. If the Kings could manage to take Onur as well, they would likely do so, though the fact remained that he was one of their own. Had they invited him to join them? Would they work together to obliterate the thirteenth tribe and come to some arrangement afterward? Onur the Feasting King had seemed intent on taking Sharakhai down from outside its walls, but coming so near death could change a man. If the Kings had made an overture, Onur may very well have had a change of heart.

As was to be expected, the mood around the fire was grim. Ishaq always seemed to project strength, but now the decision to summon the thirteenth tribe seemed to be weighing on him. No one believed they could win in a direct assault against the Kings, least of all him.

"We should push on as soon as the wind returns," Shal'alara said. She had a bloody bandage over one eye.

"We cannot flee," Hamid replied. "If we do they'll pick off our ships one by one and have us in the end anyway. But make as though we're preparing to run, as they'll expect, and attack at the right moment . . . Then perhaps we have a chance at victory."

The words sounded foolish to Çeda, and most looked despondent, but not Emre. There was a fire in him that she hadn't seen in a long while. Not since they were children, not since before his brother, Rafa, was murdered. "We have allies in Onur's camp," he said. "We should use them. We *must* use them, or we'll be abandoning them to suffer beneath Onur."

Standing by his side was a stunning Malasani beauty named Haddad, who had joined the council after Emre petitioned Ishaq to allow it. For some unfathomable reason, Ishaq had agreed. She had so far been silent, but she didn't have to say a word to distract Çeda. She was studying Emre as if she hung on his every word. Çeda ignored her as best she could and addressed the circle.

"Onur is the key," she said. "If we kill Onur, his warriors will fight for us. Kadri certainly will, likely Masal as well, even if Salmük won't."

Emre agreed. "They'll not sit by as the Kings of Sharakhai come for us. Not after what Onur has done to them. Not if he's dead."

The circle parted to make room for Macide. "It will be more complicated than that." He had two others in tow, men Çeda thought she might never see again, certainly not together, and certainly not *here*.

The first was Ramahd Amansir, looking thinner than she remembered, more haggard. His eyes scanned the gathering, and then, when they landed on her, he stopped, frozen, as if he regretted finding her here. Or regretted *something*, in any case.

The other was Brama, the thief she'd recruited to help rid her of the eh-rekh, Rümayesh. To Çeda's great regret, it had gone awry, and had led to the riddle of scars that covered nearly every square inch of his body. When their eyes met, he looked suddenly young again, fragile and fearful, as if his thoughts had returned to that time of imprisonment and torture.

"Hamzakiir is with Onur now," Macide went on.

The flickering fire made Ishaq seem to waver, as if he were insubstantial. "How do you know?"

"I saw it," Brama cut in.

"And who are you?" Ishaq shot back.

"His name is Brama Junayd'ava," Çeda said, "and I trust him to tell me the truth."

Brama gave her a sharp nod before continuing. "Only a few hours ago, I saw Hamzakiir leave Kiral's own ship, masked by a spell of the Queen of Qaimir's making. When he left, he headed east, and later, when King Kiral and Queen Meryam were talking, they spoke of an accord with Onur. To-gether, they hope to close in on you when the wind rises."

"My queen has been in league with King Kiral for months," Ramahd added. "They're hoping to use Onur to rid themselves of you, and perhaps of Onur, but especially Hamzakiir. Kiral considers him his greatest threat."

Ishaq took Ramahd in from head to toe. "And why would *you* betray your queen by coming to us?"

"She tried to have me killed for defying her. She is a mage, like Hamzakiir, but she's also found a sapphire that contains an ehrekh, a creature Brama and Çedamihn are familiar with."

All eyes turned to Çeda. She nodded. "Years ago, with Brama's help, I trapped the ehrekh named Rümayesh in a sapphire. I didn't know that Meryam now has it."

"She does," Ramahd went on. "And the only thing stopping her from using it is another ehrekh, Guhldrathen, to whom she owes a blood debt. To whom *I* owe a blood debt. Meryam plans to honor it by delivering Hamzakiir to the ehrekh."

Ramahd was staring at Çeda strangely.

"What is it?" she asked him. "What haven't you told us?"

"Guhldrathen will come for Hamzakiir," he said, "but *your* blood was used to summon it."

A gasp ran through the gathering. Çeda raised her hand for silence, and slowly their voices settled. "Why would it want me?"

"You remember when Meryam and I were in the desert?" He paused, suddenly fumbling for his words.

"Get on with it."

He licked his lips. "Hamzakiir left me and Meryam in the desert as a sacrifice to Guhldrathen. He thought it would appease the ehrekh."

"It took King Aldouan," she said, recalling how she'd stumbled across his body in the desert, "but spared you both. Why?"

"I pleaded for our lives," Ramahd said. "I begged for more time to find Hamzakiir, and it demanded your blood."

The people around the fire faded from Çeda's consciousness. Only she and Ramahd remained. A thousand things played through her mind. Foremost was the appearance of yet another ehrekh in her life. Rümayesh had been entranced by her. Now Guhldrathen as well.

"Why?" she asked, more to herself than Ramahd.

"I cannot say," Ramahd answered. "It seemed fascinated by your tale when we first met. It knew of you even then, and when I stood before it the second time and offered my own blood as payment for our failure, it asked for yours instead."

"And you agreed."

Ramahd's jaw tightened, then he nodded.

"I would hear it from your lips."

"I was afraid, Çeda." He could hardly meet her eyes. "I wanted to leave that I might find Hamzakiir and rid us all of Guhldrathen's curse."

"Say it . . ."

"I agreed. But I never thought . . . We'd planned to find Hamzakiir."

"So you said," Çeda replied evenly. "Did you?"

Ramahd shook his head in shame. "I tried. We'd planned to find him by taking Brama's stone."

"Find him, or protect yourselves from Guhldrathen's wrath," Çeda said, piecing the puzzle together. "Isn't that the right of it?"

He nodded. "That was Meryam's plan, yes. I only wanted to save you."

The confusion in Çeda was turning to rage. "Stop saying you wanted to protect me! You're the one who placed me in danger in the first place." He started to protest, but Çeda spoke over him. "So now, after all you've done to *protect me*, Guhldrathen has been summoned here to partake of the feast Meryam has prepared."

Ramahd nodded again, and this time, Çeda gave him some credit, he stared her directly in the eye. "Yes. Which is why I've come to warn you and to do what I can to prevent it."

Suddenly the crowd around them swept back into Çeda's awareness. Emre was charging headlong for Ramahd, who must have been as caught up as Çeda was, because he hardly reacted before Emre's fist caught him across the jaw. He went down, and then Emre was on top of him, pummeling his face over and over.

Frail Lemi was nearby, shouting with boyish glee, "Get him, Emre! Cut him! Bleed him!"

Çeda grabbed Emre's arm, holding back another undefended swing. "Enough!"

Emre ignored her and managed to get in a couple more punches with his left hand before Çeda dragged him off Ramahd's limp form.

"He gave you up to that thing!" Emre shouted when he'd regained his feet.

"I know, Emre. So it's up to me what we do with him."

"No!" he drew his kenshar. "He *sacrificed* you, as if you were his to give up!"

He made for Ramahd again, but Çeda stepped between them, her hands on his chest. Emre stopped, looking as frustrated as she'd ever seen him.

Çeda spoke slowly, and only to Emre. "If what he said is true, the ehrekh is on its way. We have precious little time to decide what to do. I am not his property, Emre, but I'm not yours, either."

Emre deflated before her, and was clearly embarrassed, but Çeda didn't care.

"He is *mine* to deal with," she continued, "not yours. Do you understand?"

Emre blinked. After a deep breath, he seemed to relax, though not much. He motioned to Ramahd, who was now rolling to his feet. "Then deal with him."

Only when Emre had sheathed his knife and stepped back did Çeda turn to face Ramahd. "Is that everything?"

"Yes, but—"

"Good," Çeda said, and slapped him. Not as hard as she could have, but enough for him to remember it. "You've warned me of the dangers we now face, and I let you walk away only because it may save the lives of some of my tribe. But if I lay eyes on you again, Ramahd Amansir, we will cross blades, and it won't end until your blood feeds the Great Mother. Do you understand?"

Ramahd looked as though he wanted to say more. But when he looked around at the cold faces surrounding him, he nodded soberly and walked away.

Brama watched him go. "You're making a mistake," he said. "We need him."

Despite everything she'd just learned, she wished there was a way Ramahd could stay. She felt some of the same feelings for him as she'd had since first meeting him. But how foolish would it be for her to allow it? His loyalties were to Qaimir. She couldn't trust him not to betray her or the tribe again. "I don't need Ramahd," she said to Brama, "nor anyone like him."

The look that Brama gave her was inscrutable. He was disappointed, perhaps. Or angry. Or both. Without another word, he followed Ramahd.

Chapter 60

A TERRIBLE SENSE OF foreboding spread among the gathering as Ramahd and Brama left. Ishaq and Macide and Shal'alara all began
talking heatedly, but Çeda could hardly think. She looked upon those gathered, upon the ships lit by the firelight. This was *her* tribe. These were *her*
people. She'd hardly come to know them, and now they might be swept away
like grains of sand, never to be seen again.

*How could you have led us to this, Nalamae? How could you have aban-
doned us?*

It was then that she felt something stir. An awareness inside her grew,
indistinct at first, but slowly she realized it was emanating from the bracelet
on her right wrist. There was sorrow still, as there had been before, but there
was something else, a glimmer along the horizon.

Why, though? And why now?

At the far edge of the circle, the crowd parted and a column of women
and men, led by Salsanna, came to the center of the gathering. Leorah walked
by Salsanna's side, holding not her cane but Nalamae's staff.

"I would speak," Salsanna said. She stood resigned, even hopeful. The other men and women standing in the column behind her had the same stance, as if they were preparing for something momentous.

Salsanna faced Çeda. "I found the purpose of the bracelet." She motioned to Çeda's wrist. "I know how we can free them."

She meant the souls of the asir trapped within. "Go on," Çeda said.

"At first I thought we might release the souls in the bracelet, as Mesut did in your battle with him. But neither of us has been able to, and I fear it was a gift the gods gave only him. Then I thought perhaps we could be transformed, as you saw happen to the woman in Eventide who was forced from her own body that an asir might be remade. You told me King Mesut transferred the asir's soul, but that beforehand, King Cahil prepared her."

"He did." Something was twisting over and over again inside Çeda's gut. She didn't at all like where this was headed.

"I thought, as you did, that Cahil merely prepared her body to accept another soul. I thought we would need to make our bodies ready that the asirim might share our physical forms." Salsanna motioned to the site of the battle. "I felt the moment when Kerim died today. I was bonded to him, and it made me realize what must be done for the asirim in Mesut's cursed stone to be freed."

With sudden clarity, Çeda understood what Salsanna meant to do, and why she had brought so many to the fire.

"We cannot share this mortal coil," Salsanna went on, "but a single soul may fill a body. We must make way that the asirim might live, that they might protect us." She turned, her gaze taking in all those behind her. "We are here for that purpose. We have come that you, Çedamihn Ahyanesh'ala, might lead them once we are gone."

Tears came unbidden to Çeda's eyes. She blinked to clear them. "You mean to die that the asirim might live."

Salsanna nodded. "We will pass to the farther fields and those whose lives were taken through no fault of their own might live once more. We will pass to give them one last chance at revenge, and that our tribe might survive the coming day."

A surge of protests rose all around the fire, pleading for Ishaq to deny Salsanna's request—but Salsanna never took her eyes from Çeda's. She strode forward, Leorah's hand in hers. "It must be so." Her voice carried above the growing fervor. "And you must do it."

The protests grew louder. The asirim were feared in every corner of the desert and rightly so. They were the Kings' servants and, if such a transformation could even be accomplished, the newly made asirim might be beholden to the Kings. They would have given up lives for nothing—worse, to give the Kings fresh weapons.

"What of it?" Ishaq asked. "Why should we believe that these asirim would fight for us and not the Kings?"

All eyes turned to Çeda. Moths fluttered in her chest as she struggled to find the right words. "We've seen it already in Kerim, an asir not only willing to fight for us, but die to protect us. The first asir made from that bracelet in Eventide was forced into a new form by Kings Cahil and Mesut. Neither the woman who died in that ritual, nor the asir who took her form, wished for it. I believe it poisoned them and kept them beholden to the will of the Kings. It may be that the souls in that bracelet, when given new life, will still live beneath the yoke of the Kings. But if so, we will know it and we can stop the ritual. And remember, when they were summoned on the Night of Endless Swords and I managed to give them free will, they stormed over Mesut. They took their revenge against him and ended his life. I tell you, they want more. I say we give them that chance."

The arguments broke out again. Ishaq was calling for order. Macide and Emre and Frail Lemi were pushing some back, making room for the elders to speak. Salsanna, ignoring them all, took Çeda's right wrist and held it tenderly. "You must do this, Çeda."

The raised voices became a riot of shouts. All around her were worried faces, even angry.

"Enough!" Çeda called.

But they didn't listen, not until Ishaq held up his hands and joined her. Slowly, the noise subsided. Çeda thought Ishaq would reject Salsanna's request out of hand, but to her surprise, he waved one hand to her.

"Speak, Çedamihn."

Çeda took in the crowd anew. The moths inside her were gone, replaced by cold determination. "A grim day lies ahead," she began. "We've all taken a strange path. Wherever your families' tales have led you, they bear two things in common. They began on the night of Beht Ihman, and they all led you here."

She held the golden band high and turned it so that all could see the dark stone. "This was once King Mesut's. I cut it from his wrist. I watched him die as the souls trapped within used their brief freedom to tear the skin from his bones. They are trapped still, but Salsanna has found a way to free them, and she and the others gathered here are willing to sacrifice their lives so these unfortunate souls, your own forebears, might release their rage against the Kings. Do any here think she would say this lightly?"

The gathering was silent.

"Would you die for your tribe?" Çeda asked them.

A long moment passed. The fire played across their grim faces. No one replied, until—

"*I* would die." It was Emre, with the most serious expression she'd ever seen on his face. "I would die for my tribe," he repeated.

Behind Emre, the looming form of Frail Lemi stepped forward. "I would die beside him."

"I would die as well," said a deep voice.

Everyone turned. Macide had spoken, and it was tacit approval of what she and Salsanna were planning to do.

"Would you die that your tribe might live?" Çeda asked again.

"We would." The reply had become a refrain. It had come not only from Emre, Frail Lemi, and Macide, but several others in the crowd.

"Would you die that the name of Khiyanat might be heard across the desert?"

"We would!" This time, many more joined in.

"Would you die that your children might sail where they want, free beneath the sun?"

"We would!" Nearly everyone had now joined the chorus.

She removed the golden band from her wrist and held it against the starry night sky. "When the sun rises, we do not go to *die!* We go to *live! That* is what Salsanna offers us. That is what the asirim, trapped for so long, will deliver. They offer us *life.* Let us take it and use it against the Kings!"

Çeda paced before them. "They come for us on their galleons. They come for us with ebon steel. They come for us, their spears tipped with silver and savagery and spite. For centuries have we feared them, but tomorrow the tide will turn. *They* will know the name of fear! *They* will hear our voices raised in freedom! And they will never forget the name of Khiyanat!"

As one, they threw their hands into the air and shouted, "Khiyanat! Khiyanat!"

Everyone was caught by it. Macide, Dardzada, Shal'alara, Frail Lemi. Emre, instead of looking at her with worry—always so much worry—watched her with pride. Even Hamid seemed filled with purpose. All because of *her*. Sümeya did not shout with the others, but there was surprise in her eyes, as if she hadn't expected this from Çeda. Ishaq watched with clear pride, which somehow made Çeda keenly aware of herself, and she had to look away lest she lose her nerve.

"Go, my kinsmen," Çeda called to them. "And prepare for war!"

A great roar rose from the gathering and the crowd began to break apart at the edges. There were only a few hours left to make final preparations. The wind was starting to come to life, and more would likely come with the rising sun. They needed to be ready to sail.

Çeda wanted to speak with Emre, but he was already deep in conversation with Ishaq, Macide, and Shal'alara. It was clear that Ishaq had come around to her way of thinking. For better or worse, they would attack Onur's camp with their fleetest ships and hope to slay him. If they could do that, they might gain help from the tribes Onur had strong-armed to fight beneath his banner. Meanwhile, a larger contingent led by Macide and Emre would go after the Kings, hoping to slow them down long enough for Çeda and the others to succeed.

Her heart sinking just a little bit, she let them be, and left with Salsanna, Leorah, and all those who'd volunteered. She'd not gone ten steps into the darkness, however, when she felt a tug on her hand. She turned to see Emre.

"Go on," Çeda told Salsanna. "I'll be along shortly."

Salsanna nodded and led Leorah across the sand. For a time, Emre and Çeda merely held hands, neither sure what to say. "I always thought it would be easier," he finally said.

She knew what he meant. The Kings. Their downfall. "At least we're still alive."

His dark eyes twinkled as he shrugged. "We'll live to see the sunrise. That's no small thing in the desert."

An uncomfortable silence followed. Çeda wanted to ask Emre to join her. She wanted to abandon her plans to make for Onur like an arrow when the sun rose. She wanted to *be* with him, but she knew she couldn't. He seemed to sense it as well.

"Whatever happens," he said, "we've done this much. Whatever happens, the Kings will fall."

"You're underestimating their resourcefulness."

"No, I'm not. The mountain has been chipped away at the base. Nothing will stop it from crumbling now. That's thanks to you, Çeda. *You* did that."

"It wasn't me."

He went on as if she hadn't spoken. "I should never have doubted you. I should have stopped trying to protect you a long time ago."

This was what he'd come to say, she realized. She kissed his neck, then held his face in both her hands and kissed him full on the lips. He warmed to it, and when he kissed her back, *really* kissed her, time froze for a moment. She felt the desert wind, cool on her skin. Heard the soft jingle of rigging. Felt the sand shift beneath her feet, while their lips shared stories.

At last she pulled away. "Time marches on, Emre. We must too."

"I know." He jutted his chin toward the fire. "What you did back there. What you're about to do. It's what they needed. What we all needed."

She felt tears coming to her eyes. "I should go." If she didn't, she wasn't sure she could leave his side.

"Not yet," he said, reaching into a pouch at his belt. "I have something for you." He retrieved a small metal flask, no larger than a walnut, and held it out to her.

"What is it?"

He unscrewed the top and tipped the flask toward her. It was a clear liquid that *glowed* a faint blue.

"Emre, what is it?"

"It's one of the elixirs that were hidden away in Eventide."

"You said they were all destroyed."

That roguish grin of his broke across his face. "One of them must have slipped into my pouch." He screwed the cap back on and offered it to her again.

She was already shaking her head. "No, Emre."

"You're always saving me, Çeda. Let me do something for you."

"No. Whatever I do, it will fail unless *you* succeed. Take it with you, knowing your mission against Kiral has a better chance of succeeding."

"Çeda—"

"I won't take it, Emre." She started backing away.

He looked crestfallen, but not as much as she would have guessed. "Mule."

She couldn't help it. She smiled. "Ass."

"I'll go, but the price is another kiss."

"You don't want one from your precious Haddad?"

Emre's head jerked back. "Haddad? I'm surprised you noticed her."

"Breath of the desert, Emre, she's pretty enough for *everyone* to have noticed her."

"She is but a rough stone compared to you."

It was a terrible attempt at flattery, but it warmed her heart like nothing had in many months. She swept forward and kissed him again, more passionately than before.

When she broke away, his smile was broad as the sunrise. "Well then! I'll have another when I see you again!"

"Oh you will, will you?"

He smiled his old smile, the one that made her melt. "See if I don't!"

A sigh escaped her as he jogged across the sand. She didn't wish for them to part, but it had been the perfect time to see him. How better to bolster her heart before the dark, terrible business ahead?

She rejoined Leorah and the others, who had found a place along the top of a dune near the center of their fleet. In the hour that followed, Çeda spoke to each of the volunteers in turn. She learned their names and their stories. Seventeen souls, the same number as those within the bracelet. She was constantly aware of the jet stone. She listened to the souls within, felt them stir as a man told of his time in the northern reaches of the desert, and another spoke of working as a shipwright. With Salsanna she took particular care. As the daughter of a weaver and a hunter, as a girl who took to both swords and music at an early age, who was later introduced to Leorah and became fascinated with stories of the thirteenth tribe, Salsanna's story summoned the strongest of the souls within the stone, and by far the most violent.

Salsanna's sacrifice will grant you life, Çeda whispered to it. *Remember her, and let your enemies quake.*

The wind, as many had predicted, began to lift with the coming dawn. The tribe gathered in a circle. All around, the ships had been prepared. A bell began to ring, warning that Onur's ships were on the move. It was quickly silenced by Ishaq as the thirteenth tribe gathered around Çeda and the Forsaken, as they'd already been dubbed. They wore no sandals, nor any other adornment. Each was wrapped in white gauze, to help their passage to the farther fields. Leorah had painted ancient symbols over their faces and along their palms. Save for the flush in their skin, they already looked like the gathering of wights that had risen from Mesut's stone on the Night of Endless Swords.

With Leorah by her side, Çeda moved to the first, Fahrel, a woman no older than Çeda, with bright brown eyes and rose-petal lips. She was breathing so quickly Çeda thought she might lose heart.

"You are the light that guides us," Çeda said to her, then kissed her forehead.

The woman, heartened, squeezed Çeda's hands, and tipped her head back. And with that, Çeda summoned the first of the souls. As she had on the Night of Endless Swords, she opened her heart wide and gave herself to them. Slowly, the soul came forth. The amethyst on Leorah's right hand shone like a beacon as she helped to guide it.

Fahrel gasped. A moan escaped her, one filled with pain and sorrow. And then, like the quieting of a winter breeze, Çeda felt Fahrel's soul depart. Her skin turned ashen. Her eyelids fluttered as the color in her eyes turned to ice. In her place stood another. Çeda could see it in the intensity of her eyes, which had been cast anew. That unchained soul stared about the circle. Her nostrils flared. Her lips drew back to reveal a row of perfect teeth. Everything about her spoke of the desire to fly over the desert, to expend her rage upon her enemies.

Çeda moved to the next in the circle, Stavehn, a stout man with a misshapen face and a bulbous nose. "You are the light that guides us," Çeda said and kissed his forehead.

He did not stare at the sky as his soul departed, but at Çeda, his impotent fury plain to see. The asir that filled his form kept that intensity, but the mood had changed. He was a vessel filled with power: trapped lightning, ready to be unleashed.

One by one Çeda and Leorah walked along the circle, and one by one an asir took the form of the man or woman before her until only Salsanna remained. Çeda wanted to spare her. She'd hardly come to know this valiant woman and now she was leaving. But to question her would be to insult her gravely, so she nodded, and Salsanna nodded back.

"Go well," Çeda said to her.

"May we meet again," Salsanna replied.

Çeda guided the last, and Salsanna departed these shores. In her place stood someone who sent a chill along Çeda's spine. The other asirim held power, but this one held more. Like Sehid-Alaz, like Kerim, like Havva, she was so intense she burned from within.

Çeda heard a crack, like the breaking of fine porcelain. She looked down and saw the jet stone had broken down the middle. As she watched another fissure appeared, and another, dark fragments breaking away and falling to the amber sand until none remained in the bracelet's artful setting.

As Çeda removed the bracelet and tossed it among the black fragments, the sun crested the horizon. It shone bright and beautiful upon all those gathered. Çeda thought the Forsaken would be bent as the asirim. But they weren't. They stood tall, holy avengers unsullied by the taint of the Sharakhani Kings.

All those gathered stared in awe and no one appeared ready to speak, as if doing so might change their nature, might bend their backs and turn them into the servants of the Kings once more.

When another bell rang, the spell was broken.

"The Kings' ships are moving!" the lookout called.

The wind was strong and growing stronger. "Battle is upon us!" Ishaq called.

The thirteenth tribe obeyed and spread to their assigned ships. Çeda was about to move toward hers when she saw how bent Leorah was, how weak. "Come, grandmother," Çeda said. "You and your sister have done well."

Leorah looked up with surprise in her eyes. "You know?"

"I suspected, ever since Salsanna told me the story of Devorah. As I feel the asirim, I felt Devorah within the amethyst, though at first I didn't recognize it as such. Once I did, I began to sense changes at dusk and dawn, when your souls shift between body and stone." Çeda gripped Leorah's right hand, the one with the great amethyst ring. "It's how you were able to help shepherd the Forsaken into their new forms, yes?"

Leorah nodded, her eyes suddenly misty. "I'm glad you know, child."

"I am too," Çeda replied. "I feel both of you now, lending one another strength. She's carried you for some time, but she doesn't do so alone. I'll help as I can."

"Very well, child." Leorah smiled a grandmother's smile, and motioned to her yacht. "Come with me. I've fight in me yet."

Me too, Çeda thought, and led her onward.

Chapter 61

THE *AUTUMN ROSE* SAILED the morning sand. Shaikh Aríz's crew was tense but ready. None of the grim determination they'd shown by the fireside had diminished. If anything, it seemed more intense now that the time for battle was upon them.

Well and good, Emre thought. *We'll need all the bravery we can get.*

He stood amidships, watching their fleet of thirty sail ever closer to the Kings' line of navy ships. *Thirty against their seventy-three.* Impossible odds already, but there was Çeda's mission to consider as well. She hoped to press deep into the Black Spear fleet and kill Onur, then rally the other tribes to join their cause against the Kings. Emre saw her fleet sailing in the opposite direction: nine ships readying their attack against Onur.

"Nine bloody ships," he said under his breath. "What madness have we given birth to?"

It wasn't only that they were facing similar odds against Onur. It was that they had to move quickly if any of this was going to work. Wait too long and the Kings' ships will have decimated Macide's cadre of ships.

The only saving grace was that the Kings had spread their fleet thin before the wind dropped. They must have been counting on the thirteenth tribe to flee, perhaps in many directions at once. Their spread formation would allow them to divert two ships to every one that fled and still have ships left over. And if the tribe chose to flee in a tight cluster, the Kings' faster ships would be able to slow them down while others sailed in behind to finish them off.

Haddad stood near Emre with a bright red scarf wrapped around her head. The tail blew in the early morning wind. "This isn't a bad way to die."

"I'd prefer not to die at all."

"Who doesn't? But the lord of all things comes for us all. Wouldn't you rather that day be grand?" She waved her arms wide. "However it ends, this is a day the desert will sing about for a thousand years."

"Perhaps, but if we lose, we'll be painted as the villains. Is that what you want?"

"The victors may spin their tales, Emre, but the truth will find its way free. So be bold. Be brave. Let the fates see to the rest."

Emre's laugh was cut short when a shout came from belowdecks. Moments later, three crewmen emerged with two familiar faces coming up the ladder behind them: Ramahd and Brama. Frail Lemi trailed behind them, cracking his knuckles with a look like he hoped they would try something.

Emre met them near the hatch. Haddad joined him, as did Aríz, Tribe Kadri's young shaikh. "Surely my eyes deceive me," Emre said. "Brama Junayd'ava and Ramahd bloody fucking Amansir? I'd wager my left nut you were both told to leave the desert behind."

Frail Lemi laughed. "Left nut . . ."

Brama stared at Emre with that same cocksure look he'd had when he was young, the one that dared him to say something smart to him again. It had always been a bit of a joke back then. No one had ever mistaken Brama for a fighter—he'd been nothing but a thief, a second story man—but this was not the same Brama. The scars over his face spoke of a different man, as did his expression, which reminded Emre of the massive rats that plagued the west end. They were bold, those things. It sent chills down the spine just to look at them.

Ramahd was different. He was staring at Emre as a man lost in the desert views an oasis. He wanted something, but just then Emre didn't care what. He pulled his knife and advanced on him.

"Stop, or Çeda dies," Ramahd said quickly.

Emre stayed his hand. He gripped the knife, certain that whatever Ramahd had to say would be a lie. But what if it wasn't? He was many things, but he'd never struck Emre as a liar. "This had better change my mind."

"You heard me at the council. Every word of it was true. Before the sun has set, Guhldrathen will be here. Çeda's in grave danger, but there's a way we might save her."

In the distance, the Kings' fleet loomed. It wouldn't be long before they met in battle. "How?" Emre said.

Ramahd's relief was clear, not only in his face, but in the way his words almost tripped over themselves. "You've heard the stories of the ehrekh. How dangerous they are. How angered they become when betrayed."

Emre brandished his kenshar. "We have no time for *stories*, Lord Amansir!"

Ramahd tipped his head toward Brama. "He has an obsidian stone with him. If we break the sapphire that traps Meryam's ehrekh, it will be freed, but with the stone, he can control it. Can you imagine the devastation it might wreak upon the Kings' fleet?"

"*Is* there a stone?" Emre asked the men holding Brama.

They patted Brama down and found a pouch inside his trousers. Inside was a disc of black, glasslike obsidian. Emre took it, but felt nothing special about it. "How can this free the ehrekh?"

"No," Brama replied, "we must break the sapphire around Queen Meryam's neck first. That"—he nodded toward the obsidian—"will make her bend to my will."

Emre shook his head. "I don't understand."

"Believe me when I say it will work," Brama said. "But even if you choose not to believe me, I'm offering you a powerful tool, one the Kings would surely use against you."

"This smells, Brama." Emre held the stone to the morning light and saw the sun shine through it like a silver coin in sepia ink. "It smells of ox dung and goat piss. The ehrekh cannot be *controlled*."

"Perhaps you're right," Brama replied. "But what's your alternative? Run the Kings into the sand beneath the skis of your mighty fleet?" He made a show of looking along the line of the tribe's ships. "Setting aside the Kings themselves, and the blood mage, Meryam, they still outnumber you three to one. They boast the finest ships in the desert and crews who know them better than you know your own cock. Are you ready to stand against a thousand Spears and a hundred ebon blades? Your hope of Çeda and Ishaq overcoming Onur in time to turn the tide is a mummer's fancy. *None* of you will last. Not you, not Macide"—he looked to Haddad—"not your pretty friend from Malasan, and not Çeda."

Brama's eyes burned like a demon in the night. "But consider this alternative. I know the ehrekh, Emre. There's a reason the Kings fear them. There's a reason spells were put upon the city walls to keep them out. But imagine if one were to land in the middle of their precious fleet. We'll likely die either way, but at least we'll have pissed in their soup before we feed the Great Mother. Imagine telling *that* story to Rafa when you reach the farther fields."

There was a manic glee in Brama's grin that gave Emre hope. A normal man would quake at what lay before them, but Brama stood unafraid.

No, not merely unafraid. Eager.

The deck shifted as they crested a shallow dune. In that moment Emre noticed the crew. Truly noticed them. He'd been so intent on the day, ignoring everything else—the ship's crew, her warriors, the old, the children, the wounded—that they'd become background, a part of the coming battle instead of what the battle was about. He dearly hoped he could save Çeda, but this battle was about so much more than her.

All those on deck and in the rigging stared at him, awaiting his decision, looking to *him* for orders. He wasn't prepared for this. He wasn't prepared for any of it.

Arfz would normally look to his vizir, Ali-Budrek, but he didn't this time. He nodded to Emre, as if he sensed Emre's indecision. "Whatever you decide, Tribe Kadri will follow."

Emre couldn't lead them blindly into a battle they would lose, not without taking every opportunity to help them first. But gods, the battle was nearly on them already. The *Autumn Rose* was not a small ship, but the Kings' galleons dwarfed it.

"Do you know which ship they'll be on?"

Brama turned and pointed. "The sapphire is aboard that one, behind the line."

One of the Kings' ships sailed a quarter-league back from all the others. Several other galleons along the navy fleet's grand arc were doing the same.

These were the Kings' ships, Emre understood now, and they'd be well protected from the initial onslaught.

How to reach Queen Meryam's, then? The chances that the *Rose* would
be stopped were high, and he couldn't leave it to chance.

He turned, looking over the ship's deck, staring out across the quarterdeck
to the ships sailing in a line behind them. And then his eyes fell upon the skiff
secured to the ship's stern.

It struck him then, a crazy idea that seemed crazier by the moment. "Here,"
he called to the flagman. "Hurry. We need to send a message to Macide."

Chapter 62

ÇEDA COULD FEEL the morning's wind gaining in strength. The *Amaranth*'s sails were full, the angle was favorable as well, and the captain was taking full advantage of both. It felt angry, the wind, even eager. Surely Thaash himself had come to witness the coming battle. *Though if so, does that mean he'll grant his favor to the Kings?*

Eight ships followed in the *Amaranth*'s wake. Nine ships in all had been fielded to do battle against the Black Spear fleet. Çeda had to laugh, if only to break the tension. "I don't know if you're listening, Nalamae, but we need you. This day of all days, guide our steps."

How she wished she could speak to the goddess directly. But she couldn't. The goddess was in hiding.

She glanced over to the bowsprit, where Leorah was standing with one hand holding the jib sheet for balance. She was peering at the line of Black Spear ships as if her very gaze could peel away the hulls and reveal all that lay within. Her right hand gripped Nalamae's staff. Her whole body was quivering.

Ishaq and Çeda had both questioned her about the staff. She admitted that Nalamae had given it to her, and that it had been done to even the scales for Yerinde's granting of the wyrm to Onur. Beyond this, she refused to say more, and Çeda had the impression Nalamae herself had forbade her from speaking of it.

The goddess saw far, Çeda knew, and the stakes were clearly larger than this one battle. If it was true Yerinde had granted Onur power over the wyrm, it meant the other gods were involved, *actively* involved, in this conflict, and that Nalamae must tread with utmost care lest her brothers and sisters find her. Had Ihsan himself not asked after Nalamae? Were the other gods meddling on Tauriyat as well as the desert? It would explain Nalamae's hesitance, but knowing made it no less frustrating.

She gazed west and took in the long line of Kings' ships, some of which were now breaking away from the battle with Emre's small fleet and heading toward their looming conflict with Onur. *We might lose this war before it's truly begun.*

Sümeya and Melis joined Çeda on the foredeck. All three had their veils pulled across their faces, to ward against the biting wind. Seeing them there, Ishaq stepped up to the foredeck. His pepper-gray beard blew over his shoulder as he considered the ships ahead. He seemed content as if, after running his whole life, he was grateful for the chance to stop and turn and strike at the heart of the Kings.

"You're strangely calm," Sümeya said to him.

He ignored her and called to Leorah, "Have you found him?"

Leorah shook her head violently. "No." The wind tugged strands of hair from the bun atop her head as she shook her head again. "Now leave me be!"

She was crying, Çeda realized. She wished desperately to help, but it was too much. She'd been pushed to the point of exhaustion.

"Mother, it's time to go." Ishaq tried to lead her away, but she remained, the fingers of her left hand refusing to let go of the jib line. "It's time to go below. The battle's about to begin."

Bent like a dying tree, she swiveled her head to stare at Ishaq. "I'm not afraid of *battle.*"

"Have no fear," Çeda said to them both. "We'll find him. He'll come to survey the battle sooner or later."

Ishaq's attention was caught by something along the horizon. Sidewinding through the sky like a pennant on the wind was the sand wyrm. It flew toward the ships, surely summoned by Onur.

The crew tensed. All eyes followed the wyrm, even as they readied the ship for battle. If it were possible, Leorah became more intense, her look more desperate. She scanned the ships ahead and tried to blink away the tears streaming from her bloodshot eyes. Then, without warning, her eyes rolled back in her head, and her limbs went slack.

Ishaq and Çeda caught her, and gave her to Frail Lemi, who lifted her as if she weighed nothing. The big man whispered tenderly to her as he carried her away. "It's all right, grandmother. All will be well."

The first of the cat's claws were launched a moment later. The thud of their launching filled the air as dozens more followed, arcing across a pale blue sky to catch the struts of the oncoming ships. Burning pots flew as well, trailing black smoke. The Black Spear ships responded in kind, moments before the amber wyrm arced down toward the *Amaranth*.

A jolt of fear ran through her to see the beast undulating across the pale blue sky, its wings spread wide, the morning sun lancing through the magenta veins that streaked its translucent skin. Terror set Çeda's heart to pounding, but her fear was tempered by relief. She'd reasoned that Onur would send the wyrm at Ishaq's ship. Ishaq had agreed and allowed all seventeen of the Forsaken, their asirim, to lie in wait belowdecks.

She could feel their hunger in the hold below. *Not yet,* she said to them, *but the time has nearly come.*

Closer and closer came the Black Spear ships. Closer and closer came the wyrm. Just as it spread its wings and arched its taloned feet forward, Çeda called, "Now, my brethren! Now!"

The crew slid back the hatch over the hold and the Forsaken sprang forth. They wore their white gauze still, refusing to be encumbered by armor. Each carried two long fighting knives. It was strange to see them so. Çeda was used to seeing the asirim crouched like animals, in pain from the constant torture of serving the Kings and the magic the gods had laid upon them. But these were different. Theirs was a righteous purpose, fearsome to behold.

The Forsaken had been warned about the wyrm's terrible breath. The first of the asirim, who had once been Salsanna, lifted her hand, and a gout of sand lifted from the desert around the ship. It swirled upward, toward the wyrm, and struck as the beast drew breath, blasting its eyes and open maw.

The wyrm swung its head back and forth, the stream of its deadly black spray fouled by its instinctive reaction to protect against the sand that scoured its mouth and throat.

Çeda, Ishaq, Melis, and Sümeya retreated from the foredeck as the wyrm landed with a crash. The Forsaken stormed forward, clambered the masts and rigging, and their white forms swarmed over the wyrm, clawing its fine scales, tearing its skin, ripping the translucent skin of its long wings.

The wyrm clamped its massive jaws over one, bashed another aside as it swung its head around. A fine spray of black liquid issued from its mouth with a strange, rumbling roar. Two of the Forsaken were caught in it. Their white raiment blackened and smoked; their flesh liquefied, yet still they drove their knives into the wyrm's flesh, tearing wide, gaping holes. Blood streamed from those wounds, steaming where it hit the foredeck.

The enemy ships were nearing. Çeda heard something loud clank beneath the ship and then a thud resounded through the decking. Suddenly the ship was leaning starboard and turning in that direction.

Just as she was bringing her ebon blade down against the wyrm's front leg, she saw something dark and massive looming off the port side. Her mind told her to brace, but it was too late. The prow of a ship crashed into theirs, sending her flying. She lost her sword as she was thrown along the body of the wyrm and over the port bow. She struck something that burned her left side, and then she was down, sliding against the deck of the other ship.

She pulled her knife and twisted, slamming the point into the deck. It bit, scraping against the decking, slowing her down, but not enough. She slammed into something hard, then fell to the main deck of the ship that had struck hers.

Suddenly she was among the enemy. Fighting, slashing with her knife, trying to hold them off as she looked for her sword. She saw it near the pilot's wheel, and fought her way toward it.

She reached it at last, and was up again, swinging River's Daughter in vicious arcs.

Among the clashing, she heard a whistle. *To me!*

It was Sümeya. She was surrounded and barely holding her own.

Çeda charged across the deck, screaming "Lai, lai, lai!" as she went, and fell among the Black Spear soldiers. As Sümeya's attackers retreated, the two of them stood back-to-back. She tried to locate Melis, but couldn't. She worried she'd been thrown to the sand, or worse, that she lay dead on the deck of one of the ships.

She and Sümeya fought fiercely, helping one another time and time again. But Çeda knew that the longer they fought, the worse this was for the desert tribes. They were playing into the Kings' hands.

Up! Çeda whistled.

And Sümeya took her meaning. Together, they fought away their attackers, of which there were thankfully few. The crash between ships hadn't been planned, and many now lay stunned, wounded, or unconscious.

They made their way up along the shrouds as, only ten paces distant, the wyrm continued to thrash, half its sinuous body on the Black Spear ship, half on the *Amaranth*. The Forsaken still fought it, but many were gone or lay unmoving on the deck or the sand. As the wyrm roared once more, Çeda scanned the ships, many of which had come to a stop.

They were surrounded by chaos. Ships sailing on, curving around for another pass. Others halted, some crashed into one another, their skis locked or their sails and booms caught up in the other's rigging. There were clusters of fighting all around. Any plan of attack had been forgotten as men and women from both sides fought with wild abandon.

A whistle came, not from Sümeya, but from the sand below. Melis was there, limping, her sword pointing south. Çeda swung her gaze in that direction and saw what Melis had: a ship, a three-masted schooner, with something massive standing on its deck. It was hard to get a gauge on it, as distant as it was, but it was easily twice the size of a man and was tearing at the ship's deck, ripping up boards and flinging them away as arrows came biting in from all directions.

"Onur is there," Çeda said.

"So is the ehrekh," Sümeya replied.

Çeda shrugged and grabbed a rigging line. "So it is," she said, knowing that everything Ramahd had said was true. The ehrekh, Guhldrathen, had come for Hamzakiir, who was surely on the very same ship, and it had been lured by Çeda's own blood. Her throat tightened at the thought of what it would do when it had finished with Hamzakiir.

It demanded your blood, Ramahd had said.

Bakhi's bright hammer, the strength of the thing. It was deeper into the ship, killing any foolish enough to come near. *But what is there to do about it?* Çeda thought. *If the lord of all things has come for me, so be it.*

She slid along the rigging line, somersaulting as she neared the ship's edge and rolling on the sand to break her fall. With the roar of battle still spreading around them, Sümeya landed next to her. Melis approached, limping, but seemed ready as ever to swing a sword. Before Çeda could take another step, Sümeya grabbed Çeda's arm and turned her around. "There's no need for you to go nearer a beast such as that, not when we know it thirsts for your blood. Remain with your tribe. Let me and Melis find Onur."

Çeda motioned toward the distant ship. "Look at it, Sümeya. If it finishes with Hamzakiir it will surely come for me, and there's nothing we can do about that. But we might take Onur. We can kill him for all he's done to Zaïde and a thousand others in his time walking the desert."

Sümeya hesitated, but Çeda refused to wait. She began running toward the ship where the ehrekh had clawed its way to the deck below. Without looking, the beast lashed its tails at a woman who was charging with a spear held high in both hands. One tail batted the spear aside while the other caught her across the throat. She was thrown over the far side of the ship as Guhldrathen tore a massive beam from the deck. It was as large as a skiff, but the ehrekh launched it into the air toward a group of Black Spear archers as if it were kindling. The archers were crushed, and the ehrekh dropped down into the hole it had created. Much of it was lost from view as it tore deeper and deeper into the ship like a bone crusher tearing into a hapless hare's den.

In that moment, the shutters of the captain's cabin at the rear of the ship were thrown wide. An ornate spear was tossed down to the sand, and Onur's bulky frame levered itself out to fall unceremoniously to the sand, landing just beside the spear. Using the spear to support himself, Onur propped himself up. He looked as though he were drunk as he lumbered forward, looking wild-eyed over his shoulder at the ship he'd just escaped.

A moment later, he pulled up as he spotted Çeda, Melis, and Sümeya. He had his spear at the ready, but appeared so weak he could hardly hold it.

Behind him, another form dropped from the same cabin window. He sprinted after Onur, but then pulled up as he saw Çeda and the others. It was Hamzakiir, Çeda realized. Blood ran from a cut on his forehead and stained his golden clothes. Like Onur, he seemed concerned by the sudden presence of a trio of Blade Maidens standing before him, but before he could speak a great roar came from behind him.

Hamzakiir turned, petrified, as the ehrekh lifted itself from the hole it had torn in the ship and leapt down to the sand. With his landing came a deep booming sound that rose above the chaos of the battle. Çeda felt it in her chest. The ehrekh charged straight for Hamzakiir. The blood mage ran, his eyes crazed with fear.

"Save me!" he called to Onur, stumbling toward him.

Onur looked as if he were considering it, but as Hamzakiir came close, he brought the butt of his spear up in a sharp cross-strike to the side of Hamzakiir's head. As Hamzakiir fell, stunned, Onur backed away as if a leper lay before him.

Hamzakiir reached his knees, clasped his hands, and stared at the sky. "Tulathan, save me!"

But the silver goddess was deaf to his pleas. The ebony-skinned beast fell upon him and lifted him into the air. The pair of them looked like a mirage, a twisted reflection of father and child. Hamzakiir screamed, arms flailing, legs kicking against the beast's face and horns as the ehrekh's thumbs drove into the center of his chest. Hamzakiir's rib cage was pierced and torn wide. The glistening ropes of his intestines spilled to the sand, while other viscera shook within the rapidly widening cavity. A moment later, Hamzakiir's screams were cut short, though his limbs continued to quiver like a man stricken with palsy.

"Now take *her*!" Onur bellowed at the beast. He was pointing his spear at Çeda. "Take her, Guhldrathen, as was promised!"

Chapter 63

Brama sat in the center of a skiff as it flew across the sand. The mast and sail were laid down, still held in their clamps. The sails would not be needed. They were only going to have one chance at this.

Brama held a bow in one hand. The quiver, resting in the crook where hull met thwart, bristled with arrows, though he doubted he'd have time to loose more than one. And in any case his responsibility lay not in his skill with a bow, which was moderate at best, but in the two items on the boards between his feet. At first glance it looked like a single mound of rope, but closer examination revealed two separate implements: one, a coil of thick silk rope, to one end of which was tied a triple-hooked iron grapnel. The second, lying beneath, was a boarding net woven like a ship's shroud with small hooks secured along one side.

Emre was at the front, one knee on the forward thwart, holding an axe. The wind whipped the free strands of his long, braided hair. Ramahd sat at the tiller, guiding them as they trailed the two large ships that towered ahead of them—the Kadri ship, *Autumn Rose,* and the *Errant,* Macide's ship.

The wind was gusting, and the sails of both ships were full. The ships sailed so near one another it looked as though their hulls would strike, or that their sails and rigging would get caught, but their pilots were masterful. They worked the wheels, guiding the ships carefully over the sand as they sped toward the dark line of navy ships ahead.

A thick rope hawser was looped through a hook at the front of the skiff. The hawser trailed ahead of the skiff, up and over the gunwales of both the *Autumn Rose* and the *Errant*. The hawser's ends were looped around each ship's foremast, effectively towing the skiff along the sands while at the same time—because the ships sailed so close to one another—hiding them from view. It was necessary. If the Kings' crew worked out what they were about to do, their gambit would be over before it began.

A horn blew on the *Errant*, a sound as bright as the sunrise. It was a call to all the ships trailing behind to prepare for battle, but also a signal for the skiff to be ready.

Emre pointed across the bow. "Steady now. Watch the rise there."

"I see it." Ramahd adjusted the skiff's course to avoid the steep dip along windward side of the misshapen dune.

Beyond the *Rose* and the *Errant*, the Kings' ships were only a quarter-league away. Then an eighth-league. And still the Kings' ships held their course. Brama's heart was beating like a racing akhala's when another horn finally blew, loud and long and clear.

The *Rose* and the *Errant* immediately adjusted course, their lines diverging. The trailing ships began to drift into two separate columns as well—a gambit to confuse the Kings' ships and mask what was about to happen. As the hulls of the *Rose* and *Errant* drifted farther and farther apart, the hawser was drawn tighter, and the skiff accelerated, adding to its already considerable speed.

Faster and faster it went, the wind whipping Brama's hair against his face. The ride became bumpier as Ramahd guided them steadily over the sand.

Bells rang on the Kings' massive galleons, looming ahead. They adjusted course as well. Flame pots flew from both lines of ships, arching across a robin's egg sky. Imperfect lines of black smoke trailed behind. Arrows flew. Countless dark, fletched shafts streaked between the ships. They looked like the swarms of insects that plagued the Haddah in the thick of spring.

The hawser drew tighter and tighter. Emre raised his axe, preparing to bring it down at just the right moment. But gods, dead ahead, one of the Kings' galleons, having realized the path between the *Rose* and the *Errant* was the only way to avoid a collision with either ship, was now hurtling directly toward them. A Maiden stood near the galleon's bowsprit. Brama thought he heard a series of sharp whistles, at which point two more Maidens joined her, each bearing a bow with arrow nocked.

The hawser went tight. Brama heard a creaking sound as it stretched and the front of the skiff lifted from the sand. With a sharp grunt, Emre brought the axe down. By then the skiff was moving so fast Brama was certain they'd turn and tip and be flung free. But Ramahd guided them with uncanny instincts between the oncoming galleon's long skimwood skis.

Brama loosed an arrow at the Maidens, managing nothing more than making the one who'd whistled twist from its path. The other two drew their bowstrings and let fly. One arrow grazed Brama's thigh and thudded into the skiff's hull. The other flew just past his head.

As the pain in his leg began to register, he heard a grunt behind him. He turned to see Ramahd's right forearm shot straight through, pinning him to the tiller itself. His left arm was looped through a heavy shield he was holding at the ready, but the Maiden's aim had been sure enough to slip past the shield's edge. Brama tried to reach for the arrow, but abandoned the plan when Ramahd growled, "Leave it!" his eyes fixed determinedly ahead. "Just get the bloody grapnel ready!"

Before the Maidens could shoot again, the skiff hurtled beneath the galleon's hull. Emre, Brama, and Ramahd all ducked to avoid having their heads clipped by the ship's keel. The sound of battle dimmed, replaced by the sharp hissing of the galleon's great skis. The rudder clipped the rear of the skiff, jolting them, but then they were flying out onto open sand once more.

Brama handed Emre the bow and took up the grapnel. They were headed straight for the capital ship behind the lines now. King Kiral's ship. The ship where Queen Meryam was hiding and where, Brama was certain, Rümayesh's sapphire hung around her neck.

Brama marveled at Emre's skill with a bow. The man was a wizard. He'd taken up four arrows between the knuckles of his right hand. As the three Maidens reappeared at the ship's stern behind them, he released one then another and another, all four flying in such tight sequence the Maidens hardly had time to duck before the next was on them. He appeared to catch one in the neck with the fourth arrow. She dropped from sight and wasn't seen again. The other two, however, lifted their bows and aimed while Emre grabbed more arrows.

Ramahd had lifted the heavy shield onto the thwart and ducked behind it. Just in time. Two arrows crashed into it. Both would have taken him in the back. His right arm, the arrow still driven through the meat, was bleeding badly now. "It'll come fast," he said through gritted teeth, his gaze guiding Brama to the Kings' galleon ahead.

Indeed, despite losing some speed, they were still hurtling forward. The galleon was adjusting course, perhaps trying to avoid the skiff. But Ramahd adjusted right along with them. Brama stood. He let the rope out and began spinning the grapnel. A dozen Silver Spears stood along the galleon's starboard side, most with bows at the ready. Emre loosed a volley of arrows, all four striking home. Then the Spears let fly.

Amid streaking arrows, Brama saw a wisp of a woman in a rusty red dress standing by the Kings' soldiers. Queen Meryam. She was staring at the skiff with eyes that glinted in the sunken hollows of her face. "You shouldn't have come, brother!" she shouted.

Ramahd ignored her as the galleon adjusted course so that its starboard ski headed straight for them. The ship's captain was hoping the ship itself could do the work of the Silver Spears for them. But Ramahd, grimacing, his breath coming in sharp huffs, pushed at the tiller until they were running alongside the galleon again. As the Spears, and now a pair of Maidens, fired straight down at them, Brama spun the grapnel one last time and flung it toward the rearmost shroud.

"It's caught!" Brama called. "Turn, turn, turn!"

Ramahd swung wide, then brought the line of the skiff about, curving them around so that they came nearer and nearer to the galleon's line of sail. The rope coiled out, then snapped tight. The skiff curved around the galleon's stern. The rope creaked, and Meryam appeared at the aft gunwales, her hand lifted high, and launched a ball of bright fire at the skiff. It flew straight for them, but as it neared, it diminished and flew off course, striking the sand to their starboard side.

A thundering boom accompanied a geyser of sand lifting high into the air, but Brama was paying more attention to Ramahd. His free left hand was lifted, palm facing outward. Sweat had gathered on his brow. He'd said he could protect them from Meryam, but Brama hadn't really believed him until now.

Another tight ball of fire came streaking in, but it was off target. The skiff was moving so swiftly it swung around to the galleon's port side. From there, Brama and Emre both hurled the net up and across the gunwales. Quickly, they leapt upon it, then turned to help Ramahd.

Abandoning the tiller, Ramahd snapped the arrow and yanked his arm free. Just as the skiff was beginning to pull away, he leapt across the gunwale to land on the lower portion of the net. He groaned, and his left arm slipped free, but Brama held him tight by his shirt until he could begin climbing, right behind Emre and Brama.

Brama and Emre reached the quarterdeck a moment later and engaged the squad of Silver Spears who met them, but Brama was already on the lookout for Meryam. Everything depended on her. Or rather, on his ability to take the sapphire from her.

He could feel her somewhere forward. Behind him, Ramahd reached the deck. The three of them fought viciously, keeping the Silver Spears away, but then several of the Spears retreated, making room for the Blade Maidens in their black battle dresses.

That was when Brama saw Meryam climbing the stairs to the quarterdeck. King Kiral stood beside her, with a bright two-handed shamshir in his grasp. The necklace hung from Meryam's throat, the facets of the sapphire glinting in the sun.

In that moment, Emre managed to cut down one of the Silver Spears between them, and Brama saw his chance. He rushed toward Meryam, shouldering aside the last Silver Spear between them, but he'd not taken two strides before a figure in black came rushing in from his right. He turn in time to see the Blade Maiden, her ebon blade blurring toward him.

He felt something burn along his shoulder and continue down his side, through his ribs. He fell to his knees, a sensation more painful than he'd ever experienced with Rümayesh boiling the whole of his right side. He felt a boot on his back, which shoved him forward as something *tugged* at his insides. He collapsed to the deck. Above, yards of canvas glowed the color of lemon pith. Beyond them, the sky burst in a brilliance of blue. The dark, scratched wood of the bulwark stood like a curtain reaching down toward the deck boards. As footsteps thudded loudly in his ears, a warm sensation traveled along his left side. A stream of red crept across the deck boards. Thin at first, it widened. A stream became a river became a lake.

You've come, as I knew you would.

He wanted to smile, but found it impossible. Something gurgled in his chest as he whispered, "I've arrived a dying man."

Dying? Rümayesh said. *Your eyes are lit with life!*

I yearn for life, yes. But I'm failing.

No, Brama, she said in honeyed tones, *not with the gifts I've bestowed. It would take more than this to carry you to the farther shores.*

He blinked. Heard muffled words. He had trouble understanding what she was saying at first. Yes, she'd given him the ability to heal but there were secrets hidden in her words.

Suddenly his feelings about her made sense. How he yearned for her, how he ached, how he felt as though he could not be complete without her. *Part of you,* he began. *A shard of your soul lies within me.*

It does.

More began to come clear. *You were trying to free yourself.*

Since the moment I was trapped within the sapphire, Brama. It merely took me a while to find the way out.

Through me.

Through you.

He wanted to laugh. He wanted to cry. For so long he'd thought *he* was the master. But for years Rümayesh had been working him like clay, forming him into an image that pleased her. Had she not been stolen away by Ramahd for Meryam's purposes, he wondered how long it would have been before she had him.

Not long, she replied.

Not long . . . He'd been under her spell for months, a time that seemed impossibly distant, impossibly long. And he'd nearly given himself to her again.

It won't be the same, she promised. *I came to know you, Brama. And you came to know me. We were not one, but had begun walking that path with one another. Can you say it wasn't so?*

There was no denying it. With the sort of perspective that years granted, it was clear as the rising moons.

Footsteps approached. A dress dyed in rust passed before him. As did a man wearing fine leather boots and a rich kaftan.

Come, do you not believe me now? How much we might do together? We can, Brama. If you but stand. If you but free me.

In the end, there was no refusing her. He could no more deny her than he could will his heart to stop beating. The pain it brought on was excruciating, but he rolled to one side and reached for the pouch where he'd secreted away the obsidian stone, the one he'd use to give Rümayesh her new name.

You won't need it, Rümayesh said. *I've changed.*

Good, Brama thought. His fingers were shaking too terribly for such delicate movements in any case. He turned his head and saw Ramahd being held by two Silver Spears, Meryam standing before him. He had a deep gash along his forehead. And poor Emre grunted and twisted on the deck like a wild badger. He quieted when one of the Maidens crouched and crashed the hilt of her ebon blade against the side of his head.

Someone spoke. It sounded like burbling water. Immediately after, they wrestled Emre to his feet. Ramahd stared straight at Meryam, the woman in the red dress. Emre was *forced* to do so, the Maiden grabbing a hunk of his long black hair and lifting his head until he was staring drowsy-eyed at the queen.

Brama tried pushing himself up, but his right hand slipped on the blood. He tried again. Managed to make it to his knees. So many were gathered. Surely they would spot him.

Their eyes are on the queen, Rümayesh whispered. *Only the queen.*

He pushed himself up. How his legs shook. He felt like a pile of leaves stacked high, ready to tip the moment the next breeze struck. But he managed it at last and saw that Rümayesh had spoken the truth. Every single person standing on the deck, two dozen souls, couldn't seem to take their eyes from the queen. It was Rümayesh's doing . . .

"In truth," Meryam was saying to Ramahd, "I wish you'd fled. I wish you'd returned home. I might have let you live if you'd been willing to remain in Viaroza and tend to your estate. But no. You were always so stubborn."

Brama managed a step forward. He felt something shift inside him. Heard a crunching sound and tried not to think what it meant.

A bloody, gruesome smile broke across Ramahd's face. "Not so long ago you appreciated my stubborn streak."

Brama took another step, concentrating on reaching Meryam. He could see the chain around her neck, only two steps away now. But gods how it pained him to move. A furnace burned along his right side, turning him to ash.

"I did, once," Meryam replied. "But all things come to an end."

He took one more quavering step and slipped his knife free from its sheath.

As Meryam raised her hand, one of the Maidens shouted, "Queen Meryam!"

The Maiden had somehow broken the spell, but he was so focused on Meryam he hardly spared her a glance. The Maiden was looking straight at him, breaking away from Emre's side.

Brama lunged, grabbed the chain, and fell.

The chain snapped. Something heavy thudded to the deck. The amulet. Dear gods, the amulet, only an arm's reach away.

Meryam's rusty red dress slid aside. The Maiden loomed, lifting her ebon blade high.

Crying out in pain, Brama crawled forward, brought the knife up and drove it down with all his might. The point struck the center of the amulet. Brama felt it give.

Tiny shards bit into his hands and face as the gem shattered. He was blown back, caught in a gale stronger than the desert's fierce autumn sandstorms. He rolled away, trying to shield himself from the pain, and was blown farther still. The air all about was a roar unlike anything he'd ever heard, a storm of such intensity that it felt like the first gods had returned to sunder the desert they'd left behind.

The wind swept him down the stairs to the main deck. He landed hard and slid along until he came to a stop facing the quarterdeck. Behind him, near the mainmast, a tight swirl of dust and sand was forming. The soldiers and Maidens had all backed away, Emre and Ramahd with them. Meryam and King Kiral had both fallen. They stared aghast at the dark form within the maelstrom.

The wind ebbed, blowing outward in a sudden gust, and Rümayesh stepped forward. Kiral was a tall man, but the ehrekh towered over him. Her three tails swished hypnotically behind her. A crown of thorns adorned her head, from which two ram's horns swept up and curled behind her head. Ebony skin shimmered in the morning sunlight, which grew brighter as the dust and sand drifted on the day's considerable wind. It was her eyes, however, that drew one's attention. They were filled with little save malice and wrath and vengeance. When combined with the amused smile on her lips, it sent a chill deep inside Brama. He'd known what Rümayesh's return would mean for Meryam and her accomplices, but that didn't mean he wanted to see it played out.

As Rümayesh took her first step onto the quarterdeck, Meryam leapt over the side of the ship. Kiral came right after. They arced down toward the sand, and where they struck, massive explosions followed. Sand flew outward from the twin points of impact, *thoom, thoom*. When the sand settled, there was no sign of them in either of the large, cone-shaped craters.

For several breaths Rümayesh merely stared, her black-crowned head swiveling as the ship sailed on. Everyone else, all across the decks, in the rigging, the soldiers, the crew, the pilot, the Maidens—even Emre and Ramahd—were silent and unmoving. They stared with wide eyes at the towering ehrekh before them. None moved to stand against her. None dared take a step for fear of drawing her attention.

Rümayesh turned to face Brama. As she stalked forward, footsteps booming over the deck, Brama managed to sit on the foredeck stairs.

The smile on Rümayesh's face was something he could hardly bear to look at. He'd worked long and hard to forget the memories it dredged up, but he'd been fooling himself all along. They'd not been forgotten. They were merely hidden, lurking, waiting to step into the light once more.

His heart beat madly. His breath came so strongly his throat burned from it. It felt as though his chest was ready to burst. But then Rümayesh waved one taloned hand.

"No more," she declared, and just like that, the nightmares receded, faded, until they were more like daydreams, half remembered and impotent. "Not while we are one."

Brama's mind was too muddled to discern if that was a threat of some sort, but the pain within him was easing at last. Only then did he realize that they'd sailed beyond the battle line. The bulk of the fighting was taking place behind the ship. While ahead, off the starboard bow, a second battle raged. His purpose here slowly returned to him.

"Guhldrathen is coming," Brama said.

"Guhldrathen, my brethren, has already arrived," Rümayesh corrected.

Brama lifted his arm and pointed toward the second line of battle. "Save them. Save Çeda and the others."

Rümayesh smiled a wicked smile. "You need not worry over them"—she waved her hand to Ramahd and Emre—"nor these. We may do whatever you desire. Return to Sharakhai and live the life of a King. Sail the desert. Feast among the tribes. Or go to Malasan and dine in the halls of their mad king. We might dance on the night of a thousand lanterns in Tsitsian or visit the grasslands of Kundhun, where the smell of the wind, just before a storm strikes the hills, renews the spirit. All that we can do," she said, "and leave your pain behind."

"Leave *them* behind, you mean," Brama said, nodding toward Ramahd and Emre.

"What care have you for them?"

"The Great Shangazi is worth fighting for."

"The Great Shangazi will be here whether you fight for it or not."

"Save them," Brama repeated. "Save Çeda from Guhldrathen, and you'll save the rest."

Rümayesh paused. Her tails whipped behind her in rhythms of three. When she spoke again, a distinct wryness tinted the low timbre of her voice. "Very well, my master."

Before Brama knew what was happening, Rümayesh's form burst into a thousand black beetles. They buzzed around him. They bore him into the air. He heard shouts of surprise through the deafening, chittering sound, but could spare no thought for others. He shut his eyes, as he felt something *shift*. It felt as if the world itself were altering in some unknowable way.

When the clatter of the beetle's wings receded and he dared open his eyes, he found himself in the skiff once more. It still trailed behind the galleon on the rope he'd launched over the gunwales earlier. Ramahd and Emre were there as well. All three of them were plagued by the black beetles, but in a moment the swarm was lifting up and away and speeding toward the battle in the distance.

"Cut the line," Brama said, "quickly."

Emre already had his knife out. He used it to cut them free. As the galleon drifted away, those standing at the gunwales watched them with open mouths and widened eyes. Not a single one still holding a bow made to nock an arrow.

Soon their skiff had come to a sighing halt. The galleon's looming profile and the swarming cloud of beetles both dwindled along two divergent paths. Without another word, the three of them set about the task of setting the mast and lifting the sail.

Chapter 64

OVER THE SAND, Guhldrathen stalked Çeda.
Onur watched, gleeful as a boy on Beht Revahl. A scattering of his warriors, who'd been separated when he'd fled the ship, were approaching from behind. Çeda knew she had only moments to act before Guhldrathen was on her, and she refused to flee. It was vital to take Onur down before Guhldrathen could reach her.

She sprinted left, whistling for Melis and Sümeya to flank her as she went. She wanted to warn them not to attack Onur—not yet—but the chance that he would decipher her instructions was too great.

Guhldrathen moved faster now, a black laugher charging its prey. As she'd hoped, it adjusted course as she ran, its path bringing it closer and closer to Onur.

Onur, too late, realized what she was doing and tried to move out of the way, but he was weakened, from battle but surely from having tasted of human flesh as well. As he trudged through the sand, he looked as though millstones had been bound to his ankles. Guhldrathen, focused squarely on Çeda, clubbed Onur with one of his great fists, and Onur, despite his bulk, went flying to fall unmoving against the amber sand. For a moment, Çeda could only stare. She'd meant for it to happen—the joy of seeing Onur fall set her fingers to tingling—but the ease with which Guhldrathen had done it, as if the felling of a King was but an afterthought, made her heart go cold.

Çeda, Melis, and Sümeya stood at the ready as the ehrekh neared. Surprisingly, it slowed and approached with care. Its taurine eyes stared warily at the ebon swords, as if it had faced such a threat before. It began moving its hands in strange ways. Outlining symbols in the air.

Çeda felt herself slowing. Her body became leaden, and she knew the beast would have all of them in moments if she didn't act. She charged, hoping to distract the beast, to foil its spell, but she'd not gone two steps before Guhldrathen raised a hand to her. She came to an immediate stop. Something pressed on her from all directions while a high-pitched tone sounded loud in her ears.

"My wish is not to see thee dead," it said in a voice so low it made her skin itch. "Not yet. I would bring thee to the desert. Study thee before I decide how and when to deliver thy soul to the farther fields. I would follow thy path, oh White Wolf. I would reach across the divide to touch the land of my maker's maker once more."

It stretched one arm out, reaching for her neck, but just then a spear streaked through the air from Çeda's right and pierced Guhldrathen's skin. Another struck its neck. A third sunk deep into one thigh. Çeda could not move, but she saw a line of desert-garbed warriors hurtling forward. Ishaq led them. The ghostly white forms of the Forsaken followed, wailing as they streaked toward the ehrekh. Leading the way was Salsanna, her body now occupied by the soul of an asir; behind her came Fahrel and Stavehn and a half-dozen more. They bore spears and swords and shields. The Forsaken engaged Guhldrathen, moving with blinding speed and ferocity while others encircled the beast.

As they fought, Çeda felt her limbs slowly loosening. It was the presence of the Forsaken—she could feel the brightness of their souls pushing away the darkness of the ehrekh's magic—but it didn't all happen at once. She felt as if she were trapped in honey, so she fought to hasten the process; the more she worked her muscles, she soon found, the looser they became.

The need for haste was paramount. Guhldrathen was already winning his battle. One of the Forsaken had taken a blow to the head. Fahrel was lost when one of Guhldrathen's tails skewered her chest. Blood so dark it was nearly black burst from the wound, and then she was gone as Guhldrathen whipped his tail and sent her flying through the air.

A third was crushed beneath one of Guhldrathen's cloven hooves. Another was gored and flung away with a vicious lift of his terrible curving horns. Ishaq, releasing a long battle cry and wielding a spear, distracted the ehrekh as Salsanna swept in and pierced Guhldrathen's right eye with the tip of her own spear.

In that moment, Çeda was released. She fell to the ground, but was up again in a blink and rushing toward the ehrekh. Stavehn was lost when Guhldrathen's great jaws clamped over his right shoulder and tore half his chest away. Another soul dimmed when Guhldrathen picked him up and tore his body in two.

As it flung the halves of that poor soul's body aside, Ishaq rushed in, yelling as he stabbed the spear up beneath Guhldrathen's chin. The spearhead was partially lost as it sunk deep into Guhldrathen's flesh.

Guhldrathen staggered back, eyes blinking in confusion at the sky. But the next moment, it grabbed the spear and snapped it in two. And then Ishaq was driven against the sand by a mighty downward blow.

"No!" Çeda cried.

She reached the ehrekh's side and swung River's Daughter once, twice, backing away quickly when the ehrekh rounded on her. Each swing of her blade cut deep, some artifact of the ebon's steel allowing it to bite deeper than mundane weapons seemed to.

Melis and Sümeya fought by her side now. Together they attacked, in constant flow, one retreating while the other two blooded the beast. Black blood flowed from the wounds, slicking the ehrekh's skin, making it glisten yellow in the mid-morning light.

Salsanna had lost her knives, but she leapt, trying to claw her way up the ehrekh's back, only to be thrown off. Another white asir took her place, stabbing a knife deep into the ehrekh's shoulder.

Guhldrathen reached over its shoulder, grabbed the white-clothed asir, and flung him against a ship's bowsprit. As he fell lifeless to the sand, Guhldrathen reared up and bellowed so loudly it brought pain to Çeda's ears. Then it brought both fists down.

Suddenly the world tilted. Çeda saw sky then desert then sky again. She fell hard and rolled across the sand, her ears ringing. She felt pummeled where the unseen force had struck. Slowly, she lifted herself up, only to find those who'd been fighting Guhldrathen lying, like her, ten paces distant. They were stunned and slow to rise, even the Forsaken.

Guhldrathen limped toward Çeda, its eyes filled with rage, which made her wonder whether it still wanted to take her away and kill her at its leisure or slay her now for her defiance. Çeda reached across the sand for River's Daughter. She thought it had fallen next to her. She realized it hadn't. She couldn't see it anywhere. She still had her knife, though. She drew it and tried to stand, but fell to the ground as a wave of dizziness struck.

One of the ehrekh's hooves stepped on her right arm, pinning her hand and the knife. She heard the bones break as white hot pain burned along her forearm. A scream tore from her throat, which seemed to please Guhldrathen.

It reached one clawed hand down and said, "Now—"

But got no farther before a buzzing, rattling sound made it lift its head. Çeda turned in time to see a black cloud sweeping over the desert. It swallowed Guhldrathen and *lifted* the ehrekh, sending it flying backward. And then the cloud resolved into a tall figure, nearly of a height with Guhldrathen. Its silhouette had feminine notes, but retained all the other hallmarks of the ehrekh—curving horns, a mane of thorn-like hair, serpentine eyes and taurine legs that ended in cloven hooves.

Rümayesh. The last time she'd seen her had been in Nalamae's temple in Sharakhai, moments before she'd been trapped in the sapphire. Somehow, she'd escaped her prison. *Or had been released,* Çeda thought, *likely by Brama.* She couldn't guess how, but just then she was glad for it.

Cradling her right arm, gritting her teeth against the pain, Çeda took up her knife and watched the battle unfold. The ehrekh struck one another mightily. They fought like animals, sometimes rolling across the sand. For many long moments they seemed equally matched, but it soon became clear Guhldrathen was weakening. It staggered backward, raising its hands to draw more arcane symbols, but Rümayesh saw and charged.

Guhldrathen dissolved like smoke. In response, Rümayesh crumbled, returning to the cloud of black beetles. The swarm swept up the black smoke, the two twisting as one, flying farther and farther away, surging and swelling until they were lost behind the line of ships.

Suddenly the rest of the battle reentered Çeda's awareness. All around them, tribesman fought tribesman. On the decks of ships, over the sand. Nearby, a fight had broken out between Onur's personal guard and Ishaq's best warriors. Çeda sheathed her knife and found River's Daughter at last, half hidden in the sand several paces away. She picked it up, and then saw Ishaq, lying facedown in the sand, unmoving.

She swallowed—*there will be time to grieve when the battle is done*—and staggered toward the fight, pulling her veil from her face as she went. "Stop!" she called, pointing to the horizon with her sword. "Stop! We cannot fight one another, not if we wish to live!"

The cries of steel continued to ring.

"Stop!" she cried again. "Onur is dead! But the other Kings have come! And they're waiting." She pointed River's Daughter toward the advancing ships. "Look at them!"

At this, some few paused. With tentative glances, they looked. Beyond the battle, dozens of the Kings' ships were arrayed like soldiers. Their sails were at the ready, but they were unmoving, which meant they had anchors set, a maneuver used when a ship wished to get on the move quickly.

"Look at them!" she repeated. "They wait like jackals. They wait for us to kill each other that they might take us at our weakest, with little loss to their own numbers. But we need not give them what they want."

Çeda walked down the line of the fighting. Slowly, they lowered their guard, combatants stepped away from each other. Seeing the lull in the battle, more stayed their swords. Men, women, the old, the young, many of them wounded, all held their weapons still, perhaps hoping for an end to the hostilities.

"The lure of the Kings is strong," Çeda went on, shouting so that all could hear. "I know this more than most. You were *drawn* to him, Tribe Salmük. We can all see that. Tribe Masal was as well. Even Tribe Kadri saw in the King of Spears a chance to strike at the heart of Sharakhai. You were lured by Onur's false promises. Beguiled by the same magic the gods placed upon his shoulders like a mantle. But now his dark presence has been lifted! We need not fight one another." She lifted River's Daughter and described an arc that encompassed the whole of the Kings' line of ships. "Not when our true enemy lies there!"

Reversing her grip on her ebon sword, she sheathed it with her left hand, then walked toward the warriors from Tribe Salmük. She held out her good hand in peace to the nearest of them, a woman with a wary expression in her kohl-rimmed eyes. "We need not fight one another. Not while we can grasp hands and free the desert from the yoke of the Kings of Sharakhai."

The woman stared at Çeda's hand. She looked to the others from her tribe. None gave their assent to take Çeda's hand, but neither did they deny her. Slowly, the woman reached out.

"Çeda!" Sümeya called, just as Melis whistled, *Enemy! Behind!*

Çeda turned just in time to see Onur charging toward her. He held his spear in both hands. Çeda tried to dodge, but Onur was too quick. He took her in the belly and the spear sank in. Sank *through* her. It pinned her to the sand. A pain as vast as the desert gripped her as Onur's greasy face hung above her, smiling through the cuts, the streaking blood, the lank hair. Çeda managed to pull her knife from her belt with her good left hand, but the weight of his chest was against her.

"At least I'll have you," he rasped at her, his eyes crazed. He fell across her, nearly exhausted. "At least I'll have you!"

Screaming, Çeda tugged her arm free, and the knife with it. With all her might, she drove it against the side of his neck. It plunged all the way to the hilt. Immediately she sawed it free, cutting his throat along with it.

Onur blinked. His mouth worked. His blood pulsed against her, a river, hot against her chest and neck. And then all his weight fell against her.

Çeda's body fell slack. Her toes tingled but she could no longer feel her hands, nor the broken bones of her right arm. Nor, she realized with a strange sort of curiosity, the spear wound that had traveled all the way through her gut.

A weight was lifted from her. Faces staring aghast appeared in a halo around her.

She tried to speak to them. Her mouth worked, but nothing came out. They spoke as well, but she heard nothing more than a warbling, a susurrus, an inscrutable tumult of sound that made her wonder if they were uttering farewells, speaking her rites, guiding her to the world beyond.

Someone knelt by her side. A woman in a black dress wearing a turban. Her veil was off, revealing a beautiful face, bright brown eyes. She nodded to another dressed like her. Something tugged at her belly. She felt the stabbing pain once more, but only for a moment—as though, with that last offering of pain, the cost of her passage had been paid in full.

The woman with brown eyes held something. A metal flask, no larger than a walnut, which she opened with shaking fingers. Some of the soft blue, strangely bright liquid within spilled.

And then the flask was being pressed to her lips.

Something cool touched her tongue. Gods, how sweet it tasted. An elixir distilled from the light of the stars themselves. Down her throat it traveled, creating something like warmth within her.

As the feeling spread, the pain came once more. And the world around her went dark.

Chapter 65

ÇEDA'S EYES FLUTTERED OPEN.

Above her, over the roof of a tent that fluttered in the wind, the brightness of the sun shone through, a golden disk on a field of ivory. She blinked and looked away, taking in her surroundings. She lay on thick bedding over a beautifully woven carpet. A dozen tin censers were arrayed around her. One still burned, filling the air with the rich scents of copal and myrrh. More carpets covered the rest of the interior. The center was left clear for a small fire pit.

The wind was playful, sending the tent's walls in and out in a rhythm that made Çeda want to sleep again. She fought the urge, trying to lift herself and grunted at the sudden pain in her gut. Lifting the blanket that covered her, she saw she was wrapped in bandages from her hips all the way to her chest. She let the blanket fall and gripped her right arm, turning it this way and that. Only the smallest twinge of pain accompanied the movements. It had been broken, though. Guhldrathen had stepped on it, shattering her bones.

She lifted the blanket again. There was some blood on the bandages, but it was dried and old.

Gritting her teeth against the pain, she rolled onto her side and pushed herself up. She unwrapped the bandages around her chest and waist to find a faint pink scar running across her stomach. The center was puckered slightly, like a larger version of the wound from the adichara's kiss on her right thumb.

"You have a big sister," she said as she ran her right hand over the new wound. She was no stranger to wounds. To scars. This could easily have been mistaken for one that was months old. She had little doubt that over the next day, it would heal further and grow fainter.

The tent flap opened and Dardzada stepped in. Seeing her standing there naked, his eyes went wide and he turned around. "Forgive me," he said as he stepped back outside.

Çeda smiled. As surly as Dardzada always seemed to be, it was funny to see him chastened. She pulled on the dress that lay folded on the carpet, a blue dress made of fine linen with beautiful embroidered panels stitched along the chest, skirt, and voluminous sleeves. She found a mirror on a small wooden chest, winced as she bent to pick it up, and held it high to examine herself. Her face was clean. There were cuts she remembered receiving during the battle that were now as faint as a star at sunrise. Her hair was unbound, clean, and well combed. There was not a speck of dirt in it, nor was there any trace of blood in her hair or along her scalp. Dardzada's doing?

Gods, you've looked better, Çeda.

Her eyes were haggard. Her hair was disheveled from having slept on it for—who knew, a day or more? But what matter was that? She was alive. They had apparently survived the battle with the Kings. They had lived to fight another day.

After setting the mirror back on the chest, she took one of the chairs. "Come."

Dardzada returned, rubbing his hands over his belly, as if he were suddenly worried about his appearance. His left arm was still in a sling. Smiling awkwardly, he took her in, his eyes drifting to *her* belly. "How does it feel?"

"I should be dead," she replied. "So by any measure that matters, it ought to feel wonderful."

In a blink, the old Dardzada returned. He gave her a wooden stare. "How does it *feel?*"

"Like I took a good punch, and little more."

Dardzada shook his head in amazement, as if he could hardly believe it.
"I have Emre to thank for this, don't I?"

Dardzada nodded. "Apparently he gave the elixir to Sümeya when you refused him."

"Where is he now?" She tried to make it sound as if she didn't truly care, though she felt foolish for doing so. She was a child no longer. And she didn't have to hide her affection from anyone, Dardzada included—perhaps *especially* Dardzada.

"Just returning from a patrol. There's still concern that the Kings will return, but we suspect they'll be content with the damage they've done to the tribes and return to Sharakhai."

Çeda wondered at it all. By her reckoning, five of the Kings were now dead: Azad by her mother's hand; Külaşan, Mesut, and Onur by her own; and Yusam, though who might have killed him remained a mystery. And yet the task before her still seemed so daunting. Those who lived—Kiral, Ihsan, Husamettín, Sukru, Cahil, Beşir, and Zeheb—were hardly less powerful than before. *They may be fewer in number,* Çeda mused, *but that only means they've consolidated the power the dead had left behind.*

"Why would the Kings leave?" she asked. "Even if the four tribes banded together, they could have destroyed us."

"True, but there was the ehrekh, Rümayesh, to contend with. After you fell, Masal and Salmük *did* join us. When the Kings saw the end of our battle, they began to close in, but paused when Rümayesh returned."

"But they'd risked so much," Çeda said. "They'd come so far. They had numbers, even with Rümayesh on our side."

"Guhldrathen lay dead a half-league away, and many of the Kings' ships witnessed that battle. They had lost both King Kiral and Queen Meryam in Emre's bold gambit."

Çeda shook her head, confused.

"You'll hear the stories over the fires these coming nights. Suffice it to say that Emre, Brama, and Lord Amansir pulled off a story for the ages. The three of them made their way to Kiral's own ship and destroyed the sapphire that trapped Rümayesh. Even I will admit it was daring. It likely saved us all." Dardzada's chest rumbled as he laughed. "Don't tell him I said so."

"We wouldn't want Emre thinking you care about him."

"I wouldn't want delusions of grandeur making him think he's better than he is."

"For the love of the gods, Dardzada, let the man rejoice in doing something good."

He shrugged and scratched at his beard, which had quite a bit more salt in it than it used to. "He can rejoice all he wants. Just don't expect me to dance around the fire with him while he does it."

Çeda rolled her eyes. "Kiral and Meryam are dead, then?"

"That's doubtful. I hear they leapt from their ship and were ensorcelled away."

"Of course. The heavens forbid a star might shine upon us."

"No doubt. But we've done well. Four tribes have agreed to band together. Macide has sent ships carrying emissaries from all four tribes—ours, Masal, Salmük, and Kadri—to treat with the others in the desert. Some will resist, no doubt, but some will join us. And the others . . . well, we hope that by showing our strength now, they'll at least not support the Kings lest they make enemies of *us*."

Çeda wondered at the turn of events. "Our future was balanced on a knife's edge."

"And will be for some time. But there is hope now. The truth will be revealed. Some will cast doubt on it. Many will refuse to believe that we're anything more than the Moonless Host trying to find a place for ourselves in the desert after being run out of Sharakhai. Thieves, they'll call us. Barbarians. They'll label us the villains. But others will not." Dardzada's eyes twinkled as she'd rarely seen them do.

"Could it be, Dardzada?" Çeda asked him. "Are you *hopeful*?"

He considered the question, lips pursed. "I wouldn't put it so. The road ahead is long. But the gods have given us a chance. We have but to take it, and take *care*. And then, with a bit more luck, perhaps we'll see this through."

Footsteps approached the tent flap. "They're ready," a voice called.

Macide's voice, Çeda realized.

"A moment," Dardzada said, then pushed himself up off of his chair and held his hand out to Çeda.

"What's happening?"

He flicked his fingers at her. "You'll see soon enough."

She took his hand and he helped her to rise. She stepped gingerly over the carpets to the flap, where Dardzada held it wide. She saw as she ducked down that there were many gathered outside, but she didn't realize *how* many until she stood up again. There were hundreds upon hundreds arrayed in a fan before her tent. They stood facing her. Men in thawbs and kaftans. Women in desert dresses. Babes held in mothers' arms, children by their sides. They bore the designs of their tribes in the colors they wore, the cut of their clothes, the tattoos on their faces and hands. Tribes Khiyanat, Kadri, Masal, and Salmük. All watched Çeda.

Macide stood nearby. Behind him were Emre, Melis, and Sümeya. Leorah was there with an unabashed smile on her face, though she also looked older than Çeda ever remembered. Shal'alara stood by her side in the role of care-taker. There were dozens of others from the thirteenth tribe. Hamid, Darius, Frail Lemi, and more.

"I don't understand," Çeda said.

Macide stepped forward. "Two nights ago, the Kings left the field of bat-tle. Yesterday we tended to our wounded. We built a great pyre for the dead and celebrated all who fought. But you were not there. We had no chance to honor you. We do so now, Çedamihn Ahyanesh'ala."

With that he stepped back and knelt. Emre, Hamid, Leorah, and every-one nearby did the same. Even Melis and Sümeya, after a pause, nodded to her and knelt on the sand. Then the other tribes did the same, those at the front first, then moving progressively farther back, until all of those gathered, the survivors of the deadliest battle the desert had seen since the days of Beht Ihman, were on the ground, their ships curving in an a grand arc behind them.

The sight brought tears to her eyes. But it wasn't merely their presence here, nor the fact that they'd somehow managed to survive the Kings. This was what her mother had been hoping to achieve. She'd wanted to help carve out an existence for the thirteenth tribe. Çeda had played a part, but it had all started with her mother's going to Sharakhai, uncovering three of the bloody verses, and killing King Azad. It felt, more than ever, as if Ahya had passed a candle to Çeda. It was a beautiful thing to behold.

Wiping tears away, she said, "Rise," but it came out so weakly, she was forced to say it again. "Please, rise."

Those nearest did, then more and more, until all had risen. Then, as one, they began to shout and hold their hands high, many jumping where they stood or releasing melodic ululations that rose above the deafening sound of the gathered crowd.

A celebration was held that night. Araq was passed around the many fires, and people danced. A thousand songs were sung. Çeda was tired from her long sleep, and she still ached, but she refused to sit for long. She wandered among the many carpets, sitting here for a time, listening to the music played, even joining in, and then she'd move to the next.

She heard many tales of woe, but also of bravery, of selflessness. There was anger between the tribes yet, for all that had happened while they had lived beneath Onur's rule, but those wounds were beginning to heal. The threat of the Kings had finally bound them together.

She came finally to a fire where Melis and Sümeya were talking with Emre and Macide. Çeda sat and listened for a while. She danced with Frail Lemi and Macide and even Sümeya. And then she grew tired and took Emre's hand. Pretty Haddad of Malasan was nearby, and she took note of it, but Çeda paid her no mind. She took Emre to her tent, and together, amid all the sounds playing out beyond the tent's walls, they held one another. They told their own tales of the battle, sat by a small fire, dined on olives and bread and wine, just like they'd said they'd do.

"You're smiling too much," Emre said to her as the celebrations outside were beginning to dwindle.

"How can one smile too much?" she asked.

He shook his head, as if he knew he'd made a mistake by saying so. "It's just that there's still so much danger. And . . ."

"What?"

"Macide has asked me to go with Aríz. To be our eyes among Tribe Kadri."

Çeda tilted her head. "I think you'll be good for him."

Emre poked at the fire. "I thought you'd be more upset."

She leaned forward, ignoring the pain along her belly, and kissed him. "I am. But I've reconciled myself to us being apart. There's too much to do, Emre. But one day, when all this is done, we'll do as we said, yes? Sail the Great Shangazi together?"

He tried to smile. "I hope we can."

"We will," she said, and with that she stood and held her hand out to him. "For now, though, we leave all that behind."

He stared at her hand, suddenly unsure of himself, so she reached down, took the stick he'd been using to poke at the fire, and threw it into the flames. She took his hand and pulled him up until the two of them were standing chest to chest. She could feel the warmth coming off him. How good it felt, despite the heat of the tent.

She kissed him. The whiskers of his mustache and beard tickled as he placed more kisses along her cheek, her neck. Their hands roamed, and soon they moved to her blankets, where the two of them *did* leave everything behind. The sounds of the celebration played around them, mixing with the heady effects of the araq she'd drunk. Emre removed her clothes, taking great care for her wounds. She removed his, taking much less care. And then she reveled in his shape, noting just how many more scars he had than when they were young.

They made love. Simply. Sweetly. The music and voices felt otherworldly, the perfect counterpoint to how real Emre felt in her arms, and when they were done, they lay side by side, Emre's head cradled along her shoulder as she ran her fingernails up and down his back. Like that, they fell asleep.

Çeda woke some time later with a dread inside her. Feeling watched. All had gone dark outside the tent. The fire within was little more than embers. She looked around the tent and shook when she realized a silent figure was sitting beside the fire.

As she sat up, pulling the blanket up to cover her nakedness, the figure reached down and stoked the fire back to life with a triple-bladed knife. A bloody light was shed across the tent's interior, especially on King Ihsan himself. He blew upon the blades of the knife, clearing them of ash, and set it across his knees.

Çeda realized both her sword belt and Emre's, which had been lying near the bed earlier, had been moved to the far side of the tent. When she nudged Emre, he didn't stir, and his breathing retained the even rhythm of a man in the depths of slumber.

"I think it would be best if it's only the two of us," Ihsan said, "wouldn't you agree?"

"What are you doing here?"

Ihsan feigned surprise. "Why, I've come to see the fruits of your labor!" A smile lit his fine features as he gave a wave that encompassed the entire camp outside the tent's walls. "It's quite a tale. Four tribes to call to your banner, with more likely on their way, especially if I whisper in their ears. And meanwhile, the Kings' vaunted navy returns to Sharakhai, thwarted."

"If you're not careful, my Lord King, you'll have nothing left to rule."

"That's truer than you know," he said with a wink.

"What do you mean?"

"Forgive me, but were you under the impression the Kings left because they feared *you*?"

"Then why did they leave?"

"It may not surprise you to learn that the young King of Malasan and the Queen of Mirea both covet the Amber Jewel of the Desert. In a new development, fleets flying their colors now sail the desert. They're making for Sharakhai as we speak." He paused. "We've entered a new phase in the struggle, Çedamihn. The Four Kingdoms were always going to play a part in this war, and now it has begun. Mirea, Qaimir, and Malasan have all shown their hands. The Thousand Territories have yet to make a stand, but I'm certain they'll play their part."

"War comes to Sharakhai," Çeda said breathlessly, feeling as though her world were no longer expanding, but shrinking.

"To its very doorstep. We have to tread carefully now, Kings and tribes both, lest we lose it all."

Çeda's eyes snapped back to Ihsan's. "*We?*"

"Do we not still have common ground?"

"You tried to have me killed in Sukru's palace!"

"I can assure you that was not me." Ihsan frowned. "I can only think Davud was promised some reward should he manage to kill you. He's gone missing. Did you know?"

She shook her head.

"He's not been seen since he left through that strange device. We're all most curious where he's gone. Whoever is hiding him . . . They have the answers to your riddle."

"You call it a *riddle*?"

"I name it so because it *is* one. Why in the great wide desert would *I* wish you dead? You're the answer to my prayers."

"Until I prove an obstacle to your plans."

"Granted, but I think we can agree that you are not that yet." He paused, one hand waving to where she and Emre lay. "Come, if I'd wished you dead I would have done it by now."

There was no denying that. She softened her tone. "I'm weary, Ihsan."

"Then I shan't occupy you much longer. There are but two points of business that remain. The first: Have you seen the goddess Nalamae since the Night of Endless Swords?"

Now that was an unexpected question. "No. Why do you ask?"

"Because I fear she is in danger."

A sudden spike of fear ran through her. "Yerinde . . ."

Ihsan peered more closely at her, his face lit a ghastly crimson from the fire. "You said you haven't seen her."

"I haven't." She told him what Leorah had done with the wyrm, how Nalamae had come to *even the scales*, as she'd put it. "Onur found the gem among the treasures of Tribe Masal, but it was Yerinde who granted him the power over the wyrm."

"Well, well, well . . ." Ihsan's eyes searched the embers of the fire. "The sands hide many secrets, do they not? Let me ask you, would you find it strange to learn that Yerinde herself asked the Kings for Nalamae's head?" He didn't wait for a reply. "*I* did. I also find it strange that the gods have seen fit to watch this conflict from afar. They granted gifts that secured the Kings' our power over Sharakhai and the desert. Now it crumbles before our very eyes, and the gods have not lifted a finger to shore up that which they helped build. Moreover, they seem ready to employ us as *servants* to destroy the goddess they've hounded and killed many times before. Why?"

Indeed. It was a puzzle Çeda had been trying to unlock since learning the truth about Beht Ihman. "They know something we don't."

"If you're right, and I've no doubt you are, it would be in our best interests to discover what it is. And so I ask you again, Çedamihn, have you seen Nalamae?"

"Even if I had, I wouldn't tell you. She is the thirteenth tribe's greatest ally against you and the other Kings. And now, apparently, the other gods of the desert as well. So what was your second point?"

Ihsan picked up his knife. "You may level many charges against me, but

I do not wish the goddess dead. Your assessment of the other gods, however, may prove all too accurate." He examined the edges of his knife. "Promise me you'll think on it."

Çeda merely stared.

"I'll take that as agreement." He stood and with an easy move sheathed the knife. "Very well. The second: we made a bargain on the mount of Sharakhai."

Çeda's heart tripped, then began racing. She hadn't forgotten the bargain, but she hadn't dreamed that Ihsan would follow through on it.

Return to me, he'd told her on Tauriyat, *and I'll grant you something I know you want.*

What could you grant me? she'd asked.

Why, the name of your father . . .

She sat there unwilling to move, almost unwilling to speak, lest Ihsan change his mind. "Who is he?" she finally asked.

He made his way to the tent flap, pulled it aside, and stepped halfway through. "Your sire," he said, looking back, "caught your mother after she took her knife to Azad's throat. He was the very one who sought to stop you in the blooming fields. The one who granted you your blade." He stepped out, and the tent flap closed behind him. "Your father, Husamettín, the King of Swords."

His footsteps shushed against the sand, slowly fading. And Çeda's heart began to beat again.

Chapter 66

ROM THE DECK OF THE *BLUE HERON*, Ramahd pointed to a spot of clear sand just short of the eight ponderous wrecks ahead. "Anchor there."

"Aye," Vrago replied, and guided the ship in while Tiron and Cicio began pulling in the sails.

As the ship slid to a halt, Ramahd dropped the heavy anchor over the prow. It fell against the sand with a resounding thud. Shovels in hand, the four of them leapt over the gunwales. The nearest of the wrecks was a caravel that had already been denuded of everything useful. Sails. Rope. Weapons. Equipment. The ship itself had a rotted hull, half-eaten decks, and a collection of blackened masts—the work of the great wyrm's acid. It had rightly been left behind as useless. As deeply as the acid had eaten into the beams below, it would have been dangerous to sail. Two other sandships had been abandoned for similar reasons. Another four had been burned by fire pots. All seven had been stripped of anything of value.

Ramahd vaguely wondered where the wyrm was now. It had appeared mortally wounded after the attack by the Forsaken. It had fled, its wings no longer able to bear it aloft, slithering over the ground like a desert asp. No one had wanted to chase it.

Ahead lay the eighth ship, a schooner that had been treated in an entirely different manner from the other ships. The deck and starboard hull amidships was little more than a shambles of shattered bulwarks, torn-up planks, and broken beams, exposing much of the ship's interior. It might still have been repaired, but the tribes had been too fearful to go near it, for this was not the work of the dragon but of Guhldrathen, the fearsome ehrekh.

"That thing puts a chill in my bones," Cicio said.

Ramahd agreed. It looked like a ghost ship. The canvas and rigging were intact. The full complement of ballistae and bolts and catapults and fire pots were all still there. A good bit of sand had built up over its deck and skis, but otherwise looked little different than it had a week ago, after the battle had ended.

Between the abandoned ships was the spot where Çeda had fought both Onur and Guhldrathen, where the Forsaken had swarmed to protect her. It was where Ishaq Kirhan'ava of the Moonless Host and the thirteenth tribe had died. It was also the place where Hamzakiir had been run down and slain by Guhldrathen.

"Here," Ramahd said, pointing to an unremarkable patch of sand. And the four of them set to, shovels biting in a rhythmic pattern.

Nearly three hundred had died in the fierce battle. Ishaq, the foremost among them, had been given back to the desert, wrapped in white linen with the weapons of his enemies, placed in a skiff, and set adrift, for the desert winds to take him where they would. Other skiffs held several warriors to each skiff, some up to a dozen. Too many had died, however, to perform the ritual for all of them. Most bodies had simply been burned in a great pyre, their remains buried in the sand.

There had been two notable exceptions: Onur, the Feasting King, and the blood mage, Hamzakiir.

The tribes would not risk angering Bakhi by leaving them to rot beneath the sun, but neither had been given shrouds, nor had a single word been uttered over their graves. They had simply been dumped into a hole and covered, to be forgotten by man and god alike.

Ramahd was not normally in the business of disturbing graves, but there was a mystery that needed solving. Before the battle, Brama had told Ramahd what he'd seen in the cabin of Kiral's ship. Kiral had been there, as had

Meryam and Amaryllis. But so had Hamzakiir. Something odd had occurred just before Brama had arrived.

"They'd been pulling on their clothes," Brama had said.

"Why?" Ramahd had asked.

Brama hadn't been sure, but Ramahd had an inkling. He'd kept his thoughts to himself, however. It was the sort of information that, if true, an outsider like Brama should never have.

They dug for a long while, missing the mark several times before Cicio called, "Here."

They dug around the bodies and slowly but surely uncovered the tall figure of Hamzakiir and half of the ox-like frame of Onur.

Ramahd knelt by Hamzakiir's side. He could detect no difference between his memories of the man and the dusty, sunken corpse he found lying before him, but that meant little. Meryam's magic had always been impressive.

Taking a deep breath, Ramahd placed his hands on Hamzakiir's face. He'd never tried to *unwork* a spell once it had been wrought, but he tried now. He ran his hands over Hamzakiir's features—cheeks, nose, mouth, even his hair—and tried to guide the magic *away*, as he'd done with Hamzakiir in the temple, and again with Meryam as she stood on the deck of the galleon.

After long moments nothing changed, nor could Ramahd sense the fabric of woven magic. Over and over again he tried, to no avail. Hamzakiir looked the same as he ever had. Pulling out his knife, he cut Hamzakiir's robes down the front to expose his chest. The corpse's skin was pasty white with various blemishes and a pattern of hair across chest and stomach that reminded Ramahd of a sword hilt. He tried there as well, wondering if working closer to his heart would have more effect. But here, too, he failed to find any trace of magic.

"Is it Hamzakiir, then?" Tiron asked after a time.

Ramahd realized how long he'd been staring. The men were nervous. They wanted to leave. "I don't know," he said. "Give me more time."

Could I have been wrong about Meryam? About all of this?

He refused to believe it. Like stones across a stream, he could trace a series of events all the way from the abduction of Hamzakiir near Külaşan's desert palace to Meryam's order to have Ramahd killed.

The most important of them was the battle for Hamzakiir's mind in

Viaroza. But then came Aldouan's death in the desert at the hands of the ehrekh, Guhldrathen. And later, after they'd reached Sharakhai, Meryam's refusal to return home to Qaimir, even when her duties as queen became ever more urgent. The trail ended with her insistence on dealing directly with Kiral to rid the desert of Hamzakiir, the price of which was nothing less than Malasan itself, and a chance to rule those lands once their armies had been crushed in the looming war.

Over the months Meryam had become more harried. She'd become ever more eager to distance herself from Ramahd. But then came the event that had opened Ramahd's eyes for good. The sapphire. After stealing it from Brama, they'd performed the ritual to bind it anew. They'd cut away the leather cords and cleaned it. Meryam had applied a mixture of goat fat and smoke from her own burning blood so that Rümayesh would be chained to her will.

At the closing of that ritual, the ehrekh had nearly caught Ramahd in her spell. Meryam had clipped her locket closed to prevent it, but in that moment, Rümayesh had summoned up a memory: Meryam sobbing in the desert oasis after they'd escaped Guhldrathen.

I've done a terrible thing, Ramahd.

Meryam's father had just died. She'd been despondent, nearly inconsolable. Rümayesh had clearly done it in hopes of causing discord between them, enough that she might free herself or ensorcel one of them to do it for her, but Ramahd hadn't understood. How would *that* particular memory help Rümayesh?

During the battle, after Brama had shattered the sapphire and freed Rümayesh, Ramahd had been petrified, even more than while standing before Guhldrathen. Even so, he'd had every intention of asking the ehrekh about Meryam. He needed *proof.*

His chance never came, however. The last he'd seen of Rümayesh and Guhldrathen was when they'd flown from the battle in an undulating cloud of smoke and black beetles. Brama had followed them numbly. Neither he nor Rümayesh had been seen since.

Ramahd had tried to convince himself that the memory was nothing more than a desperate attempt by Rümayesh to save herself—a lie, in essence. But there was the rub. For the implications of that memory to create any sort of rift between Ramahd and Meryam, it had to be true.

I've done a terrible thing.

Had Meryam planned all along to break Hamzakiir's mind and *pretend* she'd been ensorcelled by him? Might that give her the perfect excuse to remove her father from the throne? If so, it would be a simple thing to draw Ramahd into her plans in Viaroza, and to force him to play his part in covering up her crimes.

He recalled how eager she'd been at the thought of breaking Hamzakiir. She'd *already* broken him, Ramahd understood now. She must have. The rest had been for Ramahd's benefit, so he'd believe that Hamzakiir had in fact dominated them both.

The only part Ramahd didn't understand was her father's death. If she meant to kill him, why not do it in the capital—why take them to Guhldrathen? Perhaps it was unforeseen, a miscalculation on Meryam's part. Or for her plans to work did Hamzakiir need *some* free will, and he'd chosen the method of Aldouan's death? Or maybe she'd foreseen it all and hoped to trick Guhldrathen into killing Kiral, disguised as Hamzakiir.

Whatever the case, after Aldouan's death, Hamzakiir had begun laying the groundwork of her plans in Sharakhai. He'd made overtures to Kiral to give up the identity of the Moonless Host's leaders. Kiral had taken the bait, for it served his purposes, but it served Meryam's as well. She had weakened the Moonless Host even as she made her bargain with Kiral to ensure her eventual place in the House of Kings.

That was her goal all along. The throne of Sharakhai.

Hadn't she said as much? How better to take it than as a woman who controlled Kiral himself, or the man who looked like him?

As Ramahd stared at Hamzakiir's face once more, a cold dread inside him began to expand. He'd been certain Hamzakiir and Kiral had switched forms, but he could sense none of Meryam's magic. Was he wrong? Was this, in fact, Hamzakiir?

"My lord," Tiron said as he glanced to the dead ships. "Perhaps we should bury them."

"Yes." Ramahd stood and picked up his shovel. "Very well."

They began covering the two men once more. Sand piled higher and higher, covering legs, arms, chests. When Vrago tossed some onto Hamzakiir's face, however, Ramahd started.

"Stop!" he called, raising one hand.

In a rush, he dropped to Hamzakiir's side and brushed away the sand from the left side of his face.

There, along his jaw, was a lone pockmark. Ramahd ran a finger over it. Peering close, he saw the barest signs that there were more, but they were extremely shallow.

He pressed one hand against Kiral's cheek, closed his eyes, and used his power to feel for that lone mark on Hamzakiir's face. Rümayesh had done this, he realized, not Meryam, which was why he'd been unable to sense it. It was more subtle than Meryam's magic, but now he'd found the way to unravel it.

Like a knife through a chink in armor, he pressed and found his way through. Slowly, the whole of the spell was revealed, and he rubbed his hands over Hamzakiir's face once more. He ran his fingers through his wiry hair and beard. With each movement, the face before him changed just a little bit more. The beard sloughed from his chin and cheeks. The hair atop his head did as well, leaving it closely shorn. Bones popped and cracked as his face widened, transforming from Hamzakiir's narrow face to one with broad cheeks and a strong jaw. The pockmarks were plain to see now. And although the eyes were cloudy, they were Kiral's steely gray.

For a time, the four of them simply stared. "Blessed Alu," Cicio said.

Ramahd had shared his fears with all of them. They knew what this meant: that all of it was true. Meryam had dominated Hamzakiir from the start. She'd forced him to kill Aldouan, her own father and the rightful king of Qaimir. She'd killed Kiral, the King of Kings, and put Hamzakiir in his place.

"What shall we do?" Vrago asked.

Indeed, what *should* they do? Ramahd had been asking himself the same question over and over. Should he return home to Qaimir? Surely Meryam had returned to Sharakhai. Should he go there and confront her? Present proof to the Kings and let *them* deal with her treachery? And whatever he chose, he had to consider how Qaimir would suffer. Each option came with a price, and some would be steeper than others.

Taking out his knife, Ramahd sawed through Kiral's neck. He cut the head clean away, then wrapped it in the shreds of the robes he'd cut earlier.

Climbing out of the hole, he set the head of the King of Kings aside and motioned for the others to take up their shovels.

They buried the bodies, then headed back to the *Blue Heron*. Once aboard, his men looked to him. "Where to, my lord?"

Taking the wrapped head with him, Ramahd made for the ladder leading belowdecks. He needed to think. But there was a plan starting to form in his mind.

"Set sail for Sharakhai."

Acknowledgments

Sometimes authors struggle mightily with books. Sometimes we don't. This one, thank goodness, was more the latter than the former. Not that it came *easy*, mind you—only that it came easier than some of the books I've written. And as always, I had a ton of help along the way.

I'd like to thank Paul Genesse for pushing me to make this story better. Your keen eye helped me innumerable times in course correcting this story. Just as importantly, though, your enthusiasm for the series has helped me stay positive when things got rough. To Rob Ziegler, thank you for the read, our chats, and your advice. I've always appreciated how you can cut through the noise and get me back to the only thing that really matters in the end: the *story*.

To Renée Ann Torres and Femke Giesolf, thank you for taking a look at the manuscript and providing your valuable insights. It's wonderful to have that sort of feedback as things are nearing their final form.

I am indebted to the DAW and Gollancz publishing teams for shepherding both the story and the manuscript from its early, protean stages all the way through to this, its final form. To Betsy Wollheim, thank you for the wealth of knowledge, experience, and insights you've shared with me and brought to bear on this book and the larger series. To Gillian Redfearn, thank you for your invaluable feedback, particularly in showing me how trimming can amplify a scene's impact without losing meaning. To Marylou Capes-Platt, thank you for your keen eye and your insights into writing. I don't know where I'd be without you! (I'm learning, slowly but surely, Marylou.

Don't give up on me!) And thank you to all the unsung heroes in the DAW and Gollancz production, marketing, sales, and back office support teams. I see you, and appreciate all that you do.

I am indebted to my agent, Russ Galen, not only for this book, but for helping to ensure that the full series will see the light of day. Many thanks to Danny Baror and Heather Baror-Shapiro as well for your tireless efforts in bringing this series to readers all over the world.

Last of all, I'd like to thank you, the fans of this series. We've made it through three books and reached the halfway point in this sand-filled epic. I hope you'll stick with me to the end.